West
of the
Moon

Also by Katherine Langrish:

Dark Angels

KATHERINE LANGRISH

HarperCollins *Children's Books*

WEST OF THE MOON is abridged from *Troll Fell*, *Troll Mill*, and *Troll Blood*

HarperCollins *Children's Books* is a division of HarperCollins*Publishers* Ltd,
77-85 Fulham Palace Road, Hammersmith, London W6 8JB

Visit us on the web at
www.harpercollins.co.uk

1

WEST OF THE MOON

ISBN 978-0-00-739523-1

Printed and bound in England by
Clays Ltd, St Ives plc

This book is for
my mother and father

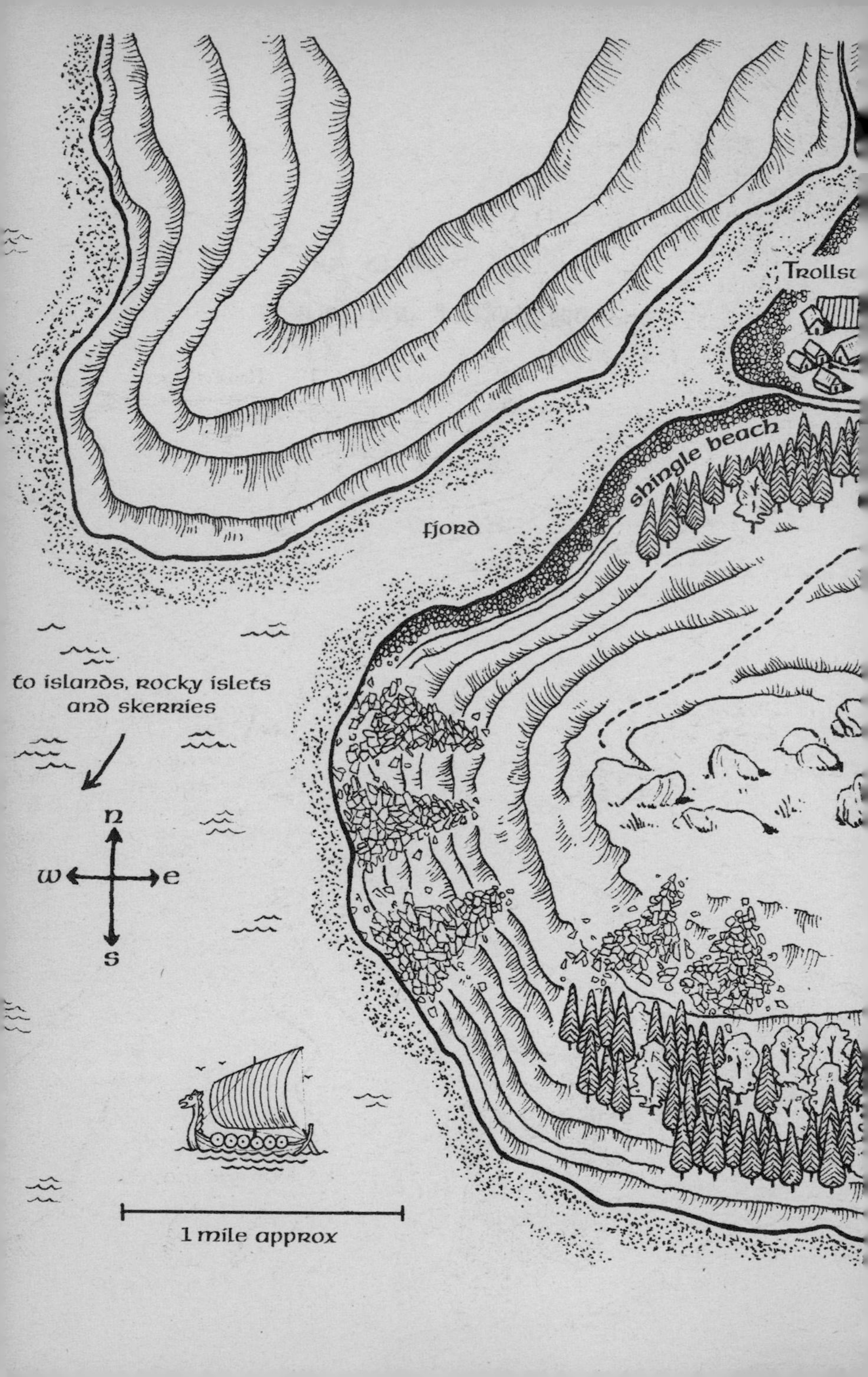
Trollst
shingle beach
fjord
to islands, rocky islets
and skerries
n
w
e
s
1 mile approx

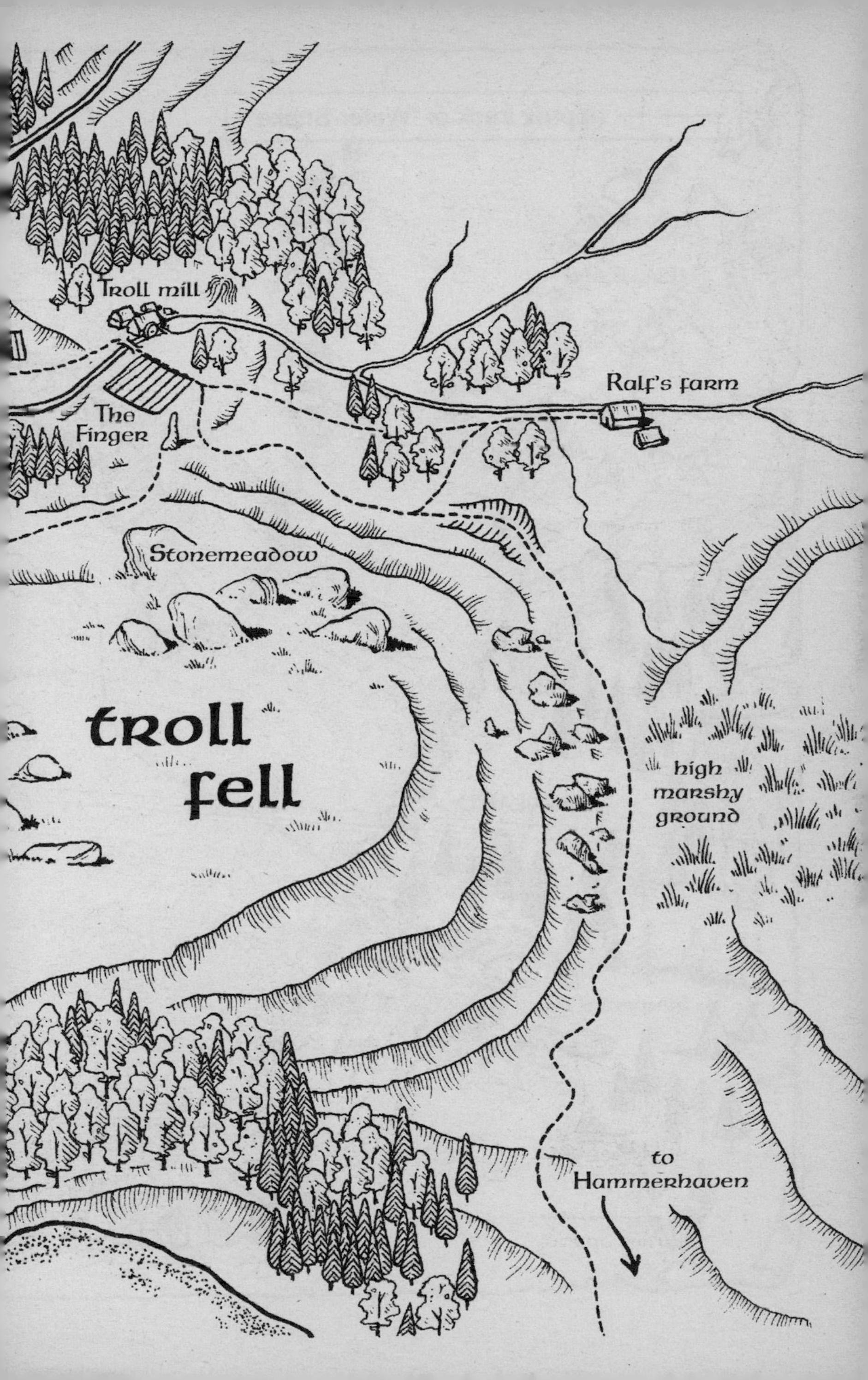
Troll mill
Ralf's farm
The Finger
Stonemeadow
troll fell
high marshy ground
to Hammerhaven

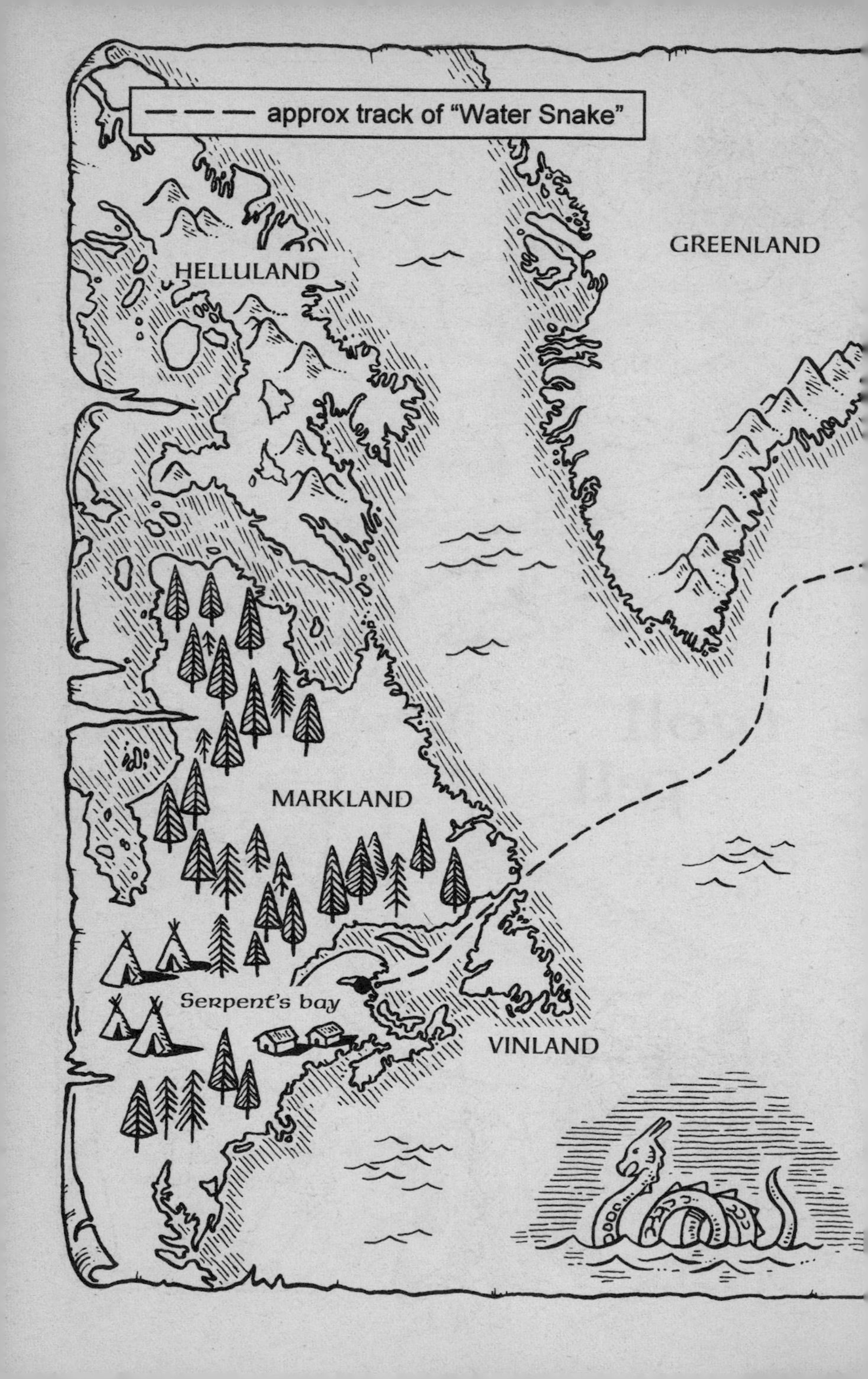
approx track of "Water Snake"
GREENLAND
HELLULAND
MARKLAND
Serpent's bay
VINLAND

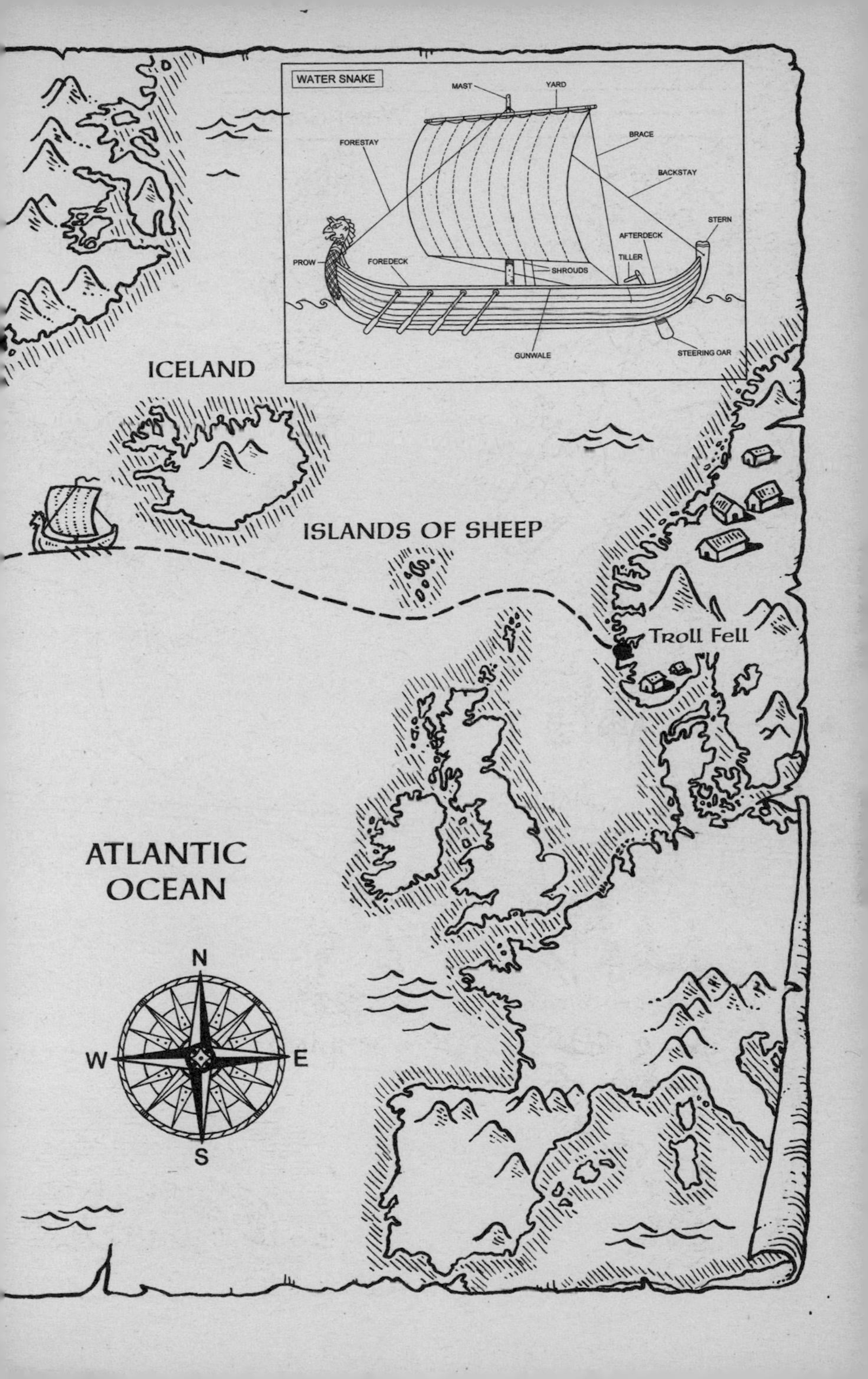
WATER SNAKE
MAST
YARD
FORESTAY
BRACE
BACKSTAY
STERN
AFTERDECK
TILLER
PROW
FOREDECK
SHROUDS
GUNWALE
STEERING OAR
ICELAND
ISLANDS OF SHEEP
Troll Fell
ATLANTIC
OCEAN
N
W
E
S

Part One

CHAPTER 1

The Coming of Uncle Baldur

Peer Ulfsson stood at his father's funeral pyre, watching the sparks whirl up like millions of shining spirits streaking away into the dark. The flames scorched his face, but his back was freezing. The wind slid cold fingers down his neck.

Surely this was all a bad dream? He turned, almost expecting to see his father standing behind him, his thin, tanned face carved with deep lines of laughter and life. But the sloping shingle beach ran steep and empty into the sea.

A small body bumped Peer's legs. He reached down. His dog Loki leaned against him, a rough-haired, flea-bitten brown mongrel – all the family Peer had left.

The pyre flung violent shadows up and down the beach. Friends and neighbours crowded around it in a ring. Their faces were curves of light and hollows of darkness: the flames lit up their steaming breath like dragon-smoke. Above the fire, the air shimmered and shook. It was like looking through a magic glass into a world of ghosts and monsters – the world into which his father's spirit was passing, beginning the long journey to the land of the dead. Was that a pale face turning towards him? A dim arm waving?

What if I see him?

Beyond the fire a shadow lurched into life. It tramped forwards, man-shaped, looming up behind the people, a sort of black haystack with thick groping arms…

Peer gave a strangled shout.

A huge man shoved his way into the circle of firelight. Elbowing the neighbours aside, he tramped right up to the pyre and turned, his boots carelessly planted in the glowing ashes. He waited, dark against the flames, until an uneasy silence fell. Then he spoke, in a high cracked voice as shrill as a whistle.

"I've come for the boy. Which is Ulf's son?"

Nobody answered. The men close to Peer edged nearer, closing ranks around him. Catching the movement, the giant turned. He lifted his head like a wolf smelling out its prey. Peer stopped breathing. Their eyes met.

The stranger bore down on him like a landslide. Enormous fingers crunched on his arm. High over his head the toneless, reedy voice piped, "I'm your uncle, Baldur Grimsson. From now on, you'll be living with me."

"But I haven't got an uncle," Peer gasped.

"I don't like saying things twice," the man said menacingly. "I'm your Uncle Baldur, the miller of Trollsvik." He challenged the crowd. "You all know it's true. Tell him – before I twist his arm off."

Brand the shipbuilder stepped forward, shaking his head in distress. "Dear me! This – that is to say, Peer, your father did mention to me once—"

His wife Ingrid pushed in, glaring. "Let go of the boy, you brute. We all know that poor Ulf never had anything to do with you!"

"*Is* this my uncle?" Peer whispered. He looked up at Uncle Baldur. It was like looking up at a dark cliff. First came a powerful chest, then a thick neck, gleaming like naked rock. There was a black beard like a rook's nest, and a face of stony slabs with bristling black eyebrows for ledges. At the top came tangled bushes of dark hair.

Against Peer's legs Loki pulsed, growling. Any moment now, he would bite. Uncle Baldur knew it too. He looked down, and Peer read the death penalty in his face.

"Loki, quiet!" he cried in sharp fear. The little dog subsided. Uncle Baldur released Peer's arm and inspected him. "What's *that*?"

"He's my dog, Loki." Peer rubbed his bruised arm.

"Call that a dog?" Uncle Baldur grinned. "My dog could have 'im for breakfast!"

Brand put a protective arm around Peer's shoulder. "You don't need to take the boy away. We're looking after him."

"You are, are you? And who are you?"

"He's the master shipbuilder of Hammerhaven, that's who!" Ingrid snapped. "Peer's father was his best carpenter!"

"Best of a bad lot, hey?" sneered Uncle Baldur. "Could he make a barrel that didn't leak?"

Brand glared. "Ulf did a wonderful job on the new ship. Never put a finger wrong."

"No? But he sliced himself with a chisel and died when it turned bad," scoffed Uncle Baldur. "Some carpenter!"

With a bang, a piece of wood exploded in the heart of the pyre. Peer leaped forwards. "Don't talk about my father like that! You want to know what he could do? Look there! *That's* what he could do!" He pointed seawards. Uncle Baldur rocked back, off balance. High over the crowd, the fierce head and snaky neck of a dragon emerged from the darkness. The firelight glinted on its red scales and open jaws, and its goggle eyes glared threateningly at Uncle Baldur. The neck curved down swanlike and became the swooping lines of a ship, chocked upright on the beach. Behind it, ranks of dark waves rushed up the shingle.

Uncle Baldur recovered, though sweat glistened on his face. He forced a laugh. "A dragonship! A pretty toy," he jeered, and a mutter of anger ran through the crowd. He seized Peer's arm again. "Come along. I'm a busy man. I've a mill to run and no time to waste."

"You'll not drag the boy away from his father's funeral?" Brand exclaimed. "Why, it's not even over!"

And the villagers surged around, crying, "Shame!"

"Show some respect!" said Brand hotly.

Uncle Baldur grunted. Summing up the crowd with his sharp black eyes, he said at last, "Very well. I'll stay a day or two. There's stuff to sell, I suppose." Jerking his head at Brand he demanded, "Has he paid your dad's last wages – eh?"

"Of c-course he has," Peer stammered in fury. "He's been very k-kind – he's arranged everything."

"Nothing owing?" Uncle Baldur scowled. "I'll look into that. Nobody cheats *me*."

Behind him, Ulf's funeral pyre collapsed into a pile of glowing ash and sighed out a last stream of sparks which sped away for ever.

Eager as a pig digging for truffles, Uncle Baldur set about selling off Peer's home. Benches, pots, blankets, Ulf's cherished mallets and bright chisels – he squeezed the last penny out of each deal.

Brand dared to complain. Uncle Baldur stared at him coldly and jingled the silver and copper in his pocket. "It's mine," he said. "Ulf owed me money."

"That's not true!" cried Peer.

"How would you know?" jeered his uncle. "And what's that ring on your finger? Silver, eh? Boys don't wear rings. Give it here."

"No! It was my father's!" Peer backed away, fists clenched. Uncle Baldur grabbed him, prised his fingers open and wrenched the ring off.

"Silver," he nodded. It was too tight to fit over his own hairy knuckles, so he stuffed it in his pocket.

Fat comfortable Ingrid took Peer in and tried to mother him. "Cheer up, my pet!" She pushed a honey cake into his hand. Peer dropped it, and it disappeared into the eager jaws of Loki, lurking under the table.

"Ingrid," he asked in desperation, "how can that fat beast be my uncle?"

Ingrid's plump face creased into worried folds. "Oh Peer, it's a sad story. Your father was just a boy when his own father died. His mother married the miller at Trollsvik, the other side of Troll Fell. Poor soul, she lived to regret it. The old miller was a cruel hard man. He used his fists on both of them."

Peer flinched. "He never told me. What happened?"

"Your father ran away and never saw his mother again. But she had two more boys, and this Baldur is one of them. He's your father's own half-brother, though as far as I know, they never met." Ingrid lifted her wooden bread bowl from the hearth and poured a yeasty froth into the warm flour. "But that was all long ago. I know your Uncle Baldur is very rough-spoken, and not a bit like your father, but blood is thicker than water. Surely he'll look after you, you poor boy!"

Peer was silent. He cleared his throat. "Couldn't I stay here with you?"

"Oh my dearie!" Ingrid cried. "We've thought of it. But we can't. He's your uncle. He's got a right to you, and we haven't."

"No," said Peer bitterly. "Of course not."

Ingrid tried to put an arm around his shoulders. "Give your uncles a chance," she pleaded. "Don't you think your father would want you to try?"

"Maybe..." Peer shut his eyes on a sudden glimpse of his father, turning over a piece of oak and saying as he often did, "You've got to make the best of the wood you're given, Peer. And that's true of life, too!" He could almost smell the sweet sawdust clinging to his father's clothes.

Loki sprang to his feet barking. The door opened and Uncle Baldur thrust his head and shoulders in. "Boy!" he squealed. "Are those chickens in the yard yours? Catch them and put them in the cart. We're leaving. *Run!*"

A fine row blew up indoors as his uncle accused Ingrid of trying to steal the chickens. Peer fled outside and began stalking a fat speckled hen. Loki joined in. He dashed at the hens, which scattered, cackling. "Bad dog!" cried Peer, but Loki had lost his head and was hurtling around the yard with a mouthful of brown tail feathers.

Uncle Baldur burst out of the house. He bent down, heaved up the heavy stone doorstop and hurled it at Loki. There were two shrieks, one from Peer and the other from Loki who lay down suddenly and licked his flank, whimpering.

"You could have killed him!" Peer yelled. His uncle turned on him. "If he ever chases my chickens again, I will. Now catch them and tie them up with this." He threw Peer a hank of twine. "Be quick!"

As Peer captured the last of the hens, Uncle Baldur tied a string around Loki's neck. "Fasten 'im to the tail of the cart. He can run behind."

"Can't he ride?" Peer asked. "He's limping..." But his voice died under Uncle Baldur's unwinking stare, and miserably he did as he was told. Then he clambered into the cart himself.

Ingrid came out to see him off, mopping first her hands and then her eyes on her apron. "Poor lamb," she wailed. "And Brand's down at the shipyard and can't even say goodbye. Whatever will he say when he hears?"

The cart creaked as Uncle Baldur climbed aboard. He took a new piece of twine from his pocket and tied one end around the rail of the cart. Then he tied the other end around Peer's right wrist. Peer's mouth fell open. He tried to pull away and got his ears slapped.

"What are you doing to the boy?" Ingrid shrieked.

Uncle Baldur looked round in surprise. "Got to fasten up the livestock," he explained. "Chickens *or* boys – can't have 'em escaping, running around loose."

Ingrid opened her mouth – and shut it. Peer looked at her. *See?* he told her silently.

"Gee! Hoick!" Uncle Baldur cracked his whip over the oxen. The cart lurched. Peer stared resolutely ahead. He did not wave goodbye.

The steep road twisted up into low woods of birch and spruce, then into high meadows, and then stony and boggy moorland. "Garn! Grr! Hoick, hoick!" The oxen snorted, straining. The cart tilted like the deck of a ship and the chickens slid about, flapping.

"Shall I get out and walk?" Peer suggested.

His uncle ignored him. Peer muttered a bad word. He sat on a pile of sacks, his arm awkwardly tethered above his head. Over the end of the cart he could see Loki trotting along with his head and tail low. He looked miserable, but the limp had gone – he'd been faking it, Peer decided.

They came to a bend in the road. Peer looked, then pulled himself up, staring. In front, dwarfing Uncle Baldur's bulky shoulders, the land swooped upwards. Crag above crag, upland beyond upland, in murky shouldering ridges, clotted with trees and tumbling with rockfalls, the flanks of Troll Fell rose before him. At the summit he glimpsed a savage crown of rocks, but even as he gazed, the clouds came lower. The top of Troll Fell wrapped itself in mist.

A fine cold rain began to fall, soaking through Peer's clothes. He dragged out a sack and draped it across his shoulders. Uncle Baldur pulled up the hood of his thick cloak.

Shadowy boulders loomed out of the drizzle on both sides of the track. They seemed to stare at Peer as he huddled in the bottom of the cart. One looked like a giant's head with shallow, scooped-out eyes. Something bolted out from underneath it as the cart passed, kicking itself up the hillside with powerful leaps. Peer sat up. What was that? Too big for a hare – and he thought he'd seen *elbows*...

A wind sprang up. Mud sprayed from the great wooden cartwheels. Peer clutched the sodden sack under his chin and sat jolting and shivering.

At last he realised that they were over the saddle of the hill and beginning to descend. Leaning out, he looked down into a great shadowy basin. A few faint lights freckled the valley. That must be the village of Trollsvik. He thought longingly of dry clothes, hot food and a fire. He had hardly spoken to his uncle all the way, but now he called out as politely as he could, "Uncle? How far is the mill?"

Uncle Baldur pointed. "Down among the trees yonder. A matter of half a mile. Beside the brook." He sounded quite civil for once, and Peer was encouraged.

"Home!" his uncle added, in his shrill toad's croak. "Lived there all me life, and me father before him, and *his* father before *him*. Millers all."

"That's nice," Peer agreed between chattering teeth.

"Needs a new wheel, and the dam repaired," complained his uncle. "If I had the money – if I had my rights –"

You've got my money now, Peer thought bitterly.

"– I'd be the most important man in the place," his uncle went on. "I'm the miller. I deserve to be rich. I *will be* rich. Hark!"

He hauled on the reins. The track plunged between steep banks, and the cart slewed, blocking the road. Uncle Baldur twisted around, straining his thick neck and raising one hand.

"Hear that?" he muttered. "Someone's coming..."

Who? What had Uncle Baldur heard on this wild, lonely road? What was that long burbling cry, drifting on the wind?

"You hear it?" Uncle Baldur hissed eagerly. "Could be friends of mine, boy. I've got some funny friends. People you'd be surprised to meet!" He giggled.

Stones clattered on the track close behind. Loki shot under the tail of the cart and Peer could hear him growling. He braced himself, skin crawling, ready to face anything – monsters or trolls.

A small, wet pony emerged from the drizzle, picking its way downhill, carrying a rider and a packsaddle. On seeing the cart, it stopped with a snort.

"Hello!" shouted the rider. "Move the cart, will you? I can't get past."

With a deep breath of fury, Uncle Baldur flung down the reins. He surged to his feet, teetering on the cart's narrow step.

"Ralf Eiriksson!" he screamed. "You cheating piece of stinking offal! How dare you creep up on me, you – you crawling worm?"

"Baldur Grimsson," the rider groaned. "Just my luck! Shift the cart, you fat fool. I want to get home."

"Liar! Thief!" Uncle Baldur swayed, shaking his fist. "You watch out. If the trolls don't get you, I will! You'll steal no more. That's finished. If the Gaffer—"

A blinding whip of lightning cracked across the sky, accompanied by a heart-stopping jolt of thunder. The rain came down twice as hard. Uncle Baldur threw himself back on his seat and shook the reins. The oxen plodded forwards. The rider trotted past without another word and struck off along an even rougher track that led off to the right.

Peer clung to the side of the cart.

Well, that's it, he said to himself. *Uncle Baldur is mad. Completely crazy.*

Sick with cold, he tried to picture his father's bright, kind eyes – his thin shoulders hunched from bending over chisel and plane. What would he say now, if only he knew?

He'd say, 'Keep your heart up!' After all, I've got another uncle at the mill. Maybe he'll take after my side of the family. Maybe – just maybe – he'll be a little like Father. There can only be one Uncle Baldur...

The cart rattled down the last slope and trundled over a shaky wooden bridge. "Gee!" howled Uncle Baldur, his voice almost lost in the roar of the water hurtling beneath. On the other side of the bridge, Peer saw the mill, crouching dismally on the bank with dripping thatch and sly little black windows. Wild trees pressed around it, tossing despairing arms in the wind. Uncle Baldur drove the cart into a pinched little yard. Ahead was a line of mean-looking sheds, and on the other side lurked a dark barn with a gaping entrance like an open mouth.

The weary oxen splashed to a halt. A wolf-like baying broke out from some unseen dog. Uncle Baldur dropped the reins and stretched his arms till the joints cracked.

"Home!" he proclaimed, jumping down. He strode across to the door of the mill and kicked it open. Frail firelight leaked out. "Grim!" he called triumphantly. "I'm back. And I've *got* him!" The door banged shut. Peer sat out in the rain, shivering with hope and fear.

"Grim," he muttered. "Uncle Grim will be different, I know he will. There can't be another Uncle Baldur."

The latch lifted with a noisy click. A new, deep voice said loudly, "Let's take a look at him, then!"

The mill door swung slowly open. Out strode the burly shape of Uncle Baldur. At his heels trod someone else – someone unbelievably familiar. Flabbergasted, Peer squinted through the rain. It couldn't be true! But it was, and there was nothing left to hope for. He shook his head in horrified despair.

CHAPTER 2

The Departure of Ralf

In a small damp farmhouse higher up the valley, Hilde threw down her knitting. Her eyes ached from peering at the stitches in the firelight. And she was worried.

"Ma? He's so late. Do you think he's all right?"

Before Gudrun could answer, the wind pounced on the house as if trying to tear it loose from the hillside. Eerie voices wailed and chattered outside as rain lashed the closed wooden shutters. It was a night for wolves, trolls, bears. And Hilde's father was out there, riding home over the shaggy black shoulder of Troll Fell. Even if he was hurt or in trouble, she and her mother could only wait, anxiously listening, while her grandfather dozed fitfully by the fire. But then she heard the clop and clatter of the pony's feet trotting into the yard.

"At last!" said Gudrun, smiling. And Hilde ran out into the wild, wet night.

"I'm back!" Ralf threw her the reins. His long blond hair was plastered to his head, and his boots and leggings were covered in mud.

"You're soaking! I'll rub the pony down. You go in and get dry," said Hilde, leading the steaming animal into the stable. Ralf came with her to unbuckle the packs. "How was the trip?"

"Fine! I got everything your mother wanted from the market. It's been a long day, though. And I overtook that madman Baldur Grimsson coming back over Troll Fell."

"What happened?" asked Hilde sharply.

"Oh, he yelled a few insults, as usual. That's not my news. Hilde—" Ralf stopped and gave her a strange look, excited yet apprehensive.

"What? What is it?" Hilde stopped grooming the pony.

"There's a new ship in the harbour! A new longship, ready to sail! And I – well, no, I'd better tell your mother first. Be quick as you can, now, and you'll soon hear all about it." He tugged her long hair and left her.

What was he up to? Hilde rubbed the pony dry and threw down fresh straw, hurrying so she could get back to the family. It was creepy in the stable with the wind howling outside. The lantern cast huge shadows. Whistling to keep up her courage, she turned to the door – and saw with horror a thin black arm come through the loophole and grope about for the latch. She screamed and hit it with the broom. It vanished.

"Trolls!" Hilde hissed. "Not again!" Clutching the broom she waited a moment, recovered her breath, tiptoed to the door and peered out.

Falling rain glittered in the doorway. A black shadow shifted in the mud. Squatting there, its knees up past its ears, was a thing about the size of a large dog. She saw a fat paunchy body slung between long legs, and damp bald skin twitching in the rain. Glowing yellow eyes blinked from a wrinkled pug face. For one fascinated second they stared at each other, troll and girl; then Hilde was splattered with mud as the troll sprang away in a couple of long, liquid jumps.

Hilde flew across the yard and wrenched open the farmhouse door to tell everyone about it. She tumbled straight into a colossal row.

"I never heard such a ridiculous idea in my WHOLE LIFE,"

Hilde's mother was yelling at Ralf. "You're a FARMER, not some sort of VIKING!"

Hilde let go of the door. It slammed behind her with a deafening bang. And so she forgot about the troll, and didn't see it leap as suddenly as a frog on to the low eaves of their thick turf roof and go scrambling up to the ridge.

"Why should it be ridiculous?" Ralf bellowed back. "That's what half these fellows ARE – farmers *and* Vikings!"

"Ma – Pa – stop it!" cried Hilde. "What's happening? Stop it – you'll wake the little ones!"

In fact the twins were already awake – and bawling.

The wind managed an extra strong blast. All the birch trees growing up the sides of Troll Fell reeled and danced. Up on the roof the troll clung on, whimpering, and one of its large black ears blew inside out like a dog's. It squirmed along to where a hole had been cut out to let smoke escape, and peered over at the fierce red eye of the fire. It pulled back, coughing and chattering to itself: "Hutututu!" But the sound was lost in a rattle of sleet that fell hissing into the flames.

"Very well," said Gudrun, suddenly deadly quiet. "Let's see what your *father* thinks about his only son sailing off on a longship into storms and whirlpools and goodness knows what. It will break his heart!"

"Why don't you let him speak for himself?" Ralf roared. "And why don't you give us both some supper? Starving us while you nag at me!"

Hilde glanced at her grandfather, Eirik, and saw his eye brighten at the suggestion of supper. Gudrun saw it too. She fetched them both a jug of ale and a bowl of groute, warm barley porridge, served as Eirik liked it with a big lump of butter.

"Eirik, tell Ralf what you think of this mad idea," she

demanded, twisting her hands in her apron. "He'll listen to you."

But Eirik's face lit up. "Aha, if only I were a young fellow again. A brand-new ship! *Long Serpent*, they're calling her. Oh, to sail away east of the sun and west of the moon! To follow the whales' road, seeking adventure!" He tasted his groute. "The whales' road – d'you know what that means, Hilde, my girl?"

"Yes, Grandfather," said Hilde kindly. "It's the sea."

Eirik broke into a chant from some long saga he was making about Harald the Seafarer, waving his spoon to the beat. While Hilde clapped softly in time, Ralf tiptoed over to the twins, five-year old Sigurd and Sigrid. He sat down between them, an arm round each, and whispered. Suddenly they came jumping out of bed.

"Pa's going to be a Viking!" they shrieked.

"He's going to bring us presents!"

"An amber necklace!"

"A real dagger!"

"Ralf!" Gudrun whirled around. "Stop bribing those children!"

Eirik's poem reached its climax, all dead heroes and burning ships. He sat back happily. Ralf cheered. Gudrun glared at him.

"Oh, that's a fine way to end, isn't it – floating face down in the water? And who'll look after the farm while you're away? What about the sheep? You know somebody's stealing them: three lambs gone already. It's the trolls, or those Grimsson brothers down at the mill. They're all troublemakers. We can't spare you!"

Up on the roof the troll remembered the flavour of roast lamb. It licked its lips with a thin black tongue.

"Speaking of the millers," Ralf began, clearly hoping to change the subject, "did I tell you I met Baldur Grimsson tonight as I came home? The man's a fool. He sat in his cart in the pouring rain, shouting at me."

"Why did he shout at you, Pa?" asked Sigrid, wide eyed.

"Because he doesn't like me," Ralf grinned.

"Why not?"

"It's all because of Pa's golden cup," said Hilde wisely. "Isn't it?"

"That's right, Hilde," said Ralf with relish. "He'd love to get his hands on that. My troll treasure, my lucky cup!"

"*Unlucky* cup, more like," Gudrun sniffed. But Sigurd and Sigrid jumped up and down begging, "Tell us the story, Pa!"

"All right!" Ralf scooped the twins on to his knees. "One wild night just like this, about ten years ago, I was riding home from the market at Hammerhaven, and halfway over Troll Fell, wet and weary, I saw a bright light glowing from the top of the crag and heard snatches of music gusting on the wind."

"Curiosity killed the cat," Gudrun muttered.

"I was in one of our own fields, the high one called the Stonemeadow. I trotted the pony up the slope to see what was happening. Well, if you'll believe me, the whole rocky summit of the hill had been lifted up, like a great stone lid! It was resting on four stout red pillars, and underneath was a space shining with golden light, and hundreds of trolls, all shapes and sizes, skipping and dancing."

"How *could* they lift the whole top of Troll Fell, Pa?" asked Sigurd.

"As easily as you take off the top of your egg," joked Ralf. He sobered. "Who knows what powers they have, my son? I only tell you what I saw with my own eyes. They had all sorts of food spread out on gold and silver dishes, and little troll servingmen jumping about between the dancers, balancing great loaded trays and never spilling a drop. It made me laugh out loud!

"I was so busy staring, I never noticed this troll girl creeping up on me till she popped up right by the pony's shoulder. She held out a beautiful golden cup brimful of something steaming hot – spiced ale, I thought. I took it gratefully, cold and wet as I was."

"Madness," muttered Gudrun.

"Just before I gulped it down," Ralf said slowly, "I noticed a gleam in her slanting eyes, a wicked sparkle! And her ears – her *hairy, pointed* ears – twitched forwards."

"Go on!" said the children breathlessly.

Ralf leaned forward. "I lifted the cup, as if to take a sip. Then I threw the whole drink out over my shoulder. It splashed out smoking on to the pony's tail and singed off half his hair! There's an awful yell from the troll girl, and next thing the pony and I are off down the hill, galloping for our lives. I'm still clutching the golden cup, and half the trolls of Troll Fell are tearing after us!"

Soot showered into the fire. Up on the roof the troll lay flat with one large ear unfurled over the smoke hole. It lashed its tail like a cat, and growled. None of the humans noticed. They were too wrapped up in the story. Ralf wiped his face, trembling with remembered excitement, and laughed.

"I daren't go home," he continued. "The trolls would have torn your mother and Hilde to pieces!"

"What about us?" shouted Sigurd.

"You weren't born, brats," said Hilde cheerfully. "Go on, Pa!"

"I had one chance," said Ralf. "At the tall stone called

the Finger, I turned off the road and galloped across the big ploughed field above the mill. The trolls found it slow going over the furrows, and the clay clogged their feet. I reached the millstream ahead of them, jumped off and dragged the pony through the water. There was no bridge then. I was safe! The trolls couldn't follow me over the brook."

"Were they angry?" asked Sigurd.

"Spitting like cats and hissing like kettles!" said Ralf. "But it was nearly dawn, and off they scuttled up the hill. I staggered over to the mill, and as I banged on the door I heard – no, I *felt*, through the soles of my feet, a sort of far-off grating shudder as the top of Troll Fell sank into its place again."

"And then?" prompted Hilde.

"The old miller, Grim, threw the door open, swearing at me for knocking so early. Then he saw the golden cup. A minute later he couldn't do enough for me. He kicked his sons out of bed, sent his wife running for ale and bread, and it was, "Sit down, Ralf, toast your feet and tell us everything!"

"And you did!" said Gudrun grimly.

"Of course I did," sighed Ralf. He turned to Hilde. "Fetch down the cup, Hilde. Let's look at it again!"

The troll on the roof skirmished around the smoke hole like a dog at a rabbit-burrow, trying to get an upside-down glimpse of the golden goblet, which Hilde lifted from the shelf and carried to her father.

"Lovely!" Ralf whispered, tilting it. The bowl was wide. Two handles like serpents looped from the rim to the foot. The gold shone in the firelight as if it might melt over his fingers like butter.

"It's so pretty!" said Sigrid. "Why don't we ever use it?"

"Use that?" cried Gudrun in horror. "Never! It's real bad luck, you mark my words. Many a time I've asked your father to take it back up the hill and leave it. But he's too stubborn."

"Gudrun!" Ralf grumbled. "Always worrying! Who'd believe my story without this cup? My prize, won fair and square. Bad luck goes to people with bad hearts. We have nothing to fear."

"Did the old miller like it?" asked Sigurd.

"Oh yes! 'Troll treasure!' said old Grim. 'We could use a bit of that, couldn't we, boys?' The way he was looking at it made me uneasy. After all, no one knew where I was. I got up to go – and there were the boys in front of me, blocking the door, and old Grim behind me, picking up a log from the woodpile!" Ralf looked grim. "If it hadn't been for Bjørn and Arne Egilsson coming to the door that moment with a sack of barley to grind, I might have been knocked on the head for this cup."

"And that's why the millers hate us?" said Hilde. "Because we've got the cup and they haven't?"

"There's more to it than that," said Gudrun. "Old Grim was crazy to have that cup, or something like it. Next day he came round pestering your father to sell him the Stonemeadow. He thought if he owned it, he could dig it up for treasure."

"I turned him down flat," said Ralf. "'If there's any treasure up there,' I told him, 'it belongs to the trolls and they'll be guarding it. Leave well alone!'"

"Now that was sense," said Gudrun. "But what happened? Old Grim tells everyone that your father's cheated him – taken his money and kept the land!"

"A dirty lie!" said Ralf, reddening.

"But old Grim's dead now, isn't he?" asked Hilde.

"Yes," said Ralf, "he died last winter. But do you know why? Because he hung about on that hill in all weathers, hoping to find the way in, and he got caught in a snowstorm."

"His sons found him," added Gudrun, "lying under a crag, clawing at the rocks. Weeping that he'd found the gate, and could hear the gatekeeper laughing at him from inside the hill. They carried him back to the mill, but he was too far gone. They blamed your father, of course."

"That's not fair!" said Hilde.

"It's not fair," said Gudrun, "but it's the way things are. Which makes it madness for your father to be thinking of taking off on a foolhardy voyage. Ralf," she begged, "you know these trips are a gamble. Don't go!"

Ralf scratched his head. "I want some adventure, Gudrun. All my life I've lived here, in this one little valley. I want new skies – new seas – new places." He looked at her pleadingly. "Can't you see?"

"All I can see," Gudrun flashed, "is that you want to desert us, and throw away good money on a selfish pleasure trip."

Ralf went scarlet. "If the money worries you, sell this!" he roared, brandishing the golden cup. "It's gold, it will fetch a good price, and I know you've always hated it! But I'm sailing on that longship!"

"You'll drown!" Gudrun sobbed. "And all the time I'm waiting and waiting for you, you'll be riding over Hel's bridge with the rest of the dead!"

There was an awful silence.

Ralf put the cup down and took Gudrun by the shoulders. He gave her a little shake and said gently, "You're a wonderful woman, Gudrun. I married a grand woman, sure enough. But I've got to take this chance of going a-Viking."

The gale buffeted the house. Draughts crept moaning under the door. Gudrun drew a long, shaky breath. "When do you go?"

Ralf looked at the floor. "Tomorrow morning," he admitted in a low voice. "I'm sorry, Gudrun. The ship sails tomorrow."

"*Tomorrow!*" Gudrun's lips whitened. She turned her face against Ralf's shoulder and shuddered. "Ralf, Ralf! It's no weather for sailors!"

"This will blow itself out by morning," Ralf consoled her.

Up on the roof, the troll lost interest. It sat riding the ridge, waving its arms in the wind and calling loudly, "Hoooo! Hutututututu!"

"How the wind shrieks!" said Gudrun. She took the poker and stirred up the fire. A stream of sparks shot through the smoke hole, and the startled troll threw itself backwards and rolled off the roof. Then it prowled inquisitively round the buildings, leaving odd little eight-toed footprints in the mud. The farmhouse door had a horseshoe nailed over it. The troll wouldn't go near that. But it pried into every other corner of the farmyard, leaving smears of bad luck, like snail-tracks, on everything it touched.

CHAPTER 3

Talking to the Nis

AFTER THE FIRST stunned moment, Peer began to laugh – tight, hiccupping laughter that hurt his chest.

Uncle Grim and Uncle Baldur were identical twins. Same barrel chests and muscular, knotted arms. Same mean little eyes peering from masses of black tangled beard and hair. Uncle Baldur was still wrapped in his wet cloak, however, while his brother seemed to have been eating supper, for he was holding a knife with a piece of meat skewered to the point.

"Shut up," he said to Peer. "And get down." Only the voice was different – deep and rough.

With a stitch in his side from laughing – or sobbing – Peer held up his wrist, still tethered to the side of the cart. Uncle Grim snapped the twine with a contemptuous jerk. He sucked the meat off his knife, licked the blade, and severed the string holding Loki. "*Now* get down," he ordered through his food. He turned to his brother as Peer jumped stiffly into the mud. "Not much, is he?"

"But he'll do," grunted Uncle Baldur. "Here!" He thrust the lantern at Peer. "Take this. Put the oxen in the stalls. Put the hens in the barn. Feed them. Move!" He threw an arm over Grim's shoulder and as the two of them slouched away, Peer heard Baldur saying, "What's in the pot? Stew? I'll have some of that!" The door shut.

Peer stood in the rain with the lantern. All desire to laugh left him. Loki whined, his head on one side. "Come on, boy," said Peer wearily. "Let's get on with it."

He unloaded the hens and set them loose on the barn floor, where an arrogant black cockerel came strutting to inspect them. Then he unhitched the oxen and gave them some hay. Loki curled up in the straw and fell asleep. Peer decided to leave him there. There had been a big dog barking inside the mill, and he hadn't forgotten what Uncle Baldur had said about his dog eating Loki. Taking the lantern, he set off across the yard. It had stopped raining, and tatters of cloud blew wildly overhead.

Not a glimmer of light escaped from the mill. Peer hoped his uncles hadn't locked him out. Cold, damp and hungry, he hesitated on the step, afraid to go in. Voices mumbled inside. *What were they saying? Was it about him?* He put his ear to the door and listened.

"There wasn't much," Baldur was saying.

"Count it anyway," said Grim's deep voice, and Peer realised they were counting the money Baldur had made from the sale.

"Twenty-nine, thirty, thirty-one, in copper and silver," Baldur finished. "Lock it up! We don't want the boy finding it."

"It's *my* money, you thieves," Peer whispered furiously. A lid creaked open and crashed shut. They had hidden the money in some chest. If he walked in now, he might see where it was.

"About the boy," said Baldur, and Peer glued his ear to the wet wood. Unfortunately Baldur was walking about, for he could hear feet clumping to and fro, and the words came in snatches.

"...time to take him to the Gaffer?" Peer heard, and, "...no point taking him yet. Plenty of time before the wedding."

What wedding? And who's the Gaffer? Peer applied his ear to the door again. A succession of thuds sounded like both of his uncles taking their boots off and kicking them across the room. He heard Grim say loudly, "At least we'll get some work out of him first," and this seemed to end the discussion.

Peer straightened up and scratched his head. But it was too cold to stand around wondering. The wind bit his ears and a fresh rain shower rattled out of the sky. Inside the mill Baldur was saying, "Hasn't that pesky lad finished *yet?*" Hastily Peer knocked and lifted the latch.

With a blood-curdling bellow, the most enormous dog Peer had ever seen launched itself from the fireside directly at his throat. Uncle Grim stuck out a casual hand and yanked the monster backwards, roaring, "*Down, Grendel!* Come in and shut the door," he added roughly to Peer. "Let him smell you. Then he'll know you."

Grendel was taller than a wolf. His brindled coat stood up in a thick ruff of fur over his shoulders and down his spine. He smelled Peer's outstretched fingers, grumbling distrustfully. "Best dog in the valley," boasted Uncle Grim, giving him an affectionate slap. "Wins every fight: a real killer!"

Thank goodness I didn't bring Loki in, Peer thought with a shudder as he looked about. The narrow smoke-stained room was a jumble of rickety furniture, bins, barrels and old tools. A sullen fire smouldered in the middle of the floor, and Uncle Baldur sat beside it on a stool, guzzling stew from a bowl in his lap and toasting his vast hairy toes over the embers. Two bunk beds, set into alcoves, trailed tangles of dirty blankets on to the floor.

At the end of the room a short ladder led up to a kind of loft with a raised platform for the millstones. In the shadows Peer could make out the mill machinery, hoists and hoppers, chains and hooks. A huge pair of iron scales hung from the roof. Swags of rope looped from beam to beam.

Cobwebs clung everywhere to the walls, loaded with old flour. Underfoot, the dirt floor felt spongy and damp. A sweetish smell of ancient bran and mouldy grain mingled with the stink of Uncle Baldur's cheesy feet and a lingering odour of stew.

Peer swallowed. He said faintly, "I did what you said, Uncle. I fed the animals and put them away. Is – is there any stew?"

"Over there," his uncle grunted, jerking his head at a black iron pot sitting in the embers. Peer looked in. It was nearly empty.

"But it's all gone," he said in dismay.

"*All gone?*" Uncle Baldur's face blackened. "*All gone?* This boy's been spoilt, Grim. I can see that. The boy's been spoilt."

"Plenty left," growled Grim. "Wipe out the pot with bread and be thankful!"

Peer knelt. He found a dry heel of bread and scraped it around inside the pot. There was no meat, barely a spoonful of gravy and few fragments of onion, but the warmth of the iron pot was comforting, and he chewed the bread hungrily, saving a scrap for Loki. When at last he looked up he found Uncle Baldur staring at him. His uncle's dark little eyes glittered, and he buried his thick fingers in his beard and scratched, rasping slowly up and down.

Peer stared back uneasily. His uncle's face turned purple. He convulsed. He doubled up, choking, and slapped his knees. "Hee, hee," he gasped. "Ha, ha! Oh dear. Look at him!" He pointed at Peer. "Look at him, Grim! Some might call him a bad bargain, but to me – to me, he's worth his weight in gold!"

The brothers howled. "That's good!" Grim roared,

punching Baldur's shoulder. "Worth his weight in – oh, very good!"

Peer gave them a dark glance. Whatever the joke was, it was clearly not a friendly one. He pretended to yawn. "I'm tired, Uncle. Where do I sleep?"

"Eh?" Uncle Baldur turned to him, wiping tears of laughter from his hairy cheeks. "The lad's *tired*, Grim. He wants to *sleep*."

Uncle Grim lumbered to his feet. He burrowed into a corner under the loft, kicked aside a couple of dusty baskets and a crate, and revealed a small wooden door not more than three feet high. Peer followed warily. Uncle Grim opened the little door. Behind it was blackness, a strong damp smell, and a sound of trickling water.

Before Peer could protest, Uncle Grim grabbed him and thrust him through the door into the dark space beyond. Peer pitched on to his face. With a flump, a pile of mouldy sacks landed on his legs. "You can sleep on those!" his uncle shouted.

Peer kicked his legs free, scrambled up and hit his head a stunning blow. Stars spangled the darkness. He felt about and found a huge rounded beam of wood and the cold blunt teeth of some enormous cogwheel. He was in with the machinery under the millstones! A thin line of light indicated the closed door. "Let me *out!*" He pounded on it, shrieking. "Let me out, let me *out!*"

The rotten catch gave way. The door sprang open, a magical glimpse of firelight and safety. Peer crawled out and leaped to his feet. Uncle Baldur advanced upon him.

"No!" Peer cried. "Don't make me sleep in there! I'll sleep in the barn! Please! Don't make me!"

Uncle Baldur stopped. "What's wrong with it? It's not that bad."

"It's too dark! Too dark and cramped. I can't breathe," panted Peer, his heart still pounding.

His uncles stared. Baldur began to grin. "Too dark?" His grin developed into a chuckle. "D'you hear that, Grim? He's afraid of the dark. The boy's *afraid of the dark!*"

For the second time that night, the brothers roared with laughter. They pounded each other on the back and choked and staggered about. At last Uncle Baldur recovered. The old bad-tempered scowl settled back on his face.

"So go sleep in the barn, Faintheart!" he snarled, throwing himself into his bunk.

With flaming cheeks, Peer tiptoed to the door. He had to step over Grendel, who opened a glinting red eye and wrinkled his lip to show a tooth. He shut the door as quickly and quietly as he could, and crossed the yard. The sky had cleared and the moon had risen.

The barn felt high and sweet and airy. Peer pulled crackling straw over his knees and woke Loki, who gobbled the crust Peer had saved. A few bright strips of moonlight lay across the floor. Cold and exhausted Peer lay back, his arm around Loki, and fell into uneasy dreams.

He dreamed of a little voice, panting and muttering to itself. "Up we go! Up we go! Here we are!" There was scrabbling, like rats in the rafters, and a smell of porridge. Peer rolled over.

"Up we go," muttered the hoarse little voice again, and then more loudly, "Move over, you great fat hen. Budge, I say!" A roosting hen fell off the rafter with a squawk and minced indignantly away. Peer sat up. He could see only black shapes and shadows.

"Aaah!" A long sigh from overhead set his hair on end. There came a sound of lapping or slurping. Peer listened, fascinated.

"No butter!" the little voice complained. "No butter in me groute!" It mumbled to itself in disappointment. "The cheapskates, the skinflints, the hard-hearted misers. But wait! Maybe the butter's at the bottom. Let's find out." The slurping began again. Then a sucking sound, as if the person – whoever it was – had scraped the bowl with its fingers and was licking them off. There was a pause.

"No butter," sulked the voice in deep displeasure. A wooden bowl dropped out of the rafters on to Peer's head.

"Ow!" said Peer.

There was a gasp and a scuffle. Next time the voice spoke it was from a far corner.

"Who's there?" it quavered.

"I'm Peer Ulfsson," said Peer. "Who are you?"

"Nobody," said the voice quickly. "Nobody at all."

"I think you're a Nis," said Peer. A Nis was a sort of house spirit. Peer had heard of them, but never expected to meet one. "Are you a Nis?" he persisted.

There was a bit of a silence. "What if I am?" the voice asked huffily.

"Didn't they give you any butter?" Peer asked, hoping to make friends.

This set the creature off. "Plain groute!" it exclaimed. "Nary a bit of butter for poor Nithing, but plain barley porridge. Me that does half the work around here, me that sweeps and dusts, me that polishes away cobwebs!" Recalling the dirt he had seen earlier, Peer doubted that it did any of these things well, but he did not say so.

"And they has mountains of butter," went on the Nis, working itself up, "in the dairy. In a wooden barrel," it added darkly, "to keep off cats and mice and the likes of me. Plain groute they puts in my bowl by the fire, and I sees it, and I fetches it away, and I tastes it – and no butter!"

"I know how you feel," said Peer, "they didn't leave me any stew, either."

"No butter." It was still brooding over its wrongs. "Could you get me butter?"

"I shouldn't think so," said Peer gloomily, "if they caught me stealing butter I should think they'd half kill me. I don't suppose I'm going to get much to eat here. I'm sorry," he added.

"Have an egg!" said the Nis with a squeak of laughter. And it spoke no more that night.

In the morning when Peer woke up, he wondered if it had been a dream. Then he felt something in the straw just under his hand. It was a smooth brown hen's egg. Loki looked eagerly at it, ears pricked. He knew what an egg was.

"Thanks!" said Peer to the rafters. He broke the egg for Loki, who lapped it up as noisily as the Nis, while Peer stretched and brushed straw from his clothes.

"Come on, Loki," he said, pushing the barn door open. "Let's go and explore!"

CHAPTER 4

Meeting Hilde

THE SKY WAS fresh and clear. It was still very early. Peer splashed through the puddles, keeping a wary eye on the silent mill with its blind shutters and tattered thatch. A dismal thread of smoke wavered from the roof and trickled into the yard. There was no sign of anyone about.

Peer walked around the end of the building to the bridge. He leaned on the rail, looking upstream at the big wooden waterwheel. It towered higher than his head, its dark teeth dripping. A cold breath came off the water, which flowed listlessly under the bridge in inky creases.

He crossed over and turned up the bank to visit the millpond. It was a gloomy place, even on this bright morning. Patches of green slime rotated on the dark water, which seemed hardly to move except at the very edge of the weir. Peer sniffed. There was a damp reek in the air.

He walked further, till his way was blocked by a narrow, deep-cut channel, fed by an open sluice in the side of the millpond. The water sprayed in a glittering arc over a sill slotted between wooden posts, and dashed noisily away to join the tailrace below the bridge.

Loki had run off, nosing into the reeds with his tail high. He dashed back and jumped at Peer with muddy paws.

"Down!" Peer pushed him off. "Phew. That stinks!" It

was thick, black mud, the sort that dries to a hard grey shell. He tried to wipe Loki's paws with a handful of grass, and Loki tried to help by lavishly licking his own paws and Peer's fingers. In the middle of this mess Peer heard a pony coming down the lane towards the mill.

A girl of about his own age was riding it, brightly dressed in a blue woollen dress with red stitching. On her head she wore a jaunty red and yellow cap, and her hair was done in two long plaits tied with pieces of red and blue ribbon. She sat sideways on the shaggy little pony, with a basket on her knee. Her eyes widened when she saw Peer, and she pulled the pony to a stop. "Hello! Who are you?"

Peer tried to wipe his muddy hands on his clothes. "My name's Peer. Peer Ulfsson."

"*Ulf's* son?" said the girl. "Now wait, I know everyone, don't tell me. I'll get it. Yes! There was an Ulf who was old Grim's stepson. Is that him?"

Peer nodded. "But he died last week," he told her.

"Oh, I'm sorry! I'm so sorry, Peer. Is that why you're here? Have you—"

"I've come to live with my uncles. Yes."

"That's terrible for you!" the girl cried. "Whoops!" She clapped a hand over her mouth, but her eyes gleamed. "Perhaps you like them?"

"Not much," said Peer cautiously. "Who are you?"

"Hilde, Ralf's daughter," said Hilde with a flourish. "Ours is the highest farm in the dale; we own most of the north side of Troll Fell. Come and visit! You won't meet my father, Ralf, though, because he went away this morning. He's gone off to Hammerhaven to join some wretched new dragonship they've built, and my mother's really upset. What's wrong? What have I said?"

"Nothing," Peer growled. "My father helped to build that ship. That's all!"

Hilde went red. "Sorry," she said awkwardly. "Pa says the ship is wonderful. He's so proud to be sailing on her... Is that your dog?" She pointed suddenly at Loki. "Don't let him near the millpond."

"Why not? He can swim."

"I know, but Granny Greenteeth lives in there. That's why there aren't any ducks or moorhens. She pulls them under and eats them. So people say."

"Really?" Peer looked at the sullen brown water with its oily reflections. It was easy to believe that Hilde could be right.

"What's she like?" he asked.

"She has green teeth, of course," said Hilde. "Pointed. Green weedy hair. I've never seen her, but a man in the village has. He met an enormous eel one night, sliding along through the grass – and that was her, too!"

"How did he know?" Peer asked reasonably.

"He just did! And that's not all," said Hilde. "There are all sorts of spooky stories about this mill. I don't envy you, living here. The Grimssons think they are *so* important, just because they're the millers, and yet the mill only runs once in a while. They're always cheating people and not giving fair measure. They won't touch our corn any more. We have to grind it at home with the hand mill."

"Why's that?" Peer began to think he didn't like this girl. Couldn't she say anything good about the place?

"We have a feud with them," said Hilde. "They claim they own one of our fields. They don't, of course." She grinned at him. "If you're their nephew, I suppose that means we have a feud with you, too."

"A feud!" Peer exclaimed. "And your father's called Ralf? I think I saw him last night. Didn't he come over Troll Fell in all that rain?"

"You were there? Pa never said. What happened exactly?"

"It was so dark he probably didn't see me," Peer told her. "I was in the bottom of the cart, getting soaked. As soon as my uncle saw your father, he went crazy. He jumped up and started calling him names—"

"What sort of names?"

"A crawling worm, and a thief—"

"*Did he?*" Hilde flashed.

Peer shrugged. "You asked. It's not my fault. Anyway, if you hate the millers so much, why are you here this morning?"

Hilde laughed. "I'm not coming to your precious mill. I'm riding down to the village." She patted her basket. "I'm going to see Bjørn the fisherman, and trade some cheese and butter. Mother wants fish, and my grandfather fancies a roast crab for his tea."

Cheese! Butter! Roast crabs! Peer swallowed. He realised how terribly hungry he felt. His downcast look must have touched Hilde, for she said in a more friendly way, "I hope you'll like living here. Your uncles will give you an easy time at first, won't they? I know! I can bring our barley to you now. If you don't tell your uncles who it's from, maybe they'll grind it for us. That would be a joke!"

"I don't think I could," said Peer, alarmed. He felt sure that her jokes could get him into a lot of trouble.

"I didn't mean it," said Hilde impatiently. She gave him a look, plainly wondering how anyone could be so dull and serious, and Peer flushed. Hilde waved. "I'll be seeing you!" she cried.

She rode over the bridge and on down the hill. Peer blew out his cheeks.

"Who cares what *she* thinks?" he muttered. "Eh, Loki?"

He called Loki to heel and trailed back to the yard. The mill door was open, and he saw one of his uncles standing dishevelled in the morning sunshine, scratching under his arms and staring at Hilde as her pony picked its neat-footed way down the road to the village. He summoned Peer with a jerk of the head.

"Were you talking to that lass?"

"Yes, Uncle Grim," said Peer meekly.

He received a slap that made his head ring. "That's for chattering and wasting time," growled his uncle. "What did she say?"

"If you don't want me to talk to her, why do you want to know?" asked Peer angrily, rubbing his ear. Uncle Grim lifted his hand again.

"Oh well, let me see," said Peer with an edge to his voice. "She asked me who I was. I told her my name. Then she said her name is Hilde, and she welcomed me to the dale, which she seems to think she owns. Isn't this interesting?"

Uncle Grim didn't seem to notice sarcasm. "What else?"

Peer wasn't going to repeat what Hilde had said about the millers. He racked his brains for something else. "Oh yes," he remembered. "She said her father went away this morning. He's going a-Viking for the summer, on the new longship."

Uncle Grim's black beard split open in a wide grin, showing a set of brown and yellow teeth. "Has he, indeed? Baldur!" he bellowed. "Ralf Eiriksson has gone a-Viking. Leaving his family *all alone*!" He clapped Peer on the back. "Maybe you'll be useful after all, sonny!"

With a sinking heart Peer followed his uncle indoors. Loki

trotted at his heels. And Grendel, sprawled out beside the fire, saw Loki. He surged to his feet like a hairy earthquake and crept forwards growling, eyes riveted on the intruder, strings of saliva drooling from his jaws. Peer whirled in alarm. Loki stood there, his tail wagging slower and slower as he lost confidence.

"Down Grendel! Down!" cried Peer.

"He'll not listen to *you*," said Uncle Baldur scornfully from the table.

"Tell him Loki's a friend," Peer begged, trying to bundle Loki backwards out of the door. "Can't we introduce them, or something?"

In no hurry, Uncle Baldur finished his mouthful. "Down, Grendel," he ordered. The huge dog flicked a glance at his master.

"Get *down*, sir!" screamed Uncle Baldur, slapping his hand on the table. Grendel shook his great head, spattering Peer with froth, and lowered himself to the floor, still glaring at Loki with unforgiving menace.

Peer got the door open and Loki vanished into the yard.

"Come here," said Uncle Baldur to Peer, cutting himself some more cheese. Peer approached reluctantly till he was standing between his uncle's outstretched legs. Crumbs of bread and cheese speckled his uncle's beard. His stained shirt gaped open at the throat, exposing another tangle of black hair. A flea jumped out. Uncle Baldur caught it, cracked it, wiped his fingers on his shirt, and reached for more bread.

"That dog," he said, nodding at Grendel. "That dog only obeys me and Grim. Right? He hates other dogs. He's a born fighter."

"Killed half a dozen," agreed Grim in a sort of proud growl.

"So if you want to keep *your* dog in one piece, you watch your step and make yourself very, very useful." Uncle Baldur stared Peer straight in the eye. "Otherwise we might organise a little dogfight. Understand?"

Peer understood. He compressed his lips and nodded, as slightly as he dared.

"Good." Baldur explored a back molar with a dirty fingernail. "Now what's all this about Ralf Eiriksson?"

"I don't know," said Peer sullenly. "No!" he added. "I mean, all I know is what I've told you. His daughter says he's walking to Hammerhaven this morning. He's going a-Viking for the summer. I didn't ask any more."

His uncles winked at each other, and Uncle Baldur kicked Peer on the ankle. "Where did the girl go?"

"To the village," said Peer in a small voice. "To buy fish."

"I want to see her." Uncle Baldur jabbed Peer in the chest. "Watch for her coming back. Bring her straight to me. Right?"

He turned to the table, not waiting for a reply, and tossed him the end of a loaf. "Eat that and get on with the chores," he said abruptly. "Grim'll show you what to do. And remember – fetch me that girl!"

CHAPTER 5

Trouble at the Mill

HILDE'S SHOES SANK into the wet sand. She rubbed her arms, willing the sun to climb higher. It was chilly here on the beach in the shadow of Troll Fell. The tide was going out, and cold grey waves splashed on the shore.

"Half a dozen herring and a couple of crabs? Done!" agreed Bjørn cheerfully. He shouted to his brother who sat in the boat sorting the catch, "Find us a couple of good big crabs, Arne!" He turned back to Hilde. "Any news?"

"I should say so," said Hilde gloomily. "My father's left. Gone off for the whole summer on the new longship they've built at Hammerhaven."

Bjørn whistled, Arne clambered out of the boat, and Hilde discovered that explaining it all to two interested young men cheered her up – especially when Arne fixed his vivid blue eyes on her face. "Lucky Ralf," he said enviously. "I wish I'd heard about it. What's the ship like?"

"Lovely," Hilde assured him. "She's got a dragon head, all carved and painted."

"Yes," Bjørn laughed, "but how long is she? How many oars?"

Hilde didn't know. "That boy at the mill could tell you. His father built her."

"What boy?"

"The millers' nephew. I met him this morning. They've taken him in because his father died."

Bjørn's eyebrows rose. "The millers have taken in an orphan? What's he like?"

"He's all right," said Hilde without enthusiasm. "He seems a bit nervous."

"I'd be nervous in his shoes," said Bjørn darkly. "Arne! Dreamer! Give the girl her fish!"

With her basket full of herring and the two live crabs wrapped firmly in a cloth, Hilde rode whistling back up the steep path out of the village. Her good mood lasted until she came in sight of the mill. Even the spring sunshine could not gild its slimy black thatch. The brook rushed away from it, tumbling over itself in a white cascade. Nobody happy had ever lived there.

Hilde felt sorry for the boy, Peer, but she didn't want to stop. She gathered up the reins and trotted, hoping to get past without being seen, but as she reached the bridge, Peer dashed out of the yard. "Hilde! Hilde!" He ran up, looking pale and miserable. "I'm sorry. My uncles want to talk to you. Will you come?"

Hilde rode warily into the yard. Both the millers were there, lounging on the doorstep. They lowered their heads threateningly – like a couple of prize bulls, Hilde thought.

"What d'you want?" she demanded.

"A little *bird* told us," Baldur sneered in his high voice, "that Daddy's gone away. The great Ralf Eiriksson, who thinks he's so important. Is that right? Eh?"

"Only for the summer," said Hilde icily. "He'll be back before winter with a bunch of his Viking friends, so don't give me any trouble, Baldur Grimsson."

"Vikings!" said Baldur. "I don't give *that* for Vikings."

He spat. "Besides, what with storms and whirlpools and sea serpents, he'll never come back."

"Is that all you have to say?" snapped Hilde.

"No!" Baldur snarled. He came up close and grabbed the pony by the bridle. "Tell your *mother* – and your *grandpa* –" he emphasised the words with a stab of his thick forefinger, "to keep off that land on Troll Fell that belongs to us. You ask your mother which she'd prefer. Those fields – or that golden cup? The land is ours. And so are the sheep you've been grazing on it. You and your family keep off the Stonemeadow!"

He let go of the bridle and whistled. Grendel came hurtling out of the mill.

"See 'em off!" shouted Grim.

Hilde grabbed the mane. The terrified pony whirled out of the yard and bolted over the bridge and up the hill. Clinging to her bouncing basket, she hauled on the reins and slithered off sideways as the pony came to a snorting halt. "It's all right! It's all right." She patted its steaming neck. "The dog's not after you now..."

But the pony rolled a wild eye as a little brown dog burst out of the bushes. There was a crackling, crashing noise as someone tackled the steep and brambly shortcut up the side of the hill. Hilde shook back her hair. "Who's there?" she challenged.

Peer's pale and dirty face became visible as he parted some branches. "Are you all right?" he puffed.

"No thanks to you!" Hilde scowled at him. "Was it you who told those – those *oafs* – that my father has gone away?"

"Yes, it was," said Peer miserably. "I didn't mean any harm – I didn't know it was important. I'm sorry, Hilde."

"Oh, don't worry." Hilde recovered her temper. "Stop

apologising. You haven't done anything. They'd have heard soon enough. Everybody knows everything in a little place like this." She gave him a sharp look. "Why are you hiding in the bushes, Peer? Are you scared of the millers? Or are you scared of me?"

Peer flushed. He didn't answer.

"Well," Hilde went on, "I expect there's going to be trouble. I'm sorry, Peer, but I absolutely detest your uncles."

"So do I," said Peer in a low, savage voice. "I don't know why they want me. There's something going on that I don't understand. Some strange plan. They stole my father's money. I heard them counting it and talking about someone called the Gaffer – and a wedding. And if I don't do everything they say, they'll set their dog on Loki. He'll be killed."

"That's terrible!" Hilde cried. She patted Loki, who collapsed on to his back and folded up his paws to let her rub his tummy. She scratched his chest. "Money, and a wedding?" she repeated, frowning. "I can't imagine. Of course, old Grim, their father, was always poking about looking for the trolls' treasure."

"*Was* he? Why?"

"It's a long story. Have you got time? And anyway, whose side are you on?"

"On your side," said Peer with determination. "Even if they are my uncles. But I can't help living with them. I've got nowhere else to go."

Hilde patted the ground beside her. "Sit down and I'll tell you about the trolls. It's a good story, and it's true. Years ago, my father was riding over Troll Fell late one night when he stumbled on a troll banquet..." She told Peer what had happened, and how Ralf had raced to the mill for shelter, and old Grim had seen the golden cup.

"Mother swears it's unlucky," she went on, "and it certainly was for Grim. He spent the rest of his days wandering around Troll Fell, looking for the gate into the hill."

"What gate? I thought you said the whole place was up on pillars?"

"I think they only do that for special occasions. But there must be a gateway into the hill. We have trolls the way other people have rats and mice, and they're all getting out somewhere. And wherever it is, it seems Grim found it, only it was winter, and he collapsed up there and died later."

"So my uncles must know where it is," said Peer thoughtfully.

"Yes, but what good is that? The trolls aren't going to come out and just give them presents," said Hilde. She was still scratching Loki's tummy. "Goodness, Loki, how much more of this do you want?"

"Oh, he'll go on for ever," said Peer, laughing. Just then a distant bellow floated up from the mill. He stopped laughing and jumped up. "I'd better go."

"Yes, you'd better." Hilde looked sorry for him. "Watch out for yourself, Peer." She offered her hand, which Peer took shyly. "See you soon!"

Peer raced for the mill, Loki bounding ahead. He reached the yard to find his uncles talking to a carter, a surly-looking man who had just unloaded some sacks of barley. Grendel lay in a patch of sunlight by the mill door, gnawing a bone. He growled at Loki, who pottered past and cocked a cheeky leg on the corner of the barn.

"Grind it small," shouted the carter as he drove his cart out into the lane. "We want fine meal. I'll collect it tomorrow."

"You're going to learn about the mill, boy," said Uncle Baldur to Peer. "Grim's just a farmer, but me – I'm the miller!"

He rapped his chest. "You're a lucky lad to have me to teach you. I hope you're thankful."

Something flamed up in Peer's heart. "Thankful? What have I got to be thankful for? You treat me like a slave, you can't even remember my *name!*"

Baldur raised a fist the size of a ham and clouted Peer casually over the ear. Peer found himself sitting on the ground, clutching his ringing head. Loki streaked across the yard, teeth bared for Uncle Baldur's leg. Grendel rose silently from the doorstep and hurled himself at Loki.

"Loki!" Peer screamed. Loki saw Grendel out of the tail of his eye and veered off around the corner. Grendel dropped his hackles and slouched back to his bone.

"Come inside," said Uncle Baldur as if nothing had happened. "I'll show you what to do. Pay attention. You'll be doing a lot of this."

"You're not going to take me to the Gaffer, then?" said Peer on impulse.

Uncle Baldur swung round, fast for such a big man.

"What?" he said in a menacing whisper. Their eyes met. Peer thought fast. "Something Uncle Grim said," he invented. "He said, er, if I didn't work hard, you'd give me to the Gaffer." Come to think of it, it sounded exactly the sort of thing Uncle Grim *would* say.

Uncle Baldur clearly believed it. He muttered something about Grim being a chattering fool, then grabbed Peer. "The Gaffer," he whispered, "is the King of Troll Fell. He lives up there under the crags, not far away. And naughty boys, why, he likes to tear them in pieces! So watch your step, laddie."

He pulled Peer into the mill and climbed the creaking ladder to the loft. Peer followed, overhung by his uncle's bulky bottom, and found himself standing on a dark, dusty platform, badly lit by one little louvred window high in the apex of the roof. In front of him in the middle of the floor sat two millstones, one above the other, cartwheel sized slabs of gritstone rimmed with iron.

"Power!" Baldur wheezed, slapping the upper millstone. "See how heavy that is? But finely balanced. What drives it? Water power. Ah, but who controls the water? Me, the miller!

"The brook *obeys* me, boy. I control it with my dam and my sluice gates. It turns my waterwheel and drives my millstones.

"It all comes down to power. The power of the water, the power of the stones and me. I'm the most powerful man in the valley." He gave the millstone another affectionate pat.

"See that?" he went on, straightening up. Peer banged his head on the corner of a big wooden box with sloping sides that hung suspended over the millstones from four thick ropes. "The hopper," his uncle grunted. "You fill it with barley, which runs out through this hole in the bottom, and shakes down through *this* hole in the upper millstone, which is called the runnerstone. Because it's the one that turns. Understand?"

To his own surprise, Peer did. He tried to show an interest. "Does everyone bring their corn here?" Perhaps Hilde had been exaggerating. Perhaps the mill was doing quite well.

But Uncle Baldur scowled. "They soon will," he growled, "now that blackguard Ralf Eiriksson has gone. Spreading lies...Telling everyone I put chalk in the flour – or dirt –" He shook his fist. "This will be the best mill in the valley. I'll put in another wheel – another pair of stones. They'll come to me from miles around. But first—" He stopped. "But first," he said in a different tone of voice, "get that hopper filled, boy. I haven't got all night!"

To lift the sack high enough to pour the barley into the hopper was quite beyond Peer. With a bad-tempered grunt, Uncle Baldur hefted the sack in his thick arms and let the glossy grain pour effortlessly into the hopper. Then he took Peer outside to open the sluice and start the wheel.

It was getting late. The sun had set and it was cold by the stream. Peer looked anxiously for Loki as he followed his uncle up to the dam. The millpond seemed more sinister than ever as darkness fell. A little breeze shivered the surface and the trees sighed sadly. He hoped with all his heart that Loki had kept away from this dark water.

Uncle Baldur showed Peer how to work the sluice gate. He stood on a narrow plank bridge and simply tugged the gate up. It slid up and down between grooves in two big timber posts. He banged in some wedges to keep it stuck in place. A rush of water boiled from under the gate, filling the air with thunder, and the great black waterwheel stirred into life. The mill machinery began to clack.

"You'll do that job next time," Uncle Baldur said. "And don't hang about here after dark. Or Granny Greenteeth will get you."

As if he cared, thought Peer. Aloud he asked, "Who *is* Granny Greenteeth?"

"She lives at the bottom of the pond," said Uncle Baldur briefly. "She likes to come out at night – the old hag. So watch yourself."

It was now almost quite dark. Peer looked over his shoulder as they walked back to the mill. What was that dark patch floating in the shadow of the willows? Weeds? Or the spreading hair of Granny Greenteeth rising from her slimy bed? A fish splashed, and ripples lapped against the bank... He hurried after his uncle. Something crashed through a nearby bramble bush and leaped on to the path. Peer's heart nearly stopped – then he saw what it was.

"Loki!" he gasped in relief. "You crazy dog!" Loki leaped and lashed his tail. Peer hugged him. "Come on," he said, and they ran into the yard together.

CHAPTER 6

Trolls from the Dovrefell

A MILE OR so further up the valley, Hilde was eating supper. Through mouthfuls, she told her family about meeting Peer, and the Grimsson brothers' threats.

"I knew there'd be trouble," Gudrun exclaimed. "Your father should never have gone."

"You could always give them the golden cup?" Hilde cocked an eyebrow at her mother.

"Over my dead body," said Gudrun promptly. "I never wanted the thing, but it's your father's pride and joy. They can't have it."

"I thought you'd say that. I'd better keep an eye on our sheep, then, hadn't I? In case the Grimssons steal them. I'll ride up to the Stonemeadow tomorrow."

"Oh no, you won't."

"Why not?" Hilde tossed back her hair, fancying herself as the family's gallant guardian, patrolling the hills. "Don't *you* think I ought to, Grandpa?"

"Well," began Eirik, working at a meaty crab claw with the point of his knife.

"I utterly forbid it," Gudrun interrupted. "She's just a girl. What could she do against those two ruffians and their savage dog? Off with you, Hilde, and milk the cow before it gets too dark."

Hilde picked up the milking bucket and stool and went, banging the door a little harder than necessary. But once she began climbing the steep pasture behind the farm, she felt better. The wide western sky was full of light. It was a perfect spring evening, very quiet, except for far-off sheep bleating, and the sounds of the cow and the pony tearing up grass.

Then she heard a new sound, the unmistakeable high-pitched rattle of milk squirting into a metal pan – accompanied by a weird growling hum like a very large bee. Goosebumps rose on her skin. She broke into a run and saw a small hairy troll squatting beside Bonny the cow, milking her into a copper pail.

"Oi!" shouted Hilde. The troll snatched up its pail and scampered up the hillside into the twilight. Hilde stood panting, hands on hips. She had to soothe and stroke the cow before Bonny would stand still. But the troll had milked her nearly dry, and Hilde went back to the house with no more than a cupful at the bottom of her pail. As she came to the door her mother called, "Bring the broom in with you, Hilde."

"What broom?" Hilde asked.

"Isn't it there?" Gudrun came out. "But I left it right by the door," she said, vexed. "I can't lay my hands on anything... Is that all the milk?" She was even more put out when she heard Hilde's tale.

"They probably stole the broom too," said Hilde. "You see, mother? It's not so easy to keep out of trouble."

"The varmints!" Eirik shook his head. "Worse than rats. They wouldn't be so bold if my son was here: no, they wouldn't come robbing us then!"

"They're becoming a perfect plague," said Gudrun.

"When I was a young fellow," said Eirik gloomily, "I could

have thrown anyone who so much as stepped on my shadow clean over the barn. No pack of trolls would have bothered me. Now I'm just a useless old man."

"Nonsense," Gudrun scolded him. "We need you very much, Eirik. We depend on you for – for wisdom, and advice."

"Advice! Women never listen to advice," scoffed Eirik, but he looked pleased.

"And stories! Tell us a story, Grandpa," little Sigrid piped up from the floor where she was playing with the kitten. Eirik tugged her plait with his gnarled old hand.

"A story, missy? What is it to be about?"

"Trolls!" said her brother, Sigurd. The twins scrambled up and pressed close to Eirik's knees.

"Let me think," Eirik began. "Let me see. How about a story from a place far to the north, the wild mountains of the Dovrefell, where there are even more trolls than here? And some of them giants, by what I've heard!"

"Giants?" Sigurd's eyes grew wide.

Eirik nodded. "Trolls come all sizes; and the one in this story was a big one, a little taller than a man. She was pretty, I daresay—"

"A pretty troll!" Sigrid interrupted, laughing.

"Yes, she had yellow hair and a nice long tail that wagged when she was happy. And she married a young farmer and wagged her tail at the wedding."

Gudrun and Hilde were laughing now.

"Well, this young farmer's friends and neighbours were disgusted. They thought he was out of his mind to go marrying a troll. They wouldn't talk to his bride, or visit her. She sat by herself in her nice new house and was very lonely."

"Poor troll," said Sigrid.

"Huh," said Sigurd. "I think he was stupid to marry a troll."

"See what happened," said Eirik. "One day, her father paid her a visit. He was a grim old troll from under the Dovrefell, and when he found his daughter sitting crying he said, '*What's all this?*'" Eirik deepened his voice to a growl. "'If your husband isn't kind to you, I'll tear his arms and legs off!'

"'It's the neighbours,' said the troll bride. 'They won't have anything to do with me, and I'm so-o-o lonely!'

"'Come with me,' said her father, rolling up his sleeves, 'and we'll have a little game of catch.'

"The grim old troll went stamping round the village chasing people out of their houses, and when he got hold of them he threw them right over the Hall roof. And his daughter rushed around the other side and caught each one of them and put them back on their feet.

"When everyone in the village had been thrown over the Hall roof, the old troll shouted, 'You'd better start being very nice to my daughter. Because if not,' he glared, 'if not, I'll come back and play with you again – only, this time, my daughter will throw, and *I* will catch!'"

Sigrid looked puzzled. "I don't understand," she began.

"Do you think the old troll would really have caught them?" Hilde asked.

"Oh!" Sigrid's face cleared. "He would have let them fall!"

"Or eaten them up," said Sigurd with relish.

Eirik nodded. "So after that you'd never believe how polite the neighbours were. They called to see her every day and brought flowers and cakes and baskets of eggs. She was as happy as the day was long, and wagged her tail merrily. And that's a story from the Dovrefell!" He smiled and stopped.

"Bedtime," said Gudrun. As the twins hugged their grandfather and said goodnight, Hilde felt sudden sadness wash over her. *If only Pa were here*, she thought. *But at least he's alive. Not like Peer Ulfsson's father. Poor Peer, he must hate living at the mill. I wonder what he's doing right now?*

Peer was eating his frugal supper. His uncles had given him some stale bread, a raw onion, a small piece of dry cheese and the end of a rancid sausage, and gone off somewhere taking Grendel with them, leaving Peer to mind the mill alone – except for Loki, who lay asleep by the fire...

The mill was noisily alive. Everything vibrated. The waterwheel thumped like a dark heart beating. The machinery clacked. Old dust trickled down the walls. Up in the loft, finely ground meal was snowing from the rim of the millstones and piling up on a wooden platform. Peer's job was to climb the ladder from time to time and sweep it into sacks. It was dark up there, full of spooky shadows and old junk: worm-eaten cogwheels with half the teeth missing, a worn old millstone propped against the wall.

Peer gave the sausage to Loki and looked about, still hungry. The table was cluttered with dirty dishes, bacon rinds and crusts. On the floor by the fire his uncles had left a bowl full of cold, congealed groute, but it did not look very appetising.

I suppose that's for the Nis, anyway, thought Peer. *Even Grendel hasn't touched it.*

He prowled round the room. His uncles hadn't said how late they'd be. He suspected they had gone out drinking. It was time to try and find where they had hidden his father's money.

He lifted the lids of several wooden bins, built on either

side of the ladder to the loft. Most were empty except for a few dusty grains at the bottom. One held a tangle of old leather harness. And one would not open. The lid was secured with an iron padlock. Peer rattled it. By the fire, Loki raised his head inquiringly. "I'm sure this is the one, Loki!" Peer told him. But knowing that did not help very much.

Reluctantly he climbed the rickety ladder to the grinding loft. A soft ring of flour encircled the millstones. Peer shovelled it into the waiting sack. He peeped into the hopper, which was getting low, and refilled it from a half-full sack of barley, which he could just lift. Pleased with himself, he was about to climb back down, when Loki leaped from his place by the fire and burst out barking, hackles up. Peer looked over the edge of the loft in alarm. Were his uncles coming back? Was it thieves?

Loki pranced, growling, then jumped and snapped at something above his head. He backed a few steps and barked some more, watching the rafters.

Peer slid down the ladder. "Loki, shut up! It's only a rat." And he sat on the dirty rush mat and reached out his hands to the fire. Slowly his eyes closed. His head nodded forwards. But Loki barked again, and he sat up with a jerk.

"Stop it!" he complained. Loki flung him an apologetic glance but continued to stand braced and staring upwards. Peer's head drooped again, but as his eyelids closed he heard a familiar voice. "See my leg?" it giggled. There was another flurry of barks from Loki, who jumped about as if on springs.

Peer's eyes flew wide. By the flickering firelight he saw something sitting on one of the cross beams. A spindly little leg covered in a worn grey stocking dangled temptingly just over Loki's head.

"See my little leg?" teased the voice again. Loki leaped again in frustrated frenzy.

"It's only the Nis, silly!" Peer got up and grabbed his pet, closing his hand around Loki's muzzle to keep his mouth shut. "Now be quiet." He stared up into the beams. The leg had been withdrawn. He could just see a dim shape sitting with its arms wrapped round its knees. "Hello!" he said.

"You spoiled the fun," the Nis sulked.

"I'm sorry."

The Nis shuffled round on the beam till it had its back turned.

"How's the groute this evening? Have they given you any butter?" asked Peer cunningly. The Nis came to life at once.

"I doesn't know, Peer Ulfsson. Has they? Let's see."

It ran briskly along the beam and down the wall like a big spider. Peer watched, delighted. It was a little grey, whiskery thing with big hands and long knobbly fingers. Its ragged grey clothing seemed part of it, but it wore a little red cap on its head. Loki backed away grumbling.

The Nis scampered to the bowl of groute and lifted it. "Cold!" it muttered. "Cold as their cruel hearts, and lumpy, too!" It stirred the bowl, scooping up the groute in messy splodges, then sat distastefully licking its fingers.

"Was there any butter?" asked Peer. The Nis shook its head.

"Now for the housework!" it said suddenly. "I has to do the housework, Peer Ulfsson. As long as they feeds me, I has to do the work. But I doesn't have to do it well. See me!"

The little creature seized a broom bigger than itself and went leaping about the room like a grasshopper, sweeping up great clouds of floury dust. Sneezing, it cleared the dishes from the table and hid the bones under Uncle Baldur's pillow.

It polished the plates with one of Uncle Grim's shirts, and shook the stale crusts and crumbs into his best boots. The pieces of bacon rind it dropped in front of Loki, who ate them suspiciously. Finally it put three wooden spoons and the frying pan tidily away under Uncle Grim's mattress.

"Well done," said Peer, laughing. "Do you always tidy up like that? Won't they be furious?"

"What can they do?" asked the Nis. "I doesn't want much, Peer Ulfsson. Only a bit of butter in my groute. Or a drop of honey to keep me sweet." Loki had fallen asleep. The Nis began sneaking up on him with the obvious intention of pulling his tail.

"Don't do that," Peer said. "Tell me about my uncles. I'm sure you know all about them. Where have they gone tonight?"

"To the Stonemeadow. Ssh!" The Nis laid a long finger to its lips and tiptoed closer to Loki.

"Oh, leave him alone! The Stonemeadow? Where's that?"

The Nis gave up. "High up on Troll Fell!" it snapped.

"I thought they'd gone drinking. What are they doing there?"

The Nis looked at him out of the corner of one eye.

"Talking to trolls? Please tell me," Peer begged. "I heard them say something about trolls, and taking me to the – to the Gaffer, the King of the Trolls. Is that right? And something about a wedding? Do you know anything? Can you help me?"

The Nis ran into the corner where the big scales hung, and jumped into one of the pans, which hardly moved. It sat there bouncing gently and would not look round.

Peer saw he had gone about things the wrong way.

"Nis," he called quietly, "I think you're very clever."

The Nis sniffed.

"I know a girl who lives on a farm near here. She has lots of butter. Shall I ask her to give me a big lump all for you?"

The Nis twitched and the scales swayed.

"Please be my friend, Nis, and I'll be yours." Peer stopped as his voice shook. He so badly wanted a friend.

The Nis relented. It sat cross-legged in the pan and leaned on the chains to make the scales swing. "What does you want to know, Peer Ulfsson?"

Peer didn't know where to start. "Well – what's this wedding?"

"Oh!" The Nis got very excited. "A very big wedding indeed! At midwinter, the Gaffer, the old King of Troll Fell, will marry his son to – guess who?"

"I can't guess," said Peer.

"Guess! Guess!" the Nis insisted.

"I can't," Peer laughed. "Tell me!"

The Nis paused, and said in a hushed voice, "To the King of the Dovrefell's daughter!" It sat back.

It meant something to Peer after all. Even he had heard of the trolls of the Dovrefell, the wild mountain range to the north. "That's an important match?" he suggested.

The Nis nodded. "Everyone is going, Peer Ulfsson. They say the bride is very beautiful. There will be such a feast!" It wriggled with delight and cracked its knuckles.

"Are you going?"

The Nis's face fell. "I doesn't know," it admitted. "Food and drink, as much as you can hold, music and dancing, and the hill raised up on red pillars – but they hasn't invited poor Nithing yet."

"Oh, there's plenty of time, if it's not till midwinter. But what has the troll wedding got to do with Uncle Baldur and

Uncle Grim? What are they up to on Troll Fell in the middle of the night?"

"Middle of the night is daytime for trolls," the Nis pointed out scornfully. "If Grimssons go knocking on the troll gate at noon, what will they hear? Snores."

"I see that. But what do they want with the trolls at all?"

The Nis was getting bored and fidgety. "Treasure," it yawned, showing a pink tongue and sharp little teeth like a kitten's.

"Troll gold? Yes, but why," said Peer, struggling to make sense of it, "why would the trolls give them any? I don't understand."

With a loud squeak, the scales tipped as the Nis leaped into the rafters like a squirrel. Heavy feet sounded at the door. In tramped Uncle Baldur and Uncle Grim, stamping mud from their boots, cold night air pouring from them like water. They looked sour and displeased. Grendel loped behind them, and Loki nipped quickly outside.

Peer scrambled up. Uncle Baldur took him by the ear, led him to the door and booted him out. "Make yourself useful, you idle young layabout. I want the wheel stopped now."

"But I don't know how," Peer called at the closing door.

Uncle Baldur paused with the door a couple of inches open. "Go and lower the sluicegate, of course. And then get off to the barn. Don't come knocking and disturbing us – it's late!"

And the door slammed shut.

CHAPTER 7

Granny Greenteeth

IT WAS PAST midnight. A star fell over the barn roof. Peer shivered, wrapping his arms across his chest.

"They didn't look too happy, did they?" he muttered to Loki. "Perhaps their interview with the King of Troll Fell didn't go too well. No need to take it out on us, though. Lower the sluicegate? At this hour?"

Loki whined softly. Peer didn't know which was scarier, to disobey Uncle Baldur or go up near that dark millpond by himself.

"Into the barn with you," he told Loki, dragging him there by the collar. "Sit. Stay! I'm not risking you." Loki's eyes gleamed in the dark and again he whined gently.

Peer crossed the yard and turned on to the wooden bridge. The mill clacked steadily. The wheel churned, chopping the water with dripping blades that glinted in the starlight. Peer leaned on the rail, trying to gather courage to go on.

A black shadow moved at the corner of his eye. He whipped around, heart beating wildly. But it was only a woman plodding up the road, dressed in dark clothes with a scarf over her head. She was using a stick to help herself along.

She saw him and stopped. Realising that she too might be nervous, Peer called out softly. "It's all right. I'm the – the millers' boy. Only the millers' boy."

"The millers' boy!" repeated the woman. "And what is the millers' boy doing out here so late?"

"I have to close the sluicegate," said Peer.

"Ah!" The woman looked at him. It was too dark to see her face properly, but her eyes glittered in the starlight. "So late at night, that's a job for the miller himself. He shouldn't be sending a boy out. They say Granny Greenteeth lives in the millpond. Aren't you afraid of her?"

"A bit," Peer confessed, "but if I don't go my uncles will be angry."

"And you're more afraid of them." The woman nodded angrily. "Ah, Baldur Grimsson, Grim Grimsson, I'd make you sorry if I had my way!" She shook her finger at the lightless mill before turning to Peer again. "I'll come along with you, my son, if you like."

Peer hesitated. Something about the old woman made him shiver, but his father had taught him to honour old people, and he didn't know how to refuse. And it was true he would feel braver with company, though the path to the sluice seemed no place for an old lady to be hobbling along at night. He made her a stiff little bow and offered her his arm. She took it with a chuckle and a cough.

"Quite the young lord! You didn't learn your manners from the Grimssons. What's your name, boy?"

"Peer Ulfsson – ma'am." Peer winced as her cold claw dug into his arm. She was surprisingly smelly too, now he was close to her. Her clothes must be damp, mouldy, or something.

But he was glad she was there. As they passed the millrace, he knew he would have been terrified by himself. The threshing wheel and racing water made him dizzy; there was a cold draught fanned by the wheel, and a smell of wet stone and black slime. He tripped, and the old woman steadied him, hugging his arm to her side. She felt strong, and cold.

At the edge of the millpond she released his arm so he could step on to the narrow walkway above the sluice. The pond was so black he could not see where the surface lay. If only there was a guardrail! He shuffled out and grabbed the handle of the sluicegate, remembering it acted like a simple shutter. He leaned his weight on it, driving the gate down against the pressure of the water. The wheel slowed, its great vanes dripping. The rattle and grumble of the mill faltered and ceased. Only the sound of the water was left, tumbling over the weir.

"Well done," said the old woman. She stretched out a hand to help Peer off the bridge. He took it and then let go with a cry. It was clammy – and wet – and webbed.

The late moon was rising. She stood quietly at the end of the plank, leaning on her stick. Her long skirt and cloak weren't damp but wet – soaking wet. How had she got so wet? She pulled her scarf away from her head in fronds of trailing weed. She smiled. Even in the moonlight he could see her teeth were sharp points. Peer's hand shook on the sluice handle. He had walked here with Granny Greenteeth herself!

The woman chuckled, like the brook gurgling. "Yesss... I like to take a stroll on a fine evening. Poor boy, didn't you know me? Shall I tell you how?" She leaned towards him. "Watch for the sign of the river," she whispered. "A dripping hem or sleeve. Wet footprints on the doorstep."

Peer nodded, dry-mouthed. Granny Greenteeth drew back, as if satisfied that she had scared him. "I hate the miller," she hissed. "Oh, how I hate him, thinking he owns my water, boasting about his mill. Now I will punish him by taking you."

Peer clung to the post of the sluice. "But he doesn't care anything about me. Neither of them does. The only thing they care about is their dog, Grendel. Please!"

"Ssso?" Granny Greenteeth paused. Peer waited, shivering. At last she smiled, showing dark triangular teeth. "Then I shall send that dog, Grendel, with an apple in his mouth, as a dish for my friend the Dovreking's daughter, at her midwinter wedding. But as for you! Don't you know the miller has plans for you?"

"Plans?" Peer's heart thudded.

Granny Greenteeth leaned both hands on her stick, like the old woman he had supposed her to be. "We'll have a little gossip, shall we? I hear it all, you know. Every stream on Troll Fell runs into my river!

"After the old miller died – bad riddance to him! – the two young 'uns knew where the troll gate was. And they wouldn't let it alone. Knocking and banging, day after day! Hoping to get at the gold, weren't they? Even tried bribes. Imagine! They left fine white bread there, and trout stolen from my water. Ah! Yet they never gave me anything." Granny Greenteeth worked her mouth as though chewing on something bitter. She spat.

"And this went on and on, didn't it? And at last the Troll King got tired of all this hammering and shouting outside his gate. Not seemly was it?

"So to get rid of them he thinks up something difficult. He sends word: *My eldest son will be married at midwinter. He wishes to present his bride with a slave boy, as a betrothal gift. Bring me a slave boy, and you shall have your gold.*"

Granny Greenteeth nodded spitefully at Peer. "And that's where you come in, my son. Your precious uncles – your flesh and blood – will sell you to the trolls."

Peer's heart turned to ice.

"So now you'll come with me, won't you?" Granny Greenteeth coaxed. "You'll help old Granny. Baldur Grimsson wants that gold to build a bigger mill. I'd drown him sooner! But he never puts a foot wrong. He knows I'm after him."

"Let me go," Peer croaked. "Please…"

"Ah, but where?" she cried. "Come to me, Peer, come to me." She stretched out her arms to him and her voice became a low musical murmur like the brook in summer. "I'll take you – I'll love you – I'll look after you. Who else will? I'll give you an everlasting bed. Come down under the water and rest. Ressst your weary bones."

White mist rose from the millpond, flowing in soft wreaths over the plank bridge and swirling gently around Peer's knees. His teeth chattered and his head swam. How easy it would be to let go, to fall into the soft mist. No one would grieve. All for the best, maybe.

"All for the bessst," Granny Greenteeth agreed.

Far away a dog barked, sharp and anxious. Peer blinked awake. "No!" He looked at the old woman. "Loki loves me," he said thickly. "No, I won't!"

In a whisper of wind, the mist blew away into the willows.

Granny Greenteeth nodded. "You're stronger than you look, Peer Ulfsson. Not this time, then," she said softly. "But I'll wait. One day you'll call to me. And I'll be listening. I'll come!"

She jerked, twice, threw her stick away and fell sideways. Her cloak twisted and clung to her body; she lay on the ground kicking – no, flapping: an immense eel in gleaming loops as thick as Peer's leg. It raised a head with narrow glinting eyes and snapped its trap-like jaws before slithering over the bank into the pond. The black water closed over it in silent ripples.

Peer leaped off the plank. He raced down the path, drummed across the wooden bridge, hurled himself into the barn, dragged the door shut behind him and leaped into the straw. He grabbed Loki and hugged him.

"If you hadn't barked, Loki – oh!" Loki licked his face. At last Peer stopped shaking. "I got away. But what shall I do? They're going to sell me under the hill. Under the hill!"

Suddenly he was hot with anger. The Grimssons had sold his home, taken his money and treated him worse than their dog – and now they were going to sell him? Trade their own nephew for troll gold?

"We'll see about that!" he exclaimed to the dark barn. The oxen munched indifferently. The hens, roosting in the beams, clucked in disapproval and irritably ruffled their feathers. Peer no longer thought of them as his hens. They had transferred their loyalty to the black cockerel, who plainly despised him. He hugged Loki again.

"Featherbrains! Traitors!" he called.

The hens squawked in shocked surprise. For a moment, Peer wondered if they had understood. But it was only the Nis, in high spirits, tipping them off their comfortable perches. He could hear it giggling. Loki's hackles bristled under his hand. Hen after hen fell clumsily from the rafters and ran about in the straw. One ran right over him, digging its hard claws into his stomach.

"Stop it," he called.

The Nis pranced about in the beams, kicking down dust and feathers. "News!" it carolled.

"I don't care," Peer groaned. "All right, what news?"

"News from Troll Fell!" said the Nis slyly.

"All right, I'm interested – go *on*!"

The Nis hopped. "The Gaffer's son will marry the King of the Dovrefell's daughter," it said.

"You told me that already."

"But now there's more, Peer Ulfsson. Much more! I hear your uncles saying that now…" it took a deep breath, "the King of the Dovrefell's son will marry the Gaffer's daughter!"

Peer tried to work this out. "Instead?"

"No!" the Nis said impatiently. "As well!"

"Ah. So it will be a double wedding?"

The Nis nodded in ecstasy. "Even bigger wedding! Even bigger feast!"

Peer rubbed his eyes. He understood that the Gaffer of Troll Fell had pulled off an important alliance for his son and daughter, but he didn't see why he should care. Still, one thing puzzled him. "Why would it bother the Grimssons, Nis? Why did they look so cross?"

The Nis had gone skipping off over the stalls. It answered from the other side of the barn. "Now they has to find a girl as well as a boy."

"What!" Peer sat up.

"A girl to serve the Prince as well as a boy for the Princess," explained the Nis. "Or the King of the Dovre will be offended."

"You mean you knew all the time that Baldur wants to sell me to the trolls?" Peer gasped. "And you didn't tell me?"

The Nis stopped scampering about. "Doesn't you want to serve the trolls?" it asked, amazed.

"No!"

"Why not?"

Peer struggled to reply. "I'm a human," he said at last. "I can't work for trolls."

"I'm a Nis," said the Nis huffily, "and I works for humans."

"Sorry," said Peer, a little ashamed. "But you can't *like* working for Uncle Baldur and Uncle Grim."

"No, because of cold groute with no butter," the Nis agreed. "But for them that gives me hot, sweet groute with a big lump of butter, or a bowl of cream – for them, Peer Ulfsson, I works willingly." It sighed.

"It'd take more than a bowl of hot porridge to get me working for the trolls," muttered Peer. "Under the mountain? In the dark?" He shuddered.

"Under the hill is rich and splendid!" the Nis insisted.

"I'm sorry, Nis, it doesn't appeal to me." Peer was overcome by an enormous yawn. "So you're saying the trolls want a girl as well as a boy, or the deal's off? Good news for me. Lucky I don't have a sister." He lay back in the straw. Moonlight was blending into dawn. "I'm so tired." He yawned again. "I wonder what my uncles will do now...?"

"They has to find a girl, of course," the Nis replied – but Peer was already asleep.

The black cockerel woke him with a falsetto shriek of "cock-a-doodle-doo!" right beside his ear. Peer sat up with a gasp. The cockerel gave him a malicious glance and stalked away, tail feathers quivering.

"I'll tell the Nis to pull them out," Peer threatened, pushing the barn door open. As the morning sunlight streamed in, he remembered everything he had learned.

If the trolls want a girl as well as a boy, I'm safe, he thought. *Uncle Baldur and Uncle Grim don't have a niece, or any female relations. Did they even know any girls*?

His eyes suddenly widened in horror.

Hilde was a girl!

They couldn't. They wouldn't.

Could they?

No! thought Peer. *But – all the same – I've got to warn her!*

CHAPTER 8

A Day Out

But Peer did not see Hilde again for a long time. Weeks passed. White windflowers sprang up in the birchwoods on the flanks of Troll Fell; the ploughed field above the mill sprouted with green barley, and still Hilde did not come riding down to the village, and Peer was kept far too busy to go walking up the valley to find her. He woke each morning sore and tired, and fell asleep at the end of each long day half dead with exhaustion.

One fine afternoon Hilde decided to take her little brother and sister down to the sea.

It was washday. Gudrun and Hilde had carried nearly every piece of clothing in the house to a place where a waterfall tumbled into a little pool. They had kilted up their skirts and trodden the clothes down till their legs were blue and aching. Bringing the dripping load back to the farm they found that Eirik, sitting outside the door in the sunshine, had nodded off. Unwatched, Sigurd and Sigrid had taken it into their heads to try riding the cow. They had untied her picket rope, scrambled on her bony back and allowed her to amble down the steep little valley where the wild garlic grew. She had gorged herself on the pungent leaves and flowers.

"The milk will taste of garlic for a week!" Gudrun scolded.

"We can make cheese," suggested Hilde. "Ma, you need a rest. Let me get the children out of your way. We'll take the pony and go down to the fjord, and you can sit in the sun and spin."

"That would be lovely," Gudrun agreed thankfully.

As Hilde led the pony downhill through the wood, the white trunks of the birch trees shone as if newly scoured and the brook flashed in the sunlight. Sigrid sang one song, Hilde another. Sigurd pounded the pony with his heels to make it trot. On leaving the woods the path slanted across the fields to the wooden bridge. The mill was working, clattering busily, and Hilde looked eagerly for Peer.

As it happened, Peer saw her first. He was cleaning the pigsty, a lean-to shed at the back of the mill on the other side of the millpond. Stripped to the waist, his ragged trousers rolled up, Peer shovelled out mud and smelly straw and cabbage stalks, while Bristles the boar basked against the wall, his hairy sides heaving. Resting for a moment to wipe sweat from his eyes, Peer saw Hilde and the children coming out of the woods. He almost ducked out of sight. Why did Hilde always have to see him this way, covered in dirt? But there were things he needed to tell her. He climbed out of the sty and waved.

Hilde waved back. "Hello! We're going to the sea. Want to come?"

To the sea! Suddenly Peer didn't care what his uncles did or said. A sunny afternoon with Hilde would be worth almost anything that could happen afterwards. He threw down his shovel. "I'll catch you up," he called, and Loki, who had been lying in gloomy boredom with his nose between his paws, jumped up wagging his tail.

Peer ran around the back of the barn, skirting a bank of green stinging nettles, and crept through the bushes till he was out of sight of the mill. He emerged on the path breathless, and fell into step with Hilde.

"Good for you!" she greeted him. "I hope you won't get into trouble."

"Oh, I will," said Peer grimly. His face hardened. "I just don't care any more."

Hilde glanced at him. He was burned brown from working in the sun with his shirt off. He was covered with mud, and his trousers were nothing but rags. He looked thinner, taller and older. And Loki's coat was rough, and his ribs showed.

"Oh!" she said, shocked.

Peer scowled, as though daring her to comment. "Loki doesn't get enough to eat," he said curtly. "Grendel gets it all."

Hilde took the hint and changed the subject. "Meet the mischief-makers," she said cheerfully. "My little brother Sigurd and my little sister Sigrid. Say hello to him, brats!"

"Hello," said Peer, smiling. The two little children looked very alike, with pale fair hair and blue eyes. "Are you twins, by any chance?"

They nodded. "But I came first," boasted Sigrid. "So Sigurd has to do what I say!"

"I do not!" Sigurd pulled her hair. They fell off the pony and wrestled in the road. Hilde and Peer dragged them apart. "Behave!" Hilde threatened. "Or Peer won't come with us."

"No, I'm coming all right," said Peer. "I want to swim."

Trollsvik was tiny compared to Hammerhaven, just seven or eight houses with streams of white smoke rising from their grassy roofs. A gang of dogs rushed up to sniff at Loki who instantly made five new friends. A woman came out from her door and threw a pail of water over her vegetable patch.

Seeing Hilde she called out, asking how her mother was and whether they'd heard from Ralf. Peer stood shyly apart while they talked, but Hilde dragged his arm.

"This is Kersten, Bjørn the fisherman's wife. This is Peer Ulfsson, Kersten, who has come to live at the mill." Kersten smiled; she was very pretty, with long dark hair and green eyes, but Peer was embarrassed because he was so dirty, and glad when the conversation ended and she went back inside. Hilde tethered the pony, and together they crossed some low grassy dunes to the shore.

The wide fjord sparkled. Baby waves lifted themselves an inch or two and turned over with a clear splash on a narrow beach where every pebble seemed a different colour. A couple of faerings, narrow fishing boats, lay on the shingle. The twins squealed with delight and ran to pick up shells and seaweed. Peer breathed deep and gazed at the bright water and high mountains.

"I'm going in," he said happily.

"It'll be cold," Hilde warned him.

"Who cares?" He ran into the water with a whoop. "You're right! It's freezing!"

Loki dashed up and down, barking at the waves in case they attacked his master. In a few moments Peer came wading out. "I'm clean," he said through chattering teeth, "but I can't stay in any longer. Let's find a nice sunny boulder and sit down. There's something I need to tell you."

Wrapped in an old cloak which Hilde had brought to sit on, and munching bread and cheese which she had packed, Peer told Hilde about the flighty little Nis, and how he had promised to bring it some butter. He told about his meeting with Granny Greenteeth, and how she had revealed his uncles' plan to sell Peer to the trolls.

Hilde was horrified. "They couldn't!"

"Oh yes, they could. And that's not all. The Nis found out that now it's to be a double wedding. The old Gaffer's son and daughter," he explained carefully, "are marrying the Dovreking's daughter and son."

"Well?" asked Hilde, as he stopped.

"And it seems my uncles were very angry, because the Gaffer told them that the deal was off unless they could bring him a girl as well as a boy. You see, if he gives the Dovre prince a servant, he has to give the Dovre princess a maid."

"So no gold for the Grimssons without a girl?" Hilde laughed in relief. "Then you're safe."

"I don't know," said Peer softly. "I think they're going to find a girl. I think you ought to be very careful, Hilde."

Hilde whistled. There was silence, except for the lapping of waves and the cries of gulls.

"So Troll Fell wants to impress the Dovrefell," she said.

"With two human wedding presents," Peer nodded.

"It's unusual. I wonder what a troll servant has to do?"

"I don't want to find out. I couldn't bear—" Peer bit off his words. No need for Hilde to know how he dreaded being shut up in the dark.

Hilde began to speak, but was interrupted by excited shouts from Sigurd and Sigrid, who were playing around the boats. "Look! Look!" Another small boat was dancing in from the sea. Hilde jumped up, shading her eyes.

"That's Bjørn's faering. Look – can you see the seal following behind him?"

Squinting, Peer made out a dark dot in the waves.

"There's always a seal or two following Bjørn," Hilde told him. "People say they drive the herring to him. Some people even say that his wife Kersten was a seal woman, but my pa doesn't think that's true. Still, Bjørn and his brother Arne know more stories about the sea than anyone else. I wonder where Arne is? I can't see him."

Together they ran to help pull the boat up the beach. Bjørn was a short, stocky fellow with a strong friendly face, blue eyes, and untidy hair falling over his shoulders.

"Hello Hilde, my lass, who's your friend? Hello sprats," he said to Sigurd and Sigrid.

"Hello Bjørn. This is Peer Ulfsson, who now lives at the mill."

Bjørn put out a calloused hand and Peer took it, liking him already. "The mill, eh?" was all he said, but his smile was sympathetic.

"Where's Arne?" asked Hilde.

"Haven't you heard?" Bjørn scratched his head. "He's gone off south, and it's your doing, Hilde, you and your father between you. He went on so much about how he wished he could have sailed on that blessed longship, that in the end I told him to go after it. 'Take your boat,' I said. 'Ten to one you'll catch them up, and even if you don't, you'll find another one to join. It's the sailing season.' So off he went. He'll be back before winter." He smiled at Hilde's disappointed face. "But what's this? A holiday? Light a fire, and I'll join you. We can cook some fish."

Sigrid and Sigurd ran to collect armfuls of driftwood and dry seaweed. When they had assembled a tangled pile, Bjørn struck sparks from his strike-a-light, and a fire was soon blazing. The fish were delicious. They all burned their fingers, but it was worth it. Even Loki gobbled his fill of the rich white meat and flame-blackened skins, and lay contentedly afterwards, licking his paws.

"Tell us a story," begged Sigrid.

Bjørn lay on his back with his arms behind his head, soaking up the sunshine. "What sort of story?"

"A scary one!" said Sigurd.

Bjørn looked sideways under his lashes. And he told them about the draug, the phantom fisherman who sails the seas in half a boat and can be heard wailing in the storm winds when someone is about to drown. "Have *you* ever heard him?" breathed Sigurd. But Bjørn refused to say.

A cloud passed over the sun and a chill breeze sprang up. Hilde rubbed her arms and shivered. "I wish you hadn't told that story," she said to Bjørn, half-laughing. "I shall think about it now, and worry. I wish…" But she didn't finish. "We'd better go. Thank you for the fish, Bjørn."

"You're welcome," said Bjørn. He tousled the little ones' heads, patted Hilde on the shoulder and clapped Peer on the back. "Good luck, friend!" he said.

"Thanks, I'm going to need it," said Peer ruefully. He didn't like to think what his uncles would do to him when he got back.

CHAPTER 9

More Trouble at the Mill

HILDE WAS UNCHARACTERISTICALLY quiet as they led the pony away from the village. "What's the matter?" Peer asked at last.

"Nothing." Hilde hesitated. "To tell you the truth," she admitted, "I know it's silly, but when Bjørn told that story I started thinking about Pa. I'm not worried! I'm just—"

"Worried!" Peer finished. "But don't be, Hilde. I'm sure he's all right."

"I know," she agreed, still rather glum. "But nothing's really gone right since he left. And the trolls – besides what you told me - they're such a nuisance. They're round the house every night, stealing and spoiling things."

"A pity your father didn't know that before he left," offered Peer.

"He did know," said Hilde. "I mean, it's got worse, but he did know."

"Ah." Peer paused, and Hilde imagined him thinking, *Ralf knew, and he left all the same? What kind of a father is that?* She bit her lip. Peer gave her a sideways look and suddenly squeezed her hand.

"You're just missing him," he said gruffly. "I know how it feels."

Hilde smeared a hand across her eyes. "I'm not crying, I

never cry. Don't tell the twins." She looked back at Sigurd and Sigrid, coming along behind with Loki, teasing him with a slippery ribbon of seaweed. "At least they're having fun."

"And Loki and I got something to eat today," said Peer. "I don't suppose we'll get much supper tonight. Not that we ever do."

Hilde flashed him a glance, opened her mouth, sighed, and shut it again. They plodded on up the track, the pony clopping beside Hilde with its neck low. "I wish you could live with us," Hilde muttered at last.

"Thanks," said Peer sadly, "but it wouldn't work. They'd only come and get me."

Hilde stopped suddenly. "Yes – they would *now*. But Pa will be home by midwinter. Of course!" She danced in excitement. "Pa won't let them sell you to the trolls. You can stay with us and be perfectly safe. He'll be home long before then!"

Peer lifted his head. "Really? Would your father really take me in?"

"I know he would." Hilde assured him. "Loki too. Don't worry any more, Peer."

Peer drew a deep breath. He could hardly believe the problem had been solved so easily. Hilde beamed at him and they talked cheerfully as they went on up the path. By now the little ones were straggling.

"I'm tired," Sigurd complained. "My feet ache."

"Get on the pony," said Hilde, lifting him up.

"I'm tired too," wailed Sigrid.

Peer felt strong and capable. "I'll give you a ride!" he said, bending down, and Sigrid gleefully scrambled on to his back. She was very light. He bounded up the track, bumping to make her laugh, till they came in sight of the mill. A figure like a dark stone tower stood at the entrance to the yard, glaring down the road.

Heart thudding, mouth dry, Peer uncurled Sigrid's warm little hands from their stranglehold around his neck and lowered her gently to the ground.

"I'm for it," he whispered to Hilde. "Better get out while you can."

"Boy!" Uncle Baldur's voice cracked, shooting into a scream. "Come here AT ONCE!"

"Who is that nasty man?" asked Sigrid in a high, alarmed little voice.

"The miller," said Hilde crisply. "Come here, Sigrid."

"Go *home*," said Peer distractedly. "Go on, Hilde – go!"

He went warily forwards. Behind him Sigrid was asking piercingly, "Why is the nasty man angry with Peer?"

"Just *wait* till I get my hands on you," Uncle Baldur shrieked. "Corn to grind and work to do, and you run off to *play*?" He lunged, and Peer instinctively dodged him. Even madder, Uncle Baldur grabbed again, got Peer by the wrist and twisted his arm behind his back. Peer gasped.

"Wastrel!" Uncle Baldur shook him. Through the drumming blood in his ears Peer heard Loki barking, Hilde shouting, "Let go of him!" and above it all little Sigrid screaming, "I don't like that nasty man! I hate him!"

"Hilde!" he yelled, struggling to see through a red flood of shame. Uncle Baldur had him doubled over now, and was raining blows on him. And Hilde was witnessing it all! "Hilde, for goodness' sake, *get those kids away from here!*"

The noise attracted Uncle Grim. He stood watching for a moment and then roared, "Let go of 'im, Baldur. Let 'im go!"

Uncle Baldur stopped in astonishment. He looked at his

brother. Grim simply jerked his head towards Hilde, who was hurriedly lifting the shrieking twins on to the pony. Then he turned and walked away.

"Ha." Uncle Baldur let Peer go. Peer fell to the ground. Baldur's little piggy eyes twinkled, dark and calculating. He scratched his beard.

"Maybe I was hasty," he puffed. "A boy has to have friends, eh? I like a lad of spirit. Don't you be scared of me, my dear," he cooed to Hilde, who was dragging the pony towards the bridge. "This lad of mine is the apple of my eye. He is! I used to play truant myself, once, and my dear old dad used to beat me for it. Made me the man I am today!"

"Goodbye," said Hilde quickly to Peer.

"Boys will be boys," went on Uncle Baldur, following her around the end of the building. "Don't go yet! How about a bite to eat, or a drink of, er – a drink of – of buttermilk?" He stopped, watching as Hilde urged the pony across the bridge and uphill towards the wood.

"Come again to play with the boy!" he shouted after her. "Bring the kiddies. Don't be shy!" Sigurd and Sigrid were still crying. Uncle Baldur stood staring after them until they disappeared into the trees. At last he turned on his heel and strode back to the yard.

"I'm a fair man, see," he said to Peer, showing his teeth. "You deserve a bit of fun. Bring your friends here any time you like. Make sure you tell them. Any time! Show them how the mill works. They'll like that."

"Yes, Uncle." Peer was determined to do no such thing. Baldur opened his mouth as if to say something more, and changed his mind. He swung away, aiming a kick at Loki, who jumped deftly aside.

⊗

Peer lay in the straw that night, wrapped in the worn old cloak Hilde had given him. Though his bruises hurt, he didn't mind them, because now he had a future. At midwinter – or sooner, as soon as Ralf Eiriksson came home – he and Loki would escape up the valley.

Ralf would protect them. Secretly Peer hoped that Ralf would let him stay. Surely a boy could help on the farm? Peer wouldn't eat much. He would train Loki to herd sheep. As for his uncles – well, perhaps once their plan had failed, they would not care enough to try and recapture him.

He pulled the cloak over his head and fell asleep. But dark water came spilling into his dreams. He was swimming in the middle of the millpond, far from the bank. Below him, Granny Greenteeth came rising through the water. She wrapped long skinny arms about his neck and pulled him down for a kiss. "Come to me," she crooned. "Come to your old granny. Nobody else cares!" "No, no!" cried Peer. But tangled in her strong arms he sank deeper and deeper.

He woke sweating, all wound up in the cloak. The barn was completely dark. Loki pushed a cold nose into his hand, a mouse whisked over his foot, and a scuffling overhead suggested the Nis. Peer stood up. He needed to go outside.

It was raining. A sweet smell of new hay puffed from the damp fields. The rain came on harder, as if it had been just waiting for him to step outside. Peer could not afford to let his only cloak get soaked. He felt his way along the side of the barn to the privy, a small stone shed built against the wall, pushed at the creaky old door and slipped inside.

Here it was warm and smelly. Some Grimsson ancestor had built it years before, dug a deep trench and erected a plank seat with three holes in it. Peer wrinkled his nose. But it was a dry place to go. He sat down on the first seat.

It was too dark to see much. *Just as well*, thought Peer, *or I might start imagining things.* There was a black shadow away to his left that was just the shape of a person sitting there. Probably a stain on the wall. He stared at it harder. Actually it wasn't so like a person. No one could really have such a short body and lumpy head, with one ear much, much bigger than the other. No one could really—

The shadow sitting on the third seat coughed quietly, and Peer's hair stood upright on his head. He burst into the yard trying to run and haul his trousers up at the same time. He had the nasty impression, though he could not swear to it, that a second misshapen head had popped up through the middle seat as he rushed out.

He went quickly behind the barn, among the wet nettles, and returned to Loki, zinging with nerves.

It was a relief to hear the Nis skipping about again after all that. Peer called to it, and in a trembling voice, asked what he had seen.

"Lubbers," replied the Nis with a contemptuous sniff.

"Not trolls?" Peer cleared his throat. "What's a lubber?"

The Nis would not come down. It was chasing spiders, and he heard it muttering to itself: "Butter! They all promises butter to poor Nithing. But promises melt easy in the mouth."

"I'm sorry." Peer saw he was out of favour. "I did ask my friend to get you some butter, but she hasn't been able to. Please, what's a lubber? Would they hurt me?"

"Hurt you? Only if they catches you. Lubbers is stupid, slow," said the Nis impatiently. "Lubbers is low. Look where they live!"

Peer shuddered. "Are there any more nasty creepy things living here? I hate this place."

The Nis refused to tell him anything more. It stole about overhead with sudden flurries of activity and snatching movements, keeping Peer awake.

"What *are* you doing?"

"Collecting spiders." Its voice floated down.

"Would you stop it and let me sleep?"

"Very well!" said the Nis, highly offended. "Everyone must hush, everything keep still as a stone while Peer Ulfsson sleeps!" It flounced away and silence fell.

Next day there was an unaccountable plague of spiders in the mill. Big, small and medium-sized, they scuttled here and there across the floor, ran out from every crack and cranny, and wove webs in every corner. Uncle Baldur set Peer to get rid of them. It took him all day.

CHAPTER 10

Bad News

AUTUMN ARRIVED WITH crisp biting winds and skeins of wild geese flying south. The birch leaves turned a clear pale yellow and fluttered to the ground.

The trolls grew bolder. Things went badly at Hilde's house. Animals strayed, rain came through the roof, the children quarrelled, and things were mislaid. As autumn grew older the trolls became very bold indeed. The family saw them often now at twilight, hiding near the walls, sending looks of ill will on the house. The twins met one scuttling short and squat around a corner one evening, and were frightened by its pattering feet and slate-grey skin and odd eyes like live pebbles. And sleepless at night in their warm beds, the family lay worrying about Ralf. Nobody spoke of it, but everyone knew he was late, late, late.

One frosty morning Bjørn Egilsson knocked at the door with his brother Arne. They came in and Arne stood awkwardly while Gudrun fussed and exclaimed and offered them breakfast.

Arne looked tired and weatherbeaten; his clothes were waterstained and faded. When Hilde smiled at him he looked at the floor. Alf, the old sheepdog, ambled stiffly to greet him, and Arne stroked his ears as if grateful for something to do.

"Tell us your adventures, Arne," said Gudrun brightly, but

her hand shook as she poured ale for the visitors.

Bjørn and Arne exchanged glances. Arne cleared his throat. "Well – you know I wanted to join Ralf's ship but missed the sailing? I followed in my own boat, hoping to catch her at some place further south. For a while I got plenty of news of her from villages along the coast. I was sure I'd catch up. Then – well, then the news dried up. Nobody knew anything about her."

"'All right,' I thought, 'they've struck out to sea at last, and I've missed them.' I was disappointed, but I got a place on one of those pot-bellied cargo ships instead. But now..."

He stopped and went on with a rush. "I hate to tell you this, Gudrun. I'm afraid there's been news of a wreck. Part of a dragon-prowed longship was washed up on rocks south of Hammerhaven. No survivors."

Gudrun flinched, and Eirik suddenly looked very old. "Is Pa dead?" wailed Sigrid. Hilde hugged her.

"We don't know that," said Bjørn hastily. "We just thought you ought to hear it from Arne before the story gets garbled all around the dale."

"Thank you," said Gudrun quietly.

"I wouldn't have brought such news for the world," Arne muttered.

"It may not be true," said Bjørn.

"We must wait to hear more," said Gudrun, knowing full well that more news was unlikely ever to arrive.

"I hope I'm wrong." Arne took Gudrun's hand. "If there's anything we can do, anything..."

Gudrun stifled a sob. The two brothers looked very troubled as they departed.

Hilde took a pitchfork out to the cowshed. Where no one could see her, she leaned on the smooth wooden rail of Bonny's stall, and buried her head in her arms.

Now I know how Peer felt when he lost his father.

Hot-eyed, she thought about Peer. She remembered that day in early spring when they had first met. The day Baldur Grimsson had threatened her; the day he had told her to keep off the Stonemeadow; the day he had claimed Ralf's sheep. He had said Ralf would never come back; and he had been right. Drearily she realised how different everything would be from now on. She wouldn't even be able to help Peer escape from his uncles. The Grimsson brothers had won.

She gritted her teeth. "No they haven't! They shan't have the sheep, for a start. I'll go up to the Stonemeadow and fetch them down myself!" And she marched straight back into the house to tell Gudrun so.

Her mother gasped in horror.

"Go up the mountain by yourself? At this time of the year, with trolls about? And wolves, and bears? And the Grimssons, up there all hours of the day and night, thick as thieves with the Troll King himself? I won't allow it. Hasn't this house seen enough trouble?"

"Then what will we do?" asked Hilde in a low voice. "Hand everything over to the Grimssons on a plate? And what about poor Peer Ulfsson?"

"I'm sorry for the boy, but he's not our problem," cried Gudrun.

"All right!" said Hilde, very white. "But those are our sheep up there, on our land. And the Grimssons have had the wool off them already this year – and it was Peer who told me. Oh Ma! If I don't bring them down to our sheepfold, we'll lose them altogether. Pa would have done it weeks ago – if he'd been here."

Hunched over the fire, old Eirik stirred. "The girl is right," he said unexpectedly. "The sheep *do* have to be brought down. She's a brave girl, and sensible. She can manage."

"I'll be all right," Hilde added eagerly. "I'll take Alf. He'll look after me."

"He's too old!" Gudrun protested.

"Ma, he knows every inch of the hills, and he knows the sheep. I can't get lost with Alf. Look at him!"

The old dog had heard his name and was looking up enquiringly. Eirik slapped his thigh. "Knows every trick. The old ones are the good ones!"

With bad grace Gudrun gave way. "I suppose you may go, Hilde – since your *grandfather* approves... But be careful. Get back before dark!"

"I'll try." Already Hilde felt better, wrapping herself up in a sheepskin jacket and pulling on a pair of soft leather boots. She grabbed a stick. "For cracking trolls on the head," she joked.

"Oh dear." Gudrun looked anxiously out. The sky was overcast and a chill wind swept the farmyard. "It looks like snow."

"Get inside and keep warm," said Hilde impatiently. "Keep Grandpa off the ice. And don't worry about me. Come, Alf!" She set off, the old sheepdog trotting beside her.

Hilde knew that long hours of tramping hills lay before her. The tough, independent little sheep roamed where they pleased and were often widely scattered. As she climbed the shoulder of Troll Fell, the wind hit her, burning her ears and forcing tears from her eyes. More ominously, the first grey flakes of snow came whizzing past.

The sheep seemed to have disappeared. Hilde listened for the sound of bleating, or the clonking of the sheep bell worn by the old ewe who led the flock. A flurry of snow whirled down from the north-east, erasing the hillside, leaving nothing visible but a few blurred yards of wet bent grass already turning white.

Hilde trudged on, unwilling to give up. She began to wonder if Baldur and Grim had already taken the sheep away. Perhaps there were none to find. Then it dawned on her that the sheep would shelter from the weather on the western side of the crags. She turned in that direction. Alf trotted ahead, the wind blowing up his thick fur to show the pale skin at the roots.

A blue, unfriendly twilight descended on Troll Fell, and the snow grew deeper. Grey shapes were slinking and sliding about on the edge of sight, and Hilde remembered the trolls. And then Alf barked, once. He stood with one front paw raised, listening intently.

"Have you found them?" Hilde gasped. "Good lad! Go on, then – fetch 'em down!" Alf sped away into the gloom.

Hilde waited, stamping her feet. In a moment a couple of sheep came jogging into view. Snow was piling up on their backs, but Hilde knew they couldn't feel it under their thick fleeces. Two more arrived at their heels – black faced and scrawny, but to Hilde a beautiful sight.

She whistled. Alf came running, head low, snaking along behind another little group of startled, put-out looking sheep. A bell clonked dismally – he had found the old ewe. Alf looked extremely pleased with himself and grinned at her, panting.

"Good lad!" Hilde did a quick head count and decided there should be some more. "Go on Alf. Seek 'em out!" Alf whisked around the sheep he had gathered, nudging them into a compact group, and dashed off into the storm.

Hilde was smiling to see the old dog so proud of his work, when something small and solid hurled itself into her back and knocked her down. She grovelled on the wet ground, twisting and grappling. The unseen attacker let go, and she scrambled up dizzily, looking for her stick, which had spun away into the snow. Before she could find it, the creature scuttled back and gripped her around the thighs. She looked down into the enigmatic yellow eyes of a small troll, doing its best to heave her off her feet. She hammered it on the head and yelled, then stuck two fingers in her mouth and blew a piercing whistle.

Alf came streaking downhill so fast that he overshot. His back legs slid from under him as he turned, snarling, to attack. The troll let go abruptly and melted into the darkness. Alf pursued it for a few yards, hackles up, before returning to Hilde to check that all was well.

"Hey," said Hilde gently. "You brave old boy, what a good dog!" She rubbed his chest and neck. His heart was thudding against his ribs, but his eyes were bright. It was Alf's glory to be useful, and this was his great day.

"Let's just round up the ones we've got, and go." They were near the western edge of the Stonemeadow, where the ground broke up into dangerous clefts, rocks and cliffs. It was now too dark to see where she put her feet. The best thing was to go slowly and let Alf and the sheep pick their own path.

A gust of wind parted the whirling snow. Not too far ahead a light waved, dim and smeary, such as might come from a traveller's lantern. Hilde's heart lifted. Perhaps Arne or Bjørn had come looking for her! "Over here!" she shouted, and heard an answering shout, blurred by the wind.

"Coming!" If only she had a lantern to signal back. The wind flung snow in her face like handfuls of grey soot. Alf barked, and the sound was whipped away.

The light glimmered again, further off and weaker. "Wait!" Hilde cried. She struggled on, panting. Each gasp filled her mouth with snowflakes like feathers. She coughed. "Wait for me!" She ran, Alf bounding at her heels, overtaking the sheep. The ground sloped. She slowed, afraid to go too fast. "Where are you?" she bellowed between cupped hands.

Alf sprang up and grabbed her sleeve in his teeth. He tugged, and she sat down hard. "What on earth –!" But the far-away light was returning, impossibly fast. No human being could run so smoothly over such rough ground. The light hurtled towards her, growing brighter and brighter, and halted in the air overhead. Hilde threw herself flat. Alf cowered beside her, growling. With a soft *puff!* the light went out. There was a wild laugh. Something rushed past them in the darkness and receded up the slope.

Hilde stood up on wobbling legs. She was on the edge of a cliff. If Alf hadn't caught her sleeve, she would have pitched straight over. The creature, whatever it was – troll or mountain spirit – had led her completely astray.

Alf shook himself, as if telling her the danger was over. She patted his rough coat. "Good old Alf! They haven't done for us yet. That's the second time you've saved me tonight."

As she turned to follow the old dog back to the sheep, the dark night and racing snow lit up as if a door had opened. And indeed it had. A few hundred yards up the slope, yellow light poured from a rift in the crag. In fear and amazement, she watched a dark silhouette approach the lighted gap and disappear inside. Spindly limbs and a large head – was that the troll-thing which had misled her? And was it going home?

Icy fragments of hail flew into her face. She shielded her eyes and looked again. The light was failing. A huge stone door swung ponderously shut. The hillside trembled at the shock, and all was dark.

Hilde touched Alf's neck. "Come!" she murmured.

At the bottom of the Stonemeadow the snow lay only ankle deep, and Alf drove the little flock briskly along the road till they reached the track to the farm.

Gudrun had the farmhouse door open in a flash. "You clever girl! You found them! Come inside at once!" She began to hug Hilde but then held her off. "Get those wet things off – you're frozen! I'll put the sheep away. There's hot soup in the pot."

"Alf shall have some," declared Hilde. The old dog lay stiffly down by the fire. He gave a perfunctory lick to his bedraggled fur and laid his head between his paws.

"Dry him and give him some soup," Hilde called to the twins, rubbing her hair vigorously. "He was marvellous. He saved my life! Ma, just wait till you hear our adventures. We found the door into Troll Fell!"

CHAPTER 11

The Dogfight

Peer was sitting by the hearth one dark afternoon, cleaning his uncles' boots. Several pairs lay scattered about and he was scraping the mud off and greasing them to keep them waterproof and supple. The best pairs were thick, double-stitched reindeer hide with the fur inside.

Peer handled them enviously. His own shoes were worn and split, wrapped around with string and stuffed with hay to try and keep his feet warm. They were always wet. His toes were red with chilblains.

He sat as close to the fire as he could. He'd been out for hours shovelling snow and carrying feed to the animals. There were a lot of them now. Grim had taken Grendel one morning and brought down some sheep he claimed were all his, though Peer, looking suspiciously, spotted a variety of different marks. The sheep were penned behind a wattle fence in a corner of the yard, where their breath hung in clouds over their draggled woolly backs.

The mill had been silent for a week. The millpond was freezing. Already the weir was fringed with icicles, and the waterwheel glazed with dark ice. No power. While the ice lasted, Uncle Baldur was a miller no longer. Only a farmer.

Bored and lonely, Peer smeared more grease on to the toe of the fifth boot. Uncle Grim lay snoring in his bunk. Baldur was out. Peer guessed he was down in the village, drinking with his cronies – if he had any.

There was no one to talk to. He hadn't seen Hilde for weeks, and since the spider episode, the Nis had ignored him, though he often heard it skipping about at night. Peer remembered last winter's fun, snowball fights and skating with the other boys in Hammerhaven. It felt like another life.

The door crashed open, and Uncle Baldur stamped in, beating snow from his mittens. "He's dead!" he cried.

Uncle Grim jerked awake in mid-snore. He struggled up. "Who's dead?"

"Ralf Eiriksson. It's all around the village," shrilled Uncle Baldur. "His ship was wrecked and they were all drowned. Just as I thought!"

The brothers flung their arms around each other and began a sort of stamping dance. Peer dropped the boot he was holding and sat in open-mouthed horror.

"Dead as a doornail," chortled Uncle Baldur.

"A *drowned* doornail," Grim wheezed, and Grendel leaped around them shattering the air with his barks.

"Is this sure?" asked Grim, sobering suddenly.

"Certain sure," Baldur nodded. "Arne Egilsson's been saying so. I went specially to ask him as soon as I heard. He didn't like telling me, but he couldn't deny the facts. The ship's long overdue, and her timbers have been washing up further down the coast. She sank, it's obvious."

Grim smacked his brother on the shoulder. "Then the land's ours! No one will argue about that if Ralf's dead."

Baldur laughed. He paced up and down, slapping his great thighs. "We'll be rich, brother. We'll own the best half of Troll Fell. And after tonight, with the Gaffer's gold—"

Uncle Grim nodded at Peer. "The boy's listening," he growled.

"Who cares?" Uncle Baldur caught Peer by the scruff and shook him. "He don't know what I'm talking about. We'll get the goods for the Gaffer now, all right. Who's to stop us? With Ralf out of the way, we can do whatever we like!"

He whacked Peer on the ear and dropped him. Peer felt sick. Poor, poor Hilde. Poor Ralf! And his father's lovely ship, smashed on the rocks and lost for ever! Then with a stab of fear he saw what this meant for himself. No safety up at the farm. No escape from Baldur and Grim.

"This calls for a drop of ale!" Baldur declared, rubbing his hands.

"Mead," Grim suggested.

"You're right." Uncle Baldur licked his lips. "Something strong!"

Soon the two brothers were singing noisily, banging their cups together. Mechanically, Peer finished cleaning the boots. He lined them up by the door and sank to the floor. Something gnawed at his mind. Tonight? Had Uncle Baldur said "*tonight*"?

Midwinter! He'd been talking and thinking and planning about it for months. Now, with a shock like icy water dashed in his face, he realised he had no idea how close midwinter was. He thought back, counting on his fingers. How long since the first snow? Weeks? It seemed a long time. And the days were so short now; it was dark outside already. Midwinter must be nearly upon them.

There was a bang at the door. Peer looked at his uncles. They were singing so loudly that neither they nor Grendel had heard. Peer shrugged and went wearily to open it. With his hand on the latch he paused. What if it was Granny

Greenteeth, come to pay a visit before the ice locked her in for the winter? Well, let her come! He jerked the door open.

A cutting wind whirled in. There stood two ordinary men, muffled up against the cold. They stepped quickly in and shook snow from their clothes.

"Shut that DOOR!" Uncle Baldur yelled. Then he saw the visitors and staggered to his feet. "Look who's here." He prodded Grim. "It's Arne and Bjørn."

"Give 'em a drink," hiccupped Grim.

But Bjørn's good-natured face was stern. "Hey, Peer," he said quietly, dropping a friendly hand on Peer's shoulder. "Grim, Baldur," he went on, "we've not come to drink with you. We've come to say one thing. Leave Ralf's family alone!"

Uncle Baldur sprawled back on the bench. He gave an unpleasant laugh. "I don't know what you mean."

"Yes you do," said Arne. "You're after Ralf's land on Troll Fell."

"But you won't get it," said Bjørn. "Arne and I will stand witness against you. It was never yours, and you know it!"

Peer felt like cheering. He glowed with admiration for the two young men. They looked like heroes to him as they stood there together, their faces tight with anger. Baldur and Grim exchanged glances.

"Why are you interfering?" asked Baldur with a suspicious scowl. "What's in it for you?"

"*Why?*" exploded Bjørn. "Because Ralf was our friend. Because the land was his. Because you're a couple of cheating pigs who'd rob a widow and her family!"

"Don't bother trying to understand," added Arne.

"Get out!" Baldur surged to his feet. "Out, before I set the dog on you!"

"Oh, we'll go," said Bjørn coldly. "I wouldn't stay in your stinking mill for all the gold on Troll Fell."

He strode for the door, but Uncle Baldur grabbed his arm. "Gold?" he croaked. "What do you mean? What do you know about troll gold?"

Bjørn stared at him and whistled. "That's your game, is it? Don't you worry, Grimsson. The only thing I know about troll gold is this: it's unlucky and I don't want anything to do with it. And if you'll take my advice, neither will you. Goodnight!"

Peer stepped hopefully forwards. If he could only catch Bjørn's eye; if he could only go with him! But this time, Bjørn did not notice Peer. He and Arne slipped through the door and vanished into the night.

Uncle Baldur sat down heavily. He tried to pour himself another drink, but the bottle was empty. He swore.

"There's no fun for a man round here," he grumbled. "Nothing but trouble and work—"

"Let's have a dogfight," suggested Grim. Peer looked up.

"What with?" asked Uncle Baldur scornfully. "That thing of the lad's? He wouldn't last a minute with Grendel."

"He's nippy," offered Grim. "Bet you he'd last five."

A grin spread over Baldur's face. "All right!" he said.

"No!" Peer shrieked. "You can't! You can't, you bullies!" He hurled himself at Uncle Baldur, kicking and biting.

"The boy's mad!" Uncle Baldur twisted Peer's wrist up behind his back. "Keep still, or I'll break yer arm. You go and fetch the dog, Grim. The boy might turn him loose."

"Let go of me," panted Peer, still struggling as Grim nodded and went out. "Let me go!"

Loki trotted in at Uncle Grim's heels, looking wary and puzzled.

"They can't fight in here," said Uncle Baldur over Peer's head.

"No," Grim agreed, "we'll have it in the yard. I give you ten to one he lasts a good five minutes before Grendel grips him. He's quick, you see."

"Done!" Baldur grinned. "Speed won't save him from Grendel. One good crunch and it'll all be over." Peer couldn't believe they were talking about his beloved dog.

"Loki can't fight, he won't fight," he cried. "He doesn't know how."

Paying no attention, Uncle Baldur dragged him outside with Loki, while Uncle Grim brought Grendel along by the collar, holding a flaring torch in the other hand to light the dogfight. The snow had stopped falling, but was blowing about the yard chased by a cruel little wind. It was an unbearably cold night.

Peer looked at the two dogs in despair. Grendel dwarfed little Loki. He was built like a wolf, but thicker and taller, with massive head and powerful jaws. Loki curled his tail between his legs and trembled.

"Three… two… one! Eat him, Grendel!" yelled Uncle Baldur, releasing Loki. At the same moment Uncle Grim let go of Grendel, who sprang forward snarling.

Loki took one look and ran for his life. But Grendel's long legs gained on him. At the edge of the sheepfold Loki doubled back, his front and back legs crossing each other in his efforts to escape, and the two dogs merged in a rolling tangle near the barn wall, falling over and over in a spray of snow. "Gren-del! Gren-del!" shouted Baldur.

"Loki! Run!" screamed Peer.

Suddenly an avalanche of snow slumped off the barn roof on top of the two dogs, burying them. There was a moment's surprised silence as they struggled to rise, shaking themselves free. Peer caught a flicker of movement running along the barn roof, and was sure it was the Nis. "Oh, thank you," he breathed.

Loki got his wits back before Grendel did. He jumped out of the drift and raced across the yard towards the road. "Head him off!" shouted Uncle Baldur, and Grim tried to bar his way, swinging the blazing torch. Loki whizzed between his legs and was out of the yard and over the wooden bridge before Grendel could catch him. Grim slipped and fell, cursing. Peer and Uncle Baldur ran past, following the two dogs over the icy bridge. They were already out of sight. Where, oh where was Loki?

A shivering howl of triumph quivered up and up until it seemed to reach the frosty stars. It lingered in the cold air, holding Peer motionless till it died away. Uncle Baldur too, was frozen in his steps. Grim came limping up, the blazing branch in one hand, the other hand pressed to his hip.

"He's got the little beggar," he said.

Tears of horror rose in Peer's eyes. He stumbled along the kicked-up path to the millpond, and his uncles followed, Baldur grumbling: "Didn't get to see anything. No fun at all. Call that a fight?"

Peer blundered out of the bushes on the edge of the millpond, and stopped dead. A few yards away Grendel stood with his back to Peer, hackles raised and head lowered threateningly. At the very brink of the millpond, Loki faced him at bay. Loki's head was up and he looked this way and that with quick, desperate movements.

No wonder Grendel had howled in triumph. Loki was cornered. Behind him, the millpond reflected the starlight with a thin layer of milky ice. To his left, the dark waters of the sluice poured in icicles down to the rapidly freezing stream.

Grendel's breath steamed. The flames from Grim's torch lit the snow to rosy warmth and glistened on every yellow tooth in Grendel's head. He was waiting for his master's signal to bring the fight to its end. Even across the yards of snow, Peer could see Loki shaking.

"Good lad, Grendel," puffed Uncle Baldur. "Get him!"

Peer clapped his hands over his eyes, but lowered them at a shout from Baldur. Loki had turned and leaped out on to the ice. Amazingly, it held him. He slithered across it, paws scrabbling.

"Oh Loki – go on, go on," panted Peer. Uncle Grim gave a bellow of alarm. "Grendel! Stop!"

He was too late. Grendel launched himself after Loki. With a splintering crash he went straight through the fragile ice and was struggling in the black water.

Grim ran to the edge. He plunged the branch he held into the water. The flames sizzled out. "Here Grendel! Grip hold!" he shouted, but Grendel took no notice. He tried to follow Loki, snarling and raking at the ice with his claws. It broke into crazy pieces. He could smash his way across!

Loki had reached the far bank. It was steep; he scrambled up, clinging desperately with his front paws, kicking with his back legs, but the loose snow collapsed under him and he tumbled back on to the ice.

"Pay up," said Grim to Baldur.

"He'll catch him yet," said Baldur, watching Grendel crashing his way across.

Loki flung himself a second time at the bank. Again his twisting body fell back on to the ice. Grendel was halfway over by now, his great strength breaking a jagged passage. Peer could not stand it. Without even thinking he filled his lungs and ran forward. "*Granny!*" he yelled, so loudly his voice cracked. "*Granny Greenteeth!*"

Baldur and Grim glanced at him in angry surprise. Then Baldur bit off an exclamation and pointed.

Something was happening to Grendel, out there in the middle of the pond. He writhed, splashing, biting at something that seemed to have risen beside him. It was hard to see in the bitter starlight. Could those be skinny white arms twining about Grendel's neck, pulling him under? The chunks of broken ice danced and clashed. There was a thrashing struggle just below the surface, a choked-off bark – and Grendel was gone.

"*Granny Greenteeth!*" Peer whispered, hugging himself and shuddering.

There was a loud wail from Uncle Grim. "Grendel!"

"She's got him," said Uncle Baldur, shrugging, but his mouth was set.

On his third try, Loki reached the top of the bank and hurtled away into the woods. Uncle Grim forgot his sorrow. "You owe me, Baldur. Pay up!"

"Later," said Baldur. "When we're rich. And we'd better get on with that." He stared at Peer, who quailed, expecting to be blamed for Grendel's awful fate. But it seemed that Uncle Baldur had taken Peer's shout for a warning, and wasn't thinking about that.

"Tonight is midwinter's eve," he said softly, still staring at Peer. "Don't forget, Grim, we're invited to a wedding. It's time we went to get the presents!"

Peer tried to dash for it, but Uncle Baldur caught his arm. "What shall we do with him, Grim? We don't want to take him along with us."

"Lock him up. Shut him up in the privy," Grim growled.

"There's no window, and we can block up the door."

Peer struggled, but the two big men dragged him down the path to the mill. Uncle Baldur hauled open the privy door and thrust him inside. "You'll not die of cold," he joked. "Where there's dirt there's warmth." He shoved the door shut and Peer heard logs being piled against it. With a last effort he beat his fists on the rough planks, screaming, "Let me out! Where are you going?"

"To pay a little visit to Ralf's farm, of course," came Baldur's muffled voice. They clumped away, leaving Peer to gasp for his breath in the cold and stinking darkness.

CHAPTER 12

Stolen in the Storm

"THERE'S A HEAVY snow coming," Eirik said to Gudrun. "I can feel it in my bones."

"And what if there is?" Gudrun slapped the dough she was kneading. "I don't have to worry about the weather any more."

Hilde, pulling on her thick-fur lined boots, looked anxiously at her mother. Gudrun was very pale these days.

"It's not snowing yet," she said. "Just freezing hard." She belted her sheepskin jacket with a piece of string, and took the lantern from its hook. "I'm going to feed the cows."

Eirik looked up. "I'll help," he offered.

"Oh, I don't need any help, Grandpa..."

"Don't be an old fool, Eirik," Gudrun snapped. "Stay in the warmth."

Eirik was offended and hurt, and Hilde saw it. "If Sigurd and Sigrid come out with me, Eirik could keep an eye on them. They need some fresh air."

"No we don't," objected Sigrid.

"You'll do what you're told!" Hilde hissed.

"Can we have a snowball fight?" asked Sigurd.

"Certainly, if you don't go out of Grandpa's sight," said Hilde briskly. She pushed their boots on and pulled their woolly caps over their ears. Gudrun wrapped up Eirik till he was almost circular.

Hilde filled her pockets with stones – handy for throwing at trolls – and bundled the little ones ahead of her out of the door. They screamed with delight and slid off across the icy yard. Gudrun appeared in the doorway supporting Eirik, who shook her off irritably and stepped after Hilde. He staggered, and Hilde leaped to help him. "Leave me alone, girl," he growled at her. "I can manage!"

"Now Father-in-law, do take care!" shrilled Gudrun.

Eirik really lost his temper. "Women, women," he shouted, "cluck, cluck, never leave you alone. I wish my son was here. He'd know I'm not in the grave yet!" He slipped on a particularly glossy patch of ice and sat down hard.

Hilde rushed to pick him up. Sigurd and Sigrid threw snow about, quarrelling. Gudrun clung to the doorpost, calling out instructions. Eirik sat puffing with shock.

There was an apologetic cough. "Can we help?" Hilde looked up to see Bjørn and Arne climbing over the gate. The two young men pulled Eirik to his feet and dusted the snow off him tactfully. Eirik dabbed at himself, muttering.

"It was the ice," Hilde explained awkwardly. "It was so slippery that he – he slipped."

"Ah yes, it's slippery stuff, ice," said Arne with a grin. He became serious again. "We've brought some news."

"Come inside then, before you freeze," snapped Gudrun, holding the door open. "Hurry! I'm losing all the warmth."

They all trooped into the house. "It's nothing much," Bjørn began, but Gudrun stopped him. "Not a word! Not a word of your news do I wish to hear till we've shown you some hospitality. We still know how to welcome our neighbours here, I hope. Hilde, where's your manners? Fetch some ale."

"In some houses," Eirik grumbled under his breath, "it's the man who calls for ale!"

The ale was drunk in an atmosphere of polite discomfort. "Well," said Arne, when Gudrun finally allowed him to speak, "we spoke to the Grimsson boys today. We came straight on from the mill, in fact. They've heard about Ralf. They were – celebrating, I'm afraid."

"Boasting about how they're going to steal Ralf's land," Bjørn added.

"We wiped the smile off Baldur's fat face. We told him to leave you alone."

"Did you see Peer? Was he all right?" asked Hilde anxiously.

Bjørn looked thoughtful. "Yes, we saw him. I hope so. There was a little noise going on when we left, and I forgot to speak to him."

"Bjørn lost his temper," Arne grinned.

Gudrun's eyes were wet. She mopped them quickly with her apron. "You're such good friends," she exclaimed, stretching out her hands. The young men flushed.

"So we'll keep a close eye on the Grimssons for you," Arne went on hastily, "if Eirik has no objection, that is?"

Everyone looked at Eirik. "What?" said Eirik. "No, er – of course not. Keep an eye on them for all you're worth, young fellow!"

"Good," said Arne. "If they start any trouble, let us know." He stood up.

"I'll come out with you," said Hilde. She slipped out ahead of Bjørn and Arne, surprising three small trolls who were sneaking across the yard.

"Get out!" she yelled, scrabbling in her pocket for stones. They bolted under the gate, and Arne and Bjørn ran up. "Are you all right? We heard you shout."

"Quite all right, Bjørn, thank you. I was frightening away a few trolls."

Arne looked at her admiringly. "So you know how to deal with trolls?"

"I'm a pretty good shot," Hilde boasted.

"But where are you going? To feed the cows? Can I help?"

"No, no!" said Hilde, blushing as Bjørn nudged his brother and grinned. "You should both get home. Grandfather's bones tell him a snowstorm is coming." As she spoke she realised it was already snowing again. "And it looks as if he's right," she added.

Arne and Bjørn said goodnight, and Hilde dived into the dark cowshed. She pulled down hay for Bonny and her calf, and threw down fresh straw. When the animals were comfortable, she left the sheltered shed, tramped across the wild white yard and banged on the farmhouse door. She waited, shivering, while Gudrun unbarred it, and then jumped inside, gasping and laughing and brushing off snow.

"Brrr! Shut the door, mother! Whatever are you waiting for?"

"The twins, of course. Aren't they with you?"

"No!" said Hilde, alarmed. "Weren't they with you?"

Gudrun slammed the door. "I thought they went out after you the second time. They went out just before Bjørn and Arne."

"They never joined me. I've been in the shed."

They looked at each other.

"Listen," said Gudrun in a low voice. She pointed to Eirik, asleep by the fire. "Don't wake him yet. Take the lanterns and go round the steading – call them. They may be building a snow fort or something. If not – ah!" She moved her hands despairingly. "What then?"

"What *next?*" said Hilde grimly. "Don't worry, mother. I'll find them." She plunged back out into the darkness.

The lantern shone on to snow whirling on the ground,

picked up and flung about by the wind. It was hard to walk in a straight line.

"Sigurd?" she shouted. "Sigrid? Where are you? Come in at once, supper's ready!

"Sigurd! Come here *now!*

"Children! I'll smack you if you don't come!"

A night bird shrieked. What bird would be out in such a night? *Huuu – hutututu!* She shivered. That was no bird; the trolls were out. The wind swept snow into her eyes. She went round to the sheepfold, swinging the lantern. The sheep lay huddled in the shelter of the fence, drifted snow on their backs.

"Sigurd? Sigrid?"

She held the lantern close to the ground, searching for tracks. Her own were obvious, and there were a lot of larger half-filled prints which must belong to Bjørn and Arne. The small light tracks of the little children had disappeared as completely as they had themselves.

"Oh where *are* you?" she cried – and stealthy movements caught her eye. She whirled. Trolls were creeping up to the very edge of her lantern's pool of light, and their eyes reflected flashes of green and red. Hilde stamped her foot and shouted. They scattered, but a moment later a hail of snowballs flew at her, some loaded with stones. She stumbled back to the house.

Gudrun pulled the door open. "Have you found them?"

"No! Ma, the trolls are out there. They've been snowballing me. Ma, can the trolls have stolen them?" She clutched her mother's arm, and they stared at each other, white-faced.

"We must tell Eirik," said Gudrun. She ran to shake his shoulder. "Eirik, wake up! Wake up! Sigurd and Sigrid are missing!"

Eirik opened his eyes with a start and listened, bewildered, while Hilde and Gudrun gabbled.

"They're missing!"

"It was after Bjørn and Arne left!"

"No, it was before!"

"They went out with you the first time."

"I know, but—"

"Did they ever come back in?"

"I don't remember. Did they, Grandfather?"

Eirik slapped his knee in irritation. "What are you talking about?" he asked.

Hilde repeated the story in desperation. "They're *lost!* In the *snow!* And the *trolls* are out! And I made them go! Oh, if only they come back, I'll never be mean to them again!" She began to cry.

"Have you looked for them?" Eirik asked. Gudrun's control broke.

"Of course she's looked for them! Why can't you listen? Oh what shall we do? My poor little twins, lured away to die in the snow! I told Ralf there'd be trouble with the trolls, I *told* him, but would he listen? Oh, what shall we do?" She threw her apron over her head and sat down crying hysterically.

Eirik struggled upright in his chair. "Hush, Gudrun, hush," he began, but as she paid no attention he cleared his throat and thundered, "Woman!"

It worked. Gudrun raised a startled face.

"Will you be quiet?" Eirik demanded. He got to his feet in great excitement. "It's not the trolls. It's not the trolls, I say. It's the Grimssons who've stolen our children away!"

"The Grimssons?" Gudrun asked in wonderment.

"Of course it is!" Eirik raised his stick and whacked it down. "What did you tell us about them, Hilde? Didn't they want a pair of children? And isn't tonight midwinter's eve?"

"They've taken *Sigrid?*" screamed Hilde. "They've taken *Sigurd* and *Sigrid*?"

Alf sprang up, barking. "I'll kill them!" Hilde yelled.

Eirik was still explaining. "...crept up under cover of darkness – probably followed Arne and Bjørn – lay in wait –"

"All that fuss when you fell over," gasped Hilde. "Perhaps they grabbed them then. There did seem a lot of big footprints, but I never thought! Oh, I can't bear it! They'll be so frightened!" She turned. "Mother, where are you going?"

Gudrun, white-lipped, was wrapping herself up. "To look for them, of course. You stay here and look after Grandpa."

"By Odin," shouted Eirik furiously, "you take me for a dotard, you do. Hilde will stay here. Gudrun, you will come with me. We shall go to Arne Egilsson's and raise the village. Ha!" He stamped his foot down into a boot and broke into an old battle chant.

Gudrun shrugged. Her pale face softened into a very faint smile.

"He's exactly like his son," she remarked proudly.

CHAPTER 13

The Nis to the Rescue

PEER CROUCHED ON the frozen privy floor, wrapping his arms around his knees. He was so cold that in spite of Uncle Baldur's last words to him, he rather thought he might die before morning. That would spoil their plans, he thought bitterly.

The only comfort was that Loki had got away. Everything else was a disaster. He imagined Baldur and Grim kicking open the door of Hilde's house and dragging her out – her mother and her old grandfather would be unable to stop them. With Hilde in their power they would return to the mill for him, Peer, and take the pair of them away up Troll Fell. The Grimssons would collect their golden reward, and he and Hilde would become slaves of the trolls.

As for Loki, he would probably die in the woods, lost and cold and starving. Peer groaned in anguish…

…and heard a slithering sound somewhere over in the corner. He went very still. New fear tingled through him. He had completely forgotten about the other inhabitants of this privy.

The sound came again, accompanied by a creaking noise. Peer could imagine somebody hoisting themselves through one of the holes in the wooden seat. He tried not to breathe.

A voice spoke suddenly. "'Oo's there?" it squeaked.

Peer dared not answer. A second voice spoke up from the pit below, hollow and muffled. "What's up?"

"There's someone 'ere!" squeaked the first voice.

"Light coming up," boomed the second voice. In utter amazement Peer saw the three holes in the long wooden seat light up, throwing three round patches of light on to the rough roof. An arm came up through the middle hole, carrying a bluish flame.

The creature in the corner reached out and took it; the flame transferred easily from the first hand to the second and seemed not to belong to any oil lamp or taper. It was just a flame, flickering away by itself.

The second creature's head now appeared through the hole. It spotted Peer and squealed. "Ooh! Look at that!"

"It's a boy," declared the first one in deep disgust.

Peer had never seen such strange beings. Their heads reminded him of turnips. They were lumpy and blotchy and bewhiskered. The one in the corner had an ear that stuck out like a cabbage leaf on one side of its head, while the other ear was small and knobbly. The one peering out of the hole seemed to have no ears at all. And the nose on it! And the mouth! Like a thin line with no lips.

"Are you – lubbers?" Peer quavered.

The first one jumped and the flame swerved and nearly went out. "It talks!"

"Of course it talks," growled the second lubber. "All boys talk, you fool. Give me that!" It clambered nimbly through the hole and snatched the flame back. Then it crossed its legs and sat on the edge of the seat, looking at Peer.

"Whatcher doing here, then?" it asked chattily, but its bald turnip head and slit-like features did not reassure him.

"My – my uncles locked me in," Peer explained.

The lubber seemed astonished. "You mean you can't get out?"

"N-no," Peer faltered, aware of making a mistake. The lubber in the corner nudged its friend.

"He can't get out," it said.

"Yeah," said the lubber with the light. "I heard."

They both stared at Peer, and then as if by unspoken agreement they both shuffled a bit closer to him along the bench.

"So," said the lubber with the light. "Right cosy little party, this."

There didn't seem any reply to that. During the next minute's silence, both lubbers came a little bit closer again.

Peer shifted anxiously. He pushed the door, testing it. It would not move. The Grimssons must have stacked half the woodpile against it.

"That's an interesting trick," he said quickly. "Your light, I mean. H-how does it work?"

"Watch this," said the lubber with the light. He opened his mouth, wider and wider, till it looked as if his throat had been cut. He placed the flame inside his mouth and shut it. For a moment his cheeks glowed purple and red like a lantern. He gulped, and the flame went out.

In the ensuing darkness Peer felt both the lubbers scuffling much, much nearer.

"Then I snap my fingers," said the lubber's voice, close to his ear, "and back comes the light. Neat, or what?"

The bluish, bobbing flame appeared not far from Peer's nose.

"It's his party trick," said the other lubber. They were now one on either side of Peer, and he did not know which way to look.

"It's very clever," he said desperately.

"It *is* clever," agreed the lubber. "It's very, very clever, but you know what? It always – makes me – *hungry!*"

Its mouth yawned open next to Peer's shoulder. He leaped aside, cannoning into the other lubber. The touch of it made his flesh crawl: it was clammy and cold.

"Grab him," shouted the lubber with the light, "the first square meal in ages, I'm sick of beetles and slugs—"

It would be like being eaten by frogs. Mad with loathing, Peer raised his arms to ward the hideous creatures off – and felt something hard being slipped into his hand from above. His fingers knew what it was, they closed over the hilt instinctively.

"Look out!" shrieked the second lubber. "He's got a knife!"

The two lubbers rushed for the holes. There were two splashes, and the light went out. Peer was alone in the dark, though a mumbling, grumbling conversation was going on in the pit below.

A small pearly light dawned near the roof. Peer looked up. "Thank you, Nis!" he said in heartfelt gratitude.

The Nis giggled. "Lubbers is fools, no match for me!"

"I'm sure they're not." Peer's legs gave way and he sat down.

"Get up! Get up!" hissed the Nis.

"What for?" Peer groaned.

"What for?" The Nis clicked its tongue in disbelief. "For to escape, of course. Hurry! Hurry!"

Peer didn't move. "Nis, I can't get through little holes like you do. The door's barred. I can't get out."

"*The door is barred, I can't get out!*" the Nis mimicked. "What is the knife for? To cut your way out through the thatch, of course!"

"Of course!" cried Peer. He climbed on to the wooden seat, hoping no lubber would grab his ankles, and began chopping at the bundles of reeds that made up the low roof. They were almost rotten, riddled with rat-runs, bird's nests and passages. He soon broke through, cursing as the thick snow outside fell down his neck and on to his shoulders, and half slithered, half fell down into the yard, where a bundle of hysterical doggy joy leaped upon him and pushed him flat.

"Loki!" spluttered Peer. "Loki, you're safe! All right now, stop it. Let me get up!"

He got up, gulping fresh air in freezing lungfuls. It was snowing again. The Nis scampered past like a little whirlwind and opened the mill door. Peer and Loki ran inside, and the Nis closed the door behind them.

It was blessedly warm. For a few moments all Peer could do was lean shuddering over the long hearth. The fire was dying; the red and violet embers gave little light, but they were still hot. His uncles must have been away for at least an hour. Peer was afraid they would soon be back. He turned around to get warm all over, and saw the Nis perching on the back of Uncle Grim's big chair. It looked at him steadily, eyes gleaming.

"You saved my life," said Peer. "And you saved Loki earlier, didn't you? You pushed that snow off the roof."

The Nis scratched itself. It skipped to the floor and spread its long spindly fingers over the fire.

"Why did you do it?" Peer asked. "I thought you were so keen on this wedding."

"They hasn't invited me," said the Nis sadly.

"Oh..."

"Such a big wedding." The Nis looked miserable and its mouth turned down. "The hill to be raised on red pillars. So much food… but they forgets to invite the poor Nis."

"Perhaps they're only inviting trolls."

But the Nis shook its head. "Stromkarls, nixies, merrows even, all are going!"

Peer bit his lip. "I'm sure it's been a dreadful oversight. But Nis – Loki and I have to escape before my uncles come back. They've gone for Hilde, so they can take the two of us up Troll Fell and give us to the trolls. But it's not going to happen!" he went on fiercely. "If I'm not here, they won't have the pair they need. And I'm leaving! I've had enough of Uncle Baldur and Uncle Grim! I'm going back to Hammerhaven." Brand and Ingrid would take him in for a while, he was sure. "But first I want what's mine." He strode over to the locked bin where the money was and rattled the lid. "I need to break into this. Any ideas?"

The Nis darted him a mischievous look. It reached out a long arm and hooked its wooden bowl out of the ashes. It was empty. Baldur and Grim had forgotten to fill it. "I has had enough too, Peer Ulfsson," the Nis announced importantly. "See me!"

It scampered up the ladder and disappeared over the edge into the loft, where it began puffing and groaning. Bewildered, Peer climbed up to find it heaving away at the upper millstone, trying to lift it from its spindle.

"What on earth?" Peer began, and then he saw. If they could roll the millstone over the edge, it would fall on the chest below. But it must weigh half a ton. They could never lift it.

The Nis doubled limply over the millstone and lay panting. Peer looked about for something else to use. He clenched his fist in triumph. Standing upright against the wall, dark with dust, was the old worn millstone that had been replaced in

Baldur's father's time. No need to lift it: it was already on its rim, with just a couple of chocks driven in on the underside to stop it rolling.

The Nis saw, and the sparkle came back into its eyes. It probed under the old millstone, pulling out the chocks. Peer grabbed the top of the stone and felt it roll forward. Between them, they guided it to the edge of the loft. At the very brink they paused and looked at each other. The Nis giggled. Peer grinned and pushed.

There was an ear-splitting crash, and pieces of wood flew like daggers. Loki fled under the table. Peer looked over to see the damage. The millstone had cracked in two, and the wooden bin was firewood. He jumped down, reached into the wreckage, and pulled out a soft leather bag.

It was all there, his father's hard-earned wages – thin copper pennies, and worn silver pieces that slipped gently through his fingers. At the bottom of the bag was his father's old silver ring. He shut his eyes and pushed it on to his own finger. *Father, are you there? Can you hear me? I'm doing what you did, Father. I'm running away.* He waited, as if there could be an answer, before opening his eyes.

He pulled on one of Uncle Baldur's old tunics. It was smelly but warm, and came down to his knees. He seized the best of the blankets from Grim's bed and wrapped it around his shoulders like a cloak. Next he chose the smallest pair of boots. They were still huge, so he stuffed the toes with straw and laced them up tightly.

"We need some food," he said, taking a loaf from the bread crock. He tore some off to munch and gave half to Loki. The Nis watched, bright-eyed.

"Want some?" asked Peer. The Nis sprang into the rafters and sat nibbling like a squirrel. Peer took a last look at the dark room, the glowing bed of the fire, the shattered millstone and broken bin. "I'm off. Goodbye, Nis. I'll never forget you. But I have to go now, before they get back."

Snow was falling thickly in the yard. Peer crossed the bridge and decided to leave the road. He did not want to meet his uncles on the way home. Somewhere behind the snow-laden clouds the moon had risen, and he could pick his way up over the glimmering white fields. In spite of the cold and the dangerous journey ahead, he felt he had come to life.

"I'm free!" he said, savouring the word. It was a pity he was leaving the Nis behind. And Hilde. He desperately hoped Hilde would be all right. But leaving seemed to be the only thing he could do for her now. Hilde and her family belonged here: the neighbours would look out for them. Arne and Bjørn would, for example. But Peer? He was nobody's business. *We're just strays, Loki and me. We'd better look out for ourselves. Nobody else will.*

At the top of the big field above the mill, the same field Ralf had galloped across escaping from the trolls all those years ago, he stopped for breath, leaning against the tall stone called the Finger. Out of the steadily falling snow, a white fox came trotting downhill. Loki pricked his ears, whining, and Peer caught his collar. The fox froze with one foot lifted and looked sharply at the boy and his dog.

"Hello!" said Peer, amused. "Going down to the farms to see what you can find? There's a black cockerel at the mill. You can have him and welcome!"

The fox shook its head and sneezed. It sprang away with flattened ears, disappearing into the white world in seconds. Peer laughed. But beside him, Loki growled. A moment late, Peer realised why.

Only a few yards away, two huge shapes emerged from the greyness, plodding uphill. He heard the grumble of two familiar and hated voices. His heart nearly stopped.

Uncle Baldur and Uncle Grim!

CHAPTER 14

Peer Alone

PEER CROUCHED, HIS mind spinning. Were they after him? How could they know where he was?

Had they caught Hilde? Were they taking her to the Troll King all by herself?

Cheek pressed to the stone, he looked around the edge. And one thing was clear: his uncles had no idea he was there. Their hoods pulled well down, they trudged past his hiding place without looking left or right. And Hilde wasn't with them. He sighed in relief. But each of them carried a large bundle over his shoulder.

What *were* those bundles? Was it just the poor light, or were they moving? Peer strained his eyes. With a jolt of horror he suddenly saw what they were. Two small children, bundled in sacking and swathed in ropes.

"Sigurd and Sigrid!" Peer breathed. A girl and a boy. Twins.

A matching pair!

He stood in the snow, in full view if his uncles turned around, his mind racing. What could he do? What could he possibly do, all by himself? How could he rescue the twins from two huge, powerful men – or from a whole hill full of trolls?

If he had been slower leaving the mill, or if he had gone

by the road, he would never have known – never have seen what his uncles were doing. He gazed after their disappearing backs. It was nearly too late. In a moment they would vanish into the dim night and falling snow. He could go on to Hammerhaven as if nothing had happened.

But into his head slipped a memory, the memory of Sigrid's high little voice in the summer, screaming at Uncle Baldur: "I don't like the nasty man! I hate him!" Sigrid and Sigurd were only little, but they were his friends.

Peer stood as still as the big stone. He knew what he should do. He should follow, and see where his uncles were taking the children. He should tell the whole village what they had done. If he didn't he would blame himself for ever.

"Loki!" he said with a furious sob. "*This* way!"

Loki gambolled along at his heels, thinking this was a game. Peer was terrified he would bark and give them away. He was afraid of losing his uncles, and afraid of getting too close. Already their shadowy shapes were disappearing into a little valley. Peer ran, as if in a bad dream. His cumbersome boots dragged half off at each stride.

The valley was no more than a dimple on the hillside, but it was full of drifted snow. Both Peer's boots came off as he ploughed through it. There was no time to empty out the snow; he just shoved his numb feet back in and plunged on. The tracks turned uphill again. Peer dropped into a plod, forced himself to run, fell to plodding again. On and on he went. It stopped snowing, and the moon sailed out over a landscape of white slopes and black rocks. Deep dragging marks showed where his uncles had turned aside towards the foot of a cliff – twenty feet or so of glistening stone capped with a snowy overhang. The tracks continued along the base to a place where a rockfall of boulders offered a way up. Peer and Loki picked their way, slipping and bruising themselves on half-buried stones.

At the top of the cliff, the ground levelled out into a wide ledge. Peer reached it, gasping. A few hundred yards ahead, clear in the moonlight, two dark figures strode towards a narrow ravine. If they turned around, Peer would be in plain view. But they didn't turn.

He looked back, realising he was not far from the top of Troll Fell. The land fell away in all directions, and he could sense the bulk of the mountain below him. Other lonely peaks reared up white in the dark sky to the north. An inhuman silence reigned.

Loki pawed at his legs. Peer was suddenly very thankful for his dog. "Good boy. Come on!"

The snow was shallow here, combed thin by the wind. Peer hurried up the slope in his uncles' tracks, determined to keep them – and the twins – in sight to the end. They were heading into the ravine. Steep cliffs leaned over, slashed black with shadows. And then a shrill yell rang out, ringing off the rocks. Uncle Baldur was shouting to the gatekeeper of Troll Fell: "Open! Open up!"

The troll gate opened.

A hairline of light appeared in the dark root of the cliff. Silently and swiftly it widened as the stone door turned on unseen pivots. Spellbound, Peer crouched in the snow as golden light spilled down the mountain.

The dark shapes of his two uncles, carrying the bundles that were Sigurd and Sigrid, stood out black for a moment against the gold, then vanished inside. Smoothly, silently, the door swung shut. The rectangle of light shrank to a line, narrowed to a filament, and was gone. The shock passed through the ground as though Troll Fell shivered, and prickled over Peer's skin.

He ran, scrambling over the pebbles at the base of the cliff and threw himself at the cold face, patting and fumbling for the door. Nothing. Solid stone without a crack. His legs gave way. He sank to the ground, ashamed to have come so far and been so useless. His hand felt something in the snow beside him. It was Sigrid's woolly cap, gritty with melting snow crystals, but still warm.

Peer bent his head on to his knees.

Loki sensed Peer's despair. He lifted his muzzle to the sky and let the misery within him float away in a long, musical howl. The eerie sound echoed in the cliffs, and brought Peer back to his feet. "Quiet, Loki. Hush!" But Loki, surprised and impressed by the noise he had made, was doing it again.

"*Oooo...ooo...ooo...!*" The sound trailed away. To Peer it seemed as though all the mountains were looking at them. It was awful. The rebounding echoes came fainter and fainter. And then came an echo that was not an echo.

Peer froze. "Was that – a bark?"

Unmistakably, a second bark came from somewhere below them on the hill. Loki shot off. Moments later he reappeared, leaping crazily around another dog – an old sheepdog, by the look of it – that was trotting steadily uphill. Peer couldn't believe his eyes. A shepherd? On top of Troll Fell at this hour?

Somebody was coming, all right, puffing up the slope. Somebody too small to be a shepherd...

"Loki!" cried a clear, incredulous voice. "Peer? What are you doing here?"

"Hilde!" yelled Peer. He rushed to meet her; he grabbed her hands. Words tumbled out. "It was Uncle Baldur – Uncle Grim. I was escaping – I saw them carrying the twins. They went into the mountain, Hilde, I couldn't stop them. What shall we do?"

Hilde pulled off her cap and pushed the hair out of her eyes. "You saw them? And you followed? Oh well done, Peer!"

"How did you know where to come?" Peer still couldn't believe it.

"Alf and I discovered this place when we were gathering sheep at the beginning of winter," Hilde told him. "Alf. My dog." Alf licked her mittened hand. "Tonight, when we realised the twins had been stolen—" her voice shook, "Mother and Grandfather went to the village to rouse everyone. I was supposed to stay behind in case – in case the twins came back; but I knew they wouldn't. I couldn't bear to wait. I decided to come here. Alf knows the way."

"The door's shut," said Peer. "I didn't know what to do. I still don't."

"Well, if the door's shut, let's go and knock on it," said Hilde.

"I found this," said Peer unhappily. He handed her Sigrid's cap. Hilde looked at it silently and tucked it into her pocket.

"But even if they hear us knocking," Peer went on, "why should they let us in?"

"They'll let us in," said Hilde with strange confidence, "when they know I've got this!"

She pulled out a small bundle wrapped in cloth and unrolled it. Peer gasped. "Is that—?"

"The famous cup? Yes," said Hilde. She turned it this way and that. The gold gleamed pale in the moonlight and the moulding winked white fire. "Let's see how badly the Gaffer of Troll Fell wants it back! Let's go. It'll soon be dawn, and they won't open the troll gate after sunrise. Hurry!"

She picked up a stone and pounded the rock face, shouting. "Open up! Open up! I'm Hilde, Ralf's daughter!"

"Open up!" Peer joined in. They hammered on the cliff.

The dogs barked.

"Wait a minute," panted Hilde. They listened. The echoes died away. It was growing lighter every moment.

"Open up!" called Hilde. "Tell the Gaffer I've brought his cup. Remember? The cup Ralf Eiriksson took, years ago!"

Years ago! Years ago! The echo sprang to and fro. Hilde bit her lip. "It's not working." Her face was wan in the cold pre-dawn glow.

Peer caught her arm. A vertical black seam ran down the rock face. It split apart. They smelled sparks. The soles of their feet tickled. The stone door swung slowly inwards, revealing nothing but a gaping darkness.

Hilde stepped forwards, but Peer dragged her back. "You can't go in there!"

"Yes I can. Let go!"

"Not in the dark! You'll get lost – trapped!" He hung on. She twisted a foot behind his leg and tripped him. They fell together, sobbing and struggling.

"*Let – me – go!*" Hilde shrieked, her face inches from his. "*You* don't have to come! They're not *your* brother and sister! If you're such a coward, go home!"

Peer let go. He lay back on the ground, chest heaving. Tears leaked from under his eyelids. Hilde scrambled up. "I'm sorry," she said between gasps. "I'm sorry."

Behind her loomed the cliff and the tall black slot of the troll gate. The thought of disappearing into it filled Peer with terror, but he got to his feet. "You're not going alone," he said fiercely, "I'm coming with you."

"Oh Peer!" Hilde wiped her eyes on the back of her hand. "Come on then. Wait! Just a minute." She bent to the dogs. "Go home, Alf. Good boy. Go home, you hear me? And take Loki. You can't come with us."

"Off you go, Loki," said Peer, clenching his teeth.

Alf sniffed Loki. He turned and trotted a few paces downhill. He stopped and looked round. "Go home, Loki!" said Peer loudly. The old dog barked, and slowly Loki began to follow him. "Goodbye!" muttered Peer. He watched the two dogs going away down the hill and felt lonelier than ever before in his life.

"Come on!" Hilde beckoned anxiously. The moon was paling and the sky was pink.

Sucking in a huge gasp of the cold, fresh air, filling his lungs as if it was the last breath he would ever take, Peer turned his back on the sunrise and followed Hilde into Troll Fell.

CHAPTER 15

Torches by the Fjord

GUDRUN STEADIED EIRIK as he slipped. With arms linked, they waded through the drifts, encouraging each other – Gudrun with breathless gasps of, "Well done," and "Slippy here – hold up!" and Eirik with battle cries of "Bring on the wolf's brood! Rouse the steel-storm!" The pine trees whistled overhead and snow whirled through the branches.

When they came out of the woods above the mill, it looked deserted. The buildings glimmered grey and ghostly in the snow. Not a light showed. No smoke rose from the roof.

Eirik paused, wheezing, and Gudrun hugged his arm. "Father-in-law! Are you all right?"

Eirik shook himself like a dog. "I'm fine," he growled. "Fine!" And he plunged on down the path.

The black waterwheel was toothed with icicles. As Gudrun and Eirik shuffled over the icy bridge, they heard the excited bark of a fox from the mill yard, followed by an unearthly cackling.

Fox among the hens, thought Gudrun at once, but she didn't care. Serve the Grimssons right if they lost their hens! And Eirik thought the same, he was nodding at her. "Foxes! I'll give 'em foxes," he roared. "I'll *feed* them to the foxes, in tiny pieces. On we go!"

He was getting very tired though, Gudrun could tell,

leaning more and more heavily on her arm. Still, the path was smoother now. It wasn't so far to the village. Oh, but what was she doing here, when Sigurd and Sigrid must be far up the mountain? Why hadn't she sent Hilde with Eirik and gone after them herself? She began to cry, big tears spilling over her cheeks. Her woollen skirt dragged, clotted with snow.

"Snow's stopped," Eirik shouted. "Dawn's on the way." It was true.

Wiping her tears, Gudrun saw the first houses and smelled the heavy tang of woodsmoke. She let go of Eirik's arm and ran stumbling to the nearest door. "Einar!" She beat on it and pushed it open.

There was no one there. The fire burned cheerfully, the blankets on the sleeping bench were disturbed as though the sleepers had flung them back and left suddenly. "No one's here!" cried Gudrun as Eirik hobbled up behind her.

"Try next door," Eirik gasped.

Gudrun flew past him. "Arne – Harald! Where are you?" she begged. "Bjørn – Kersten?" House after house was empty, though cats yowled from corners and in one a baby cried, alone in its cradle. Gudrun came out looking bewildered. "Where are they all? Is it some evil spell?"

Eirik held up his hand. "Listen!" Gudrun obeyed. It seemed she could hear a far-off shouting.

"Is it an attack?" she gasped. "Is it war?"

"Onwards to battle!" shouted Eirik. "Let's go see!"

Alf and Loki trotted briskly down the hill. As they came in sight of the tall stone where Peer had sheltered the night before, the sun rose over the hill. The snow glittered, and the stone's long shadow fell across the slope.

Light-footed up the hill, the white fox came dancing, dragging something by the neck. Close to the big stone it stopped to lay down the burden and get a fresh grip. Limp and bedraggled, the black cockerel lay dead on the snow.

Alf circled the fox, glaring and growling. But Loki trotted nimbly right up to it, and touched noses. His tail moved in a tentative wag, and the fox's brush twitched in reply. Then its sharp ears pricked. It glanced up. The dogs stiffened. A breath of wind brought to their acute hearing a distant clamour. Far away on the shore, many voices were shouting.

The fox grabbed the cockerel and slunk off up the hill. Alf stood rigid, his muzzle raised, snuffing the wind, straining at those sounds floating from the fjord. With a hoarse bark he bounded forwards, his bushy tail waving. Loki dashed after him. Side by side the two dogs crossed the wooden bridge and disappeared into the trees on the path to the village.

Torches flared by the fjord, pale in the dawn. Beached on the shingle, dwarfing Bjørn and Arne's boats, an elegant longship reared its proud neck. The fierce dragonhead was covered in sacking, so as not to frighten the timid land spirits of the homeland.

The whole village had turned out to greet it. Clinging together, Eirik and Gudrun made their way on to the pebbles, where Gudrun shrieked, let go of Eirik and ran into the water to seize the arm of a tall burly man who vaulted laughing out of the ship.

"Ralf! Ralf, my man, is it really you?" She pounded his chest with her fists, laughing and crying. "Is it really you?"

"Yes, my girl!" Ralf scooped her off her feet and gave her a bristly kiss. "It's really me!"

CHAPTER 16

In the Hall of the Mountain King

THE TROLL DOOR closed with a boom and a suck of air, as if a giant mouth had breathed in.

It was dark.

Peer's breath shortened. "Hilde! Where are you?"

"Here!" Their groping hands met. "I thought there would be lights," she whispered, gripping him. "Why is it dark?"

Her touch steadied him. "It's daybreak." Peer remembered something the Nis had once said. "That's night-time for trolls."

"If they're all asleep, who let us in?"

"Ssh!" said Peer, freezing. They listened, tense. Was anyone there? Peer heard water dripping, and his own harsh breath. He closed his eyes, opened them wide. It made no difference. The darkness moulded to his face, clung to him, caught in his throat like black glue...

"Hello!" Hilde's bold voice rang out. "Gatekeeper! We've come to see the Gaffer. Bring us a light!"

There was a soft clap and an explosion of light. The tunnel blanched. Painfully, through watering eyes, Peer saw a spindly figure twirling a bright sphere, like a little sun, on one crooked forefinger. It laughed quietly: "*Ho, ho!*"

"We want – to see – the Gaffer," Hilde gasped.

A dark hooked arm bowled the ball of light towards them.

They dodged, and the quivering light rolled past, illuminating the first few yards of a long passage. They looked back at the stone door, trying to see the gatekeeper, but their own shadows blotted it out – except for a long clawed foot, like a bird's, scraping along the floor.

Peer and Hilde turned and ran. "Oh my goodness," panted Hilde. "It must have been standing right behind us in the dark!"

"What now?" Peer demanded. "What do we do?"

"Follow the light, I think. Come on!" She tugged his hand. Peer came, throwing a nervous glance over his shoulder. But only darkness followed them.

At first, the passage was wide enough to walk abreast. Peer clumped along in his wet boots, trying not to shiver. Troll Fell had swallowed him and here he was in its long stone gullet. The air was chill. The floor rose and fell, with unexpected puddles.

Sometimes the passage twisted, or branched into side passages, which corkscrewed up or dived into darkness. Sometimes the roof dipped, and they had to duck. Or the walls bulged, nipping the passage into a tight waist. "One at a time here," muttered Hilde, sliding sideways. "Come on!" Peer squeezed after her: the stone felt wet and smooth, slick as a cow's tongue.

On the other side Hilde clutched him, shouting. "Look at that!"

A rough cataract of yellow water shot from a hole in the ceiling and hurtled into a pit. The only way past was along a slanting ledge on the left-hand wall. Peer looked down the shaft. The water careered into darkness.

"I'll go first!" he said grimly. He needed to keep moving. When he stood still, he felt as though the whole weight of

Troll Fell was pressing on his shoulders. "It's not too bad," he shouted. "Keep near the wall like this, and – ah!"

His foot slipped and in panic he snatched at the rocks. One hand curled over a sharp rim and he hung over the drop, kicking. Water drummed on his back. Hilde screamed; then her hand caught his flailing wrist and she hauled. He dragged his knee up and over, and clawed his way further up the slippery shelf. Together they crawled out of the spray to where the passage opened again on the far side of the shaft.

The ball of light was loitering there, bluish and fitful. As they scrambled to their feet it turned a couple of brisk spins, brightened, and whirled off down the tunnel. Bruised and bedraggled, Peer and Hilde limped along. They stumbled up a flight of shallow steps. At the top the light sprang up and hung overhead, rotating lazily.

Deep in the rock of the left-hand wall was a crevice, shaped into a rough archway. Set back into it was a solid wooden door.

Peer looked at Hilde. She gave him an anxious nod. He knocked.

In a moment the door opened a crack and small troll looked out, holding a smoking pine branch in one fist. It saw them and hissed, exposing needle sharp teeth and began to shut the door again, but Peer stuck his foot in the way.

"We want to see the Gaffer!"

The troll jerked at the door. Peer got his fingers around the edge and dragged it back. Feverishly, Hilde unwrapped the golden cup.

The troll's eyes grew round and black. It let go of the door and sprang up and down, tail lashing. "Give! Give!" it squeaked.

"It's not for you." Hilde held the cup high in the air. "It's for the Gaffer. We want to see him – now!"

The little troll's claws shot out and its ears folded flat like an angry cat's, but it stood back and opened the door wide. Side by side, shoulder to shoulder, Peer and Hilde stepped in.

It was a large chamber, gloriously warm and smelling of pine needles. In the middle of the floor a brazier glowed red, filled with logs. The troll pitched the burning branch back into the flames.

Beyond the brazier was a stone bed. Its four crooked posts seemed to have dripped from the ceiling and grown from the floor. Peer and Hilde tiptoed closer. On it, snoring loudly under a pile of sheepskins, the old Gaffer of Troll Fell lay – apparently asleep. His mouth hung open, showing two long brown curving teeth like tusks. His eyes were closed. But in the middle of his forehead a third eye glared, red-rimmed and weeping. It rolled around and fixed on Peer and Hilde.

"I see strangers," the Gaffer mumbled in his sleep. He yawned, stretched and sat up, opening his other eyes – and as he did so, the eye in the middle of his forehead fluttered slowly shut.

"*Hutututu!* What's this, what's this?" growled the Gaffer. Peer and Hilde grabbed hands.

"I'm Ralf Eiriksson's daughter." Hilde spoke up bravely. "I've come for my little brother and sister. The millers of Trollsvik stole them."

"We brought you something in exchange," Peer added as the Gaffer scowled.

Hilde held up the golden cup. "This! You lost it years ago. Give me back my brother and sister, and in return—"

"*Lost* it?" the Gaffer interrupted. "It was stolen! Stolen by your father, a thief if ever there was. How dare you make bargains with me?"

"How dare you call him a thief?" Hilde cried. "You trolls tried to poison him!"

"Hilde—" said Peer.

"It wasn't poison!" shouted the King of Troll Fell.

"Then why did it burn all the hair off his pony's tail?" Hilde yelled.

"Hilde—"

Hilde grabbed a sheepskin from the Gaffer's bed and shook it in his face. "See that?" she panted. "See that mark? That came from one of our sheep – and so did this!" She seized another fleece, and another. "Who's the thief now?" She threw them down and stood glaring at him.

Peer expected the Gaffer to call his trolls and have both of them torn to pieces. To his immense relief, the huge old troll began to laugh. He screwed up all three eyes and rocked to and fro on the edge of his bed, choking.

"Well, what's a little borrowing between neighbours?" he coughed, slapping his knees. "Give me that!" He snatched the cup and turned it in his claws, admiring it.

"Nice timing," he grinned at Hilde. "We need this for the wedding. It's the Bride Cup of Troll Fell, always used at weddings. Traditional! Belonged to my grandmother. Skotte!"

The little troll in the corner gave a shrill squeak and stood to attention.

"Get everyone up," said the Gaffer. "If I'm awake, no one else sleeps. There's plenty to do. I want the Hall ready before midnight. Wake up the princess. I want to see her." The little troll doubled over in a bow and scuttled out.

The troll king reached for his coat, which was made of sewn-together cat skins, mostly tabby. There was a slit in the back for his cow-like tail. He thrashed about. "Help me!" he growled, and Peer gingerly bent and hooked the tail through.

"Follow me," the Gaffer commanded. He threw open the door and stumped out. The ball of light, idly drifting against the ceiling, brightened rapidly and bounded ahead of him as he marched along the tunnel.

Peer and Hilde began to hear noises ahead: bangs, crashes and whoops. The passage ended in some steps, and they found themselves looking into the splendid Hall under Troll Fell.

It was a huge cavern. The roof was an arch of darkness, patrolled by many floating lights, golden and blue. Their own ball whirled aloft to join the others.

Opposite them, a waterfall found its way in white threads down between rocks. At the foot of the waterfall was a stone chair. The water divided around it and flowed away in a channel under an archway.

The Hall was filling with trolls. Some tumbled from dark chimneys in the roof and dropped to the floor like bouncing balls. Others scrambled out from underneath boulders. Gangs rushed in with tables and benches, dragging them here and there, setting them in order. Over by the river a group of dripping water spirits, or nixies, scoured a pile of golden plates with handfuls of fine white sand. Everyone was shouting at once:

"Fetch a high-seat for the King of the Dovre!"

"A special table for his son and daughter!"

"How many tubs of water for the merrows?"

"We need to have just as many for the nixies!"

"Couldn't they sit on wet stones…?"

Peer scanned the crowd for a sight of Sigurd or Sigrid. He saw trolls with pigs' snouts, trolls with owls' eyes, trolls with birds' beaks. There was not a human face among them – except for the nixies whose beautiful faces were narrow and sly with curious slanting eyes.

Then he saw them – slouching on rocks at the bottom of the waterfall – not the children, but the burly, black-haired figures of the Grimsson twins. He winced.

"Don't worry, Peer," whispered Hilde beside him.

"I'm not," he lied. The Gaffer set off across the uneven stone floor. They followed. The trolls fell back for them, muttering.

Cold with fright, Peer threw his head back and stared at his two uncles. They hadn't seen him yet, and he wasn't looking forward to the moment when they did. Baldur noticed the Gaffer and got to his feet, jogging his brother's elbow – and then he spotted Peer. His jaw dropped. So did Grim's. Their faces registered blank astonishment changing to pop-eyed fury. Scared though he was, Peer had to giggle.

The Gaffer walked past the Grimsson brothers, ignoring them, and climbed on to his throne. He swept his tail out of the way and settled himself. But as Peer and Hilde drew near, the two men came out of their trance. Baldur shot out a thick arm. He caught Peer by the scruff and shook him like a puppet.

"Let him go!" Hilde shrieked, trying to pull him free. Grim kicked her, and there was a hiss of delight from the assembled trolls: "Bite them and tear them! Pull them to pieces!"

"QUIET!" bellowed the Gaffer. He folded his arms. "*Huuuu!* If we're not ready by midnight for the King of the Dovre, I'll look at you all with my other eye and shrivel you into earthworms! Get on with your work." The trolls began to bustle about very busily.

Baldur dropped Peer and turned blustering to the Gaffer. "Whatever the boy's said to you, don't listen to him! We've done what you asked, haven't we? We've got you those children – just what you wanted!"

"S'right!" added Grim. "Give us our gold – as much as we can carry!"

"I'll *do* as I *please*," said the Gaffer, growling.

With a discordant blast, horns sounded in a corner of the Hall. The little troll came hurrying in and bowed several times, out of breath. "The princess!" it gasped. "And the prince!"

Into the Hall came the Gaffer's eldest daughter. She was in a bad temper, for the occasion was so great: she had never been married before! She was pretty; her mother had been a nixie. Her eyes were large, slanted like birch leaves, and her tail was as delicate as a cat's.

"The spiders haven't finished my wedding dress," she complained. "And look at all the dust! You should have raised the hill yesterday and aired the place. Then North Wind could have swept in here. We shall never be ready in time, and the King of the Dovre will think I'm a bad housewife."

"He won't think that as long as there's enough beer," chuckled the Gaffer. "Besides, my dear, look what I have for you! The Bride Cup you so foolishly lost, long ago."

The troll princess looked at it carelessly. "That old thing? You've got it back? So at last you'll stop fussing?"

"It's an heirloom, my dear!"

Up came her brother the troll prince, a sulky expression on his piggish face. "Those two children you've got for us are terrible," he burst out. "They won't fetch or carry or dance or sing. They won't do anything but scream and cry. I can't possibly give the girl to my bride."

"I can't possibly give the boy to my husband!" agreed the troll princess.

They glared at their father who in turn scowled at the Grimssons.

"'*Just what I wanted*,' eh?" he growled, and the eye in the middle of his forehead flickered in a red blink. The two big men shuffled their feet.

"How can they *sing* when they're unhappy? Where are they?" cried Hilde, imagining the children locked in some dark cave. But Peer pulled her arm and there, creeping into the Hall, holding hands tightly, were Sigurd and Sigrid. Their dirty tear-streaked faces brightened as they saw Hilde, and they raced to meet her. She grabbed one in each arm and hugged them close. "This'll teach you to go running off," she choked. "I *told* you to stay with Grandpa!"

Sigrid sobbed. Peer tousled her hair, a brotherly lump in his throat. "Don't scold, Hilde," he whispered.

"I'm not," sniffed Hilde. "Don't cry any more, Siggy. We're taking you home."

"Are you, now?" asked the Gaffer drily.

Hilde turned on him. "I brought you the cup!"

"And the prince and princess don't want the children," Peer added.

"It's what *I* want that counts!" the Gaffer snarled. "And it boils down to this. I want a pair of you for the Dovreking's son and daughter. So two of you may go – but two must stay.

"I'm feeling generous," he added genially, "so I'll let you choose."

"You don't mean it," said Hilde in horror.

The Gaffer looked at her.

"But—" She stopped, gasping. "How *can* we choose?"

"Take your time," the Gaffer advised merrily. "Think hard. Don't decide in a hurry!"

"Can't we go home?" Sigrid wept, her mouth turned down. "I want to go home!"

"So do I!" cried Sigurd. They buried themselves in Hilde's clothes. She looked down at them and bit her lip.

"I – I suppose I had better stay," she whispered.

Sick with shock, Peer opened his mouth, and closed it again, unable to say the words that would condemn him to a life of slavery. He imagined living here, trapped – never seeing Loki again, never seeing anyone but trolls – and choked. He looked at Hilde and she turned away. Peer thought it was scorn. He gritted his teeth. It was easy for her to be brave. The twins were her family!

He stole another glance. Hilde's head was bowed, her fists clenched. Peer was ashamed of himself. Of course it wasn't easy.

He stared dizzily around the Hall – the scurrying trolls, the white strands of the waterfall, the moving lights in the dark roof. It all seemed horribly strange and meaningless. *I've got to get out! Out, where the sun shines and the wind blows!*

Again he looked at Hilde, who still would not look at him. And then his eyes came to rest on the stupid, brutal, calculating faces of Baldur and Grim. A cold thought penetrated. What sort of life would it be, to go back to the mill with those two? How could he live, knowing he had abandoned Hilde?

I'd be as bad as they are, he thought in revulsion.

He pressed his hands over his eyes. It was the same choice he had made on the mountain, but this time it was much harder. Who would have thought you had to keep on choosing and choosing? *I can't keep running away, Father*, he said silently in the blackness behind his closed lids. *It doesn't work. It's time to stand up to them.* And he opened his eyes.

"I'll stay here too."

Hilde shot him a look of amazed and shining gratitude. Peer turned to the Gaffer. "I'll stay," he repeated, bleak but firm. "So don't give my uncles any treasure. They haven't earned it. Sigurd and Sigrid are no good to you, and *we're* staying of our own free will."

The Gaffer howled with laughter, opening his mouth so wide he showed every jagged tooth. "Good boy – excellent!"

"Our reward – our gold!" Baldur squeaked in horror. "Besides, that boy's my own nephew. You have to pay me for him."

"Not – a – penny!" said the Gaffer, and his mouth snapped shut. The Grimssons looked completely confounded, Peer saw. It was some consolation.

"When can the children go home?" Hilde demanded.

"After the wedding," said the Gaffer. "We're busy till then."

"And keep them quiet," ordered the troll princess. "Or I'll bite them!" She cast a critical eye over Hilde and Peer. "Come here!" She looked them up and down. "Humph! These two are bigger and stronger. I suppose that's better. Oh! Look at her boots! Why, they're better than mine!"

Hilde looked down. It was true she was wearing a good pair, made by her father and embroidered round the tops in blue and red thread.

The princess hoisted her skirts and showed a foot shod in a clumsy wooden clog.

"Let her have 'em," Peer advised from the corner of his mouth.

"Take them," said Hilde quietly. She pulled them off and gave them to the princess, who kicked off her clogs. Hilde slipped her own feet into them with a slight shudder.

The princess tugged the boots on. She stuck out her feet. "Now I shall be finer than the Dovreking's daughter. They pinch, it's true – but that's the price of elegance!"

"Now there's plenty to do!" the Gaffer shouted. "Has the beer come in yet?"

"Not yet. The bog wife has been brewing for us all week. I ordered twelve barrels of strong black beer. When the steam rises from her vats, the humans say, 'Oh, there's mist on the marshes!'" laughed his son.

The Gaffer licked his lips with a long red tongue and turned to his daughter. "Take the girl away. She can help you to dress. As for you, boy—" he waved at Peer, "roll barrels or move tables. Make yourself useful."

They were being separated! As Hilde was led reluctantly away, Peer startled at a touch on his shoulder. He looked round into the face of a small troll with huge eyes and a long thin beak like a curlew. "Come to the kitchens!" it piped. "Help the cooks!"

It rushed him over to a dark crack in the floor. Hot air rose from it, and the strangest smells. Peer teetered on the edge; the troll pushed him, and with a cry he shot into the darkness, whipping down a natural slide, and was spat out into a lower cavern filled with a red mist of steam and smoke. The troll popped out beside him.

Peer got up, rubbing his bruised knees. "Whatever are they cooking?" he coughed. The troll piped something hard to hear – had it really said, "*Frog soup, eel pie, spittle cakes – bone bread?*"

Hot fires blazed. Frenzied trolls rushed about with ladles, spoons, colanders and platters. From one corner came a rhythmic thumping where a couple of trolls were working a huge pestle and mortar, pounding a pile of bones into smaller and smaller fragments. Nearby was a stone quern for grinding them into flour, and a series of wooden troughs where several small trolls danced up and down on the dough. Batches of gritty bread were being lifted out of ovens.

Great pots hung over the fires. Peer glanced into one. It

held a bubbling mess that looked like frogspawn. And a greasy little troll turned the handle of a spit on which a whole pig was roasting. Or was it a—?

"Dog!" squeaked the troll. That wasn't – *Grendel*, by any chance, he wondered? It looked big enough. He backed away, feeling ill. How would he and Hilde live? Never, never could they eat such food.

We'll escape, he swore to himself. *They can't guard us for ever. Perhaps we can follow the stream. It must find its way out somewhere!*

Through streaming eyes he spotted a flight of steps. His troll had forgotten him, and he darted across and ran up the twisting spiral. Emerging into the cool Hall he blinked. He must have been in the kitchens longer than he'd thought, for the tables were all prepared and the guests were arriving and being shown to their places. Everywhere, gold gleamed and silver shone. Jewels winked in the crowns of the Gaffer of Troll Fell and his son and daughter, who stood in front of the throne, welcoming the arrivals.

Where was Hilde? Over there, sitting forlornly on the rocks by the waterfall with Sigurd beside her and Sigrid on her lap. And there were Baldur and Grim, seated at a table, heads together, deep in some grumbling conversation. They wouldn't go without their gold. Peer smiled grimly. He thought they would have to wait for a very long time. A group of pig-snouted musicians struck up. One blew a twisted ram's horn; another sawed notes from a one-stringed fiddle. The third rattled a stick up and down a sheep's jawbone. There was a shout.

"The King of the Dovrefell! He's arriving, he's here!"

"Raise up the hill!" shouted the Gaffer of Troll Fell. "Time for some fun!"

CHAPTER 17

Raising the Hill

WITH A RUMBLING and a rattling of all the dishes on the table, the roof began to rise. All around the Hall a gap appeared, a widening strip of night sky fringed with trailing roots and ragged earth. Clods rained from the edges, and a draught of cold air rushed into the Hall, smelling of snow, fresh earth and freedom. Hoisted up on four strong red pillars, the hill stood open to the midwinter night, spilling light to all sides.

As the musicians launched into a lively jig, the King of the Dovrefell and his party swept down into the Hall on the night wind. They landed in a chattering group, collecting themselves and adjusting their clothes. The King of the Dovrefell was tall and dignified. He threw back the hood of his white bearskin cloak and strode forward with his son behind him and his daughter clutching his arm. Peer couldn't see her face. Hadn't the Nis said she was beautiful? She lifted her veil, and a murmur of admiration ran around the Hall. The Troll Fell princess was looking as cross as two sticks. Peer edged around curiously.

The princess had three tails. Two were draped elegantly over her elbows; the third sprouted from the middle of her forehead and was tied up in a bow to keep it out of her eyes. The Troll Fell prince greeted her eagerly, looking smitten already. Peer closed his eyes and shook his head.

The Gaffer and the Dovreking clasped hands. "Welcome!"

boomed the Gaffer. He slapped the Dovreking on the back. "A drink to warm you after your journey! And we'll let the young people get to know each other, hey?" He laughed loudly.

The two princesses bristled at each other like a couple of cats.

"What a funny little place you have here," observed the Dovre princess. "Quite rustic. I see you have a sod roof. At home in the Dovrefell, our hall is so high that the roof is carved from ice."

"That must be very chilly," the Troll Fell princess smiled. "Here we enjoy simple comfort, and despise ostentation."

"I imagine you have to," replied the Dovre princess.

"Will you dance?" asked the Troll Fell prince hastily. But his bride said she was tired and would rather sit. The couples sat stiffly down together, and the Troll Fell princess yawned.

"Now then! Brighten up!" shouted the Gaffer. He and the Dovreking were laughing and drinking, and seemed to be getting along famously. "You're not allowed to quarrel till *after* you're married, remember. You boys, give your brides a hug and a kiss. Don't be shy!"

"Vulgar old fellow," muttered the Dovre princess.

"Let's exchange gifts," boomed the King of the Dovrefell. "That'll cheer them all up. We brought a few small things from the Dovrefell."

He snapped his fingers. Two stout trolls stepped forward with a heavy sack. The untied the neck and poured out a stream of jewels. Diamonds, rubies, amethysts, emeralds, rattled out like peas and lay on the floor in a shimmering drift – or bounced and rolled under the tables. Baldur and Grim crashed heads as they lunged to pick up a skipping diamond.

"Very pretty," said the Gaffer. He beckoned to various

servants who came staggering out with piles of gold: necklaces, rings, bracelets, chains and crowns. "Part of a dragon's hoard," said the Gaffer, waving a casual hand. Peer glanced at his uncles. Their mouths were wet with excitement.

The Dovreking frowned and snapped his fingers again. This time his trolls laid out heaps of beautifully woven and embroidered clothes, each one of which would have taken a human seamstress a year to make. But these were not made by mortals. There were scarves snipped from the trailing ends of the Northern Lights; petticoats trimmed with the most delicate frost; seven-league boots lined in ermine. The Troll Fell princess got a cloak of moonshine that pleased her so much she threw her arms around the Dovreking and gave him a kiss.

"Aha!" said the Dovreking, pinching her cheek. But the Gaffer grinned triumphantly and signalled to Peer and Hilde.

"Now for a little extra – a special present," he gloated. "You won't have brought anything like *this* from the Dovrefell!"

Peer caught Hilde's eye. Together they stepped forward. *Better make a good job of it*, thought Peer gloomily, and he bowed low. Hilde curtsied. The three-tailed princess screamed in mock terror and clutched her bridegroom's arm. "Oooh! What is it? What are they for?"

"Something you don't see every day," the Gaffer boasted. "Your new servants!"

"Humans!"

"Yes, of course," broke in the Troll Fell princess. She pushed the pile of jewels with a contemptuous toe. "We see so much of this kind of thing. We wanted to be original!"

The two free tails of the Dovre princess swished angrily; the one knotted up above her face could only twitch. "What a strange idea. They're very pale. All that unhealthy daylight, I suppose. Is this the girl? Turn around. I thought so! This ugly creature has no tail at all. Take her away at once and fix one on!"

"No!" Hilde cried.

"We don't have tails," Peer shouted. "We think they're ugly!"

The Dovre princess screamed. "Oh, what an insult!"

The Gaffer stepped in, bowing as gallantly as he could. "Now, now," he rumbled. "No cause for concern. We all appreciate your beauty, my dear. I myself have three eyes," he coughed modestly, "but three tails are rare indeed."

His own daughter scowled. The Dovre princess simpered.

"No," the Gaffer went on, "we've simply neglected one small ceremony. After that, these humans will see things as *we* do. Here, you two!" He snapped his fingers and led them aside.

"Ceremony?" asked Peer apprehensively.

The Gaffer nodded. "You haven't yet tasted our beer. A single sip of the bog-wife's brew, and you'll see things our way for ever and ever!"

"For ever?" Peer repeated slowly.

"Excuse me – but we'll think the Dovre princess is beautiful?" asked Hilde.

"You will indeed," said the Gaffer.

"And the food?" Peer was too shaken to mince his words. "We'll enjoy eating frog soup and rat stew? And the music? It sounds like – like a cat on the roof, or a cow in pain."

"It's giving me a headache," Hilde added.

"I'm getting annoyed!" The Gaffer squared up to them. "See here! We can't have servants that don't admire us. Once you've drunk our brew you'll think black is white. You think night is day and day is night. And so they are! It's only another way of seeing."

"But then," said Hilde, appalled, "we won't be *us*. We *are* what we think!" She looked around wildly. "We won't be humans any more. Inside, we'll be trolls!"

"AND WHAT'S THE MATTER WITH THAT?" roared the Gaffer.

Peer and Hilde stared at the glittering crowds, and then at each other. Everything was very sharp and clear, and also a little distant. Peer tasted fear, sour in his mouth. Between the red pillars supporting the roof he could see the dark spaces of the night sky. Out there lay freedom, the snowy slopes, the stars. But he would never reach it.

We'll never escape, he thought. *We'll never follow the stream out of the hill.*

Once he and Hilde had drunk a drop of the bog-wife's beer, they wouldn't even want to leave. They would live the rest of their lives like earthworms buried under Troll Fell. They would still look the same, but on the inside they would have changed completely. Peer thought he would rather be dead.

One of the Gaffer's trolls came trotting up. Dimly Peer recognised it: the kitchen troll with the long beak. It bowed to the Gaffer, presenting a golden cup. The cup was Ralf's cup – the Bride Cup – and it was half full of brown beer.

"Right!" Briskly the Gaffer lashed his tail. "Who's going first?"

Hilde met Peer's eyes, despairing but steady. "I'm sorry I got you into this, Peer."

"You didn't," said Peer. "I wanted to come."

She reached for the cup, but Peer was quicker and snatched it up. "Wait!" he said breathlessly.

He looked into the cup. The dark liquid swirled, a bottomless whirlpool. He glanced up, to see the world for the last time as himself. His throat closed up. There was a drumming in his ears – or was that the Gaffer growling? He bent his head, lifting the cup reluctantly to his lips, spinning out the seconds…

The moment dragged past. There was no time left.

And Hilde shouted. "Peer! *Stop!*" He lowered the cup.

Out in the dark beyond the pillars, he saw lights. Lanterns! People were out there, real people, struggling through the snow! Voices shouted; a dog barked. The trolls began to turn around, chattering uneasily. More shouts, closer! A scuffle broke out, a clang of metal, and then uproar as a band of rough-looking men came shoving their way into the Hall. Hey, that was Bjørn! And there was Arne! But who was the big man in front, wearing a dented iron helmet over his long hair? He was looking about anxiously and shouting, "Hilde! Hilde!"

"Peer! That's my *father!*" Hilde's face was shocked and white, her eyes like stars.

"Pa! *Pa!*" Sigurd and Sigrid picked themselves up from the corner where they had been sitting, quiet as mice, and flung themselves into Ralf's arms. Gudrun appeared behind him, bundled in furs, her thin face alive with gladness. Two dogs dashed through the crowd. Alf threaded his way up to Hilde, followed by Loki, who threw himself on Peer.

"The dogs knew!" bellowed Ralf, thrusting his way towards Hilde. "By thunder, they knew! They've dragged us all the way up from the fjord – ripped my clothes, see? We had to leave poor old Eirik behind – he'd have killed himself trying." He reached Hilde and wrapped her in a bear hug. "We've been desperate – searching the slopes for hours. Thank God they opened the hill!"

Trolls howled, squeaked and grunted. The Dovre princess fainted. The Dovreking drew himself up, outraged and alarmed. The Gaffer of Troll Fell raised his arms and tried to speak. No one listened. His tail coiling with fury, he grabbed a horn from the nearest musician and blew a deafening blast.

"QUIET!" he roared, and silence fell.

"Get out of here, Ralf Eiriksson," yelled the old troll, glaring at Ralf like a spider out of all three eyes. "Out! It's all settled. You can take your younger children home, but the elder girl stays. And the boy, too."

Ralf held on to Hilde. He looked tall, strong and dangerous. Peer, sitting on the ground with his arm around Loki's neck, looked up in hope. Surely Ralf could save them? He spared a glance for his two uncles. They were staring at Ralf with horrified, bulging eyes, as if they had seen a ghost.

"Do you think I'd leave any of my children?" Ralf demanded. "How dare you trolls steal them?"

"Trolls didn't steal them!" shouted the Gaffer. "Men did!" He pointed at Baldur and Grim. Ralf, who had not noticed them before, swung round.

"Men?" he asked contemptuously. "*Men?* Those aren't men. Those are animals – beasts!"

"Don't get high and mighty with me," snarled the Gaffer. "They're men – your own sort. And you can take away the children they stole. The other two are staying of their own free will."

"That's a lie," said Ralf.

"We did promise," said Hilde faintly, "but it was to save Sigurd and Sigrid. He said he had to have two of us as – as servants. Wedding presents – for them!" She nodded towards the princes and princesses. Ralf's eyes followed, and he spotted the Troll Fell princess with a frown of recognition. "I know you," he said slowly. She gave him a sly, curling smile. Ralf's fist clenched. "By thunder, that's it! You're the one who gave me the cup, all that time ago. Aren't you? Well, here's a deal." He swung round on her father. "Give me the children and you shall have your golden cup!"

The Gaffer picked up the cup from where Peer had put it on the table in front of him. He raised it to Ralf in a mocking toast, slurped the beer in one greedy gulp and set it down with a bang.

"I already tried that, Pa, and it didn't work," said Hilde miserably. Ralf rubbed a big hand over his face. "What's to prevent us grabbing the children and leaving now?" he enquired.

"What's to prevent us tearing you all to pieces?" the Gaffer asked with a grin.

Ralf looked around, poised tensely on the balls of his feet, as if ready to attack. Arne, Bjørn and the other men edged nearer to him. Peer and Hilde looked around too. There were too many trolls to be counted, all waiting with teeth and claws and hooves and horns, their glittering eyes fixed on the village people. The odds were hopeless. Peer held his breath, preparing himself for a frightful battle. But then Ralf sighed deeply and his shoulders slumped in defeat. The Gaffer saw it and clapped his hands.

"But no fighting at a wedding," he roared. "Beer all round! It's time to pledge the health of the two happy couples."

All the guests broke into cheers and laughter. With a rumbling sound the big barrels were rolled forward and broached. Little trolls sprang into action with cups, jugs and pitchers and rushed to serve the tables. Up from the kitchens poured a stream of even more trolls bearing trays of smoking and steaming food.

Peer felt a nudge at his elbow. A small troll was impatiently shoving a jug of beer at him and making signs that he was to pour it out for the top table. Peer took it uncertainly and held it for a moment.

I suppose I'm still a servant, he thought. He sniffed the beer cautiously. It smelled all right, though it looked very dark. Perhaps there was a slight marshy whiff.

He glanced around. The royal party was recovering: the princes and princesses were seating themselves at their tables. The Gaffer laid an arm over the Dovreking's shoulders and led him to his place.

Uncle Baldur and Uncle Grim were happily sitting on their benches again, comparing fistfuls of jewels, which they had collected from the floor. Their bushy beards wagged as they argued about their shares. Peer hoped the Gaffer would notice they were stealing, but none of the trolls seemed to care. The Gaffer was not going to fuss about losing a few jewels when he wanted to impress the Dovreking.

"We won't go without you!" Ralf was swearing to Hilde.

"Pa, what can you do?" Hilde asked despairingly.

Ralf clenched his fist. "We can fight! We can form a shield wall – go down like heroes—"

"Don't be silly," said Gudrun bitterly. "You don't *have* any shields."

Peer looked back at his two uncles and absolutely hated them. They had caused all this misery, and they didn't care a fig. In fact Baldur was chuckling now, and rubbing his hands. They would walk out of here with all those jewels and go home to the mill. Ralf couldn't stop them, unless he killed them. And somehow Peer knew Ralf wouldn't kill them. Ralf wasn't the type.

If anyone's going to get them, Peer thought, *it'll have to be me.* And the very next moment, he saw how to do it. Simple, obvious and beautiful.

Had Baldur and Grim overheard what the Gaffer had said about the effects of troll beer? Peer didn't think so. They hadn't been close enough. He walked quietly to the table and picked up the beautiful golden cup. No one was watching. And even if they were, he was only doing what a servant should. He gave it a quick polish on his sleeve and filled it with beer.

The bog-wife's brew rushed foaming into the cup, a rich, bitter broth with a tang of moss. Careful not to splash, Peer carried it smoothly to his uncles and set it down between them.

They didn't even look up to see who he was. Arguing over a big emerald, Uncle Baldur seized the cup in one hairy hand. He tipped his head back. The bog-wife's beer glugged down his throat.

"Give me some of that!" His brother snatched the cup and swirled it. "There's only half left!" he snarled, gulping it down and pushing the cup back at Peer. "It's good! Here boy – fill that up!" Peer gladly obliged.

As Baldur once again raised the cup to his lips, it jarred and slopped. It had struck something hard. Peer backed away, holding his breath. Something was growing through Baldur's beard. Something hard and curved and pointed. Baldur grabbed at his face. He stared at his brother. Grim too was feeling his face. From the hairy tangles of black beard protruded two curving white…

"Tusks!" Peer's yell of delight echoed through the Hall. "Look! Uncle Baldur and Uncle Grim have got tusks!"

Everyone looked. And from both trolls and men came a mighty roar of laughter, as Baldur and Grim stood rubbing their jowls in bewilderment, their treasure quite forgotten.

"Like pigs! We always thought they looked like pigs," Hilde called to Peer, laughing between her tears.

The Troll Fell princess came slipping up to Ralf. "That would have happened to you too, if you had drunk from it," she murmured, pinching his arm. "What a pity you didn't stay with me. So big and strong!" Ralf brushed her off angrily, but then his eyes widened. "Hey, your Majesty, or whatever you call yourself?"

The Gaffer turned.

"You wanted two?" Ralf asked. "Two human servants? A matching pair?"

"You know I do," scowled the old troll. Ralf pointed at Baldur and Grim. "Then there they are," he roared. "THERE'S YOUR MATCHING PAIR!"

"Oh yes," cried Hilde in delight. "Twins! And they've already drunk your beer. Oh Peer, well done!"

She beamed at him. Peer grinned. Breathlessly, they looked at the Gaffer, who looked at his guests. "I *wanted* a boy and a girl. But it's for the bride to say," he remarked, staring at the Dovre princess who rose to her feet with an ill-tempered shrug. She took a look at Baldur and Grim, who still stood there swaying and fingering their faces. She flicked her napkin. "Yes, yes, they'll do," she said pettishly. "Better than the others in fact. They have such nice, trollish faces."

"Yes!!!"

Peer rushed at Hilde and swung her off her feet. Laughing and crying, she hugged him back. And then Peer found himself surrounded by friendly villagers, all trying at once to shake his hand and rumple his hair and bang him on the back. He came face to face with Gudrun. "Oh Peer! You blessed boy!" She kissed him on both cheeks. Beside him, Loki leaped, jealous for his share. Lovingly he nipped Peer's fingers.

And now Ralf and Bjørn and the villagers were shepherding them out. The trolls fell back to open a path for them. Peer cast a backwards glance over his shoulder. Goodbye, the glittering splendour of the Hall under Troll Fell. The musicians were already striking up again. Couples ventured on to the dance floor. Wasn't that the Troll Fell prince, doing an astounding somersault to impress his bride? And there were Uncle Baldur and Uncle Grim, sitting down, reaching for more of the beer that had turned them into trolls. Much good those jewels would do them now!

"Perhaps they always were trolls, on the inside," Peer murmured. "Perhaps it won't change them very much."

A dark figure flitted through the throng. Could that be Granny Greenteeth? He tried to wave, but Hilde had his hand and was dragging him along. "What's the matter with you, Peer? Come on!"

His foot sank into snow. A chill wind curled around him and his breath smoked. He had crossed the boundary and was outside, on the slopes of Troll Fell.

CHAPTER 18

Home

"BUT WHERE HAD you been?" Hilde asked Ralf the next day.

It was late morning, and the little farmhouse seemed very full. Gudrun was baking oatcakes on the griddle. She put a dab of butter on the first one and handed it to Peer over the heads of Sigrid and Sigurd. "For the guest of honour!"

It was smoking hot. The butter ran over his fingers. Peer juggled it from hand to hand before taking the first nibble. It was delicious, crumbly and buttery and salty, the best food he had ever tasted.

"Mmmm!" he exclaimed, finishing it rapidly. Loki materialised beside him, thumping his tail and gluing greedy eyes on the last piece.

"Go on!" said Peer, giving in. It vanished like lightning.

"Give Loki an oatcake, Ma," begged Hilde. "He deserves it. Alf too."

"Waste good food on the dogs?" asked Gudrun. But she patted Alf as she passed him and said, "Good boy!" to Loki. "It's amazing how they found us," she said, shaking her head. "How could they tell we were down by the fjord? We shall never know."

Everyone looked at the dogs in silence. The dogs looked embarrassed.

"They *do* deserve an oatcake," said Hilde.

"They can have the one Sigurd dropped," said Gudrun. At that, Sigrid deliberately dropped hers, so that the dogs could have one each.

When Gudrun had finished scolding (and trying not to laugh), Hilde asked Ralf, "But Pa, where had you been?"

"Now *there's* a story," said Ralf happily, "that will last us for many a winter's night." He stretched his arms and looked around the room.

"We know you went down the coast, southwards," said Gudrun. "Arne told us that. But, afterwards – and he said there'd been a sinking—"

Her voice trembled and she stopped abruptly.

"Poor old girl," exclaimed Ralf, squeezing her hand. "How I wish Arne had never told you that. He meant well, I know, and some poor sailormen must have drowned. But it wasn't us, you see. We were right as rain."

"So *what happened?*" asked Hilde impatiently.

"We sailed west," said Ralf. "West for the Shetlands and then northwest for the Faroes. They live by keeping sheep and catching whales. Aye, they drive the whales on to the beaches and kill them there. We helped! And seabirds! I've never seen so many.

"But our skipper Thorolf – you saw him yesterday, he's staying with Bjørn and Kersten – he has a brother in Iceland, on Breidafjord. So from the Faroes we set off again, north-west for Iceland. And this would be late summer.

"Now here it gets exciting!" He winked at Hilde. "We never made Iceland. We were struck by a terrible gale and driven west. Three days it blew; we spent all our time bailing and hoping to make Greenland. But after the storm we had a north wind, and then fog. For days we were lost, helpless."

"Go on," gasped Gudrun.

"At last the sun came out," said Ralf, "the fog cleared and there we all were, hanging on to the ropes, staring out for a sight of where we might be – and we saw it. Land!"

"Greenland!" said Hilde knowingly.

Ralf shook his head. "No. Greenland is all ice and mountains. We saw low hills, covered in green shaggy forests." He leaned forward impressively. "*We had found the land that lies west of the moon – the land at the other end of the world!*"

The family sat with their eyes and mouths wide open.

"And you set foot on it?" gasped Hilde.

"Aye, that we did! We longed for fresh water and dry ground. But as we rowed in we all wondered if the land was real or an enchantment. Would it vanish as we set foot on it, and leave us struggling in the grey sea?"

He looked around at their faces and said mischievously, "I'm still hungry, Gudrun. Any more of those oatcakes?"

Gudrun jumped up. "I'll make some, Ralf. But keep talking!"

"This is the stuff of a fine saga," said old Eirik in a voice quivering with excitement. His bowl of groute was going cold and he had dropped his spoon.

"You've got to make a poem about this, Grandpa," Hilde encouraged him. Eirik slapped his knee. "I will. What a story – *what* a story! A new land, with no people in it! Go on, my son."

"But there were people." Ralf spoke through a mouthful of oatcake. "Lots of people! Villages, with houses made from the bark of trees... What a wonderful place! The rivers full of trout and salmon. Beavers and reindeer in the woods. How I wished you were all with me. We decided to call it Wood Land, and the days just slipped by..."

He jumped to his feet. "But why spoil a good story by rushing at it? This should last us for many nights. Not another word now!" His eyes twinkled at their disappointed faces.

"Just one more thing," begged Hilde. "These people – what were they like?"

"Brown faces!" declared Ralf dramatically. "Brown all over, like smoked oak. And black hair – black as jet. With feathers in it."

"Ohhh!" wailed Hilde. "I can't wait. You have to tell us more!"

"Tonight," Ralf promised. "Now I want to go and look all round the farm – check the sheep – visit the cow – look at the fences. I want to feel I'm really home. I want to get down to some good solid work."

Peer glanced up. Perhaps this was his chance. "Ralf," he said shyly. "You don't happen to want a boy, do you?"

"Oh yes, Pa!" said Hilde quickly. "Can't Peer live with us?"

Ralf looked quizzically at Peer. "A boy?" he said, turning the words over in his mouth as though seeing how they tasted. "A boy? No, I can't really say that I need a boy. I've got Hilde, you see, and the twins growing up, and it's a small place – no, I don't really need a boy."

"Ralf!" cried Gudrun reproachfully, while Peer bit his lip. But Ralf was still talking. "So, I don't need a boy, as such," he went on. "But Peer Ulfsson, who went after the twins – Peer Ulfsson, who stood by Hilde and helped her – Peer Ulfsson, who offered to stay in Troll Fell to rescue Sigurd – I think we certainly need him!"

Hilde cheered. Peer blushed scarlet. Ralf took Peer by the shoulders and shook him gently.

"It's not for the work you can do, my lad," he said, "though

I'm sure you'll be useful. It's not because we need you – it's because we want you."

Peer tried to speak. To his horror, he felt his eyes filling with tears. Gudrun put her arms around him, and he was glad to hide his head against her apron.

"You belong with us now, and we're proud of you," she said briskly. "Yes, and you too!" she nodded to Loki, who gave a surprised sneeze. Peer managed a shaky laugh and went to fuss Loki till he had control of himself again.

"That's a good little dog," Ralf approved. "Smart and loyal. We'll train him into a fine sheepdog, won't we, Alf?" Alf gave his master an adoring look. And as Ralf reached down his old coat and headed for the door, Alf followed him like an extra shadow.

Peer watched Ralf go out and then reached for a cloak himself. He was happier than he could have imagined, but he was not yet quite comfortable just sitting there chatting. And there was something he needed to do.

"Where are you going?" asked Hilde.

"To the mill," said Peer quietly.

"I suppose it belongs to you now," said Hilde in surprise. "Does it?"

"I don't know," said Peer, startled. "But there's animals there. Someone has to feed the sheep…"

"Shall I come?"

Peer hesitated. He really wanted to go alone, or his idea might not work. Still, it was only fair to tell them about it.

"You see," he stammered, "there's the Nis."

Hilde put a hand to her mouth. "The poor Nis! I'd forgotten about it. Nobody lives at the mill now, do they?"

"So I wondered," said Peer, "if it might like to come here. Would that be all right, Gudrun?"

"Goodness," said Gudrun. "I suppose so. Is it well behaved?"

Peer thought. "Well, not very. But I think it would be if we treated it nicely. With Baldur and Grim it wasn't."

"That's no surprise," Gudrun sniffed. "Very well, Peer, you can try. But mind you tell it to be good!"

Warmly wrapped in a thick cloak, Peer set off down the valley. It wasn't snowing, but the wind was keen and the skies were grey. He tramped down through the wood till he came in sight of the mill.

So much had happened since he had been there. But he saw the broken ice on the millpond, frozen over again but still visible as the spot where Grendel had gone through. Was it really only two nights ago?

In the yard the penned sheep were bleating hungrily. He pushed open the barn door to fetch their hay, and stepped into a starburst of black feathers.

Peer squinted into the rafters and saw the huddled shapes of his chickens. He counted them. All nine were there, but not the black cockerel. There were feathers everywhere, and a strong smell of fox. The hens had clearly had a terrible experience.

"Hmmm!" said Peer. He scattered grain on the floor. "Come down and eat, you silly things. I'll come for you tomorrow, with a basket, and take you somewhere safe." Repentant, humbled, the hens scrambled from the rafters and began picking away gratefully.

Peer fed the sheep and oxen, and tossed a few armfuls of hay to Bristles and the sow, though he could hardly bear to look at them for being reminded of his uncles. *Maybe Bjørn or Arne would like to have them*, he thought.

Finally he ventured into the mill. The fire had long gone

out. The wreckage of the millstone still lay where it had fallen on the splintered wooden chest. There was no sound.

"Nis?" called Peer quietly. "Are you there?" He looked around, hoping to see a small shadow flit from beam to beam, or catch the gleam of its eyes. There was no sound.

"Nis?"

It was growing dark. The short day was done. Peer backed out of the cold and lonely mill, wondering with a sigh where the Nis had gone. He stood for a moment looking thoughtfully into the yard. Did all this really belong to him now? It wasn't something he was ready to think about. The pile of snow that the Nis had pushed off the barn roof still lay in the yard, and he remembered the dogfight with a shudder.

It was then that he heard a light sound. A white fox came skipping into the yard. It was playing games in the snow, chasing its tail, running in rings, dashing about. Peer watched, enchanted. So this was the culprit, probably back for a few more hens! He resolved to make sure the barn door was firmly shut.

He blinked. There seemed to be a little whirlwind blowing about the yard – a little, swirling column of snow, playing with the fox. He rubbed his eyes. Or was it a little, wispy grey creature with big hands and feet?

"Nis?" he called. Something ran across the yard kicking spurts of snow from its heels. The fox sat down and turned its sharp, laughing face towards him. Something jumped on to the mill roof, and a chunk of snow flumped off the eaves on to his head and shoulders, and went down his neck.

Peer yelped and wriggled, and a cross little voice muttered above his head: "They all forgets the poor Nis!"

"Nis!" said Peer firmly and kindly. "I haven't forgotten

you. Listen. You don't have to stay in the cold mill. I'm living at Ralf Eiriksson's farm now. Please come too! There'll be hot groute with butter every day, I promise!"

He heard no reply. But the wispy little wind whirled itself on to the fox's back, and the white fox straightened out and went streaking out of the yard and over the wooden bridge.

Peer followed its tracks in the snow all the way home, grinning to himself.

Hilde greeted him at the farmhouse door. "Suppertime!" she called. "And it's a funny thing, but the floor seems to have swept itself in the last half-hour, and the logs have stacked themselves neatly, and it didn't take half as long for the kettle to boil. I think your Nis has come home!"

Gudrun peeped over her shoulder. "It's a marvellous help, Peer. I hope it stays. What do you say it likes to eat?" And she poured out a full bowl of groute, carefully stirring in the butter, and set it on the warm hearthstone. As a final touch, she spooned in some honey.

From then on, the Nis was positively spoilt.

That evening, and for many more to come, they listened spellbound to one another's stories. Peer and Hilde had much to tell of the wonders they had seen under Troll Fell. Eirik spun the tale of how he and Gudrun had struggled down to the fjord, of their despair at finding the village deserted, and their joy at discovering the longship. He made such a good job of it that Gudrun herself shook her head and declared, while they laughed at her, "What an adventure!"

But the best and newest story of all was Ralf's. With his arm round Gudrun and the little ones on his knee he told them more and more about the green forests at the other end of the world, of the dark-haired people who spoke a strange language, of the bright feathers in their hair, of their bark houses built deep in the woods. And he told of the long journey home.

"Will you ever go back?" asked Hilde curiously. Gudrun clutched Ralf's hand, shaking her head. Ralf paused a long moment and sighed.

"East, west; home's best," he said at last. "But who knows? It's a wonderful land out there, Hilde. A wonderful land."

Part Two

CHAPTER 19

What Happened on the Shore

THE BOAT DANCED ungracefully in from the fishing grounds. Her crew, a man and a boy, reached steadily back and forth, working their two pairs of oars through the choppy water. Out beyond the islands, the wind tore a long yellow rift in the clouds and the setting sun blinked through in stormy brilliance.

Dazzled, the boy missed his stroke. The oars sliced through air instead of water, and he flew backwards off his seat into a tangle of nets and a slithery heap of fat, bright fish.

"Resting?" teased his friend Bjørn. "Had enough for one day?"

Peer laughed, then gasped as spray slapped his face. He scrambled up with dripping hair, snatching for the loose oars.

"Bad weather's coming," said Bjørn. The breeze stiffened, carrying cold points of rain. "But we'll get home before it catches us."

"You will," Peer said. "I'll get soaked on my way up the hill."

"Stay with us," offered Bjørn. "Kersten would love to see you. You can earn your supper by admiring the baby." He glanced around, smiling at Peer's sudden silence. "Come on. Surely you're used to babies, up at the farm? How old is little Eirik now? About a year? He's a fine little fellow, isn't he? It's sad his grandpa never saw him."

"Yes... although actually," said Peer, "he might have lost patience with the noise. Dear old Eirik, he was always grumbling, 'A poet needs peace and quiet!' Little Eirik screams such a lot. Babies! I never knew they were so much trouble."

"Ours is a good little soul," Bjørn said proudly. "Never cries."

"So how is Kersten?" Peer asked, his eye on the shore. Bjørn pulled a couple of hard strokes on one oar to straighten up. "Fine, thanks." The boat shot in on the back of a breaking wave, and Peer sprang out into a welter of froth and seaweed. Bjørn followed and together they ran the boat higher up the stony beach.

"A grand day's work," Bjørn said. Reaching into the boat, he hooked his fingers into the gills of a heavy, shining cod and hefted it in his blunt, capable hands. "Plenty of eating on that one. Take it with you." He handed it to Peer, long strands of sea-stiffened fair hair blowing across his face. "Or will you stay?"

"I'll stay," Peer decided. "They won't worry. They know I'm with you." Absurdly, he hugged the fish, smiling. Three years ago he'd been a friendless orphan, and he could still hardly believe that he had a family now, who cared about him.

"Good choice!" said Bjørn. "Kersten can fry that fish, then, and we'll have it with lots of warm bread and hot sizzling butter. Hungry?"

"Starving." Peer licked his lips.

"Go on ahead while I finish up. Off with you! Here comes the wet."

Cold rain swept in from the sea as Peer dashed across the clattering shingle, dodging boulders and jumping over inlets where the tide swirled and sloshed. It was fun, pitting himself against the weather. Soon he came to the channel where the stream ran down to the sea. Beside it, the path to the village wound up through the sand dunes. Rain hissed through the long wiry grass. He slowed to a plod, looking forward to sitting snugly by the fire while Kersten cooked.

Footsteps thudded on the path. In a flurry of flying hair and swirling cloak, a woman ran headlong out of the mist and slammed into him. Peer dropped the fish, and the woman grabbed him, struggling for balance. He tried to push her off and his hands tangled in her wet hair. Her hood fell back.

"*Kersten!*" Peer's voice rose in cold fright. "What's wrong?"

She clutched him fiercely. "Is Gudrun still breast-feeding?"

Peer gaped. "What?"

She shook his arm angrily. "Is Gudrun still suckling her baby?" She threw back a fold of her huge cloak. It flapped heavily in the wind, slapping his legs like wet hide. In the crook of her arm, wrapped in a lambskin—

Her baby? Peer blinked in horror. She thrust it into his arms; he had to take it before she dropped it.

"Take her to Gudrun – Gudrun can feed her—"

"Kersten," Peer croaked. "What's happened? Where are you going?"

She looked at him with eyes like dark holes. "Home."

Then she was past him, the cloak dragging after her. He snatched for it. Sleek wet fur tugged through his fingers. "Kersten! Stop!"

She ran down the path, and he began to run too, but the baby jolting in his arms slowed him to long desperate strides.

"Kersten!" His feet skated on wet grass, sank into pockets

of soft sand. She was on the beach now, running straight for the water. He could never catch her. Peer skidded to a crazy halt. He saw Bjørn bending over the boat, doing something with the nets. Peer filled his lungs and bellowed, "*Bjørn!*" at the top of his voice. He pointed.

Bjørn turned, staring. Then he flung himself forwards, pounding across the beach to intercept Kersten. And Kersten stopped. She threw herself flat, and the wet sealskin cloak billowed over her, hiding her from head to foot. Underneath it, she continued to move, in heavy lolloping jumps. She must be crawling, drawing the skin cloak closely around her. She rolled. Waves rushed up and sucked her into the water. Trapped in those encumbering folds, she would drown.

"Kersten!" Peer screamed. The body in the water twisted, lithe and muscular, and plunged forward into the next grey wave.

Bjørn was racing for his boat. He hurled himself on it, driving it down the shingle into the water, wrenching the bows around to point into the waves.

"Bjørn!" Peer cried into the wind. Spray filled his mouth with salt. He stammered and spat. "Your baby – your baby!"

Bjørn jumped into the boat. The oars rattled out and he dug them into the water with savage strokes, twisting to scan the sea. Peer heard him shout, his voice cracking, "Kersten! Kersten, come back..." The boat reared over lines of white breakers, and was swallowed by rain and darkness.

Peer stared. A sleek head bobbed in the water. He ran forward in wild hope. It was gone. Then he saw another – and another, rising and falling with the swell. Swift dark bodies swept easily between wave and wave.

"Seals!" he whispered.

In his arm the baby stirred, arching its back and thrusting

thin fists into the rain. Its eyes were tight shut, but it moved its head as if seeking something to suck. Soon it would be hungry. Soon it would cry.

Peer's teeth chattered. Clumsily he tried to arrange its wrappings, dragging the blanket over its arms. It seemed tiny, much younger than little Eirik up at the farm. Was it a boy or a girl? He couldn't remember. It felt like ice. Didn't babies die if they got too cold?

Gudrun, he thought. *I've got to get it to Gudrun. Kersten said.*

Holding the baby stiffly across his chest, he trudged up the path through the dunes. The sound of the sea was muffled, and he left the spray behind, but the keen rain followed, soaking his shoulders and arms, trickling down his back. The first house in the village was Bjørn's. The door stood wide open. Peer hesitated, then stepped quickly in. He pushed the door shut, shivering.

The fire was out. The dark house smelt of cold, bitter ashes. Angry tears pricked Peer's eyelids. He remembered Kersten's warmth and gaiety and good cooking. Whatever had gone wrong?

He blundered across the room and cracked his shins on something wooden that moved. It swung back and hit him again, and he put a hand out to still it. A cradle.

Thankfully, Peer lowered the baby into the cradle. Now what? He tried to think. Did anyone else in the village have a young baby? No. Gudrun was the only person who could feed it. *But what will Bjørn think if he comes home and the baby's gone? Should I wait for him? But he might capsize, he might never come home at all…*

Peer crushed down rising panic. *When he does come, he'll be cold,* he told himself. *I should light the fire.*

He knew where Bjørn kept his strike-a-light and a box of

dry wood-shavings, but in the dark he knocked the box to the floor and had to feel about for the knob of flint and the wedge of cold iron. He struck flint and iron together, showering sparks. The wood-shavings caught. When the fire was burning steadily, he got stiffly to his feet and looked around.

The house had only one room, and little furniture. The firelight gleamed here on a polished wooden bowl, there on a thin-bladed sickle hanging on the wall. In a corner stood Bjørn and Kersten's bed, the blankets neatly folded. Peer felt like an intruder. And there was nothing to show why Kersten had suddenly rushed out of the house, carrying her baby.

His foot came down on something small and hard. He picked it up and held it to the light. A small iron key.

His eyes flew to the darkest corner of the room. A long wooden box stood there, a chest for valuables. Bjørn always kept the lid padlocked shut. It was open now, dragged out crookedly from the wall, the padlock unhooked and the lid hurled back. Peer knelt, plunging his arms into the solid black shadow that was the interior, feeling into every corner. The chest was empty.

It didn't make sense. Peer tried to imagine robbers arriving, forcing Kersten to find the key, open the chest… but Kersten need only scream to raise the entire village. And why would she run into the sea? And what could Bjørn possibly own, that anyone might want to steal? He paced about in growing anxiety, waiting for Bjørn to return. At last he gave up. He covered the fire, and bent to scoop the baby out of the cradle. It was awake, and hungry. It had crammed its tiny fingers into its mouth and was munching them busily. Peer's heart sank.

"I haven't got anything for you!" he told it, as if speaking to his dog, Loki. "Let's get you wrapped up." He grabbed an old cloak from a peg behind the door, and as he bundled it around them both, the baby looked straight into his eyes.

It didn't smile – Peer didn't know if it was even old enough to smile. It gazed into his face with a serious, penetrating stare, as if his soul were a well and it was looking right down to the very bottom. Peer gazed back. The baby didn't know about robbers, or the wild night outside, or its missing parents. It didn't know that it might die or grow up an orphan. It knew only what was right here and now: the hunger in its belly, and Peer's arms holding it, firmly wrapped and warm. He drew a shaky breath.

"They left you," he said through gritted teeth. "But I won't. You come with me!" Pressing the baby to his shoulder, he elbowed the door open and strode furiously out into the pitch-black night.

The wind spat rain and sleet. Peer splashed past Einar's house, and a goat, sheltering against a wall, scrambled to its feet and barged past, nearly knocking him down. As he cursed it, the doorlatch clicked and Einar looked out. "Who's there?"

"It's me," began Peer, but he couldn't explain. Kersten had thrown herself into the sea. Bjørn's house had been robbed. He was holding their baby... He left Einar puzzled on the doorstep, and slunk out of the village like a thief.

Driving rain followed him up the hill. Every gust of wind blew his cloak open. The baby wriggled. Afraid it would slip, he stopped, trying to find a dry edge to wrap around it, but the woollen fabric seemed all muddy or sodden, and he gave up in despair. The baby's head tipped back and those dark eyes stared at him again. Uneasily Peer stared back. Something was wrong. This baby was too good, too quiet. *Little Eirik would be screaming his head off by now,* he thought. Was the baby too cold to cry? Too weak?

Frightened, he plunged on up the path. Gudrun could give it warmth and milk. But at the moment he could hardly see where to put his feet; and there were a couple of miles of rough track to go, past the old mill and up through the leafless wood.

Ahead of him the black roofline of the mill appeared between the trees, the thatch twisted into crooked horns above narrow gables. It was on just such a wild night that Peer had first seen it, three years ago. His uncles had long gone, but the mill had a bad name still. Odd creatures were said to loiter in its dark rooms and squint through the broken shutters. A splash from the mill pond might be Granny Greenteeth, lurking under the weed-clogged surface, waiting to drag down anyone who strayed.

Peer clutched the baby tighter. There was no way of avoiding the place: the road led right up to it, before crossing the stream on an old wooden bridge. As he passed he glanced up. The walls leaned over, cold and silent.

The river snarled over the weir in white froth. He looked upstream at the waterwheel, in the darkness hardly more than a tall looming bulk – and was instantly giddy. *The wheel's moving!* Only the water tearing underneath, perhaps; or were those black, dripping blades really lifting, one after another, rolling upwards, picking up speed?

An unearthly squeal skewered the night. Peer shot off the bridge. The anguished noise went on and on, far too long for anything with lungs. It came from deep within the mill. Peer fought for his wits. *The machinery!* It was the sound of great wooden axles screeching into life.

The wheel was turning. The mill was awake! Peer flinched, half expecting the lopsided windows to wink open with yellow light. He got a grip on himself. *The mill can't start by itself. Someone's opened the sluice, started the wheel. But who?*

The path that led to the dam was overgrown with a wilderness of whispering bushes. Anything might crouch there, hiding... or watching. From high up the fell came the distant shriek of some bird, a sound broken into pieces by the gale.

He drew a deep, careful breath. *With all this rain, perhaps the sluicegate's collapsed, and the water's escaping under the wheel.*

That'll be it.

He hurried on. The cart track slanted uphill into the woods. Often, as he went, he heard stones clatter on the path behind him, dislodged perhaps by rain and weather. And, all the way, he had the feeling that someone or something was following him, climbing out of the dark pocket where the mill sat in its narrow valley. He tried looking over his shoulder, but that made him stumble, and it was too dark to see.

CHAPTER 20

A Brush with the Trolls

A FEW HOURS earlier, just before sunset, Hilde stood on the seaward shoulder of Troll Fell, looking out over a huge gulf of air. Far below, the fjord flashed trembling silver, between headlands half-drowned in shadow. A tiny dark boat was creeping along on the brightness.

"*Hiillde!*"

She turned to see her little brother racing down the hill towards her, a small brown dog running at his heels. Braced for the crash, she caught him and swung him round.

"Oof! You're getting pretty heavy for an eight-year-old. Where's Pa and Sigrid?"

"They're coming. What were you staring at?"

"See that boat down there? That's Peer and Bjørn."

Sigurd craned his neck. "So it is. Hey, Loki, it's Peer! Where's Peer?" Loki pricked his ears, barking.

"Don't tease him!" said Hilde. Sigurd threw himself down beside Loki, laughing and tussling.

Fierce sunlight blazed through a gap in the clouds. The hillside turned unearthly green. The long drifts of tired snow lying in every dip and hollow woke into blinding sparkles, and the crooked thorn trees sprang out, every mossy twig a shrill yellow. Two more people came over the skyline: a tall man in a plaid cloak and a little fair-haired girl whose red hood glowed like a jewel.

Sigurd jumped up, waving to his twin. "Sigrid, we can see the boat! Lucky things," he added. "Peer gets to go fishing with Bjørn, and we have to count sheep. Why can't Sigrid and I have some fun?"

"You can, when you're older," said Hilde. "I didn't go fishing, did I?"

"You didn't want to," Sigurd muttered.

"I know who she'd like to go fishing with!" said Sigrid slyly. "Bjørn's brother, Arne! Wouldn't you? Wouldn't you, Hilde?"

"Not very likely," said Hilde calmly, "since Arne doesn't even live in the village any more. You know perfectly well that he works a fishing boat out of Hammerhaven—"

"And it's bigger than Bjørn's!" Sigurd interrupted. "Bjørn's boat is a faering, with a mast but only two sets of oars. Arne's boat is a six-oarer!"

"That's right, and he has a partner to help him sail it," Hilde said.

"You know a lot about him," Sigrid giggled.

"Don't be silly. Arne is twenty-two; he's a grown man."

"So? You're sixteen, you're grown-up, too! When he came to say goodbye to you, he held your hand. You went all pink."

Hilde gave her little sister a withering glance, and wrapped her arms around herself with a shiver. Out at sea, the clouds had eaten up the sun.

"It's going to rain, Pa," she said as Ralf joined them.

"We can see Peer," Sigrid squeaked, pointing at the boat. "Look, Pa, look!"

"Aha!" Ralf peered down the slope, scanning every rock and boulder. "Now I wonder if our lost sheep have gone over this edge. I don't see any. But they wouldn't show up against all the grey stones."

"How many are missing?" Hilde demanded.

"Let's see." Grimly, Ralf ticked them off on his fingers. "The old ewe with the bell round her neck, two of the black sheep, the lame one, the speckled one, and the one with the broken horn. And their lambs. It can't be wolves or foxes. They'd leave tracks."

"Stolen?" asked Hilde. "By the trolls?"

"That thought does worry me," Ralf admitted.

The wind blew rain into their faces. The fjord below was a brooding gulf of shadows. Sigrid tugged Hilde's sleeve. "The boat's gone. Where is it?"

"Don't worry, Siggy. They'll be coming in to land. We can't see the shore from here; the hillside gets in the way. Pa, let's go. Those clouds are coming up fast."

"Yes." Ralf was gazing out to sea. "The old seawife is brewing up some dirty weather in that cookpot of hers!" He caught their puzzled looks, and laughed. "Did Grandfather never tell you that story? It's a sailor's yarn. The old seawife, Ran, sits in her kitchen at the bottom of the sea, brewing up storms in her big black pot. Oh, yes! All the drowned sailors go down to sit in rows on the benches in Ran's kitchen!"

Hilde gave an appreciative shudder. "That's like one of Bjørn's tales – about the draug, who sails the seas in half a boat and screams on the wind when people are going to drown. Brrr!"

"I remember. That's a good one," said Sigurd. "You think it's an ordinary boat, but then it gets closer and you see that the sailors are all dead and rotten. And the boat can sail against the wind and catch you anywhere. And the draug steers it, and he hasn't got a face. And then you hear this terrible scream—"

"Well, Peer and Bjørn are safely home," said Ralf. "So let

him scream! But we won't see Peer tonight. He'll stay with Bjørn and Kersten, snug and dry. Like we want to be: so let's be off." But he stood for a moment staring west, as if straining to see something far away, though all that Hilde saw was a line of advancing clouds like inky mountains.

"It's dark and I'm hungry." Sigurd hopped from foot to foot. "What are you waiting for?"

Reluctantly, Ralf turned away. "Only trying to catch a glimpse of the islands, but it's too murky now." Sigurd and Sigrid dashed ahead with Loki.

"I passed those islands once, you know," Ralf said to Hilde, following the twins. "In the dragonship, the summer I went to sea."

"I know you did, Pa." Hilde wasn't listening. There was no real path, only a sheep track twisting between outcrops of rock, and she had to watch where she put her feet.

"I'd never seen them so close before," Ralf called over his shoulder. "Never been so far from home. Some of them are big, with steep cliffs where seagulls nest. A wild sort of people live there. Fishermen, not farmers. They climb on the cliffs for gulls' eggs, and gather seaweed and shellfish—"

"Yes, you've told me." She'd heard the story many times, and just now she wished he'd be quiet and hurry up. This rain and early darkness made her nervous. She started. Had something just peered out from behind that big stone?

Ralf was still talking. "But many of the islands are just rocks, skerries, with the sea swilling over them and no room for anyone but seals. They'd lie basking in the sun, watching us. It's tricky sailing. The tides come boiling up through the channels, sweeping the boat along, and there's rocks everywhere just waiting to take a bite. But we got through. And further out, and beyond the horizon – many days' sailing

– well, you know what we found, Hilde. The land at the other end of the world!"

The old thrill prickled down Hilde's spine. "East of the sun and west of the moon," she said softly. "Like a fairytale."

"No fairytale," said Ralf. "To think I've been so far away! Why, by the time I passed the islands again on my way home, they seemed like old friends. How I'd love to… but I've promised your mother… and there's the baby. Ah, well!"

He strode on. Hilde squelched after him, looking affectionately at the back of his head. She knew part of him longed to go off again – to sail away to that wondrous land, adventurous and free. *He'll never be quite contented here*, she thought. *It worries Ma, but I understand. I'd go there too, if I could – to the lands lying west of the moon… Why, even Peer's seen more of the world than I have. He used to live miles away, in Hammerhaven. I've spent my whole life here.*

Hammerhaven… Her mind skipped to the day, last year, when Arne had made a special visit to the farm. He'd come to say goodbye: he was moving his fine new boat to Hammerhaven, where he could sell his catch for a better price. He'd taken her hand and asked her not to forget him. Surely that meant something?

I wonder how he is. I wonder—

She tripped over a rock. Thunder rolled. Scraping the wet hair from her eyes, she glanced up. The storm stretched black wings over Troll Fell.

"I think we left it a little late," shouted Ralf, half-turning. "Sigrid, Sigurd – keep close!" He caught Sigrid's hand, and they hurried on together past the base of a long, low crag. Blackthorn trees craned over the edge like a row of spiteful old women.

A bird screamed from somewhere on top of the crag, a

long liquid call that ended in syllables: "*Huuuuutututututu!*" An answering cry floated up the slope from their left, and a third, distant and quavering, came from far below. Hilde caught Ralf's arm. "Those aren't birds. Trolls, Pa! On both sides of us."

With a gasp, Sigrid shrank close to her father, and Hilde cursed herself for speaking without thinking. Sigrid was terrified of trolls.

Ralf cocked his head. The bubbling cries began again, relayed up the hill like a series of signals. "You're right," he muttered. "My fault. I should have got us home earlier. Never mind, Sigrid, the trolls won't hurt us. It's just the sort of night they like, you see – dark and wet and windy. Let them prance around if they want – they can't scare us."

"Are they stealing the sheep?" Sigurd whispered.

"Can't we get home?" Sigrid's voice was thin.

"Of course we can," said Hilde.

"We'll slip past," said Ralf. "They won't bother us."

"They will!" Sigrid clutched him with cold hands. "They stole Sigurd and me; they wanted to keep us for ever!"

"No, no, the Grimsson brothers stole you," Hilde tried to reassure her, "and the trolls kept *them* instead, and serve them right. Don't worry, Siggy. Pa's here; and me. You're safe with us."

There was a sudden blast of wind. Rain lashed the hillside.

"Nothing can see us in this," shouted Ralf. "Let's go!" Swept along by wind and weather, they stumbled half blind down a sudden slope into a narrow gully. At the bottom a thin stream rattled over pebbles. Something ran out of the dense curtains of drifting rain. Sigrid shrieked.

Trolls were all around them: tails, snouts, glow-worm eyes.

Dim lines of trolls louping and leaping from the raincloud. A pair of thin, thin legs that raked like a cockerel's, and a round hairless body on top. Ralf and the children skidded to an appalled halt. Hilde grabbed the twins and bundled them back the way they had come. But the trolls stampeded, racing up the slope with gobbling yells. Hilde slipped. The wet hillside reeled and hit her. She lay, winded, as a troll bounded over her. Its rat-like tail slashed her legs. A horny hoof drove hard into the small of her back. A hot, sharp smell prickled her nose. Then the trolls were gone. Loki tore after them in hysterical fury.

Covered in mud, Hilde sat up. Ralf pulled her to her feet. The world steadied. Here was Sigrid, curled up on the ground, sobbing. "It's all right, Siggy, they didn't mean to hurt us. We frightened them just as much as they frightened us..."

"Loki chased them!" Sigurd arrived at his father's side. "Where is he? I have to find him!" He made a lunge for the slope, but Hilde caught him. "Loki can look after himself." And she stepped on something that crunched and splintered.

"He can't, he can't! Peer told me to look after him!" Sigurd wrestled free; but just then Loki came sliding and scrabbling down the stony gully, wagging a jaunty tail. Sigurd grabbed him. "Good boy, Loki! Brave dog!" he choked into Loki's fur. Loki shook himself.

"Siggy, don't cry, they've gone." Hilde hugged her little sister, "The trolls have all gone."

"Carrying off my sheep and lambs, I'll swear!" Ralf growled.

Sigurd shook his head. "No they weren't. Didn't you see? They were carrying sacks and baskets, Pa. But what was in them?"

Sigrid raised her head from Hilde's shoulder. "Bones," she gulped.

"What? Bones, Siggy? Are you sure?"

"Some fell out." Sigrid buried her face again. "They fell on me. A bundle of bones, tied up like firewood."

"Bones?" Slowly, Ralf shook his head. "I don't like the sound of that."

Something else snapped under Hilde's foot – something thin and curved that gleamed faintly in the dark. She bent to look. Nearby, Ralf was kicking at a greyish tangle, barely visible in the grass. He nodded to her. "*Bones*," he mouthed.

"Let's get home," Hilde shivered, and Ralf swung Sigrid on to his shoulders.

"What about the trolls?" asked Sigurd. "What if they follow us?"

"They won't," said his father easily. "Loki here has chased them all into their foxholes amongst those rocks. Forget them. I wonder what your ma has for supper?"

Talking cheerfully, he set off at a rapid pace. Hilde followed, Sigurd tramping manfully at her side. At last they came to the proper track that led down to the farm. Far ahead in the dim wet night they saw a speck of light. Gudrun had lit the lantern to guide them home.

CHAPTER 21

A Warning from the Nis

"BONES?" EXCLAIMED GUDRUN, ladling out four bowls of hot mutton stew. "What kind of bones?"

"Dry ones." Ralf took a long gulp of ale and wiped his mouth with a sigh. "Old dry bones," he repeated. "I kicked some with my foot. Looked like bits of a sheep's ribcage, years old. Sigrid got a fright, but so long as it's dry bones and not ones with meat on them, the trolls can have them and welcome." He looked at Gudrun over the rim of his mug, and his eyes said, *Let's talk about this later.*

For more than a year after being trapped underground, Sigrid had woken every night, screaming about trolls. *Best not make a fuss,* thought Gudrun, sighing. "Well, Ralf, as you say, it's hard to see what harm dry bones can do. Unless the trolls killed the sheep in the first place, the thieves! Come and sit down, Hilde."

Hilde was admiring her baby brother. He lay breathing quietly, long lashes furled on the peaceful curve of his cheek. The firelight glowed on his golden curls.

"Has Eirik been good today?"

Gudrun laughed. "I can't turn my back on that child for half a minute. He tried three times to crawl into the fire, and screamed blue murder when I pulled him back. If it weren't for the Nis, I'd be tearing my hair out."

"The Nis?" Hilde asked, intrigued. "Why, what does it do?"

"Haven't you noticed? It croons away and dangles things over the cradle; it's very good with him! Of course I don't see it properly, only out of the corner of my eye, but I hear the baby coo, and I know he's all right for a while. It was a blessing when Peer brought that creature into our house."

Wind rattled the shutters, and smoke swirled over the fire. The family bent over their meal. By the hearth Loki lay, watchful, resting his chin over the back of Ralf's old sheepdog, Alf. Suddenly he raised his head and pricked his ears. Alf too woke from his dreaming, turning his grey muzzle towards the door.

Which burst open. In staggered a tall, white-faced boy, streaming with water, dragging a ripped and flapping cloak like stormy broken wings. He turned dilated, desperate eyes on Gudrun, and shoved something at her.

"Take it!" he gasped. "Please, Gudrun! Take the baby!"

They all jumped up. Gudrun stared at the bundle he held out. She reached for it as if half afraid – then snatched it and peeled the wrappings back. The dark head of a tiny baby lolled on to her arm, and she clutched it to her chest and stepped back, mouth open.

"Merciful heavens, Peer! Whatever…?"

Peer sank on the bench. "It's Kersten's baby." His voice quivered. "She gave it to me – she said—"

"Kersten's? Where is she? What's happened?"

"She fell into the sea," Peer buried his face in his hands while they all gasped, then looked up again with miserable eyes. "At least – that's not true. She ran into it. I couldn't stop her. Bjørn went after her. Gudrun, I think that baby's terribly cold!"

Gudrun, Hilde and Ralf looked at one another.

"First things first," said Gudrun, becoming practical. "Peer, take off those wet things. Sigrid will bring you some hot stew. Hilde, warm a blanket. Let me look at this child." She laid the baby on her knee, gently unwrapping it and chafing the mottled little arms and legs.

"Poor creature," she said softly. "Dear me, it must be weeks since Kersten had her. I've been meaning to get down and visit. But there's always something else to do. There – there, now!" She turned the baby over and rubbed the narrow back. "Do you know her name, Peer?"

"I didn't even know she was a girl." Peer was struggling into a dry jerkin. His head came out, tousled. "Is she all right?" He came over and stared down at the baby in silence. "She looks like a little frog," he said at last.

"She is rather cold, but she'll be all right." Gudrun swaddled the baby in the warm shawl that Hilde brought. "Now she's warming up, I'll try and feed her."

"Will you, Gudrun?" Tears sprang into Peer's eyes, and he turned away. "I think she *is* hungry. She was chewing my collar bone half the way home," he said over his shoulder.

Hilde laughed at him. "That wouldn't do her much good!"

The baby's dark hair fluffed up as it dried, and she nuzzled into Gudrun's breast, sucking strongly and blinking upwards with vague bright eyes.

Ralf blew his nose. "Now – Peer. Tell us what happened!"

"We were on the shore. I was going to stay with Bjørn, and he gave me a fish to take to Kersten – we were going to have cod for supper. Then—" Peer broke off, trying to make sense of his memories. "Kersten came running down through the sand dunes. It was pouring with rain. She ran smack into me! She had the baby. She said – I can't remember exactly what, but she pushed the baby at me and told me to take it to you, Gudrun. She said, 'Is Gudrun still giving suck?' And then she ran past me and down the shingle. I shouted for Bjørn, but—" He stopped again. "She was wearing this big fur cloak," he whispered. "Before Bjørn could get to her, she'd thrown herself into the sea."

Gudrun's eyes were bright with tears.

"She's gone back to the sea," she said softly. "Do you remember, Ralf, how we all said Bjørn's bride was a seal woman?"

"Nonsense." Ralf punched his fist into his palm. "Utter nonsense. I've never believed it, and I never shall."

"Don't you see?" Gudrun persisted. "That fur cloak will have been her sealskin."

"Explain," demanded Hilde.

Gudrun went on talking quietly, almost singing, crooning over the baby. "It's the grey seals I'm talking about. They can be seals in the water, but people on land, shedding their skins like fur cloaks. If a man meets a seal woman while she's in her mortal shape, and he hides her sealskin, he has power over her. Then she must marry him and bear his children. But if ever she finds her sealskin again, then woe betide! She'll return to the sea and break his heart."

Hilde was horrified. "Did Bjørn do that to Kersten?"

"No, he did not!" said Ralf angrily. "Don't fill their heads with this nonsense, Gudrun. Kersten and Bjørn were an ordinary loving couple."

"Then why did she throw herself into the sea?" asked Hilde. She touched Peer's hand. "What happened, Peer? What happened to Kersten?"

But Peer was no longer certain what he remembered. He

rubbed his hands over his eyes, pressing till coloured lights danced on the darkness. "I don't know," he groaned. "She rolled into the sea. The waves broke over her. It was getting dark, and I was yards away. I thought... I don't know what I thought. I thought she'd drown."

"What did Bjørn do?" Sigrid asked in a small voice. Peer put an arm around her. "He went after her, Siggy. He jumped in the boat and went rowing out..."

"Will he find her?" Sigrid's eyes were round and scared. "Will he?"

Ralf stood. He paced up and down, shaking his head. "I can't bear to think of it!" he exclaimed. "I ought to go down there now – see if there's anything I can do. Didn't you raise the alarm, Peer? Bjørn needs help."

Peer went a painful red. "I—" he stammered. "I never thought of it! I'm sorry! I just – I only – I wanted to bring the baby home!"

Hilde rolled her eyes. "You'd better get down there straight away, Pa!"

"I will." Ralf was already pulling on his boots. "Now, don't worry, Gudrun – but I won't be back tonight. I'll get some of the men together – we'll comb the shore. If Bjørn hasn't found her, we'll search again when it's light."

"I'll come!" Peer got up, staggering slightly.

"No, stay and rest," said Ralf kindly. "You did the best you could, Peer. You can join the search tomorrow. Right – I'm off!" The door slammed behind him.

Hilde puffed out her cheeks and sat down. "How awful."

"Why didn't I tell everyone?" Peer beat his forehead with the heel of his hand. "How could I be so stupid? I even saw Einar, and I dodged him, because I was too embarrassed to explain..."

Hilde patted his shoulder. "Same old Peer! But listen: you brought the baby safely home."

Peer caught her hand, but she drew it away. Gudrun looked up, closing her dress and tucking the shawl more tightly around the baby.

"There, she's had enough. She's falling asleep. Peer, don't upset yourself. Ralf has rushed off like this because he can't bear sitting still, but really, there's nothing useful anyone can do till daybreak. Now eat your stew before it goes cold. Hilde, get the twins to bed. We'll put this little one in the cradle with Eirik."

"Can I?" Sigrid asked, stretching her arms out.

"Yes, but be careful," said Gudrun, handing her over. Sigrid grappled the bundle of shawl and baby with exaggerated care. "She's sweet. I wish I had a little sister." She lowered her into the wide cradle. "I'll put her on her side. Isn't she tiny? Doesn't Eirik look big beside her?"

Peer came to look. The two babies lay side by side. Eirik's fair skin and rosy cheeks made the new baby look sallow. Her thin little wrists looked delicate and fragile compared with Eirik's sturdy dimpled arms.

"Is she sickly?" asked Hilde dubiously.

"No, no," said Gudrun. "She's much younger, that's all. Hardly three months old, when I come to think. I wish now I'd visited Kersten. 'Never put things off,' my mother used to say. But I've been so busy, and little Eirik is such a handful."

"Yes, and he's in for a surprise tomorrow," said Hilde. "Twins! Bedtime." She chased them under the blankets, but Sigrid stuck her head out to call, "I like the new baby, Ma. Can we keep her?"

Gudrun whirled, eyes snapping. "Not another word from you, miss!" She beckoned Peer and Hilde to the other end of the long hearth. "Tell me again," she whispered. "What happened when Kersten ran down to the water?"

Peer closed his eyes. "She saw Bjørn coming, I think," he said slowly. "And she just dived to the ground, and rolled herself up in the cloak and crawled into the water. And I looked away then because Bjørn was pushing the boat out. He rowed out, shouting for her – but it was so wet and misty, I lost sight of him."

They sat in a huddle with their heads together.

"I couldn't stop her!" Peer cried. "I was holding the baby..."

"Hush." Gudrun took his hand. "No one blames you, Peer. And Kersten trusted you with the baby. But the seals – didn't you see any seals?"

"Yes," Peer admitted. "After Bjørn disappeared, the water was full of them. But – Gudrun!" He swallowed. Was such a thing possible? And if so, did it mean Bjørn had trapped Kersten – kept her against her will?

Gudrun wiped her eyes. "It's sad, either way," she said quietly. "And worst of all for that poor little mite over there. Well, we'd better go to bed. There'll be plenty to do in the morning."

They wished one another a glum good night. Peer had been given old Eirik's sleeping place, a bunk built into the wall with a sliding wooden panel for privacy. He clambered in, but as usual left the panel half open so he could see out into the room. Loki pottered over to jump up on Peer's blankets. He turned around three times and settled down behind Peer's knees, yawning. The familiar weight was comforting. Peer slid a hand down to scratch his dog's ears.

He lay, bone weary, staring out into the darkened room. Gudrun had covered the fire with chunks of turf to keep it burning till morning. Small red eyes winked hotly from chinks and crannies, and he smelled scorching earth and woodsmoke. Rain tapped on the shutters. Each time he closed his eyes he saw Kersten, rushing past him, hurling herself into the sea. *I should have stopped her. I should have raised the alarm. I did everything wrong.* Was Bjørn still out there, rowing hopelessly over dark wastes of heaving water?

Peer dropped into an uneasy doze. A cobwebby shadow scampered out to sit hunched on the hearthstones. Peer woke. He heard a faint sound, a steady lapping. The click of a wooden bowl set stealthily down.

Peer watched between his lashes as the Nis set the room to rights, a little rushing shadow, swift as a bat. He hadn't seen it in a long time. Sometimes he glimpsed a wispy grey beard or a little red cap glowing in the firelight, but when he looked closer it was always just a bit of sheep's wool escaped from Gudrun's spindle, or a bright rag wrapped around Sigrid's doll.

Now here it was again, as if to comfort him for this terrible day. It frisked over the hearth, sweeping up ashes, damping the cloth over the dough that Gudrun had left by the fire, and turning the bowl so that it should rise evenly. Finished, it skipped lightly on to the edge of the creaking cradle, and perched there. With a furtive glance over one shoulder, it extended a knobbly forefinger into the cradle to prod one of the sleeping babies, then snatched it back, as if it had touched red-hot iron. It chirruped disapprovingly and hopped down.

Peer raised himself on one elbow. "Nis!" he called softly, half expecting the Nis to vanish like a mouse whisking into its hole. Two beady glinting eyes fixed on his. Behind him, Loki broke into a grumbling growl: Loki had never liked the Nis.

"Quiet," whispered Peer. "Nis, I'm so glad to see you. It's been ages!"

The Nis glared at him. "What has you *done*, Peer Ulfsson?" it demanded.

"Me? What do you mean? I brought Kersten's baby home, that's all."

"Yes! It is all your fault!" the Nis squeaked. Its hair and beard frilled out into a mad ruff of feathery tendrils. "Foolish, foolish boy! What was you thinking of, to bring such a baby here?"

"Wait a minute!" Peer sat right up. "That little baby has lost her mother. What did you want me to do – leave her?"

"Yes!" hissed the Nis. "She doesn't belong here, Peer Ulfsson. Who is her mother? One of the savage sea people, all wild and wet and webbed. Brrr!" It shook its head, a whirr and a blur of bright eyes and whiskers. "The likes of them doesn't belong in house, Peer Ulfsson. Besides, how can the mistress feed two childs, eh? Poor little Eirik. He will starve."

"No he won't," said Peer. "Eirik's nearly weaned. He eats all sorts of things."

The Nis covered its face with two spidery hands. "Poor, poor Eirik!" it moaned, peeping through its fingers. "No milk for him! No food! The little stranger eats it all, steals his mother away. Like a cuckoo chick!"

"I thought you liked babies. What's wrong with her?"

"Everything!" fizzed the Nis. "This is not a proper baby, but a seal baby. Not one thing, not the other." With its head on one side, it added more cheerfully, "Maybe she will pine, maybe she will die!"

Peer almost choked. "A seal baby? You've been listening to Gudrun, but she doesn't *know*. Kersten wasn't – and even if it's true, what are you saying? If her mother's a seal woman, you want the baby to go – yet it's quite all right for you to live here?"

The Nis nodded vigorously. "The Nis is very useful in a house. Often, often, the mistress says she can't manage without me!"

"Does she now?"

The Nis simpered, plaiting its long fingers. "So the baby will go?" it chirped.

"No – actually, the baby will stay."

The Nis's lower lip stuck out, and its eyes glittered. "Peer Ulfsson is so clever," it hissed. "Of course he is right. He knows so much more than the poor Nis!" It turned its back.

Angry though he was, Peer still owed the Nis a lot.

"Come, let's be friends," he said.

"Huh!" snapped the Nis without turning.

"Oh, really, Nis – let's not quarrel."

"If the baby stays – I goes." The Nis delivered this ultimatum over its shoulder, its face still half-averted.

"You're being——" Peer halted. He'd nearly said, "You're being silly," but he thought better of it. "You're being very difficult."

"I means it, Peer Ulfsson," the Nis insisted.

"I'm sure you won't do anything to upset Gudrun," said Peer after a moment. "Now tell me what else is happening."

"What does the Nis know? The Nis knows nothing," the little creature sulked.

"No news?" Peer asked. "When it's so long since we talked?" He faked a yawn. "Very well; I'm tired. I'll go back to sleep."

This worked almost too well. The Nis turned round, stiff with fury. "What sort of news does Peer Ulfsson want?"

"I was only joking!" But Peer saw he had gone too far. While the Nis loved to tease others, it hated to be teased itself.

"News of the trolls – the merrows – the nixies?" it

demanded with an unforgiving glare.

Peer sighed. "Tell me about the trolls?"

"Great tidings from Troll Fell," announced the Nis in a cold, huffy voice. "Remember the Gaffer, the king under the mountain? His daughter, who married and went to live with the trolls of the Dovrefell, has borne a son."

Peer remembered the Gaffer and his sly daughter only too well. "So the Gaffer has a grandson?" he said without enthusiasm. "Let's hope it doesn't take after him, then, with an extra eye, and a cow's tail. Will there be a feast?" He knew the Nis was always interested in food.

A reluctant sparkle appeared in the Nis's eyes. "Oh, yes, Peer Ulfsson," it began. "You see, the princess is visiting her old father under Troll Fell. How grand she is now! Nothing is good enough for her! And such fuss over the new prince. Such a commotion! They'll be having the naming feast on Midsummer Eve."

"And are you invited?" said Peer – but just then, at the dark end of the room, Sigrid stirred in her sleep. "Trolls!" she wailed. "Help! Help, Mamma!" Gudrun stumbled sleepily from the blankets to comfort her. A piece of turf slid on the fire and a bright flame shot up.

The Nis was gone.

"Drat the creature," Peer muttered to Loki. "Why does it have to be so touchy? Troll princes, indeed!"

He lay down again, sighing, dragging the blankets round his neck. But strangely, it wasn't the Nis who haunted his sleep, or even Kersten, running down the shingle to throw herself into the water. All through the long night, as he slept and woke and slept again, the great black waterwheel at Troll Mill rolled through his dreams, turning and turning relentlessly in the darkness.

CHAPTER 22

Bjørn's Story

PIERCING YELLS FROM Eirik woke Peer next morning. Sticking a bleary head round the edge of his sliding panel, he saw that the rest of the family was already up. He bundled Loki off the bed and dressed, thumping and bumping his elbows in his haste. As he scrambled out, Hilde came in with the milk pail, taking short fast steps to prevent it from slopping.

"I should have done that," Peer said, taking it from her. How pretty she looked, he thought, in her old blue dress and unbleached milking apron. Her fair hair was twisted into two hasty braids, wispy with escaping tendrils.

"Oh well, you were tired." She gave him a sunny smile and his heart leaped. "Besides, it's a beautiful morning. My goodness, Eirik! Such a noise!"

"Take him, Hilde." Gudrun handed him over with relief. "I've fed him. He just wants to get down and create mischief. Keep him out of the fire, do! I'll have to feed the other one now."

Hilde seized Eirik under his plump arms and swung him on to her hip. "Come to Hilde, you bad fellow. What a bad boy you are!" Eirik stopped screaming long enough to grab her nose. She pushed his hand away and joggled him up and down. Just as he filled his lungs to yell again, he caught sight of Gudrun lifting the other baby from the cradle, and his angry face smoothed into blank astonishment. He stretched out, leaning away from Hilde, trying to reach the baby girl.

Hilde and Gudrun laughed. "Oh, what a surprise," Hilde teased. "Just look at that expression!"

"Ha, ha!" Sigurd danced around, hooking his fingers into the corners of his mouth and pulling a horrible face – something that usually made Eirik gurgle with laughter. "You're not the littlest one any more!" This time, it failed. Eirik craned past him, yearning towards the little baby.

"They were both asleep when I lifted him out," explained Gudrun, sitting down to feed the new baby. "It's the first time he's noticed her."

Eirik began to writhe and kick, determined to find out what this new creature was. Hilde carried him away and tried to spoonfeed him. Eirik spat milky groute down his chin in angry dribbles. She tried again. Purple with fury, Eirik smacked the spoon out of her hand.

"Just bring him here," said Gudrun wearily, "he's curious, that's all." By now, Eirik's eyes were screwed shut. Tears poured down his cheeks. "All right, all right," Hilde cried. "You can see her. Stop screaming!"

Gudrun righted the baby and sat her upright on her knee, holding her tenderly. The baby hiccupped. She gazed solemnly around. Peer watched her. What had the Nis been complaining about? She seemed like any other baby to him.

"There's nothing wrong with the baby, is there?" he asked.

"She's fine," Gudrun reassured him. "She hasn't even caught a cold. You looked after her very well, Peer. There's no need to worry."

"I didn't mean that. I talked to the Nis last night."

"The Nis?" Gudrun looked up. "What did it say?"

"It was cross," Peer said with a short laugh. "It told me off for bringing the baby here."

"Why?" asked Hilde, amazed.

"Jealousy, I think. It said she's a wild seal baby, and doesn't belong here, and Gudrun won't be able to manage. Something like that."

"Wild?" Hilde started to laugh. "She's as good as gold. If anyone's wild it's young Eirik here." She tickled Eirik's tear-stained cheek.

Gudrun was watching Peer's face. "Is there something else?"

Peer hesitated. "It threatened to leave if the baby stays. But you know what it's like. It probably wasn't serious."

Gudrun tightened her lips. "I managed when the twins were little, so I suppose I can manage now. And the Nis must learn to cope as well."

"But it won't be for long, Gudrun," Peer tried to comfort her. "I mean, even if they don't find Kersten, Bjørn will soon come for the baby."

"But Peer," said Hilde impatiently. "Bjørn can't feed her."

"Oh, of course!" Peer felt himself flush.

"Yes," said Gudrun, "if they don't find Kersten, poor Bjørn will lose his child as well as his wife. Even when she's weaned, he's still got to go out fishing. He can't leave her behind, and he can't take her along."

"How could Kersten leave her own little baby?" Peer wondered aloud.

"Perhaps Ma is right," said Hilde. "What if she was really a seal woman all the time, and Bjørn caught her and kept her prisoner?"

"I don't believe it!" Peer cried. "Bjørn wouldn't do that."

"No?" Hilde flashed. "Then what do *you* suggest? Did Kersten desert her baby – and Bjørn – for nothing? Bjørn's a man, so *he's* not to blame – is that what you're thinking?"

Hurt and angry, Peer was about to snap back. But there were voices in the yard and the doorlatch lifted. Ralf came in, dark against the daylight, bowing his head under the lintel. "Come along, come in," he called over his shoulder.

Bjørn stepped uncertainly after him, narrowing his eyes to see through the indoor shadows. Hilde and Peer exchanged shocked glances and forgot their argument. Could this really be steady, practical, cheerful Bjørn? He looked like a stranger – as if what had happened to him had changed him, or put him on the other side of some barrier of knowledge, so that the old Bjørn was gone, and this new Bjørn was someone they must get to know all over again. There were blue shadows under his eyes, and he did not smile.

Without a word, Gudrun put the baby into his arms, kissed him, and drew him forward to sit down at the fire. "Has he eaten?" she whispered to Ralf. Ralf shook his head. Gudrun hurried to fetch a bowl.

Hilde grimaced at Peer. Still carrying the wriggling Eirik, she went to kneel beside Bjørn. "We're all so sorry," she said quietly.

"Thanks." Bjørn's voice creaked. He cleared his throat. "And here's young Eirik Ralfsson!" he added, with an almost natural laugh. "That fine chip off the old block!" He looked down at his own baby, and his face tightened. He handed her back to Gudrun as she brought his food.

"It's only groute, but it's sweet and hot. Eat up, Bjørn, you'll need your strength," she said anxiously, lulling the baby against her shoulder.

They tried not to stare as Bjørn ate, at first wearily, but then more hungrily as his appetite returned. Ralf said in a low voice to Gudrun, "He needed that. He was out searching all night. When we saw him coming in this morning, he could barely hold the oars."

Bjørn put the bowl down, and looked at Peer. "So what happened?" he asked.

There was no way of softening the bleak tale. In a low voice Peer described yet again how Kersten had come running over the dunes, how she'd pushed the baby into his arms and rushed past him to the sea. Bjørn listened in silence. Under the force of his attention, Peer scoured his mind for extra details. He recalled the cold touch of Kersten's fingers, and the dark tangles of wet hair caught across her face.

"She looked so wild, I thought something dreadful had happened. I said, 'What's wrong, Kersten? Where are you going?' And all she said was, 'Home'."

Bjørn caught a tense breath. Gudrun coughed. "Well now, Bjørn. What might she mean by that? Where was home, for Kersten?"

"She wasn't from round here, was she?" Ralf joined in. "A pretty lass, but foreign? Those looks of hers..."

They all thought of tall beautiful Kersten with her dark hair and green eyes.

"She came from the islands," said Bjørn reluctantly.

The family nodded. "The islands!", "Ah...", "So that explains it!"

But it doesn't, thought Peer, *it doesn't explain anything, and we all know it. Why aren't we talking about what really happened?*

"I must go." Bjørn got up, stiff as an old man. "Must try and find her..."

Ralf shook his head in rough pity. "She's gone, Bjørn. Accept it, lad. Oh, we can search along the shore, but whatever we find, it won't be your Kersten any more."

Bjørn's face set, so hard and unhappy that Peer jumped to

his feet. "But we'll help him. Won't we, Ralf?"

"Of course we will," began Ralf, but Bjørn laid a hand on his arm. "Kersten's not dead, Ralf. I know she hasn't drowned."

With a worried frown, Ralf blew out his cheeks and ran his hands through his hair. "Well – if that's how you feel, Bjørn, we won't give up yet. What's your plan?"

Peer clapped a hand to his mouth. "I forgot!" He looked at Bjørn, stricken. "I completely forgot. When I went to your house last night, you'd been robbed! Your big chest was open, and it was empty. The key was on the floor."

Bjørn stared at him. Peer rattled on, afraid to stop. "And so – maybe that upset Kersten?" He faltered. "I should have told you before, but it – it went clean out of my mind. Have you lost something precious?"

"Don't worry, Peer, I'd already guessed," said Bjørn quietly. "Precious? You could say so. Kersten stole the key. She robbed the chest..."

Gudrun interrupted, her eyes fixed on Bjørn. "She took her sealskin, did she? You kept her sealskin in that chest!"

"Oh, now come on," began Ralf, but Bjørn cut across him. "Was it wrong, Gudrun? Do you blame me?"

"Blame?" said Gudrun. "It's not for me to judge. Did Kersten blame you?"

Bjørn shook his head. Locks of his fair hair swung across his face, hiding it. "She never said so. Maybe. Perhaps she's angry with me. I've got to find her. I've got to know. It's out to the skerries I'm bound, and looking for a bull seal with a scarred shoulder..."

"Why?" Peer rose to his feet, half angry, half incredulous. He imagined Kersten kneeling before the chest, flinging the lid back, dragging out the heavy sealskin, stroking it, wrapping herself in it. "What's going on? Tell us the truth, Bjørn. Was Kersten really a seal woman? Did you trap her?"

"*Trap* her?" Bjørn went white. "We were happy!"

"Then why did you keep the sealskin locked up?"

For a second Bjørn looked as if he might hit Peer. "Because I—"

He gulped and started again. "At first I was afraid she would leave. Then, later, I didn't think it mattered any more. She was my wife! She wasn't a *prisoner!*" The last word was almost a shout.

"But she ran away!" Peer was breathless. "She ran away from you."

"Gods, Peer, what do you take me for?" Bjørn cried. "You don't know what you're saying. All right, listen! This is how I found Kersten – and I've never told the story to another living soul."

Gudrun made a murmur of protest, but Bjørn ignored it.

"Seven – yes, seven years ago, when Arne was a lad about your age – we were out in the boat, the faering, hunting seal among the skerries. I told Arne to land me on the rocks. I'd hide with a harpoon, waiting for the seals to come, and he could go fishing and come back for me later.

"So I scrambled ashore on one of the big skerries where the seals lie and watched him row away. It was fine – and fresh – and lonely, when the boat had gone. No seals yet, only a few black cormorants diving for fish, so I found a sheltered place and lay down in the sunshine on a litter of seaweed and sticks and old gulls' feathers, with my harpoon near at hand."

His voice relaxed into a quiet, storytelling rhythm.

"No sound but the sea and the cries of the cormorants. The rocks felt warm in the sun, winking with bits of crystal. I lay still, so as not to frighten the seals when they came. You know how they float, with their heads just out of the water, watching for danger?

"And I suppose I dropped off to sleep. When I woke it was low tide. The skerry was bigger, going down in rocky steps to a wide broken platform on the western side. And there they were! I could see the seals basking, scratching themselves in the sunshine. I took my harpoon and climbed over the rocks as quietly as I could."

"Go on," prompted Ralf, as Bjørn fell silent.

"I was sun-struck, perhaps," he said slowly. "At least, as I crept over the rocks, I felt dizzy, and my head ached, and I remember seeing and hearing odd things. White bees buzzing around my head. Faces in the stones. The sea gurgling in secret holes under my feet. Voices… And then, on the flat rocks where the seals lay, I saw three fair women sitting. Their dark hair blew in tangled strands, and they combed it out with long fingers. At their feet, three sealskins lay in wet gleaming folds."

The family sat spellbound. Bjørn stared at the wall as if seeing right through it to the far-distant skerry and the washing waves.

"I leaped down the rocks," he went on in the same far-off voice. "The air was singing and ringing. The sun winked off the water, sharp as needles. In the blink of an eye the women were gone. All but the nearest! As her sisters threw on their skins and plunged into the water with the seals, I snatched up her sealskin. Heavy, it was – glossy and greasy and reeking of the sea.

"She screamed like a seagull, and her hair fell over her face and her white shoulders. She stretched out pleading fingers. How she wept! I almost gave it back to her – for pity! – but it seemed wrong to wrap such beauty in a stinking sealskin…

Then I heard a shout. It was Arne calling, and the boat came knocking along the side of the rocks. And I knew I had to choose."

Bjørn's square brown hands knotted. "I'm just a fisherman!" He looked up defiantly. "There I stood with the catch of my life. Suppose I let her go? I already knew that I was caught, too. I'd never forget her. I'd grow old, still dreaming of her, wishing I'd had the courage to do... what I did then.

"I threw the sealskin down to Arne. And I put my two arms around her, and wrapped her in my cloak, and lifted her into the boat."

Gudrun breathed a long, wistful sigh. Ralf shuffled his feet. Hilde sat frowning, her eyes intent on Bjørn. Even the babies were quiet. Peer's head ached fiercely. So Bjørn admitted it – he had stolen Kersten! In the silence, Sigrid piped up in a puzzled voice. "Is this a true story, Bjørn?"

Bjørn gave a brief, unhappy smile. "A true story?" he echoed. "There are so many stories, aren't there, sweetheart? Who knows which are true? I told Arne a different story, and it may have been a better one. He was sixteen, no older than Peer is now, and I could see he was scared. 'Who's this, brother?' said he, and his teeth chattered. So I told him I'd found the girl stranded on the skerry. 'Likely, her boat went down,' I said. 'But no wonder if she's a bit dazed. Who knows how many nights and days she's spent on that rock, with only the seals and the seabirds for company?'

"Arne accepted it. Even to me, it sounded reasonable. But the weather suddenly changed, with a black squall driving over the sea, and the waves clapping against the skerries in spouts of foam.

"As the boat tossed and Arne rowed, a face rose out of the water, a face that looked half-human with furious eyes and snarling teeth. A great bull seal it was, that charged at the boat, roaring. He'd have tipped us over. I still had the harpoon. I threw it without even thinking. It sank deep into his shoulder. He screamed, and the line burned though my hands as he dived, and the water around us was streaked with dark blood and red bubbles. Arne gave a shout, and the girl flung herself at me, screeching like a wildcat. I had to hold her off, and we fell down together in the bottom of the boat as it pitched and swung. I was nearly as crazy as she. The seal in the water, what was it? Her father, her brother? I knew I'd done her wrong.

"At last she lay quiet. Her long hair trailed in the water, over the side of the boat. I looked at her and it came to me that" – Bjørn hesitated – "that I was in love with a wild thing out of the sea. With no name. What words could there be between us? What understanding? And so I gave her the only gift I could. I named her, 'Kersten'.

"Kersten," he repeated gently. "Well, the sea calmed as though we'd thrown oil on the water. And she leaned towards me, shivering and smiling. Yes, she smiled at me and took my hand, and she spoke for the first time. 'Do you really wish me to be Kersten? Can you pay the price?'

"I said I would, I would pay anything. She put her fingers on my lips.

"'Hush! It will be a hard price,' she said, 'hard as tearing the heart from your body; and we will both pay it. *For as long as you keep the sealskin safe, I will be your Kersten.* And while I am with you, the seal folk will befriend you, and drive the mackerel to your nets. But beware of the day we part.'"

There was quite a silence.

"So that's the story." Bjørn got up, his face bleak. "I kept the sealskin locked away, but the years went by and I got careless. I stopped carrying the key about with me – I left it on the shelf. Surely Kersten knew, although I never told her. I thought she loved me. She did love me! But she took the key and unlocked the sealskin. They've called her back, the seal people. Why did she go? Why, without a word to me? After seven years, how could she leave me?

"I'm going to search for her among the skerries, and I'll search for that bull seal too, for I'm sure he lives and hates me. If I find him, I'll see what a second blow can do. I've nothing to lose now."

"Nothing? What about the baby?" asked Peer.

"What?" Bjørn sounded as though he hardly understood the question.

"Your baby," Peer repeated. A thrill of rage trembled in his voice as he remembered the stumbling nightmare of the journey home. "I brought her back for you last night. You've hardly looked at her. We don't even know her name."

Bjørn looked away. "She's called Ran," he said flatly. "Her name is Ran."

"What sort of an outlandish name—?" Gudrun's hand flew to her mouth.

"Kersten wanted a name that came from the sea," said Bjørn wearily. "Change it, if you don't like it. Call her Elli. That was the name I would have picked."

Gudrun was horrified. "Oh, I couldn't, Bjørn. It wouldn't be right."

"Listen to Peer, Bjørn," Ralf urged, "You're a father now. You mustn't take risks."

"A fine father who can't even give his child a home." Bjørn stood. "I must go. You don't mind me coming to see her – from time to time?"

"What a question!" Gudrun exclaimed.

Bjørn nodded. His blue gaze travelled slowly over all of them, seeming to burn each of them up. At Peer, he hesitated, silent appeal in his face. Peer stared back stonily. Bjørn turned away. The door closed behind him.

CHAPTER 23

The Quarrel

RALF ROSE. "I'LL go after him. We mustn't leave him alone. Besides, I left Einar and Harald and old Thorkell searching the tide-line. They may have found poor Kersten by now."

"But Pa!" Hilde cried. "What about Bjørn's story? Don't you believe it?"

"No, Hilde, I don't." Ralf looked down at her. "Even Bjørn's not really sure, is he? Oh, I believe he found Kersten on the skerry. But he talks about sunstroke. That can do strange things to a man – make him see things that aren't there. Most likely, what he told his brother was true, and she'd been stranded there after a wreck. Those waters are dangerous."

Halfway out of the door he added, "And don't go repeating that story of Bjørn's. No good encouraging him to hope. It's best to face up to things. Drowned men and women don't come back."

"Leave the door open," Gudrun called after him, as the sunshine streamed in.

Hilde looked at Peer, sitting at the table with his head in his hands. She reached to touch his shoulder, but changed her mind and carried Eirik outside. She put him down to crawl about. "Look, Eirik! A dandelion! The first this year." She snapped it off and gave it to him to play with. Eirik's fingers closed deliberately around the stem and he sat inspecting it.

The sky was pale blue, with a high layer of fine-combed clouds. Hilde gazed around at the well-loved fields and skyline. Only one thing had changed since last year: the new mound on the rising ground above the farm, where old Grandfather Eirik had been laid to rest. "Where he can keep an eye on us all," Ralf had said gruffly. "Where he can get a good view of everything that's going on!"

Why did sad things have to happen? Why should old folk die and young folk mourn? On a sunny spring morning like this, old Eirik should have been sitting on the bench beside the door, his stick between his knees, composing one of his long poems, or nodding off into one of his many naps. Hilde brushed her eyes with the back of her hand.

Gudrun came out, the dogs trotting at her heels. "Well, if any work at all is to be done this morning, I suppose we women must do it. Goodness, we're behind! Why haven't the twins let the chickens out?"

"Where's Ran?" asked Hilde, going to open the shed.

"Asleep again. Tired out still, I expect. What a nice fresh morning! But I must get on."

Sigurd and Sigrid ran out together.

"Where are you two going?" cried Gudrun.

"Just playing," Sigurd called back.

"All right, but don't go too far." She watched them, and shook her head at Hilde, who was chuckling. "I know, I know. They ought to do their chores. But they're still little enough to have some time to play, especially after last night..."

"Ma," said Hilde, suddenly serious.

"Yes, Hilde?"

"Do you really think Kersten was a seal woman?"

"It doesn't matter what I think," said Gudrun. "The poor

girl's gone, either way. But it matters what Bjørn thinks. It could be easier if he thought she was dead."

"But Ma. If she really was a seal woman – and Bjørn caught her and kept her – well, how could he do that? It's… it's as bad as when Peer's uncles stole the twins away from us. Isn't it?"

Gudrun snorted. "You've got a lot to learn, my girl," she said cryptically.

"And if it's not true," Hilde went on, "if Kersten was just ordinary, just like me or you, then it's almost worse. How could she leave Bjørn and her own little baby, and go and drown herself?"

"You want to know which of them to blame, is that it?" asked Gudrun. "It's none of our business, Hilde. There've been times in my life when I could cheerfully have walked out on the lot of you. Not for long, mind, and I'd draw the line at drowning myself. But having a baby upsets a woman. Sometimes it takes 'em oddly."

Hilde leaned against the farmhouse wall, picking at the fringe of her apron. "But don't you want to know the truth?"

"Hilde, I know enough to be going on with. I know Bjørn loved his wife, and I believe she loved him. I know he's in trouble, and I know he's our friend." She paused. "And I also know that we haven't enough flour for tomorrow's bread, so you'd better begin grinding the barley."

Hilde groaned.

"As for Peer –" Gudrun lowered her voice. "He's upset about this. I don't want him going down to the shore. Imagine if they find her, drowned! Better if he has a different sort of day. Let him take the cows up the fell, and keep an eye on the twins if he can. And the sheepfold wall needs mending."

"All right," said Hilde. "I'll go and tell him."

In the dark farmhouse, Peer was still staring at the fire. She sat beside him.

"Ma wants you to take the cows up the fell, and look after the twins, and patch up the sheepfold."

"I think I should go down to the shore," said Peer gloomily.

Hilde hesitated. "Don't you think there are enough people searching? In any case, if Bjørn's story is true, they won't find her."

"I didn't believe Bjørn could have done such a thing – but I was wrong. He did trap Kersten!"

"Yes," said Hilde carefully, "but I've just been asking Ma, and she seems to think it's more complicated than that."

"I messed everything up last night."

"No, you didn't!" Hilde began to feel annoyed with him. "What more could you have done? Ma's right, nobody could have found Kersten in the dark."

"I should have grabbed her," he said furiously. "I'm taller and stronger than Kersten. I could see she was upset. I should have grabbed her and hung on to her. But first I was holding that stupid fish. And then the baby. I should have put the baby down, and run after her…"

"That's just silly," said Hilde. "Nobody in their right mind would put a little baby down in the sand dunes."

"And I dropped the fish," he added. "It's probably still there."

"The gulls will have eaten it," Hilde said without thinking. Peer winced, and she could see him imagining what else the gulls might be eating. *Why does he have to torture himself so?*

"Hilde!" Peer put a shy arm around her shoulders. Sighing, Hilde returned him a sisterly squeeze. Next moment, to her astonishment, Peer turned towards her, put both his arms around her, and dropped a damp, fumbled kiss somewhere near her right ear.

"*Peer!*" she shrieked, shoving him away.

He sprang up, scarlet in the face. "Don't be angry! I'm sorry, I'm sorry. Oh, Hilde!"

Hilde didn't know whether to laugh, or be furious. He stared at her dolefully, tall and thin and gangly, with hunched shoulders and drooping neck. She burst out laughing. "Oh, stop it, Peer. You look exactly like a heron!"

Peer's head came up. "Fine, make fun of me! I suppose it's true, then, what Sigrid says."

"What does Sigrid say?"

"That you're always thinking of Arne Egilsson!"

Hilde's eyes narrowed. "*For your information*, Peer Ulfsson, I'm not *always thinking* of anyone, but if I were, it certainly wouldn't be a little boy like you!"

Peer's mouth straightened, and his face went pale. "I'm very sorry to have bothered you, Hilde! I won't do it again. And now I'm going down to the shore."

"But Mother said—" Hilde began rashly.

"I don't care what she said!" Peer yelled. "I'm going where I'm needed!" He blundered past and stormed out into the yard.

Hilde put a hand over her eyes.

Gudrun looked round the door. "What's the matter with Peer? Have you been teasing him?"

Hilde exploded. "Me, teasing him? He just tried to kiss me, and got all upset when I told him off. I said he looked like a heron. And he does!"

"That was rather unkind," said Gudrun mildly.

"Mother!"

"Well, he's a good boy, and he's fond of you."

"I know he is! I'm fond of him – I suppose – but not like that! And now I've hurt his feelings. Why can't he be more – more *sensible?*"

"He'll get over it," Gudrun sighed.

Peer marched down the hill in huge strides.

So that was that. Hilde despised him.

He loved Hilde. If he knew anything, he knew that. He loved her fresh face and clear eyes, her ready laugh and sure step. He loved the way she flicked her long braids back over her shoulders when she came to a decision about anything. And now she seemed to have made up her mind about him!

Why did I do it? I shouldn't have risked it. But she was being so sweet to me, trying to cheer me up.

He screwed his face up in agony. What a fool he was! Of course she wouldn't think of him. Who was he, anyway? Just a homeless stray the family had taken in. Not much more than a herd-boy.

That's not fair, he told himself. *Gudrun and Ralf treat me like a son.*

But I'm not their son. That's the point, isn't it? The farm will go to Sigurd one day. What future have I got?

"Why should she think anything of me, Loki? All I've got is you." Loki wagged his tail, scampering to keep up.

How could he make Hilde take him seriously? *You look like a heron.* It had been the flash of real laughter in her face that had stung the worst.

Hardly aware of what he was doing, he came stumbling out of the wood and saw the path unfolding down the slope and into the dip by the mill. Between the branches of the willows, the mill pond looked like Gudrun's bronze mirror winking at the sun, brown with sediment from last night's rain. He could hear the water roaring over the weir.

The mill! With everything else that had happened, he'd forgotten to tell anyone about seeing the waterwheel turning. Indeed, on this bright windy morning it seemed like some strange bad dream.

I'll go and look. Grateful for something different to occupy his mind, he ran down the slope to the bridge and squinted across at the huge wheel.

The broad wooden vanes looked slimy and wet, but that wasn't surprising after such a rainy night. Constellations of bright orange fungus grew on the wood. *Maybe the wheel's rotting… but it still looks fairly solid. Anyhow, it was turning last night. But it isn't now. And that means…*

He frowned. That meant that the sluice gate hadn't burst. If it had, water would still be coursing along the mill race, and the mill would still be working – if the wheel hadn't shaken itself to pieces first. So last night, while he'd been coming up the track in the wild dark, carrying the baby, someone had deliberately opened the sluice gate. And later, they had closed it again. There was no other explanation. But who would have done it, and why?

Frowning, he pushed along the overgrown path beside the dam. As he expected, the sluice gate at the head of the mill race was firmly lowered, shutting off the water. There was no way that the waterwheel could turn.

Peer scratched his head and looked at the swollen mill pond. The current had opened a brown channel down the middle, sweeping the green duckweed to the calm stretch at the far side. Somewhere underneath all that, he knew, lived Granny Greenteeth. What was her dwelling like, down in the cloudy water? He imagined a sort of dark hole, ringed with snags, and Granny Greenteeth lurking in it like an old eel. He remembered the dark figure he'd half seen, half imagined, creeping after him up the hill. Had it been Granny Greenteeth? Had she opened the sluice?

No wiser for what he'd seen, he wandered back to the wooden bridge and stopped halfway over. There was nowhere to go. If he joined the search party on the shore, Bjørn would be there, and Peer didn't want to meet him. He couldn't go back to the farm yet, either – he couldn't face Hilde.

He stood, restlessly peeling long splinters from the wooden handrail and dropping them into the rushing water. *Kersten ran away from Bjørn. She doesn't want to be found.*

The stream babbled away under the bridge, as if arguing with itself in different voices. Listening, he caught a few half-syllables in the rush. *Gone. Lost, gone.* Or maybe, *long ago...* And was someone sobbing?

It's just the water, Peer thought. But he shivered. Could the mill be haunted by the people who had once lived here? None of them had been happy, including his own grandmother. "A thin little worn-out shadow of a woman," Ralf had once described her. She'd come here after her first husband died, and married the old miller. And the miller had ill-treated her; and her young son Ulf, Peer's own father, had run away and never come back. And then she'd had two more sons, who had grown up to become his violent, selfish, bullying half-uncles, Baldur and Grim.

Instinctively, Peer twisted the thin silver ring he always wore on his finger, the only thing of his father's that he still owned. Ulf had been a thin, quiet man, whose slow rare smiles could warm you from top to toe. *If only I could talk to him. He wouldn't say much, but he'd put his arm around me. He'd...*

I miss him. Why did he have to die?

Peer crashed his fist down on to the rail.

What's wrong with me? he wondered, and suddenly realised. *I'm angry!*

He considered it, amazed. Peer never lost his temper. For three years now he'd lived with Gudrun and Ralf, grateful to the family, glad to live among decent kindly folk who treated him well. And he'd admired Bjørn. Bjørn was the sort of person Peer wanted to be – cheerful, self-reliant, always willing to help – but with a steely streak that meant nobody pushed him around.

And ruthless enough to keep Kersten against her will?

Peer swallowed a lump in his throat and trailed off the bridge towards the entrance to the mill. The mill and the barn faced each other across the narrow yard, with a line of rough sheds and a pigsty to the north, backing on to the millpond. A cluster of trees grew around the buildings; bare brown brooms just softening into green. Above the dilapidated thatch of the mill roof, the clean edge of Troll Fell rose against the sky.

Go on. Go in!

Peer hesitated. It was all so very quiet, and he was by himself.

Scared? In broad daylight? Faintheart!

He walked slowly into the yard, his feet sinking into soft, untrodden leaf-mould and moss. Underneath were cobblestones, buried by years of neglect. Peer padded warily towards the barn and looked inside. There was a smell of damp, mildewed straw, a litter of bird droppings, and a breathless, dusty silence. He backed out, trying to look over both shoulders at once.

Something bitter rose in his throat. A rush of memories

swept over him. He was thirteen years old again, cringing half defensively, half defiantly under the harsh hand of Uncle Baldur.

He'd slept in that dusty barn, in the straw with the hens. Over there by the mill door, Uncle Baldur had knocked him down. Peer remembered every inch of the yard. One hot summer's day, Baldur's twin brother, Uncle Grim, had made him sweep it twice over, first with a broom, and then on his knees with a hand brush. He could still see his uncle's red face, oozing little beads of sweat, gloating as he pointed out tiny bits of twig and chicken feathers that Peer had missed.

Clean it up, boy! No supper until you do…

Peer's fists clenched, the nails digging into his palms.

Nobody, nobody, was going to treat him like that again!

CHAPTER 24

Exploring the Mill

NOBODY'S EVER GOING *to treat me like that again!* The words rang out in Peer's mind. He straightened his shoulders, letting the anger drain away. A subdued Loki looked up at him, pressing closely to his legs.

They stood in front of the mossy mill door. It leaned on its hinges, half open. Peer pushed, and it scraped inwards over a rubble of earth and stones and decayed leaves. He stepped through.

With a shriek and a clatter of feathers, a frantic starling swept out over his head and disappeared over the barn roof, chattering hysterically. Loki rushed after it.

Peer sank against the doorpost, his heart thundering. "It's all right, Loki!" he managed to say, as the dog returned at a stiff trot, hackles high. "Just a bird! What a couple of cowards we are. Come on!"

It was dark inside. The shutters were closed. Peer trod carefully. There was a strong damp smell, and his nose prickled. As his eyes got used to the gloom, he saw spectral weeds growing in the long-dead ashes of the central fireplace. Pale and unhealthy, they straggled upwards on hopeless spindly stalks, trying to reach the weak light filtering through the smoke-hole. Peer brushed past them, shuddering.

The place was smaller than he remembered. At the far

end, a ladder led up into the shadowy grinding loft, and at its foot lay a worn old millstone, cracked in two, amongst a litter of splintered and broken wood. On either side of the hearth were the two bunks that his uncles had slept in, built into dark alcoves in the wall. A lump of some pale fungus was growing over the pillow end of the nearest. The ruckled blankets trailed in damp, dirty folds and looked as though they had been nibbled by mice. Peer bumped into a huge pair of scales, dangling from the rafters on a rusty chain. They squeaked and swung: there was a bird's nest in one of the pans. Alarmed by the noise, Peer tried to steady them. They bobbed and ducked and seesawed into stillness.

He let out his breath, turning around. It didn't look as if anyone had been here. Loki nosed about the spongy floor. He growled at the bedding, sniffed and sneezed.

Peer struggled with one of the shutters, brushing away a tangle of cobwebs and dead bluebottles. A narrow column of daylight slanted in and lay in a pale stripe across the ghostly hearth and the filthy floor. Dusting his hands together, Peer lifted the lid of one of the old grain bins. It was a third full of some sort of coarse grey flour. It didn't look edible any more. He lowered the lid and craned his neck to see up on to the floor of the grinding loft, where the millstones rested. It looked dark and creepy up there, and he fought a wish to get out into the open air.

I'd better look, he thought. He couldn't see why anyone should have been up there – yet the mill had been working. *I'll nip up the ladder and see.*

He climbed the rough ladder, leaving Loki sitting below. The big grain hopper loomed over him, hanging from the rafters on ropes. It was made of blackish oak, blending with the darkness, and he misjudged his distance and hit his head.

Muttering curses, he crouched to inspect the millstones. A tiny gable window, half blocked with an old flour sack, provided a glimmer of daylight, but not really enough to see by. He ran his hands over the upper millstone, and then round the edges, covering his fingers with gritty powder. He sniffed. It smelled of stone and dust, nothing like the yeasty smell of freshly ground grain. He stood, and gave one of the hoists an experimental tug. The rope ran easily over the squeaking pulley.

"I don't know, Loki. Everything works, but nobody's been grinding corn. The place is a mess. It's a pity somebody doesn't fix it. We could all do with a proper mill again..."

Why not me?

Peer stood still, high up under the rafters, staring at the room below. Baldur, he remembered, had been fiercely proud of his mill. He and Grim might have lived like pigs, but they'd kept the machinery in good order. Peer vaulted down from the loft, not bothering with the ladder. Clearing aside a stack of old crates and some mouldy baskets, he exposed a small door that led to the cramped space directly under the millstones. He dropped on his knees to open it. A crude wooden swivel kept it shut. He paused.

Uncle Grim, opening this door, forcing him through into the blackness beyond. Himself screaming, panting for breath, bursting his way out, and begging, pleading, not to be thrown back in again...

His mouth hardened. Deliberately he turned the catch, dragged the door open, and stuck his head through. Even in daylight, it was very dark in there, and full of the noise of the stream. He could dimly see the great axle of the waterwheel, piercing the wall on the right, and the toothed edges of the pit wheel and lantern gear that drove the millstones.

Peer got up slowly, dirty patches on his knees.

"It's my mill now," he said aloud. Loki whined unhappily,

but Peer felt furious excitement welling up. "It *is* my mill. It belonged to my uncles, and I'm the only one left. I can get it working again. I can be independent."

His words sank into the damp, unhealthy siftings that covered the floor. The walls seemed to squeeze inwards like a tightening fist. He hurried for the door, tripping over the hearth and kicking up wads of damp ashes.

The yard seemed bright after the darkness indoors. Loki shook his ears till they rattled, and trotted towards the lane, but Peer called him back. "No, boy, we're not leaving yet."

Arne may have a boat, he thought. *But I've got a mill!*

He imagined the yard cleared and swept, with gleaming cobbles. Shutters and doors mended; sheds and outhouses rebuilt. Everything tidy and cool and clean. He saw himself welcoming the neighbours as they brought their sacks of barley and rye. For a second, he even allowed himself to imagine Hilde standing in the doorway, smiling at him, and throwing corn to the chickens from the pocket of her apron…

He found some old tools leaning in a corner of the barn, a collection of toothless hay rakes and rusty scythes. He picked a battered old shovel and began scraping moss from the cobbles.

Loki watched, his tail swinging slower and slower. He seemed to realise that they would not be going to the village after all. He settled down with his nose on his paws, keeping one wary eye open.

"That's right, Loki," panted Peer. "On guard!" The edge of the shovel rattled noisily over the cobbles, and he knew he wouldn't hear anyone coming up behind him… but that was a foolish thought. Baldur and Grim were gone.

He worked on, falling into a stubborn rhythm. The sunshine faded: thin clouds spread across the sky like spilt milk. Loki rose, his short fur bristling. He barked once, sharp and loud, staring at the mill door. Peer looked up.

But the mill was empty! Wasn't it…?

Holding the shovel like an axe, he tiptoed over the cobbles. Had something slipped into the mill while he wasn't looking? He listened and heard nothing. After a second or two he gave the door a push and jumped back. Still nothing.

Probably Loki had seen a rat. Peer stepped inside. It was even darker than it had been earlier, and for a moment he was half blind. The fusty, mouldy smell rose into his nostrils. He blundered a couple of paces, and scanned the room. This end, by the door, didn't bother him. The feeble daylight showed him it was empty, except for a couple of worm-eaten stools and a pile of sacks. But the far end was a different matter. Anything might be crouching up in the shadow-draped loft, or hiding in the big square grain bins with their slanting lids.

He took another tense step, level now with the hearth. *Aaahhh!* There was a sound like a shifting sigh. Peer stared at the dirty bunk beds against the wall. Nothing moved, but the whole shadowy room had the feeling of a joke about to be played, a trap about to be sprung. He prodded the greasy bedclothes nearest to him. They were so snarled together and rolled up, it looked as if a body was lying there – a long, thin body. And that pale fungus made a sort of shapeless head –

"*BOO!*" The fungus opened two glittering, hungry eyes and a wide, split-like mouth. It sat up. The other bunk bed heaved. A second shape catapulted out and leap-frogged towards him. Peer shrieked and struck out with the shovel. It connected with a satisfying *ding*! With an anguished yelp the creature rushed past on flat, slapping feet. The other one followed. Colliding at the door, they wrestled briefly, elbowing and pushing to get out first. They fell into the yard and dashed off in different directions. His blood up, Peer charged out in time to see Loki chasing one of them around the end of the barn. He joined in.

Trees grew close up to the back of the building. Peer raced through a sea of young nettles, leaving great bruising footmarks. More marks showed where someone had dashed on ahead.

Peer wasn't going to play tag around the barn – not when they might circle round behind and grab him. He whistled to Loki, sweeping his arm back towards the yard. Loki streaked off, and Peer hurried the opposite way, hoping that he and Loki would catch the creatures between them. But as he rounded the other end of the barn, Loki was casting about, clearly at a loss, and the yard was empty.

So the lubbers were loose! He shivered, recalling their skinny limbs, clammy hands and blotchy features. They had lived in the old lean-to privy of wattle and daub, built against the end of the barn nearest the road.

And that was the answer, he realised. The lubbers had taken over the empty mill. They must have been playing about with the machinery. *That's why the wheel was turning: that's who followed me up the hill!*

If he wanted the mill for himself, he had to get rid of them. But how?

He stared at the privy. They were sure to be hiding there now. The door was blocked by a stack of firewood. No one could get through it – but there was a ragged hole in the mouldering thatch. Peer stood back and looked at it. He'd made that hole himself, the night he'd escaped from his uncles. But it seemed to have got bigger. He squeezed up close to the wall and listened.

He heard creaking sounds, huffing and puffing. An agitated voice broke out: "Ow, me leg hurts, it hurts! He got me with his shovel. It's bleeding. Look at that gash!"

"Lick it, stupid," the other one growled. "Why did you get in the way? I was just going to grab him."

"Why didn't you lie low?" the first voice snuffled. "He'd never have spotted us, if you hadn't jumped out like that. He didn't the first time."

"'Cos I couldn't stand it, see? I'm highly strung. Me nerves couldn't take it."

"There I lay, hardly breathing," the first lubber hiccupped, "while he prowls up the room with his dog and his shovel."

"Yeah. He's vicious, that boy is. Vicious!"

There was a short silence.

"It's all slimy in here," lamented the first lubber. "I wish I'd brung me blanket. Where's yours?"

"Left it behind," said the other in a hollow voice. "Heartbreaking, innit? First blankets we ever had. Blankets and beds, all cosy and nice, and what happens? Thrown out. Evicted by a nasty young thug with a dog and a shovel." Its voice sharpened. "Oooh – a snail!"

"I want it! I oughter have it, 'cos I cut my leg," shrieked the wounded lubber. "Got it!" it added, with a slurping crunch.

"Bet you never see your blanket again," said the other spitefully. "Kiss goodbye to it. It's *his*, now."

"But it's mine! I wa-a-ant it!"

Peer turned and ran through the nettles, across the yard and into the mill. He groped his way to the nearest bunk bed, felt for the blanket and jerked. It came up in stiff, stinking folds. It felt like something that had died and was rotting. He could hardly bring himself to touch the other one, but he did, and dragged them both out into the yard. Black stuff showered off – woodlice, and pieces of decaying wool, and mouse droppings.

"I've got your blankets here," he yelled at the top of his voice. "And if you don't come out, I'll throw them in the millpond!"

There was a shriek of alarm.

"So come and get them!" Peer shouted. "Both of you! I know you're in there. Do you want me to come after you? *With my dog and my shovel?*"

He stopped, panting. With a thud and a scrabbling sound, a shape appeared through the privy roof. It clambered out, becoming a spindly figure with a very large head and one flyaway ear, just visible against the dark trees.

Peer backed a few steps. "Where's your friend?" he called roughly. "Come on, I want both of you out of there!"

A second head emerged from the hole in the privy roof. It was pale and bald, and glimmered horribly in the dusk. He couldn't make out any eyes, and didn't know if it was looking at him or not. He took another step back and nearly fell over Loki. Recovering, he brandished the blankets, and more pieces dropped off. "Here they are! But you can't have them till you're out of the yard."

The lubbers twisted over the edge and slithered into the nettles. They crouched, gaping at Peer with dark, frog-like mouths, and he stared back, quivering with revulsion. One of them hissed, a loud, startling noise. He flinched, and both lubbers twitched forwards. A moment's loss of nerve, and they would rush him.

"Out!" he yelled, waving the blankets like a banner. "Come on, Loki!" He ran at them, gripping the shovel in his left hand like a sword. Loki hurtled ahead, barking. The lubbers fled. Peer drove them before him, right out of the yard, across the lane and into the wood. With all his strength, he flung the reeking folds after them. In a flash, the nearest turned and snatched up both blankets. It gambolled away into the trees, lifting its bony knees high. The other limped after it, screaming. The crashes and cries and howls grew fainter and further away.

Peer burst out laughing. "What cowards! We've done it, Loki, we've cleared them out of the mill!"

It was the perfect ending to a difficult day. He turned back towards the mill, smiling. As he did so, there was a step behind him. A twig crunched; a heavy hand fell on his shoulder. For a second his heart stopped. But Loki was wriggling and wagging in ecstatic welcome – and Ralf's voice said in hearty greeting: "Peer, my lad! What on earth have you been doing?"

CHAPTER 25

A Family Argument

RALF LISTENED IN amazement as Peer rattled off an account of his day at the mill.

"Well, I'm blowed," he exclaimed. "You chased off those lubbers by yourself?"

"Loki helped!" Peer dragged Ralf into the yard and showed him the cleared cobbles. "See, only a few hours' work, and I've made a big difference. It's my mill, Ralf, and I'm sure I can do it. I remember how the machinery works. What do you think? Isn't it a good idea?"

Ralf looked at the dark buildings and hesitated. Peer's high spirits sank. An owl hooted from the woods. The trees around the mill whispered, rubbing their branches together as though plotting something unpleasant. And something scuttled along in the shadow of the wall.

Peer realised that he was hungry and cold, and his back ached.

"Let's talk about it at home," Ralf suggested, leading him out of the yard. "It's late, and I've had a hard day."

"What happened?" Peer asked awkwardly. "Is there any news?"

"No," Ralf said as they crossed the bridge. "We combed the shore, right round under the south cliffs. Not a sign of the body. And Harald Bowlegs took his boat across the fjord to search the Long Strand on the other side. He found nothing. But Bjørn keeps insisting Kersten isn't dead. I wish he wouldn't. All sorts of rumours are flying around."

"Like what?"

Ralf snorted. "Dreams, omens – all kinds of rubbish. There was a white fog on the fjord first thing this morning, and what must old Thorkell say but that he's seen a boat gliding through it – but only half a boat, if you please, with a ghostly sail like shreds of mist, all tattering and curling. 'The draug-boat,' he says, 'coming for Bjørn now his luck is gone!'"

"Really?" Cold fingertips touched Peer's spine.

"No one else saw it," said Ralf, "and we all know Thorkell's eyesight isn't what it should be. And then Einar got going. He says he heard a voice crying in the dark last night, but when he looked out, there was no one there."

"That would be me," said Peer, shamefaced.

Ralf nodded. "But now everyone's at it. They've all seen or heard something strange. Raps and noises and strange messages."

"Don't you believe any of it?" asked Peer.

"There was a storm last night," said Ralf. "Of course people heard noises!"

"But, Ralf," Peer didn't quite know how to say it. "You know there are trolls – and lubbers – and Granny Greenteeth in the millpond down there. Why shouldn't these other things be true, too?"

Ralf stopped. "They may be, Peer. Indeed they may. But we don't need to rush to believe in them. Some folks enjoy looking for bad luck everywhere. A man makes his own destiny. That's what I think."

He gripped Peer's shoulders, gave him a little shake, and strode on uphill. Peer walked after him, deep in thought.

A man makes his own destiny. And I will. I'm going to take Troll Mill, and make myself a future!

They were nearly home. Ahead was the farm, snuggling against the black hillside. Loki ran ahead, eager for his supper. Peer slowed down, and let Ralf go into the house without him. He felt awkward about meeting Hilde.

What should he do? Apologise again? Or pretend the quarrel had never happened? *Hello, Hilde*, he could say. *Had a good day? I did!*

"Hello, Peer!" came a crisp voice behind him. Peer leaped like a deer and swung round. Hilde stood there, carrying the milk pail. "Back at last?" She raised an eyebrow. "You've missed evening milking. I shouldn't have to do *all* your chores."

"I'm sorry!" he stammered, reaching for the pail. "Let me carry that in."

"No, never mind," she said, setting it down. "I'm glad I saw you. I want to say something. I was rude to you this morning, Peer. I shouldn't have said what I did. And I'm sorry."

You look like a heron! If I did think about anybody, it certainly wouldn't be a little boy like you!

The words buzzed in the air around Peer's head, and they stung just as much as they had that morning. He flushed and mumbled something, looking down.

"Ma said it was wrong," continued Hilde. "She said it was unkind."

Peer looked up, horrified. "You *told* your *mother?*"

"Oh, Peer, she overheard most of it!" said Hilde impatiently. "We weren't exactly whispering, you know!"

"Yes, but—" He needed to impress her. He said boldly, almost boastfully, "I've been cleaning out the mill all day. I'm going to start working it again."

"The mill?" Hilde stared. "You're joking!"

"No. I've cleared half the yard already. And I know the machinery still works, because—" He stopped suddenly, unwilling to describe the fright he'd had when the empty mill started working by itself in the dark. "I'm sure it does – it looks all right. I'm going to be the new miller. What's wrong with that?"

"What's *wrong?* Do you need me to tell you? What about Granny Greenteeth? The lubbers?"

"No problem," said Peer airily. "I've thrown the lubbers out."

"What do you mean?"

Peer explained. She gave a satisfying gasp as he told how the lubbers had jumped out at him. And when he got to the bit about the blankets, she laughed out loud. "Brilliant! But did it work?"

"Oh yes." Peer couldn't help grinning. "One of them grabbed both the blankets, and the other one chased it into the woods."

Hilde became serious again. "But they're bound to come slinking back. Why be a miller? What for? You don't have to do this, Peer. You live with us."

"For ever?" asked Peer. He watched as Hilde hesitated. "I've made up my mind," he went on. "You don't believe I can do it; but just wait and see!"

"Don't be silly," Hilde snapped. "I'm worried about you, that's all."

The last of the evening glow had faded. An owl hooted from the farmhouse gable. Hilde's face was a pale splash. In the dark it was easier to say what he wanted.

"At the mill this morning, I remembered what it was like to live there. How scared I was of my uncles. The way I crept about. I was a coward."

"But they were great big men, and you were only thirteen years old. It wasn't your fault!"

Peer shook his head. "I want to take something back from them."

"What?"

"My self respect," he said through gritted teeth.

The owl called again, a wild, quivering note. Hilde sighed. "And you can only do that by taking over the mill? All right." She half-flapped her arms. "All right, Peer, I can see you have to try. So I'll help you. Count me in!"

Eirik was crying again when Peer and Hilde entered the farmhouse, and this covered the sound of their low-voiced, furious disagreement.

"If it's safe for you, it's safe for me." Hilde held the door for Peer as he carried in the milk pail.

"Well, perhaps it isn't safe!" Peer poured the milk into the shallow skimming pan so that the cream could rise. "But it's my business, Hilde, not yours."

Hilde looked ready to say something sharp, but before she could open her mouth, Gudrun's voice rose above the clamour.

"You rowed to the skerries in that little boat!" She stood, joggling Eirik in her arms and looking down at Ralf, as he sat in his big wooden chair. "*Ralf!* You could have capsized – drowned!"

"No, no." Ralf stretched his legs to the fire with a groan of relief. "Whew! I'm stiff. Bjørn knows every inch of that water, Gudrun. We were quite safe, but he was too tired to go alone. I haven't rowed so far in ages. Blisters, look! But nothing else to show for it."

Gudrun looked unconvinced. "Everyone says it's so dangerous out there when the tide is running."

"We were there at slack water," Ralf reassured her. "We tossed around between the stacks, scaring the gulls, shouting like fools for Kersten. And yes, we saw some seals. They took no notice of us, as far as I could tell.

"I've been thinking," he went on. "Seems to me someone should cross to Hammerhaven and find Arne. Bjørn needs his brother at a time like this."

Arne? Peer glanced at Hilde.

"That's a good idea," Gudrun agreed. "Who'll go for him? Harald Bowlegs, in his boat?" She looked Ralf with suspicion. "Not you, Ralf? We're so busy. Surely it doesn't have to be you?"

"No-oo." Ralf shifted uncomfortably. "But everyone else is busy, too. Einar hasn't sown his oatfield yet, and Thorkell's too old."

"So you've offered already!" Gudrun's eyes snapped sparks. "I might have guessed. You should ask me first before you go promising all sorts of things. Here I am, with an extra child to care for—"

"She's no trouble, is she?" Ralf demanded. "You've got plenty of help – Hilde and Peer, and even the Nis."

"Oh, have I?" Gudrun cried. "Not today, I haven't! The Nis has been sulking. It hasn't so much as swept the hearth."

"Why are you making such a fuss? I'd only be gone for a couple of days."

Gudrun tossed her head. "And suppose Arne's not there? Suppose he's away? What if he's joined another of these Viking ships? I expect you'd sail after him, and leave me for months wondering whether you were dead or alive – like last time."

"Now you're being ridiculous!" Ralf shouted.

Eirik struggled, screaming in sympathy. Gudrun passed him to Hilde. "Take this child and find him something to chew." She turned on Ralf, braids flying. "I sometimes think I'm the only one with any sense round here. Worry about us for once, Ralf Eiriksson! What about the trolls, stealing our sheep?"

Ralf paused. "That's true," he said more calmly. "That's true, Gudrun. I'd forgotten about that. I'll have to move the sheep off the Stonemeadow. Very well. I'll wait a while and see how Bjørn gets on."

CHAPTER 26

Voices at the Mill Pond

NEXT MORNING, THE high Stonemeadow rang to Ralf's whistles as Loki raced about, rounding up the sheep.

"A beautiful day!" Hilde called to Peer and the twins. It was true. The last snow had melted, and the ground trickled with water. The mountains to the north and east seemed curled like cats, basking in the sun. To the west, the sea was a warm blue line, smudged with islands.

Peer felt light-hearted, glad to be walking on Troll Fell in the spring sunshine, rather than toiling away at the mill. Lambs played tag around the rocks. An early bee zoomed past. It was hard to believe in trolls – or mills, or wicked uncles! But as they tramped down from the high fields, the sheep trotting ahead of them, Hilde pointed out a low, rocky crag, with a line of thorn trees along the top.

"See the little gully under it, where the brook runs? That's where we met the trolls, the night before last," she told Peer. "Just under that scar."

"When they saw us, they bolted uphill," said Ralf.

"Scattering bones!" added Hilde.

Peer frowned. "Are they butchering sheep on the hillside?"

"That's the odd part," said Hilde. "The bones we saw were old and dry."

Sigurd broke in. "Perhaps they're hiding the bones so we won't know the sheep have been stolen."

Sigrid shook her head. "Remember when we were kidnapped?"

"Nobody ever lets us forget," he muttered. "*Be careful, twins – don't go too far – stay with Hilde – get back before dark!* What about it?"

"Remember the old Gaffer, the king of the trolls? He wouldn't bother hiding bones from us. He just wouldn't care." She shivered. "I had a nasty dream about him last night. He had those three red eyes, and he jumped out at me like a spider."

Peer felt a tug at his memory. Someone else had said something, recently, about the Gaffer…

The crag glinted like a line of grey teeth in the hillside. The summit of Troll Fell was out of sight, hiding behind its own ridges. Peer remembered that winter night three years ago, when he'd seen the rocky cap of the hill hoisted up on stout pillars for the midwinter banquet.

"Got it!" He snapped his fingers. They all stared. "I know what's going on! The Nis told me, the other night. Remember the Gaffer's daughter, Ralf, who gave you the golden cup, and married the Dovreking's son? She's had a son of her own, a new troll prince. And she's back from the Dovrefell, visiting her father. They're naming the child on Midsummer Eve. There's going to be a feast!"

Ralf's eyes widened. "That'll be it," he growled. "They've got extra mouths to feed, and a feast coming up – and they're dining off our sheep. I suppose they prefer roast mutton to that awful food you told us about, Peer – frogspawn soup, and the like. Who'd be a farmer around here? This hill must be riddled with their rat-holes and burrows. Let's get going." He whistled to Loki, for the flock had slowed and was beginning to scatter.

Glancing downhill, Peer felt poised like a bird, high above the world. The woods below looked soft enough to stroke, like the tufts of wool in Gudrun's scrap basket. Here and there a white sparkle betrayed the stream, flickering with waterfalls. There was a dark spot buried amongst the trees. He pointed. "Look! You can see the roof of the mill from here!"

But Ralf was already moving on.

By noon, the meadows around the farm were dotted with ewes and their lambs, and the farmstead echoed with raucous bleating. Only the home field, walled and fenced, remained empty so that the grass could grow there.

"A good job well done," commented Ralf, munching bread and cheese. But he looked dissatisfied, and they all knew why. Ralf depended on hay cut from the meadows as well as the home field. If the sheep grazed down here for too long, there would be nothing left for winter feed.

"Well," he continued, stretching his arms. "What do you say, Peer? We've time to look at this mill of yours – if you still want to?"

"Yes," answered Peer, although yesterday's enthusiasm had worn off. *I can't give up*, he thought, stiffening. *I've hardly started yet. A man makes his own destiny!*

"What's this?" asked Gudrun.

"The lad wants to do up the old mill," Ralf explained, and she gasped.

"The mill? Oh, Peer! I really don't think that's a good idea."

"We'll help!" said Sigurd eagerly. "I've always wanted to see inside."

"No, you won't," said Gudrun quickly.

He glared at her. "Why not?"

"Because it isn't safe."

"Hilde's going!"

"That's different," said Hilde, as Gudrun exclaimed, "We'll see about that!"

Hilde stared defiantly at her mother, her flyaway hair glinting in the sunlight, her colour high. Gudrun gave in. "Very well. Hilde may go. But the twins may not: and that's the end of it."

"It isn't fair," yelled Sigurd. "You never let us do anything!"

Ralf held up a big hand. "Don't speak to your mother like that. You'll stay at home and do as you're told. Hilde and I will help Peer. There's no reason why the place should be dangerous – in daylight, at least."

They trooped down through the wood, carrying brooms, spades and sickles. Ralf had a pickaxe over his shoulder. No one had much to say, and Peer led Ralf and Hilde into the mill yard with a mixture of bravado and nerves. As Ralf went poking through the sheds, Hilde stood in the centre of the yard, arms crossed, peering up at the sagging rooflines and sliding thatch.

"It's horrid. All those dark doorways. And look at the holes in the roof. The lubbers might be hiding anywhere. I'll bet they just waited for you to go and then came creeping back."

"They probably did," said Peer. "But they're scared of me now. I've got the measure of them, Hilde. You don't have to worry."

"Hmm." Hilde looked sceptical.

Ralf emerged from the pigsty. "All clear," he shouted. "The sheds are empty. Let's start by tearing down that old privy. No sense in leaving any bolt-holes!"

"Hush, Ralf," Peer said instinctively. "Not so loud."

"No need to tiptoe around whispering," Ralf said, surprised. "We'll make plenty of noise as soon as we start work."

"Pa's right," said Hilde. "The Grimssons have gone." She laughed suddenly. "Peer, relax! Look at you – you're all hunched up!"

"Am I?" Discovering it was true, he straightened. "I'm expecting Uncle Baldur to come and start screaming at us. It's as if the last three years have been a dream, and I'm going to wake up," he said uncertainly.

"You're awake," Hilde told him. "I'll pinch you, if you like."

Ralf set about the privy with the pickaxe. Hilde came into the mill with Peer, and helped force back the shutters. Sunshine and fresh air streamed in, lighting up the dismal interior. She looked around in disgust.

"You should have seen the blankets I threw out," Peer told her. "But it won't be so bad when it's swept and cleaned."

"Won't it?" Hilde kicked at a pile of sacks that had rotted together into a thick mat. A cloud of mould spores rose into the air, and she choked, covering her nose. "Peer, what an awful place. You can't live here!"

"The machinery's all right," said Peer, to avoid answering. "Let's get all this rubbish outside."

They emptied the mill. Out went the stinking sacks, the armfuls of mouldy baskets, the worm-eaten stools and the broken table. "Everything on the heap!" called Ralf, as they passed in the doorway.

A huge pile of rubbish built up in the centre of the yard. Inside the mill, nothing was left except the rectangular hearth in the middle of the floor, and, against the wall, the two bunk beds and the tall grain bins with their sloping lids. Hilde weeded the fireplace. She swept the walls free of cobwebs – disturbing ancient, floury dust which settled in their hair, their eyes, and their lungs. They retreated into the yard, sneezing. Loki lifted his head. He was lying tightly curled up in a patch of sunshine near the lane, and his eyes implored, *Are we leaving yet?*

"Poor Loki," said Peer, wiping his face with his arm. "He hates this place."

"You can't blame him," coughed Hilde. "Nothing nice ever happened to him here."

A cloud passed over the sun. Uncle Baldur's shrill voice echoed in Peer's mind: *What d'you call that? A dog? Looks more like a rat. You know what we do to rats round here? Set Grendel on 'em! One chomp – that's all it takes!*

"Back to work," he said fiercely. He would sweep away every trace of his uncles. He would never think of them again.

He dived back in. Hilde followed, shaking her head. "What's in the grain bins?" she asked, chasing a large spider across the floor with her broom.

Ralf knocked on the nearest, and opened the lid. Delving in, he brought out a handful of greyish, crumbly meal. He pulled a face. "What's this?"

Hilde shrugged. "Some sort of oatmeal?"

"Whatever it was, it's gone off," declared Ralf. "We'll have to throw it out and leave the bin in the sun to sweeten. What's in the others?"

There were three more large grain bins. One contained a tangle of mouldy harness, one was empty, and in the third…

"Oh, yuck," cried Hilde. "Something's died in here!" The bottom of the bin was covered with little skeletons.

"Rats!" said Ralf. "They must have got trapped somehow, and starved."

"Horrible," Hilde shuddered. "I hate this place! Brrr! I'm going outside."

Peer remembered his daydream of a smiling Hilde, living happily with him at the mill. Thank goodness she didn't know. He gnawed a knuckle. If only he could impress her. If only the lubbers would creep up on her, so he could chase them off! But as soon as he thought of it, he knew that Hilde was perfectly capable of chasing them off herself.

"I'll go after her," he muttered to Ralf. "Just in case. It might not be safe for her to wander about alone."

"Thanks, lad," said Ralf gravely. Was he hiding a smile?

Hilde was standing on the bridge, undoing her plait and running her hands through her hair, shaking it loose. Peer watched, thinking how long and pretty it was, as she combed it with her fingers and tidied it. He had a sudden idea. *I'll make her a comb! Carved out of ash wood, with patterns on the back. It'll be useful, and she'll like it, and…* He cleared his throat. "Are you all right?" he asked gruffly. "I'm sorry about the rats."

"Never mind," said Hilde. Finishing off her plait, she flipped it over her shoulder and looked at him. "Peer, think again about this. The place… feels wrong. Where are the lubbers? Where's Granny Greenteeth?" She paused. "Dare to walk up to the mill pond with me?"

"We'd better be careful," said Peer. "It'll be dusk soon." But he followed her to the dam, and Loki came too, trotting along with his nose down. The pond was calm today, and the duckweed spread across it, temptingly flat, like a green floor. Peer imagined walking on it, and then, with a shiver, plunging through. There was a glossy streak in the middle, where the current wandered towards the weir. Midges danced in the mild air, and the sullen willows were combing tangled tresses into the water.

"She's in there, somewhere," said Hilde.

They listened to the endless music of the water hurrying

over the weir. "It's funny," said Hilde after a while. "It's like voices, in a language you can't quite understand. What do you think they're saying?"

"Sad things," said Peer.

"Listen again." Hilde's finger went to her lips. "Ssh!"

Peer closed his eyes. Almost at once he began to hear a low conversation. There was a lapping, gurgling voice, as though the owner was speaking through a mouth half-full of water; and two snivelling, flat, nasal voices.

"They've driven us out," one of the flat voices whimpered. "We've nowhere to go. I want my blanket. I'm cold, cold!"

"'Cold, cold,'" the watery voice mimicked with a chuckle, "'and nowhere to go!' I'll remember that when I sit under the weir, singing my songs. All my sad songs, I took from the people who came to me. People who cried at night. All lost now; all gone, but I still sing their songs under the weir. Lost… long ago."

"I want my blanket!" croaked the first voice.

"Finders, keepers," sneered the other flat voice. "Ouch – gerroff!" There was the sound of a scuffle, and the willows shook.

"I can give you a fine green blanket, nice and thick," said the watery voice slyly.

"Where is it?" squeaked the first lubber.

"Here – take your old blanket. I want a new one too!" croaked the second lubber greedily.

"Not so fast," gargled the watery voice. "You'll have to do something for me first. You'll have to be helpful…"

The three voices fell into a low murmur, and mingled with the steady rush of the weir. A dog barked far off in the wood: a sharp and lonely sound. Loki flung up his head, whining. The willows sieved darkness through their branches. A bat flicked past, quick as an uneasy thought.

Hilde touched Peer's arm. "Let's go."

"Wait," Peer breathed. What was that, rustling in the dark bushes? Loki pricked his ears and uttered a little grumbling woof.

"What's the matter?"

"The Nis!" Something small and spindly, with a wisp of hair like grey smoke, dashed along the edge of the pond and scuttled into the trees. "Loki always makes that noise when he sees it..."

"It can't be," Hilde whispered. "What would the Nis be doing here?"

She was right. Why should the Nis come down to the mill? Peer hesitated, and then they heard a distant, surging splash, as though someone had clambered out of the water at the far end of the millpond, where the stream ran in through a tunnel of matted and woven willows.

"Quick!" Hilde pulled him away. They ran back to the bridge, Loki bounding behind them with his hackles up.

"I'm sure I saw the Nis," Peer panted.

"Never mind the Nis!" said Hilde. "What about Granny Greenteeth? That was her, wasn't it, talking to the lubbers? Plotting. There'll be trouble. She hates the mill, doesn't she? She hates the miller, whoever he is!"

She yanked on his hand and tugged him round to face her. Her hair was coming loose again in tousled strands. Bits of willow twig were stuck in it, and her eyes blazed dark in her pale face. Peer stared at her, transfixed. He found his voice.

"Maybe she does," he said. "But we knew that already. My uncles managed to run the mill with Granny Greenteeth and the lubbers about, so why shouldn't I? I'm going to do it, Hilde. I'm not giving up!"

CHAPTER 27

The Nis Behaves Badly

"HUSH, BABY, HUSH-A-BYE, can you see the swans fly?" Gudrun sang as she sat at her loom near the open door. She was weaving, and keeping an eye on Eirik who had crawled outside and was busy in the dirt by the doorstep, digging with a stick.

In the big cradle next to the loom, little Ran slept. Sigrid sat by the fire wielding a pair of knitting needles, while Sigurd peeled rushes, extracting the long white pith to use for lamp wicks.

"*Hush, baby, hush-a-bye, far away the swans fly. Over hill and over river, white wings waft together...*" Gudrun's voice sank into a low humming.

"You used to sing that song to us," Sigrid yawned, tangling the wool round her fingers. "Bother! I've dropped a stitch."

"I used to sing it to Hilde," said Gudrun. She rose to take Sigrid's knitting. "You've both worked well today. Go out and play before it gets dark. Take Alf," she added as the twins headed gladly for the door.

"Oh Ma, do we have to? He's so slow!" wailed Sigurd.

"Never mind," said Gudrun, coming to the doorway. "He'll look after you."

"We don't need looking after," muttered Sigurd.

"Don't go up the hill. Play in the wood!" Gudrun called.

She watched as they ran eagerly out of the yard and down the track.

"Now then, pickle," she sighed, looking down at baby Eirik. "It's your turn." Eirik raised his face. He dropped the stick and put up his arms. "Ma!" he cooed.

Gudrun swooped on him with a gasp of delight. "Say it again! Say, 'Ma!'"

"Ma!" said Eirik boldly. He stared at her and laughed.

"My gorgeous boy!" said Gudrun, carrying him in. She wiped his fingers and gave him a piece of bread to chew while she washed and changed him. "Let's get you fed before little Ran wakes." Holding him on her hip, she peeked into the cradle and saw the baby girl was wide awake, but lying quietly. Eirik leaned to see her too. He pointed. "Ba!" he exclaimed.

"Baby," cried Gudrun. "That's right, Eirik. Baby!"

"Ba," said Eirik with deep satisfaction. Gudrun hugged him, while Ran stared up with dark, unreadable eyes.

"Clever little boy!" said Gudrun. She took Eirik on her knee and fed him sweet milky groute. The house was peaceful, full of quiet, pleasant sounds. Somewhere in the background, the Nis was busy. She was half aware of it whisking the floor, giving the pot a stir, tweaking the bedclothes. *It's got over its sulks,* she thought. *That's good!* At last, Eirik's head nodded and his eyes closed. Gudrun lowered him into the cradle beside Ran. To her surprise, little Ran rolled her eyes towards Eirik. Her thin arms waved, and she kicked feebly. She looked scrawny and brown beside him; her hair grew over her round head in a soft dark – *pelt* was the word, Gudrun thought suddenly, startled.

The baby seemed to be clutching something. She uncurled one of the tiny hands. There was nothing in the palm, but between all the fingers was a thin web of skin.

Gudrun tucked the fingers closed again and picked the baby up. "You strange little creature," she murmured. "I wish you'd smile. Or even cry!"

Ran looked back with her still, vague gaze. Gudrun gave her a little shake. "Well? Aren't you hungry?" she asked, and sat down to nurse her.

Something jumped across the room like an angry grasshopper. A string of onions tumbled from the wall. The cookpot capsized into the fire. Gudrun dumped Ran unceremoniously back in the cradle, and rushed for a cloth to lift the pot back on to its trivet. Barley broth scorched and bubbled in the flames.

"Drat!" Gudrun panted, righting the pot. There wasn't much left, and sighing she tipped in more barley and extra water.

Something tugged the hem of her skirt. Gudrun stopped dead. She didn't see anything, but a little humming voice buzzed like a sleepy bee: "The mistress mustn't feed the seal baby!"

"Let me go!" Gudrun snapped. The hem swished free. "Now," she went on in the same sharp voice, "like it or not, I'm going to feed this baby. Behave!"

She lifted Ran and sat down. The Nis whirled into the rafters where the soot fluttered like black rags, and kicked down a shower of smuts to settle on Gudrun's face and arms, on the floor, the bedding and the scrubbed table.

"Stop it!" Gudrun shrieked. Through falling flakes like a swarm of black butterflies, she glimpsed a small figure, swinging rebellious legs. "Stop it at ONCE!"

With an angry squeak, so high and sharp it made Gudrun wince, a shadow pattered down the wall and dived under the table.

Gudrun pressed the baby against her. "I won't have any more of this nonsense," she announced in a cold voice. "Sweep up the mess you've made. If you can't behave better than this, you'll have to go!"

She bent her head over the baby, aware of a small shape creeping about in the corners with a brush. She ignored it, and it slunk out of sight like a scolded puppy.

Ran fed hungrily. *The seal baby,* Gudrun thought. She looked down at the small dark head butting her breast. For a moment she saw a sleek little animal that snuffled and sucked, and spread out cold webbed fingers against her skin. She almost plucked it away.

Then she thought of the joy of cuddling Eirik, and the way he laughed and cried and made endless trouble. "She's not my own," she said to herself. "That makes enough difference without looking for more. I'll love her yet."

She put Ran back in the cradle and looked around. The soot had been swept up. The brush was laid tidily near the hearth. The barley broth was bubbling gently. Gudrun lifted the pot into the ashes to keep warm for supper. She poured some milk for the Nis and placed it under the table.

"There now," she said. "You see? Live and let live. There's plenty for everyone." She went back to her knitting, glancing at the bowl from time to time, but the milk remained untouched.

The fire was low. Draughts blew over the floor. Gudrun stepped outside to fetch logs and call for the twins. No one answered, but down in the dark spaces of the wood, a dog barked. It sounded like Alf, and the twins would be with him. They would soon be home.

Back in the house, a steady lapping came from the bowl under the table. Gudrun smiled to herself, and pretended to pay no attention. Then, as she built up the fire, one of the cats strolled out from under the table, licking her whiskers.

Gudrun's hands flew to her face. "Oh, my goodness!" she wailed. The Nis was fiercely protective of its food. All the household animals had learned to stay well clear of its dish, on pain of pinched ears and tweaked whiskers. The complacent cat sat down by the hearth for a good wash – and Gudrun knew that the Nis had gone.

Run away? For good? She turned to the door quickly, with the idea of calling it back; but before she got there the latch flew up, and the twins tumbled in with Alf, slamming it behind them.

"There are trolls in the wood! We saw a little dark thing slinking between the trees!"

"Trolls? No, it must have been the Nis," said Gudrun. "I scolded it and it ran off. It's been very naughty."

"The Nis?" Sigrid's face cleared. "Why? What's it done?"

"Only spilt the broth! Only thrown soot all over the place!" Gudrun began, but was interrupted by a knock at the door.

"I'll go!" cried Sigurd. Using both hands, he lifted the latch and opened the door a few inches, blocking it with his body. Gudrun and Sigrid heard a voice mumbling questions, and Sigurd's polite answers:

"Yes, this is Ralf Eiriksson's house. I'm his son. A new baby? Yes, we have!

"I don't know, I'll ask." He turned, with the door still in his hands. "It's an old lady, Ma. She wants to see the baby. Can she come in?"

For ever after, Gudrun wondered what prevented her from saying yes. Had it been Alf, facing the door with his lips curled over his teeth? Or the draught, like a breath from the weedy bottom of a well? Or had she simply been unwilling to let a stranger into the house after sunset? She placed a hand on Sigurd's shoulder, moved him aside, and confronted the visitor herself.

And indeed it was only an old woman leaning on a stick. Her bent body was a dark outline against the last of the light, and a greenish-black scarf was wrapped around her head.

"Good evening," said the old woman. "A fine boy you have there, mistress. And the little girl, too! I was watching them, the pretty pair, as I came up through the wood. Running ahead, they were, and never saw me. Aren't you afraid to let them play so late?"

"Who are you? What do you want?" Gudrun asked.

"I've been told about this baby you've taken in, mistress. I'd like to see her."

Gudrun shook her head. "She's asleep, and I won't wake her."

"Old granny won't wake her, dearie. I've rocked many a baby to sleep."

"I'm afraid I'm too busy," said Gudrun. "Goodnight." She tried to close the door, but the old woman thrust her stick in the way. "Of course you are. A mother's always busy. You look tired, mistress. And no wonder, wearing yourself out, looking after all these children, and a man who's always roaming, never home."

"He'll be home soon enough!" Gudrun pushed at the door, but the old woman's stick appeared to have taken root, and she couldn't shift it.

"And isn't it good of you to take in another bairn," crooned the old woman. "Another child to wake you at night, to clean and carry and nurse and sing to!"

Gudrun bit her lip.

The old woman shifted the grip of her hands on the stick.

Her voice dropped. "I know how you feel, dearie. I know how your heart sank when the boy brought this baby home."

"No..." Gudrun protested. The cold draught blew colder.

The old woman leaned forward. "And who could blame you?" she muttered. "After all, the child's barely human. But the seal folk don't want her. As for the fisherman, every time he looks at her, he'll be reminded of what he's lost. Give her to me."

Barely human? Gudrun remembered the touch of Ran's cold little fingers.

"Give her to me," coaxed the old woman. "I'll take good care of her! The stream can sing to her all night long. She'll have the softest, softest cradle. And I'm lonely, mistress. I'm lonely... Give me the child to rock to my bosom at night."

Water dripped. Gudrun looked down. A pair of very large bare feet protruded from the hem of the old woman's dark dress. They were gnarled and sinewy and streaked with mud. Water leaked around them, pooling and spreading.

"Let me in," whispered the old woman. One of those big, wet feet shuffled forward over the threshold. As hard as she could, Gudrun stamped on it.

The old woman yelled and snatched her foot back. Gudrun slammed the door and began dragging the heavy wooden bar across. "Help me, twins!" Sigurd flung himself beside her. The bar clattered home into the slots. Sigurd yelped and sucked his thumb.

There was a shriek from outside. "Very well, my fine mistress! You'll soon weary of a bairn that's half a seal pup out of the sea. She'll come to me at last, to darkness under the water. And I'll dandle her in my arms..."

Gudrun put her arm round Sigurd and hugged him tightly.

Her hair was coming down, and she swiped a strand out of her eyes and looked up, across the room. Sigrid was backed against the far wall, with Ran in her arms. Her eyes were wild, her lips trembled. "Has it gone? It can't have her, Mamma. It can't have her!"

"Yes, yes, it's gone," soothed Gudrun. There were no more sounds from outside, but she wasn't going to open the door and check. She let go of Sigurd and came towards Sigrid, her arms out. "That's right, Sigrid! Ran's *our* baby! It can't have her!"

Her knees gave way, and she sat down.

CHAPTER 28

The Nis in Disgrace

PEER, HILDE AND Ralf stopped on the doorstep to take off their boots. Ralf tried the door, and then thumped on it. "We're back!"

There was a muffled cry from inside. Gudrun and the children unbarred the door. "Ralf!" Gudrun wailed.

Ralf made for her at once, one boot on and one off. "What's wrong?"

Gudrun clutched him. "Granny Greenteeth was here!"

"Granny Greenteeth?" Hilde screeched.

"What?" exclaimed Ralf. "Are you all right, Gudrun? Sure? What happened? Tell me quickly."

Gudrun gripped his hand. "An old woman came. She was dripping all over the doorstep. Look, it's still wet! She came for Ran. She wanted to take her away. I wouldn't let her in. Oh, Ralf! I stamped on her foot!"

Ralf began to laugh. "You stamped on old Granny Greenteeth? Good for you! My, the sparks must have flown."

Instead of answering, Gudrun gulped on a sob. Ralf looked into her face.

"I'm sorry." He hugged her again. "I'm a fool. I wish I'd been here. But you're safe, and I'm proud of you. Proud of you!"

Gudrun cried into his shoulder. Then she pulled herself together. "The twins were so brave! Sigurd helped me bar the door, and Sigrid – why, she picked up little Ran and stood there like a – a…"

"Wolf at bay!" supplied Sigurd, and Sigrid dissolved into shaky giggles.

"However did Granny Greenteeth find out about Ran?" Hilde muttered to Peer. Gudrun heard the question. "I think I know!" she cried, nodding.

"Just let me get my other boot off, and then tell us everything." Ralf turned to shut the door, but before he could close it, something small shot in from outside and hurtled between his legs. He gasped and swore. "What in thunder—?"

Over by the fire, the cat rose up in an arch, spat, and dashed outside. Under the table something clattered and fizzed. The Nis's empty dish came careering out on its rim and bowled to a giddy standstill against the wall.

"The Nis is back." Gudrun gave a hysterical laugh. "That's the sort of tantrum I've been putting up with today. And there's your answer, Hilde. The Nis has been jealous of little Ran ever since she came. This evening it upset the broth and threw soot about, and when I scolded, it rushed out of the house in a temper. The twins spotted it, going down through the wood. I believe it went straight to Granny Greenteeth!"

"Oh no," breathed Peer.

With a stab of dread, he remembered the scuttling shadow he had seen near the millpond. So it must have been the Nis! But why? He tried to think of an innocent reason why the Nis might want to visit the mill, and failed. The Nis hated the place as much as Peer did, and for the same reason: it had been badly treated by the Grimsson brothers. It would never go there, unless for some special purpose.

He had to tell. "I think I saw it this evening," he began in a troubled voice, and broke off as something nudged him under the table. He glanced down, expecting Loki. Instead, light dry fingers caught at his knee. Two beady eyes glinted pleadingly up at him.

He stopped. But everyone was looking at him, waiting for him to finish. Should he lie? *But Hilde was there too. And it is very jealous of Ran. What if it went to Granny Greenteeth in a fit of temper?*

"Down by the millpond, I saw it," he stammered. "But I'm sure there's an explanation, Gudrun. I mean, I know it can be vain and quarrelsome, but I'm sure it wouldn't be treacherous."

The clutching hand abruptly let go. Ralf wore a dark frown on his usually pleasant face. "The Nis was at the millpond? It rushed down there in a temper, just before Granny Greenteeth turned up? That's bad, Peer. That looks very bad."

Everyone looked into the corners of the room to see where the Nis was lurking.

"What will you do?" Peer felt a complete traitor. The Nis was his oldest friend. He'd met it even before he'd met Hilde. *It saved my life, and it saved Loki. I was the one who brought it here.*

"I don't know," said Gudrun wearily. "I think it may have to go. I don't see how we can trust it again."

"Don't feel bad, Peer," said Ralf in a kind voice. "It isn't your fault." He looked at his wife. "Shall we talk about it later? After supper?"

Gudrun whirled with a cry of alarm and lifted the pot of barley broth from the embers. "Oh dear!" She was almost in tears again. "It's been keeping warm for hours, and now look at it! All dried up."

"Blame old Granny Greenteeth for that, not yourself," said Ralf.

"Blame the Nis," Gudrun muttered.

They both believed the Nis was guilty. Peer looked at Hilde, who was rocking Ran on her knee, murmuring old nursery rhymes. "What do you think?" he asked in a low voice. She shook her head, avoiding his eye.

"This child is asleep. Why don't you put her in the cradle for me? Come on, Peer. Take your baby!"

"Why mine?" asked Peer gruffly, allowing Hilde to hand Ran over.

"Yours, because you rescued her." She added quietly, "And I wonder, Peer, if you hadn't been there, what Kersten would have done with her?"

"I've wondered that, too." Peer remembered the cold waves crashing on the beach. He looked down at the sleepy face, and felt his heart squeeze. Little Ran seemed surrounded by dangers. Did he have to protect her from the Nis as well?

Peer woke in the middle of the night.

"No groute!"

It was a thread of a voice, the tiniest whisper. There was a hiccupping sniff. Peer's eyes flew wide. A dismal little shape was crouching by the hearth. Gudrun had forgotten to put out food for the Nis.

He lay, wondering what to do. Should he get up? Gudrun had never forgotten before. Perhaps this was its punishment.

"No groute! Everybody hates the poor Nis." There was a bitter little sob.

Whether the Nis was guilty or not, Peer couldn't bear it. He called out gently. "Nis, we don't all hate you, truly we don't. But I did see you down at the mill. What you were up to?"

"The mistress wants me to go." The Nis sounded

heartbroken and Peer wasn't sure it was even listening to him. "And so – I goes!"

With a faint flutter like falling ash, the small humped shape vanished.

I'd better get up and fill its bowl... but it didn't answer the question...

He lay back, groaning. Why did the Nis have to be so difficult all the time? He was stiff, aching from hours of work. The bed was warm. He didn't fancy blundering around in the dark, and maybe waking the family. And Loki was lying across his legs; and besides, he was sleepy... so sleepy...

"Well, the Nis is gone!" snapped Gudrun next morning, slapping breakfast on the table.

"How do you know?" asked Hilde.

"I just do," said Gudrun. "And look at Eirik: crotchety, mardy – he knows too. If the Nis were here, it'd be keeping him happy. It adored Eirik, I will say that. Still, if it's gone, it's gone."

"It's upset," said Peer. "I heard it last night. You forgot to put its food out."

Gudrun flushed. "I cannot think of everything. I've a house to run, and two babies to look after. When's Bjørn coming to see his daughter? I hope he doesn't suppose he can just leave the child to me."

"I'll feed the Nis, Ma," said Sigrid. "I'm sure it didn't mean to do wrong." She measured a ladleful of groute into a bowl, and looked at her mother. "Shall I put in some butter?"

"If you must," said Gudrun. Sigrid cut a very small lump. She placed the bowl in the hearth among the warm ashes, and the family watched as if she were doing something very important. It was easier than talking, with Gudrun in this mood.

Next day, to Sigrid's sorrow, the Nis's bowl was still full of congealed groute. She scraped it out for the dogs, poured a fresh one, and wandered round the farmstead with the bowl in her hand, calling for the Nis as though it were a lost kitten. And although Gudrun muttered that it was a shocking waste of good food, she didn't try to prevent Sigrid from putting food out in various different places around the farm. The bowl she left in the cowshed seemed to get cleaned out most regularly.

"I'm sure it's the Nis," said Sigrid wistfully.

"It's rats," snapped Gudrun. "I don't know why the cats don't get them."

"The cats won't go in the cowshed any more," said Sigrid – so quietly, that nobody heard her.

CHAPTER 29

Success at the Mill

"I WISH THE Nis *would* come home," Hilde sighed to Peer one afternoon, as she spread wet washing over the bushes to dry.

"So do I," Peer agreed. "I'm sure it didn't talk to Granny Greenteeth."

Hilde dried her hands on her apron. "*I* think it probably did. It's got such a quick temper. But I wish it would come back, all the same. Ma never meant it to go. She's missing it. She's angry, and hurt that they've quarrelled; and neither of them knows how to make friends."

"Do you think it's hiding in the cowshed?"

"I don't know. Have you looked? I have. And I've seen Ma and Pa going in there too, when they thought no one was around."

Peer nodded gloomily. He'd been in, early morning and late at night, and found nothing but a few cold dusty nests in the straw, that might have been made by cats. "I feel bad about it," he said. "I hated giving it away like that, and it would never understand why…"

Hilde gave him a significant glance. "Speaking of quarrels, what about you and Bjørn? Isn't it time you made friends again?"

"What have I done to Bjørn?" Peer asked harshly. "Only rescued his daughter. Not that he seems to care. He never comes to see her."

"After the way you glowered at him?" murmured Hilde. "I'm not surprised."

Peer turned away. But Hilde's words smouldered in his mind. Slowly, reluctantly, he began to remember the good times he had spent with Bjørn, the easy companionship of their fishing trips. With the Nis and Bjørn, he had lost two out of his three best friends. And he missed them.

At least the sheep were safe, although they had nibbled the meadows down to a short, dry sward. It seemed the trolls dared not venture this far down the hillside. "We'll move the flock back up to the Stonemeadow after midsummer," Ralf told Peer. "Once the trolls' feast is over, perhaps the danger will be past."

And the spring days followed one after another: the grass in the home field grew deep, the birch trees on Troll Fell glittered with new leaves, and the larches put out tender green fingers. It was a pleasure simply to be out of doors. And the swallows arrived, skimming about the farmyard faster than the eye could follow. Hilde's heart sang as she watched them flashing to and fro. Summer was here!

But the sunshine had no effect on the mill. A clammy chill lingered inside the building, and although they had fixed the doors and shutters and mended the holes in the roof, it didn't look much like the neat, trim place of Peer's dreams. The new patches in the old thatch gave the mill a scabby, piebald appearance. And there was an odd, sickly smell about the place, which no amount of daylight and fresh air could cure.

"Let's light a fire!" said Hilde in desperation one morning. "That might bring the place back to life!"

If anything can, Peer thought.

"I've got a better idea!" Ralf rubbed his hands. "There's

only one way to bring a mill back to life – isn't there, Peer?"

Peer looked at him. "You mean – set it going? But we don't have any grain."

"Aha." Ralf beamed. "I brought some. Just a little, a quarter of a sack. Seems to me it's time we found out if the machinery still works."

"It works all right," said Peer at once.

"How do you know?" Hilde asked.

His mouth fell open. He'd never told her. And if he tried to explain now, it would sound as if he'd been hiding it. What could he say?

Ralf saved him. "Feeling confident?" he asked, his eyes twinkling. "I like that. Well, you're the miller. Show us how it's done. What first?"

"Fill up the hopper," said Peer quickly.

"Lead on!" Ralf picked up the quarter sack of barley. They climbed the rickety ladder and crowded together in the small space beside the millstones. Above them loomed the dark bulk of the hopper, suspended from the rafters on four thick ropes.

"Mind your heads!" warned Peer.

Ralf slapped his hand against the hopper's sloping wooden sides. "That's solid!" he exclaimed, impressed. He raised the sack to tip the barley into the open top.

"Wait," said Hilde. "It'll be dirty. After three years, that hopper must be full of dust and cobwebs. Let me sweep it out." She scrambled down the ladder and returned with a small brush, but discovered that the sides of the hopper were too high for her to get her hand inside. Peer found a crate. Standing tiptoe, Hilde bent over the edge of the hopper and started brushing. "I was right!" they heard her muffled voice. "What is this? It must have dropped from the thatch. Almost like gravel. Cover your eyes!" She peered down at them. "I'll flick it out!"

Peer and Ralf looked away as a gritty shower pattered over the edges of the hopper. They couldn't see what it was, but it crunched underfoot. Finally Hilde was satisfied.

"Good enough. Go ahead, Pa!"

Ralf poured the barley into the hopper. A few grains dribbled through the hole in the bottom and ran down into the eye of the upper millstone.

"Right!" said Peer breathlessly. "Now we go and open the sluice."

"Simple as that?" asked Ralf. "No levers to pull, or wheels to turn?"

"If it was hard to work a mill, my Uncle Baldur couldn't have done it," Peer said with a sudden grin. "The only wheel that has to turn is the waterwheel. As soon as that moves, the mill starts grinding. Come on!"

They ran over the bridge, past the mill race to the brink of the dam, where a narrow plank was suspended over the weir. Peer stepped on to it carefully.

The plank was slimy. There was no handrail, just a couple of posts spaced along it. Peer felt his foot slip, and grabbed the nearest to save himself. For a second he stared into the rumbling white cauldron where the water tumbled over the weir. Was Granny Greenteeth down there? He imagined her in the whirling waters, her grey-green hair flying around her face, mixed with silt and bubbles. Or maybe she was in the quiet millpond, sliding through the brown peaty water with barely a ripple – till her hand emerged to seize his ankle and jerk him under…

"Are you all right?" shouted Hilde from the bank.

"Fine," he called back. "My foot skidded, that's all."

He went on along the plank. The waterwheel loomed over him, dark and dripping. Long ago, thick timbers had been driven into the stream bed, fencing off the mill race from the dam. He needed to raise the sluice gate, a simple wooden shutter running in grooves between two squared-off posts.

Peer grabbed it and tugged. It rose easily. Water roared into the race, rising up the sides and kicking against the blades of the mill wheel with spurts of foam. One after another, the paddles slashed down, picking up speed. On the bank, Hilde and Ralf clapped and cheered.

"It's working!" Hilde yelled. "Let's go and look at the millstones!"

"Right!" Peer shouted.

They hurried over the bridge. The mill was clacking, rumbling, vibrating. Dust shook from the rafters. Peer snatched open the door leading to the dark underloft, and glimpsed the wooden pit wheel turning, the gears revolving, the drive shaft twirling. He scrambled up the ladder to the grinding floor. The upper millstone was revolving. Peer blinked and laughed to see how the iron-bound rim flew past. Barley shook down into the eye of the millstones, and flour showered from the edges in a rich sprinkle.

"It works!" he cried again. "We've done it!"

Hilde and Ralf were climbing the ladder, eager to see. Peer grabbed Hilde's hand and hauled her up. Without thinking, he pulled her into a joyful hug. For a second, he had Hilde in his arms. Her hair tickled his chin. Then he let go, amazed and thrilled. Was she annoyed? But it seemed not, for she met his anxious glance with a wry smile. Noticing none of it, Ralf pounded him on the back. Breathless, triumphant, they watched as the millstones whirled and the flour poured out.

"But that's enough," said Peer, suddenly practical. "There

can't be much left in the hopper, and we mustn't let the millstones grind on nothing."

"And we'll take a bag of flour home to Gudrun," observed Ralf. "What a day!"

Hilde gave Peer a quizzical look. "Well? How does it feel? You've got what you wanted. You're the Miller of Troll Fell!"

CHAPTER 30

Rumours

"You do look smug," Gudrun teased. "Like the cat that got the cream."

"And so he should," put in Ralf. "He's going to be a rich man. A successful miller!"

Peer grinned shyly. He sat, as he often did now, holding Ran in the crook of his arm. The baby looked about with her dark, solemn eyes, stretching her hand towards anything that interested her. By now, everyone in the family had noticed the fine webs lacing between her tiny fingers. No one talked about it.

Eirik hauled himself up against Peer's knee. He grabbed Ran's hand and planted a wet kiss on it, looking at her with an impish smile. Ran blew bubbles. Gudrun turned, rubbing dough from her fingers.

"Did Ran make that noise? I suppose it's something. I've wondered if she's deaf. She never smiles. She never cries."

Peer looked down at the baby. "She'll learn, won't she?" he asked. "I thought she smiled at me the other day – she sort of crinkled her nose."

Gudrun sniffed. "Peer, if she had really smiled, you wouldn't *think*. You'd *know*."

I'll make her a toy!" said Peer, suddenly. He handed Ran to Hilde, and spent the next half hour constructing a little wooden whistle with two stops. When blown, it produced a pretty, warbling note. Ran's eyes opened wide and she reached for it, but still she didn't smile.

"How clever of you, Peer!" exclaimed Hilde. "Look, she heard it. Now we know for sure she's not deaf."

Peer smiled, thinking of the comb he was carving for Hilde. It was nearly finished, but he didn't want to give it to her in front of everyone. He was waiting for the perfect moment. "My father showed me how to make whistles," he said, aloud. "I haven't made one for years."

"I'd forgotten your father was a woodcarver," said Ralf. "Didn't he make the dragonhead for our ship, the *Long Serpent*?"

Peer nodded slowly. "He was working on it just before he died." He fell silent, his hands between his knees, remembering how they had burned his father's body on the beach at Hammerhaven, with the dragonship drawn up on the strand close by. He had watched the flames shooting into the cold sky, and the ship had seemed to arch its proud dragon neck, glaring over the crowds like a sentinel. That dragonship had sailed all the way to Vinland and back again.

"Thorolf's still the skipper," Ralf said. "He takes her voyaging every summer. They'll be sailing soon. I wonder..." And he gave a long, unconscious sigh.

Gudrun stared at him, biting her lip. Suddenly she burst out, "It's no good dreaming, Ralf. There's too much work to do. Sheep shearing next, and then harvest time. Nearly every morning, you're off to the mill, and here I am, coping with two babies and the children. You can't go."

Ralf looked at her in surprise. "Why, Gudrun!"

"It's all very well for you, Ralf!" Gudrun's voice shook. "I haven't set foot off the farm in weeks. I can't remember when I last spoke to one of the neighbours."

"You're right." Ralf got to his feet. "By thunder, you're right, Gudrun. We've been working so hard, we've forgotten how to have fun. Here's a plan! We'll take a holiday tomorrow, children, babies and all. We'll go down to Trollsvik. You can visit the womenfolk and have a good chat, and I'll find Bjørn. It's time he clapped eyes on his daughter. The children can play on the beach. How does that sound?"

Gudrun sniffed and smiled.

Next morning, the children were scrubbed and paraded.

"You can't go to the village with a neck like that!" Gudrun pushed up her sleeves and dunked the spluttering Sigurd for a second time. "And put on a clean tunic!" she added, opening the chest where the best clothes were kept.

"Gudrun, they'll only get dirty on the beach," Ralf tried to say. His wife tossed him a comb. "Use this, Ralf. And clean your nails! Hilde?"

"Yes, Ma?" asked Hilde meekly, winking at Peer.

"Come and help me pin my cloak. Are we ready?"

"This is more trouble than any Viking expedition," Ralf joked. He lifted her on to the pony, put Ran into her arms, stood back and saluted. "Lead on, Captain!" And with Peer and Hilde leading the pony, the twins and Loki running ahead, and Ralf bringing up the rear with Eirik on his shoulders, the family set off.

Peer sneaked a look at Hilde round the end of the pony's nose. Her fair skin was flushed and freckled, and her golden plaits shone. She was swinging along, humming to herself. Over her best blue dress she wore an embroidered linen apron, almost blindingly white in the sunshine, and a white linen hood.

He felt in his pocket. He'd sat up half of last night, straining his eyes in the firelight, finishing Hilde's comb. He explored it with his fingers. The teeth were a bit thick, perhaps. But the curved back was nicely carved. He gripped it tightly. "You do look pretty, Hilde," he said shyly.

Hilde glanced at him. "Thanks," she said curtly, and stopped humming. With a sigh, Peer let the comb slide into the depths of his pocket.

The mill came in sight. Even Peer felt secretly glad to be going somewhere else. "Would you like to see what we've done, Gudrun?" he offered half-heartedly. But Gudrun, swaying downhill on the pony, clutched Ran more tightly to her chest and said in alarm, "Another time, perhaps!"

He lowered his head and trudged on.

"It's a strange business!" said Einar, shaking his head.

"What is, Einar?" Gudrun finished a morsel of his wife's salted cheese. "Try this, Ralf, it's so good! What do you put in it, Asa?"

"Just a little thyme!" As fat as Gudrun was thin, Asa beamed at her. "But then our goats forage along the seashore, you know, and they eat the seaweed. I think that gives the cheese some of its flavour."

"This business of Bjørn Egilsson," persisted Einar.

"Oh, terrible!" Asa joined in. "You wouldn't believe what's been going on." Her voice dropped. "Day and night, he's out there, rowing and calling for his wife – if wife she was!"

"What else might she be?" Ralf asked, his hand suddenly suspended between mouth and platter.

Asa tittered. "Well, Ralf, you know as well as I do. A seal woman she was – and the seals have called her back. To think of a neighbour of ours taking a creature like that between his sheets!"

Ralf laid the piece of cheese back on the platter. "I believe I will go and find Bjørn," he said, rising. "Come with me, Peer? Excuse us, Einar!" Peer followed him out. Einar and Asa watched them go, and Einar raised a hand to silence Gudrun, who was about to speak.

"Don't say a word! Ralf's a decent man. I can see he doesn't want to believe it, but it's true enough."

"And what do you mean by that?" asked Gudrun.

Einar leaned across the table. "Bjørn's a marked man!" he said importantly. "We've all seen the signs. In the last seven years, think of the luck he's had! The best fisherman on the fjord, for sure. That's all changed now. His wife's gone, and taken his luck with her. And there's worse."

"They say," whispered Asa, "that the draug boat follows him now, every time he goes out."

"Harald's seen it," Einar continued. "Out beyond the point, three days ago. He saw Bjørn's boat, sailing in, and beyond it another. But this second boat *wasn't always there*."

"That's silly," said Hilde, who was listening, with Ran swaddled on her knee. "Harald got spray in his eyes, I should think."

"No," said Asa. "It was a six-oarer, with a dark sail, and it flickered in and out of sight like a butterfly's wings. There, and then gone.

"And what about the odd thing Thorkell saw on the beach? Only a week ago – late evening, nearly dark. He's coming along past the boats, and he hears something cough. He looks around, and he sees this big, dark shape heaving itself up out of Bjørn's boat. It topples over the side and starts to drag itself along on the shingle, scrunching and moaning.

"Like a huge black seal it was, as far as he could see in the gloaming: but there's something uncanny about it, and it's coming closer and closer, and he can't hobble fast, old Thorkell. So he picks up a rock and flings it straight at the creature! Up it jumps, taller than a man; and clatters off on two legs, away down the shingle!"

Gudrun raised a sceptical eyebrow. There was a short silence. Asa wriggled on her seat and changed the subject. "So this is Bjørn's baby, Gudrun," she said, avidly studying Ran. "Is it true she's a freak?"

"A freak?" Hilde gasped. "She's quite normal!"

Asa's face fell. "But I heard she has hair all over her body! And seal's paws, instead of hands. Surely that's why Bjørn won't have anything to do with her?"

Protectively, Hilde's hands flew to cover Ran's.

"You shouldn't believe all you hear, Asa," said Gudrun in a calm voice.

"Well!" Asa bridled. "*I* wouldn't dare to bring up a baby like that along with my own children: but you've always been bold, Gudrun. At least I suppose you've given up thinking of Bjørn's brother Arne for young Hilde. There's a curse on that family now!"

"Hilde!" said Gudrun swiftly. "Why don't you join the twins on the beach? Take Ran and go for a walk. It's lovely out there in the sunshine!"

With a burning face Hilde scrambled up and blundered thankfully out into the hot sunlight. Behind her, she heard her mother begin in scorching tones: "Now just you listen to me, Asa…"

"Give it to her, Ma!" Hilde stuck out her tongue at the house, hitched Ran up in her arms, and walked through the village and up over the sand dunes. Down on the beach Sigurd and Sigrid were playing with Einar's two little boys, throwing pebbles into the water to make them skip. A couple of boats were drawn up on the shingle, and she could see Ralf and Peer talking with a small group of the village men: she couldn't see Bjørn.

Hilde turned the other way. She kicked off her shoes and paddled through the stream where it fanned out over the sand. Ahead, the cliffs under Troll Fell rose steeply out of the water, and the strand narrowed to a jumble of rocks at the point where the fjord met the open sea.

It was noon, boiling hot, and the tide was in. Splinters of light flew off the water like darts. Hilde trod gratefully into baking banks of seaweed, brittle on top, soft and slippery beneath. Sand fleas hopped over her toes. The sea curled over on to the strand and drained out through the pebbles with a crackling sound.

Further along, a ridge of rocks extended into the water like a knobbly backbone. With an effort, Hilde clambered on to a big one and sat down with Ran in her lap, thinking poisoned thoughts. *Is it true, what Asa said? Bjørn doesn't want Ran because she's got seal blood? Is that why he doesn't come to see her?* It seemed horribly possible. She dropped an angry kiss on Ran's silky dark head.

Waves tilted casually against the rocks and burst, spattering her with their cold salty spray. Then they sank back, and an embroidery of foam swirled after them. Further out, seabirds were diving: guillemots, cormorants and gulls quarrelling in great tangled knots on the surface, screaming over the fish.

Hilde longed to scream too – at Asa *(stupid woman!)* – at Arne *(because he's forgotten me)* – at Bjørn *(why should we have to bring Ran to him? He should have come to us!)* – and at Peer *(still gawping at me with sheep's eyes!)*.

Suddenly the gulls lifted, scattering into the air. Where they had been – Hilde's heart gave a great skip and a thud – a shape drifted in the water, as long as a man… or a woman.

Kersten! Oh no, I don't want to see! Kersten drowned weeks ago! Hilde scrambled to her feet. She stood upright on the rock, clutching Ran and staring, staring into the sea, all the skin on her body prickling with horror. There it was again, a dark mass glancing through a wave, floating just under the surface. Slick, slimy, glistening, it broke through in a formless curve. Hilde drew her breath to scream.

Then she saw. The shape bunched, twisted. A flipper smacked the water. There was a sharp exhalation of breath. A head rose from the waves, small, glossy, with huge shining eyes.

And looked at her.

Balanced on the rock, Hilde gazed into those wild, joyful eyes. Ran leaned forward in her arms, struggling. The sea swung upwards, sank back. Overhead, the gulls screamed in circles, and the cliffs seemed to lean over, watching.

"K-Kersten? Is that you?"

Hilde's whisper was too soft, too tentative, to be heard over the clap and crash of water on the rocks. She waited, trembling. Now something would happen. Some enormous secret would be told, some sorrowful, dark message delivered.

At last we will know. At last we will understand!

Then, as she held her breath, the seal was gone. She did not even see it go. The bright waves danced over the place where it had been, and the spray flew.

"Ran!" She turned the baby to her cheek, and both their faces were salty and wet. "Was that your mother?" Feeling Ran grasp her hair, she caught the little hand, holding it up. The sun shone scarlet through the thin, almost transparent webs of skin looping between finger and finger. Hilde closed the hand and kissed it.

"You, a freak?" she muttered. "How dare they! Come on, baby. Let's go and find your father."

CHAPTER 31

More Rumours

PEER AND RALF sat on an upturned boat talking to Harald Bowlegs and old Thorkell.

"I just think someone ought to sail with Bjørn," Ralf argued.

"Bjørn's doomed," wheezed Thorkell. His white hair and beard fluttered in the breeze, and his pale blue eyes blinked and watered.

"That's right!" Harald nodded. "He stole from the sea. Now he'll pay the price. You think any of us want to pay it with him?" He glanced up and saw Hilde crossing the shingle towards them. He paled. "She's got that creature with her, hasn't she? The seal brat! I'm off!" And he hurried away up the strand.

Hilde watched him go, with a disgusted toss of her head. "Where's Bjørn?"

"At home, they tell me." Ralf got up. "Well, Thorkell, we'll go and knock on his door. Won't you come too?"

Thorkell shook his head. "No, no. I'll have nothing to do with him." His pale eyes grew wide. "The draug boat's a-following of him, Ralf, drawn after him like a raven to a fresh carcass! Aye, it's a-smelling out death; and it's drawing closer. But you won't be told. You're rash folk. Even the lad!" He shot a sharp look at Peer.

"Me? What have I done?" Peer asked in surprise.

"Meddled with Grimsson's mill, that's what," said the old man.

"It's mine now," said Peer. "You'll soon find out, Thorkell – it'll be a great thing for the village. We worked it yesterday and it ran perfectly."

"Oh, aye." Thorkell pointed a gnarled finger at him. "Working at night, too, are you?"

"At night?" Peer stammered. "No."

"I thought not!" Thorkell slapped his knee. "I thought you didn't know! Well, it does work at nights, laddie! I've heard it, when the wind blows off Troll Fell; I've heard it clack-clack-clacking away. Working all by itself! You've stirred up a heap of trouble there. I wouldn't go past that place at night for a pocketful of gold!"

"And you've heard this often?" Peer enquired. "Recently?"

"Many times," nodded Thorkell fiercely. "Many times!"

Peer didn't believe him. But he made up his mind to slip down to the mill that evening and see if anything happened.

"Working, all by itself!" Thorkell repeated, glaring at them.

Ralf clapped him on the shoulder. "Thanks for the warning! Peer will keep his eyes open, won't you, Peer? And now we'll be off. Good day to you!"

He strode off so fast, Peer and Hilde had to run to catch up. "Daft old fellow," Ralf was muttering. "What an old nanny-goat he is."

"P-Pa," Hilde stammered. "Asa says Bjørn doesn't want Ran. Asa says—"

"I don't want to hear what Asa says!" Ralf bellowed. "I want to hear what *Bjørn* has to say!"

"Yes, Pa. And…" Hilde hesitated, trying to frame her thoughts. *I saw a seal. We saw a seal, and I thought it would speak to us. I asked a seal if it was Kersten.* It sounded mad, put into words. But she tried. "I was up near the point, Pa, sitting on a rock with Ran, and a seal came. It was watching us."

"Yes? Well, they're curious beasts."

"I know, but I thought – I did wonder…"

"Did it speak?"

Hilde blushed. "No."

"I thought not," said Ralf. "Don't mention it to Bjørn, Hilde. It really wouldn't be fair."

All the same, thought Hilde, *something special happened. Something I can't explain.* She hurried after her father, distressed, as though she'd been given a message that she couldn't deliver.

Outside Bjørn's house, Ralf knocked, and knocked again. Finally he pushed the door open and stepped in. Hilde and Peer followed. A thin column of smoke dawdled up from the hearth. Bjørn lay on the bed, propped against the wall, as if he had fallen asleep while trying to keep awake. Ralf shook him gently.

Bjørn groaned. He sat up, scrubbing his fingers into his eyes. "Ralf?" Then his eyes opened properly and he snatched at Ralf. "Is there news?"

"No! No, lad. We've come to see you, that's all. Me and Hilde – and Peer. We've brought the baby; seems a while since you saw the little lass. She's doing fine, as you can see…" Ralf talked on, in the soothing tone he would use to a startled animal, and Bjørn relaxed.

"Sorry." He sounded more awake now. "Haven't slept much, lately…" He got up, stifling an enormous yawn, and saw Ran in Hilde's arms.

"She's grown!" was all he said, but even through the indoor gloom, Hilde saw his face soften.

"Go to Pappa!" she exclaimed, passing the baby over. Bjørn held her easily, tipping her back in the crook of his arm and tickling her. He sat on the edge of the bed. "Hello!" he whispered, bending his head over her. "Hello!" The baby waved her arms and gurgled.

Ralf put his arm around Hilde's shoulders. "So much for Asa's spiteful gossip," he whispered.

Hanging back behind the other two, Peer watched. Bjørn sat barefoot, the sleeves of his old blue jerkin pushed up, crooning to his child, who gazed back at him with wide eyes.

He's not so much older than me, after all, Peer realised. *And he's not some hero. He's a fisherman. He's never claimed to be anything more. But he's brave, and he's always been kind to me. Why couldn't I see he was shocked, last time we met? Why did I lose my temper?* There was a painful knot in his chest as he remembered some of the things he'd said.

"Thanks for coming," said Bjørn. His eyes met Peer's. All of a sudden his face split into the old smile, tired but welcoming. "Hey, Peer!"

The tight knot in Peer's chest shook loose. Whatever had happened between Bjørn and Kersten, whatever had been said or done, it didn't matter any more. This was just Bjørn, the same as ever. He held out his hand. "I'm sorry, Bjørn. I was wrong. I didn't understand." Bjørn gripped it, hard enough to stop the blood flowing.

"Ouch!" Peer yelped, laughing, glad to excuse the tears in his eyes.

Bjørn let go. He said sadly, "I don't blame you for getting angry with me. I've been angry with myself. And most of the village is finding it hard to understand. They say the draug boat's following me."

"Yes, we've heard that from certain people," Ralf growled.

"You mean Harald and Thorkell." Bjørn shut his eyes, as if there was something he didn't want to see. "I'd like to disbelieve it. But I don't sleep very well. I hear things outside the house at night."

"What things?" asked Hilde.

Bjørn shrugged. "They come wading to shore after dark and cluster round the house, dripping and whispering, picking at the door. I can never quite hear what they say. That's why I haven't come up the valley. In case they follow me."

Peer felt cold.

"Dreams," said Ralf gently. "You're not sleeping well, you've said so yourself."

Bjørn looked down, stroking Ran's hair. "No, they're real."

"Bjørn." Hilde dropped to her knees beside him. "What's this all about? What is the black seal Thorkell saw?"

"Ah, him," said Bjørn with a slight shiver. "I've seen him too. That's the one I have to watch out for, Hilde. That's the one I threw the harpoon at, seven years ago."

Ralf snorted. "How can you know that?"

Bjørn looked at him steadily. "Because the other evening, I went to take the boat out. But when I tried to run it down the shingle, it wouldn't budge. It might as well have been filled with stones. I looked over the gunwale, and there was a big man lying down inside. He bared his teeth at me, and I gave a shout, and he bounded out of the boat and ran. I saw then the broken harpoon sticking out of his shoulder."

Hilde clutched Ralf's arm. Bjørn added, "It was after sunset.

He ran into the sea. And I heard splashing and wallowing in the shallows. And if that's what Thorkell saw, you can understand why I'm not too popular in the village right now."

Ralf sat silently. "A strange story," he said at last. "I don't know what to say, Bjørn. If there's anything in it, you need help."

At that moment, the latch clicked noisily. They all jumped. Gudrun elbowed in, a basket over her arm.

"Gudrun!" said Ralf. "I thought you were still with Asa. Where's Eirik?"

"I've given Asa a piece of my mind that she won't forget in a hurry," Gudrun said. "I pinned her ears back, I can tell you! Eirik's on the beach, playing with the twins." She laid the basket down. "How are you, Bjørn? I've brought some of our eggs. You sit there with the baby, and I'll cook them for you."

"Eggs?" said Bjørn appreciatively. "Now this is nice. This is very nice!" He leaned back, letting Ran sprawl on his chest, as he watched Gudrun scramble the eggs on a black iron skillet. A dreamy smile curled the corners of his mouth.

"Did I ever tell you what happened to Kersten once? She'd been out on the cliffs, climbing after gulls' eggs. She'd got a tidy collection, and put them in her apron. So she was coming home, really carefully, holding up her apron with all these eggs in it. I didn't know what she'd been doing, and I came around the back of the house and put my arms round her to give her a great big hug. And the eggs went everywhere!" He laughed at the memory. "Splat, splat, splat! She called me a clumsy bear – but she couldn't help laughing." The merriment died from his face. "I still can't believe she's gone. No explanation. No goodbyes. Just – gone!"

Hilde caught her breath. Now – now was the moment. It

had been so clear, so strong, that moment of joyful certainty. She knew she was meant to tell Bjørn about it. *But what can I say? We saw a seal, and it seemed to be telling us that everything's all right? That the world is beautiful, and life and death are in their proper places? What will Pa think? He'll be angry with me for raising Bjørn's hopes.*

She hesitated too long. Gudrun wiped her hands. "Give Ran to me, Bjørn, while you eat your eggs, and then you can have her back. The little thing needs you. You've been a stranger for too long. Surely by now you've given up looking for her poor mother?"

Bjørn took a mouthful of the hot, buttery eggs. "I've not given up, Gudrun. She's out there among the skerries. Even if she's forgotten me, even if she's wild now and doesn't remember – perhaps, if she saw me, she'd come back. I'm hunting her, and the black seal's hunting me. One day soon, the boat will capsize, or a wave will swamp me. That's how it will be. But I don't regret a thing. Not many fishermen live to be old, anyway."

Gudrun threw down the skillet with a crash.

"Shame on you for talking like that! You may well drown, if you keep taking your little boat out alone in all weathers, but as for black seals and draug boats, fancy believing a word of anything dreamed up by old Thorkell and Harald Bowlegs!"

"I've seen the seal myself," said Bjørn gently.

"Anybody can see a seal!" Gudrun cried. She swung round. "Ralf, the boy needs help. Tell him! I'm surprised you haven't already."

Ralf blinked. "Tell him what?"

Gudrun put her hands on her hips. "Tell him you'll go with him to Hammerhaven to fetch his brother, to fetch Arne. What are you waiting for?"

Ralf's face cracked into a huge grin. "Gudrun, you're amazing!" He sprang up like a dog set loose. "She's right, Bjørn. What do you say? If you and I go in the boat, we can reach Hammerhaven tonight. If Arne's at home, we'll bring him back. If he's out fishing, we'll wait for him. Two, three days, that's all it will take."

Bjørn began to object. "I can't bring Arne into this."

Gudrun rolled her eyes. "It's very simple, Bjørn. If Arne was in trouble, wouldn't you want to help him?"

"She's right again," said Ralf. "He's your brother."

Very slowly, Bjørn nodded. "I should like to see him," he admitted.

"Then we're off!" Ralf stuck his head out of the door. "A light wind coming down the fjord, and the tide was high an hour ago. Get your boots on, man!"

"Be careful," said Gudrun, suddenly nervous. "The faering is such a little boat."

"Don't worry." Bjørn looked happier already, as though glad to be given a job he knew how to do. "I know the waters, Gudrun."

"You're the skipper," said Ralf cheerfully. "I'm just the muscle power."

Peer stepped forward. "I'll come too."

"Better not," said Ralf. He put a hand on Peer's shoulder. "We can't have all the men going off together. Look after the family for me."

"I will, Ralf!" Peer felt inches taller.

"Oh good," said Hilde, "then you get the job of carrying Eirik back up the hill."

They stood watching Bjørn and Ralf drag the little faering down the dark bank of wet pebbles and into the water. The sail flapped as the two men jumped in. Bjørn scrambled into the stern, and grabbed the steering oar.

"We won't be long," Ralf called. "Look for us tomorrow, or the day after."

"Bye, Pa!" screamed Sigrid.

"Goodbye!"

The faering flew away from the shore. They saw Ralf turn his head, listening to something Bjørn was saying behind him. He was laughing.

Hilde turned to look at her mother. "Ma, don't worry. They'll be all right."

"I had to do it!" Gudrun's face was white but resolute. "When I think of what those two boys did for us, the year Ralf was away – the way they stood up for us against your uncles, Peer – and when I heard Asa saying that Bjørn brought all this upon his own head by marrying a seal woman, as though poor Kersten had been some kind of monster – well, I couldn't stand it, that's all."

"Of course you couldn't," said Hilde.

"I only hope Arne can talk some sense into him," Gudrun added.

"Then you don't believe the stories?"

Gudrun sighed. "I don't know, Hilde. But believing them isn't doing Bjørn any good."

They watched the faering cut out into the middle of the wide fjord. There was a bloom of haze over the opposite shore. The mountains there looked flat and shadowy, against a sky the colour of tin.

"Look!" Peer exclaimed. "Another boat."

"Where?" Hilde squinted under her hand.

"I've lost it. No, there – see?" There it was, just a scratch on the brilliance. As they watched, it seemed to blur and vanish. Hilde shivered. *A six-oarer, with a dark sail,* she thought, suddenly cold as Asa's words returned to her mind. *And it flickered in and out of sight like a butterfly's wings…*

Bjørn and Ralf were sailing confidently towards the mouth of the fjord.

"Well, there they go," said Hilde. As they turned to begin the long walk home, Peer heard her say quietly, "And it's too late now to call them back."

CHAPTER 32

The Mill Grinds

CARRYING A STOUT stick, Peer crept stealthily across the farmyard. He was nearly into the trees when he heard the brisk clap and thud of the house door, and Hilde came out. "Peer!" she called. "Where are you off to?"

"Just for a walk."

"Without Loki?" She came across to join him. "And what's the stick for? Is this something to do with what Thorkell said? Are you going down to the mill?"

"Yes, but I thought I'd go alone."

"Not a chance," said Hilde cheerfully. "I'll come too."

"No! Look, if the mill's really working at night, it's probably only the lubbers messing about, like before. I just want to go down quietly and see…" His voice faded.

"'Like before?'" Hilde narrowed her eyes. "What do you mean?"

Peer flushed. "You might as well know. The night I brought Ran home, the mill started grinding as I was crossing the bridge." He didn't want her know how it had felt, that awful moment in the rain and darkness, when he had half-believed the mill was somehow alive…

"You saw the mill working at night – all by itself? And you never told me?"

"Not *all by itself*," said Peer. "It's the lubbers, and I did tell you about them."

"Yes, but only to say you'd chased them off. You never said a word about the mill grinding. It's important, Peer. You should have told me."

"Hilde, let me deal with it. I'm not afraid of the lubbers."

"What a hero!" Hilde flashed. "Never mind that the lubbers are loathsome, treacherous, nasty things that might creep up from behind and throttle you. Tra-la! What fun. I'll just come along and watch."

Peer gave in. "Please yourself." He turned on his heel, then swung back. "Hadn't you better tell your mother?"

"She knows I'm going for a stroll," said Hilde.

They set off briskly. But soon their quick pace slowed. It was peaceful under the trees. Scents of flowers and fresh leaves floated past on currents of deliciously warm air. A big beetle hurtled by with a rattle of wings. And always there was the brook, sometimes a gossiping voice among the trees, sometimes chattering boldly beside the path.

"All right, I'm sorry," Peer said after a while. "I should have told you. I didn't want to worry you."

"Let *me* decide whether to be worried or not. Don't keep secrets, Peer: it doesn't suit you." Peer swung his stick and whistled quietly between his teeth. He had Hilde's comb in his pocket, but he wasn't going to give it to her while she was telling him off. They walked on.

Hilde changed the subject. "I wonder if Pa and Bjørn have got to Hammerhaven yet!" She sounded casual, but Peer knew her too well to be fooled.

"Ages ago. The sun's nearly down." He hesitated. "You're not worrying about that sail we saw? It was just some fisherman."

"Maybe. But if Thorkell's right about the mill, what if he's right about the draug boat, too? Those are creepy stories, Peer. It's terrible bad luck to see it. At first it seems like a real boat. But there's only half, split along the keel from stem to stern. The crew are drowned men, all blue and stiff, and the draug sits at the steerboard. He looks like a man, but—" her voice dropped to a whisper "—he hasn't got a face – only a bunch of seaweed."

Before Peer could answer, there was a loud splash from the stream, now running hidden on their left behind a screen of hazels. Peer whirled with a shout and brought his stick thrashing down through the leaves. Something leaped the stream, scrambled up the opposite bank and dived away under the trees. Branches shook. A clod tumbled back into the water.

"What was that?" Hilde cried. "A troll?"

"It was one of the lubbers!" Peer said. "It was dragging a tatty old blanket, didn't you see? So the other one won't be far away."

"Lubbers, this close to the farm?" Hilde sounded uneasy. "I must warn Ma. The twins play in the wood. We never told them about the lubbers; we didn't want to scare them. What are you grinning about?"

"You shouldn't keep secrets, Hilde," Peer teased. "People have a right to know!"

"It's not the same thing at all," she protested. "Sigrid's terrified of trolls, and then there was Granny Greenteeth – Ma and I thought that was enough for them to cope with."

"Fair enough," Peer agreed. "But come on. If the lubbers are slinking about up here, we can get to the mill ahead of them. Then we can lie in wait."

"Bad idea," said Hilde. "No one goes into the mill at night."

"It's my mill," Peer argued. "I'll have to live there one day. How can I be the miller if I only ever go there in daylight?"

"All right," Hilde sighed. "But we can't be long, or Ma will start to worry."

They crept down the lane as quietly as they could, and tiptoed over the bridge and into the yard. Stinging clouds of midges swirled in the dusk.

Peer put out a cautious hand and pushed the mill door.

"I won't go in without a light," hissed Hilde.

"A light would give us away. Take this." He retrieved the rusty old shovel from the barn porch. "To scare away the lubbers!" he whispered with a grin.

"Thank you so much," said Hilde drily. They slipped through the door.

The darkness seemed absolute. Peer heard the folds of Hilde's dress sway, the faint rub of her sleeves, the creak of her shoe. "What now?" Her breath fanned his cheek.

"Wait for a while…"

"I'm going to sit." The shovel rang faintly as she settled to the ground. "It could be midnight before the lubbers come back. We can't wait that long."

"Thorkell's asleep by midnight," said Peer. "If he's really heard anything, it must start happening long before then."

She sniffed. They sat in silence. Peer listened to the sound of his own heart beating. The darkness was grainy, as if made up of thousands of speckled seeds. Though the moving airs of evening were just beyond the door, he began to feel uneasy, breathless, trapped. *Maybe this wasn't such a good idea. Maybe we shouldn't have come.*

Hilde sat up. "What's that noise?" she breathed.

It came from outside, a sweeping, pattering rush like the onset of a rainstorm. Louder and louder it came, closer and closer. Peer and Hilde leaped up, leaving stick and shovel on the ground.

With a piercing squeal – with an anguished wooden groan – with a roar of muffled waters, Troll Mill woke from its sleep.

"Somebody's opened the sluice!" Peer shouted. Up in the grinding loft, the millstones screeched and sparked. "But the hopper's empty! There's nothing for the millstones to grind. We've got to stop it."

He sprang to the door and looked out. For a second his eyes couldn't take it in. The ground outside was seething with dark shapes, surging with energy like a nest of maggots. "Huuuutututututu!" The shriek rose into the night, and he understood.

"Hilde! The yard is swarming with trolls!"

He dragged her away from the door, treading on something that clanked, spun round and bashed his ankles. The shovel! He kicked it aside, cursing, and pushed Hilde into the darkest corner. They crouched there, panting – and the door flew wide.

A mob of trolls rushed in, flooding across the floor. The dark space filled with bangs and crashes, with jabbering, hooting, chuckling cries. Through the jiggling, sparking light, a furry face snarled, a white-rimmed eye glittered, a thin beak stabbed. The loft ladder was clotted with trolls. Scaly feet scraped on the rungs; a naked, rat-like tail clung and twitched. Some leaped straight up into the grinding loft with huge kicking jumps. Peppery dust showered down, and Peer and Hilde shrank back, wiping their eyes.

With a long, rattling roar, the trolls emptied something

into the hopper. The terrible shriek of stone on stone ceased, and the sparks vanished. Ears ringing, Peer and Hilde knelt listening to the millstones' rasping grumble.

Red light bloomed in the doorway. Now they could see the trolls, working away. They could see baskets being carried in, passed forward from hand to claw. A short, fat troll with long naked arms and splayed fingers flipped up the lid of the nearest grain bin. Two others lifted a basket and poured into it a rattling stream of—

"Bones!" Hilde whispered in horror. "They've been grinding bones, Peer! Bone-meal for troll bread!"

But Peer's attention was fixed on the doorway. The light blushed brighter. Shadows raced one another round the walls. "Someone's coming!" he said, hoarse with dread. "Somebody's – coming!"

The shadows fled to quiver in corners. A fiery torch was thrust through the doorway, a pine branch flaring with orange and blue flames. It lit up an arm – thick, bare, hairy, bulging with muscles. The arm was followed by a shoulder, clad in a ragged tunic. The creature – troll – whatever it was – ducked under the lintel and straightened up, up, and further up until its head nearly vanished among the rafters.

Peer's fingers bit into Hilde's arm. He saw a mane of shaggy black hair. Wicked little eyes, blinking in the torch light. A small red mouth, half-buried in masses of bushy black beard: and on either side of that mouth, two glistening white tusks curving upwards, as sharp as meat-hooks.

Baldur Grimsson!

The man spread his arms, fists clenched, lifting the torch high so that the light played over the walls. Again the shadows dashed for cover, as if the mill were full of dark, sliding, desperate ghosts. Shaking his fists over his head, the man let out a wild howl. *"Huuuuuutututututu! Huuuuuutututututu!"* Yellow froth gathered at the corners of his mouth and dripped from his tusks.

"Peer." Hilde pinched him. "Peer!"

"It's my uncle," said Peer stonily. "Baldur Grimsson."

"I know, I *know*. And we've got to run before he sees us!"

Too late! With a slow gesture, Uncle Baldur bent down, sweeping the torch low towards the corner where Hilde and Peer crouched. The streaming flames lit his face from below, so that nostrils and brows were bright, while his eye sockets turned into black holes. The tusks threw sharp stripes of shadow up his face and into his hair. Hilde and Peer stiffened, hoping against hope that somehow he would miss them.

"Well, well, well!" The high whistling voice of Peer's nightmares was accompanied by a gust of hot, bad breath. "My nephew. Scared, as usual. Crouching in a corner like a rabbit, as usual. And his girlfriend, too. Two rats in a trap!"

Peer got up. He pulled Hilde to her feet.

Sometimes, in daydreams, he'd imagined facing Uncle Baldur again. In those daydreams, Peer had grown, while Uncle Baldur had shrunk. Tall, strong and capable, he'd been able to stare his uncle straight in the eye. He'd not been afraid.

This wasn't a dream.

Uncle Baldur waved the torch in front of their faces gloatingly. "I ought to break your necks. That's what you do with rats and rabbits. One quick snap. Or I could hand you over to this lot!" He waved at the shifting, sniggering, rustling crowd of trolls. There was a pause, while the millstones overhead continued sullenly chewing up bones, and Peer tried to push Hilde behind him.

"But I won't." A thick smile appeared on Uncle Baldur's lips. "Because you've mended the mill for me. For me, do you hear?" He raised both hands above his head, yelling, "Did you think you could take the mill from me? I'll always be the miller! I'm miller to the Troll King himself! *Huuuuuutututututu!*"

Hilde shoved Peer in the small of the back. "Run!"

Peer snatched her hand and tugged her under Uncle Baldur's outstretched arms. He swooped on the rusty old shovel and backed towards the door, waving it in threatening arcs. "Go, Hilde! Run! I'll hold them off." Hilde vanished without argument.

Peer reached the door, flung the shovel at the approaching trolls, and hurtled out. "Come on!" Hilde screamed from the end of the bridge. He pounded across and tore up the hill after Hilde's flying figure. Distantly, he heard Uncle Baldur calling the trolls off the chase: "Get back to work!"

He caught up with Hilde under the eaves of the wood. "Are you all right?" She nodded. Holding hands tightly, they hurried into the sheltering darkness.

"Rat bones, sheep bones," panted Hilde. "Even bird bones. Do you think they use them to make different sorts of bread?" She shuddered. "All that gritty stuff in the hopper. It was crushed bone, for grinding up small."

"I ought to have guessed." Peer was sick with shock. "That crag where you saw the trolls, Hilde. The mill is straight down the fell from there. That's where the trolls were heading. Why didn't I guess?"

"Why should you?" Hilde demanded. "We thought Baldur Grimsson was gone for good. How could anyone guess he'd persuade the Gaffer to let him out and start using the old mill for grinding *bones*?"

"Hilde!" A terrible thought struck Peer. "If Uncle Baldur's down at the mill – then where's Uncle Grim?"

They stood for a second, staring at each other.

"Run!" said Hilde, breaking away and starting up the path as fast as she could. But it was too late. They ran out of the trees, and saw the dim outline of the farmhouse roof; and even from this distance, they could hear Gudrun screaming.

CHAPTER 33

The Lubbers at Large

AFTER PEER'S STICK came whistling down through the leaves, the lubbers dived into the undergrowth and began creeping stealthily uphill. At the edge of the wood they parted the last twigs with their clammy fingers, and stuck out their heads, peering with greedy eyes at Ralf's farm.

The door was shut. Loki was visible on the doorstep, lying with his nose on his paws, waiting for Peer to come home.

The lubbers blinked at him. "See?" muttered one. "It's no use. There's always a dog somewhere about. I hate dogs."

"Patience," said the other in a hollow whisper. "They'll get careless. They've drove out their Nis already, right? Think of those thick, green blankets waiting for us – if we do the job!"

"Aaah..." The first lubber dragged the blackish threads of its old blanket around its sharp shoulders. "You're right. We'll wait." It flung itself down like an abandoned scarecrow.

The other crouched, clawing at the leaf mould for beetles and small worms. After a while, there was a hooting and a pattering in the wood. Hidden in the bushes, the lubbers listened intently.

"Trolls," mumbled the crouching lubber. "A whole bunch of trolls going down to the mill. Pah!" It spat out a mouthful of shiny black wing-cases and legs, and ran an exploratory finger around its teeth. "That'll give that boy a shock. Him, and his dog, and his shovel!"

"Hark!" The other lubber tensed. "Here's someone else. Coming this way. Someone big. Someone heavy!"

With slow thudding footfalls, a man as huge as a marching tree-trunk came up the path. He clutched a club. Shaggy black hair hung over his shoulders, and as he flung back his head, the lubbers saw the pale flash of tusks.

The first lubber sank back with a sigh of relief. "It's only one of them man-trolls from the mill."

"What d'you mean, 'only'?" hissed the other. "Look at him! Big enough to tear us limb from limb."

"But he's not after *us*, is he?"

Over by the farmhouse door, Loki raised his head, suddenly alert. He sprang up, barking. The man broke into a run. With Loki snarling at his heels, he loped past the farmhouse and out of sight, heading for the sheep pastures. A chorus of terrified bleating rose into the air.

The woman who lived in the farmhouse ran out into the twilight, the old brindled sheepdog trotting after her. A couple of fair-haired children followed, a boy and a girl. "Loki? Peer?" cried the woman. "Hilde? I'm coming!" She turned to the children. "Get back inside. It'll be trolls, after the sheep. The three of us can deal with it."

"Let me come," the boy pleaded.

"*Do as I say*," said the woman fiercely, and, with the old sheepdog following at a shambling canter, she picked up her skirts and ran towards the pasture. Instead of obeying her, the children climbed on the gate, trying to see.

The farmhouse door stood open, unguarded. Nudging each other, the lubbers crawled out of the bushes and slipped like shadows into the house.

The fire was as bright as a bar of red-hot iron, and it hurt their eyes. A reek and fug of humans swirled about them: peat smoke and salt fish, dogs and leather and oil, broth and cheese and onions. They stood snuffling, blinking and gaping.

From a sort of box near the hearth came a sleepy wail. The lubbers' mouths spread into wide slit-like grins, and they tiptoed nearer.

"Keep a look out," whispered one. "I'll grab the baby."

"Oh no you don't; *I'll* grab the baby," the other pushed in front.

"Let me!"

"Let *me*!"

There was a scuffle, and then, as the lubbers ended up with their heads over the cradle, an astounded silence.

"There's *two* babies!"

"Which one does she want?"

"Don't be more stupid than you can help," growled the first lubber. "We'll take 'em both! And if old Granny doesn't want two, we'll keep the extra one!" It plunged skinny hands into the cradle and picked up Eirik. The other lubber shouldered in greedily, snatching up Ran. "Here, that's not fair – yours is bigger!"

For about a second, Eirik's tousled head nodded sleepily on the first lubber's bony shoulder. Then he woke. His eyes flew open. His body went rigid. Drawing a gigantic breath, he threw back his head and began to scream and scream.

"Shut him up!" The other lubber danced in terror. "Shut him up!"

The one carrying Eirik tried to get a hand over the little boy's mouth. Eirik bit it and went on screaming.

"Run for it! Quick!"

They burst out of the farmhouse door. Eirik's yells faded

as his lungs emptied. Sucking in another enormous breath, he began again.

Balanced on the gate, Sigurd and Sigrid turned in time to see two grotesque figures dashing away from the house. One had some sort of bundle tucked under its scrawny elbow. On the shoulder of the other bounced the face of their baby brother, his eyes screwed shut, his mouth wide.

Adding their screams to his, the twins leaped from the gate and tore after him.

"MA!" shrieked Sigrid. "COME QUICKLY! THE TROLLS HAVE GOT EIRIK!"

"MA! PEER! HILDE!" Sigurd yelled. Ahead of them, the lubbers swerved into the wood and vanished into black shadows.

"Which way? Which way?" Sigrid sobbed.

Among the trees, it was hard to tell the direction of Eirik's terrible screams, and they were getting fainter. Sigurd looked wildly this way and that.

"Uphill!" he cried. "They'll be taking him back up Troll Fell. Quick!"

Scrabbling, panting, crying, the twins clawed their way up through the birch forest, clutching at branches, heaving themselves higher and higher.

"MA!" Sigurd's voice cracked.

"It's no good," wept Sigrid. "She can't hear. Oh, oh, we've got to find him!"

"Listen." Sigurd jerked to a halt. "Is he still screaming?"

Over their thumping hearts and rasping breath, they thought they could still hear a distant cry. Then an owl swooped past with a long, shivering hoot.

"We've lost him!" Sigrid burst out. Sigurd punched the trunk of the nearest birch tree as hard as he could. He nursed his broken knuckles.

A lonely wind sighed through the boughs. Then there was a rustling, a pattering, a crackling, as if the undergrowth was on fire, as if all the creeping things in the wood were stirring and scurrying and hurrying up hill. Sigurd caught his sister's hand.

"We haven't lost him yet, twin. See, here come the trolls."

Something bounded out of the bushes. It was too dark to see very well, but the twins thought it had a longish beak. Its arms seemed far too long for its body. It let out a deafening cry: "*Huuuutututututututu!*"

Sigrid hid her face. The crackling and pattering got closer. Then the leading troll bounded on, and after it in a long file came other shapes, eyes dimly gleaming green and red; snuffling and snorting, panting and wheezing, carrying baskets and bundles and sacks. But the gangling figures with the big heads, which had carried Eirik away from the farm, were nowhere to be seen.

"Where is he?" Sigrid choked. "What if he's in one of those sacks?"

It was an unbearable thought. "We'll follow," Sigurd whispered. "Come on! We mustn't lose them again."

They fell in at the back of the odd procession. The trolls never looked round, but jogged on with their burdens. Sigrid and Sigurd struggled after them. They clambered beside steep little waterfalls, splashed ankle deep through boggy pockets of marsh. Suddenly they were out on the bare hillside. Troll Fell reared up ahead, featureless against the sky. A bright, thumb-nail moon was edging over the crest.

From far up the hill came the warbling cries of the trolls.

With bursting lungs, Sigurd and Sigrid ran, and trotted, and ran again, falling further and further behind. "Come on, Siggy," gasped Sigurd.

"I'm – trying," panted Sigrid. "But I've – got a – stitch."

Sigurd dashed the hair out of his eyes. The column of trolls was out of sight, but there was one lone, lame straggler. "Come on, Siggy, we can keep up with that one!"

They puffed on. Presently Sigurd gave an exclamation. "I see where we are. That's the crag where we bumped into the trolls before. And this is the stream that runs out from it."

The twins dodged up the slope, taking cover in the black moon-shadow at the foot of each grey rock. The troll was in difficulties. It was a smallish furry creature, with a long stripy tail. The pale moonlight showed two little knobby horns on top of its head. Its ears were folded flat, and it was hissing and spitting to itself, as it worked to get its heavy sack up the rocks. First it tried pulling. Then it clambered awkwardly down – "Poor thing, it's limping!" breathed Sigrid – and tried pushing the sack from below, head and shoulders almost buried. This was better. It got the weight balanced on a ledge, and scrambled up – just as the whole thing tumbled off.

Sigurd whispered, "It makes you want to go and help!"

With a sizzling noise exactly like water drops scalding in a hot frying pan, the troll jumped down again. It wrestled the sack up the cliff, clinging on somehow to invisible cracks and crannies. It reached the top, and its whisking tail disappeared over the edge.

"Quick! We mustn't lose it."

There were plenty of ledges and footholds: even in the shadow it was easy to climb. With grazed knees and knuckles the twins pulled themselves up.

The top of the scar was split, as though a giant axe had chopped through the rocks in a criss-cross pattern. In the moonlight, the clefts were very black. Small thorn trees grew out of them, their dry roots clinging to the stones.

The troll had vanished, but the twins could still hear muffled noises. They hunted about between the rocks. One of the clefts was particularly deep. They knelt side by side on the edge, peering in, and sounds of bumping, squeaking and snarling floated up to them.

"It went down there," said Sigurd.

They looked at each other, ghostly in the moonlight. Sigurd squared his shoulders. "Go home, Siggy. Tell Ma and Peer what's happened. I'll go on."

"No!" said Sigrid.

"But you're frightened of trolls."

"No I'm not. I was before we started chasing them, but now, I don't know why, I've stopped." She stuck out her bottom lip. "I'm not afraid of them any more. I want to find Eirik."

Sigurd looked undecided. "I don't know, Siggy. I think you should go back."

"Well I won't!" hissed Sigrid. "You can't make me! And we're wasting time!"

Sigurd shrugged. "All right then. Follow me."

And he swung his legs into the hole.

CHAPTER 34

Under Troll Fell

ELBOWS BRACED, SIGURD kicked for a foothold. "It goes down a long way!"

"Don't get stuck," whispered Sigrid as he sank into black shadow.

"There's loads of room. Ouch!" he added. Sigrid heard gasps and grunts. "Your turn," he called softly. "I'm down."

With Sigurd guiding her, Sigrid joined him at the bottom of the crevice. It was completely dark, except for the narrow streak of sky overhead, fringed with ferns.

"This way!" Sigurd pulled her hand. "It keeps going. There's a passage into the hill." He twisted round and squeezed himself into a gap at the end of the crevice. With a shiver, Sigrid followed.

The passage was not wide. They had to slide along crab-wise, bruising knees and elbows on projecting ribs of rock. Sigrid didn't realise at first that the troll was only just ahead of them. It was twittering and swearing as it yanked the sack along.

A wider space opened out. The troll dropped the sack with a thump. It whistled; shrill and impatient. A slow light dawned. The twins saw the passage walls, streaked with water, and, only a few yards away, the small hunched back of the troll, sitting on the sack with its tail twitching. A globe of swirling bluish fire sped around a distant bend in the tunnel, whirled up to the troll, and hung, dancing up and down in the air.

The troll jumped up. "To the kitchens!" it squeaked, heaving the sack on to its shoulders. The light began floating down the tunnel, and the little troll hobbled after it, still muttering and complaining. Its claws scritched on the stones as it trotted away.

Sigrid started forwards, but Sigurd caught her arm. "Let it go, Siggy. We don't want the kitchens."

"But we can't find our way in the dark!"

"I know. I've got an idea." The troll turned a corner, and huge shadows squeezed back down the tunnel. Sigurd fumbled in his pocket and produced Peer's little wooden whistle. "We'll call for our own light," he said.

"Can we?"

"Let's see!" Night swept over them again as Sigurd blew. Two pure little notes warbled out, mimicking the sound the troll had made. Blinking uselessly in the darkness, Sigurd waited a moment and tried again.

"It's working!" Sigrid saw a cold glow far down the passage. They turned dirty faces to each other in triumph. Another of the blue lights came dashing up like a dog answering the whistle, and drifted around their heads, crackling. Fine strands of Sigrid's hair floated up towards it, and their scalps prickled.

"Take us to Eirik!" Sigurd demanded. The ball of light flickered. It sank, pulsing nervously.

"You can't ask that," Sigrid said. "It doesn't know who Eirik is. You're confusing it. Eirik's a baby," she explained to the light. "We want to find him. Can you take us? Where's the baby?"

The ball of light brightened. It zoomed off, and the twins hurried hopefully after. The stone floor rose and fell, and sometimes narrowed to a deep V with water at the bottom, so that they had to scuffle along with a foot braced on each side. Cold air breathed from cracks and splits in the tunnel wall. Through one opening they heard a sort of pounding rumble, and smelt spray: an underground waterfall pouring invisibly from darkness into darkness. Through another, they heard distant voices. Sigurd glanced at their guiding light. "I hope it's taking us by the back ways," he muttered. "Hey, you up there! We don't want to meet anyone."

The light winked, and vanished through a black hole in the ceiling.

"How do we get up there?" Sigrid wailed.

Her brother pointed. A dead pine tree had been propped against the wall. Its roughly trimmed branches formed a crude ladder. Sigurd shook it dubiously. "I'll hold it for you," he suggested, "and then you hold it at the top for me."

Prickly pine needles showered on Sigurd as Sigrid clambered up. Then it was his turn to climb the sharp spokes of the branches. They sat at the top, sucking their sore fingers.

"I'm *so* tired," Sigrid moaned. "How long have we been in here?"

"Seems like hours. It must be daybreak, outside. Ma will be frantic."

"I'm thirsty." Sigrid licked her lips.

"So am I. But," warned her brother, "we mustn't eat or drink any troll food."

"Or we'll turn into trolls. I know. That's what happened" – Sigrid's face went suddenly white – "to the Grimsson brothers. Oh, they're down here, too! What if we meet them?"

"Let's hope we don't."

"I wish Peer was with us," said Sigrid.

"So do I. But wishing's no good. Let's find Eirik!"

They got up, looking around at the new tunnel. It was smaller, and warmer, and the walls were smoothly cut.

As though sensing their tiredness, the ball of light bobbed along slowly. Sigurd and Sigrid followed, holding hands.

Somewhere down the passageway, a door opened and closed. They heard footsteps, briskly approaching.

Sigurd whirled. "Hide!"

"Where? Keep walking," Sigrid ordered urgently. "With any luck, they'll think we're trolls. Pull up your hood and keep your head down!" She beckoned the light with a fierce gesture, and obediently it spun behind them, so their faces were in shadow. Hearts pounding, the twins walked on.

Stealing a look under the edge of her hood, Sigrid saw a new light approaching, a greenish one this time. A bulky figure trotted along behind it, wearing hard shoes that clicked on the floor. It was carrying something that looked like an enormous stack of folded linen. As it got closer, they heard it complaining to itself in a thick, muffled voice: "'*Fetch this, nursie! Fetch that, nursie!*' Ooh, my poor feet. Now, let's see. Green nettle coverlets, half a dozen. Sheepskins, a score. The best silk spiderweb sheets for my lady's bedchamber, or she'll make trouble. Nothing but work, work, work! – and never a chance for poor nursie to sit down and drink a drop of beer with her old friend the bog-wife!"

The green light and the twins' blue light met in the tunnel roof and whirled around like a couple of friendly puppies. The twins shrank close to the wall as a strange figure came hurrying past: a large troll with a piggish face, pressing its chin into the teetering pile of linen. A white cap perched on its head, with little peaks like curly horns. Without so much as glancing at them, it tapped by on horny, cloven hooves – not shoes at all – muttering, "Rush here, rush there – not a moment's peace since my lady came back from the Dovrefell! And the washing bills from the water nixies – *scandalous!*"

It was gone.

Sigrid and Sigurd scuttled on, while their blue light disentangled itself from the green one, and sped after them. And a moment later, they had arrived in a square hall. To the right, and straight ahead, were the dark mouths of two more tunnels. To the left was a carved doorway, set with a stout oak door. The light floated towards it.

Sigrid trembled. "Is this it? Have you brought us to the baby?" The light flashed brightly. "Yes! We've found him, Sigurd! Quick!"

"Ssh. Not too fast." Sigurd leaned his ear against the thick oak planking, and listened. "Can't hear a thing." He lifted the latch as carefully as he could, and the door swung silently open. They slipped inside.

It was a large chamber with an arched roof. The entire roof and walls sparkled with sharp white crystals. In amazement, Sigrid put out a finger to touch the glittering crust. A bead of blood sprang on her fingertip.

To one side of the door was a stone platform covered with fleeces, obviously a bed. On the other side was a plain wooden chair with a straw seat and a carved back, and next to it, a high chair with a bar across the seat to stop a child from falling out.

At the foot of the bed, near the brazier, was a stout wooden cot, carved in woven patterns with little snarling faces. A string of pine cones dangled over it.

"It's a nursery," Sigurd said. "He must be in the cot. Hurry!"

Sigrid peered into the cot, her heart banging with hope and terror. She drew a joyful breath. There at the bottom was a soft humped shape, just Eirik's size: an infant sleeping on its side, rolled up in black lambskins.

"Oh, he's safe! We've found him." She reached in.

"Stop!"

"What's wrong?" She turned a frightened face to her brother, who was staring into the cot as if he'd seen an adder.

He said in a choked whisper, "It isn't him."

The infant rolled on to its back, and the blue glow from the light played over its sleeping face. Sigrid pressed her hands to her mouth.

It was the ugliest baby she had ever seen.

Its skin was crumpled, wrinkled and damp, like hands that have been in the wash too long. A squashed little snout twitched and snuffled in the middle of its face. Above the tightly shut eyes, long hairs sprang from its brows, like bristles on a pig's skin. Its mouth was extremely wide, and its ears were hairy.

Sigurd looked sick. "It's a troll. We've come all this way for nothing!"

"Where's Eirik?" asked Sigrid faintly.

"How should I know?" Sigurd kicked the floor. "We'd better go."

"But we haven't got Eirik!"

"How can we find him now?" Sigurd asked in despair. "He might be anywhere." He tried to drag her towards the door.

Sigrid resisted. "But the light was taking us to him!"

In the cradle, the troll baby cautiously opened one eye.

The twins didn't notice. "Don't you see?" Sigurd jigged with panicked impatience. "We asked the light to take us to a *baby*. So it brought us here, to the only baby it knows."

The troll baby quickly closed its eye. Then it opened the other a slit, and peeked through its lashes.

"That's not a baby, it's a monster," Sigrid cried.

"It's a prince," said Sigurd gloomily. "Remember what the Nis told Peer, about the troll princess's son?"

Sigrid stiffened. "A prince!"

"What does it matter, Sigrid – just come, now, before we get caught!"

But Sigrid seemed to catch fire. She jerked free from Sigurd, flew back to the cradle, and scooped the troll baby into her arms, swaddled up like an enormous cocoon, with its wizened face sticking out at the end.

"What are you *doing?*" Sigurd screeched.

"We're taking it with us." She gripped the baby – which appeared to be sound asleep – and faced Sigurd with hot cheeks and flashing eyes. "If they've got our baby – we'll take theirs!"

Sigrid's mouth fell open. "We can't do that."

"Yes, we can!" Sigrid stamped her foot.

Their eyes met. Slowly, Sigurd's stunned expression altered to one of mischievous delight. He laughed excitedly. "We'll do it. We'll trade their prince for Eirik. Let's go!"

They stole out into the corridor, the ball of light bouncing gently after them. Sigurd looked up, his face stark in the blue glow. "Back the way we came, please!" he ordered, with a slight quiver to his voice. What if it realised what they were doing? But obediently it began rolling along the ceiling.

They hurried after. Sigrid kept stopping to hitch up the troll baby. "It's awfully heavy," she whispered.

"Let me take it." They shuffled the baby from Sigrid's arms to Sigurd's. Its cold, hairy ear twitched against his cheek, and he shuddered. "Is it awake?"

A diamond glint squeezed through the troll baby's flickering lashes. Next second, its eyes were tightly shut again. The twins exchanged scared glances. "Hurry!" said Sigurd. "We're done for if it starts yelling."

Moments later, they reached the dark pit in the floor of the tunnel. The light hovered, sinking slowly.

"Here we go," panted Sigurd. "Back down the pine tree. Listen. You climb down halfway and I'll try and lower the baby to you. Then I'll climb past you, and we'll do the same thing again."

Sigrid nodded. She sat on the edge and dipped her legs into the darkness, feeling about for the first spokes of the pine tree. She turned on her stomach and slithered down, till she was neck deep in the hole.

"All right?" whispered Sigurd.

"I can't see my feet. And my skirt's catching!" The dead tree shivered and rustled as she kicked her way lower.

"Stop there!" Sigurd hissed. "Are you ready? Reach up as high as you can. Here it comes!" He knelt awkwardly on the brink of the pit, and, getting a good grip of the swaddled bundle, lifted it out over the drop.

The troll baby's eyes flew open. It grimaced in alarm.

"Don't drop me!" it squawked in a shrill, harsh voice.

Sigurd almost let go.

CHAPTER 35

The Nis Confesses

GUDRUN AND ALF ran. Beyond the farm, the ground lifted in a series of shallow rises, with the fells closing in on either side. In the cool evening air, raucous bleating and frenzied barking echoed off the slopes. Gudrun had no doubt as to what was going on.

"Hilde! Peer! I'm coming!" she cried again, wondering why she couldn't hear them shouting. She scrambled up the last rise, and saw why.

Hilde and Peer were nowhere to be seen. There were no trolls, either. Just twenty yards away, a monstrous figure was stalking the sheep. A mane of hair grew over his shoulders, and a heavy club swung in his right hand. Suddenly he broke into a deep-throated shout: "Ho! Ho!" Loki skirmished furiously at his heels.

Gudrun felt as if the ground had split open in front of her. "That's one of the millers! That's Grim Grimsson!"

Grim advanced upon the sheep, thwacking his club into the palm of his hand. Trapped against the slope, the frightened ewes and their lambs bunched together. They milled restlessly – then scattered, dashing for freedom. Some sprang up the hillside. One galloped straight past Grim's legs, her lamb following close. Grim lunged. He sank a massive hairy hand into the tangled wool of her back. He hoisted her up, struggling and kicking. His arm rose and fell.

Gudrun heard the dull knock of his club. She ran a few paces, shouting, "Grim Grimsson! Leave our sheep alone, you thieving rascal!"

The big man turned, hitching the dead sheep under his arm, and Gudrun saw the curling tusks, winking from his mouth like white knives. She'd made a mistake. This was no longer merely their bad-tempered neighbour from the mill. This was a troll creature from under the fell!

Grim stared at her, and she stared back, frozen. She could never outrun him. Suddenly Grim threw back his head, exposing a throat as pale as the underbelly of a slug, and howled like a wolf. It seemed the wild sound must reach to the lonely top of Troll Fell. The dogs whimpered.

Grim waited till the echoes died. Then, with the sheep tucked under his arm, he strode up the side of the valley. The orphaned lamb ran uncertainly after him.

A distant cry came from the farm. "Ma... Ma!"

The twins!

Gudrun plunged back down the slope. It was almost dark, and she couldn't see where she was going: she tripped over tufts of grass, skidded on stones. Loki shot ahead; Alf panted at her heels. It was like a nightmare: the valley swung from side to side as she ran; the stars jolted in the sky. The farmyard was silent and still.

"Twins!" Gudrun shrieked. "Sigrid! Sigurd!"

No answer. No one called from the house, no one ran out to meet her. The farmhouse door stood half open. Even before she shoved it wide and stumbled into the warm, homely gloom, Gudrun knew that the twins were gone.

Every muscle melted with terror. She staggered over to the cradle and looked in. It was empty. They had all gone, all been taken! She sank beside the cradle, dizzy and sick.

Time passed. The dogs were poking cold noses into her face. Then Loki sprang away. He was barking again, excited, welcoming barks. The door scraped. Feet clattered on the floor. There were voices: "Ma!" – "Gudrun!" – "Ma, are you all right?"

Hands grasped her, dragged her to her feet. "Lean on me, Gudrun." A man's voice – no, it was Peer's, deep with concern. He supported her to a bench. Their faces swam into focus, Peer and Hilde, staring at her with frightened eyes. She tried speak, but her breath wouldn't come right. She managed a shuddering wail. "The – the *children!*"

"Listen." Hilde held her mother's cold hands. "Ma, listen, this is important. The Grimsson brothers are back. Baldur Grimsson is down at the mill. Have you seen Grim? Has he got the children?"

Gudrun shook her head. "No. S-seen him, yes. But he took – a sheep. H-heard the twins shouting. When I came back – they were gone!"

"Not the Grimssons." Hilde was pale. "In that case – Granny Greenteeth?"

"How could she take all four of them?" Peer asked in a low voice.

"I don't know. If only we'd been here! If only we knew what happened!" She buried her face in her hands. "Peer – what shall we do?"

Hilde needed him. Peer's blood ran warmer and quicker. He tried to be strong, to think. The haze of shock, from seeing the trolls and Uncle Baldur in control of the mill, cleared a little. He said slowly, "Perhaps the Nis saw what happened."

"The Nis!"

"If it's really in the cowshed…"

"Oh, quick!" Hilde jumped up. "Go on, Peer, it only speaks to you. Go! Find it!"

She pushed him out. He hurried across the yard. The cowshed, with its thick walls and turf roof, was very dark indeed.

"Nis!" he called urgently. "Nis, we need you!"

Silence, but Peer felt it was a listening silence. "We need you," he repeated. "The twins have gone, and both the babies. It's desperate. Gudrun's beside herself. Did you see what happened? Please help us!"

There was a rustle of straw. A small dark figure crept out of one of the stalls. It drew an unsteady breath. "This is all my fault," it said brokenly.

"Of course it isn't." Peer tried to curb his impatience. "Nis, just tell me if you saw anything or not."

But the Nis was off. "Aieeee!" it wailed. "What is a Nis for? To protect the house. Now the children is lost! Gone, and it is all my fault. Here I was, Peer Ulfsson, curled up in my cold, dark corner, because the mistress doesn't want me any more. I hears screaming, Peer Ulfsson, and I looks out, and there is the thieves, running, running. And I thinks, *Good, the seal baby has gone!* But then I looks again, and I sees little Eirik, they has taken little Eirik as well, and it is *all my fault!*"

Peer tried to interrupt, but the Nis gabbled on. "And the twins, I sees the twins chasing after, and I tries to follow, Peer Ulfsson! I tries, but I loses them in the woods – the woods is so dark. And then the mistress comes home, and she is screaming too. How can I face her? She will be so angry with the poor Nis! I will – have to – go – awa-a-ay!" It buried its head in its arms and howled.

"NIS!" said Peer. "For goodness' sake tell me – WHO TOOK THE BABIES?"

The Nis looked up, gulping. "You doesn't know? It was the lubbers, of course."

"The lubbers!" Peer breathed. "Nis, *did* you tell Granny Greenteeth about Ran?"

"Lubbers did," it sniffed. "The Nis never talks to Granny Greenteeth, though nobody believes me."

"Then why did I see you at the millpond that night?"

"I tells the mistress," hiccupped the Nis, "not to feed the seal baby. And she gets angry, and she throws me out. And then, then I sees the lubbers sneaking around the farm, peeking and prowling. And I follows them to see what they are up to, protecting the house, like I should. And nobody believes me, they all think poor Nithing is bad, is wicked. And I thinks, why shouldn't Granny Greenteeth have the seal baby? They are both wet, both watery. Why not?"

"So now the lubbers have taken Eirik, too," Peer finished. The Nis bowed its head, and its thin shoulders heaved.

There was no point in scolding it, and no time to lose. "Nis," he said solemnly, "We need your cleverness more than ever, now. The lubbers have taken the babies for Granny Greenteeth. You have to help us save them."

The Nis looked up with drenched eyes. "Both babies?"

"*Both* of them!" said Peer sternly.

The Nis sat up and mopped its wet cheeks with the end of its beard. It waved a finger in the air. "What does the lubbers want most, Peer Ulfsson?" it enquired.

"What? Oh! *Blankets?*"

"Yes! We needs blankets to bargain with," squeaked the Nis.

"We'll get them. Come on, back to the house. Hurry! The lubbers could be throwing Eirik and Ran into the millpond, any minute."

"They won't do that, Peer Ulfsson," the Nis chirped.

"Why not?"

"For two things. Lubbers is stupid," it explained, "but not so stupid as to trust Granny Greenteeth. A fine, green blanket, she promises! They'll want to see it, first."

"I wondered about that," said Peer grimly. "I expect she meant the pondweed, did she? What's the other reason?"

"Lubbers is cowards," pointed out the Nis. "Afraid of the trolls, afraid of the Grimssons. Is the mill working? Then they'll keep away, slink about in the woods till the trolls go home."

"Good thinking. Come on, we'll go and tell the others." Peer strode out into the moonlight, and collided with Gudrun and Hilde, huddled together against the cowshed door, listening. The Nis scampered across the yard and shot happily into the warm house.

"We heard it all," said Hilde.

"I'll get the blankets now," said Gudrun in a trembling voice, "Oh, if the Nis can find the children for us, I'll never know how to thank it. What shall I say to Ralf? How can I face Bjørn if we lose his little girl?"

"We'll find them," Peer swore. "Let's go. We'd better head straight for the mill pond, but be careful!"

"Careful?" Hilde laughed bitterly. "Trolls, lubbers, the Grimsson brothers, Granny Greenteeth – and you want us to be careful? Well, we can try."

The lubbers had gone crashing downhill through the wood, but once they were sure that the twins were no longer following, they swung north, crossing the stream a good way above the mill, and striking up into the woods opposite Troll

Fell. They had a lair up there, an old badger sett under a bank, half buried in leaves.

They careered up through the moonlit wood, Eirik still roaring, and pushed the babies into the drifted leaves. Ran lay quietly, her fingers curling and uncurling. The moon shone in her eyes.

Bright tear tracks gleamed like snail trails down Eirik's fat cheeks. But the change from movement to stillness took him by surprise. He stopped crying, and kicked experimentally. The leaves rustled. It was a nice noise. He kicked again.

"Peace at last," said one of the lubbers, with immense relief. "Why couldn't you have stopped him before? Mine was quiet enough."

"You try it!" snarled the other.

"You just ain't got a way with babies," said the first.

"If Granny Greenteeth don't want him, I'll soon show you my way with babies!" returned the other. "Listen. Has the mill stopped? I can't hear it clacking."

They cocked their heads, large black silhouettes against the moonrise. The night was silent, except for the sound of the stream in the valley bottom.

"The trolls have gone," exclaimed the second lubber in satisfaction. "Now we can pop down and deliver madam's order. A baby? Two babies! Take your choice."

"Wait a minute." The first lubber placed a clammy hand on its companion's shoulder. "I'll carry the big one, this time. You'd only set him off again." It crawled through the leaves to where Eirik was lying, and hung its big head over him.

Eirik's shock and anger at being woken and taken out of his warm cradle had worn off. He was becoming interested in his new surroundings. Ran was nearby, and that felt right. There was a bright, shining light in the sky. The dry leaves were crinkly and they smelt nice. He scrunched them in handfuls, and nobody told him not to.

Now a face was looking down at him, a new face, a funny one. It had tiny little eyes, and a wide slitty mouth, and a big ear like a cabbage leaf that blew out to one side. Eirik was used to funny faces. Sigurd pulled them to make him laugh.

"Man!" he said clearly, trying to snatch at the lubber's bulbous nose.

The lubber froze. "Did you hear that?"

"Man!" gurgled Eirik.

"He called me a man." The lubber drew back and stared. "Me, a man! Fancy! Fancy that!"

"Well you're not a man," the second lubber remarked sourly. "You're a lubber, same as me."

The first lubber flexed its arms and puffed out a ribby chest. "Rather a fine figure, I do believe!" It leaned back over Eirik and prodded him. "Say that again!"

"Man," Eirik obliged.

The lubber gazed at him, and a dark mottled flush spread slowly over its face. It whirled, crouching in the leaves, and faced its friend.

"I wants this one!" it panted. "We'll keep him. Old Granny'll never know. She asked for a baby, and a baby she'll get."

The other lubber licked its lips. "Good enough," it grinned. "We'll keep the one with the most eating on it, eh?"

"No, you fool!" the first lubber spat. "We'll just… keep him! He'll – he'll be ours, see? He'll grow up, and he'll teach us things."

"What things?" the other asked blankly.

"Teach us to be… human," mumbled the first lubber. "I've always wanted to be human. See, then we'd have nice beds, and houses – and all that."

There was a pause.

"I never heard such drivel!" said the second lubber with conviction. "Come on, pick him up. Let's go."

"I won't!" The first lubber began to snivel. "Nobody ever – *ever* – called me a man before..."

The second lubber grabbed at Eirik. The first one lunged. Next they were rolling down hill in a tangled ball, trying to strangle each other. They ended up in a bramble bush, the second lubber sitting astride the first lubber's chest and banging its head rhythmically backwards into the soil.

"Listen to me, stupid!" it snarled. "We take both babies to Granny Greenteeth, or we take her one and eat the other. I don't care. But we are not – keeping – either of them, get it! DO YOU KNOW HOW LONG THEY TAKE TO GROW UP?"

"No..." gasped the first lubber.

"YEARS! THAT'S HOW LONG! YEARS!"

There was another pause.

"I didn't know that," said the first lubber sulkily at last. It dabbed an oozing nose. "All right, lemme go. We'll do it your way."

"Hark!" the second lubber raised its hand. From far down the valley came the spindly cry of a cock. Both lubbers raised their heads. The moon was pale. Dawn was in the sky.

"Cock-crow!" spat the second lubber. "See what you've done? We've left it too late. Now we'll have to wait till it's dark again."

Down by the mill pond, the three desperate watchers saw the sky lightening. Birds began to sing; the midges came out to dance over the sullen green water. Gradually the sun toiled up over the edge of Troll Fell, and golden shafts struck down between the trees.

It was going to be a long, hot day.

Up in the old badger sett, cuddled together amongst the leaves, Eirik and Ran had fallen fast asleep.

CHAPTER 36

The Troll Baby at the Farm

SIGURD STRUGGLED UP out of the cleft in the rocks on the side of Troll Fell, pale and dishevelled, scratched and bleeding. A low crimson sun shone straight into his eyes, as if to welcome him home. Gratefully he sniffed the warm air, scented with turf and sheep and wildflowers. Then he turned and called into the darkness.

"All right, Sigrid. Pass up the baby!"

"Mind my head," complained a shrill voice from the bottom of the narrow chasm. "Ouch! Look out. You nearly took my nose off on that rock."

Sigurd shuddered. He heard his sister answering, tired and tearful: "I'm sorry. I'm doing my best. Can you reach it, Sigurd? Here it comes!"

With a boost from below, the extraordinary face of the troll baby popped up into the sunlight, mewing. Sigurd hoisted it out, while Sigrid scrambled after. Her face was bruised and filthy; she rolled over and lay exhausted on the rocks.

Sigurd prodded her. "We can't stop, twin. The trolls will be after us as soon as it's dark, and look, the sun's sinking. We must have been underground for ages – all night, and most of the day."

"It feels even longer," Sigrid groaned. "I'm so hungry!"

On shaking legs they descended the scar and hurried along

the track, delighting in the warm sun on their backs. Sigurd carried the troll baby over his shoulder. It kept up a constant chitter-chatter, horrid to hear.

"I spy wiv my little eye – somefing nasty coming after us. A monster... It's red and glaring and all on fire. Run, run!"

The twins turned in alarm.

"Where's the monster?" said Sigurd scornfully. "That's the sun!"

"What's the sun?" squeaked the troll baby.

"It's – well, it's the sun, that's all! Like one of your glowing lights, I suppose – but bigger and yellow, and it lives in the sky."

"But it ain't yellow. S'red."

"Yes, it's red *now*, but that's because it's setting."

"What's *setting?*"

"Going down. Going away. Sunset. That's when it gets dark."

The troll baby jeered. "What's the use of a light that goes away just when it gets dark?"

Sigurd opened and closed his mouth like a fish.

"Don't argue with it," said Sigrid. "Here we are! Home at last. Ma, Hilde! We're back..."

They broke into a run, only to come to a puzzled halt in the yard.

"Where are they? No one's here."

"*Knock, knock, knock! Nobody's at home, only a little rat chewing on a bone,*" chanted the troll baby in a sing-song voice.

"I expect they're all looking for us," said Sigrid bleakly.

Disappointed and weary, the twins trudged into the farmhouse. The fire was nearly out, and it was clear that no one had been home for some time.

"*Rock-a-bye baby, mammy's not here, she's out in the woodshed making a bier...*" sang the troll baby.

In furious disgust, Sigurd held it out at arm's length. "At least I don't have to carry *this* thing any further." He plonked it into the cold cradle. It seized the sides with both hands and pulled itself upright to peer over the edge, looking about with interested malice.

"I'm hungry," it announced. "Hungry, hungry, *hungry*!"

"All right, we heard," Sigurd shouted.

Sigrid seized a pot and the scoop. "I'll make it some groute – perhaps that will keep it quiet. Build up the fire, Sigurd. And bar the door."

The troll baby sniggered. "Ooh, aye, bar the door. I wouldn' like to be in your shoes when my mammy catches you!"

"Is that so?" Sigurd glared at it. "Your *mammy* and her trolls shouldn't have kidnapped my little brother. Why didn't you make a fuss when we stole you, anyway? If you'd yelled, your nurse would have come running."

The troll baby looked sly. "I know. But jus' fink of the fuss when they find I'm missing. What fun, what fun!" It threw itself backwards in glee. "Ooh, the rushing about! Ooh, the screaming!" It popped up over the edge again. "My mammy will be *so-oo* mad with you. Better be nice to me. Or she'll scratch your eyes out."

Unable to bear looking at the little troll for a moment longer, Sigurd threw more wood on the fire. Sigrid was stirring the groute as if her life depended on it. Her brother saw a tear fall glittering into the pot, and he put his arm around her neck.

"What's the matter, sis?"

"What's the *matter*?" Sigrid turned on him. "I want Ma and Pa, and Peer and Hilde. I want Eirik. And nobody's here, and that creature is sitting – sitting in Eirik's cradle, and..."

With a sob, she smeared her hand across her eyes. "I wish we'd never brought it back with us!"

The troll baby sat bolt upright in the cradle, gripping the edge with long, hairy fingers. Its broad pointed ears stuck out on each side of its head, and its eyes glinted green and slanting in its wrinkled face.

"She's crying," it remarked.

"Leave her alone!" snarled Sigurd.

The troll baby's eyes glittered. "I'm hungry. Feed me."

"It isn't ready," Sigrid began, but the troll baby screamed, "Feed me, feed me, *feed me*! Or tell me a story."

"We don't know any stories!" Sigurd shouted.

"Ye're a liar," the troll baby shrieked, jerking to and fro in fury. The cradle rocked, and its eyes opened wide. "Save me! It's an earthquake. The whole world moved!"

"Only because you were having a tantrum," said Sigrid sharply. "Sit still."

"Did I do it?" The little thing smirked. "Be nice to me, or I'll do it again."

"Ooh, I'm so scared," said Sigurd. Sigrid nudged him.

"*I* know a story," the troll baby boasted. "It's one my mammy tells, to send me off to sleep." It winked, coughed, wriggled, and began: "An old wife was spinning away one night, and 'Oh,' said she, 'I wish I had some company.' So the door creaked open, and in came a pair of big flat feet, slapping across the floor to the fireside."

The twins looked at each other uneasily. The troll baby grinned, and chanted: "In came a pair of thin shanks, and sat down on the big flat feet. *And still she sat, and still she spun, and still she wished for company*!

"In came a pair of great big knees and sat down on the thin shanks.

"*And still she sat, and still she spun, and still she wished for company*!

"In came a pair of thin, thin thighs and sat down on the great big knees.

"*And still she sat, and still she spun, and still she wished for company*!

"In came a pair of great big hips and sat down on the thin, thin thighs.

"*And still she sat, and still she spun, and still she wished for company*!"

At every verse, the troll baby looked at the door, and then followed something across the floor with its eyes. The twins gazed, dry mouthed. "I don't like this story," said Sigrid.

"In came a narrow waist and sat down on the great big hips.

"*And still she sat, and still she spun, and still she wished for company*!

"In came a pair of broad shoulders and sat down on the narrow waist.

"*And still she sat, and still she spun, and still she wished for company*!

"In came a pair of thin arms and sat down on the broad shoulders.

"*And still she sat, and still she spun, and still she wished for company*!

"In came a pair of great big hands and sat down on the thin arms." With gleaming eyes, the troll baby flapped its own hairy hands at the twins.

"*And still she sat, and still she spun, and still she wished for company*!

"In came a thin neck and sat down on the broad shoulders.

"*And still she sat, and still she spun, and still she wished for company*!

"In came a great big head and sat down on the thin neck.

"*And still she sat, and still she spun, and still she wished for company*!"

Sigurd cleared his throat. "Is that the end?"

"No!" the troll baby whispered, as if sharing a secret. "I'll tell you the rest! But firs', go an' look. Is it dark outside?"

Sigurd peeked through the shutters. "Getting dark, yes."

"Good," the troll baby giggled, "'cos this is a story you have to tell in the dark. So the old wife looked up from her spinning and she said, 'Why have you got such big flat feet?'

"'With walking, with walking!' says the thing as it sits by the fire.

"'Why have you got such thin shanks?'

"'*Aiiii – late – and wee-eee moul*!'" The troll baby threw back its head and let out a wailing scream that made Sigrid nearly jump out of her shoes.

"'Why have you got such big knees?'" the troll baby went on. "'With kneeling, with kneeling!'

"'Why have you got such thin thighs?'

"'*Aiii – late – and wee-eee moul*!'

"'Why have you got such big hips?'

"'With sitting, with sitting.'

"'Why have you got such a narrow waist?'

"'*Aiii – late – and wee-eee moul*!'"

"Thanks," broke in Sigurd. "We've got the idea. Why don't you just stop, right now? Is the groute ready, Sigrid?"

"Nearly," quavered Sigrid, slopping some into a bowl.

"I'll have some in a minute," said the troll baby. "So the old wife asked:

"'Why have you got such broad shoulders?'

"'With carrying brooms, with carrying brooms.'

"'Why have you got such thin arms?'

"'*Aiii – late – and wee-eee moul!*'

"'Why have you got such big hands?"

"'Threshing with an iron flail, threshing with an iron flail.'

"'Why have you got such a thin neck?'

"'*Aiii – late – and wee-eee moul!*'"

Sigrid had her hands over her ears. "Make it stop, make it stop!"

"Take this, and shut up," said Sigurd roughly, thrusting a bowl of groute and a horn spoon at the troll baby. The little troll put its head to one side. "Can't feed meself," it said coyly. "I'm a *baby*! You got to do it for me. Uggh!"

It choked as Sigurd, provoked beyond endurance, shoved a large spoonful into its gaping mouth. A large tongue came out and swept up the dribbles.

"Good," it spluttered greedily. "More! More!" With his face screwed up, Sigurd spoon-fed it the rest of the bowlful. The troll baby jigged up and down. "Now I'll finish the story. So the old wife asked:

"' Why have you got such a big head?'

"'With thinking, with thinking.'

" 'WHAT HAVE YOU COME FOR?'"

"'I'VE COME'" – the troll baby opened its mouth wide, wide, wide, and Sigurd and Sigrid saw for the first time that it had a full set of very sharp, very pointed teeth – "'**FOR YOU!**'" it yelled at the top of its voice.

Sigrid screamed. Sigurd jumped. The house was very dark, the fire struggling and sinking. "Listen!" The troll baby leaned towards them with its hairy ears waggling. "Can you hear footsteps? I can. Little feet, going pitter-patter, pitter-patter. My mammy's coming down the hill to fetch me. An' she won't be alone."

"Oh, no!" Sigrid's voice shook. "What shall we do?"

"They can't get in. Don't worry." Sigurd was very pale. The troll baby curled up like a caterpillar and rolled around and around inside the cradle, giggling.

Then with a muffled noise, someone outside seized the door and shook it. The twins caught at each other. A voice called.

"Children, are you there? Open the door! Let us in!"

"It's Ma!" Sigrid flushed with relief. She started forwards to undo the bar; but Sigurd was looking at the troll baby, which pulled itself upright, ears pricked.

"Tee hee," it sniggered. "Are you sure?"

"Wait, Sigrid," said Sigurd quietly. She froze. "Why?"

"It might not be Ma."

"But that's her voice!"

They crept up to the door, listening intently. All at once Sigurd shouted, "Who is it?"

"It's me, it's all of us!" the voice reverberated through the thickness of the wood. It *sounded* like Gudrun: but how to be certain? "Quickly, let us in!"

"Who's afraid of the big, bad wolf?" the troll baby sang tunelessly. It screeched with laughter. "What are you waiting for? Let them in!" Still the twins hung back in agonised uncertainty. Fists beat on the door in an urgent tattoo.

"Open up, let us in! Open the door, twins, *quick*! The trolls are coming!"

CHAPTER 37

Granny Greenteeth's Lair

PEER CROUCHED AMONGST tangled willows and elders, down the bank from the old pigsty, scratching his midge bites. Loki lay beside him. It had been a hot, thirsty, endless day. But the sun was down behind the trees now, and the shadow of the mill stretched far across the bland green water. Soon, surely, the lubbers would come creeping out of the woods.

Gudrun and Hilde were out of sight in the bushes on the other side of the millpond. As for the Nis, it had vanished. Maybe it was scouting in the woods or hiding in the brambles.

Peer couldn't bear to think of the babies, alone with the lubbers. How terrified they must be! And he had a darker fear, one he hadn't shared with Gudrun or Hilde. *What happens if the lubbers get really hungry*?

The last glowing warmth on twigs and branches vanished. A cold breath ruffled the water and the leaves whispered. Darkness gathered under the trees.

Just along the bank, two twisted willows leaned together. Their long branches quivered and parted. Out hobbled an old woman in a dingy black cloak, her head wrapped in a scarf.

Granny Greenteeth! Peer scrambled up, his heart leaping with dread. Was she here to meet the lubbers – or to gloat? Loki pressed against his legs, growling.

The old woman beckoned. "Peer Ulfsson," she called softly. "Come closer. Let me take a look at you. Why, what a fine young man you've grown to be. But rash and foolish, eh, like all young fellows? I've got a bone to pick with you!" Webs of greenish skin stretched from the skinny forefinger she pointed at him.

"The babies – where are the babies?" Peer's mouth was so dry, the words came out as a croak.

"For three years, Troll Mill was empty," Granny Greenteeth said dreamily. "And I'm patient, very patient, my son. I can wait for the mill to *rot*." The last word was louder. "I can send my winter floods sucking at the foundations. One day, the wheel will break, the walls will tumble, and my waters will run free.

"But you came back. Meddling. Interfering. Patching and mending and building up. You'd have the mill clattering away day and night, night and day, with never a moment's peace for me in my water – you and Baldur Grimsson."

"I've nothing to do with him," said Peer fiercely. "Don't talk as if I have!"

"I'll say what I like, my fine young cockerel. Let's come to an understanding. A poor boy, alone in the world, has to take what he can. I can help you, if you'll help me."

"How?"

She gave a low chuckle. "A life, just a little one. Nothing you can't spare. The seal child. You're waiting here for her, aren't you? But she's mine. You go quietly away now, and leave her to me."

Between revulsion and relief, Peer couldn't reply. *She hasn't got Ran! So the babies aren't drowned!* Granny Greenteeth misunderstood his silence. She rubbed her twitching fingers together, like the pale, whiskered things that crawl at the bottom of ponds. "Good boy. See how easy it is? You don't have to *do* anything. Just go away. The others will never know. Let old Granny keep the bairn, and Granny will give you the mill."

Clammy white mist formed over the mill pond, drifting up the banks in clinging wreaths. Surely it was full of ghosts.

She thinks it's just Ran the lubbers have got. She doesn't know about Eirik or the twins. What does that mean? Keep her talking.

Peer dragged out the words slowly. "What you're asking me to do would be murder. The baby would drown."

"Yesss..." Granny Greenteeth sighed. Her shallow jaw opened, showing rows of narrow sloping teeth. "Yesss, they only stay warm for a little while. Then they go cold and silent, and the stream tumbles them out of my arms... but this one's different. Like me!" She spread out her webbed hands. "A seal child, a water baby. Only half human. I'll hold her tight, till the mortal part... dissolves, and she'll be mine for ever. Mine to bring up as my own."

"Turn little Ran into a creature like you?" Peer choked.

Granny Greenteeth hissed. "Don't cross me, boy. Think. How will you like it, alone there at night, afraid to look round in case old Granny's *behind you*?"

Her voice hushed to a rippling lilt. "But Granny's always had a soft spot for you. We won't quarrel. We'll deal with your uncles together. We'll make your dreams come true. The mill will be yours. Yours. And I'll have my child."

Before Peer could answer, something small and excited rushed through the undergrowth, chirping, "Quick, Peer Ulfsson, quick! The lubbers is coming!" And from somewhere up the hillside came a rustling and crackling, and the unmistakeable sound of Eirik yelling.

"Stand aside!" Granny Greenteeth pointed at Peer.

"HILDE!" Peer bellowed. "Gudrun! Get over here, quickly! Bring those blankets!"

The lubbers burst through the trees. In the dusk their limbs gleamed like white roots. Granny Greenteeth swung round greedily. Her pale tongue flickered, tasting the air. "At lassst! They've brought my child."

Peer saw Eirik, riding on the second lubber's shoulders, and realised in amazement that his screams were not screams of terror, but yells of delight at this fast, romping ride. He saw Ran, her face a dim blob, tucked under the arm of the second lubber.

Hilde and Gudrun arrived, pelting through the mill yard and slithering down to the brink of the mill pond. Seeing Eirik with the lubbers, Gudrun shrieked and dropped the blankets. Peer snatched them up.

"Hey!" he shouted, flapping them, and the lubbers flinched and jumped. "We've got blankets for you. See? Lovely blankets, right here!"

The lubbers gaped at Peer, and at the dark figure lurking in the mist. "We got an agreement with Granny Greenteeth," one of them croaked. "Gennleman's honour – and all that..."

"It's a trick," screeched Hilde. "She hasn't got any blankets. She'll only drown you!"

"Meddling little miss!" Granny Greenteeth drew herself up, swaying. Her eyes widened into white circles, and her voice thickened and slurred. "That child is my price. Sssssss! My price. I'll have the ssseal baby."

Gudrun rushed at her. "You shan't have *any* of my children!" But she clutched at a moving wraith of mist. Granny Greenteeth had fallen to the ground. Her arms melted to her sides in long dark ribbons. Her body twisted and thrashed. A huge eel lay coiling in the grass, snapping at Gudrun's ankles.

As Gudrun jumped back with a cry, it slid swiftly over the bank and into the mill pond. The water closed over it with a swirl of oily ripples.

"She's gone," Peer cried. "All right, you lubbers. Hand over the babies, and we'll give you the blankets."

The lubbers looked at each other.

"Do as he says," growled the first. "I'm sick of carting them around." It turned to Peer. "Throw us the blankets!"

Peer hesitated, then tossed the blankets so that they fell halfway between the lubbers and himself. The second lubber lowered Eirik to the ground and drew back. Eirik crawled towards Gudrun, who darted at him. "My darling!" She caught him up, but Eirik twisted round to look back.

"Man," he cooed. The second lubber whimpered, and its eyes gleamed.

The first lubber hung back, holding Ran up like a shield.

"Put her down," demanded Peer.

"You don't need 'em both!"

"Both babies, or no blankets." Peer's voice shook with tension. He stepped forwards.

"All *right*, all *right*!" the first lubber screamed. Without warning it tossed Ran into the air, and dived for the blankets.

Then everything happened at once, and it seemed to happen very slowly. Peer saw Ran arcing towards him, her arms flying wide, her head tipping back. He seemed to stare for hours into her eyes. At the edge of sight he saw Gudrun turn, her mouth opening in terror; he saw Hilde lunge forward, but yards out of reach. His own arms came up. He plucked Ran out of the air. Trying to protect her from the impact, he reeled, and then was falling, falling slowly backwards, the baby clutched to his chest. He still had time to see everything as he fell: Gudrun and Hilde screaming, the lubbers grovelling for the blankets, Loki barking, the Nis jumping about. He fell through a layer of white mist, and all the people on the bank faded like phantoms. Then the mill pond hit him in the back.

There was a crash of water in his ears, and water filled his eyes and rushed up his nose, and covered his face. He lost hold of Ran.

Everything was black. Which way was up? He thrashed for air and light. With terror he felt a muscular body bend briefly against his side and glide on past.

He slipped into a colder layer. His groping hands touched something impossibly soft, melting ghost-like from his fingers. Mud – the mud at the bottom of the mill pond. He could sink into it and go on sinking for ever.

He was strangling. Stars tingled in the water. Something caught in his clothes: a hard root or tangle of branches. He wrenched desperately, feeling clouds of mud billowing past him like smoke.

Then he saw her, or thought he did: Granny Greenteeth in human form, sitting on the bottom of the mill pond with Ran in her arms. A greenish light clung around them. Granny Greenteeth's hair was waving upwards in a terrible aureole as she bent over Ran, rocking to and fro.

The flashing stars turned red. He could see Ran's face by them, blood red and sickly green. Her dark eyes stared out into the water, expressionless, hopeless.

So this was the end of little Ran's short life. She might be a seal baby, she might last longer underwater than another child, but she would still drown. And then? Would some inhuman part of her linger in the mill pond, to be brought up as Granny Greenteeth's child – another malignant water spirit to haunt the mill? He thought with fierce sorrow of Bjørn tickling Ran, Sigurd whistling to her, Gudrun feeding her.

She never had a chance.

But she has me! Rage crackled through him. He struggled like a madman. The obstruction holding him gave way. Plunging his arms into the mud, he pulled himself forwards, stirring up more sediment. Granny Greenteeth, her head bowed, did not see. He reached for Ran. His hands clamped around her small body, and he pulled her away. Granny Greenteeth looked up. Her eyes fixed on him, lidless and blank and terrible. She lunged at him jaws wide. He gave a last, desperate, flailing kick, and a flash of scarlet lightning blotted out his sight.

With a roar and a rush, the other world came back: the world of air and light and sound. His head broke through into a mild, twilit evening. He stood, staggered, nearly fell, floundering waist-deep in the pond. Pain stabbed his chest, and he clasped little Ran as though a knife skewered them together. Any minute now, Granny Greenteeth would grab his legs. He choked, choked again. Half the mill pond seemed to pour from his throat and nose.

"Peer! Over here!" Hilde was halfway into the water, clinging to a willow branch with one hand and stretching out the other. "Back!" Peer spluttered. "Or – she'll get you!"

Against his chest the baby jerked, convulsed, opened her mouth. She scrunched up her face, clenched her tiny fists, drew in a mighty breath, and let out an ear-shattering scream. Peer wallowed towards the bank, holding her: a cold little dripping morsel, hiccupping and kicking, and screaming again and again her indignation and fury and fright. Ran had found her voice at last!

He hauled himself up the bank, feeling as though he had

been underwater for hours, though it could have been no more than minutes. Loki and Alf dashed up to welcome him. Peer hugged them, and climbed shakily to his feet.

Eirik was crying. "Man!" he wailed, pointing in the direction the lubbers had run off, taking the blankets with them. "Man gone!"

"Home, right away." Gudrun set off through the mill yard, tight-lipped. Neither she nor Hilde looked happy, Peer realised. "What's th'matter?" he asked Hilde foggily as he stumbled along beside her. "We got the babies back."

She raised an eyebrow. "But not the twins."

The shock woke him right up. "I forgot!" He was tongue-tied with shame. *How could I? What must she think?* And he'd fallen into the mill pond, nearly drowning Ran. What an idiot!

"Oh, Peer!" Hilde's voice was low. "It was so awful when you went into the water. You were gone for ages. I thought you'd never come up. There, there," she added distractedly to Ran. "Poor little thing, you'll soon be home, and dry… If only the twins have got back. If only…"

They hurried up the path, Eirik and Ran trying to out-do one another. The wood rang with their uncontrollable grief, but as Peer lagged behind, he began to notice other noises. What was that whooping, high up in the birchwoods?

Gudrun was almost running, and Hilde hurried to catch up. The group was strung out along the track. As Peer came out of the wood, Gudrun was pushing at the farmhouse door.

"It's barred!" she called.

"Barred!" Hilde turned to Peer with excited eyes. "Then the twins must be here. They've come home!"

"Children, are you there?" Gudrun put her ear to the

door. "Open up! Let us in!" They waited, shifting restlessly in the dusk. Eirik had quietened, but Ran was still producing sniffling sobs. A boy's muffled voice, loaded with suspicion, called from inside, "Who is it?"

"That's Sigurd!" Gudrun sagged with relief. She turned back to the door. "It's me, it's all of us. Quickly, let us in!"

"Whatever's that noise?" Hilde broke in. Someone in the house was singing or chanting in an odd squeaky voice, and it didn't sound like either of the twins. The hairs prickled on Peer's neck. And there was that whooping in the wood…

He looked over his shoulder. Troll Fell reared against the sky like some enormous wave. A light shone from the crest, yellow as the evening star.

"Troll Fell's open! They've lifted the top of the hill. But… why?"

A yell sounded amongst the trees. There was a prolonged echoing crack of splintering branches. More cries – and a dark flood, pricked with torches, spilled from the edge of the wood.

"The trolls are coming," Peer shouted. "They've sent a whole army!" A stone flew past his head.

"Trolls!" Hilde hammered on the door. "Open up, let us in! Open the door, twins, quick!" More stones thudded against the house wall.

A wild figure came leaping over the foremost trolls, skirt kilted up, mouth wide open in a skirling yell. *The troll princess!* Peer thought dizzily. *What's she doing here?* Torch flames streamed over the attack.

"Let us in!" Gudrun beat on the door with the flat of her hand. At last there was a rattle and a clunk as Sigurd removed the bar. The door opened a crack. "It's them," they heard him shout, and the group of them pushed inside, the dogs squeezing between their legs. The door clapped shut. Peer and Hilde crashed the bar back into its slots and leaned on it, breathless.

Next second, it jumped and shuddered under an enormous blow.

"*Give me my child!*" screamed the voice of the troll princess outside the door.

"Her child?" Gudrun said. "What does she mean? We haven't got her child."

"That's what you fink, missus!" said a scratchy voice. Out of the cradle rose the wrinkled face and protruding hairy ears of the troll baby. It gave Gudrun a slow grin, showing every single one of its teeth.

"Oh my goodness!" shrieked Gudrun. "What in the world is that?"

CHAPTER 38

The Miller of Troll Fell

BEFORE ANYONE COULD answer, stones rattled on the wooden planking. The farmhouse trembled as the trolls stormed around the walls, plucking at the shutters and yelling.

Sigurd clung to Gudrun, shouting explanations. But Sigrid seized Eirik and hugged him tight. Tears poured down her face.

"Here," said Hilde into Peer's ear. She shoved a dry jerkin into his arms, and turned to strip Ran of her sodden clothing. Peer put it on, shivering. The noise outside was terrific. The dogs crept under the table.

Gudrun turned on the troll baby. "You! What's your name?"

"Me?" smirked the troll baby. "I'm jus' meself. No name yet, missus!"

"Is that your mother outside?" demanded Gudrun. In a lull in the racket, the troll princess's voice soared shrilly skywards: "I want my child!"

The troll baby winked. "That's her."

"I see." Gudrun's lips thinned. "The twins did very wrong to steal you away. No!" – as Sigurd tried to protest – "I'll speak to you later. She must have her child back *immediately!*"

"Ma," protested Hilde, "if we open that door, they'll tear us to pieces!"

At that very moment, someone leaped on to the roof with a tremendous thump. Heavy footfalls thudded from one gable end to the other, and back again. Crash, crash, crash! The rafters groaned in warning.

A fearsome face plunged through the smoke hole and twisted about, glaring. The mouth was at the top; the eyes were at the bottom: it shook a ruff of sooty hair and screeched, "I can see him, princess! I knew they'd be hiding him here. I'll punish them for you. I'll rip their arms and legs off!"

It was Baldur Grimsson, looking in upside down. Hilde jabbed a broom at him. He disappeared, but they heard contemptuous laughter. What if he came through the roof?

"Rock-a-bye, baby," giggled the troll in the cradle. Gudrun advanced on it, rolling up her sleeves, and it squealed. "Don't hurt me!"

"I wouldn't dream of it," said Gudrun. "But you're not staying here another minute."

"Wait, Gudrun." Peer caught her arm. "Let me out first. I'll try and draw Uncle Baldur off."

"Peer, are you mad?" Hilde shouted.

"No. I've got an idea. No time to explain." He seized a pinewood torch – Ralf kept a collection of trimmed branches near the door – and shoved it into the embers. It crackled and flared. He looked round at the family. *His* family.

Ralf told me to look after them. And I will. He slipped his free hand into his pocket. It was half full of wet silt, but the carved comb was still there.

"Here, Hilde. I made this for you. Sorry it's got a bit dirty – but you'd better have it now. When I tell you, open the door." He cupped a hand around his mouth and yelled. "Uncle Baldur! Can you hear me? Who's the miller of Troll Fell? You… or me?"

He nodded to Hilde. "Now!"

She flung herself at the door. As soon as it was wide enough, Peer slipped out. As it slammed behind him, he charged through the assembled trolls, waving his torch so fiercely that they fell back.

"UNCLE BALDUR!" he yelled again. "COME AND GET ME!" He turned and looked, poised to run.

The Grimsson brothers were outlined against the sky, monstrous riders sitting astride the ridge and kicking great wounds in the turf roof. But now they saw him. They both rose, towering against the stars.

"COME AND GET ME!" Peer taunted once more, and waited till he saw both his uncles run down the slant of the roof and leap into the crowd of trolls. Then he took to his heels.

Gudrun swung the troll baby out of the cradle. It eyed her with alarm, flattening its ears. "Don't squirm," she told it grimly. "I'm going to have a word with your mother."

"No, Ma!" said Hilde.

"Well? Surely you don't want to keep it?"

"No, but—"

"And you'll agree that the trolls didn't steal the twins? Or Ran, or Eirik?"

"No, but—"

"Then this time, *we're* at fault, and I'm not afraid to admit it. Lift the bar."

"But..." The words died on Hilde's lips. She did as she was told.

"Stand back!" commanded Gudrun. She marched out with the troll baby in her arms.

A shout went up from the trolls. Looking over her mother's shoulder, Hilde saw them swarming round the doorway, thick as angry bees. In front of Gudrun stood the troll princess, her wild hair floating out, a coronet of leaves slipping from her head, her slanted eyes flashing. "*Aha*!" she hissed.

"Mammy!" said the troll baby feebly.

"My precious princeling!" The troll princess snatched her child from Gudrun and squashed it against her bosom. "My little king!" She glared at Gudrun. "How dare you steal him from me?"

"Mmmf. *Mmmf*." The troll baby struggled to breathe. It bit. The princess loosened her clutch, squealing.

"Mammy, don't fuss," it complained. "Anyway, it wasn't her that took me. It was her children. No, stop it – get off..."

It disappeared into another stifling embrace. The princess stepped forwards, snarling, "*Your children stole my baby?*"

"He's been perfectly safe," Gudrun cried. "They meant no harm. They took your – your son – because they thought the trolls had stolen their own little brother and sister. Believe me, I've been as upset as you have."

A muffled howl came from the troll baby. It popped out its head, tousled and breathless, with crumpled ears. "Let *go*! I want those children, Mammy. I wanna – I wanna – I wanna play with them!" It bared its teeth and bit her again.

"Ouch!" The troll princess snatched her fingers away. "Naughty little – poppet! It's all in fun," she added hastily to Gudrun. "He doesn't mean it."

"Just so," Gudrun agreed with an odd smile. The crowd of trolls pressed closer to the door, buzzing. The princess lashed her tail suspiciously, breathing hard. Gudrun maintained her smile. The troll baby crossed its eyes, sticking out a long purple tongue.

Then the princess sprang forwards. Gudrun recoiled, stepping on Hilde's toes. But the princess cast herself into

Gudrun's arms, crying dramatically, "I was wrong! My baby needs you. Your children shall be his little playmates. We must be friends. Who but a mother can understand a mother's heart? Ah, the little ones. What a trial they are! How one suffers!"

Open-mouthed, Hilde watched her mother patting the troll princess on the back, the troll baby awkwardly squished between them.

"It's your first, isn't it?" Gudrun was asking. "Of course. Now don't you worry, my dear, it's – he's – fine. Never mind his tantrums. He's been fed, so he can't be hungry. He's – um – he's very *advanced* for his age!"

"Oh, do you think so?" The troll princess drew back and looked at her infant with tearful pride. "I was a little worried – he only has thirty teeth."

Ma clearly had things under control. Hilde slithered past her mother, out of the door, and threaded her way through the squeaking, jostling, chattering trolls. She broke into a run. She had to find Peer.

Peer burst out of the woods and raced down the track to the mill. The wind blew the torch flames shrunken and small: he was afraid it would go out. He was afraid of tripping. He was afraid the Grimssons would catch him. Worst of all, he was afraid that they would give up the chase and go back to the farm.

He reached the mill pond and risked a glance back. Were they behind him? *Come on, come on!* He jogged anxiously from foot to foot. Had he out-run his lumbering uncles?

Start the mill! That would bring Uncle Baldur like a wasp to honey. He dashed up to the sluice and sidled along the plank. Holding the torch high, he pulled up the sluice gate one-handed: it came crookedly, and then jammed open. Water rushed through. With a creaking rumble, the mill clattered into life.

Angry yells echoed from the edge of the wood. Peer bounded back to the path and ran to the bridge, where, suddenly inspired, he waved the torch over his head and shouted, "Come on, you fat fools!" They came thundering down the hill, and he ran into the yard and waited, head high, heart pounding. The torch drooped in his hand, and the flames crept upwards, unfurling bright yellow petals.

Footsteps battered the bridge. Baldur and Grim charged around the end of the mill and into the yard. Baldur yelled with triumph and punched Grim in the shoulder. "We've got him, brother! He didn't even try to hide." Grim threw back his head and howled. Chests heaving, they moved towards him and Peer retreated, step by step.

"In a minute," Baldur growled. "I'm going to break every bone in your body. But before I do, you'll answer that question you asked me." He paused, trembling, and his eyes glowed in the torchlight, red as a rat's.

"Yes, you'll answer that question," he repeated, licking his lips, savouring the words. "And you'll answer it loud and clear. Who's the miller of Troll Fell, boy? You – or me?"

Peer backed another step. "Neither of us," he said quietly. The flames streamed from the end of his torch, twining towards his hand.

"What's that? Speak up, boy! WHO IS THE MILLER? WHO?"

"NO ONE!" Peer lifted his arm and hurled the torch – but not at Uncle Baldur. He sent it spinning up in a fiery arc. End over end it wheeled through the air and plumped down on the mill roof, amongst the thatch.

A fierce column of fire sprang into the night.

Uncle Baldur stood speechless, while the flames lit the yard a glaring orange. "Fire, Grim! Fire! Fetch water! Fetch water, you!" He whirled a fist at Peer, knocking him to the ground. "Fetch water! Buckets in the barn!" He trampled towards the mill pond, yelling.

While his uncles charged to and fro, Peer dragged himself up on his elbow. He gazed at his handiwork.

It was beautiful. A tracery of smoke trickled from the edges of the thatch, as if the whole roof were slowly breathing out its last, grey breath.

The smoke thickened. It came in dense, billowing clouds, which boiled, and climbed, and doubled. There was a sudden sucking *whoomph*. Flames and smoke rushed upwards. The whole roof crept and crackled. The eaves dripped glowing straws, which fell to the cobbles and started little fires of their own, or were caught in the updraught and whirled away burning into the night. And still the mill clacked stubbornly away, and under the blazing roof the millstones grumbled round and round.

The smoke spread across the yard, choking and blinding. Peer struggled to his knees, and then to his feet. Uncle Baldur had hit him hard, and when he put his hand to his forehead it came away dark with blood. He stood unsteadily, awed by the speed with which the mill had gone up. With stinging eyes he staggered towards the bridge.

Running down through the wood, Hilde smelled smoke on the air. She emerged from the trees and stared, transfixed. The mill roof was a bright lozenge of fire. Convolutions of smoke twisted up from it, their undersides lit a lurid orange. The trees around the mill seemed to shrivel in the blaze, their leaves withering. Sparks fell around her, even this far up the hill. The mill pond was a mirror of black and gold ripples. Figures were dashing about down there, dipping bucketfuls of water and flinging them at the mill roof. Hilde shook her head in disbelief. *Can't they see it's hopeless?*

Where's Peer?

She tore down the hill, coughing in gusts of smoke, terrified Peer might be inside the mill. Torrents of water rushed past the blazing walls; the waterwheel chopped the mill race into blood-red foam. Hilde raced to the bridge. Someone loomed up out of the smoke cloud.

"Peer!" She seized him. "What happened?"

"I set the mill on fire."

"*What?*"

"Stop, Hilde – you've got a spark in your hair." He disentangled it and pinched it out.

"But Peer, why?" Hilde cried. "All that work! Your dream of being a miller! What will you do?"

Peer put an arm around her shoulders. "It would never have worked," he said. He gazed at the mill, and the flames filled his eyes. "I see that now. The mill brings nothing but trouble. Let it go."

Hilde gave a shout. "The roof!"

With an exhausted sigh, the centre of the roof collapsed. Chunks of blazing thatch tumbled into the racing water. One piece fell on to the wheel and was carried round till it plunged into the sluice and was extinguished.

"*Burned! All burned!*" The wild figure of Baldur Grimsson came charging though the clutter of flying sparks. He seized Peer, sobbing. "You! You destroyed it! I'll burn you, too.

You'll burn!" He dragged Peer towards the dam. Peer fought, punching and kicking, and Hilde grabbed Baldur's arm. He threw her off and forced Peer on to the plank above the weir. It sagged under their combined weight. At the far end of the plank roared the open sluice. The heat of the burning walls beat on their bodies. Under them raced the hungry water.

Peer hooked his free arm around one of the posts of the plank bridge, but Baldur jerked him away. They wrestled, right above the open sluice, Baldur trying to wrench Peer off his feet and pitch him into the burning building. Peer grabbed at the handle of the sluice gate.

"Hold on, Peer! Hold on!" Hilde screamed.

Baldur tore Peer loose, lifting him, his muscles bulging with effort. He flung his head back, hair and beard spangled with sparks, his tusks gleaming in the flames. Hilde hid her eyes, then looked through her fingers. Peer twisted out of Baldur's arms like an eel and threw himself flat along the plank, his arms wrapped round it, almost in the water.

What was that glistening swirl in the mill pond?

A green hand slid out of the scummy water and closed around Baldur's ankle. There was a sharp splash, and Baldur was toppling forwards. Like an oak tree struck by lightning, he crashed over into the sluice. The dripping vanes of the mill wheel struck him down, shuddering. Hilde rushed on to the plank. Peer pushed himself up, trying to scramble to his feet. There was nothing they could do. The wheel drove Baldur Grimsson deep into the black water, and he rose no more.

CHAPTER 39

Kersten

IN THE SMALL, cold hours before dawn, Hilde woke.

They had got back to the farmhouse to find the babies asleep, the trolls gone, and Gudrun tucking the exhausted twins into bed. She listened wide-eyed to their story. "Baldur Grimsson, drowned? What about his brother? Didn't Grim try to help?"

"We shouted for him," said Peer. "But I think Grim's more like an animal now. He came across the bridge, but he didn't seem to understand us. He just howled, and ran off up the hill."

"The mill's still burning," said Hilde. "There'll be nothing left by morning."

"Oh, Peer!" said Gudrun. "Your precious mill!"

Peer dropped wearily on to a bench. He closed his eyes.

Hilde coughed and turned to Gudrun. "What happened here? I left you gossiping with the troll princess, for all the world like a couple of neighbours chatting over a fence."

"Well," Gudrun said defensively, "she's not very old. I just gave her a few tips about bringing up children."

"I knew it! *Early to bed and early to rise* – that means *late* for trolls, of course – and the importance of settling them into a good routine," Hilde teased.

"She was quite grateful," said Gudrun with dignity. "And

the little prince spoke up and said what fun he'd had with the twins. Still, I felt that the twins didn't have as much fun as he had."

Sigurd sat up in bed. "Fun? It was awful. And then she invited us to his naming feast."

"Very gracious, I dare say," said Gudrun, "but it wouldn't have been wise to accept... So I told her our contribution would be the sheep they'd taken. That made her blush!" She yawned. "And then the Nis came back, happy as a dog with two tails, and lapped up its groute."

A spatter of rain struck the shutters and drove the smoke back down through the smoke hole. Gudrun cast an anxious eye at the rattling door.

"The weather's worsening. Oh, I do wish Ralf was here!"

Peer looked up. "Don't worry. Bjørn and Ralf and Arne know what they're doing. They won't set out unless it's safe."

So that had been that, and they had all gone to bed and slept like the dead – although in that case, Hilde thought, the dead must dream very strange dreams...

The wind blustered outside, like some big animal trying to get in. Was that why she'd woken? Then something moved on the bed, something light that pattered quickly across her legs. One of the cats? She opened her eyes.

The Nis was so shy of being seen, Hilde had never more than glimpsed it. Now it crouched beside her, pin-prick eyes gleaming, trembling as though all its bones had come loose.

"What's the matter?" Hilde breathed, enchanted but concerned. She lifted the bedclothes, and the Nis crept under them and burrowed down into the darkness. It went right to the bottom of the bed: she could feel it somewhere near her toes, shivering as continuously as a cat purrs.

Hilde lay stiff, unwilling to look into the room. *What could possibly frighten the Nis so much?* There was something there, she could feel it.

There was a sound, too, now she was listening. An eerie wordless humming mingled with the rushing wind outside. With it came a slow creaking that Hilde recognised. Somebody was rocking the cradle.

Skin prickling, Hilde sat up and peered around the panel of her bed. Across the dark room she saw the outline of a woman, rimmed in pale flickers, bending over the cradle. *Granny Greenteeth?* Her back was to Hilde, and she crooned that mournful, unearthly lullaby.

The crooning ceased. The woman turned. Her face was dark, shrouded in tangles of long hair. A cloak trailed to the floor from her naked shoulders, and the sea water ran from her in rivulets of blue fire.

"*Kersten*?" Hilde's heart banged.

The woman nodded. "My name was Kersten."

The air smelled of salt and seaweed, and there was a rushing sound in the room, like the tide creeping up the beach, or the sea in a shell. Hilde remembered the seal in the water, strong and happy in its own element. She knew without being told that the old Kersten was gone for ever.

Why did you leave Bjørn, Kersten? Why did you leave your baby? What happened to the girl who used to laugh and spin and cook the fish Bjørn caught, and joke with me in the summer evenings?

"Why…?" Hilde began, and couldn't finish. There was something hard in her throat.

"Everything ends as it must. And then begins again, like the waves," the seal woman whispered. "But get up quickly, Hilde, and come with me, if you want to save your father."

"What?"

"The black seal has tempted them out to the skerries. He

will sink the boat. Come now. Wake Peer. Leave your bed."

"The black seal! Who is he? What is he to you?"

"My husband, Hilde, my seal husband. I had a mate and children in the sea before ever I married Bjørn the fisherman." She wrung her hands. "Aiee! Seven years they were lost to me, seven long years I loved a mortal man. But the sea called me home. Never again for me the cradle and the hearth. Never again will I take my little child in my arms. Aiee!" She leaned over the cradle, and her hair fell across it in a loose curtain. "Farewell, my sweeting, my mortal darling. Look after her well, Hilde.

"Now come. There is no time to lose."

"How will we get there?" Hilde was scrambling out of bed.

"I will lead you. Hurry! You are needed, needed, out amongst the skerries… skerries…" How long that last word was, a lingering sibilance like a wave washing over the sand! The figure was fading, holding out two arms from which the sea fire splashed and spilled and vanished. Hilde rubbed her eyes. Not a glimmer remained; not so much as a wet spot on the floor.

But the warning was true; it ran in her blood like a fever. She pulled her dress over her shift, and jumped across the hearth to wake Peer. As she dragged back the panel of his bunk, Loki lifted his muzzle from Peer's legs and thumped his tail. *And that's why the Nis came to me. It doesn't like Loki.*

"Peer, wake up." He groaned, flung an arm over his face, tried to roll over. She shook him ruthlessly. "Wake up!"

"Wha'sa'marrer? 'S not morning yet…"

Hilde dipped a cupful from the water jar and threw it into his face. He sat up, shocked and gasping. "What's that for? I'm soaked!"

"Ssh! Don't wake mother. We've got to get up, Peer. I've just seen Kersten. She says Pa and the others are in danger, out by the skerries!"

Peer shook his head. "*Kersten*? Are you sure you weren't dreaming?"

"Ask the Nis! It's hiding at the bottom of my bed."

She peeled the blankets back to a muffled shriek. The Nis scuffled away from her, further and further down, pressing its face into the straw mattress. "Has she gone? Has she gone?" it kept asking piteously. Finally it hopped out, cross as a cat that has made a fool of itself, hair and beard straggling everywhere, and leaped straight into the rafters, tutting and muttering.

"Was it a ghost?" Peer asked. But the Nis refused to answer.

"It doesn't matter," Hilde whispered impatiently. "It was a warning. We've got to go, now."

"Out to the skerries?" Peer looked at her.

"*Yes!* If you don't come with me, I'll go alone."

"You know I'll come."

They opened the door together, lifting the bar down as quietly as they could. Wind whirled into the house. "On guard, Loki! Stay!" Peer ordered, as Loki tried to follow. Alf was still asleep, flat out by the fire. Perched high on the cross beam, the Nis watched them go, its little eyes glowing.

Clouds tore across the face of the moon, and wild shadows flew. Hilde crossed the yard, her cloak billowing. As Peer caught up with her, she caught his arm and pointed. "Look! There she goes, slipping between the trees. Come on. She'll guide us."

The wood roared about their heads, and the path was no more than a dim trace in the darkness, but Hilde seemed able to see her way. "She's ahead of us," she shouted over the noise of the wind. "She's beckoning."

They came down the hill to smell ash and burning. The mill was a patch of glowing red and black that creaked and ticked; and flurries of golden sparks chased in circles as the wind woke the embers. The handrail of the bridge was still hot to touch. Not even the great wheel had survived. Falling debris had jammed it solid, and the top half was burned away.

They hurried past the entrance to the yard and ran down to the village, past the sleeping, shaggy-roofed houses where the smoke blew to and fro, and up over the soft sand dunes, and down to the shore. Here the wind was even stronger. The fjord tossed and snored like an uneasy sleeper. Waves crashed on the pebbles. It would be very rough, beyond the point. "She's going into the sea!" Hilde cried, and the memory of Kersten plunging into the waves was so strong, that Peer almost saw her himself.

Hilde seized the prow of Harald's boat. "We'll take this one!" The wind whipped her hair across her face. "Can we sail her, Peer?"

"We'll try," Peer answered grimly. He jumped into the boat as it lay tilted on the shingle. It was a six-oarer, Harald's pride and joy: bigger than Bjørn's faering. He hauled the yard to the masthead. Hilde hurried to help him untie the tags which held the sail reefed. It unfurled, flying loose.

"Jump out and push!" They leaned on the boat, driving it down over the stones. The first cold wave caught Peer around the knees, and he felt the boat lift. Hilde sprang in. He followed, grinding an oar into the shingle to send them surging out, bucking over the wave troughs. Hilde hauled on the sheets and braces and the sail bellied out with a crack. Instantly they were yards from land.

"Sit down!" Peer yelled, and sat down hard himself, leaning

to grab the steering oar. The moon dashed out from between the clouds, the water rushed past the sides of the boat in long silky stripes. With a snort and a splash, something broke from a wave on the starboard side. Hilde cried out and pointed, but Peer had already seen the sleek head, pointed muzzle and dark eyes. The seal plunged past, leading them onwards: dancing ahead of them towards the fjord mouth.

The boat slipped over the water, supple as a snake. Spray flew in, rattling into Peer's face. He shook his head, and suddenly wild excitement swept him away. The whole broad fjord was their racecourse, and they sped along with hurtling clouds and streaming moon, while the dark mountains pressed in on either side to see the winner.

Beyond the mouth of the fjord they sped, into rough black water that snapped and chopped in white snarls of foam. Clouds poured over the moon. Darkness rushed from the north with stinging rain. The world vanished, leaving them tossing from wave to wave.

The moment of exhilaration faded. It was crazy to come out here for nothing but a dream or a ghost... How would they find Bjørn's boat? Where was their guide? The seal had gone. Maybe it was a trap, maybe they had been lured out here to their doom. Peer clung to the steering oar, as the boat kicked over the waves.

In the bows, Hilde screamed. "Rocks, Peer! The skerries!" The sea tilted upwards: spray burst around them. Then they were pitched away and hurled on, missing the black jawbone of rock by barely an oar's length.

Peer stared into the mirk. This was the seals' kingdom: their fortress and refuge. Here they would lie on the rocks and skerries, or dart through the dangerous waters. He imagined them, plunging into whirlpools that would suck down a ship, weaving through the tangled ribbons of the kelp forests, snatching fish from the darting shoals. Some had human faces, gleaming pale in the water. And one black shape came thrusting through the weeds, trailing a broken harpoon from its shoulder, eyes glaring angrily through the gloom…

The moon floated out past a cloud edge. Hilde screamed again. "A boat! That's the faering! PA!"

Through the constant spray Peer saw it too, a long low hull wallowing between the wavebacks; the mast bare; the three men wrenching at the oars, turning blanched faces at Hilde's call. The faering was riding low. There was a dark clot clinging to her prow, a great knot of seaweed perhaps, or a tangled net. No. It was alive. It threw black arms up and wrapped them around the bows, clambering out of the sea and into the boat. Man or seal? It sat there, heavy-shouldered.

With a shout, the nearest man let go his oars. The moonlight lit his blond hair and stocky frame: it was Bjørn. Twisting, he grappled with the creature. An eye-blink later, the faering turned over, flinging them all into the sea.

Hilde struggled with the sail. It came down higgledy-piggledy. The boat drifted, pitching. With nightmare urgency, Peer ran out the oars, fighting to keep the stern to the waves. Hilde was leaning out, stretching a spare oar to someone in the water. Peer threw his weight sideways. With a shuddering lurch, a man toppled over the side and fell on to the bottom boards, coughing water. It was Ralf.

His weight lent ballast to the boat. It became easier to handle. In the bows, Hilde raked out with her oar. The prow sliced through a wave, and Peer was wet to the waist. He cried out with the shock, but somehow the wave ran past, and the boat rode up again.

Ralf pulled himself up. He helped Hilde drag her oar back

in, with someone clinging to the blade. It was Arne, gasping for air. Two, saved from the sea! Peer heaved again on the oars, his back and arms aching with the strain. *But where's Bjørn? Where's Bjørn?*

How far away the others seemed: Ralf, Hilde, Arne, shouting, coughing, choking, trying to tidy away the yard and the loose sail, leaning over the side to search for Bjørn. Wrapped in his lonely task – *lift, reach, pull*! – Peer glanced up past the crooked yard to the masthead. Dawn was coming. The sea gleamed a cold grey, broken by dark skerries and white breakers.

That was when he saw another boat, keeping pace with them across the dim water. A black sail reeled against the sky, and the crew – how could the crew sit so still? Stiff as a row of ninepins, their faces turned away.

The draug boat…

He only saw it for a moment. Then a fresh rainstorm swept between and blinded him. Something knocked against the hull and went whirling past. A face glimmered through the water.

Fingers gripped at the boat's side, and then, as Peer watched in horror, unclenched and slid stiffly under. Everyone shouted at once. And Ralf, roaring, cast himself half overboard, Hilde clinging to his legs. The boat canted horribly. Peer dropped the oars and leaned out the other way. Arne was doing the same. They almost went over themselves as the vessel righted – and Ralf was hauling Bjørn out of the sea: Bjørn, his face white and blue, his hair streaming with water, his arms lolling. Ralf laid him gently down on his side. A broken-off harpoon was embedded in his right shoulder.

CHAPTER 40

New Beginnings

"I DON'T WANT to say much about it." Bjørn told them. Sitting in Ralf's chair next day, his shoulder bandaged, he looked white and tired, but peaceful. "The faering lurched, and I thought we'd struck. I turned, and there was the black seal grinning at me. I grabbed him, and the boat went over. We sank together, into the cold – throttling, strangling each other. He drove the harpoon into me. It barely hurt; I was numb. It hurts now!" He eased his shoulder, grimacing. "He left me. I was done for. I could see things, glimmering green – drifting wreckage, and twisting sea-worms questing about for drowned sailors, and the long weeds swaying from the rocks. Then something brushed past me in the gloom, another seal. It circled, nuzzling around me, pushing me up to the surface. I saw the boat go past, and I reached for the side. That's all I remember."

"That seal was Kersten," said Hilde certainly. "You see, she *did* care for you."

"She did," said Bjørn sadly. Arne leaned forward and gripped his brother's hand. "Hilde's dream saved us," he said.

Peer gave him a dark look. His own muscles felt as though they would tear every time he moved, and he didn't like the warm, admiring glance Arne cast on Hilde.

"Peer and Hilde both saved us," said Bjørn, as though he

knew what Peer was thinking. His face cracked into a broad grin. "Though it'll be a long time before Harald forgives you for stealing his precious boat."

"That Harald," sniffed Gudrun. "Sour as last week's milk. Oh, *hush*, Eirik!" She joggled Eirik, who appeared to be cutting a tooth. He snivelled on her shoulder, wailing, "*Man! Man!*" in between sobs.

"What's *wrong* with this child?" cried Gudrun in desperation. "Whoever heard of wanting a lubber for a nursemaid?"

"Put him down," Ralf suggested. "Let the Nis look after him."

Gudrun turned. "And where are you two going?" Caught sneaking out, the twins turned innocent faces towards their mother.

"To see the mill," said Sigurd. "To see if there's anything left."

"Not now."

"But that's not fair! We didn't get to see it burning—"

"Ssh!" Hilde whispered to them. "Peer's upset about it."

"But he set fire to the mill himself!" Sigurd objected. "Why should he be upset?"

"Because—"

"Hilde, leave it," said Peer loudly. "I'm not upset, and it doesn't matter. None of it matters!" He flung out of the house with Loki at his heels, banging the door behind him.

A grey drizzle hung over the farm. Peer splashed through the mud to the empty cowshed and sat on a pile of straw, cuddling Loki for company, furious with himself and the world. *It's just you and me again*, he thought, rubbing Loki's ears. The mill was gone. Uncle Baldur was gone, too, but in a strange way that didn't make Peer feel better.

What do I do now? Go back to helping Ralf – hanging around

Hilde? Arne's back; she won't even notice me.

He considered Arne gloomily. It was obvious that Hilde would like him. Tall, broad shouldered, with brown skin and blue eyes. That long white-blond hair that looked untidy on Bjørn looked sort of – heroic, on Arne. *Heroic. Arne looks like a hero. Of course, I look like a heron.*

He bit his fingers. So many stupid mistakes; no wonder Hilde couldn't take him seriously. Hiding from Uncle Baldur! Falling into the pond with Ran! What a clown!

He went to stand in the doorway, under the eaves of the shed, watching the raindrops collect and drip from the ragged edge of the thatch. After a while, because nobody came after him, and there was nothing better to do, he went back to the house.

And Hilde was using his comb, running it smoothly through her long fair hair. She looked up. "I never thanked you for this."

"It's not much," he told her.

"Not much? It's beautiful! You're so clever, Peer." She added casually, "People would pay good money for combs like this."

"They certainly would," Gudrun agreed.

"You could make anything," Hilde went on. "You could be a boat-builder, like your father!"

"There's a thought," said Bjørn. He had Ran on his knee. "I'll have to build a new faering. Could use a hand from a fellow who knows what he's doing."

Peer stared at them suspiciously. So they'd guessed what he'd been thinking. And they'd been talking about him, and trying to find ways of making him feel better, and in fact… in fact, it was working. He did feel better.

"That's not a bad idea," he said, amazed. He thought about

it. *A boat builder like Father. Yes.* It was as if his father was there, sitting in the warm family circle, watching him with quiet pride. He touched his father's ring, turning it gently on his finger.

Hilde grinned. "I told you so. You were never cut out to be a miller."

For a second, that stung. Peer opened his mouth to snap – but he began to laugh instead. He picked up Sigrid and swung her round. "You're so right! I'll be a boat builder. I'll build my own boats, and everyone will want them."

"Build one for me," Sigrid giggled.

"I will! And it will have a neck like a swan, and gilded wings and silken cushions, and the Emperor of the Southlands will hear of it and come courting you."

"What a useless sort of boat," said Sigurd.

"All right, for you I'll build a warship, Sigurd, with a striped sail and a fierce dragonhead, and you can go off in it, fighting and raiding."

Sigurd gave him a pitying look. "No. I shall be a farmer."

"And what sort of boat will you build for me?" asked Hilde.

Peer turned to her. "A boat that will carry two," he said, and was pleased to see her redden and look away. Arne's eyebrows went up thoughtfully. Gudrun's lips twitched.

"And the babies?" clamoured Sigrid. "What about Eirik and Ran?"

"Eirik needs a washtub, not a boat," Peer laughed. "As for Ran, well, I don't quite know. Shall I ask her?" He hoisted her out of Bjørn's arms and tickled her. "Any ideas, you?" he teased – and was rewarded with the widest, merriest, most infectious smile he'd ever seen. He found himself grinning breathlessly back at her gleaming red gums and crinkled nose.

"*Look* at her!" gasped Hilde. "Ran's smiling!"

"She's smiling!"

They crowded round to see, chattering excitedly, while Ran looked from face to face, beaming at them as if they were the most wonderful people in the world.

"You got her to smile. Well *done*, Peer!" Hilde banged him on the back, and he shook his head. "But I didn't do anything. I suppose she was just – ready."

"She can smile and she can cry! She's not a seal baby any more, is she, Ma?" Sigrid said.

Gudrun's eyes were wet, and she leaned on Bjørn's good shoulder. "This is a day of marvels, to be sure. A day of new beginnings. Bjørn, my dear boy, I think it's time we changed her name. We'll call her 'Elli' from now on, the name you wanted."

"Elli," said Sigrid softly. "Elli, my little sister."

Part Three

CHAPTER 41

Far Away in Vinland

THE MIST PERSONS are busy, crouching on wave-splashed rocks out in the gulf, blowing chilly whiteness over the sea. Their breath rolls over the beach, over the boggy meadowlands near the river mouth, and far up the valley into the dark woods.

A birch-bark canoe comes whirling downriver through the fog. Kneeling in the prow, Kwimu braces a long pole like a lance, ready to fend off rocks. Each bend, each stretch of rapids comes as a surprise. Even the banks are hard to see.

The river humps its back like an animal. The canoe shoots over the hump and goes arrowing into a narrow gorge, where tall cliffs squeeze the water into a mad downhill dash. Spray splashes in, and Fox, curled against Kwimu's knees, shakes an irritated head. Fox hates getting wet.

A rock! Kwimu jabs the pole, and the canoe swerves lightly away. It hurtles down a sleek slope and goes bouncing into roaring white water at the bottom. Again and again Kwimu flicks out the pole, striking here and there, turning the canoe between the rocks. Sometimes a whirlpool catches them, but Kwimu's father Sinumkw, kneeling behind him, gives a mighty thrust with his paddle and sends them shooting on.

A bend in the river. More rocks. Kwimu throws back his wet hair, every muscle tense. They dart down, hugging the base of the cliff where the water is cold and deep. The wet, grainy stone drips, and the mist writhes in weird shapes. There's a splash and an echo, and it's not just the paddle. The canoe tilts, veers. Fox springs up snarling, showing his white teeth and black gums, and for a heartbeat a thin muddy hand clutches at the prow. A head plastered with wet hair rises from the water. It winks at Kwimu with an expression of sullen glee, and ducks under.

"Look what you're doing!" Sinumkw shouts, and they're snatched into the next stretch of rapids.

The gorge widens, the cliffs drop back, and the canoe spills out into calm water flowing between high banks covered with trees. On either side, the grey-robed forest rises, fading into mist.

Kwimu twists around. "Did you see?" he bursts. "Did you see the Water Person – the Grabber-from-Beneath?"

Sinumkw frowns. "I saw nothing but the rocks and the rapids."

"He was there," Kwimu insists. "Fox saw him too."

His father nods. "Maybe. But if you'd taken your eyes off the water for a moment longer, we'd have capsized. So his trick didn't work. Anyway, well done! That's the worst stretch over. And we'll land here, I think."

He drives his paddle into the water. The canoe pivots towards the shore.

"But I thought we were going right down to the sea. Can't we go on in the canoe? It's so much quicker than walking," Kwimu pleads as they lift the canoe out of the water.

"Speed isn't everything," says his father. "Just look around. Who's been cutting trees here?"

Piles of lopped branches lie in the undergrowth. The bank is littered with chips of yellow wood. Sinumkw picks one up. "These aren't fresh. This was done moons ago, before the winter."

"Who would need so many trees?" Kwimu asks. His scalp prickles. There are Other Persons in the woods. Sometimes, in lonely parts of the forest, hunters hear the sound of an axe, chopping – and a tree comes crashing down, though no one is visible.

But his father is thinking along practical lines. "See here. They rolled the trunks into the river to float downstream. It could be enemies: the Kwetejk, perhaps. What if they've built a stockade at the river mouth, in just the spot we want to use?"

Kwimu thinks with a shiver of their fierce rivals from the north-west woods. "What shall we do?"

His father shrugs. "This is why we came, *n'kwis*, ahead of everyone else, to find the best place for the summer camp, and to look out for danger. Imagine if the whole clan was with us now – grandmothers, babies and all! No. We'll circle into the woods and climb the bluffs above the river. We can look down on the bay from there." He turns, setting off on a long uphill slant into the forest.

Kwimu follows. The encircling fog fills the woods with secrets. The trees are looming giants that drip and tiptoe and creak and murmur. But if there was danger, Fox would sense it; Fox would warn them. Reassured, Kwimu strokes Fox's cold fur and hurries after his father.

Snow lingers under the hemlocks and firs, and the buds on the birches aren't open yet. The forest is black, white and grey. A dozen paces ahead, Sinumkw climbs through swirls and pockets of vapour like a ghost passing through world after world.

The woods are full of mysteries…

Grandmother said that, yesterday evening, her bright eyes blinking in her soft wrinkled face. Kwimu thinks of her now, as he trudges uphill under the dripping trees. He sees her in his head, like a little partridge with bright plumage, wrapped in her big beaver-fur cloak with the coloured quillwork glinting in the firelight. She's tiny, but so strong. And she has the Sight. Everyone listens when she speaks.

Long ago, in the time of the Old Ones…

All the stories begin like this.

…in the old days, two brothers go hunting. And they find a deep ditch, too wide to jump. A strange, smooth ditch, scoured out of sticky red mud, twisting along between the trees. The track of a Horned Serpent: a jipijka'm track.

And this track is full of power.

One of the brothers climbs into the ditch to see what sort of thing made it. Aha!

His body changes. It bloats and swells and pulls out like an earthworm, growing longer and longer. His eyes widen and blaze, and two horns sprout from his head. He fills the ditch from top to bottom, he raises his head and hisses at his brother, he slithers away like a snake. The track leads into the lake. He plunges deep into the water, and no one ever sees him again.

The woods are full of mysteries…

In spite of his thick moose-hide robes, Kwimu is cold. Why did Grandmother tell that story? What does it mean? Everywhere he looks he sees omens. Layers of fungus like thick lips. A rotten log like a corpse rolled up in birch bark.

Can anything good happen on such a day?

The slope steepens, broken by small ravines where icy creeks hurry down to join the river. There are voices in the creeks, Kwimu is sure, voices that squabble and bicker. Perhaps it's the Spreaders, the nasty little people who peg you to the ground if you fall asleep by the stream-side.

They cross one creek near a waterfall. Spray has coated the boulders with ice, and the pool boils and froths like a black kettle. What if a huge head crowned with twiggy horns emerged from the water, snaking towards them on a long slimy neck? In this haunted fog, anything is possible.

It grows lighter. Kwimu follows his father along a knobbly headland that juts out from the forest into the white nothingness of the mist. He feels giddy, as if walking out into the Sky World. Down below, he knows there's a fine gravel beach and grasslands beside the river. The bay: their summer home, where the women will gather shellfish, and the men and boys take canoes out past the sand bars and over deep water to the islands, to fish and to gather birds' eggs. Right now none of that is visible. A mother-of-pearl sun peers through the haze.

All is quiet. But the mist tastes of smoke, sweet dry smoke floating up from below.

Fox growls. His fur bristles, full of prickling, warning life. Kwimu and his father exchange anxious looks.

They hunker down in the wet bushes, ill at ease. Smoke means people, but a friendly camp should be noisy with dogs, children, women chattering. Why the silence? If only the mist would clear. Kwimu begins to think he can hear muffled voices. Men talking – or arguing, for the sound becomes louder and sharper.

An appalling scream tears through the fog. Kwimu grabs his father. The scream soars into hysteria, and breaks into a series of sharp, yipping howls like a mad wolf. The morning erupts in shouts of anger and alarm, and a ring-ding, hard-edged clashing. Flocks of birds clatter up from the forest.

As if their wings are fanning it away, the mist thins and

vanishes. At last Kwimu and Sinumkw see what is going on below them, down by the river mouth.

The earth has been flayed. Scars of bare red soil show where the turf has been lifted. Two lumpy sod houses have been thrown up on a rising crescent of ground between the edge of the forest and the sea. They look like burrows, for the grass grows right over them, though smoke rises from holes in the tops. Between these houses – these burrows – men are swarming.

Men? Their faces are white as paint, and they seem shaggy round the head, like a lynx or bobcat. These are not the Kwetejk, not like any men Kwimu has seen. Are they the dead, returned from the Ghost World? But some pursue others, hacking with long axes, stabbing with lances. Some lie motionless on the ground.

Sinumkw taps Kwimu's shoulder. "Look!" His voice is awed, shocked. "In the river. *Jipijka'maq!*"

Kwimu drags his eyes from the scene below. The hairs rise on his neck. Tethered in the wide shallows where the river meets the sea, are two things – bigger than the biggest canoe – and surely they are alive? For each has a head, staring shorewards from the top of a long neck. Each head is that of a Horned Serpent.

The smaller of the two is red, and the horned head snarls open-jawed from the top of a slender curving neck. The larger one is striped red and black, and it lifts a goggle-eyed head, beaked like a screaming eagle.

"Grandmother's story," whispers Kwimu. "This is what it meant."

These people are *Jipijka'maq* – Horned Serpent people, shape-changers. They come from out of the water and under the ground. Their whiteness is not paint, but the bleached pallor of things you find under stones. Perhaps, any moment now, they will slither off on their bellies into their dark earth houses. But why are they fighting, and why are they here?

"Hah!" With a cough of disdainful laughter, Sinumkw points. "See the coward there!"

A man in a green cloak is running away from the fight. He's dragging a child along with him, a young boy. Past the end of the nearest house he stops, and pushes the child, pointing to the woods. The message is clear. "Run!" he's saying. "Run and hide yourself. Go!" The child is sent staggering with a hard shove between the shoulder blades. The man whirls and goes racing back.

So he's not a coward after all; he was trying to save the child. His enemies are coming to meet him. In the lead is a burly, bear-like man, obviously a chief. By his side is a boy no older than Kwimu, with long loose golden hair that floats behind him as he runs, yelling. The burly chief shouts an order to his warriors. They spread out to catch the man in green, who dodges and dashes like a hunted animal, heading for the river. And then he trips and falls.

The chieftain shouts again and points. His men scatter. The chieftain's right arm comes up, balancing his spear. He throws.

With whoops and howls his men run forward, closing in on the crumpled green bundle. The spear stands straight up, a marker pointing at the sky. It twitches, it wags to and fro. The green bundle is still moving, trying to crawl. Kwimu's breath hisses through his teeth.

The boy with the golden hair strolls up behind the men. The others let him through; the burly chieftain puts an arm round his shoulders. Together they gaze at the man on the ground. The chieftain tugs his spear out. The golden youth hooks a foot under the body, rolling it on to its back. The man's pale face comes into view. Still alive. His fingers open and close like claws.

Warriors taunt each other when they fight. If the man on the ground can still speak, this is the moment for his final defiance. And perhaps he does gasp something. But the golden-haired youth laughs. He puts the point of his long red blade to the man's throat, and shoves it in. Kwimu shuts his eyes. Only a blink, but when he opens them again, it's over.

He looks away, and freezes. That child – the child the man in green was trying to save! He's peering around the corner of the nearest house, clutching the sod walls with both hands, craning his neck. He sees the dead man, and shrinks like a snail when you tap its shell.

The burly chieftain gives orders, pointing this way and that. His men fan out and start searching between the houses. Kwimu sucks in his bottom lip. *They're hunting for the child. And they'll find him; there's nowhere to run.*

The child presses against the wall. Any moment now the men will come around the building, and there he'll be. Then Kwimu almost shouts. The child flings himself at the soft sod wall, digging fingers and toes into the cracks and crannies. He scurries up like a mouse, reaching the roof just as the nearest man rounds the corner. He lies flat. His light hair and clothes blend with the pale grasses growing on the turf roof, but he's still completely visible to anyone who glances up. In fact, Kwimu can see one of his feet sticking over the edge.

The man doesn't look up. He strides along with his head down. Kwimu hardly breathes. *Don't move. He's gone, but another one's coming. Don't move!*

Neither man looks up. It seems crazy, but they don't. Kwimu sighs silently, surprised by the strength of his feelings for this strange foreign child. Beside him, Sinumkw shakes with admiring laughter. "That little weasel! To fool all those warriors with one simple trick! Look, they can't think where he's gone."

It is funny, in a way, seeing the men poking and prodding around the houses, and gazing into the woods, when all the time he's a few feet above their heads, as still as a sitting bird. All the same, Kwimu's nails are cutting into his palms by the time the men give up. Maybe their hearts are not really in this search for a small boy. They return to the chief and his golden son, empty-handed.

The chief shrugs. It's clear he thinks it doesn't matter much. He gestures to the bodies lying on the ground, and goes on talking to his son. The men drag the bodies to the water's edge. They wade yelling into the cold river, carrying the bodies out to the smaller, slenderer of the Serpents, which jerks at its tether as if outraged at being given such a cargo. One by one, the dead are tumbled in.

Where's the child?

Sidling up the roof like a crab.

At least he's pulled his foot in – no, don't go near the ridge!

As if he hears, the child sinks down just below the ridge, but he keeps popping up his head and peering over. Kwimu bites his lip in agony. *Stop doing that, they'll see you!*

The chief gives another order. The child on the roof understands: he flattens himself again: and the men troop back to the houses and empty them. Everything is carried out. They stagger down to the river under bundles of furs, and heave them into the belly of the second Horned Serpent, the big one with the eagle's beak. They bring out gear, pots, sacks, weapons. Shouting, they load up with timber from a pile near the beach. "They're leaving!" Kwimu says with a gasp of relief. "They're going away!"

Sinumkw makes a brushing movement with his hand: *quiet*. He watches the scene below with a hunter's intensity.

At last, all is ready. A small, fat canoe collects the chieftain and his golden son – *they* don't have to wade through the freezing water. The chieftain hoists himself aboard the big Serpent, but his son is ferried to the smaller vessel, and leaps aboard. Kwimu shades his eyes. The boy strides up and down, pouring something out of a big pot. He upends the pot, shakes out the last drops, and tosses it overboard. With an arm twined around the Horned Serpent's painted neck, he catches a rope that uncoils through the air from the bigger vessel. He knots it at the base of the neck, and jumps into the waiting canoe. In moments, he's back with his father.

The men lift out long, thin paddles. Slowly the Horned Serpent turns away from the shore, swinging with the current till it's pointing out to sea.

Kwimu has never seen paddling like this before, with all the men facing the wrong way. How can they see where to go? But it seems to work. The red and black *jipijka'm* crawls away out of the river, loaded with furs and timber, towing its companion behind it – the red Serpent of the Dead.

They're going, and they haven't found the child. Does he know he's safe? Kwimu glances down at the roof.

The child is sitting up, staring.

Get down, get down – they might still see you...

But the child gets slowly to his feet. He stands on the rooftop in full view of the river. He lifts both arms, and starts to wave and scream. He's dancing on the roof, yelling in a shrill voice.

"He mocks his enemies!" says Sinumkw in deep appreciation.

But Kwimu isn't so sure. He's got a cold feeling that if he could understand, the child might be screaming, "Come back, come back! Don't leave me!"

But the two vessels are leaving the river, heading into the hazy waters of the bay. Something else now: they're casting off the rope. A feather of fire flies through the air, curving into the red Serpent. A moment later, flames splutter fiercely up.

"Oil," Sinumkw nods. "They poured in oil to make it burn."

Kwimu can actually hear it, crackling like a hundred spits. Black smoke pours up in a tall column. The red serpent body seems writhing in flames.

Down below, the child is scrambling off the roof. He drops the last few feet and goes racing over the ravaged grasslands towards the beach.

"Let's get him!" Kwimu turns to Sinumkw. "Please, *Nujj*..."

"No."

"Oh, please, *Nujj*. He's only little, and he's brave..."

"A bear cub is little and brave," says his father, "and if you take one for a pet, it will grow up into a big bear and claw your arm off."

Kwimu swallows. "I know... but can we leave him to die?"

"*They* have." Sinumkw nods towards the bay. "He's not one of the People, Kwimu. Not one of us."

"But you like him," says Kwimu desperately. "You laughed at the way he tricked the warriors. See – Fox approves!" Fox twists his head and licks Kwimu's hand to encourage him. Kwimu's words come from deep inside him, like a spring of water that has to bubble out. "He might become your son, Nujj. My brother."

Sinumkw looks at him. He sighs. "Well. We can try. Perhaps the cub is young enough to tame. Don't be surprised if he bites you."

The slope ahead is too steep to descend. They turn back into the woods to find another way down. Kwimu looks back once more at the burning vessel, and is in time to see it tip up and slide neatly under the water. The snarling serpent head vanishes last, and nothing is left except for drifting smoke fading against the sky.

The other *jipijka'm* is already out of the bay and turning up the gulf towards the open sea: and from this distance it looks more like a serpent than ever – a living serpent, swimming quietly away through the haze.

Down on the shingle, nine-year-old Ottar, young son of Thorolf the Seafarer, stands knee-deep in the cold waves. Tears pour down his cheeks. He's orphaned, desperate, stranded in this horrible place on the wrong side of the world. He hears a shout from the beach behind him. He turns, his heart leaping in wild, unbelieving hope. Somehow it's going to be all right – it's been a bad dream or an even worse joke – and he won't even be angry. He'll run to whoever it is, and cling to them, and sob until the sobbing turns into laughter.

And then he sees. His mouth goes dry. Coming towards him on the rising ground between him and the houses are two terrible figures. Their long hair is as black as pitch, and tied with coloured strings. Their clothes are daubed with magic signs. Furs dangle from their belts. They are both carrying bows. But the frightening thing – the really frightening thing about them – is that you can't see their expressions at all. Half of their faces are covered in black paint, the other half in red.

Their eyes glitter white and black.

“Skraelings!” Ottar whispers. “Dirty Skraelings!”

He prepares to die.

CHAPTER 42

Water Snake

THE GREEN SEA slopped around Peer Ulfsson's waist, and rose to his chest. "Yow!" he yelled. As the wave plunged past, he bent to look through the water.

There! He saw it: the hammer he'd dropped. His fingers closed on the handle as the next wave swept past his ears and knocked him over. He rolled backwards in a freezing froth of bubbles and sand and struggled up, spluttering but brandishing the hammer in triumph.

"Got it!"

"So I see." Bjørn's face was one wide grin. "If you'd tied it to your wrist like I told you, you wouldn't have had to do that. Get dressed: you look like a plucked chicken."

Peer laughed through chattering teeth. He dragged his discarded jerkin over his head, fighting wet arms through the sleeves. It fell in warm folds almost to his knees, and he hugged his arms across his chest. "Aaah, that's better. I'll leave my breeches till I've dried off a bit… Who's shouting? What's wrong?"

Bjørn stiffened, shading his eyes to look down the fjord. "It's Harald. He's seen a ship. Yes – there's a strange ship coming."

Peer jumped up on the new jetty and joined Bjørn at the unfinished end, where the last few planks waited to be nailed down. Out where the shining fjord met the pale spring sky he saw a large, reddish sail, square-on, and the thin line of an upthrust prow like the neck of a snail. A big ship running into Trollsvik before the wind.

"Who is it?"

Bjørn didn't take his eyes off the ship. "I don't know the sail. Could be raiders. Best not take chances. Run for help, Peer. Tell everyone you can."

A lonely little village like Trollsvik could expect no mercy from a shipful of Viking raiders. Peer turned without argument, and saw people hurrying across the beach. "Look, Harald's raised the alarm already. Here he comes, with Snorri and Einar..."

"Hey, Harald!" Bjørn bawled at the top of his voice. "Whose ship is that?"

A bandy-legged man with straggling grey hair raised an arm in reply as he puffed across the shingle and climbed painfully on to the jetty.

"No idea," he wheezed. "You don't know it, either?"

"Not me," said Bjørn. Peer looked at the ship – already much closer – then back at the little crowd. Most of the men had snatched up some kind of weapon. Snorri One-Eye carried a pitchfork, and old Thorkell came hobbling along with a hoe. Einar had a harpoon. Snorri's fierce, grey-haired wife Gerd came limping after him over the stones, clutching a wicked-looking knife. Even Einar's two little boys had begun piling up big round stones to throw at the visitors. Peer wondered if he should join them. Then he realised he was holding a weapon already. His hammer.

He hefted it. It was long-handled and heavy. When he swung it, it seemed to pull his hand after it. As if it wanted to strike. *Could I really hit anyone with this?* He imagined smashing it into someone's head, and sucked a wincing breath.

The neighbours were arguing.

"No fear!" yelled Gerd, lowering her knife. "See the dragonhead? That's Thorolf's ship, the old *Long Serpent* that Ralf Eiriksson sailed on."

"It never is," Snorri turned on his wife. "Thorolf's been gone two years now, went off to Vinland."

"So what?" Gerd was undaunted. "He can come back, can't he?"

"Fool of a woman," Snorri shouted. "That's not his ship, I say! This one's as broad in the beam as you are – the *Long Serpent* was narrower—"

"That isn't the *Long Serpent*," Peer put in. "I should know. My father helped to build her."

"This looks like a trader," Einar said. "Built for cargo, not war."

"That's all very well, Einar. Plenty of traders turn into raiders when it suits them – doesn't mean her crew won't fight."

"What do you think, Bjørn?" asked Peer in a low voice. "Will we have to fight?"

Bjørn gave him a glance, half-humorous, half-sympathetic. "I don't know. Let's put on a good show and hope they're friendly."

Peer tensed his shoulders and took a good grip on the hammer. The ship was so close now that he could see the stains on the ochre-red sail. The hull was painted in faded red and black stripes. A man stood in the bows, just behind the upward swoop of its tall dragon-neck.

We could be fighting in a few minutes. I might die… And with a jump of his heart he thought of Hilde, up at the farm on Troll Fell. What if he never saw her again? And who would warn her – who would tell her, if these men were dangerous?

There was a flurry of activity on board. Down came the sail in vast folds. Out came the oars to row her in. The villagers bunched like sheep.

The man in the bows cupped a hand round his mouth and yelled, "Bjørn!"

Bjørn threw his head up. "Arne!" he shouted back. "Is that you?"

Arne, Bjørn's brother! The villagers broke into relieved, lively chatter. Peer unclenched stiff fingers from the haft of his hammer. He wouldn't need it as a weapon after all: he could go back to knocking in nails.

Could he have used it? Would he be any good in a fight? The word *coward* brushed across his mind. With a shrug that was half a shudder, he dismissed the idea. It didn't matter now.

"The ship's called *Water Snake*," Arne shouted across the narrowing gap of water. "Gunnar Ingolfsson's the skipper. He wants to meet Ralf Eiriksson."

"Who's this Gunnar? Why does he want Ralf?" Peer wondered, as the ship closed on the jetty.

"Gunnar Ingolfsson?" Bjørn snapped his fingers. "He's the man Thorolf took on as a partner, a couple of years ago. A sea rover, a bit of a Viking. He and Thorolf sailed off to Vinland together in two ships. So why's he here, and why's Arne with him?"

Peer shrugged. He wasn't curious about Arne.

"Vinland? Vinland?" muttered Einar. "Where's that?"

"The land beyond the sunset," Peer said eagerly, and Snorri added, "Remember? When Ralf and Thorolf found a new land all covered in forests…"

"I know that," Einar huffed, "but I thought they called it Woodland."

"They did!" Snorri waved a triumphant finger. "But other ships went there and found vines. Vines, Vinland, see? This Gunnar must be making a second trip. I've heard you can bring back a fortune in timber and furs and grapes. I've got half a mind to go myself."

"Ho, yes," scoffed Einar. "And how would you know what a grape looks like? Ever seen one?"

"Arne's a wild one," Bjørn said to Peer. "What's he done with his fishing boat? Sold it? He's crazy."

"He always wanted to go a-Viking," Peer pointed out.

Bjørn grinned suddenly. "That's why I say he's crazy!"

And that's why Hilde likes him, thought Peer. He wished he could do something exciting or brave.

The big ship came nudging up to the jetty. Seven or eight men were busy on board, lifting the oars in, collecting their gear. Arne threw a rope up to Bjørn. "Nice new jetty," he called, laughing. "Did you build it for us? It's good, this'll be easier for Astrid."

"Astrid?"

"The skipper's wife."

Everyone stared. Peer got a glimpse of a girl in a blue cloak, huddled under an awning which had been rigged up behind the mast. Arne climbed on to the jetty and wrung Bjørn's hand. He clapped Peer on the shoulder and said, "Fancy a voyage to Vinland?" before turning to offer a helping hand to the girl, who was clutching some kind of pouch or bag. A giant of a fellow with a shock of almost white fair hair tried to boost her up from the ship.

Peer watched scornfully. *Hilde wouldn't need helping out of a boat. She'd just kilt up her dress and jump out, laughing!*

Hilde, Hilde! She teased Peer, bossed him about, and drove him crazy. Last spring, he'd made the mistake of impulsively kissing her, and she'd laughed at him. He hadn't dared to do it since, except in dreams.

One day, he swore to himself, *one day when the time is right, I'll go to Hilde and ask her... or perhaps I'll say...*

No, I'll tell her: 'We just belong together.'

But would she agree?

"Hey! You!"

Lost in thought, Peer didn't notice the voice hailing him from the ship.

"You there – Barelegs!"

"Peer!" Einar jogged him in the ribs. "The young lord's talking to you."

"What?" Peer woke up. Had he heard what he thought he'd heard?

"He means you," Einar chortled, pointing. "Anyone else around here with no breeches on?"

Barelegs? Peer turned round and met the light, cold gaze of a boy his own age – seventeen or so, wearing a dark chequered cloak wrapped around his shoulders and pinned with a large silver brooch. Because the jetty was higher than the ship, his head was currently at about Peer's waist level, but this disadvantage didn't seem to bother him. He tilted up a tanned face as smooth as a girl's, but wider in the jaw, heavier across the brow. Loose golden hair fell about his shoulders and cascaded in a wind-whipped tangle halfway down his back.

But his eyes... they reminded Peer of something. Einar once had a dangerous dog with eyes like that, odd milky blue eyes, *wolf eyes*, he'd called them.

The boy snapped his fingers. "Are you deaf? I told you to help my father up on to the jetty. He's not well." And he took the elbow of a man standing beside him. This must be the skipper, the famous Gunnar Ingolfsson. His eyes were the same pale blue as his son's, but the rims were slack, and the flesh under them was pouchy and stained. Impatiently, he stretched up his hand. Gold arm-rings slid back to his elbow.

And then Peer saw with a shock that Gunnar's other hand was gone. The left arm swung short; the wrist was a clumsily cobbled-together stump of puckered flesh with a weeping red core. *One hand, look, only one hand…* the whisper ran through the crowd as Gunnar seized Peer's arm, trod hard on the ship's gunwale and pulled himself on to the jetty with a grunt of effort. He let go of Peer without a word, and turned immediately to join his wife.

The boy sprang up after him. "That's better, Barelegs," he said to Peer.

"My name's not Barelegs," said Peer, his temper rising.

"No?" The boy's eyebrows went up, and he glanced deliberately around at the villagers. "Does he actually own a pair of breeches?"

Einar snorted, Gerd giggled, and Einar's eldest boy made things worse by shouting out, "Yes, he does, and they're over there!"

There was a burst of laughter. Peer went red.

The boy smiled at Peer. "Now why did you have to take those trousers off in such a hurry? Were you caught short? Did our big ship scare you that much, Barelegs?"

Completely forgetting the hammer in his hand, Peer struck out. The boy twisted like a cat, there was a swirl of cloak and a rasping sound. Something flashed into the air. With a shout, Bjørn grabbed Peer's arm, forcing it down. He wrenched the hammer away and hurled it on to the beach.

Peer rubbed his numbed fingers. "I'm s-sorry," he stammered to Bjørn. "I lost my – I wouldn't have hurt him—"

"No," said Bjørn in a savage undertone, "you'd have been

gutted." And he nodded at the boy, who stood watching Peer with dancing eyes, holding a long steel-edged sword at a casual slant.

Peer had never actually seen a sword before. Nobody in the village was rich enough to have one. Patterns seemed to play and move on the flat steel surface. The frighteningly sharp edges had been honed to fresh silver.

That could cut my arm off.

In sudden silence the villagers gaped, their grins wearing off like old paint. The sailors from the ship edged together, watchful, glancing at their leader, Gunnar. The tall girl, Gunnar's wife, looked on with cool eyes, as if nothing surprised her.

Then the boy pushed the sword back into its sheath. He tossed his hair back and said in a light, amused way, "He started it."

"And who are you?" demanded Bjørn.

The boy waited for a second, and Gunnar interrupted. "He's my son, Harald Gunnarsson, my first-born." His voice was gruff, thick with pride. "My young lion, eh, Harald?" Affectionately he cuffed the boy with his sound right hand. "Look at him, pretty as a girl, no wonder they call him 'Harald Silkenhair'. But don't be fooled. See this?" He lifted his left arm to show the missing fist, and turned slowly around, grinning at the villagers. "Seen it? All had a good look?" His voice changed to a snarl. "But the man who did it lost his *head,* and it was my boy here who took it off him."

There was scattered applause. "A brave lad, to defend his father!"

"A fine young hero. And so handsome, too!" Gerd clasped her knobbly hands.

"But a little too quick with his tongue, perhaps," said Bjørn drily.

Gunnar hesitated. Then he burst out laughing. "All right," he coughed, "all right. We can't let the young dogs bark too loudly, can we? Harald – and you, what's your name – Peer? No more quarrelling. Shake hands."

"Yes, father," said Harald sweetly. He held out his hand. Peer eyed him without taking it. His heart beat in his throat and his mouth was sour with tension, as he met Harald's bright gaze.

Harald grinned unpleasantly. "Come on, Barelegs. Can't you take a joke?"

Peer nearly burst. He turned his back and shouldered his way along the jetty, leaving Bjørn and the others to deal with the newcomers. Down on the shingle, he pulled on his breeches while Einar's little boys peeped at him round the posts of the jetty, giggling and whispering, "Barelegs, Barelegs." He pretended not to hear, but it was the sort of name that stuck. He would never live it down.

Bjørn called to him. "Arne's taking Gunnar up to Ralf's farm. Why don't you go with them? It'll be sunset soon, anyway."

"Not me," said Peer gruffly. "I'll be along later. I've work to finish here."

He watched them pick their way across the beach. Gunnar's young wife Astrid clung to his arm, mincing across the pebbles. Her shoes were too thin, Peer thought sourly. How would she ever make it up to the farm, a good two miles of rough track? But perhaps they'd borrow a pony.

He walked back along the jetty, taking his time, unwilling to talk even to Bjørn. The tide was full. *Water Snake* had risen with it.

Against the sky the knob of the dragonhead stood black, like a club or a clenched fist. The angry wooden eyes bulged.

The gaping jaws curved like pincers. An undulating tongue licked forwards between them, the damp wood splitting along the grain.

Peer glanced about. No one was looking. He quietly jumped on board.

The ship smelled of pinewood and fresh tar. The rope he clutched left a sticky line on his palm. There was decking fore and aft. The waist of the ship was an orderly clutter of crates and barrels: luggage and supplies. A white hen stuck its head out of a wicker crate and clucked gently.

Fancy a trip to Vinland, Peer?

He clambered up the curve of the ship into the stern, where he stood for a moment holding the tiller and gazing west. The sun was low, laying a bright track on the water: a road studded with glittering cobblestones. It stung his heart and dazzled his eyes.

And Harald Silkenhair, no older than Peer, had travelled that road. Harald had sailed across the world, proved himself in battles, been to places Peer would never see.

He thought of Thorolf's ship, his father's ship, the *Long Serpent,* beached on the shores of Vinland far across the world, and felt a surge of longing. What would it be like to go gliding away into the very heart of the sun? He closed his eyes and imagined he was out at sea.

"What are you doing?" Bjørn looked down from the jetty. Peer snatched his hand off the tiller, feeling every kind of fool for playing at sailing like some little boy.

"Looking at the, oh, the workmanship." He made an effort. "The dragonhead's not as fine as the one my father made. But it's still good work."

"Mm." Bjørn paused. "And what do you make of Harald Troublemaker?"

Their eyes met. Peer said, "He just picked a fight with me. For no reason at all."

"I know."

"What was I supposed to do? Stand there and take it? Did you hear what he said to me?"

Bjørn blew out a troubled breath. "Peer, better to take an insult than a sword in your guts. You don't have to play Harald's games."

"How can your brother sail with someone like that?"

Bjørn shook his head. "Arne's a bit of a fool sometimes."

"Let me get off this boat." Peer climbed on to the jetty, feeling Water Snake balance and adjust as his weight left her.

"Don't play Harald's games," Bjørn repeated.

"I won't." Half comforted, Peer straightened and stretched. "You're right," he added. What was the point of letting Harald get to him? Let him strut. Let Arne have his evening with Hilde. Tomorrow they'd both sail away.

CHAPTER 43

"Be careful what you wish for"

HILDE RUBBED TIRED eyes. It was almost too dark to see the pattern she was weaving. Further up the room, in the glow of the long hearth, nine-year-old Sigrid was telling little Eirik a bedtime story.

"So there was a terrible storm. And Halvor's ship was blown along until he landed in a beautiful country. And he got out, and he came to a castle where there was an enormous troll with three heads."

"Isn't he rather young for that story?" Hilde interrupted. "He's only two."

"He likes it," said Sigrid. "And the troll said, '*Hutututu!* I smell the blood of a mortal man!' So Halvor pulled out his sword, and chopped off the troll's heads."

"Chop, chop, chop!" chuckled Eirik. Hilde rolled her eyes.

"And he rescued a princess, a beautiful princess, and got married to her. And they lived in the castle together, ever so happily, till one day Halvor began to miss his poor mother and father, who would think he had drowned."

Hilde wove a few more rows, half-listening while the princess gave Halvor a magical ring, which would carry him back over the sea, with a warning never to forget her. "'Or I shall have to go away to Soria Moria Castle, to marry a troll with nine heads.'"

Eirik lost interest. He squirmed eel-like over the edge of the bed. Sigrid dragged him back. "Lie still, Eirik, or I won't go on."

Gudrun was slicing onions with streaming eyes. "Thank goodness Elli's asleep. I'll be so glad when she's finished teething. All that wailing really wears you out..."

"Shall I do the onions?" Hilde asked. "I can't see to weave."

"No, go and help with Eirik, I've nearly done."

"Eirik," said Hilde, "sit on my knee and listen to Siggy's nice story. Better chop off a few more heads," she advised Sigrid from the side of her mouth.

"Halvor was so happy to get home that he quite forgot the poor princess was waiting for him," said Sigrid rapidly. "And she waited and waited, and then she said, 'He's forgotten me, and now I must go to Soria Moria Castle, east of the sun and west of the moon, and marry the troll with nine heads.'"

"Excellent!" exclaimed Hilde, trying to stop Eirik slithering off her lap. "Nine heads coming off soon, Eirik."

"So Halvor had to find Soria Moria Castle, but nobody knew the way. Oh, Eirik, I wish you'd *listen*!"

"Eirik!" said Hilde ruthlessly. "Listen to the end of the story. The prince chopped off the troll's heads. Chop, chop, chop!"

"Chop, chop, *chop*!" chanted Eirik.

"You wrecked my story!" Sigrid cried.

"I told you, Sigrid: he's too little." She let Eirik slide to the floor. "And he isn't sleepy. He wants to play. I don't blame him, either. I know how he feels."

Gudrun looked at her. "What do you mean?"

Hilde prowled the room. "Nothing. I'm sick of being cooped up indoors. Peer's building that jetty with Bjørn. Pa and Sigurd are on the fell with Loki and the new puppy. I wish something interesting would happen to me."

"Be careful what you wish for," said Gudrun. "It was 'interesting' last summer, when the house was attacked by trolls, but I wouldn't go through that again. Life isn't fair, and you may as well get used to it."

"You always say that! I'm so *tired* of being shut up in here, doing the same things, cooking and spinning and weaving, for ever and ever and ever."

"Hilde," said Gudrun in surprise. She set down the knife and smoothed Hilde's hair with a damp hand. "We all feel low at the end of winter. But spring's here, and the weather will soon be warm again. Think of sitting outside in the long evenings."

"I suppose," Hilde muttered.

Sigrid said, "Now your hair will smell of onions."

"Well, thanks!" Hilde began, when there was a bang at the door. Gudrun's hand flew to her mouth. "Who's this, knocking after dark?"

"Trolls?" said Sigrid apprehensively.

Hilde got to her feet. "*I'll* get it. And if there are any trolls out there, I'll make them wish they hadn't bothered."

"Chop, chop, chop!" shouted Eirik. With a nervous giggle, Sigrid hoisted him into her arms, and Hilde grabbed a broom and flung the door open. "Who is it, and what do you want?"

Then she threw down the broom with a cry of delight. "Arne!"

Arne Egilsson ducked in under the lintel, pulling off his cap, a broad smile on his face. "Don't hit me, Hilde! Is Ralf here? Gudrun, I've brought visitors. Gunnar Ingolfsson of Vinland, with his wife Astrid, and his son, Harald Silkenhair! Gunnar wants to speak to Ralf. Guess what, Hilde? I've joined

Gunnar's ship. I'm sailing with him to Vinland!"

Hilde gasped. "Arne, you lucky, lucky thing!"

"Yes, but I'll miss you. Will you miss me?" he whispered.

A moment later, people were crowding in. Gunnar Ingolfsson filled the doorframe, a thickset, sandy-bearded man in a heavy wolfskin cloak. After him came a tall, pale girl. Gudrun advanced to greet them, wiping her hands on her apron. And the last to come in…

Hilde blinked. In walked a boy who made Arne look like an overgrown, ruddy-faced farmhand. He wore his fine cloak with a confident swagger. Long golden hair tumbled over his shoulders and down his back.

Harald Silkenhair? He's like a young hero from a saga.

"He's just like a prince from a fairytale," Sigrid breathed. "Look, he's even got a sword!"

Eirik struggled, kicking Sigrid with his bare toes till she put him down. He ran forward, a sturdy little figure in a nightshirt, blocking Harald's way, and gazed up in wide-eyed admiration. "Show me your sword," he demanded.

Harald's lips quirked, and he went down on one knee. He slid his sword a few inches out of the sheath. "Meet Bone-Biter. No!" he warned, as Eirik's chubby hand went out. "She's sharp. Touch the handle."

Hilde watched Eirik stretch out a finger. The hilt of the sword was wrapped in silver wire. "Shiny," said Eirik, his voice soft. He looked up at Harald. "Did you cut off the twoll's head?"

Harald frowned. Hilde cut in. "It's a story. He thinks—"

"He thinks you're a prince who killed some trolls," blurted Sigrid, blushing.

Harald pushed the sword back into its sheath. "Not trolls," he said, laughing, "not trolls." He leaned forward and ruffled

Eirik's hair. "When you're a man, maybe you'll have a sword like this." And he got to his feet.

"Wasn't that was nice of him?" Sigrid whispered to Hilde.

"I… suppose so," said Hilde slowly. Sigrid was right. It was very nice of this young warrior to take notice of a small boy. *Meet Bone-Biter.* Little boys always worshipped heroes, didn't they? What could be wrong with that?

Harald turned to Gudrun. "Lady!" He bowed over her rough hand as though it were the white hand of a queen, and declaimed with a flourish:

"Far have we fared on the wide ocean,

Where seabirds scream and the whales wander.

Glad of our landfall, thanks we give

To our fair hostess for this fine welcome."

"Goodness," Gudrun fluttered as Harald let go her hand. "Poetry!"

"His own." Gunnar watched his son with a kind of rough delight.

"I'm honoured," Gudrun exclaimed. "You're most welcome. What a shame my father-in-law isn't still alive. He was such a fine poet himself. He would so much have enjoyed this meeting."

Would he? thought Hilde, watching her mother's pleased pink flush. She looked at Harald, wondering how many times he'd used that verse. Could he possibly be poking fun? Before she could consider the matter any further, Arne tapped her shoulder. "Hilde, this is Gunnar's wife, Astrid."

Hilde turned, nearly bumping into a tall girl standing close behind her, muffled in an expensive-looking dark blue cloak with the hood up. A brown and white goatskin bag was slung over her shoulder on a long strap, which she clutched with long, thin-wristed hands. She had ice-maiden skin, so white and thin that the blue veins glistened through, wide grey eyes, a neat, straight nose like a cat's with little curling nostrils, and pale, closely shut lips.

Their eyes met. For a second, Hilde felt she was looking into the eyes of a deer or a hare, a wild animal who glares at you before bolting. Then Astrid pushed her hood down. Out sprang a bright cloud of amber hair, frizzing and fizzling, catching the light in a million fiery glints. The hair transformed her cold, still face. With her hood down, she was beautiful.

Hilde held out her hand, puzzled. *Gunnar's wife? She doesn't look much older than me. She can't possibly be that boy's mother!*

Astrid touched Hilde's hand with chilly fingers. There was a pause, and Hilde racked her brains for something to say. "Have you been to Vinland, too?"

"No!" said Astrid in a low, curt voice. After a moment she added with reluctance, "Gunnar and I were only married in the fall. He's an old friend of my father, Grimolf Sigurdsson of Westfold. He came to stay with us, and – I suppose he liked the look of me. I'm his second wife."

So that's it. Poor girl. Gunnar looks older than Pa. I'm glad I don't have to marry an old man just because he's rich. Aloud Hilde said, "How exciting! And now you can travel with him right across the world."

But perhaps Astrid could tell what Hilde was thinking. Instead of answering she raised a scornful eyebrow. Then she stared at the floor.

"Not everyone wants to travel across the world, Hilde," Arne said with a smile. "Seafaring is hard for women."

"I'd love to go to Vinland," said Hilde immediately, determined to show Arne that whatever most women were like, she was different.

Astrid looked up quickly, but before she or Arne could reply, the door opened. A half-grown black puppy tumbled in and dashed around the room barking, followed by Peer's dog Loki. A cheerful voice called, "Hey, hey, what's this? Visitors?"

"Ralf," cried Gudrun. "Sigurd, control your puppy. Ralf, look who Arne's brought to see us!"

The girls were left together. Hilde was about to make an excuse and slip away, when Astrid touched her arm, and said stiffly, "Did you mean that? Would you really like to go to Vinland?"

Hilde opened her mouth to give some airy reply. Nothing came out. The warm, stifling air of the farmhouse wrapped around her throat like a tight scarf. She stared at Astrid. Here was this awful, boring girl, with her grand, snooty manners, sailing off to Vinland while Hilde had to stay at home.

Oh, if only I had her chance. I want to see something new. I want to sail far away. I want – I want to find Soria Moria Castle, east of the sun and west of the moon!

Astrid was watching her like a cat. "Come with me!"

"What?" Hilde choked.

"Come with me. Ask your mother. I'll do my best to help you. I'll tell Gunnar I want another girl for company. It's true anyway. And then you'll be on my side, won't you?"

"On your s-side?" Hilde stammered.

Something flashed at the back of Astrid's eyes. "Nobody asked *me* if I wanted to come to Vinland. Nobody asked me if I wanted to marry Gunnar. Well, my father *asked,* but he'd already agreed. He wouldn't insult a man like Gunnar."

"Was – was there somebody else you liked?"

"There may have been," said Astrid warily.

"My father would never do that to me!"

Astrid shrugged. "Lucky you. I thought of putting the

cold curse on Gunnar, but someone's done it already. He's never warm. See?"

The cold curse? Hilde twisted round. Gunnar, still wrapped in his thick cloak, was hoisting Ralf's big chair closer to the fire.

Astrid tossed her head. "You needn't feel sorry for me. I'm making the best of it. After all, Gunnar's a famous man. *You'll* never marry anyone half so well known. He treats me well. He's never once struck me. He's as tough as Tyr, who put his hand in a wolf's mouth. But he needs me. He has fevers, and sometimes he tries to stay awake because of bad dreams. And he hates being alone in the dark." Her eyes narrowed. "I haven't found out why, yet, but I will. I know herbs, I know how to mix draughts to give him peaceful sleep. I can wind him round my little finger," she boasted.

"What about Harald?" asked Hilde.

Astrid gave her a sharp glance. "Don't be fooled by his looks. His own mother died years ago, so he didn't mind me at first; he thought I was a pretty little *thing* that his father might as well have. Now he knows better, he's jealous. What do you think of him?"

"Um. Isn't he a little bit pleased with himself?"

Astrid laughed. "Oh, yes. There's no one quite like Harald Silkenhair. Well! You might do."

"Do?" Hilde decided all over again that she didn't like Astrid. "What for?"

Astrid raised her eyebrows. "Don't be like that. We could have fun together. You want to come to Vinland, don't you? Or was that just talk?" she added.

"No! I meant it." Hilde swallowed. "But..."

Astrid seemed to realise that she hadn't been making a great impression. She looked at Hilde for a moment, as if wondering what to offer her. "I want you to come. Do you like secrets? If we're going to be friends, I'll tell you one."

"Go on," said Hilde, intrigued in spite of herself.

Astrid hesitated. "Shall I? I'm taking a risk, I'm trusting you. Are you easily shocked? No? All right, listen." Her pale eyes opened wide. "*There's troll blood in me.* Oh yes there is, a long way back perhaps, but it's there. And I can see things other people can't."

"Troll blood?" A fascinated shiver ran down Hilde's back. "What do you mean?"

Astrid gave her a conspiratorial smile. "What I say." She leaned close and whispered, "My mother's mother was the daughter of Thorodd Half-Troll, and his mother was a troll out of the Dovrefell. My mother's dead now. But she passed down all kinds of tricks to me." She patted her big goatskin bag. "Gunnar thinks this is just herbs and medicines. Well, some of it is, and some of it isn't."

Hilde drew back in sudden suspicion. "You're making it up."

"Oh, am I?" Astrid looked around, but their low conversation was easily drowned by loud laughter from the men chatting by the fire. "All right then." She unbuckled the flap and plunged her arm into the bag. "Hold this."

She handed Hilde a little square box, yellowish in the firelight. Hilde rubbed her fingers over it. It was made of smooth bone, or ivory, but there were some scratchings on the lid, runes or patterns. She looked up at Astrid. "Well?"

"Listen to it," said Astrid. "Put it to your ear."

Hilde did. The box buzzed. She almost dropped it, and listened again. Yes, when her ear was pressed close, the box was buzzing or humming. Or was it even a sleepy, angry voice, singing or chanting a very, very long way off?

"What is it?" Hilde burned with curiosity. She pried at the lid.

"Don't open it!" Astrid snatched it back. "My mother gave it me. It tells me things. Now do you believe me?"

Looking at Astrid in the flickering firelight, Hilde found she did. There was a slant to her eyes, a play of shadows on the cheekbones, that reminded Hilde of the troll princess from underneath Troll Fell.

"Does Gunnar know you've – got troll blood?" she almost whispered. Astrid smiled, showing a line of sharp little white teeth. "Oh no, he's much too shockable. I told you, it's a secret. He only knows I can do a little *seidr* – magic. Are you wondering if I've got a tail? Don't worry, I haven't. But the troll blood's there. It makes me different. And I can see this, Hilde Ralfsdaughter. Like it or not, you're coming with us to Vinland." She pinched Hilde's arm. "You wait and see. Let's talk again later."

She walked away to the fire.

Hilde's fingers prickled from touching the little buzzing box. Her breath came short. A smile of pure excitement curled her lips. *The cold curse. Troll blood. Like it or not, you're coming with us to Vinland.* To think that, only a short while ago, she had thought Astrid conventional and dull!

Oh, she thought, *I do want to go with her. I must!*

CHAPTER 44

The Nis Amuses Itself

Peer hesitated by the farmhouse door. He'd hurried up the track, imagining Harald picking a quarrel with Ralf – insulting Hilde – frightening the twins. He'd pictured himself striding in to the rescue. But now his imagination failed. Harald had a sword. It would be no good trying to pull him outside for a fist-fight.

"You don't have to play his games," Bjørn had said. But Peer had a feeling that Harald was good at pushing people into games they had no wish to play. What if Harald called him 'Barelegs' in front of Hilde? *How can I stop him? What shall I do?*

He lifted the latch, and something scampered across the yard and mewed at the bottom of the door like a hopeful cat. The Nis! As the door creaked open he got a glimpse of its beady eyes, skinny outline and little red hat, before it shot past his ankles and whizzed up the wall into the rafters.

He closed the door. The room was hot, bright and crowded; the atmosphere unnaturally hushed. Peer's taut nerves twanged. *What's going on? Trouble?*

A strong voice chanted:

"The hound of heaven, the ship-seizer,
Hunted us over the wild waters.
Weary wanderers, we fled before
The wide jaws of the wind-wolf!"

It was Harald, the centre of attention, standing at the table reciting his poetry to the family. Everyone listened in apparent admiration. No one had eyes for Peer.

Peer waited, hungry and cross. In full flow, Harald chanted on. It was all about the voyage to Vinland, and he was making it sound pretty stormy and adventurous. Once he caught Peer's eye, and a faint smirk fled across his face.

Would the poem never end? Something scuffled overhead. Dust dropped in a fairy cascade. Peer rubbed his eyes. It was the Nis, poking about amongst the cobwebs, chasing spiders – one of its favourite games. Good. At least the Nis couldn't be bothered with Harald Silkenhair!

At last, Harald's voice rose in triumphant climax:

"But our sleek ship, our proud sea-serpent
Bore us swiftly to a safe haven,
An empty land, fleeced in forests,
Land for our labours, land for claiming!"

Harald flung himself back on the bench, lifted his cup and tossed down a draught of ale. "Great stuff!" roared Ralf, pounding the table. "Grand! *'Our sleek ship, our proud sea-serpent!'* I've always wished I could make poetry. My father could, but I can't. *'An empty land, fleeced in forests.'* That's not right, though. Vinland isn't empty. There are people there."

Harald's laugh was a jeer. "People? You mean the Skraelings?"

Peer didn't know what a Skraeling was, but nothing would have induced him to ask. He reached over Arne's shoulder to grab some food, and folded himself into a corner near the fire, sitting on the earth floor with his back against one of the big wooden posts that held up the roof. Loki came to greet him. Peer pulled him close and fed him a piece of cheese.

Sigurd was asking loudly, "What's a Skraeling?"

"Skraelings, laddie?" Gunnar set down his horn cup with a crack. "It's what we call those creatures who live in Vinland. No better than trolls. They live in tents made from bits of tree bark. They dress in skins. Why," he guffawed, "at one place we stopped, they were so ignorant that they bartered good furs for a few miserable pieces of red cloth. And when we ran short of cloth, we tore it into thinner and thinner strips, and still the Skraelings paid in furs."

Ralf said mildly, "I thought they were fine people. And why shouldn't they barter furs for cloth, if cloth was a rarity? I don't call that proof of ignorance."

Gunnar stared, as though he wasn't used to being disagreed with. Gudrun broke in, "But aren't they dangerous? Isn't that how you lost your hand, Gunnar – fighting Skraelings?"

"Skraelings? No!" Gunnar's face darkened. "No. It happened in Westfold before I left. An argument in an ale-house." Here his wife gave him a cold glance, Peer noticed – perhaps she didn't approve of ale-house fights. "The man jumped me before I was ready for him. Luckily I had my boy here with me, Harald."

"What did Harald do?" Sigurd asked eagerly.

"Cut the fellow's hair for him. With this," Harald winked, patting his sword. Sigurd laughed out loud, and Ralf grinned. Astrid studied her nails, and Gudrun shook her head. Peer stared at Harald in deep dislike.

Harald brushed at his shoulder, frowning. A moment later he shook his head, combing his fingers through his hair. Then Peer saw. The Nis, perching in the rafters, was amusing itself by dropping things on to Harald's head – dead spiders, and bits of grit and cobwebs. Brilliant! He tousled Loki's ears, grinning.

"Anyway, tell us about your settlement," exclaimed Ralf.

"What's it called? What's it like? And how's my old friend Thorolf?"

A glance passed between Harald and Gunnar. "We've had no news of Thorolf since we left him in Vinland last year," said Harald, yawning. "Have we, father?"

"How could we?" Gunnar shivered suddenly, and the cup shook and splashed in his hand. He set it down. "Harald's right. We left him there last year. Haven't been back since."

"So you don't know what he's up to," Ralf nodded. "He may have come after you."

Gunnar mumbled something. His face was beaded with sweat, and Astrid gave her husband a sharp, curious glance.

Harald shook his hair. "I think we'll find Thorolf and his men right where we left them," he said, smiling. "I don't think he had any plans to leave."

Ralf leaned forwards, rubbing his hands. "Didn't he? Maybe you're right. It's a wonderful land. Those green forests, full of game – the rivers bursting with fish. No wonder Thorolf wants to make a home there. And you, you're going back?"

Harald nodded. "We have two good solid houses in a sheltered bay, with a river running out of the woods, and good anchorage in the river mouth. We named it Serpent's Bay – after our two ships, *Long Serpent* and *Water Snake*."

And I suppose that was your clever idea, thought Peer, mesmerised as a dried bean bounced off Harald's shoulder and skittered across the table. Sigurd noticed it too. He nudged his sister.

Arne broke in eagerly. "Ralf, why don't you come with us? That's why I brought Gunnar here. He's looking for another man, and I told him you've always talked about another voyage."

Gudrun, going round with the jug, knocked Arne's cup

over. Ale washed across the table. Sigrid jumped up for a cloth, but Gudrun stood still, eyes fixed on Ralf.

"Arne's right." Gunnar wiped his face and looked steadier. "It's like this, Ralf. My old crew split up over the winter. On the profits of the last trip, some of them got married, or bought land, and didn't want to set out again this season. So I've been looking for new men. What do you say?"

"I knew you'd ask," said Ralf slowly. "I've been thinking about it all evening, deciding what to do..."

Gunnar sat back. "Good! Let's drink to it."

"...but I'm needed on the farm," Ralf went on. "Sigurd's not old enough to manage, and the last time I went away Gudrun had all sorts of trouble with the trolls. I can't leave her to cope alone."

Gudrun's eyes shone, but Gunnar's whiskered cheeks creased uneasily. "Trolls? You have many trolls here?"

Ralf laughed, and waved his hand. "We live on Troll Fell, Gunnar."

"Trolls." Gunnar shuddered. "I hate 'em. Unnatural vermin."

Astrid seemed to stir. Her lips parted, then shut. Another dried bean dropped from the rafters, splashing into Harald's cup as he lifted it to his lips. Harald threw down the cup.

"That's enough, you!" He pointed at Peer, who scrambled to his feet. "Do you think I'm going to put up with this?"

Everyone stared. Harald put his hands on the table and leaned forward. "You've been throwing beans at me, haven't you, Barelegs? And you think it's funny?"

"I didn't do anything," said Peer, seriously alarmed.

"It wasn't Peer!" Sigrid cried.

"No. There's something dodging about in the roof," said Astrid, to Peer's great surprise. Most people couldn't see the Nis.

Everyone looked up into the smoky, dark roof-space, cluttered with fishing nets, strings of onions, old hay-rakes and scythes.

The Nis flung down its fistful of beans. A stinging shower rattled on to Harald's upturned face, and as he cursed and ducked, the Nis followed it up by bouncing some small wrinkled apples off his back. It could be heard drumming its heels against the beam, and sniggering: *"Tee-hee-hee!"*

Astrid's face sharpened into a triangular smile. "There it is!" she breathed, fixing her eyes on a spot above Harald's head. The sniggering broke off.

"Where?" Harald spun round, golden hair spraying out. He dragged out his sword and angled it up, craning his neck to see into the rafters.

Everyone leaped to their feet. The dogs began barking. "Put that sword away," called Ralf. "Someone'll get hurt!"

"No swords in this house!" cried Gudrun.

"My apologies," said Harald between his teeth. "There's something up there. Stand back, and let me deal with it." He put a foot on the bench, obviously preparing to spring up on to the table. Peer heard a frightened squeak from the Nis.

"There it goes!" Peer shot out his arm and pointed. "Look, a troll! Running along that rafter, see?" His finger followed the imaginary troll from beam to beam. "It's over the fire – oh!" He let his arm drop.

"What? Where?" gasped Gudrun, half-convinced.

"It went out through the smoke hole," said Peer, disappointment in his voice.

"Then it's on the roof." Harald sprang for the door, Arne and Gunnar and the dogs close behind. Ralf followed more slowly, giving Peer the flicker of a wink.

Peer made for the door, too. He caught Hilde's eye. "Let's

hope they catch it!" Hilde was laughing silently. The twins were crowding out, while Gudrun tried to pull them back: "Harald's got a sword out there!"

The moon skimmed between the clouds like a stone skipping over water, filling the yard with flowing shadows. Harald was making Arne give him a leg up on to the farmhouse's thick turf roof. Gunnar stood squarely in the patch of light from the open door, squinting up under his good hand. "Go on, son," he shouted. "A roof's no place to hide. We'll not be fooled by that again..."

"I never thought he could have climbed up," said Harald over his shoulder.

What were they talking about? Peer looked at Ralf, who shrugged and said in a low voice, "I guess they've had adventures before."

Harald walked along the roof ridge, sword in hand, a sinister silhouette against the sky. Peer shivered, and Ralf too must have felt uncomfortable about this prowling figure on his own roof, for he called out, "It's gone; you've missed it. Come down."

But the dogs began to bark and growl, and make little dashes at a blackly shadowed corner of the yard near the cowshed.

"Don't tell me they've found a real troll," Ralf muttered. He crossed the yard in a couple of quick strides, Peer beside him, Gunnar close behind.

In the angle of the wall was a crawling darkness the size of a small child. "Gods!" Gunnar's voice clotted with horror. "Look at that. Where's its *head*?"

Peer's skin prickled. Then he saw the troll had merely crouched down, wrapping skinny arms protectively over its head. It was chewing, and there was a strong stink of old herrings. So it had been robbing the fish-drying racks!

Ralf clapped his hands. "Get out of here! Shoo!" he shouted.

A pair of luminous green eyes winked open. The troll produced a dry, frightening hiss, accompanied by an even stronger smell of fish. Ralf dragged the dogs away by their collars. "Stand back, Peer – give it a chance to run."

Behind them, Harald leaped into the yard. He staggered, touching a hand to the ground to steady himself; then he was up, his naked blade glinting. "Out of my way!" he shouted, running at the troll.

The round green eyes scrunched into terrified half-moons. The troll dived away, fat sides pumping, long bald tail curving and switching. But Harald was faster. He stamped down heavily on its tail, jerking it to a halt. The troll tugged and writhed, squealing dreadfully. "Let it go! Let it go!" Ralf shouted. But Harald struck.

As the blow flashed down, the troll gave a final desperate wrench and leaped crazily up the hillside, leaving its narrow, tapering tail thrashing horribly under Harald's boot. There was a sickening smell of stale armpits and rotten eggs.

Harald leaped back in disgust and slammed his sword into its sheath. Ralf and Arne broke out coughing, and even the dogs whined, wiping their noses on their paws. With a shiver of loathing, Gunnar turned away from the jerkily wriggling tail.

"I need a drink after that," said Ralf drily. He held open the farmhouse door and nodded for everyone to go in.

Gudrun, the twins, and Hilde and Astrid clustered around the door.

"Was there really a troll?"

"What happened?"

"What was that noise?"

"Poof!" Sigurd clutched his nose. "What's that *awful* smell?"

"There was a troll, all right," Peer said to Hilde.

"Harald was so fast," said Arne in admiration. "He nearly got it!"

"He got its *tail*," said Peer with bitter sarcasm. Soft-hearted Sigrid gasped. "Oh, the poor thing! Oh, that must have hurt so much!"

"It will grow a new one," Hilde soothed her.

"Why didn't you let the dogs pull it down?" Gunnar growled at Ralf. "You could have nailed the head to your barn door to scare the others."

Ralf poured himself a cup of ale, and pushed the jug towards Gunnar and Harald. "I didn't want it killed," he said at last, politely enough. "The trolls may be a nuisance, but they're our neighbours, Gunnar. We've got to live here with them. We've all got to get along."

"Get along with trolls?" Gunnar showed a set of brownish teeth through his bristly beard. "Root 'em up, smoke 'em out. That's what I'd do."

Peer thought of the labyrinthine passages underneath Troll Fell. *Smoke 'em out? We'd have hundreds of trolls down on us like angry bees. But what's the use of talking? He's not going to listen.*

Gunnar sat down suddenly. His chest heaved. "Anyway," he got out between harsh breaths, "what about my offer? Be a man. Come with us."

Ralf and Gudrun looked at each other. He reached across and squeezed her hand. "No, I can't," he said firmly. "But ask in the village. Maybe there's someone there who wants to go."

Gunnar gave him a black look. "Then I've wasted my time.

Arne swore you'd come, that's all. I warn you, if the wind's right, we'll be leaving tomorrow. I won't lose a good wind. After tomorrow, it'll be too late to change your mind."

Ralf shrugged. Peer beat his fist on his knee in silent satisfaction. *Good for Ralf! We don't want anything to do with them, any of them!*

Hilde stood up. "Ma, Pa…"

Peer saw her resolute face and his heart stopped. He knew what was coming.

"Astrid wants me to come to Vinland with her. And I'd like to go!"

In the shocked silence that followed, a half-burned log shifted in the fire like a sleepy dragon. Its bright underbelly flaked, shedding golden scales, which dimmed and died.

Gudrun found her voice. "Hilde, you can't go to Vinland. It's ridiculous."

"It's not," said Hilde. "Astrid is going, so why shouldn't I?"

"But Astrid is married," exclaimed Gudrun.

"And I'd be with her. What's wrong with that?"

Gudrun spun round. "Ralf – say something!"

"Hold on, hold on." Ralf tried to sound soothing. "Hilde, your ma doesn't like this idea, and I can't say I blame her…"

Peer stopped listening. He knew Hilde would get her own way. She would go to Vinland. There'd be no news. He'd never know if she got there safely, or when she was coming back. When Ralf had sailed away, years ago, they hadn't known if he was alive or dead until the day he came home.

He looked up and saw Harald watching him.

"Gudrun, I know you're worried." Astrid's cool voice cut across the hubbub. "But please, please let Hilde come." Her eyes opened, wide and pleading. "We've made friends already. I swear we'll be just like sisters." She laid one hand on Gunnar's shoulder. "Gunnar wouldn't take me if it wasn't safe."

Gunnar grasped her hand. "Of course it will be safe," he declared.

"See!" Hilde turned to Gudrun. "If it's safe for Astrid, it's safe for me."

Gudrun was red and flustered. "Your father and I will be the judges of that!"

Hilde flared up. "It's so unfair! You expect me to stay at home, don't you, and – and *drudge* all my life. Now I've got this chance –Vinland, *Vinland* – and you won't let me go..."

Gudrun dropped back on to the bench and put her hands over her eyes. "You know," Ralf said to Gudrun, as quietly as if no one was listening. "Hilde's like me. She wants to see the world a bit. She's nearly grown up. This is the chance of a lifetime for her, Gudrun. I think we should let her go."

"But it's so dangerous!" Gudrun looked up in tears. "All that sea – and when they get to Vinland, those Skraeling creatures, creeping about in the woods..."

"It's dangerous here, too," said Hilde more calmly. "Trolls under the fell, and Granny Greenteeth down in the millpond, and lubbers in the woods. I daresay I'll survive a few Skraelings."

"She'll be safe enough," Ralf said to Gudrun. "Gunnar's a sound skipper and the sort of man who – well, who looks after his friends. And when they get to Vinland, there's Thorolf: I'd trust him anywhere. And now I come to think of it, Thorolf's little son must be in Vinland with him. Ottar, he's called. He's about the same age as Sigurd. Isn't that right, Gunnar? Is Ottar there?"

"Of course," said Harald, before Gunnar could answer. "Remember Ottar, father, the day we left? Climbing on to the roof of the house and waving to us?"

Gunnar grinned and nodded.

"His little boy is there?" asked Gudrun doubtfully. Hilde flung her arms around her mother and gave her a squeeze. "Oh, please Ma, let me go. Please?"

Gudrun faltered. It was hard for her to resist this sudden embrace.

Peer took a breath. He ought to tell Gudrun and Ralf everything he knew about Harald. They would never let Hilde sail away with someone who had forced a quarrel on him, and threatened him with a sword. And yet… Hilde wanted to go so very badly, and he loved her for it – for being herself, adventurous and brave. How could he wreck her chances?

"Oh, Hilde." Gudrun's voice trembled. "How can we let you go when we don't know these people? Of course, they seem splendid, and I can see that Astrid ought to have another woman with her, but—" She stopped and tried again. "If your father had been going, he could have looked after you, but as it is—"

"Ma, you know Arne," pleaded Hilde.

"Arne isn't one of the family," said Gudrun desperately.

Peer's heart pounded. He looked across the table and met Harald's bright, amused, contemptuous stare. He saw himself through those eyes – *Someone who builds boats, but never sails in them. Someone who won't take chances. Someone who might dream about crossing the sea, but would never do it. Someone who'd stay behind while Hilde sails away.*

"I'll go with her," he said.

Hilde swung round with wide, incredulous eyes. "You, Peer?"

Ralf gave him a long, steady stare. "You really mean this, Peer?" he asked gravely. "You'll take care of Hilde? You'll look after her?"

"Yes." It was like swearing an oath: the most serious thing

he'd ever done. He didn't know how he'd manage, but he'd do it, or die trying. "I will. Don't worry, Ralf. Gudrun, I promise I'll bring her home again."

There was a moment's silence. Then Ralf gave Peer a tiny nod, and looked at Gudrun. With an enormous sniff, Gudrun nodded too.

"Thank you! Oh, *thank you*!" Hilde nearly danced on the spot. Then she threw herself at Peer and hugged him. "Oh, Peer, I never thought you might want to come too. But you do, and it's perfect – absolutely perfect!"

She let him go. No one else seemed very happy. Arne was scowling. Harald lifted an ironic eyebrow. Gunnar frowned. "Who *is* this?" He jabbed his thumb at Peer, as though he'd quite forgotten meeting him on the jetty. "What use will he be to me? Why should I take him on my ship?"

And Hilde said cheerfully, pulling him forward with her arm around him: "Oh, this is Peer. He's terribly useful. He can do anything with wood. His father was a boat builder. He's helped Bjørn make a new faering. And he's my brother. He's my foster brother!"

CHAPTER 45

The Journey Begins

PEER OPENED HIS eyes and saw a dark roof space pierced with sunbeams. Straw prickled under him. Behind a plank partition to his left, something large was champing and stirring.

Slowly he remembered. He and the twins were sleeping in the cowshed to leave more room for the guests. With a sinking heart, he remembered more. Had he really promised to go away for an unknown period of time, on a strange ship, to a strange land? Spring was on the way. He'd been looking forward to the lambs being born, the barley coming up, rowing out with Bjørn and Sigurd to gather seagulls' eggs from the islands. Now, all that would go on without him.

He sat up. On mounded straw between him and the door, the twins slept, cocooned in blankets. From a warm nest in the straw beside him, Loki got up, stretching and yawning.

Peer stared at his dog. Was it fair to take him on a ship, for weeks at sea? Loki lifted a paw and scraped at Peer's arm, probably hoping for breakfast.

"Loki, old fellow," Peer murmured. "What shall we do? Do you want to come with me?" Loki's tail hit the ground, once, twice.

"Good boy!" Peer was fooling himself, and he knew it: Loki always wagged his tail when Peer spoke to him. But he didn't care. He couldn't leave Loki behind, so at least that was decided. He lay back in the straw and wished he could go back to sleep – that today need never start – that he didn't have to remember what Hilde had said last night. *Peer's my brother.*

A brother! A safe, dependable brother, to be relied on and ignored. Didn't she know how he felt about her?

Perhaps not: he'd been so careful to keep things friendly all year. Perhaps she thought he'd got over it. He wished he'd kissed her again, even if she'd been angry. He wished he'd tried.

Oh, what was the use? *Peer's my brother!* It was hopeless.

"Psst," came a piercing whisper. "Peer! Are you really going to Vinland?"

He raised his hot face from the crackling straw and saw Sigrid sitting up, arms wrapped neatly round her knees.

"Looks like it," he said gloomily.

"You don't have to go, if you don't want to."

"But Hilde wants to, and I've promised to go with her."

"Oh, Hilde," said Sigrid crossly. "Why do you always do what she wants?"

"I don't." He thought about it. "Do I?"

"Yes, you do." Sigrid sat up straighter and wagged her finger at him: Peer almost smiled, but she was quite serious. "You've got to be tougher, Peer. Sometimes, Hilde ought to do what *you* want."

Peer stared at her until Sigrid wriggled and said, "What?"

"You're a very clever girl, Siggy," he said. "And you are absolutely right!"

She beamed. Peer threw back his blankets. "Time to get up!" And he pulled open the creaking cowshed door and stuck his head out.

A wind with ice in its teeth blew down from the mountains.

A seagull tilted overhead, dark against the blue and white sky, then bright against the hillside as it went sweeping off down the valley. Peer watched it go. *A fair wind for sailing west. So we really are leaving. Today.*

But Sigrid's simple words had acted like magic. He set his jaw. *I've messed about long enough, trying to be whatever Hilde wants. From now on, I'll act the way I feel!*

He stepped out, alive and determined, and trod on something shrivelled and whip-like lying by the corner of the cowshed. Loki sniffed it and backed off, sneezing. It was the troll's tail. Peer picked it up by the tip. It was heavier and bonier than he'd expected: he threw it on the dung heap with a shudder. A rusty smear stained the bare earth where the tail had lain. He scuffed dirt over it so that Sigrid would not see, and went into the house.

Gudrun and Hilde were sorting clothes. Peer put away his faint hope that Hilde might have changed her mind. Astrid sat like a queen in Ralf's big chair with little Elli on her knee. She was letting the baby play with a bunch of keys that dangled from her belt, jigging her up and down and humming some strange little song that rose and fell. Ralf, Gunnar and Harald were nowhere to be seen.

"Eat something quickly, Peer. Gunnar wants to catch the morning tide." Gudrun's voice was brittle.

"The men have gone to the ship, to load up more food and fresh water. We're to follow as soon as we can," Hilde added. Peer could tell she was bursting with excitement.

Gudrun bundled up a big armful of cloaks, shifts and dresses. "You'd better just take everything. Peer, you can have some of Ralf's winter things. You've grown so much this year—" She broke off, folding her lips tight.

"Where's Eirik?" asked Peer.

"Pa took him along to see the ship," said Hilde. "It would have been tricky to manage him and Elli and the baggage too. And of course Ma wants to come down to the ship as well, because—" She stopped.

But for once Peer wasn't interested in sparing Hilde's feelings. He completed the sentence for her: "Because she wants to be with you as long as she can."

There was a moment when no one spoke, and in the interval they heard Astrid singing to Elli, clapping the baby's hands together at the end of each line:

"Two little children on a summer's night,
Went to the well in the pale moonlight.
The lonely moon-man, spotted and old
Scooped them up in his arms so cold.
They live in the moon now, high in the air.
When you are old and grey, darling,
They'll still be there."

"I'll take her, shall I?" Peer almost snatched Elli away from Astrid.

"What a strange rhyme," said Gudrun. Astrid looked up: "It's one my mother used to sing. What a lovely baby Elli is. Why has she got webbed fingers?"

"She's Bjørn's daughter," Peer snapped, as though that explained it. His friend's tragic marriage with a seal woman was none of Astrid's business. Gudrun must have thought so too, for she said, clearing her throat, "Now, I wonder where the Nis is. I haven't seen it this morning."

Peer made a startled, warning gesture towards Astrid. But Hilde shook her head. "It's all right, Astrid knows."

"Knows about the Nis?" Peer looked at Astrid in suspicious astonishment.

"I saw it," Astrid said. "I knew it wasn't a troll. And don't worry, I haven't told Harald." She gave him a sweet smile. "You're a good liar, aren't you, Peer? You fooled Gunnar and Harald, anyway. But not me. I asked Hilde, and she told me it was a Nis. I even put its food down last night, Gudrun showed me how, after everyone went to bed. It likes groute, doesn't it? Barley porridge, with a dab of butter? And then it does the housework."

"Or not," said Gudrun. "As the case may be." She put her hands on her hips. "Well, if Gunnar wants you on that boat before noon, we'd better move."

There seemed mountains of stuff to load on to the pony. "We'll never need it all, surely?" Hilde laughed.

"I'm sure you will," said her mother grimly.

"What's this?" Peer picked up a tightly rolled sausage of woollen fabric.

"That's a sleeping sack," said Gudrun. "Big enough for two. It's for you, Peer – we've only the one, and Astrid says she'll share hers with Hilde. Ralf used it last, when he went a-Viking."

"Thank you, Gudrun," Peer said with gratitude. He hadn't thought about sleeping arrangements. What else had he missed?

"My tools – I'll need them." He dashed back into the empty house and looked around, caught by the strangeness of it all. Would he ever come back?

"Nis," he called quietly, and then, using the little creature's secret name, "Nithing? Are you there?" Nothing rustled or scampered. No inquisitive nose came poking out over the roofbeams.

"Nis?"

Perhaps it was curled up somewhere, fast asleep after the shocks and excitement of last night. "I'm going," he called, raising his voice. "Goodbye, Nis… I'm going away. Look after the family." Again he waited, but only silence followed. "Till we meet again," he ended forlornly.

He picked up his heavy wooden toolbox, and went out, closing the door. The pony lowered its head and snorted indignantly as this last load was strapped on.

"On guard!" said Gudrun to grey-muzzled old Alf, who settled down in front of the doorstep, ears pricked. Hilde carried Elli. Astrid was wrapped in her blue cloak again, shoulder braced against the weight of her bulging goatskin bag. Peer held out his hand. "Give that to me, Astrid. I'll carry it for you."

"No!" Astrid clutched the strap. "I'll carry it myself. It's quite light."

It looked heavy to Peer, but he didn't care enough to insist. "Everyone ready? Off we go."

Through the wood and downhill to the old wooden bridge: each twist of the path so familiar, Peer could have walked it with his eyes shut. Past the ruined mill, where a whiff of charcoal still hung in the damp air, and back into the trees. On down the long slope, till they came to the handful of shaggy little houses that made up Trollsvik. They swished through the prickly grass of the sand dunes and on to the crunching shingle.

The fjord was blue-grey: beyond the shelter of the little harbour, it was rough with white caps. Short, stiff waves followed one another in to land. And there was the ship, *Water Snake,* bare mast towering over the little jetty, forestay and backstay making a great inverted V. It was a shock to see her, somehow – so real, so—

"So big!" Gudrun gasped.

Astrid stopped, her cloak flapping in the wind. Her face was sombre, and she braced her shoulders. "Here we go again!"

Most of the village was there on the shore, trying to sell things to Gunnar, and getting in the way of cursing sailors manhandling barrels of fresh water and provisions.

There was Harald, his long hair clubbed back in a ponytail, heaving crates around with the crew. Peer's eyebrows rose in grudging respect: he'd thought Harald too much the 'young lord' to bother with real work. He noticed with relief that neither Harald nor Gunnar were wearing swords this morning. That would even things out a bit. Of course, those long steel swords would rust so easily: they'd be packed away in greased wool for the voyage.

Ralf and Arne came to unload the pony. Ralf seized Hilde. "Are you sure about this?" And before Peer could hear her reply, somebody grabbed him, too.

It was Bjørn, a tight frown on his face. "Have you gone crazy?" he demanded. "How can you think of sailing with Harald?"

Peer's gaze slid past Bjørn's shoulder. "I'll be all right, Pa," Hilde was saying in an earnest voice. "I really, truly want to go."

"Ah," Bjørn said. "This is Hilde's idea, is it? I might have known."

"Not entirely," said Peer, blushing.

"I thought we were going to work together. I thought you wanted to build boats, like your father."

"I do." Peer touched the silver ring he always wore, which had belonged to his father. He added earnestly, "I *do* want to work with you, Bjørn. When I come back—"

"When you come back!" Bjørn exploded. "*If* you come back! Peer, this is no fishing trip. Whatever they say, Gunnar and his men are Vikings, and that ship is like a spark from a bonfire that goes floating off, setting trouble alight wherever it lands." He added, "I'm not usually so poetical. But you see what I mean?"

"Yes," said Peer. "But your brother's going, isn't he? This is a trading voyage, not a Viking raid. Gunnar has his wife with him. He's not going to fight anyone, he's going to Vinland to cut down trees for timber. Besides—"

He broke off. *Who am I trying to convince?* Yet he still felt the unexpected longing that had squeezed his heart yesterday evening, as he looked westwards from the stern of *Water Snake*. "Bjørn," he said awkwardly. "The very last ship my father worked on, the *Long Serpent*, she's in Vinland now. Think of it, she sailed all that way! I'd like to follow after her, just once. I'd like to find Thorolf and say, 'Remember me? I'm the son of the man who built your ship.'"

Bjørn began to speak, then shook his head. They looked at each other while the gulls screamed, and the men shouted on the jetty, and the wind whipped their clothes.

"One thing you should know," Bjørn said at last. "Gunnar's own men have been gossiping that he and Harald killed a man in Westfold and had to run for it. No wonder they're on their way back to Vinland."

"That's no secret," said Peer. "He told us about it. That's when he lost his hand. It was self-defence. The other man started it."

"You mean, the same way you 'started' that fight with Harald yesterday?"

"You may be right," said Peer after a pause. "But I won't back out now."

Bjørn sighed. "Arne won't change his mind, either. He's always been crazy, but I thought you had sense. Well, stick together." He caught Peer's expression. "You can trust Arne. You know him. But keep out of Harald's beautiful hair." He clapped Peer on the back. "Come back rich! And now we'd better go and help, before Gunnar decides you're nothing but a useless passenger."

"Don't touch the sail," Astrid said to Hilde. "That red colour comes off all over your clothes."

Hilde looked around, wondering where she could sit. The ship was full of scrambling seamen.

"Keep out of their way." Astrid perched on a barrel, forward of the mast, and began to tie her hair up in a headscarf. "It'll be better when we're sailing."

"Mind out, Miss." One of the men pushed past Hilde. "Here, you, son," – this was to Peer – "give me a hand with these oars."

Hilde craned her neck to see if Ma and Pa were still watching. Of course, they were. She gave a desperate little wave. *This is awful. If only we could just get going.*

A rope flipped past her ears. Arne jumped down into the ship and pushed off aft. Bjørn tossed another rope down to him. Harald took the tiller. A gap of water opened between the ship and the jetty. Hilde stared at it. It was only a stride wide. She could step over that easily, if she wanted.

With a heavy wooden clatter, the oars went out through the oarholes: only three on each side, but *Water Snake* was moving steadily away. For a moment longer, the gap was still narrow enough to jump: then, finally and for ever, too wide.

Pa's arm lifted. Sigurd and Sigrid waved, and she heard

them yelling, "Goodbye, goodbye!" Even Eirik opened and closed his fingers, and Sigrid flapped Elli's arm up and down. But Ma didn't move. Hilde raised her own arm and flailed it madly.

Too late to say the things she should have said. *I love you. I'll miss you all so much.* Too late to change her mind. *Ma, please wave...*

And at last, Gudrun's hand came slowly up. She waved, and as long as Hilde watched she continued to wave across the broadening water, till at last the jetty was out of sight.

Hilde's throat ached from not crying. She turned a stiff neck to look round at the ship: her new world. Her new home. And there was Peer, wrenching away at one of the oars. He looked up and caught her eye, and gave her an odd, lopsided smile.

It's going to be all right, she thought, comforted.

"Oars in," Gunnar bellowed. "Up with the sail!"

Water Snake began to seesaw, pitching and rolling over steep, choppy waves. Peer laid his wet oar on top of the others in a rattling pile, and scrambled to the stern to help pull on the halyard that raised the yard.

"Hey – up! Hey – up!" Each heave lifted the heavy spar a foot or two higher. When it was halfway up the mast, Arne yanked the lacing to unfurl the sail, and swag upon swag of hard-woven, greasy fabric dropped across the ship. "Haul!" Up went the sail again, opening out like a vast red hand to blot out the sky and half the horizon: a towering square of living, struggling, flapping cloth. The men on the braces hauled the yard around, fighting for control. The sail tautened and filled, and the ship sped forwards so suddenly that Peer had to catch at the shrouds to keep his balance.

"Right lads, listen up!" shouted Gunnar. There was a better colour in his face: he straddled forwards, his good hand on Harald's shoulder to help his balance, bad arm tucked under his cloak.

"Some of us are old friends already. Magnus, Floki, Halfdan…" His eye roamed across the men, who grinned or nodded as he named them. "The way I like to run things is this: you jump when I say jump, and we'll get along fine. We're going a long way together, so if you don't like the idea, you'd better start swimming." He bared his teeth ferociously, and the men laughed. "I lost my hand a few weeks ago. If anyone thinks that makes me less of a man, speak up now." The men glanced at each other. No one spoke. "We're going to Vinland, boys, and we'll come back rich! That's all, except… we're the crew of the *Water Snake*, we are, and there isn't a better ship on the sea."

The men cheered. Even Peer felt a stirring in his blood. *The crew of the* Water Snake *– sailing to Vinland, across the world!*

Waves smacked into the prow. The dragonhead nodded and plunged. They were out of the fjord already, and the wind was strengthening.

He looked back. There was the familiar peak of Troll Fell, piebald with snow-streaks, but behind it, other mountains jostled into view, trying to get a good look at *Water Snake* as she sailed out. As the ship drew further and further away, the details vanished, and it became more and more difficult to pick out Troll Fell from amongst its rivals, until at last they all merged and flattened into a long blue smudge of coastline.

CHAPTER 46

The Winter Visitor

KWIMU IS WIDE awake and wonders what has woken him. He's in the wigwam, feet towards the fire, which still burns enough to warm the air. It's the dead of night. Around him, his family sleeps, wrapped in warm furs.

He raises himself, listening. Behind and above, his shadow rears against the sloping birch-bark walls. Everything seems well. He scans the sleeping faces near to him: Sinumkw, his father. Kiunik, his mother's brother. Beside him, the pale face of Skusji'j, the Little Weasel. Across the fire on the women's side, his mother, grandmother, aunt and sister sleep. Even the dogs are fast asleep, noses buried in their bushy tails.

An owl calls: *koo koo!* Perhaps the owl woke him. He settles back on the springy fir boughs that layer the floor, draws the warm beaverskin robe up to his chin, and folds his arms behind his head, staring up to where the slanting poles of the wigwam come together high overhead, framing a patch of black sky.

Outside, the snow is thick, the cold is strong. His stomach grumbles, but he's not truly hungry. It's been a good winter for the People, with plenty of game. No need to kill the dogs, as they had to do in the famine three winters back. Dog is good to eat, but moose is better: besides, Kwimu likes the dogs. They are good hunting companions.

The worst of the winter is over. This is Sugar Moon, the forerunner of spring. Soon the sap will be rising in the sugar maples, and it will be time to collect it and boil it into thick, sweet syrup. Kwimu looks forward to showing Skusji'j how to pour little coils of hot syrup into the snow, where it cools into chewy candy. Then the thaw will come, the rivers will melt, and it will be time to move down to the seashore again. He glances again at Skusji'j. Hard to believe that nearly four seasons have passed since he and his father took the Little Weasel away from the deserted houses of the Jipijka'm People. The child had fought like a weasel, too, biting and scratching so fiercely they'd had to tie his hands and bundle him into the canoe all trussed up – till he realised they meant him no harm.

And he'd been quick to pick up words – a gruff greeting, a *yes* or a *no*. Still, it was months before he could tell in stumbling sentences who he was and how he came in his people's ships from a land across the ocean, a journey of a moon or more. Everyone there has pale skin. It sounds like the Ghost World. But the Little Weasel is no ghost.

"He is my little brother," Kwimu murmurs, and his heart is warm.

He reaches for Fox, who doesn't stir, even when Kwimu runs his hand over the pricked ears and sharp, pointed nose. Outside, the owl has stopped calling. Perhaps it has killed. Kwimu yawns. Why can't he sleep? He's not even drowsy.

His mind roams back over a year of changes. He'd thought, after the Jipijka'm People had gone, that they could move down to the bay as usual. But Sinumkw hadn't liked the idea. "How do we know if the Jipijka'm People have gone for good? What if they come back?" The rest of the men, after discussing it, agreed with him. They arranged with the

Beaver Clan to share their shoreline and fishing grounds for the season. But what will happen this year? Grandmother says those dark earth houses are haunted. *Angry ghosts sing songs there now*, she says. It is a place of bad memories, best avoided.

Kwimu lies thinking of it: the river where they built the fish weir, the shore where he's dug for clams and oysters, the marshlands where ducks and geese gather in hundreds, and where huge brown moose sometimes wander out of the forests to splash through the boggy pools. *Is it all lost for ever? Will we never go back?*

A branch cracks: a sharp, splintering, tearing sound. Kwimu starts, although branches break all the time. They snap like pipe stems, weighted with snow or split by frost.

All the same, he holds his breath. The cold intensifies, the fire pines and dwindles. Just as he has to let his breath go in a cloud of vapour, he hears it again: another crack, and then heavy, slow footsteps in the snow. *Crunch. Crunch.*

Beside him, Fox twists into sudden life. All through the wigwam, the family wakes, eyes flying open, breath caught. No one speaks. Even the dogs know better than to yap. Skusji'j sits up. He looks from face to face. "*Muin?*" he mouths to Kwimu. "Bear?"

Kwimu shakes his head. All the bears are asleep. They won't wake, hungry and bad tempered, till late spring.

Crunch. Crunch. Something shuffles about the wigwam. Kwimu's heart beats hard. The framework of the wigwam shudders as the thing outside jostles it, then picks at the walls, patting and fumbling. Kwimu's little sister is panting with terror. Any moment now, the frail birch-bark walls will be torn away, exposing them to the bleak wind and icy stars, and to—

Skusji'j cries out loudly in his own language, and as Kwimu turns on him in furious anger, repeats it in the language of the People: "See! See there!" He points. Something is blocking the star-shaped opening at the top of the wigwam: something dark and glistening that rolls about showing a yellowish-white rim, fixing for a malevolent moment on each person below.

An eye as big as your hand.

Sinumkw seizes his lance. Kwimu's mother shrieks. But Grandmother springs nimbly to her feet, shaking off her covers. She catches up two of the fir branches that line the floor, and thrusts them into the fire. They crackle and catch, and she waves them upwards, streaming sparks.

The eye vanishes. From high above, a terrible scream rings across the forest. The sound crushes them with its weight of cold anguish. They huddle, clutching each other, expecting to be trodden and trampled. But the frozen ground shudders to the impact of huge feet running away.

Before his father can forbid it, Kwimu dashes to the door of the wigwam, Skusji'j at his heels. He peels back the hide flap and scurries out into the bitter night. Around him the village is waking. Men stumble from the doorways of the nearest wigwams and call out in alarm. The treetops are dark against a sky hazy with moon-glimmer. A few hundred yards to the south-east, something crashes away through the trees, howling, brushing the very tops of the white pines.

There are enormous, pitted tracks in the snow.

Kiunik, Kwimu's young uncle, ducks out of the wigwam and races towards the trees, yelling a war-cry, his black hair streaming loose. Some of the other young men join in, but the older ones call them roughly back: "It's gone; let it go."

"We've been lucky: you can't fight a *jenu*."

"What was it?" The Little Weasel tugs Kwimu's arm. He looks like a ghost in the white darkness. "Kwimu, *what was it?*"

"*Jenu*," Kwimu mutters. "Ice giant. We have seen the *jenu* – and lived."

CHAPTER 47

Ghost Stories

"THERE ARE NO trolls in Vinland," said Magnus confidently.

Peer sat with his back against the curve of the side, rocking to the steady up and down of the ship. He could see sky, but not sea, and it was comforting to shut out for a while the sight of all that lonely vastness. The sun had just set: the top half of the sail still caught a ruddy glow on its western side.

Water Snake was on the starboard tack, lifting and diving over the waves in a rhythm as easy as breathing. They were far from land – further than Peer had ever been before. This big ship seemed very small now – a speck of dust under a wide sky.

The day had passed simply. At home there would be a hundred things to do: ploughing fields, chopping firewood, patching boats, mending nets. Here there was only one purpose, to sail on and on into the west.

Like an enormous, slewed curtain, the sail almost cut off the front of the ship from the rear. To be heard by someone in a different part of the vessel, you had to shout across the wind. Just now, Harald was steering, and Peer was in the bows, almost as far away from him as it was possible to get. He leaned back, watching Loki scramble over the stacks of crates and barrels amidships, sticking his nose in everywhere. Loki was having no problems adjusting to his new life at sea!

And neither was Hilde. On leaving home this morning, she'd been as close to tears as Peer had ever seen her – but now she was sitting on a crossbeam, chatting to some of the men. *Trust Hilde*, he thought to himself with a rueful smile. She knew the names of half the crew already, and was busy finding out about the others.

"No trolls in Vinland?" she was saying now. "So you've been there, Magnus – you've sailed with Gunnar before?"

"That's right." Magnus was a middle-aged man, his face criss-crossed with tiny lines from screwing up his eyes against sun and weather. He beamed at Hilde. "Me, and Halfdan, and young Floki here, we were all with the skipper on his last voyage. Never saw a troll. Floki's my mate. I look out for him, and he does what I says. Like a father to him, I am, ain't I, Floki?" Floki was a youngish man with curly hair and a rather vacant expression. Magnus dug him in the ribs, and he sniggered amiably.

"What the skipper does, you see, Missy," Magnus went on, "he splits us into two watches, so we can take turns to sail the ship and rest. There's us three, and your brother here, Peer—"

"I'm not her brother," said Peer firmly. Hilde looked at him in surprise.

"Oh, aye?" Magnus showed three missing teeth in a grin. "And in the other watch there's Arne—"

"We both know Arne," Hilde interrupted.

"And young Harald Silkenhair, and Big Tjørvi," Magnus finished. He frowned at his hands and bent down gnarled fingers, muttering, "Six, seven… that's eight of us, counting the skipper, who's in charge but who don't do much hauling and rowing any more. See?"

"It makes ten of us," Hilde corrected him. "Counting Astrid and me."

"Women don't count," said a deep voice. A man ducked under the edge of the sail and straightened up – and up, and up, a blond giant like a white summer cloud, the kind that towers up against a blue sky. His hair and beard were as fluffy as dandelion seeds. He regarded Hilde with a straight-faced, solemn expression.

"Why don't women count?" Hilde demanded.

"Too weak," said Big Tjørvi.

"I like that! We may not be as strong as you, but brains count for something!" Hilde took in the men's grins and nudges. "You're teasing me. Aren't you?"

"Wouldn't dare." Big Tjørvi's eyes gleamed.

"Better not," Magnus joked. "This girl took on a whole mountainful of trolls, so she tells me."

"Not by myself," said Hilde. "Peer was there too."

"Did you, now?" Tjørvi looked at the pair of them with interest.

"Tell Tjørvi about that troll baby," urged Floki. "She saw a troll baby, Tjørvi. With a pig's snout and a purple tongue. Like this!" He pushed his nose up with his thumb, and stuck out a slobbery tongue.

"Don't tell that tale to the skipper," said Halfdan darkly.

"Why not?" asked Peer.

Several of the men looked round. But Gunnar was in the stern with Harald and Astrid, and with the wind blowing as it was, there was no chance he could overhear this conversation. The men were uneasy, vague. "The skipper's a bit – you know…"

"Edgy," said Halfdan, a small, skinny man with narrow-set eyes.

"He'd reckon talking about trolls is unlucky," said Magnus. "Lots of things is unlucky at sea. Like whistling."

"Whistling's unlucky?" asked Hilde, who could whistle nicely herself.

Everyone nodded. "'Cos it brings the wind," said Floki. He pursed his lips and mimed a breathy little whistle. There was no true sound, but Magnus aimed a cuff at his head. "Stow that, you young fool!" he growled.

It could have been coincidence, but a strong gust sped over the water. The ship put her bows hard into the next wave. Several of the men glared at Floki, and a small shiver ran down Peer's back. Out here at sea, maybe these things weren't funny.

"There'll be no good luck this trip," went on Floki, who seemed to have no sense of self-preservation. "Women on ships is unlucky, too, and here we are with two of 'em!" Hilde gasped indignantly, but the men weren't thinking of her.

"Astrid..." There was a general mutter.

"The skipper got a wrong 'un there."

"What's she got in that bag of hers?"

"I reckon she's half a witch."

"You know what I heard?" Halfdan said in low tones. "I heard she's got troll blood in her veins – it runs in the family. But her father tried to hush it up. Who'd marry a troll? Likely the skipper doesn't know. Well, who'd tell him?"

Peer tried to exchange a sceptical glance with Hilde, but she was examining her nails. Floki's rather protuberant blue eyes opened wide. Magnus sucked air in through his teeth.

Big Tjørvi stretched. "I reckon that's rubbish," he said slowly. "At least she looks after the skipper. She's got healing herbs in that bag of hers."

"Then why's he still sick?" demanded Magnus.

"What's wrong with him?" Hilde asked. "Not just his hand?"

Magnus seemed to take this as criticism. He glared at her. "The hand? Take more than losing a hand to stop an old sea-wolf like Gunnar. No. But he gets awful fevers and black sweats that shake him till he can't hardly stand."

"That's no ordinary sickness what's wrong with the skipper," said Floki in a melancholy sing-song. "There's a ghost a-following after him, ah, and it won't rest till it gets him."

"*A ghost*?" Peer sat up.

"Shut up! Shut up!" Magnus lunged at Floki. He grabbed a handful of shirt and twisted it up under Floki's chin, shaking a hard fist under his nose. "I told you not to talk about that!" he said.

Floki screwed up his face, flinching and crying, "Sorry, Magnus, sorry. I won't do it again!"

"See you don't. Or see what you'll get!" Magnus dropped him. "Don't listen to him," he added to Hilde. "He's simple, a moon-calf. The skipper would kill him if he heard. There's no ghost. *There's no ghost!*"

Peer and Hilde looked at each other. Peer got stiffly to his feet. With Loki at his heels, he made his way up into the prow, where the tall neck of the dragonhead divided the darkening horizon. Hilde murmured an excuse and came after him.

"*Well.* What do you make of that?"

"I don't know," said Peer. "It doesn't sound good." Ranks of surly waves slopped up at the ship and sank back. He wished they had never come on board: but if Hilde was here, he was glad to be with her. He leaned over the side and Hilde did the same, her left arm almost touching his right. He thought of saying, *At least we're together.* But before he could get the words out, Hilde said crisply, "Not good? I call it very odd indeed. A ghost? Whose ghost?"

Peer sighed. "Well, Gunnar and Harald killed a man in

Westfold. Maybe Floki's thinking of him. But that doesn't mean there really is a ghost," he added, seeing she looked disturbed. "I don't think Floki's very bright."

"Then why did Magnus get so upset? And Astrid said Gunnar's afraid of the dark."

"Did she?" Peer frowned. It seemed a strange thing for a girl to say about her husband. "Do you like her? The men don't. All that stuff about troll blood..."

"I do like her – I think," said Hilde. "It's odd, though: she wanted me to come, but ever since we got on board this morning she's avoided me. If I sit with her, she moves away. If I talk to her, she barely answers. It's as though she's hiding something. What's going on?"

Peer didn't really want to talk about Astrid. "Perhaps she's feeling seasick."

"A ghost," Hilde repeated. "How could a ghost follow a man over the sea?" She looked out across the heaving water and shivered. "But remember the draug?"

"Yes..." Peer thought of the fearsome sea spirit that roamed the seas in half a boat, with a crew of drowned corpses. He'd glimpsed it once – a tattered sail and a dark hull, manned by stiff silhouettes. He began to understand why sailors didn't talk about such things. That ragged cloud on the horizon – could it be a sail?

"Hey!" said a voice behind them.

They both jumped. "Time to eat," said Arne cheerfully. "Astrid wants you, Hilde. Serving out the rations is women's work!" And he winked at Peer, much to Peer's surprise.

"All right," said Hilde mildly. She began clambering back along the ship towards the stern. Peer made to follow her, but Arne held him back. "A word, Peer?"

"Well, what is it?" asked Peer after a moment.

Arne lowered his voice, fidgeting. "You know I've always liked Hilde. More than liked her. She's a grand lass, and I don't reckon I could do better when I come to get a wife. No, listen!" He threw up his hand as Peer tried to interrupt. "I know, you're thinking, *Why's he telling me this?* You see, I always thought you'd taken a sort of boy's fancy for Hilde yourself. But after what she said the other night, I saw I was wrong." He gave an embarrassed laugh. "I should have known you're like brother and sister. Shake hands – and if you could put in a good word for me with Hilde…?"

"No. Look," Peer said in confused anger, ignoring Arne's out-thrust hand. "You've got it wrong. She's not my sister. I've never felt like her brother, and I never will."

Arne recoiled. "So that's your game?" he said in a voice brimful of disgust. "And you told Ralf and Gudrun you were only coming along to protect Hilde."

"I didn't! I mean, I am!" Peer stammered in dismay and increasing rage.

"Well, *she* says you're her brother. So what's this about? Using her trust to take advantage of her?"

"Leave me alone!"

"With pleasure. And you leave her alone." Arne turned away.

Peer boiled over. "*It's up to Hilde who she spends her time with!*" he yelled, and saw Arne check and stiffen, before ducking under the sail and walking on.

The meal was cheerless: dried herring, and cold groute – barley porridge which had been cooked on shore and left to congeal in the pot. The crew sat around, scraping their spoons into the sticky mess. And although Gunnar had taken on fresh water only that morning, it already tasted odd. When Hilde suggested warming the food, Astrid said scornfully, "Light a fire? On a ship?"

"Oh, of course…"

"There won't be any hot food till we touch land."

"And when will that be?" asked Hilde, looking around. "How far is it to Vinland? And how do we find the way?"

"Depends on the weather," Gunnar grunted, through a mouthful. "Three weeks. Four. As for how…" He shrugged.

Talkative Magnus waved his spoon. "See, first we go past the Islands of Sheep, just far enough south that the mountains show half out of the sea. And then we follow the whales past Iceland. And so, west to Greenland."

"I know how to spot Greenland," said Floki eagerly. "Don't I, Magnus? Remember, last time, you pointed out the old Blueshirt Glacier? I'd know that again."

Magnus reached across and tugged Floki's ear. "That's right, laddie," he said with a grin. Floki squealed.

"That'll be our first landfall, Greenland," said Gunnar, ignoring this.

"You'll all be glad to stretch your legs by then," said Magnus, relentlessly jokey. "And then off we go, west again, till we strike a rocky, barren sort of coast, and follow it south with the land on our right, till we get to Vinland."

Peer hadn't realised it was so far. His teeth chattered. The wind struck a dash of spray flew into his face. "Such a long way," he muttered under his breath.

Harald's voice came quietly out of the dusk:

"May the white-armed women of the waves
Speed us safely through the sea-kingdom,
Through the whales' home and the heaving waters
To the far strand where the sun westers."

For a moment everyone was still. Even Peer was held by the music of the words and the rhythm of the waves. Then Harald broke the spell he himself had cast.

"Worrying again, Barelegs?" he jeered. "Wishing you hadn't come?"

Arne laughed out loud.

Peer's face flamed. Before he could think what to say, he felt a large hand grasp his arm. "Time to turn in," said Big Tjørvi calmly. "Skipper? Gunnar? Who's for the first watch?"

Gunnar chose Magnus, Peer, Halfdan and Floki. Stringy, dark-haired Halfdan took the steering oar. Magnus and Floki propped themselves against the sides, each holding one of the long braces that trailed dizzyingly upwards to either end of the wide yard. Peer went off forward for the solitary task of lookout and tacksman. The rest of the crew unrolled their wide two-man sleeping sacks wherever they could find a bit of empty deck, and scrambled in.

Astrid's sack was already spread out in a spot as sheltered as any, in the lee of the starboard side. She slid into it as neat as a knife into a sheath, and snuggled down without speaking, but Hilde sat for a few more moments, knees drawn up to her chin. Harald's jeer and Arne's laugh hadn't escaped her. Peer and Arne – they'd never got on. She half-guessed why, but pushed it out of mind. Blue-eyed Arne: she'd always liked him. But Peer – Peer was *family.* Arne had no right to laugh at him, and especially not to side with Harald against him.

I hope the other men will like Peer. I hope he'll be all right...

The sky wasn't totally dark. It had a deep colour tinged with lingering light against which the sail looked black, a great square of starless night hanging over the ship.

Lonely wonder overcame her. Whatever was she doing out here on the ocean, listening to the chuckle and truckle of water running along the sides and under the bottom boards? She imagined the close, smoky darkness of the farmhouse. *Have they gone to bed? Has Ma left the dough to rise on the hearthstone? Has she put out the bowl for the Nis? Is she lying awake, missing me?*

A feeble glow kindled in the stern. Halfdan had lit a small, horn-windowed lantern and put it at his feet.

Hilde pulled off her shoes and tried to stuff her legs into the sleeping sack without her skirt bunching up. Nobody undressed on a ship, and in any case it was too cold. She inched her way in like a caterpillar, trying not to disturb Astrid who lay with her face turned away. It wouldn't be a comfortable night. The ship tilted and tipped and swung; she heard the mumbling voices of the men on watch, and the coughs and grunts and snores of those, who like herself, were sleeping or trying to sleep.

Her bare feet touched something at the bottom of the sack. A sort of bundle, firm but yielding, with a hairy surface. She prodded it with her toes – and it jerked.

"Ouch!" Hilde twitched her feet away. And suddenly Astrid was sitting upright. "Hush!" she hissed.

"Astrid!" Hilde seized her arm. "There's something in there. It moved!"

Astrid heaved an exasperated sigh. "I suppose you had to find out. But just *keep quiet* about it, right?" She ducked into the sleeping sack, delving past Hilde's legs, and heaved out her goatskin bag by its long strap.

"Your bag?" whispered Hilde. She remembered Astrid's little buzzing box. What else did she keep in there? Something alive?

"What is it?" She drew back. The bag bulged and bounced,

as if something inside it was kicking and punching. Then came a muffled, furious squeaking: "*Help, he-elp!*"

"The *Nis*?" Hilde gasped.

"You open it." Astrid shoved the bag at Hilde. "It might bite me."

"Oh, you haven't. You couldn't." She wrenched at the buckle, tore open the flap, and almost dropped the whole thing as a frantic little whirlwind clawed its way out, fell into her lap, kicked itself away and shot up the mast with a noise like a cat fight: "*Aiaieiyooooooooo!*"

With a yell of fright, Floki let go of the port brace. "There's something on the mast! An evil spirit!"

Astrid snatched the bag from Hilde and thrust it into the sleeping sack. "Lie down," she whispered fiercely. "Pretend you're asleep."

"Asleep?" Hilde cried. In the darkness overhead, the Nis caterwauled and shrieked.

"Shut it up, then! Make it stop!" Astrid lay back and screwed her eyes firmly shut.

Hilde struggled out of the sleeping sack. *Where's Peer? I have to find Peer.* By now everyone was yelling and rushing about. Loki barked madly. From the top of the mast, the dreadful screaming went on.

"Peer?" she shouted. With a noise like a rough kiss, waves slapped into the side, and spray showered on board. Halfdan had accidentally steered *Water Snake* too far into the wind. The sail went aback, clapping and thundering, and the ship hung in the water, tossing. Hilde lost her balance and staggered into someone tall and slender who caught her and steadied her. It was Peer. She pulled his head down and said urgently into his ear, "It's the Nis – Astrid's brought the Nis!"

Peer gave her one incredulous look, nodded grimly, and

disappeared. Hilde sank to the deck. Peer was good with the Nis: he would deal with it somehow…

"Get back on the tack!" Gunnar bellowed. Young Harald sprang past her, his long hair flying, threw Halfdan off the steering oar, and grabbed it himself. *Water Snake* swung back on course. The terrible screeching stopped. What had happened? Had Peer coaxed the Nis down – or had it fallen overboard?

Big Tjørvi held up the lantern. The tiny flame made the darkness darker, the steep sides of the waves as black and glossy as coal. It gleamed on Gunnar, staring about as though he expected to see slimy hands clawing out of the sea. His face stretched, eyebrows high, mouth agape, eyes popping.

"What made that noise?" he choked. No one answered. His voice climbed. "By Thor and his Hammer! One of you must have seen it. There's something on board this ship, and I swear when I find it, I'll cut it into tiny pieces!" Spittle caught in his beard.

"I saw it!" came a cry from the darkness beyond the sail. Everyone froze. Peer came scrambling along the side, skirting the hold. "It's all right," he gasped. "It was only a seagull. A huge one, with great flapping wings – must have been attracted by our lantern."

Hilde shut her eyes and crossed her fingers. Gunnar stared; the men broke into raucous disbelief. "A gull?" "Never!" "That was no gull – no gull screams like that!"

"It was a just a gull!" Peer shouted. "Look!" He held up a fistful of white feathers, then opened his fingers and let the wind pick them away. "Didn't you see it, Astrid?"

Astrid was on her feet now. "Me? Oh, yes! My goodness, it frightened me, it flew right in front of my face. Its wings must have been six feet across!"

"Not as big as that," Hilde joined in, scowling. *Stupid girl, why does she have to exaggerate?* "Maybe four feet."

"You saw it too?" Gunnar said slowly.

Hilde returned his stare, eye to eye. "How could you miss it?"

"All right. All right!" Gunnar swung round. "A bird, lads, a great stupid bird." He clapped his good hand across his eyes, rubbing it to and fro, gritting his teeth as though in pain. "A gull!" he gasped. Laughing or crying? His whole body shook.

Astrid threw her cloak around him. "Come with me, Gunnar, I'll give you something to make you sleep." He grabbed her and for a moment buried his head against her neck like a child hiding its face. Astrid patted his shoulder. She led him away.

Halfdan coughed, apologising to Harald. "I'm sorry, master. I don't rightly know what I was thinking. I had such a shock when that great bird flew right over my head – sort of whirled round me, like, screaming..."

Hilde bit down a nervous giggle. Soon everyone would think they'd seen it.

"All right, Halfdan." Harald strode down the deck and dragged Peer aside. "That was no gull," he said in a low, hard voice.

"You saw the feathers," Peer said, his face unmoving.

"From a distance. Before they blew away. And I happen to remember that we have a white hen on board."

Hilde edged closer. Peer said, "What are you saying? You think I would open the coops, grab a couple of chickens, pull out their feathers, and then come and tell a story about a seagull? Why would I do that?"

An uncertain flicker crossed Harald's face.

"Gunnar seems glad to think it was only a gull," Peer

pressed on. "What else could it have been?"

Harald's eyes narrowed. His fingers tightened on Peer's arm. "Let's leave my father out of it, Barelegs. I don't know what it was, but I think you do; and I hope it's no longer on this ship, because if I find it I'm going to kill it. And it was *no seagull.*"

He glared at Peer and swung away.

"Why does he call you that – Barelegs?" asked Hilde angrily.

"He does it to annoy me." Peer sounded exhausted. "I'd better get back on duty."

"Using the feathers was a great idea. Where's the Nis?"

"Hiding in the chicken coop." Peer's voice was suddenly furious. "It's terrified. Miserable. What was Astrid thinking of, to bring it here?"

"That's what I'm going to find out next," said Hilde.

The two of them were standing close together. She couldn't see Peer's face very well – he was just a dark shape against the sky – but he moved towards her. She had the feeling he was about to say something more. But a second later he just said, "Good luck," and went off forward.

She climbed into the sleeping sack with a lot less care than the first time. Astrid was already there again, lying on her side. Hilde poked her.

"You stole the Nis."

"Bravo," said Astrid in a muffled voice, her arm across her face.

"Kidnapped it. What did you do? Drug it?"

"I put a tiny, tiny bit of henbane in the groute, to make it sleep," said Astrid indignantly. "That's all. And then I very carefully scooped it into my bag. It had a nice snooze, and woke up a little while ago."

"Stuffed at the bottom of the sleeping sack. How could you? And why? It belongs at home. The Nis would never, never want to cross the sea!"

"I *brought* it because it will be *useful*," Astrid whispered. "Wait till we get to Vinland, that's all. Who'll be doing the housework? We will, the only women. Cooking? You and me. Collecting firewood, carrying water? Us again. The men will be hunting and trapping for furs – guess who'll be cleaning the hides? Believe me, you'll be glad of some extra help."

"The Nis is a person, not a thing. You can't force it to help you! And what will my mother think when she finds it's disappeared?"

"Oh, stop complaining." Astrid sounded sour. "If she's as fond of you as she pretends to be, she'll be glad you've got it. I think it was very clever of me to bring the Nis."

"Clever?" Hilde's voice rose. "What about the fuss we've just had? If it hadn't been for Peer—"

"I approve of that boy," said Astrid. "He thinks quickly."

"I don't suppose he approves of you. The Nis should go home."

"Tell Gunnar to turn the ship round, then."

"I know it's too late for that," said Hilde angrily. "But when I go home next summer, the Nis will come with me."

"But you won't be going home."

"Of course I... What do you mean?"

Astrid gave a brittle laugh. "Well, you *may* go home, of course. Eventually. But it won't be next year, or the year after that, or—"

"*What do you mean?*"

Astrid stuck her face close to Hilde's. "Gunnar and Harald are outlaws. They wouldn't pay the blood price for the man they killed in Westfold, so they've been outlawed for five years. That's why we're going to Vinland. Now you know."

The ship pitched, and Hilde's stomach seemed to pitch sickeningly with it. *Five years?*

"Who else knows?" she got out. "Arne?"

"Arne? Why Arne? Oh, you think he should have told you, because he likes you? Well maybe you'd better marry him. Because we'll be living in Vinland for a very long time." She turned away from Hilde with a heave and a flounce, and lay still.

Hilde wanted to spring up and rush to tell Peer. She forced herself to lie still, biting her knuckles, thinking furiously.

It could be true. It must be. But she's lying about Arne. If he knew Gunnar was outlawed, he'd never have sailed with him.

Five years!

She became aware of a fine tremor running through Astrid from head to foot.

She's crying.

Let her cry.

But she put out a quiet hand. Astrid flinched and froze. "What's the matter?" Hilde whispered, knowing it was a stupid question.

"I suppose you hate me," Astrid muttered.

Hilde was still very angry. "You should have told the truth."

"You were warned." Astrid twisted round like an eel. "I told you I'm part troll. Of course I tell lies and steal things. How else can I get what I want?"

"And you've got it, have you? Is this what you wanted?"

"I never get anything I want," said Astrid bitterly. "It's always the same. If I like someone, I lose them."

Hilde remembered how Astrid had hinted before at someone she'd loved and lost. She said more gently, "Was there really someone you wanted to marry before your father made you marry Gunnar?"

"Yes," Astrid sniffed.

"What was he called?"

"Erlend," said Astrid. "Erlend Asmundsson. But now he's dead."

"Dead!" Hilde fell silent. Something in Astrid's gruff voice suggested an awful possibility. "Astrid. The man Harald killed in Westfold – in the fight when Gunnar lost his hand—"

"Well?"

Hilde hardly dared say it. "He wasn't the same person, was he? I mean – he wasn't Erlend? He wasn't killed in a quarrel over you?"

For a couple of heartbeats Astrid was very still. It was too dark to see her face. At last she sighed: a long, silent, stealthy breath.

"You've guessed," she whispered softly. "He was. Yes, he was. That's exactly what happened."

CHAPTER 48

The Nis at Sea

"NIS!" PEER CROUCHED on the cargo, trying to see into the chicken coop. His blood was racing. *I faced down Harald.*

More than that – standing next to Hilde in the dark, he'd nearly kissed her. At the last moment, he'd lost his nerve. What if she protested, shoved him away? Everyone would know.

He was furious with himself. So much for those bold resolutions to behave as he felt. Well, he couldn't cope with it now. He bundled the thoughts away and tried to concentrate on the Nis. He had to get it out of this coop. In the darkness he could only make out a whitish frill of feathers here, the glint of an eye there. The hens crooned softly, weird burbling sounds. But he thought he could also detect quick, shallow breathing.

"Nis, it's me, Peer. It's all right."

Loki lurked behind him, interested and suspicious. Peer pushed him. "Go and lie down. I can't have you upsetting the Nis now. Go!" Loki backed reluctantly away.

"Nis, do come out," Peer pleaded. "If I stay here much longer, someone will notice, and we need to talk. I have to explain what's happening."

No reply.

"All right, come and find me. I'll be in the prow, by myself – that's the pointed bit with the dragon head," he added.

"But don't leave it too long, or they'll change the watch, and somebody else will be there."

Before he could move, a sliver of a voice whimpered, "Wait..."

"I am waiting," Peer said after a moment, as patiently as he could.

"Has there been a flood?" the voice quavered.

"A flood? All this water? That's not a flood, Nis, it's the sea. We're at sea."

No answer, though a hen squawked, as though someone had startled it with a sharp movement.

"In a boat," Peer amplified. "I know it's very frightening for you, but come out and let me tell you how it happened."

A moment later, the hens rustled again. From under their feathers a small shadow scuttled on all fours. It slipped between the bars of the coop.

Peer led the way into the windy bows. Up here it was like balancing on a high seesaw. Spray flew past the dragon neck, and the decking was wet. He tucked himself into the angle below the dragon, next to the anchor, and the Nis actually climbed into his lap. Loki pressed jealously against Peer's knees, grumbling. Peer gently rubbed the little creature's shoulders, feeling the tiny knobbles of its backbone under its ragged grey clothes. Its heart was jumping in its sides. The wind messed its wispy hair, and it had lost its little red hat.

"Where am I?" it wailed. "Why is I here? One minute I was supping up my groute, Peer Ulfsson, nice groute with butter and a bit of cream – and the next, I wakes up in the dark bag, all hot and smothery, and then I gets out, and there's no house, and no hills. Where's Troll Fell, Peer Ulfsson? Where's home?"

"Good question," Peer muttered. He tried to explain.

"We're a long way from home, Nis. How much did you overhear, last night? This ship is going to Vinland…"

The Nis listened fearfully. At last it interrupted. "But how did I get here, Peer Ulfsson?"

Peer hesitated; he knew the Nis wouldn't like this. "I'm afraid Astrid stole you. I think she must have put something in your food."

"In – my – food?" the Nis repeated slowly, swelling. In the darkness its eyes were two angry sparks. "Something in my food, my lovely food that the mistress gives me?" Peer nodded.

The Nis took a deep breath, but at that moment Loki lost control of himself and lunged at it. With a terrified shriek, the Nis hopped up to the base of the dragon neck, where it crouched precariously, holding on by the forestay.

"Get down from there," Peer cried. "Look out!"

"Keep that dog off me," panted the Nis, "or … Oooh!" It leaped for the deck as the prow plunged into a big wave, and spray soaked them.

The Nis curled on the planking like a drowned spider, coughing and wailing. Loki tried to pounce on it. Peer grabbed his collar. "Sit!" he ordered angrily.

The Nis had been drugged, kidnapped, made to look a fool, and finally drenched. How could he salve its wounded pride? Then he saw someone clambering towards him from the waist of the ship. By the size of the silhouette, it was Big Tjørvi. There wasn't a moment to lose. Peer tore open his thick jerkin and the linen shirt under it, scooped up the limp Nis, and stuffed it out of sight against his skin. He'd done the same thing with orphaned lambs in bad weather, and the Nis was no bigger.

"Off you go, son." Tjørvi patted him on the shoulder.

"Your turn to sleep." Peer was grateful for the friendly tone. He would have stayed and talked, but he was afraid Tjørvi would notice the lump he was clasping to his chest. And the Nis squirmed about, and trickles of sea water ran down under his clothes.

He unrolled his sleeping sack one-handed and slithered in, cold and damp. What a good thing he had a sack of his own and didn't have to share with another of the men! He made a space for Loki, who crept in and turned around. The Nis crawled out of his jerkin and wrung out its beard, snivelling. Loki growled. Peer grabbed his muzzle. "Loki, stop it," he said in a low, fierce voice. "From now on, you and the Nis have got to be friends."

The Nis huddled against him, dabbing at itself like a wet cat. Peer gave Loki a warning tap on the nose, and released him. "Bad dog!" he added for good measure. Loki flattened himself in shame.

"Nis," Peer began, "I'm really sorry this has happened, but I can't tell you how glad I am to see you." As he said it, he realised he meant it. "Hilde will be glad too. We're going to need all the friends we can get." He added, hoping the Nis would be pleased, "Do you know you just scared everyone on board nearly to death? They all thought you were some kind of – I don't know, ghost or evil spirit, or something."

But the Nis took offence. "I was never bad, Peer Ulfsson, I never does anything but sweep the house and help, and I doesn't deserve to be taken away and put in a bag. And I doesn't like ghosts. All stiff and cold, they are, and they make nasty sliding draughts."

Icy fingertips tickled Peer's neck. He said hastily, "Oh, come on, Nis, you know you enjoy playing tricks." The Nis sniffed.

"I bet you're the first Nis in the world who has ever gone to sea," Peer went on. "Imagine that, the very first!" Inspired, he added, "You should have a special name. People who do important things always get given special names. Like Thorolf. They call him 'The Seafarer,' because he's such a good sailor."

The Nis stared at him, dewdrop eyes luminous with excitement. "Could I really, Peer Ulfsson? Could I really be called that?"

"'Nithing the Seafarer'?" Peer asked. "Yes, why not?"

"'Nithing the Seafarer'," the Nis breathed. It did a little hop.

"That's right," Peer said, smiling. "And when we get to Vinland you'll meet Thorolf, and you'll see he's a real hero, a real sailor – and you'll be a hero too. But listen. You mustn't let Harald or Gunnar or the others on this ship see you. Harald's dangerous, Nis. If he finds you, he'll try and kill you. He told me so."

"Don't worry, Peer Ulfsson." The Nis had completely recovered its spirits. "They can't catch me," it boasted. "Nithing the Seafarer is too quick, too clever."

Peer said no more. He didn't want to frighten the Nis, and he reckoned it could keep out of sight if it tried – there were plenty of hiding places on board. He yawned. With three of them in it, the sleeping sack was beginning to feel steamily warm, though reeking of salty wet dog. He was dropping asleep, when the Nis jerked and wriggled. He forced his eyes open – and held his breath. The disgraced Loki had wormed his way so close to the Nis that he was nosing its fluffy hair. His tongue flicked out in an apologetic lick – and another – and to Peer's utter astonishment the Nis cuddled contentedly against Loki's side and allowed the dog to go on washing him with repetitive strokes of his long warm tongue.

Friends at last! Deeply relieved, Peer closed his eyes. A moment later, he was fast asleep.

"Lee-oh! Let go and haul!"

A wet rope whipped through a hole in the gunwale, scattering icy water into Peer's hair. Someone jumped over him – he got a good view of a pair of boots just missing his head. Up in the sky, as it seemed, the yard changed angle as the men on the braces hauled it round. Peer felt the deck tip as the ship heeled and the sail filled. Gunnar was putting *Water Snake* on to the port tack.

Peer hadn't slept for more than a few hours, but it was too uncomfortable to lie there any longer. There was no sign of the Nis. He dragged a reluctant Loki out of his warm nest, rolled up the sack, and looked around.

Dawn was in the sky. *Water Snake* rode over broad grey swells, leaving a wake like a long furrow drawn across the sea. Most of the crew were up, but no one seemed inclined to talk. Magnus stood at the tiller. He nodded to Peer and spat over the side. "I hate the first night at sea," he yawned, "and that one was worse than most." Peer grinned wanly. Gunnar stood bundled in his cloak on the port side, brooding.

"G'morning," said Hilde. He turned. She looked pale and moved stiffly. Her hair was tousled. She had wrapped herself in a brown shawl, and the tip of her nose was pink with cold. He wanted to hug her to his side and warm her up. But would that be lover-like, or brotherly, or just plain affectionate? He didn't know. And suddenly he didn't care.

"You look frozen," he said. "Want to share my cloak?"

Hilde leaned on him and shivered. "What wouldn't I

give," she said through chattering teeth, "to be standing over a nice hot fire?"

"Sorry you came?" said Peer, half-teasing.

"No," she said after a second, but she didn't sound too sure. "Here – have some nice cold breakfast." She passed over oatcakes and a piece of dried fish.

Loki sat, eyes glued on the food, and Peer broke an oatcake and dropped it into his greedy jaws. "Loki and the Nis made friends last night," he told Hilde in a lowered voice.

"The poor Nis; how is it?"

"Very upset last night, but it's fine now. It's got a new name." He grinned, wanting to share the joke. "'Nithing the Seafarer!'"

Hilde's laugh sounded hollow. He glanced at her. "Is something wrong?"

She nodded, staring out to sea. "I'd better just tell you quickly. You know Gunnar said we'd be coming home next summer? Well, we won't." She stopped. "Where's Astrid? Is anyone listening?"

Peer looked over his shoulder. "I don't think so. Astrid's combing her hair. Why? What's happened?"

She began to whisper. "Oh, Peer, it's an awful story. The man Harald killed in Westfold was someone Astrid really liked. He was called Erlend, and she wanted to marry him, but he was young and poor, so her father wouldn't agree. He made her marry Gunnar instead. But Gunnar was jealous of Erlend, and when they met he picked a quarrel with him, and Erlend defended himself, but he was alone and Gunnar had Harald and it was two against one. So Erlend died. Poor, poor Astrid!"

Peer thought of Harald's long steel sword. *Poor, poor Erlend!*

"But what's it got to do with us?" he asked.

"Harald and Gunnar were blamed for the killing. They've been outlawed for five years. That's why they're running for Vinland. Five years, Peer. And no way of telling Ma and Pa. They'll think we're never coming back."

Peer's heart dropped like a stone. "I *knew* Harald and Gunnar couldn't be trusted. Bjørn even said they were running from justice. He didn't know they'd been outlawed, though."

Hilde said miserably, "It's my own fault. I wanted to come so much; I wouldn't let anything put me off. Now I keep thinking of that story Sigrid was telling, about the boy who sailed across the sea. Weren't you there? East of the sun and west of the moon, and he was away for so long his mother and father thought he was dead. And I was mean to Sigrid and wouldn't let her finish it – and now who knows when I'll see her again?"

"Hilde, don't. We'll get home – we'll find a way." Peer scowled suddenly. "But Astrid – she should have told you about this."

"She wanted a friend. It was selfish of her – like kidnapping the Nis. She wants it to help with the housework in Vinland. But she's sorry now, Peer. She was crying last night."

She cried to make you feel sorry for her, thought Peer, but there was no point in saying so. "What about the crew?" he asked. "Are they all in on this?"

"They know about the killing. Everyone does: Harald joked about it, remember? He made it sound funny. It didn't seem real. But the five years' exile – well, Arne doesn't know, Peer, or he'd have said."

"You're right." Peer looked at Hilde's forlorn face. "I promised Ralf I'd bring you home, and I will, even if I have to build a ship with my own hands," he swore. Then his eyes opened wide. "Wait, Hilde, there is another ship. The *Long Serpent*! We've forgotten about Thorolf. He's no outlaw. He'll help us."

Hilde's face cleared. "Thorolf, of course!"

"Thorolf's a good man." Peer stopped and thought. "He'll be there. He settled in Vinland, why should he leave? Even if he went away for the winter, like Gunnar, he'll be heading back there for the summer to cut more timber, just like us. One way or the other, we're bound to meet him."

"And we could come home on the *Long Serpent*. On your father's ship, Peer. Funny to think it might rescue us!" Hilde looked far more cheerful. She added rather shyly, "You always think of a way out."

It was a beautiful morning. Peer put his arm around her shoulders and said gaily, "You see? Nothing to worry about. On to – where? West of the sun?"

"East of the sun," Hilde corrected him.

"Ah, but we're sailing west—"

"Would you like to know where we are, Hilde?"

It was Arne, and Hilde turned, startled. He took her elbow, detaching her from Peer, and pointed to the north-west, where some vague clouds lay above the horizon. "See those clouds? That's where the Faroe Islands are, the Islands of Sheep. We'll be passing them later."

"Land," breathed Hilde. "I'm already missing it."

"We won't be setting foot there," Arne laughed. "Just passing by, on our way west." He gave her one of his wide smiles. His beard was already growing through; the glittering stubble gave him a raffish, attractive air. He put a foot up against the side timbers and leaned there.

Several white gulls with long black-tipped wings had

appeared out of nowhere and were flying above the ship. Arne said to Hilde, "See those gulls? That's a sure sign we're not far from land. Maybe it was one of those, screaming last night."

Hilde flicked a glance at Peer – and the grey surface of the sea shattered. Out shot three, four, five dark, curving bodies, and plunged back in wings of spray. Arne's pose slipped, and he grabbed at the gunwale to steady himself. There was a shout from Magnus at the tiller. Harald raced along the starboard side, shoving Peer out of his way.

"Dolphins!" Hilde leaned out over the side. "Look at them go!"

The dolphins were travelling faster than the ship, springing out of the water again on the starboard quarter.

Something like a long black needle flashed out from *Water Snake's* bows and sank into the waves. "Missed," came a disappointed yell. Harald leaned over the side, hauling in the line and retrieving his dripping harpoon.

"He threw a harpoon!" Hilde cried.

Astrid picked her way over the deck, dainty as a disapproving cat. "He just likes killing things." She eyed Harald. He was laughing, and his long golden hair hung loose to his waist.

"I'm out of practice," he said to the two girls.

"Yes, Harald, we noticed," said Astrid sweetly.

"I think I grazed one, though."

"Why did you do it?" Hilde demanded. Harald gave her an impertinent grin. "Sweetheart, when I'm at sea, I take every chance to amuse myself." He examined the tip of his harpoon. "Can you see any blood?" He waved it under her nose, and laughed again as she drew back.

"Fool," said Peer, not quite under his breath.

Harald jabbed the harpoon at Peer. "Did I hear you

speak?" He jabbed again, and Peer had to twist aside to avoid the point. "What did you say to me, Barelegs?"

"If you must know," began Peer, breathless—

"Yes, I must. I must!" With blank, bright eyes Harald sliced the harpoon towards him. Peer tried to dodge again, but there was nowhere to go. "Stop it!" screamed Hilde, and Arne's arm flew out to deflect the stroke. A heartbeat later, Arne was gripping his forearm tightly and cursing. Bright blood ran liberally between his fingers and dripped on to the deck.

"Arne!" Hilde gasped.

Harald stepped back one dancing pace, lowering the harpoon. "Sorry, my friend. You shouldn't have got in the way."

"Shame on you!" Astrid spat like a wildcat. She raised her voice, "Gunnar, see what Harald's done! Look what's he's done to Arne!"

Harald glared and threw the harpoon down. Gunnar came striding over. His eyebrows curled together in a thick frown, but all he said was, "Can you use the hand? Good. Take him away, Astrid, and tie that up."

"It's only a cut." Arne looked up at Peer, standing shocked by the suddenness of it all. "Get out of my way! Just clear off and keep out of trouble," he burst out in a hard, exasperated voice, adding softly, "This was a good trip till you came on it."

Peer went without a word, ducking under the sail. When Hilde came to tell him that Arne's wound was only a long deep scratch, he turned away in silence. She stared at him. "What's the matter with you? Arne saved your skin, and you haven't even thanked him." She marched off.

Peer was too angry to care. *He doesn't want my thanks. He doesn't even like me. I was trying to stand up for you…* He waited for Hilde to come back, so that they could talk properly, but she didn't.

In the mid-afternoon, the low shapes of mountains became visible along the northern horizon, greyish scarps and knobs, dark or faint, some near, some further away. Peer began to come out of his self-imposed isolation. He looked around. Floki, Magnus, Halfdan and Big Tjørvi were sitting under the taut arc of the sail, throwing dice and talking.

"Are those the Islands of Sheep?" Peer called.

"That's right." Tjørvi got up and leaned on the rail beside Peer, looking northwards. "Bare, bleak places. Nary a tree to shelter under, but good enough for sheep. Narrow waters and dangerous currents."

"You've been there?"

"I'm *from* there," said Tjørvi quietly. "That's home. Got a wife there, and a little daughter. Haven't been back for years. Always meaning to; never make it. Maybe next time..."

Many more seabirds were now flying alongside the ship. One of them swooped past and scanned Peer with its fierce, yellow-rimmed eye. "How they stare," said Halfdan, looking up at the gracefully wheeling birds.

"Gulls are strange things," Tjørvi rumbled. "Have you seen them turning and circling over the place where a boat's gone down? And that's because they're tracking the drift of drowned corpses on the seabed."

"Is that so?" Halfdan shivered. Floki said, "I've heard how the souls of dead sailors put on the form of seagulls, and go flying after their shipmates, a-crying and a-calling..." They all turned their heads to look at Peer.

"Was that really a gull last night?" Tjørvi asked.

Peer hesitated. He didn't want to reinforce the fears about ghosts. But he couldn't afford to have news of the Nis reaching

Harald. "It seemed just an ordinary bird," he said lamely.

"Ordinary?" Magnus growled. "It didn't sound like one." Remembering the Nis's screams, Peer couldn't blame him for thinking so.

"It'll be back, you'll see," said Floki with a mournful shudder. "The skipper knows. Did you see the look on his face?"

"Will you shut up, Floki," said Magnus. "I've told you before." But he sounded irresolute, as if his heart wasn't in it, and this time Floki was unabashed.

"Now wait a minute, boys." Tjørvi glanced around and put the question Peer was longing to ask. "If there's really a ghost, whose is it?"

Magnus got to his feet. "I'm out of this." He glanced at Floki, who sat stubbornly where he was. Halfdan looked at his feet.

"Don't tell 'em," said Magnus. "I'm warning you, all right? Just don't say." He marched off. Floki licked his lips. "I'll name no names," he muttered. "It'd be asking for trouble, naming a ghost. But there was a man the skipper killed..."

"It was young Harald finished him off," Halfdan put in sombrely.

Erlend, thought Peer.

"And he cursed him as he lay dying. I wasn't close enough to hear him myself, but Magnus was. Magnus heard the curse. He said—" Floki's voice dropped to a hoarse whisper: "'*A cold life and a cold death to you, Gunnar. A cold wife and a cold bed. Look out for me when you close your eyes. For I'll follow you wherever you go and bring you to a cold grave.*' And he'd have cursed Harald too, Magnus says, but Harald was too quick for him. He dealt him the death blow."

Though he knew that what they'd heard last night was no

ghost, but only the Nis, Peer was glad of the sunlight on his face, and the bright spray blowing.

"And it's working, isn't it?" added Floki. "That Astrid – she's a cold piece, all right."

"If I'd ha' thought a ghost was following this ship, I'd never have joined," said Tjørvi heavily, chewing at his thumb.

Peer said guiltily, "Where did you join the ship, Tjørvi?"

"In Hammerhaven, lad, like your friend Arne."

Peer couldn't help himself. "He's not my friend. Not any more."

The three men stared at him. "Arne stopped a harpoon on its way to you," said Halfdan. "And you say he's not your friend?"

"Yes, but—" Peer went hot to his ears.

"Anyone's a friend that stands up for you against Harald," said Tjørvi decisively. "He's not one to cross."

"Right," Halfdan agreed. "You never know where you are with Harald."

"He's a natural-born fighter," Floki said with pride.

Peer was quiet. The men went on talking about Harald with a mixture of horror and admiration. As usual, Floki's tongue chattered most freely, dropping *Magnus says* into almost every sentence. Magnus had started out as one of Gunnar's farmhands in Westfold, and knew lots about Harald. At nine years old Harald had almost killed another boy, a playfellow who'd tripped him in a ball game, by pounding his head with a rock. At twelve years his mother, Vardis, had given him his first sword. He'd killed a man with it before his thirteenth birthday. Since his mother died, he'd accompanied his father on all his voyages. It was said he was a berserker, who lost all control when he fought.

"A berserker?" Peer's skin crawled.

Berserkers could fall into a kind of mad fury. They would howl like wild beasts and hurl themselves screaming at anyone in their way. A warrior who went berserk would have terrible strength.

"Magnus says Harald's mother fed him raw wolf-meat, to make him strong," Floki whispered, wriggling with gruesome delight. "So when the fit's on him, he's as wild as a wolf. We've seen it, haven't we, Halfdan? We've heard him howling. Enough to scare you to death!" He laughed suddenly, stupidly. "Didn't they all run!"

"Shut up." Halfdan looked half angry, half sick. "Magnus is right, Floki. You talk too much." He got up and moved restlessly away. Floki stuck out his bottom lip like a child.

"I'd follow Harald anywhere," he said defiantly. "Magnus is Gunnar's man, but I'm Harald's. I'd like to put my hands between his and swear to serve him. That's what real warriors do!"

"Floki, Floki!" Tjørvi suddenly burst out laughing. He put out a big hand and ruffled Floki's tight curls. "You don't want to be a warrior, son, believe me. Stick to being a sailor." Floki's rough, red face flushed even redder. He went off in a huff, leaving Tjørvi and Peer alone.

"I'd better be more careful," said Peer gloomily. "Gunnar doesn't think much of me. Harald hates me, and he's a berserker. Floki thinks Harald's wonderful. Arne's angry with me..."

"Angry?" said Tjørvi. "Angry's nothing."

"I used to like Arne," Peer cried, out of a sore heart. "I—" He remembered how he'd admired Arne when he first met him years ago. Arne and Bjørn had seemed like heroes to him, brave enough to stand up to his bullying uncles when no one else dared. "If he won't be friends with me, what can I do?"

Tjørvi looked shrewdly at Peer. "No wonder they say women on board ships is unlucky. It's that young lass that's causing all the trouble, isn't it? And is she fond of you?"

"I don't think she knows," said Peer.

"Ask her and be done with it," said Tjørvi.

CHAPTER 49

Lost at Sea

BUT PEER DIDN'T take Tjørvi's advice. Hilde's sunny nature made her a favourite with the entire crew. If ever he found himself alone with her, someone always pushed in, and it wasn't just Arne. Everyone wanted to talk to Hilde, or sit beside her. And so he put it off. *When the voyage is over*, he thought, *when we strike land. That's when I'll tell her how I feel.*

Days passed, and the crew of the *Water Snake* grew used to the hard boards under them, the cold air always around them, the long waves rolling under the ship. They were resigned to eating cold food and drinking stale water. On bright days they were grateful for the strength of the sun warming their aching limbs. On wet days, the lucky ones donned supple capes of fine oiled leather. Those who had none wrapped themselves up in double layers of wool, and blew on their cold red hands.

There were no more fights. Peer didn't speak to Harald and Arne, even at mealtimes. Once or twice he saw Arne watching him with an odd expression, half sorry, half annoyed. But if Arne wanted to say something, he could. Peer wouldn't be the one to begin.

The Nis adapted surprisingly well to life on board. The mast and rigging became its playground, and there were all sorts of nooks and crannies where it could hide. The apple barrel in the hold was one of its favourites, but it often curled up with Loki in a patch of sunshine, hidden from view behind the coil of the anchor rope. If anyone approached, it shot for cover. The men thought there was a big rat on board.

Late one evening, Peer was in the bows, keeping ice watch. They'd passed a big iceberg at around sunset – a scary thing like a chunk of white mountain that remained in sight for an hour or more, turning to warm amber and blue shadow, and finally to a dark tooth against the south-eastern horizon.

It was a warning they couldn't ignore. So Peer stood through the long twilight, straining for the tell-tale gleam of looming ice-castles, and listening to the Nis bouncing about in the shrouds. Now it was sitting in the cross trees at the top of the mast, thin legs dangling, wispy hair blowing in the north wind – just visible against a patch of sky where a few stars burned.

Peer was hungry. He hoped Hilde would bring him his evening meal, but was disappointed to see Astrid. She handed over his food, and then didn't go, but leaned against the steep curve of the prow and looked up at the masthead.

"There it sits," she said, and her fingers drummed on the rail. "There it sits, and it won't speak to me."

"The Nis?" Peer asked through a mouthful of crumbling oatcake. He'd forgotten that Astrid could see it. "Why should it speak to you? You're lucky it hasn't tried to pay you back."

"It wouldn't dare," said Astrid coolly, and it occurred to him that she was probably right. There was something about Astrid that would make even the Nis think twice.

She moved closer to him. "It would talk to me if *you* asked it. Why don't you call it? Ask it to come down."

"Why should I?" Peer neither liked nor trusted Astrid, and saw no reason why he should do anything for her. "Besides, someone might hear."

"They won't," said Astrid. "They're all listening to Hilde, telling about your adventures under Troll Fell." She put a slim hand on his shoulder. "It's a shame you're up here by yourself, especially when it's your story too."

Peer couldn't help secretly agreeing. He imagined the gathering back there on the afterdeck, Hilde's animated face, her hands gesturing as she told the story.

"Do ask the Nis to come down," Astrid wheedled. "I'd like to make friends with it. And look! Here's its little red cap. It'll want that back."

She opened her hand and showed him the tiny cap, dark in the darkness against her white fingers. It was true that the Nis would be glad to have it back. And where had she found it? Probably inside her goatskin bag.

"All right," Peer said gruffly. "I'll try, but I don't know if it'll come."

He chirruped gently, and saw the Nis's humped outline go tall and thin as it sat up like an alarmed squirrel and looked around.

"It's only me," Peer called. "And Astrid," he added, in case the Nis thought he was trying to deceive it. "She wants to say sorry to you. Come on down."

He didn't truly think the Nis would come. However, it skipped on to the forestay and slid cleverly down. Astrid jumped, as if half afraid, then stretched out a coaxing hand.

The Nis grabbed the cap from her fingers and crammed it on its head. It made a rude noise with its lips, and jumped away to crouch on the iron fluke of the anchor, fiddling with something it held in its skinny lap, and chanting some odd-sounding gibberish:

"Half hitch, clove hitch, bowline, sheep-shank.
Sheet bend, double sheet, reef knot, splice."

Peer leaned over. "Whatever are you doing?"

"Practising knots," squeaked the Nis. Its fingers flickered like spider legs. "Make a little hole," it muttered to itself. "*Out* pops the rabbit, *round* the tree it goes, and back into the hole again." It held up a piece of looped string in triumph. "See! Bowline." It undid it busily and tried another. "Reef knot!" It held out the end. "The harder you pull, the tighter it gets," it explained importantly. "Pull!"

Peer pulled, and the knot slid apart. "That was a slip knot," he said.

The Nis snatched the string back. "*Over* here and *under* there… No, *round* here and over *there*… Pull!" Peer tweaked, and the knot came apart again. The Nis scrunched the string up. "I could do it before," it said crossly.

Astrid laughed. "Why are you learning knots?" she asked. The Nis wouldn't answer, but Peer guessed. "They're all knots that sailors use. The Nis is turning into a real seafarer!"

Astrid caught on fast. "Goodness, yes. Why, I'm terrible at knots. I'm nothing but a landlubber. However did you learn so quickly?"

The Nis could not resist flattery. Flicking her a sideways glance, it said with shy pride, "I watches, and I listens, and I sees Magnus showing Floki. And I thinks to myself, *I am a ship nis now, I must learn the things that sailors know.*"

"How clever," Astrid praised. The Nis swaggered its thin shoulders, spitting a tiny white speck over the side in uncanny imitation of Magnus. "I knows all the right words, too," it bragged. "*Ahoy there! Haul, me boys! Lee side! Luff!*"

"That's wonderful." Peer's voice shook.

The Nis nodded complacently. "Now I must go up to the mast head, like I does every night, and keep look out. Every evening I goes *aloft*" – it looked sharply to see if they had noticed the nautical term – "I goes aloft and I can see lots from up there, and I keeps a good look out for icebergs, Peer Ulfsson, so no need to worry. And I looks for storms, too, and rocks, and sea-serpentses and whales..." Its voice trailed off as it sprang for the forestay and scampered up hand over hand.

Peer and Astrid caught each other's eye.

"Well! It's forgiven me," said Astrid.

"Maybe," said Peer. "Just keep buttering it up."

"You're fond of it, aren't you?"

"Of course I am." Peer discovered that he also felt very proud of the way the Nis was coping with its sudden uprooting from everything it had ever known. "I think it's doing better than I am," he added soberly.

"You're a nice person, Peer," said Astrid softly. "Why doesn't Hilde notice?"

Peer stiffened. "I don't know what you mean."

"Yes you do." A gleam of mischief came into Astrid's eyes. "I expect I could help. Shall I?"

"No!"

"You're afraid of me, aren't you?" she teased. "Why? A handsome boy like you shouldn't be afraid of girls."

Peer was blushing so hard, he was glad of the darkness. Astrid stepped closer. Before he knew what she was going to do, she slid one hand up over his neck and kissed his cheek. "There! Now you can say a girl's kissed you."

"Astrid!" Peer felt his whole skin scalding. "You'd better go," he said furiously. "What if someone—"

"What if someone sees us?" Astrid made her eyes go big. "Oh, yes, Gunnar would kill you, wouldn't he?" She laughed. "Don't worry, Peer, you're safe with me. I won't frighten you any more. I like you. I really do. And I can't say that about many people."

Her voice was half sad, half mocking. Peer remembered what Hilde had told him, about the young man Astrid had loved. *Erlend.* The name rose to his lips, but he bit it back. He looked at Astrid. She was staring at the stars, her white skin luminous against the darkness of the vast sail. Did she know the story of Erlend's curse? He pitied her.

"Hilde told me your secret," he said gently.

"What secret?"

She rapped it out so sharply, Peer wished he had said nothing. "About – having to marry Gunnar, and then Harald killing Erlend," he stammered.

"That!" To his amazement, she sounded relieved. After a moment she said, "Well, it was dreadful. But I'm married to Gunnar now. I don't think about it any more." She was suddenly in a hurry, pulling her cloak around her. "Gunnar will miss me. I'd better go." And she whisked away, stumbling over the curved wooden ribs of the ship's side.

Peer's hand went to his cheek, and he rubbed the spot where she'd kissed him. Did she love Gunnar? Had she loved Erlend? He couldn't make her out at all.

"Floki!" Magnus yelled next morning as a line came apart in his hands. He waved the loose end under Floki's nose. "Call yourself a sailor? That was a slip knot. Came undone as soon as I pulled on it, you – you landsman, you!"

Floki examined the line as though it could tell him what had gone wrong. "I'm sure I did it right," he grumbled.

"Never mind who did what. Pull that sail in!" bellowed Gunnar. The corner of the sail had blown free and had to be recaptured. All day, knots came mysteriously loose, or undone, or were found re-tied in the wrong way, until Gunnar was driven nearly crazy, cursing his crew for a nest of unhandy landlubbers. Peer began to fear fights would break out again – but luckily, after a day of turmoil, the Nis finally got all the knots figured out, and peace was restored. Floki muttered that *Water Snake* was an unlucky ship. When Magnus heard, he threatened to throw Floki overboard.

A few days later, just after daybreak, Peer heard an excited shout from Halfdan in the bows: "Land ahead! There's old Blueshirt! Greenland, me boys!"

Everyone who was free rushed forwards. Peer was holding the starboard brace and couldn't join them, but by shading his eyes and leaning out over the side, he caught a glimpse of it: a jag of bluish-white on the iron horizon.

Gunnar ordered Magnus, on the tiller, to alter course south of west. It was a freezing cold morning, the wind gusting almost dead north. As those white, unfriendly mountains drew nearer, snow began to scud down the wind. The horizon in all directions vanished. Grey snowflakes plastered themselves against the sail and whirled away again. The wind piled the sea into great ridges, and the ship reared and plunged over them like a frightened horse.

"Reef!" Gunnar screamed. They shortened sail. Peer sat jammed against the starboard side, hanging on to the sheet and the braces. The waves rushed at the ship, foam spilling greedily down their fronts. He could see forward, under the sail, the dark neck of the dragonhead with seas bursting around it. Then hail rattled across the deckboards, knocking against his skull like elfin hammers.

Someone shook his shoulder. Arne, shouting into his ear. *Something – the steering oar?* "Broken," Arne bawled. Peer clawed his way to the stern, where Magnus waved a splintered peg-leg of wood – the remains of the tiller. A wave had wrenched it out of his grasp, twisting the steering oar upwards and snapping the tiller like a stick of firewood. Peer clung to the side. The steering oar was lifting and falling uselessly in the waves. "It's not broken," he yelled. "The withy's snapped."

The withy – the rope that pinned the steering oar against the ship – had gone. Only a broad leather strap kept the oar from floating away as the ship tossed and dropped at the mercy of wind and waves.

Gunnar appeared out of the gale. He put his face close to Peer's. "Can – you – fix – it?" He bellowed each word separately.

"Not in this weather," Peer shouted back. He was afraid Gunnar would argue, but Gunnar nodded as though this was what he'd expected, and disappeared again.

"Get me a line," Peer yelled. The steering oar was a heavy blade of oak as long as a man, scything about in the strong waves, capable of breaking an arm or crushing a hand between it and the ship. Magnus brought a length of cord which Peer knotted around the end, so that the oar couldn't wash away when he loosed the leather strap. "When it comes free, haul!"

Magnus nodded. At Peer's other side, Harald leaned over the gunwale.

"Now!"

They grabbed for the oar. Magnus heaved on the line. Peer caught the middle of the oar and was nearly tugged overboard by the deadweight as the ship rolled and the water sucked away. For a second he stared into boiling froth and evil, licking swirls, then the water rose to engulf him, but the oar rose with it, and together Harald and he dragged it over the side and fell to the deck boards with the oar on top of them. Magnus lifted it clear.

Soaked and breathless, arms nearly torn from their sockets, Peer and Harald exchanged glances. Harald was gasping, his hair plastered to his face in rat-tails. He bared his teeth in a savage smile of triumph, and Peer found himself grinning back as savagely. Harald pulled Peer to his feet, and clapped him on the arm.

For a moment, Peer almost liked him. He was ruthless, selfish, dangerous – but enjoying the danger, twice as alive as most people, with a glow to him that you wanted to be part of. *And he knows it, and he uses it.*

They moved apart, the bond already breaking. Already Harald's eyes turned indifferently away. You couldn't be friends with him. There was no warmth to his brightness. He was in love with action, and with himself.

"Peer!" Magnus yelled. Gunnar was gesticulating angrily. "Port side – get over to port!" Peer flung himself across to help balance the ship. If she turned broadside to the waves, they would be overwhelmed – sucked down without a trace.

Now Peer saw Gunnar for the shipmaster he was. With no steering oar to help him, he took his ship on a crazy ride over the rolling hills of water, bellowing orders to haul in or slacken off the braces – twitching the sail this way and that – till the touch of the harsh, soaking ropes was raw agony. With the others Peer staggered to port or starboard as Gunnar yelled at them. In flashes between periods of dazed exhaustion Peer saw his shipmates – Floki being sick, Tjørvi hauling on the yard like a giant, Astrid and Hilde steadily baling, their sopping skirts spreading around them like puddles. Loki crept to his feet and Peer stroked his cold, wet ears.

At long last the seas dropped into heaving, sullen swells.

The sun rose, poking white rays through the clouds like gigantic wheel-spokes. The mountains of Greenland were nowhere to be seen.

Peer mended the steering oar. He threaded a new rope through it, with a thick knot against the outer side. The tiller, which slotted into the end of the steering oar, was too damaged to re-use, but he made a new one by trimming down an oar-handle. As soon as it was ready, Gunnar turned the ship about. They were sailing west again.

Tjørvi slapped Peer on the back. Gunnar gave him an approving nod. Even Arne produced a faint smile. It was a good feeling. As Peer put his tools away, he heard Magnus say, "No sense trying to reach Greenland now. But where are we? That's what I'd like to know."

A brisk discussion broke out. "May as well keep going west."

"Aye, but we could be anywhere. Did anyone see the stars last night?"

"What if we miss Vinland altogether and sail over the edge of the world?" Floki piped up, conjuring in every mind a vision of the endless waterfall plunging over the rim of the earth.

"Showing your ignorance, Floki," said Magnus. "The world is shaped like a dish, and that keeps the water in. Ye can't sail over the edge."

"That's not right," Arne argued. "The world's like a dish, but it's a upside-down dish. You can see that by the way it curves."

Magnus burst out laughing. "Then why wouldn't the sea just run off? You can't pour water into an upside-down dish."

"It's like a dish with a rim," said Gunnar, in a tone that brooked no arguments. "There's land all round the ocean, just like there's land all round any lake. Stands to reason. And that means so long as we keep sailing west, we'll strike the coastline."

The crew's worn faces broke into smiles. This was a good explanation, which everyone liked. There was no chance of getting lost or sailing over a precipice. Peer looked around at a collection of bloodshot eyes, bruises, cracked lips and dull, salt-white hair. Astrid was hollow-cheeked, with purple shadows under her eyes: the storm had blown away her beauty. Hilde's looks were more robust: the wind whipped roses into her cheeks and tousled her yellow hair. Gunnar looked terrible, grey under his red, chapped skin. His good hand shook, and he clenched his fist to disguise it.

Yet almost against his will, Peer found he trusted Gunnar to get them to Vinland. Rough and tough Gunnar might be, but he knew how to sail, and how to put confidence into his men.

"Gunnar's a good skipper," Hilde whispered, and Peer nodded.

Astrid came up behind them and draped her arm over Peer's shoulder. He knew she was only doing it to tease, but he wished she wouldn't. He saw Hilde's eyebrows go up, and tried to move aside. Astrid took her arm away with a comical pout.

"We were talking about your husband," said Hilde pointedly.

"Really?" said Astrid. "What about him?"

"Just that he knows what he's doing," Peer said. "He's a good skipper."

The corner of Astrid's mouth lifted. She threw a glance at Gunnar, where he sat against the port side. He happened to look at her, and his bristly, hard-eyed face softened for a moment.

"He doesn't look well," Astrid murmured. "He hasn't slept more than a snatch since the storm began. Thank goodness you got the steering oar fixed, Peer. You're so clever." She tucked her arm through Peer's, and pinched him playfully. "Don't you think he's clever, Hilde – this brother of yours?"

"He's not my brother," Hilde contradicted – then frowned, as if wondering what she'd said. Astrid smiled.

She dropped Peer's arm and went on, "But I came to ask you: how's the Nis?"

"The Nis!"

Hilde's mouth opened in horror, and she and Peer stared at each other. "The Nis! How did it manage in the storm? Where is it?"

Astrid looked at them with scornful amusement. "Really! You two are the ones who are supposed to look out for the Nis. I'm just the wicked woman who dragged it on board. I suppose neither of you fed it, either?"

"If you were clever enough to remember about it, why didn't you do it?" Hilde snapped.

"Nobody had time to think," Peer said. He imagined the Nis lying in some cold corner, wet, seasick and frightened; or clinging to the masthead in all that wind; or being blown off into the sea. "We'd better try and find it."

He made his way along the ship, tugging at knots and knocking on beams and joints as if examining them for strain after the storm. "Nis… Nis," he called softly whenever he dared. Astrid and Hilde looked into barrels and crates, pretending to take stock of the provisions.

The Nis wasn't in the apple barrel. It wasn't in the chicken coop, though all three of them checked it, even moving the bedraggled, seasick chickens to make sure it wasn't huddling between their feathers. In growing dread they searched across the big cluttered hold. It was impossible to be sure the Nis wasn't hiding there somewhere, but it didn't answer their calls.

They met in the bows, confirming with pale faces their lack of success. Loki plodded after them, poking an enquiring nose into the cranny behind the anchor. With the nagging worry growing into real fear, Peer even lifted the loose deck boards to look into the dark, triangular space under the foredeck, though he couldn't imagine why the Nis would ever go there. There was nothing to see but a little black water spilling about.

"Oh, where can it be?" said Hilde in despair.

"Lost something?" Arne took them by surprise.

Peer jumped and clattered the boards back into place. "No! Just making sure we're not leaking."

"You seem worried." Arne sounded concerned, and for a fleeting moment, he looked like his brother. He turned to Hilde: "Something's wrong, isn't it? Why don't you tell me?"

Hilde began to speak, stopped, and flung an unhappy look at Peer. Peer squared his shoulders and lifted his chin. "Everything's fine," he said brusquely.

Arne turned on his heel and went off.

"That was convincing," Astrid murmured.

"We should have told him," said Hilde. "He could have kept an eye out for it. He might even have seen it."

"Go after him if you want," said Peer. Arne's expression had made him feel cross and guilty. "As far as I know, he's never seen the Nis in his life. And what if he tells Harald?"

Hilde raised a cold eyebrow. "Why should he? Why do you always think the worst of Arne?"

"Children, don't quarrel," said Astrid wearily. They looked at each other, ashamed. Hilde dug the heels of her hands into her eyes, rubbing hard. "Oh, Nis, Nis, where are you?"

No one answered her. *Water Snake* rocked over long swells, nodding into wave after wave with a fresh splatter of spray. The sun was slipping down into yellow haze. "I'm so tired of this ocean," said Hilde, with a dreary little laugh. She looked at Peer with red-rimmed eyes. "We've looked everywhere. Let's face it. It's lost, isn't it? The Nis is lost."

CHAPTER 50

Landfall

THEY SEARCHED TILL long after dark, hoping the Nis would come creeping out of some forgotten hidey-hole. Even after they'd given up, and were sitting with the crew over the evening meal, one or another would get up restlessly, and wander off to try again. Everywhere he looked, Peer missed seeing the Nis's skinny little silhouette hopping in the shrouds or outlined against the sunset.

At last he crawled into his sleeping sack, all hope gone. He thought of the storm, and the way the ship had leaped like a spurred horse. He imagined the Nis swept over the side like a scrap of cloth, perhaps crying out in a thin voice, then lost in the limitless waves. *The poor little Nis. After being brought all this way, and after it tried so hard to be a sailor.* A lump rose in his throat. "The Nis is gone, Loki," he whispered. The ship was a hateful place, a trap, a coop.

He lay staring up at the great swaying sail, listening to the creak as Halfdan twisted the steering oar, the whistle of wind in the shrouds, and the slap and tickle of water running along the sides. He knew all the sounds of the ship now. That loud snoring was Tjørvi. The irritating little cough followed by a sniff was Floki. But tonight there was a muttering undercurrent. Peer lay half-sleeping, hearing it running on: somebody talking, low and rapid and feverish, and then a great sobbing shout:

"Keep him off! Keep him off! Keep him off!"

Peer sat up fast, dislodging Loki who sprang up, barking. All around him, startled men struggled out of their sleeping sacks. "The skipper's gone mad!" yelled Halfdan at the helm.

The sky flashed. From unguessable heights, silent streamers unrolled across the heavens. Like the folds of some enormous garment they trailed overhead, then twisted into ropes and went snaking over the northern horizon. The ship gleamed and flickered: every upturned face reflected a pale green.

"Help me! Help!" Gunnar crouched against the rail, panting with terror. Astrid threw herself down, trying to clasp him in her arms, but he flung her off, catapulting upwards. He grabbed the backstay with his good right hand and swung from it, pivoting and peering this way and that. "D'you hear him? D'you hear him?" he mumbled.

"Gunnar, there's nothing to fear," cried Astrid.

"There is. I hear him splashing after us, splashing, splashing…" Gunnar began to choke.

"Father." Harald's long hair shone an elfin green in the weird light. He trod forward warily, hand outstretched as if approaching a wild animal. Astrid got to her feet. "Harald, he's ill again. He needs medicine."

"He doesn't need *your* medicine," said Harald fiercely. "Who knows what you've been giving him? Father, wake up. You're dreaming." He edged forwards. Peer wondered why he was being so careful, till he saw the knife at Gunnar's belt. "Wake up, Father. It's me, Harald. It's your son."

Gunnar quieted. He dropped to his knees and began rocking to and fro, arms clasped across his chest as if in an agony of grief. "Oh, oh," Peer heard him groan. "Oh, oh." But when Harald tried to touch him he screamed: "He's climbing over the side!" and scrabbled away on all fours, cramming himself into the angle of the stern.

"Help me. Quick!" Harald snapped at the men. But they hung back, and not just because of Gunnar's knife.

"He's here." Gunnar peeped between his fingers. "I heard him, I heard him s-s-splashing after the ship, and he climbed on board, black and blue and dripping. He's hiding somewhere. Arrchch!" With a retching cough he stuck his tongue out as far as it would go, shaking his head from side to side as if he had bitten something unbearably bitter. The sea burned with a million green glints.

"The ghost!" Floki burst out.

Harald spun round and struck Floki a ringing crack across the cheek. "A ghost, is it? Where? Have you seen this ghost, Floki?" Floki reeled backwards. Harald followed. "What ghost? Whose? Do you want to give it a name? Do you want to call it up? Because if there's a ghost on this ship, I want to meet it. *Hoo-ooo!*" He flung his head back with a howl. "Come on, ghost! My name is Harald Silkenhair, what's yours?

"My name is Harald Silkenhair.
I am not afraid of death or darkness,
Of white ghost or black ghost,
Of night-walker, or barrow-dweller."

Floki fell over, sobbing. With one eye on Harald, Magnus sidled in, grabbed Floki's arm and dragged him out of Harald's way. The other men backed off.

"*Hoo-ooo!*" Harald began to slap his thighs and swing his head from side to side, tossing his hair. "Come on, ghost!"

"He's running berserk," muttered Magnus.

"Do something!" wailed Halfdan, trapped at the tiller.

Peer felt a quick hand grasp his arm. "This is ridiculous!" Hilde hissed. She had a bucket in her hand, attached to a length of rope. "Help me!" She dropped the bucket over the side, and

Peer helped her drag it up again, slopping full. Before he had time to think what she would do, Hilde seized the handle, stepped forward, and threw the whole pailful over Harald.

For a long second of silence, Harald looked down at himself. He spread out his dripping arms. He lifted his head slowly and looked at Hilde. He started to giggle, uncontrollable high-pitched giggles that raised the hair on Peer's scalp.

Hilde dropped the bucket clattering between the thwarts. She stamped her foot. "*Will* you men stop making fools of yourselves? Floki, get up at once. There isn't any ghost, Gunnar is just sick. Tjørvi, help Astrid get him into his sleeping sack. As for you, Harald, Gunnar *does* need medicine, whatever you think!"

The men obeyed like children. Harald sat on a thwart and put his head in his hands. Peer gave him a wide berth and went to find Astrid's bag. Astrid delved into it and brought out a small linen pouch. She shook a dark, gritty-looking powder into her hand, threw it into a small cup and mixed in some water.

"Willow bark," she explained. "To quench the fever." She propped Gunnar's head against her shoulder and brought the cup to his lips. Gunnar drank a little. Dribbles of blackish liquid ran down his beard.

The men stood round in a nervous cluster. "Never seen the skipper this bad. What if he dies? Who'll give the orders?"

"Young Hilde, I guess," said Tjørvi, attempting a joke. But no one laughed, and Floki said with dogged loyalty, "Harald." His lip was bleeding.

The sky was pale. The flickering Northern Dancers had burned out. Peer hadn't noticed them go, but now he saw the mast and sail distinct again; the waves around the ship were no longer black and green, but grey. He shuddered in a comfortless world.

Arne came and stood a few feet away, staring out over the sea, shoulders hunched. With his untidy hair and sprouting beard, he looked more than ever like Bjørn. Peer felt a wriggle of remorse. If only things were different. If only they could be friends. He cleared his throat. "It's not good, is it?" he tried.

Arne gave him a discouraging glance.

Peer's heart thumped. He said suddenly, "I'm sorry we fell out. I ought to have thanked you – that time Harald got you with the harpoon—"

Arne interrupted. "Just tell me one thing. What *were* you looking for, when I asked?"

Their eyes met. Arne's eyes were blue as a summer sea, blue as Bjørn's, but Bjørn had never looked at him with such cool suspicion. This was it, then – the price of Arne's good opinion. Trust him, and tell the truth.

"The Nis," he said after a moment. "Gudrun's house spirit. It used to live at the old mill. Astrid stole it… stuffed it into that bag she carries. The first night at sea, remember all the noise? I said it was a seagull, but—"

"It was a Nis?" Arne's eyes widened. He shook his head. "Why didn't you say so, instead of scaring everyone stiff?"

"How was I to know a seagull would scare everyone? Would you have told Harald about the Nis? Besides, it likes – liked – to be secret. No one usually sees it, only me sometimes."

"But if you know the Nis is on board, why look for it?"

"It's missing," said Peer bleakly. "None of us has seen it since the storm. I think it got washed overboard."

"Oh."

They stood together. Presently Arne said, "Well. Thanks for telling me."

"Hilde wanted to tell you," said Peer.

"Maybe." Arne sounded rather bitter. "She didn't, though,

did she? Not without your say-so."

There was no need to answer that. Peer rewrapped his cloak, pulling it higher around his neck. *Why is it always colder at dawn?*

Tjørvi joined them. "Look at the sunrise," he said quietly. "It's like gold leaf across the sky. I saw a picture once, of a sky like that. In a book, it was."

"What's a book?" Peer asked.

"A book..." Tjørvi held his hands apart, squaring off a bit of the air. "With leaves of calfskin, all painted and covered in runes. One of the lads on my last ship showed it me. We'd been down to the Southlands and he got it in a raid. And there was this picture, bright as a jewel. A woman and a child, and a golden sky..." He gave up. "I can't describe it."

"What happened to it?" asked Arne.

"Oh, he burned it," said Tjørvi. "Didn't know what the runes said. Could have been spells, see? All he wanted was the boards – set with goldwork and stones. But I always remember that picture. And there's the sky now, just like it."

They stared in subdued silence. Behind the high stern-post, the whole eastern sky gleamed pale, chilly gold.

"My wife and child are back there somewhere," said Tjørvi. "Wonder if I'll ever see 'em again?"

"We've come a long way," said Arne.

Maybe it's time to turn round. Nobody said it, but it was what everyone was thinking. No one had slept properly for days. *Floki's right. This is an unlucky ship. Weeks at sea, out of sight of land.*

"I'd give a lot to step on dry ground," Tjørvi sighed.

"Light a fire," agreed Arne.

Hear birdsong. Smell grass. Walk up the fell and see the lambs being born...

"Land ho!" A shrill voice sang out from the bows.

"What?" Peer's world fell into bits and rearranged itself. He knew that voice…

"Land! Land ho!"

Hilde whirled past, smiling from ear to ear. Peer joined the general rush. "Where?"

"There – dead ahead!"

They crowded together. Far, far to the west, a long, uneven line lay on the horizon. It wasn't much. It was everything.

"Land!" They hugged each other, stamped their feet, pounded one another on the back. But Peer, after one irresistible glance, tore himself away to find Hilde.

"That was the Nis!"

"I know! Where's it *been*? And why didn't it answer us? Just *wait* till I get my hands on it." Tears came to her eyes. "And where is it now? I'll put out some food. Oh, I'd better not look too happy – people will wonder why."

"They won't," said Peer. "We all look happy now." It was true. Everyone on board looked different, faces washed clean by joy and relief.

All through the long day *Water Snake* cut her pathway towards the land, in long loose tacks as the wind shifted into the north west. Magnus swore he smelled forests. Seabirds soared over, the first for days. Seaweed floated in the current. Gunnar woke, weak but clear-headed. By late afternoon he was shakily on his feet.

The foredeck was no longer a private place. It was where everyone wanted to be, to see the land growing out of the sea until the sinking sun obscured it in a haze and a glory.

Peer caught the Nis as evening fell. It was bobbing in and

out of the crates near the mast, chirping happily.

"Where *were* you?"

"Me, Peer Ulfsson?" It bounced and sprang like a kitten, immensely pleased with itself.

"We looked all over for you. Didn't you hear us calling?"

"Did you hear me?" the Nis asked. It rubbed its long fingers, full of self-satisfied glee. "*Land ho*, I called. I saw it first, Peer Ulfsson. I found it!"

"Right," said Peer drily. "They'll probably call it Nisland. *Listen* to me. We were terribly worried. We thought you'd drowned."

"I never did," said the Nis indignantly. "I worked very hard in that storm, Peer Ulfsson, holding on to the forestay and the backstay, so that the mast wouldn't fall down. And the wind blew me, and the rain rained on me, but I didn't let go. And after that, I was very, very tired."

Peer cast a glance at the stout, thick cables running from masthead to prow and stern, and then at the Nis's fragile, twiggy arms. "You would be," he agreed. "*So where did you go?*"

"To my nice den. My secret place where nobody else can go. Watch how I get there."

It reached the base of the dragon neck in one flying leap, and swarmed up the criss-cross carvings to the head. It perched for a second, poised over the ocean – and vanished. Peer sucked in his breath. But the Nis hadn't fallen. A moment later it swung back up on to the top of the dragonhead.

"The dragon's mouth?" said Peer. "You've been sitting in the dragon's mouth?"

The Nis nodded. "Nithing the Seafarer can go anywhere," it squeaked. "After the storm, I curls myself up in there, and I goes to sleep. And then I wakes up, and I smells land. And I sees it, too. And so I calls out, *Land ho*, for everyone to hear. Am I famous now? As famous as Thorolf? Will they really call it Nisland, Peer Ulfsson?"

Peer hadn't the heart to tell it the land was already named. "As far as I'm concerned," he said solemnly, "that bit of the coastline will always be Nisland."

The Nis preened.

Next morning, the land was in plain view, forested hills, and beyond them white mountains like the ghosts of clouds. Everyone stared hungrily as Gunnar altered course to run south, with the mountains on the starboard side. Every hour brought new sights and sounds. The yelling clamour of a seagull colony on one abrupt limestone rock could be heard for miles. A flight of ducks passed over the ship, quacking loudly. Whales were everywhere, heaving grey or black bodies between the waves and snorting like bullocks. The day was full of mild sunshine, with a gentle haze over silver water.

Hilde looked over the side. Down in the shadow of the ship, pale frilly blossoms floated past – jellyfish, like ghostly baby's bonnets, flowing through the cold, clear water upright, tilting, side on, anyhow. Millions of them. It made her sleepy to watch.

At midday came a shout from Magnus at the helm. "The Wonderful Beaches!" Hilde saw an unbroken white line running along the coast. Sand. Wonderful, white sand. She longed to run on it.

"Now we know where we are," Magnus told her, satisfaction in every crease of his face. "The Wonderful Beaches. Go on for miles, they do; there's no mistaking them. And you know what that means? Only a few more days, and we'll be there."

Serpent's Bay! How long ago it seemed, the night she'd first heard of it, sitting at home in the snug, warm farmhouse. *And soon we'll be there. Won't Thorolf be glad to see us!* A thrill of happiness ran through her. *Oh Ma, Pa – if only you could see me now!*

CHAPTER 51

Spring Stories

THE YOUNG MEN are playing the ball game. Stripped to their loincloths they shout and jostle, throwing and catching, leaping through shafts of dusty evening sunlight. Dots of white and yellow paint flash on their faces.

The ball flies over, and Kwimu snatches it. He twists and darts, racing for the tall pole at the edge of the glade.

"Go, Kwimu!" shouts Skusji'j from the sidelines. "Run! Ow!" He winces. Another player has tackled Kwimu. It's his young uncle, Kiunik, who jerks him off balance by a handful of his glossy black hair. They fall to the ground, wrestling, and a third young man grabs the ball and reaches the post. His friends cheer, and as Kwimu and Kiunik pick themselves up, the game is over.

"That looks like so much fun," the Little Weasel says as they come over, panting, to collect their things.

"Very rough fun," Kwimu complains, laughing, slinging his soft deerskin jacket over his shoulder, and retying his belt. "Kiunik nearly pulled my head off."

"Good practice for war." Kiunik adjusts his great necklace of curving bear claws and slyly tweaks Kwimu's long hair. "This stuff is too easy to grab. Wear it like mine." He passes a hand over his own head – shaven both sides, with a stiff black crest running down the middle.

"If I wore it like you, I'd always be changing it. When Kiunik sets a fashion, he likes to think everyone will copy him," Kwimu adds to Skusji'j. "But not me. When I'm as tall as he is, I'll rub his face in the dust."

"You can try," says Kiunik amiably, disappearing into the wigwam.

Kwimu sits down outside and offers Skusji'j a lump of pine gum to chew. Fox settles down between them, tail outspread, nose between his paws.

Spring is here. Children chase around the wigwams, laughing and calling. And the woods echo to a shrill piping. Skusji'j cocks his head.

"What's that noise?" he asks.

Kwimu looks at him. It often worries him how much the Little Weasel does not know. This is Frog-Croaking Moon. In the boggy hollow down the slope, thousands of mating frogs keep up a constant, deafeningly loud, squeaky shrilling.

"That noise is frogs," he explains. "Don't you have frogs where you come from?"

"'*Sqoljk?*'" The boy looks puzzled. He doesn't know this word. Kwimu hooks two fingers in his mouth and pulls a wide frog grin. He tries to make his eyes bug out. He croaks and hops. Skusji'j falls over, laughing. "Oh, now I get it. Frogs!"

Kwimu laughs too. Fox grins. The boys chew companionably.

After a while, Skusji'j says, "What are the little ones playing?"

The small children have formed a long line, hands on each other's shoulders. The leader calls out, "Look out for Swamp Woman!"

Kwimu's little sister, Jipjawej, is creeping up on them. "I'm so-o-oo lonely," she wails. "I'm coming to get you!" She runs at the line, which swings away from her, shrieking, but trying to stay joined. The line breaks up as Jipjawej grabs one of them, and the children tumble to get away from her. "Now *you've* got to be Swamp Woman!" she cries.

"Who is Swamp Woman?" asks the Little Weasel.

Kwimu wriggles his shoulders. "One of the Old Ones. She walks in the woods, especially in the boggy places. At evening she wanders around the edges of villages, singing, trying to lure people away, because she's lonely. She doesn't mean harm, but she comes from the Ghost World, where the dead people go."

"I know a game like that," says Skusji'j. "Only in our game it's not Swamp Woman who does the chasing, it's a wolf."

"It isn't just a game."

"I know." Skusji'j hesitates, stiffens. "Kwimu – when we move from here, where will we go? Has your father decided?"

"I don't know. Perhaps to the lake."

Skusji'j spits the gum into his palm. "I'm not a baby, Kwimu. You don't have to protect me. I know what everyone's saying."

Kwimu is silent. Everyone used to speak of the bay as *we'kowpaq*, "the bay where we go in summer". Now people are calling it *skite'kmujue'katik* – "the place of ghosts".

"I've heard people talking." The boy bites his lip. "Your father and Kiunik went back there, didn't they? And they say—"

Kwimu sighs. "They say there is a great stir of the Other Ones in that quarter of the woods this spring. They heard strange singing, and the tree-cutter, Kewasu'nukwej, striking at the trees with his invisible axe. Grandmother thinks the Other Ones are angry because of your foreign ghosts."

The Little Weasel says with a shiver, "And is that why the

jenu came? You never told me anything more about it."

"I know," says Kwimu slowly. Speaking of such things may give them power.

"Is that why it came? Will it come back?" Skusji'j fixes anxious eyes on Kwimu's face.

Kwimu shifts uneasily. Perhaps Skusji'j needs to know. He scoops up Fox and strokes his head. He lowers his voice. "Well, the *jenu* comes with the cold…"

And of course, his Grandmother hears him. "Kwimu! Come inside right now, and bring your younger brother too. You know what happens if you tell stories outside in springtime? The snakes all come and listen. You want that the camp should be full of snakes?"

The boys jump up, Skusji'j red with pride at being called Kwimu's younger brother, and go in. It's warm, with a good smell of roasting meat. Grandmother has hung a big piece over the fire, suspended on a doubled cord that twists and untwists, first one way, then the other, so that it will cook evenly. Sinumkw and Kiunik are playing *waltes* at the back of the wigwam – banging the bowl down to make the dice jump, and laughing over the scores. Kiunik's young wife Plawej sits beside him, tickling the baby on her lap.

"Grandmother," Kwimu begins, "Skusji'j has a question."

Grandmother looks at the Little Weasel. Her eyes are shrewd, and her hair, bound back with strings of painted eelskin sewn with shells, is almost as thick and black and strong as a girl's. "What is this question, *nuji'j?*"

Kwimu's little brother screws up his face. He says in a rush, "*Nukumij* – Grandmother – did the *jenu* come because of what happened down at the bay?"

"Ah." Grandmother reaches out a wrinkled hand and brushes his cheek. "Don't worry, little one. Don't worry, *nuji'j*. That was not your fault."

"It was the fault of his people," Kiunik interrupts sharply, looking up from the game. "I still say we should camp there this year. Pull down their houses and drive out their ghosts."

Sinumkw shakes his head. "Then they would wander loose in the woods. People should not interfere between Other Ones and ghosts."

"Ghosts don't frighten me," Kiunik declares. He rubs his hands over his scalp, flattening his black crest and letting it spring up again. He steals a sideways glance at Plawej, looking for her approval. She smiles at him and goes on singing softly to the baby:

"Let's go up on to the beautiful mountain
and watch the little stars playing follow-my-leader,
while Grandmother Lightning lights her pipe,
and Grandfather Thunder beats his drum."

The baby gurgles. Kiunik leans across and picks up his little son, tosses him into the air, catches him, and kisses him. He rolls back on to the fir boughs and lets the baby play with the big bearclaw necklace on his chest.

Grandmother shakes her head at him. "Those ghosts are not angry with us, Kiunik. The Other Persons are not angry. But they are disturbed, like bees swarming when a bear breaks into their nest. Keep away, and you will not be stung. But the *jenu,* now. The *jenu* is different, and I will tell you how."

But her face is troubled. Instead of beginning, she takes out her slender-stemmed pipe and hands it to Kwimu. "Light it. The smoke will help me."

Kwimu fills the pipe with a pinch of red willow bark mixed with lobelia leaves. He lights it and hands it respectfully to his grandmother. She fans a little of the sweet smoke over the boys and says quietly, "This winter has been easy. There has been plenty to eat, plenty of game. Last winter, too. But we all remember the winter before that when it was not so good. There were many blinding snowstorms. The moose and the caribou were scarce. Everyone was hungry. Some of the children died." She pauses. "Kwimu's little brother died."

Kwimu closes his mouth hard. He forces his face to remain steady, emotionless. The Little Weasel shoots him a sudden round-eyed glance.

Grandmother nods. "Yes. It's good for Kwimu to have a little brother again."

She smokes thoughtfully for a while. "And that's how life is: good winters and bad ones, times of hunger and times of plenty. But in the very worst winters, Eula'qmuejit, Starvation, comes tiptoeing through the villages, lifting the flaps of the wigwams, blowing his icy breath to chill the people's hearts.

"So long as we care for one another and share what food and warmth we have, he cannot harm us. But sometimes, if the winter is very hard, we may see a terrible change creeping over one of our neighbours. He will not join in the songs we sing at the fireside to help us forget the hunger. He sits in the cold at the wall of the wigwam, glaring at the others with red-rimmed eyes, gnawing on his own knuckles, dreaming of human flesh. His heart is hardening into ice."

The thin smoke rises from Grandmother's pipe, ascending to the ghosts and the ancestors. "They say this happened to my mother's uncle. Perhaps, at first, he was afraid of himself – afraid of what he might do to his kinfolk. He ran off into the night, crazy as a wolf. At sunrise his brothers went after him, following his trail."

Everyone is quiet, listening very seriously to Grandmother's story.

"First they see his moccasins, kicked off, and the neat

marks of bare feet running through the snow. Then they find his coat tossed into the bushes. He has pulled off his clothes to run naked in the biting wind that makes his brothers shudder and pull their faces deep inside their fur hoods. Soon they notice blood in his tracks. The sharp crust of the snow has cut his feet, but instead of limping and stumbling, he's running faster and faster, till at last his footprints are so far apart he must be leaping like a moose. And it's then that the brothers see that the barefoot tracks are changing. Growing longer, larger, like a bear's, with great gouging marks at the toes.

"Deep in the woods, the brothers stop. Around them the branches rub and squeak in the cold wind. They stare at these tracks, which are no longer the marks of human feet, and the hair rises on their necks.

"From far ahead, the wind carries a bone-chilling scream. It is too late to save their brother. They are afraid to go on, afraid to follow those great clawed marks. What if their quarry has already turned, racing back down the trail with terrible speed? What if he has begun hunting them? He will tear them apart and eat them raw.

"And that is what a *jenu* is, little son. Not one of the Old Ones or the Others, but a man who has lost his humanity. Inside every *jenu*, they say, is a frozen core, a little man-shaped lump of ice. Nothing else is left."

"Then what was it doing?" Skusji'j asks in a whisper. "What was it looking for when it came to our village?"

"Food," says Grandmother simply. "A *jenu* is always hungry. It prowls in the woods all winter, looking for fat. If it finds a village, it rips the bark from the wigwams and drags us out as we would break open a beaver dam. It comes with the snow and retreats with the snow. Only fire can harm it, because its heart is made of ice."

"And is there more than one?" the Little Weasel asks. Grandmother shrugs. "Never many. When my father was a boy, he heard two *jenu* calling to each other from two blue mountain tops. *Cold heart crying to cold heart*, he told me. A dreadful, lonely sound. They are drawn to each other, and yet they hate each other. If two *jenu* met, they will fight till one eats the other up."

"They eat each other?" asks the Little Weasel.

"A *jenu* eats anything," Kiunik sits up, frowning. "See what you've brought on us – you and your people."

"That's not fair," says Kwimu hotly. "It wasn't his fault that the *jenu* came. It was bad luck. And good luck that Grandmother knew what to do."

"Did I say it was the Little Weasel's fault?" Kiunik's dark eyes flash. "I only say that the Jipijka'm People came, and the *jenu* followed. Yes: it was bad luck. Bad that his people came to the bay. Bad that they killed each other there. I think bad luck breeds bad luck. And things like the *jenu* are drawn to it – like moths to a flame."

"You are right," Sinumkw agrees. "That's why I don't want to stay there this year. We'll go to the lake instead."

"The lake's a good place, but so is the bay. We shouldn't abandon it," Kiunik argues.

"Kiunik," Plawej pleads softly. "Remember, it's the Place of Ghosts now."

"I'm not afraid!" Kiunik hands the baby back to his wife and swings to his feet. "And I'll not be driven out. Those are our hunting grounds, our traplines. I'll go there whenever I like."

He pushes out of the wigwam into the twilight.

"What a hot-head," Sinumkw complains, pretending to be annoyed. But he looks after the tall young man with affectionate approval.

Grandmother lays her pipe aside and looks at the Little Weasel's worried face.

"The *jenu* has gone now," she says soothingly. Her eyes are very kind and bright. "Gone far away into the north, to live upon mosses and grass. Now is the hungry time for the *jenu*, while we grow fat. It can't endure summer. In the summer we are safe."

"Wonderful summer," says Kwimu, smiling, and he stretches his arms wide, and wider, as if to embrace the whole green, growing world.

CHAPTER 52

Serpent's Bay

WATER SNAKE GLIDED in over the shallows. Peer looked down through clear water at thickets of groping weed, and pale undulations of sandy gravel.

"Serpent's Bay!"

"Serpent's Bay…"

It was late afternoon. With four oars out, they were rowing in to the mouth of a river. It ran from a tuck in the hills and flowed across meadowlands and a shelving gravel beach to empty into the bay.

A black cormorant flew over. The trees made a dark fringe around the bay, rising into wooded slopes. The clear voices of Astrid and Hilde echoed off the shore.

"There are the houses!"

"I see them!" Then, after a pause: "But… they look empty."

Peer cupped his hands around his eyes. The two houses he'd heard so much about squatted side by side on rising ground behind the meadowlands. They looked just like Ralf's farm: small and homely, with thick grassy roofs. The doorway of the nearest seemed to have been left half open.

No smoke rose from the houses, no voices called in excited welcome. Where was the busy, bustling settlement Peer had imagined, with Thorolf's little boy waving cheerily from the roof?

And there was no ship drawn up on the beach or moored in the river.

"Where's the *Long Serpent*?" he asked.

Arne twisted to look over his shoulder as he sat rowing in the bows. "Where's Thorolf, skipper?" he sang out. The oars swung raggedly as the other men tried to look too. "Where's Thorolf?"

"Keep rowing," Gunnar grunted. "How should I know where he is? I'm not his master."

"They've gone." Hilde's voice was hollow. Peer knew what she was thinking. *Five years.*

"They'll be back," he said, as much to comfort himself as Hilde.

"I thought you said Thorolf had settled here," Tjørvi called to Gunnar.

"He must have changed his mind," Gunnar said shortly.

Tjørvi snatched a quick glance shorewards and his oar clashed with Magnus's.

"Watch your stroke," Magnus snarled.

"Concentrate, boys," Gunnar bawled. "We'll put her aground on the beach. Harald, steer for the houses. Pull!"

Harald leaned on the tiller. The men heaved. *Water Snake* slipped towards the shore. Her prow grated into the shingle.

The crew broke into cheers. The noise was oddly thin, rebounding off the shore. Startled waterfowl clattered off across the tranquil river, honking alarms.

But the air was sweet, smelling of earth and forest – of rich soil, black bog, fresh water. Peer filled his lungs and forgot about Thorolf. *We're here! We made it! We're in Vinland!*

"First one ashore...!" Arne vaulted into knee-deep water, whooping. Peer leaped after him. Floki and Halfdan came tumbling after. Magnus methodically shipped his oar and clambered down. They splashed on to the gravel. Land! Solid footing, for the first time in weeks! It rocked under Peer, and he stumbled. Magnus laughed. "Aye, you'll be unsteady for a while… Odd, seeing the old ship from the outside again, ain't it?"

It was. How huge she'd seemed, coming in to the jetty at Trollsvik! Now Peer just wondered how on earth he'd crossed the ocean in anything so cramped and small. Her paintwork looked even more faded than before. Her sail was down, an untidy crumple of sea-stained fabric. Ropes trailed everywhere. But the dragonhead glared inland with all its old, stiff-necked arrogance.

Loki's head and two front paws appeared over the side. He jumped, hitting the water with a crash of spray, then swimming steadily to shore. When his paws touched, he bounded out and shook himself all over Magnus and Floki.

Hilde leaned out, looking down. "Is it deep? Shall I jump?"

"Your dress will get soaked. I can carry you." Peer reached up to her. "If you sit on the edge, I'll take you on my back."
"Don't trust him, Hilde," said Arne, wading up. "He'll drop you. Better come with me, I'm stronger." He flexed his arms in a mock show of strength.

"How strong do you think you need to be?" asked Hilde, laughing.

"Here's an easier way," Tjørvi called. He and Halfdan were man-handling a long gangplank. Once it was firmly settled between ship and shore, Tjørvi swept off his cap. "Would the Lady Hilde care to descend?"

"Thank you, Tjørvi." Hilde caught Tjørvi's hand and he walked her down. At the bottom she dropped him a curtsy. Tjørvi bowed. "See?" he said over his shoulder to Peer and

Arne. "She likes me best." He went back to help Astrid.

"Vinland," breathed Hilde. She staggered, and Peer saw her eyes widen. "I feel as if I'm still on the ship. Oh, that's strange."

"You'll soon get your land legs back if you walk around a bit," Magnus told her.

"Walk?" Hilde picked up her skirts. "Ha! Who'll race me to the houses?"

"Not me," said Astrid, stepping cautiously down the gangplank. "I'm not running anywhere. Oops!" She checked as something small and light rushed past her skirts. With a patter of feet, a disturbance of the gravel, it dashed into the grass. Tjørvi's head jerked round. "Did you see that damn great rat come ashore?" he exclaimed. Peer smothered a smile.

And Hilde was off too, tearing up the slope towards the houses, plaits flying. "Wait," yelled Peer. "It might not be safe." He plunged after her. On legs that seemed hardly to obey them they ran across spongy, springy meadows patched with bright green moss and pocked with boggy holes. Birds whirred up everywhere. Loki streaked ahead.

Hilde reached the nearest house and disappeared. Peer flung himself at the door. It opened inwards, protected by a rough wooden porch sticking out of the turf roof.

It was cold inside. The thick turf walls cut off all sound. The house smelled of frost-bitten earth and old smoke, and it was so gloomy Peer could hardly see. There were no windows. A little light splashed through the smoke holes in the roof, gleaming on Hilde's pale hair as she stood, looking around. The only other light came from the doorway. Gradually Peer made out two lines of wooden posts supporting the rafters. Down the middle of the house ran the fire-pit, edged with stones. At either side long sleeping benches lined the walls. At the far end, another doorway led into a small second room. That would be for Astrid and Gunnar, Peer guessed.

Or had this been Thorolf's house? He squinted about, but there was no clue to show who had been living here, no personal possessions, or bedding, or stores.

Something bounded through the rafters like a squirrel, carolling, "Ooh, a house, a house, a lovely house!"

It fetched up on a crossbeam just overhead, and peeped at Peer upside down, wispy hair trailing like old cobwebs.

"You like it?" asked Peer.

"A house!" the Nis sang. Hilde squinted up, but the Nis had scuffled into an angle of the rafters. "I likes it, Peer Ulfsson," came its muffled voice, "but it needs – spring-cleaning!" And it flung a bird's nest down at them, giggling.

"Well, the Nis approves." Peer brushed twigs out of his hair. "What do you think?"

"I can't wait to light the fire," said Hilde. "Hot food tonight!"

"Sleeping under a roof, warm and dry!" said Peer.

They looked at each other and laughed.

"I can't wait to explore. It looks so wild and beautiful. No farms, no fields. No sheep, no cows, no villages…"

"No Thorolf."

"He'll turn up," said Hilde optimistically. "You know, that first night on the ship, when Astrid told me about Harald and Gunnar being outlawed, I thought I'd made a terrible mistake. I thought we should never have come. But I like all of the men now, don't you? Even Gunnar."

"Except Harald," said Peer.

"Except Harald," Hilde agreed. "Come on, we've spent long enough in here. I wonder which house we'll use. Shall we look at the other one?"

"Hey!" Peer raised his voice. "Nithing – want to see the other house?"

With a scuttle and a rush, the Nis was at the door. It scampered out, and Peer was surprised to see that dusk was falling. The sun had sunk below the hills, and the wooded slopes looked dark and mysterious. Down by the ship, the men had lit a fire on the shore. Around the flames, the evening turned a deeper blue. One side of Water Snake gleamed, her red and black strakes warm in the firelight. On her other side lay a black shadow double. The shadows were confusing, Peer thought. There seemed too many people criss-crossing in front of the fire.

"We should go and help," said Hilde. "Look, they're bringing things up already." Someone was coming slowly up the path, as if stiff from weeks at sea. His face was indistinct in the dusk. He turned aside, heading for the other house. Hilde called out, "Hello! Is that one ours?"

Whoever it was made no reply, but turned in to the porch of the second house. Hilde shrugged. "He didn't hear me. It must be that one."

They walked across. Flat stones made a short path outside the door, which was shut. Peer lifted the latch. The Nis darted between his feet – and sprang back like a startled cat, all arched spine and splayed limbs. Peer saved himself by clutching at the doorpost. "What are you doing?" he cried.

The Nis was creeping backwards, bristling. "Not nice," it squeaked. "Not a nice house at all, Peer Ulfsson. The other one is better!" It shook itself and shot decisively away.

With an odd feeling under his ribs, Peer shoved the door wide open and looked in. He didn't step over the threshold. Hilde craned over his shoulder.

It was just like the first house. Same long fire pit, same

smoke holes, same dusty-looking benches and line of dim posts leading to a doorway at the far end.

This house was colder than the first. The air felt disturbed, as though someone had recently passed through. But it was empty.

"Surely we saw—" Hilde broke off. "Or is he in the room at the far end?"

"In the dark? Hiding?" Peer looked at her. "Do you want to find out?"

"No," said Hilde. "Let's go."

Peer tugged the door shut. "I agree with the Nis. I like the other house better."

Not quite running, they hurried back past the first of the houses. The fire crackling merrily on the beach looked like a beacon of safety.

Magnus and Halfdan were struggling over the rise, carrying a big chest. They put it down, wiping their faces, and Magnus sat on it.

"That looks heavy," Hilde called. No one but Peer would have noticed the slight quaver in her voice.

"Women's stuff," Magnus sniffed. "Bedlinen. And clothes." He looked past the houses at the steep woods, and shivered. "I'd forgotten the forest was so close. Looks like it's got nearer. Looks like—" He stopped.

"What?"

"Like it's watching us." Magnus laughed to show he didn't really think so, but Hilde and Peer both turned to look back at the dark rampart of trees.

Hilde froze. "Peer. What's that, by the second house?"

It was hard to be sure – a blackish blur that could be a tall shrub, or a forgotten woodpile. But it looked like a man, standing silently beside the door of the furthest house.

Magnus sucked air through his remaining teeth.

"I see what you mean," said Peer with dry lips. "But I think it's just the shadow of the porch."

Floki arrived, bent double under a sack. Behind him Gunnar and Astrid walked together. "Aye, aye, it all looks much as it did," Gunnar said to her, sniffing the air like an old dog. "I remember—"

He stopped and seemed to choke. Astrid caught his arm. "There…" he croaked, staring up the slope. "Who's that – in the doorway?"

The man was gone as he spoke. Peer was sure now it was only the shadow of the porch. Yet the house door was slowly opening, swinging back in a gesture of invitation. *Come in.*

"Peer, you didn't shut that door," said Hilde, alarmed by Gunnar's face. Gunnar turned straining eyes on Peer.

"Yes I did," Peer blurted. "I latched it."

Gunnar stumbled like a deer with an arrow in its heart. He clutched Astrid's shoulder. Her breath hissed as she braced him.

A white moon was rising out of the sea. The temperature was dropping. Down in the marshes a duck quacked sharply. From somewhere in the shaggy hills came a distant, thin howl. *Wolf?*

Loki pricked his ears. Magnus and Halfdan stood tensely by the chest. They made no move to pick it up again. Their breath came in clouds. Floki, who had dropped his sack, looked round as if wondering whether to run back to the ship.

Harald came loping up towards them. "What's wrong?"

Gunnar's teeth clacked. "I – I'm not well."

Harald pushed Astrid aside, dragging his father's arm over his shoulders. "You heard!" he snapped at the others. "I'll get him indoors. You women – make a fire in the house. Our own house, the first one," he added roughly, seeing Hilde about to ask. "The rest of you bring the stuff up from the ship."

Peer lay on his back, unable to sleep. Odd to lie on a bed that didn't move – odd to look up at a roof – odd to smell smoke after weeks of cold fresh air.

Gunnar and Astrid had retired into the little room at the end of the house. They had a grand bed, which had been brought up in pieces from the ship and slotted together. Astrid had covered it with linen sheets, a goosefeather bolster and woollen blankets. Hilde was shut in with them, away from the men, in a small closet bed panelled off from the rest of their room. Peer felt sorry for her. He was glad to be out here in the hall where the fire had a chance of warming the air.

The house was so cold. They'd piled branches and logs in the hearth and kindled an enormous blaze, but it would take days for the thick sod walls to warm through. The smoke hung in the rafters as though it couldn't remember the way out.

Around him his shipmates talked in whispers.

"…the skipper looks bad…"

"…what d'you think he saw?"

"…any door can swing open…"

"…aye, but it's odd it happened just then…"

"…he does look bad…"

"…the cold curse…"

"…d'you think it's the skipper it's after, or all of us?"

"…shut up, Floki, I keep telling you…"

At last the whispers died and the snores took over. Peer turned on his side and watched the fire sink to a blue and yellow flicker over whispering embers. Every so often, the powdery grey wood-ash tumbled, opening gashes of glowing red. Then, across the hearth, apple-green eyes gleamed. The Nis crept out on to the hearthstones, warming its spindly hands.

It was a comforting sight. *At least we got here, all of us, alive and well.* He tried to keep watching the Nis. But sleep pounced on him like a hunting cat, and tossed him away into oblivion.

CHAPTER 53

Seidr

HILDE LAY AWAKE in her cramped little closet. It was hardly more than a hole in the wall with a wooden lining. The bed – a straw mattress on planks – wasn't long enough to stretch out on. If she lay down, she had to curl up. The bedding, like the mattress, had come from the ship. Both were slightly damp and smelled of sea water.

It was pitch-black, not a scrap of light, and her toes were freezing. She envied Peer, asleep in the fire hall. She lay rubbing her feet together and wondered if she dared creep out to warm herself at the hearth. Surely the men would be asleep by now? But what about Astrid and Gunnar?

She fumbled for the edge of the panel and slid it back a few inches. It was as dark out there as it was in here: and just as cold. She listened for the sound of quiet breathing that would tell her Gunnar and Astrid were asleep.

Only they weren't; they were muttering together. Hilde tried to drag the panel closed again, but it stuck. She tugged at it, hearing Astrid murmur,

"Gunnar, you mustn't fret. I'll look after you."

Gunnar said unsteadily – it sounded as if his teeth were still chattering – "How c-can you protect me?"

Hilde paused silently. She knew she shouldn't, but she had to listen to this.

"You men never know how to do things," said Astrid. "You should have run needles into his feet after he was shrouded. That would have stopped him walking."

Hilde went cold all over. *Is this Erlend she's talking about?*

Gunnar's laugh turned into a cough. "We didn't bother with shrouds. Besides, it's too late now." He was silent, shivering – Hilde heard the air hissing between his teeth. "I saw him on the ship," he whispered suddenly. "All swollen up and black."

"Hush!"

"If – if anything does come, Harald's sleeping in front of the doorway."

Is he, indeed? Hilde thanked her stars she hadn't gone creeping out.

"And what can Harald do?" Astrid said softly. "You need me."

"I can't sleep. I daren't sleep."

"You can, and you will. There are ways. If you trust me."

"You're – my wife," said Gunnar. Then came an odd sound, which puzzled Hilde, till she realised, her fingers curling, that it was a kiss. There'd been no intimacy on the ship. She'd never seen Gunnar kissing Astrid, or Astrid kissing Gunnar. But in private of course they would. Frantically she wrenched at the panel. It wouldn't budge.

"Gunnar," said Astrid on a deep, purring note, "give me your soul."

Hilde's heart almost stopped. Gunnar mumbled something; it sounded like, "How?" or "Why?"

Astrid whispered rapidly, "Because I can take it from your lips with your breath, and keep it safe. I'll hide it away where no one can find it. I'll lock it round with charms. No ghost can touch you then. You'll sleep safe. No dreams. Nothing will harm you…"

Her voice sank away. There was a long, busy silence. At last Astrid murmured, "Hush. Sleep. Sleep."

Gunnar didn't answer. Soon afterwards Hilde heard a gentle snore.

The bedroom was still dark, but she heard the bedclothes stir, and a quiet footfall on the earth floor. She held her breath. In a moment she heard Astrid whispering very softly, "*Those who sleep, sleep on still. Those who wake, wake.*" The outer door creaked. A rosy glow of firelight brightened the room, and Hilde caught sight of Astrid's dark shape slipping through the door. She must be stepping right over Harald, if he lay across the threshold. Moments later she returned, carrying a smoking stick with a glowing end. She pushed the door shut, and stopped.

She's seen the open panel.

But what Astrid could see would be a black gap in the wall. Hilde shut her eyes and breathed evenly. Brightness shone through her closed lids. She felt the heat of the glowing stick very near her face. She kept still – not afraid, but intensely curious.

The stick was withdrawn. Darkness and cold returned. Hilde's eyes flew open. Astrid was on the other side of the room, using the stick to light a shallow oil lamp. Now a single flame twinkled star-like in the gloom.

Astrid sat on the bed. From under the bolster she pulled out her goatskin bag, and hugged it to herself. She reached in, and drew out something small and square that gleamed bone-yellow. Hilde thought she knew what it was. She wriggled a little closer to the panel.

Yes. The little buzzing box.

But Astrid set it aside and reached into the bag again. This time she came out with a package wrapped in a linen cloth.

She undid the linen, and inside was a mass of sheepswool. From the middle of the sheepswool she picked out something small and held it to the light. Now Hilde could see what it was: a hollow bird's egg that gleamed half-transparent against the flame. With gentle fingers Astrid lifted the egg to her lips. She seemed to blow into it, a single puff. Pattering out some charm under her breath she pulled the wool around the eggshell, and rewrapped it in the linen. Briskly now, as though everything was complete, she popped package and box back into her bag and slipped the bag back under the bolster. She reached for the oil lamp and pinched out the flame. Blackness flooded back.

Hilde knew what she'd seen. It was *seidr* – magic, that Astrid had been practising. She didn't know if she believed in it or not: or whether Astrid did. The important thing was that if Gunnar believed his soul was safely hidden, he'd be less afraid – of ghosts, or whatever he thought was threatening him.

She curled up, shivering. Why shouldn't Astrid look after Gunnar? But it was all so black and secret. "You should have run needles into his feet before he was shrouded." Hilde shuddered. *How can she talk like that? How does she even know such a thing?*

She remembered how Astrid had said, "There's troll blood in me," and, "Of course I tell lies – how else do I get what I want?"

What *did* Astrid want? Could you ever trust somebody with troll blood?

Hilde woke with a jerk of panic. Why was it so dark? She flung out a hand and felt it knock against wood.

Someone knocked back. "Did you sleep soundly?" It was Astrid. She was carrying the oil lamp, and its flame reflected little points of fire in her eyes.

Hilde sat up. She was about to say, *not very well.* Then she thought Astrid might have reasons for asking. "Yes, thanks," she said cautiously, rubbing a cricked neck. "Is it early? It's so dark."

"Only in here," said Astrid. "It's light outside. And the fire's burning well in the hall. Listen, Gunnar's feverish. He should stay in bed. Boil some water for me, will you? I'll make him another drink of willowbark."

Chilled and stiff, Hilde came out into the fire hall. It smelled of warm smoke and salty, sweaty men. Harald, Peer and Tjørvi were up. The rest were still in their blankets. Harald was combing his hair. Tjørvi sat cross-legged on the bench, spooning groute from a wooden bowl. Peer was putting more wood on the fire. He looked up at her, his fair hair ruffled, a streak of charcoal on his forehead, and his face lit with sweet, uncomplicated pleasure.

Hilde was used to people being glad to see her. Back at home, Ma, Pa, the twins, even the babies, greeted her every morning with loving warmth. Even the quarrels were loving quarrels. She'd never thought about it. She'd taken it for granted.

Now, after a night spent in Astrid and Gunnar's cold, dark room, here was Peer, simply happy to see her, and showing it. It was like stepping into sunlight and fresh air. A strange thought crossed her mind. *We belong together.*

"Hilde." He kicked a log further into the flames and came towards her. There was golden down on his jaw, the soft beginnings of a beard. His lanky frame was filling out: he was broader across the shoulders than she'd thought: he moved lightly, with grace. *I once said he looked like a heron. Not any more…*

"Hilde?" he asked, puzzled.

She jumped. How long had she been staring at him, dumb as a post?

"Is something wrong?" He threw a glance at the dark doorway behind her, ready to tackle anyone who might have upset her.

"I'm fine." She pulled herself together. "I'm fine, but Gunnar's not well. Astrid says he shouldn't get up."

"Still ill?" Harald looked up sharply. "You should have said so at once!" He vanished into the far room with a swirl of his cloak. Hilde and Peer crowded around the door.

Gunnar sat facing them, leaning against the headboard, red-eyed and pale-faced, wrapped in his wolfskin cloak. Astrid sat on the bedside, singing softly.

Harald gave her a dark glance and knelt on the other side of the bed. "Father," his voice was full of tender respect, "can't you get up?"

"He'd much better not," said Astrid.

"I didn't ask you," said Harald, with a snap. "Father?"

"I – I tried." Gunnar lifted his hand to his throat as if it hurt. "Dizzy. Listen, son…" He muttered hoarse instructions. "*Water Snake's* boat should be unloaded for use in the river. Some of the men should go hunting…"

"Yes, father. But get up! Don't lie in bed like a woman. Fight it off. Get out into the sunshine."

"Fight it off?" said Astrid scornfully. "How can he do that? There are things you can't fight with a sword, Harald." Her voice dropped into a sinister sing-song. "Bodiless things. Insubstantial things. Things you had better leave to me."

"What – things?" said Harald between his teeth.

Astrid's face was a mask of innocence. "Fever, of course. What did you think?"

They stared at each other across the bed. At last Harald said, "Just cure him quickly." He strode out. Peer and Hilde hastily drew back to let him pass.

Astrid turned back to Gunnar, stroking his forehead. "I'll sing to you again."

Gunnar nodded wearily. His head rolled back under her fingers; his eyelids flickered shut. Peer and Hilde tiptoed back to the fire.

Peer was laughing. "I think Astrid won that bout," he whispered.

Hilde nodded. "Peer, I have to tell you about last night."

But before she could begin, Magnus sat up and stretched. With his arms widely spread, he used one foot to prod Floki in the ribs. "Wake up, Floki, you lazy young brute." He gave Hilde his gap-toothed grin. "Morning, Hilde my lass. What have you got for a starving man's breakfast? Or has Tjørvi scoffed it all?" Then he cocked his head to one side, and his brow furrowed. "What's going on in *there*?"

Astrid's voice floated out of Gunnar's room, half singing, half chanting:

"I know a black stone, out in the sea.
Nine waves wash over it, three by three.
Out, sickness!

I know an oak tree, out in the wood.
Nine crows sit in it, croaking for blood.
Out, sickness!

From breast, from body, from hand, from heart,

From eyes, from ears, from every part –
Out, sickness!"

"Troll girl. Witch woman," said Magnus darkly. "Brrr! It makes you shiver."

CHAPTER 54

Disturbances and Tall Tales

GUNNAR WAS ILL for days. Astrid and Harald clashed constantly over his care, and Astrid won, but Harald became dangerously sullen. When Gunnar recovered enough to get out of bed, he spent his days shivering over the fire with Astrid in attendance. Harald kept urging him to go outside, but he seldom set foot beyond the door, though the weather was now gloriously hot. Summer seemed to arrive all at once. Wild roses, a curious bright pink, flowered in tangles around the salty marshlands, and down on the shore purple pea blossoms twined over the dry sandy stones above the tideline.

There was food everywhere. Flocks of ducks and geese nested in the marshlands, and more flew in every day. Harald and Arne took bows and shot down dozens. Salmon were spawning, running upstream in such numbers that Tjørvi joked, "You could walk across the river on their backs." Strange birds sang in the bushes. Strange animals were glimpsed in the woods. At night, flashing fireflies wandered silently in the air. The Nis went out every evening and caught handfuls, releasing them indoors to drift amongst the rafters like bright sparks. Tjørvi put one in Hilde's hair, where it winked off and on like a green jewel.

The settling in was over. With the house roof steaming and smoking, and chickens running in and out, and Loki sleeping in the sunshine, Vinland felt almost like home. But at home it would be harvest time. Here, there were no fields to tend. A lot of the time, the men just sat about, sunning themselves or talking.

And Thorolf's house remained empty, a cold, silent reminder of how alone they all were. Every morning, Peer gazed across the bay, hoping to see a square sail making its way in from the gulf. Where were they, Thorolf and his son Ottar, and the crew of the *Long Serpent*? When would they come back?

One evening as they sat around the fire, the latch flew up. Hilde burst in from outside, eyes wide and black. She doubled over, gasping. "There's someone out there! I was filling my buckets at the stream, and I heard something moving, further up the slope. And I'm sure I heard singing."

Harald leaped up, grabbing a bow and a fistful of arrows. He ran outside, and everyone but Astrid and Gunnar followed him.

It was nearly dark. The wooded slope behind the settlement was a wall of shadows, full of creeping sounds, sleepy bird calls, snapping twigs – all strange, all mysterious. As they approached the trees, the mosquitoes came out to meet them in stinging clouds.

"There's something there all right. Loki knows," said Peer. Loki was staring into the trees, hackles up. He backed off, whining and growling.

"Skraelings, perhaps," Magnus muttered. "Lurking there, watching us…"

The slope was almost as steep as a cliff. The stream cascaded down a deep cut between mossy banks, cluttered with fallen branches. The rushing water filled their ears – and then the sound of something crashing and sliding downhill.

Peer's hair stood on end. Would he see Skraelings at last?

"Bear!" Tjørvi yelled. Out from the trees plunged a shambling, sloppy-coated black bear. It saw them and reared up, paws loosely dangling. Peer saw its curved black nails, the white spot on its chest, and its small, narrow-set, blinking eyes.

Harald's arrow flew just as the bear shook its flat head and dropped on to all fours. The arrow vanished, and Harald swore, fumbling for another. But the bear was gone, melting into the dark bushes as swiftly as any deer.

"Well, now," Tjørvi said to Harald. "If you'd stung that bear, young master, it would have charged us. And then what would you have done?"

Harald's teeth gleamed. "I would have let you deal with it, Tjørvi. You look like a bear yourself. It would probably mistake you for its mother."

Halfdan and Magnus sniggered. Tjørvi pretended to scratch his head and said, "I've always fancied a bearclaw necklace."

"But I heard singing," Hilde said. They all looked at her.

Arne put his arm across her shoulders. "I don't think you could, Hilde. Bears don't sing."

"I know that, Arne. And I know what I heard."

"Mosquitoes," suggested Tjørvi helpfully after a moment.

"Don't be silly!" Hilde bent crossly for the buckets she had dropped, but Peer picked them up for her.

"Whatever it was, Hilde, please don't fetch water by yourself again."

Harald's voice sliced through the dusk. "Why don't you fetch it? You look a proper milkmaid with those buckets."

Magnus choked and slapped his thigh. A hot flush crawled under Peer's skin, but he knew it wouldn't show in the dark.

"What a shame we didn't bring any goats," Harald mocked.

"Can you milk, Barelegs? I'm sure you can."

With difficulty, Peer controlled his temper. "Of course I can. If I meet the bear, I'll milk it for you, shall I?"

There was silence, and he knew he'd shut Harald up. Tjørvi burst out laughing. He threw his arm around Peer's shoulders, roaring: "Milk the bear! Excellent! That was very good, young 'un. Here, give me one of those buckets. Bear's milk! I like it."

With a quick, dancing step, Hilde caught up with Peer. "Good for you. That showed him!" But Peer's flash of triumph was already fading.

He'll make me pay.

Was there no way of dealing with someone like Harald, and winning?

Whizz! Whizz! Whizz!

A metallic, rasping sound greeted Peer's ears as he and Floki came out of the house together next morning, heading for the fish-traps on the shore. Harald sat on a cut log near the porch, sharpening his sword. He whistled between his teeth, tilting the blade, and the sun flashed off in brilliant winks.

It was an ominous sight. Peer was going past without speaking, but Floki stopped in delight. "Your sword, Harald! You've got Bone-Biter out." He stared at the bright, dangerous thing, obviously longing to touch it, just as obviously not daring to ask. "I suppose it costs a lot, a sword like that?" he added wistfully.

Harald glanced up, shaking his hair back.

"Yes, it cost my father a pound of silver."

Floki gasped like a fish, and Peer just managed to keep his

own jaw from dropping. *A pound of silver!* He looked at his own little silver ring, the most valuable thing he had. How much silver was in that? A fraction of an ounce. How long had his father scrimped and saved to buy it?

Harald laid the whetstone down. He lifted the blade, shutting one eye to look down its length. "My father always gets me the best," he said to Floki. "Pattern-welded, see? Gilded crossbar. The hilt's bound with silver wire. And the balance – well, see for yourself." He reversed it neatly and offered the hilt to Floki.

Floki flushed till even his ears turned scarlet. He took the sword reverently, one hand clutching the hilt, the other palm out under the blade.

"Try her," said Harald. "Go on, give her a swing." He gave Peer a bright look. "Not too close to Barelegs, though. We know what happens if he gets a fright."

With sly glee, Floki prodded the sword at Peer's ankles. Peer stepped back. "Stop it, Floki."

"He's scared!" Floki grinned. "How do I look?" He bared his teeth in a ferocious snarl.

"Floki," said Harald lazily, "with a sword in your hand, you frighten even me." Peer's lips tightened. But Floki didn't notice the mockery. He raised the sword and slashed it through the air. "Hey, look at me!" he cried. "Magnus, Tjørvi, look at me."

"Mind you don't take your own leg off," growled Magnus from the porch. Tjørvi emerged, ducking low under the lintel, his shock of hair white in the sun. Yawning and stretching his arms, he watched Floki chop down invisible enemies, yelling: "Ya! Hey! Take that!"

Hilde came out with a pail of dirty water and stopped to stare. Encouraged by the audience, Floki whirled ever more wildly, till his toe caught on a loose turf, and he fell flat on his face. Everyone burst out laughing. Harald strolled forwards. Floki scrabbled for the sword on all fours, and handed it back. He knelt in front of Harald, gazing up with an expression of raw adoration on his silly red face. Peer stopped laughing. This wasn't funny any more.

"I'm your man, Harald." Floki pawed at Harald's knees. Hand on hip, Harald smiled easily down at him, the picture of nobility. Peer's toes curled. There was still a scar beside Floki's mouth, where Harald had hit him. Didn't he have any pride?

"If only I could have a sword like that," Floki mumbled. "But I never will."

"If we make our fortunes, you can buy one," Halfdan suggested.

"A lad like him doesn't need a sword," said Magnus scornfully. "He's got a knife and an axe. What more does he want? Better spend his money on a cow." Floki looked downcast.

"Here's some advice," said Tjørvi solemnly. "If you do get a sword, Floki, there's something else you ought to get first."

"A shield?" Floki asked.

"Na, na." Tjørvi winked at Peer. "You ought to get yourself a life-stone."

"What's one of them?"

"A life-stone? Ah, it's a wonderful thing to have. If you've got a life-stone, no matter what happens to you, you won't die. Sickness, battles, wounds – no matter. You've really never heard of one?" Tjørvi sounded amazed. He looked around. "*You've* all heard of a life-stone, haven't you?" The men grinned, smelling a joke.

"A mate of mine had one once," Tjørvi went on. "He

went to an awful lot of trouble to get it, too. He knew where to look – in an eagle's nest."

Floki listened, wide-eyed. Several of the men were chuckling.

"So my mate shins up to the nest and grabs the life-stone. There's a terrible fight, the eagle squealing and slashing him – but with the life-stone in his fist, he slithers safely down. Then he has a proper look at it.

"*My,* he thinks, *that's a bit small. How'm I going to keep it safe? I know – I'll get the wife to sew it into my armpit.*"

"And did she?" asked Hilde demurely.

"She certainly did," said Tjørvi, straight-faced. "Sewed it into his left armpit. He was right-handed, you see. And after that, my mate was as safe as houses. His lucky life-stone got him through all sorts of adventures without so much as a single scratch."

"Has he still got it?" demanded Floki excitedly.

Tjørvi sighed. "That's the sad part. He went on a long sea voyage. There was a terrible storm right out in the middle of the ocean, and the ship was wrecked. Everyone on board drowned. Except him. He couldn't drown, could he? He had the life-stone."

"What was sad about that?" Peer asked.

Tjørvi opened his eyes wide. "He had to walk home along the bottom of the sea, and it took him years. Oh, a horrible time he had – with sea monsters trying to swallow him, and the fish nibbling at him all the way. At long last he staggered out on shore, and the first thing he asked was for one of us to open his armpit and take out the stone. We did it, of course – anything for a friend – and as soon as it was out of him, the poor fellow crumbled into dust."

They were still laughing at Tjørvi's tall tale – and at Floki, who wanted to know where the life-stone was now, and whether Tjørvi had it – when Halfdan cried out. "Listen! D'you hear that?"

It was the unmistakeable ringing chop of an axe, far away in the forest: a flat clap followed by an echo. It repeated and repeated.

"Someone cutting wood. But who?"

"Skraelings at last." Harald was on his feet, his eyes bright and narrow, the sword swinging in his hand. "Let's go and find them."

"I'll come!" said Arne.

"And me," Tjørvi rumbled. He patted his hard, flat stomach. "Too much food and too little exercise. I'm getting fat."

Everyone wanted to come and Harald had to choose. "Halfdan, Tjørvi, Arne… Not you, Barelegs," he said to Peer, who hadn't offered. "Floki, you can come if you like."

They set off into the trees in high spirits. Magnus stood at the house door and shook his head. "There goes a lad who needs to be kept busy."

"Oh, I wish I could go," Hilde exclaimed. "I wonder what Skraelings are really like? Do you think they'll find them?"

Magnus scratched his stubbly chin. "If not, let's hope young Harald finds another bear or something. 'Cos he hasn't got enough to do."

It was oddly quiet around the houses with half of the men missing. By sunset, they had not returned. Magnus stood outside, wafting away mosquitoes and staring at the woods. "Should've thought they'd be here by now," he kept muttering. "P'raps I should'a gone along. Floki's got no sense. Still, Tjørvi'll prob'ly keep an eye on him. Don't you reckon?"

Gunnar kept sending Astrid and Hilde to the door to look for Harald coming back. At last Peer and Hilde and Magnus walked up to the spot where they'd met the bear, listening for the sounds of their friends coming out of the forest. The chopping had long since stopped. Branches cracked, birds cried in strange voices. On the edge of hearing, some creature wailed, a wordless, wistful call. It dragged on Peer's nerves. *Find me. I'm lost, I'm lonely...*

And then: "Ahoy, there!"

This time it was a real shout. Magnus sighed in relief. "That's them. Here they are, look – coming from the river. This way!" he bellowed.

Exhausted, swearing, and plastered with mud, the expedition limped out of the bogs beside the river and up on to the firmer ground below the trees.

"Gods!" said Arne. "I'm glad that's over. We've wandered for miles." He looked back and shuddered. "I've felt eyes on my back all day."

"And insects!" exclaimed Tjørvi. "Whew!" His eyes were almost swollen shut with mosquito bites.

"It's been horrible," Floki whined, scratching at an angry lump on his face.

Tjørvi gave Halfdan a shove. "It was Halfdan's fault. He kept seeing things." Peer had never seen Big Tjørvi in such a bad mood.

"What things?" asked Hilde.

Halfdan looked unhappy. "Someone beckoning between the trees. With long hair covering the face. Sort of – greenish. Arne saw it too. He thought it was a woman."

"I was never sure," said Arne quickly.

"So we followed this 'person' till we lost it," Tjørvi growled, "and ended up in a stinking bog, and floundered around for hours. Finally we stumbled across a stream—"

"He means that – Floki fell into it," Arne added.

"Which led us down to the river. And thankful I am that it's the right river." Tjørvi still seemed unusually angry. "I thought we'd never get back."

Harald had said nothing so far. He was wiping his sword in the long grass. His hair trailed over his shoulders in long muddy draggles, and his legs were mired to the knee. A spirit of mischief rose in Peer. "So you found no Skraelings. What a pity!"

Harald glanced up. "Oh, but we did. That was the one thing that went right."

"You found Skraelings!" Peer felt sudden deep alarm.

"Just two," said Arne. He sounded rather odd. "Camped a mile or so back along the river, under a sort of bark shelter. We saw the fire they'd lit."

"What happened?" Hilde cried. "Could you talk to them? Were they friendly?"

"We didn't have time to find out," said Tjørvi carefully, "before Harald killed them."

Harald finished cleaning his sword and rammed it back in its sheath. "Exciting, wasn't it?" he said cheerfully. "Floki almost wet himself. Look at this." He tapped his chest. Slung from his neck, a rope of splendid white claws gleamed in the dusk, each one as long as a finger. "Skraeling work. A bearclaw necklace: the only thing worth taking. Who said he wanted one of these? You, Tjørvi? Too bad; you'll have to be quicker next time. Come on, it's suppertime, and I'm starving."

CHAPTER 55

A Walk on the Beach

"HE KILLED THEM?" Hilde stared after Harald in disbelief. The thick dusk prickled with stars. Mosquitoes whined about their ears.

Halfdan muttered, "They might have attacked us."

"Certainly," said Tjørvi with heavy sarcasm. "It pays to be careful with odds like that. Two of them, and only five of us."

"Did they look dangerous?" Hilde asked in a strained voice.

"A couple of young fellows, cooking fish over a camp fire?" Tjørvi snorted. "They hardly had time to look around, let alone go for their weapons."

"Couldn't you do something?" Hilde cried. "Arne!"

"It was so quick," said Arne glumly. "I mean, Harald wasn't fooling around. The one with the bearclaw necklace stood up – maybe he thought we were going to say something. I thought so too, but Harald just – he just..." He stopped and looked down.

"They were Skraelings!" Halfdan shouted. "Outlaws, for all we know. Spies, even. Harald did the right thing. He kept us safe."

Tjørvi pushed him aside and stamped past. Halfdan ran after him, arguing. Magnus smacked Floki around the ear and said gruffly, "Come along, lad, and clean up."

Peer held back. He didn't want to go in with them, to the noise and the smoke and the smells. He didn't want to be anywhere near Harald. "There'll be a breeze on the shore," he said to Hilde. "Let them get their own supper. Come for a walk with me and Loki."

"All right," she said quietly.

Arne glanced over his shoulder, but Tjørvi said, "That's right, get along with the lad, Hilde. We can manage to ladle stew out of the pot by ourselves." He dropped a swollen eyelid at Peer and hustled Arne ahead of him through the door.

Peer looked at Hilde. "You're upset."

She folded her arms and hunched her shoulders. "He killed two men and stole from the bodies. And none of them stopped him…"

"It wouldn't be easy to stop him," Peer said gently, and she turned to him with a small sob.

The door reopened, and out came Astrid. "Heigh-ho!" she yawned. "Gunnar's all over his darling boy. Have you heard what he did? Horrible, isn't it?"

"It's awful," said Hilde passionately.

"That's what I said." Astrid eyed her. "Were you surprised? Harald's killed real people, you know, not just Skraelings."

"Skraelings are people!"

"Yes – well – never having seen one, I can't say. Are you going to the shore? I'll come too."

With poor grace, Peer led the way along the path they'd trodden to the shore. The two girls walked behind.

"Oof," Astrid sighed. "It's good to get out. I've been cooped up all day."

"You could have got out before," said Hilde. "There are plenty of outside jobs to do. Carrying water. Collecting firewood…"

"I'm busy looking after Gunnar," said Astrid coolly.

The grassland halted at the shore in a sudden edge of turf, a foot or two high, eroded by winter storms and cut here and there by tiny black brooks that tinkled out of the marsh to vanish in the shingle. Peer jumped on to the stones. Astrid teetered on the brink behind him. "Help me down."

"For goodness' sake," said Hilde. "Jump! It's nothing."

"I might hurt myself. Please, Peer," Astrid said sweetly. Biting his lip, he reached up and swung her down. She was lighter than he expected, despite being so tall, and her beautiful hair brushed his face. She clung to his arm as they picked their way across oval pebbles to the level beach. Hilde followed. Peer couldn't guess what she was thinking.

The sea was a glimmering curve with a milk-white rim. At the edge of the tide they walked in a film of water where the gravel stirred underfoot, sucked back and forth by advancing and retreating ripples.

"How bright the stars are," Astrid said to Peer. "Do you know their names?"

"Some." She was still holding his arm. He couldn't shake her off. He looked up. "Over the headland, that's the Wagon. See? And if you follow up from the two stars on the end, they'll lead you to the Nail. That marks north."

"Clever," said Astrid.

"The Nail's much lower here than it is at home," said Hilde.

"Because we've come south," said Peer.

"I thought we'd come west," Astrid complained.

Hilde rolled her eyes. "And south, too. How can you not know that, Astrid?"

"I leave all that sort of thing to the men," said Astrid, unperturbed. She released Peer's arm. "I think I'll go and sit on that rock."

She wandered off. Peer looked sideways at Hilde, who was staring at the softly splashing sea. "Are you upset?" he asked again.

"A bit." She crossed her arms. "*I leave all that sort of thing to the men*. Astrid doesn't care about anything, does she? She leaves nearly everything to someone else. Cleaning to the Nis. Cooking and fetching and carrying to me."

"She looks after Gunnar," said Peer.

"I thought Vinland would be a wonderful adventure. Remember Pa first telling us about the Skraelings? People with brown skin, he said, and black hair. I've tried to imagine them ever since." She shivered. "And now I'm imagining blood. I was stupid to expect adventures. I'm only here to keep Astrid company. I'm a girl: I belong in the house."

Peer almost laughed. "That's not how I think of you."

"Isn't it? How do you think of me?"

"How can you ask? I think you could do anything. I think you're braver than I am."

She gave him a grateful smile, and he glowed. "I'm not so brave," she said. "These days I'm almost afraid of going to bed at night..." Side by side they walked on, and he half-listened, entranced by her flyaway hair silver in the moonlight, her smooth skin and clear eyes. "...You don't know what it's like, sharing that little room with them. Gunnar has terrible dreams. I hear him waking, and crying out, and Astrid trying to calm him." She stopped and turned. "Peer, there's something I've wanted to tell you for ages, only we've never been on our own, I've never had the chance..."

His heart kicked. His blood leaped. Hilde loved him. She was about to tell him so...

Then he realised what she was saying: "...and Astrid was working *seidr*. She hid Gunnar's soul, to keep it safe. She has a bone box with a little voice inside that tells her things. I've heard it humming." She stared at him, waiting for a reaction. "Are you listening?"

He drew a hand across his eyes. "Tell me that again."

She did so, with dogged patience. "And Astrid does have troll blood. I was supposed to keep it a secret, but Halfdan and Magnus and Floki all seem to know; it's just that they daren't tell Gunnar. I don't know whether to trust her at all."

The letdown had been severe. Peer's voice shook as he sought for some kind of answer. "Aren't you rather hard on Astrid?"

Hilde choked. "If you'd been there – if you'd heard her telling Gunnar to stick needles in a corpse's feet—"

"Yes, it sounds bad." Since they had to talk about Astrid, Peer set his mind to it. "But what about Gunnar? What has Astrid done that's so wrong? Gunnar's *killed* somebody – him and Harald together. And the way they did it must have been pretty dreadful, or why is he so afraid?"

Hilde began to speak, and stopped.

"And you know," said Peer slowly, "the more I think about it, the more I wonder whether Thorolf left after some quarrel. We've only Gunnar's word for it that he ever meant to settle here. He might have decided that living with Gunnar and Harald wasn't worth the trouble."

"Do you think he won't come back?" said Hilde quietly.

"I wonder. And I've noticed something else. I've noticed that when we talk about Thorolf, it's always you and me, or sometimes Arne or Tjørvi. The others, who sailed with Gunnar before – they don't say anything. Maybe they know something we don't."

Hilde thought about it, and shook her head. "Oh, Peer, that can't be right. Look at Floki, he can't keep his mouth shut about anything. If Gunnar and Thorolf had fallen out, we'd have heard all about it by now."

"I suppose that's true," said Peer. "I hope so. I want to see Thorolf as much as you do."

Hilde started. Something galloped past them, kicking up splatters of wet gravel. "It's only the Nis," said Peer. He could just see it, careering across the beach in happy circles. "Out for a run."

The moon was clear of the headland, casting sharp shadows. The wet beach ticked, clicked, pattered, as though a myriad little people were busy among the stones. Peer looked harder. The gravel danced in patterns.

The Nis dashed past again, jinking and skipping, making little rushes here and there, picking up shells, "What are you doing?" Peer called.

"Playing with the *wiklatmu'jk*," the Nis cried in a high-pitched voice like a bird call.

"What?" said Hilde.

"Look!" Peer pointed. Ahead, on a patch of smooth sand, someone had laid out figures in lines of pebbles. One had legs, one had a triangular skirt. To the side was a comical short-legged animal with a stiff tail. Hilde and Peer bent over them.

"That's us," whispered Hilde. "Us and Loki. Did the Nis do it?"

Peer shook his head. He straightened up, his face alive with delight. "Hilde, the whole beach is covered with – *tiny* – people."

She stared.

"I've been seeing them all along," he went on. "I just didn't notice. They're everywhere. But I can only see them when I'm not looking straight."

Hilde half-shut her eyes and peeped out of the corners. Nothing. Wait, there was something scurrying through the gravel.

"It's crabs," she said.

"It isn't," Peer insisted. "They're all over the place, knocking and chipping at the pebbles. Don't try so hard. Try looking at them the way you look at a faint star."

The moonlit beach didn't change at all: but something happened behind her eyes. For a second she saw the stones alive with hurrying, busy little creatures, tugging and pushing and rearranging the pebbles, making patterns and scattering them again. She saw their little black shadows, the size of her thumb.

She lost the way to do it, and they were gone. The picture of the girl and the boy and the dog was gone too. In its place was a serpentine curve, with four little lines descending from it, and one tall line sticking up from the middle.

"A snake with legs?"

"It's a ship," Peer said suddenly. "See, the hull, and the dragonhead, and the mast – and those things that look like legs are the oars. It's our ship – *Water Snake*. They're making pictures of what they see."

"What did the Nis call them? The *weeklat* something?"

"*Wiklatmu'jk*."

"The weeklatmoojig?" Hilde repeated. "How does it know?"

"It comes out playing every night," Peer said. "It's made friends." He swung round, scanning the bay, forest and stars with shining eyes. "Ralf was right. This is a wonderful country."

"Let's ask the Nis about them," said Hilde. "Where's it gone?"

They had been slowly walking along the curve of the bay. Ahead of them a line of rocks ran out from the southern headland. The sea had scooped hollows around the bases of the rocks, which the retreating tide had left full of water, almost invisible in the moonlight. The Nis was scrambling about between the tide pools. Peer could hear distant splashes as it tossed pebbles into the water.

"Let's run!"

He caught her hand. They pounded across the shingle, clattered over flat stones that slid and clinked like coins, splashed, shockingly, across a flat shining stretch that turned out to be water, so that Hilde shrieked and laughed as the spray flew – tugging each other along by the swinging clasp of their joined hands, till at last Hilde stepped on the hem of her dress and fell over, pulling Peer after her. Loki pounced on them both, play-biting.

Breathless with laughter, they sat up. Hilde brushed gravel off her dress and flicked the bigger bits at Peer, till she saw that he had stopped laughing and was looking at her in a way that made the back of her neck shiver. She got up quickly. "Look, we're at the rocks. We'd better turn back. Astrid is miles behind. Let's call the Nis and go."

"Hilde." He was still looking at her. "Please listen to me."

Hilde suddenly saw two things with perfect clarity. The first was that she'd known all along that Peer still loved her. Only she hadn't let herself know, because it was easier – because she wasn't sure how she felt. The second was that Peer was no longer the gawky lad who had kissed her last year. He had changed. No, he hadn't, he was the same as ever, he had just… grown up. She faced him, twining her fingers into her apron. "All right then – go on."

She wasn't used to being shy with Peer. It came out wrong.

It sounded petulant and brusque. Peer winced. He drew in a deep breath – she saw his chest heave – but before he could speak, the Nis appeared over the rocks. It leaped on to the beach, prattling excitedly.

"Come and see what I has found!"

The breath left Peer in a defeated whoosh. The Nis skipped about, bright-eyed, cracking its knuckles. "A present for you, Peer Ulfsson! Come see, come see!" it cried, springing over a strip of water and frisking away.

"Shall we?" asked Hilde in a small voice. Without a word, Peer followed it. Hilde rubbed her hot face with both hands, and went after them.

Almost immediately, she wished she hadn't. The rocks were full of inky shadows and unexpected holes. Some were loose, tipping alarmingly. There was a reek of salt and seaweed and all the nameless things that the sea swept up and dumped. She cracked her knee and muttered a bad word.

Peer looked back. "Can you manage?" he asked curtly.

"Yes." The last thing she wanted was for him to help her. She hoisted her skirts and clambered grimly on.

Cheeping with excitement, the Nis led them to a long pool. Repeated tides had pushed up sand and gravel into a ridge blocking the entrance, so that although waves broke against the rocks a few yards away, only a few ripples ran in over the sand bar to disturb the pool itself. An old black log was jammed there too, half buried.

The Nis stopped, its grey wispy hair blowing in the wind, pointing with one long finger. "For you!" it announced proudly. "Nithing the Seafarer found it!"

Hilde heard Peer say softly, "Oh, no."

"What is it?" she asked, bewildered. "Peer, what are you doing?"

She scrambled after him as he flung himself recklessly down the sharp rocks and jumped into the water. It came up to his thighs: he waded through it, arms flailing, thrashing up spray. He stumbled up the slope where the bottom rose towards the sandbank, and threw himself upon the old black log, digging the silt away from it with his hands.

"What's the matter?" gasped Hilde, really frightened, though she didn't know why. Had Peer gone mad?

Peer put both his arms around the log, and heaved. It came out of the silt with a rush, streaming water, and he hugged it to his chest. He turned to face Hilde, holding it. His face was dark against the opal sky, his eyes glittered. She stared, knowing what she was seeing before she could frame it in words.

The black log glistened, slimy as a snail; it was horned like a snail, with two root-like stumps. It had a savage look: a twist to it like a neck, a gaping maw like some snarling animal.

"Burned!"

The word burst from Peer. He staggered back through the water and laid the thing on the edge of the rocks. He covered his face.

Hilde crouched. With a finger she gently traced the blackened carvings: the criss-cross scales, the round, charred eye.

"A dragonhead."

"It's the *Long Serpent*," said Peer from behind his hands.

"Oh, Peer!" Hilde's voice shook on a sob. She reached out and awkwardly patted his hair. "Oh, Peer!"

"Thorolf's not coming back." Peer's eyes were dark; his mouth was a white line. A tear fell down his face and he wiped it away with the back of his hand.

Hilde didn't know what to say. "Don't stand in the water.

Come on, get out." She gave him a hand and he struggled on to the rocks and stood dripping and shivering.

From the peak of a rock higher above the pool, the Nis looked down, its face crinkling in an effort to understand. "Doesn't you like it, Peer Ulfsson?"

Peer tried to speak. The Nis scuttled down the rocks and laid a knobbly hand lightly against his knee. "Doesn't you want my present?"

Peer bent down. "Yes, Nis, I do. It was very clever of you to find it. Thank you for showing us. Do you know who made this? My father made it."

"Good!" Satisfied, the Nis hopped away.

Peer said to Hilde, "I suppose it's stupid, but I feel as if my father was on the ship, too. I feel as though I just lost him all over again." He picked up the burned dragonhead and said bleakly, "Let's go."

"What are you going to do with it?"

"Take it back, of course. Show it to the others. Now we know."

"Know what?" Hilde felt slow and clumsy. "What do we know?"

He turned fiercely. "The ship *burned*, Hilde. It wasn't wrecked, it burned. And how do you suppose that happened?"

She hurried after him, fear pecking at her heart. "I – I don't know. How?"

Peer jumped off the rocks. Loki greeted him in relieved delight. "Down!" Peer snapped, striding past.

"How did the ship catch fire?" Hilde had to run to keep up.

Peer flung her a look of disbelief. "How do you think? Gunnar and Harald. They did it, didn't they? All this time, they've been lying to us. They know quite well what happened to Thorolf."

"No," Hilde said dizzily. "Surely..."

"No?" Peer swung away. "Let's go and ask them."

"Peer, don't!" Hilde caught his arm. But he broke roughly away, running towards the low sod houses by the river mouth.

"Peer!" she screamed. He was faster than she was, she'd never catch him. She sprinted after him, and the wind blew tears from her eyes. How quickly everything had gone wrong. Only a little while ago they'd been laughing, running in the moonlight, marvelling at the pictures made by the little *wiklatmu'jk*.

Astrid rose like a ghost from a stone in front of her. "What on earth have you done to Peer? Didn't I give you long enough? Has he kissed you?"

"What" – Hilde pressed a hand to her ribs – "are you talking about? We've got to stop him. He's going to... he's found..."

Astrid's eyes narrowed. "So it's Arne after all, is it? What a fool you are. Arne's quite ordinary."

Hilde nearly screamed at her. "He's found the dragonhead from the *Long Serpent*. Burned. He's going to face Harald."

"Oh, gods." Astrid's face changed. "Get after him, quick. They'll kill him."

"Then it's true? And you knew?"

"Just go!" Astrid shrieked, and Hilde flew on. The surface of the beach seemed to jump at her. Patterns, everywhere: patterns...

They danced before her eyes, in her mind, at the back of her head. A boy, a girl, a boat... she dashed through the patterns, scattering them. *Mind out, little creatures*. Stick figures flew, a leg here, an arm there. *The wiklatmu'jk make pictures of what they see.* What pictures had they made a year ago, when the beach was a battleground?

CHAPTER 56

Single Combat

PEER BURST INTO the house like a destroying wind. The men eating around the hearth looked up in amazement. He lifted the dragonhead high, like a standard. Then he hurled it to the floor.

"What's this?" Harald was the first to break silence, in his insolent drawl. "Firewood?"

Big Tjørvi came slowly forward. "That's a dragonhead," he growled in wonder. "A burned dragonhead."

"From the *Long Serpent*," said Peer harshly.

Gunnar half-rose, staring at the ruined dragonhead. Harald's lip curled.

"And how would you know that, Barelegs?" he sneered.

Peer laughed, a hard, fierce laugh. "Better than anyone, Harald. My father made it. In a way, it killed him. His chisel slipped, and the wound turned bad... You might say he put his blood into that ship."

"And so? Why should I care about your carpenter father?" Harald lounged back, stretching out his legs and propping his heels on a small stool.

The dark, smoky room blurred and narrowed to the bright, pale, hated face of Harald. Peer tore free of Tjørvi's restraining hand.

"Because my father was a maker, Harald," he yelled. "He

put something into this world, instead of taking something out of it. He made a ship, and it was a good ship. It brought Thorolf and his men all the way across the sea, not once, but twice."

He drew a sobbing breath. "And where's Thorolf now? Where's Thorolf, and his son Ottar, and all his crew? What happened to the *Long Serpent*, Harald? Why did she burn?"

He ran out of air. Harald stared up at Peer with a hard little smile. Beside him, Gunnar bent over and coughed: short, wet, hacking coughs. Harald's hand shifted to grip his father's arm.

Everyone else remained perfectly still.

Peer shouted, "They're dead, aren't they? Dead, like those Skraelings you slaughtered today. And you know it, because you killed them, and then you burned their ship and took their goods and sailed away. Thorolf's in Vinland, you told us. And we believed you. Of course we did. How were we going to check?"

The door rattled open. Hilde tumbled in out of the night, her hair falling down. "Peer, come outside. I… need to talk to you."

Peer didn't even look at her. "You murderer, Harald. You bloody murderer. Ships don't burn themselves. Thorolf's not in Vinland. Thorolf's in Valhalla."

Harald still didn't move. "You're crazy. I'm flattered, of course. You think I killed how many men, all alone?"

"Of course not alone. You and Gunnar, and – your crew…" Peer looked around and swallowed.

"You mean Magnus, and Floki, and Halfdan?" Harald mused, flicking out fingers. "At least five of us here?" He twisted round. "What about it, men? Remember killing Thorolf?"

Floki's ready mouth opened, but Magnus's elbow caught

him in the ribs. He doubled over, wheezing. Magnus turned a dark look on Harald and shook his head.

"No, Magnus doesn't remember. What about Halfdan? Can you remember killing Thorolf, Halfdan?" Halfdan pinched his lips together. "Nope," he said quickly. Arne and Tjørvi looked at each other.

"Oh dear, Halfdan doesn't remember either." Harald put his head to one side. "It can't have happened, then."

"Peer, leave it," said Hilde. Her voice crackled with fear.

Only his anger was supporting Peer, a fragile scaffolding over a pit of terror. "They're lying. I know you did it."

Harald stood up. "Prove that."

Peer pointed at the dragonhead on the floor. "There's the proof."

"I don't mean that sort of proof." Harald's eyes sparkled. "You've accused me: now let's see if you can prove it – man to man."

"No!" Hilde screamed.

All the men began shouting. "No, no!" "Yes!"

"Fight!" Floki yapped.

The door opened again and Astrid stole in, white-faced and narrow-eyed. Hilde ran to her. "Astrid, you must know what happened. It's true, isn't it? You know Peer's right. Tell them, quickly." She pulled Astrid forwards. The clamour died down. Tjørvi looked at Astrid as if expecting pearls to drop from her mouth.

Astrid's eyes flashed from Peer's face to Gunnar's. "Sorry, Hilde." The words were as cold and distinct as chips of marble. "I don't know what you're talking about." And next second everyone was shouting again.

"Enough!" Gunnar struggled to his feet. He stood, head low, glaring around the room with fierce, red-rimmed eyes.

"That's enough. *I'll* say what goes on here." He eyed the blackened dragonhead with a disgusted shudder. "Throw that thing on the fire. And you" – he turned on Peer – "apologise to my son and we'll forget about this."

Peer licked his lips. The anger was draining away. He felt he was waking from a dream into a cold daybreak. *How did I get myself into this mess? I've made all the wrong moves. Run straight into the net.*

"Apologise, Peer," whispered Hilde. "It doesn't matter, nothing matters. It's only words. Just do it."

Harald smiled at him, eyes alight with amused contempt. "You heard her, Barelegs. Get on with it. Grovel."

Peer looked at Harald. *I can't,* he thought, *I really can't.* It was a surprise to discover that he'd sooner die than do what Harald wanted. He was almost angry with himself. *Stupid, stiff-necked, stubborn…* He said doggedly, and a chill swept down his spine: "No. You killed Thorolf, Harald. I swear it on my father's life."

"All right then." Harald nodded to him. "We'll fight."

"This is crazy!" Hilde's face was white. "How can fighting prove anything? Gunnar, please!"

Peer wished she'd stop fussing: it wouldn't do any good. Harald's sword came out with a grating hiss. Floki was saying, "But what's Peer – I mean, Barelegs – what's he going to fight with? He hasn't got a sword."

"He can borrow my father's." Harald tossed a look at Peer. "Or would you prefer a hammer?" Laughter bubbled up in his face, and Peer saw in his eyes the memory of that faraway day on the jetty. He remembered, too. He remembered watching the ship come in, wondering if he would be any good in a fight. Now he'd have to find out. *Harald always meant it should come to this.*

"He gets to borrow Gunnar's sword?" Floki was saying jealously. "Lucky!"

"Shut your stupid mouth," Magnus growled.

"This won't do." Arne slammed a fist down. "Peer can't fight Harald. It's not a fair match."

Tjørvi rumbled agreement, but Gunnar picked at his front teeth with a brown fingernail and said, "Two lads, the same age, the same height?" He shook his head. "What's wrong with that?"

"Harald's experience?" said Astrid, her voice like cold water dripping.

Harald laughed. "He doesn't *have* to fight me, darling Astrid. He can back down."

"Peer," Hilde pleaded.

"But he can't," said Halfdan, shocked. "Only a coward would do that."

Someone – Floki – shoved a sword into Peer's hands. "Here, take it." His red face swam close up to Peer's, round-eyed and curious as a cow's. "You must be mad," he said on a waft of damp, warm breath. "Fancy having a go at Harald."

Peer clutched the sword. It was amazingly heavy: he had to use both hands. He stared at the blade. There were little silver scratches where it had been sharpened, and halfway down, the edge had been turned by some blow.

A space was clearing around them. Benches were being dragged back. Peer felt horribly calm, though rather weak at the knees. There was no way out. He had a sword he didn't know how to use, and Harald would kill him. It was as simple as that.

"Right." Harald stepped forward.

"Wait, Harald." Arne grabbed him. "You can't fight like this – indoors, by firelight. Look around!" He gestured. "There's hardly room to move. What's more, it's unlawful. Night killings are murder: that's the law."

Harald turned. "What law, Arne? Whose law? This is Vinland," he added cheerfully. "There are no laws here. That's why we came." He advanced on Peer.

Peer backed away, holding the sword out in front of him. He saw Big Tjørvi's troubled face, the firelight shining through his dandelion-fluff hair. He saw Hilde's horrified stare – Floki, twisting his hands together excitedly – Magnus, sour and uneasy. Astrid stood behind Gunnar, gazing intently. Gunnar's light eyes blinked at Peer and flicked away. Blink, flick.

Harald shook his sword suddenly and laughed to see Peer jump. He was moving sideways, making Peer turn to face the fire so that the light would shine in his eyes. He feinted in, a low slash. Everyone went, "Ooh!" and Peer stumbled back before realising that Harald was playing with him.

Cat and mouse, he thought bitterly. A dog barked outside the door. *Loki*. Peer's attention flickered. At least Loki was safe out there...

He dodged, barely in time. The sword struck like a serpent, stinging his arm, parting his sleeve. Harald feinted again, high, then low. Peer hopped – this way, that way. Where would the next blow come from? Harald was smiling. *I've got to fight back,* Peer remembered. *Got to use this sword*. He wagged it clumsily.

With a grunt and a cry Harald whirled his sword in an arc towards Peer's shoulder. Peer's reflexes took over. He lashed furiously upwards. There was a ringing crash, and the blades clung, biting, then slid apart with a tooth-jangling screech and a flurry of blue sparks.

Sweat and terror half-blinded Peer. His arm hurt now. There was blood on his sleeve. His fingers were numb with the shock of the blow. He stepped back, blinking, shaking his head. *I'm done for. I'll never manage to ward him off twice.*

Harald was in no hurry. He began to jeer. "Not bad for a carpenter, Barelegs. I can see you've chopped a few trees down in your time. But you'll have to do better than that."

Peer's vision cleared. Past Harald's shoulder he saw Hilde, white-knuckled fists bunched at her sides. Next to her was Arne. He was staring at Peer, as if willing him to look. Their eyes locked. Slightly but urgently, Arne shook his head.

Don't play Harald's games. As if a message had flown straight from Arne's mind to his, Peer remembered Bjørn's warning. *Better to take an insult than a sword in your guts.*

It's too late now. Or is it?

Peer glanced around. Behind him was the door. In front of him was Harald, dark against the fire, his loose hair rimming him in gold. And there on the floor lay the burned dragonhead, with its snarling mouth and blackened eye, like a legless monster creeping into the fight on its belly…

With a shout, Peer flung Gunnar's sword at Harald. Instinctively, Harald lashed out. His blow sent the loose sword cartwheeling through the air. Everyone yelled and ducked. The sword hit the stones of the hearth with a clang.

Peer hurled himself on the burned dragonhead. He lifted it like a club. "You're right, Harald," he panted, "I'm useless with a sword. This'll be better."

Harald's beautiful face contorted. He leaped towards Peer and brought his sword round in a scything sweep at neck-level. Eyes screwed shut, teeth bared, Peer swung the dragonhead. There was a thud and a jerk. His eyes flew open. Harald's blade had bitten deep into the wood and was stuck there. Glaring and snorting, Harald wrenched at it.

Peer let go. As Harald went reeling backwards, he sprang

for the door. The men were roaring. Hilde screamed, "Run, Peer! Run!"

He fumbled with the latch. Harald was up, one foot braced against the dragonhead, wrestling and tugging, working his sword free.

The door came open. Loki rushed in, tail wagging. "No, Loki!" Peer yelled. "*This* way!" He whistled, fierce and shrill, and Loki bounded after him, confused but willing. Peer banged the door shut. He was out in the cool night, running for the woods.

Loki raced alongside. Behind them the door opened again, spilling pursuit. Shouts echoed between the trees and the shore. Peer didn't bother to listen. The ground was uneven, scattered with branches, pitted with holes. He staggered, recovered, sprinted on.

Then he was at the foot of the bluff, close to the little cascade where Hilde fetched the water. He threw himself at the rise, pulling himself up. Twigs lashed his face; brambles snagged his skin. He scrambled higher, clawing handholds out of the soft leaf mould. Beside him Loki scrabbled and sprang. Sobbing for breath, Peer forced himself to keep climbing.

The shouts faded. The slope lessened, levelled. Still Peer ran, weaving under the trees. Fireflies tacked across the dark: a bright stitch here, a bright stitch there.

He ran on, not thinking, escaping. Something terrible was following, that was all he knew. And if he stopped, it would catch him. But his legs were weaker and weaker. His arm stung and throbbed. His sleeve was sticky and warm.

The ground vanished. Peer pitched forwards down a steep slope. Dry branches cracked under him. In an avalanche of dead leaves and small stones, he rolled, fell, and thudded on to rocks.

CHAPTER 57

Losing Peer

"RUN!" HILDE SCREAMED, as Peer swung the dragonhead at Harald. She screamed again as he paused to call Loki. Then he vanished, and Harald rushed after him, and all the men followed. Only Gunnar was left behind, like some crippled old spider that couldn't crawl out of its web.

Hilde ran out too. Wildly she looked to the woods, hearing the men yell as they fought their way up into the forest.

Oh, Peer – get away. Run, hide!

But where? There was nowhere for him to go. Vinland was a wilderness, a place without places. Hilde gasped as the enormity of the disaster broke over her. Peer couldn't come back.

Harald and Gunnar, outlawed for five years for the murder of Erlend, would never let Peer live to tell of an even worse crime here in Vinland – the slaughter of Thorolf and all his men. Peer had defied them, accused them outright. So he would die: either slowly in the forest, or quickly under Harald's sword.

I know as much as Peer does. I could tell everything. But a woman couldn't be a witness. Harald wouldn't care about a girl's threats. Magnus, Floki and the others were mixed up in it themselves and would say nothing. Arne or Tjørvi might speak. But Harald had been clever. He'd challenged Peer, asked him to prove his claim through combat. By breaking off the fight, Peer had lost his case.

Hilde ground her teeth. Men! What stupid rules they set up – as though fighting about something could alter the truth!

It was dreadful to be so helpless.

The dragonhead! Gunnar had ordered it to be thrown on the fire. But Peer was right. It was a different sort of proof: it showed beyond doubt that death had come to the *Long Serpent* and her crew. Perhaps, one day, it could be used against Gunnar and Harald. She had to save it.

Quickly. It may already be burning. Silent as a thief, she slid back inside. Gunnar sat at the far end of the fire hall, moodily swigging from his drinking horn. Astrid paced up and down near the door. She jumped as Hilde came in. "Where's Peer? Did they catch him?"

Hilde didn't reply. The dragonhead lay in the hearth, where Harald had thrown it after wrenching his sword free. Luckily it had fallen in the ashes. She dragged it out, giving Astrid a searing glare that dared her to say anything, and backed through the door without a word.

The dragonhead was top-heavy and awkward. The ash had stuck to its sea-slimed surface. She hugged it to her chest and thought of Peer digging in the tidepool, heaving the dragonhead out of the sand and crying for Thorolf – for his father – for the waste of it all. Tears filled her own eyes, but there was no time for that. She looked about. Where to hide it? Not near the house – someone would be sure to find it. No time to run to the shore or the woods. *Quickly, before Harald gets back…*

Then she knew. Thorolf's empty house. *Nobody ever goes there.*

She stole up the dim path. The door swung open at a touch, and a chill, damp smell came out. Squatting, she slid the dragonhead in along the floor. As she let go, it vanished into the waiting blackness so completely that she could almost believe it had wriggled away like a snake. She felt for it, patting the earth floor. If someone did look in, she didn't want them to see the dragonhead lying just inside. But she must have pushed it further than she had thought, for her groping fingers couldn't find it again.

The silence in the house was tense and emphatic… the silence of a roomful of people all holding their breath. And a *tick, tick, tick* of dripping water. Hilde's skin roughened up in goosebumps. She dragged the door shut. But the dragonhead was hidden, and she couldn't shake off a ridiculous, clinging hope that somehow, if the dragonhead was safe, Peer might be too.

The Nis scampered past her ankles with a swish of air and a heavy patter of feet. *It's still playing. It doesn't know what happened.* She called for it. "Nis? Nis, I need you." It was probably hiding in the dark porch, hoping to jump out and make her scream. "Nis, there's no time for games. Peer's hurt. He's run off into the woods. We have to find him." She swallowed a sob. "Nis, that dragonhead you found. It means that Thorolf's dead, Thorolf and all his men. Harald and Gunnar killed them, and burned their ship. Peer said so, and Harald made him fight with swords. And Harald hurt him, and Peer's run away."

The Nis appeared suddenly on the top of the porch. Its eyes glinted like angry garnets. "Thorolf the Seafarer – dead?" it exclaimed. "Dead – my namesake – and Peer Ulfsson lost? And Harald Silkenhair did it? Ooh!" It raised scrawny arms and shook its fists above its head. "I will make him pay! I will avenge Peer Ulfsson, my good friend. Avenge!" it repeated grandly.

"But..."

"You thinks I can't, but I can," the Nis bristled. "I can sneak up when Harald's asleep and tie knots in his hair, his beautiful hair he's so proud of. Ha! I can hide his clothes – put stones in his boots. I can—"

"Do all that if you like, but the most important thing is to find Peer! Before he dies in the woods, or gets lost and starves. Please, please, go and look for him."

The Nis's eyes widened. "The woods is big, mistress," it quavered. "I am a house Nis, and a ship Nis, but I isn't a woods Nis. I would get lost too. I would starve as well, no one to make me nice groute, only mushrooms to eat, and leaves, ugh! No butter any more, never again..." Its voice nearly broke at the affecting thought.

"Never mind, then," said Hilde sadly. "Just do what you can."

The men straggled back empty-handed, excited and ashamed as a pack of dogs caught doing something disgraceful but fun, like chasing sheep. Even Arne and Tjørvi avoided her eyes. Perhaps they'd gone with good intentions, to do what they could. For the moment Hilde loathed them as much as the others, for being part of the dog pack that had hunted Peer.

"Where is he?" she rapped, before even Gunnar could ask.

"Skulking," Harald grinned. "Skulking in the woods. And he can stay there."

Hilde caught her breath. "What will he do? How can he survive?"

Harald tilted his head to one side and paused. "By milking bears?" he suggested, and burst out laughing. Floki giggled, but he glanced at Magnus for approval and soon stopped. The others looked uneasily at their feet.

Hilde walked out. She sat on the log seat by the porch and folded her arms. Arne followed. "Hilde, please come in." He knelt before her, trying to take her hands. "I'll go looking for Peer tomorrow, I swear I will, but it's too dark now, I wouldn't find him. Please."

"Leave me alone."

Astrid stuck her head out. "Hilde, come in. Sitting out here won't help." Hilde stared straight ahead. There was no way she was going to shut herself up in the cold little cupboard that was her bed. She heard Astrid murmur to Arne, "Better leave her be." The door shut.

I'll stay here till he comes, Hilde thought. *He'll wait till everything's quiet, then he'll creep out of the woods. He'll see me, and we'll make a plan. We'll think of something. Peer always has an idea up his sleeve...*

The sea hushed and shivered on the beach below the houses. There was a breeze, thin and chill. Something yapped sharply in the forest, and a thrill of hope brought her to her feet. *Is that Loki? Please, oh please let it be Loki and Peer.*

Nothing happened. No tall figure of a boy with his dog came limping out of the trees.

A terrible conviction settled slowly on Hilde that the worst had happened. She would never see Peer again. She covered her face with her hands. *And we parted so badly. He tried to tell me he loved me, and I – was – so – stupid...*

She saw her behaviour as Peer must have seen it. *He must have thought I didn't care about him at all. But I did. I do. I'd just – got used to him. I suppose I took him for granted.*

The moon was setting and the sky glittered with constellations. *The Wagon,* she thought, remembering how Peer had pointed them out. *The Nail. Oh Peer. Can you see them? Where are you now?*

The stars blurred and trembled, and ran together in a luminous smear.

CHAPTER 58

"A son like Harald"

"YOU'LL HAVE TO speak to me again some time," said Astrid wearily next the day, "so why not now?"

She wiped her forehead with the back of her hand, leaving a smear of blood. It wasn't her own, it came from the pile of dead pigeons lying in her lap.

"And at least Peer got away," she went on. "Harald didn't kill him."

The girls were alone. The door was open and the men were out, either searching for Peer, or hunting or fishing. Even Gunnar had felt well enough to walk down to the shore with Magnus and Harald.

"What do you think I could have done?" Irritably Astrid tweaked out a handful of feathers. "If I'd rushed in shouting, *It's all true – Gunnar and Harald slaughtered Thorolf and his men,* would that have stopped Harald?"

Without speaking, Hilde dropped her brace of pigeons into the pot and went to rinse her hands in the pail by the door.

"Well?" Astrid insisted.

"It might have helped," Hilde said at last.

"No, it wouldn't," said Astrid flatly. "Harald wanted blood."

"Gunnar could have stopped him, and he would have if you'd asked him."

"After everything Peer said?" Astrid's eyes flashed. "Don't be silly. If I'd taken Peer's side, it would have made Gunnar even angrier. And he gave Peer a chance to back down, didn't he? And Peer could have taken it."

"No he couldn't!" Hilde's chest began to heave. "He couldn't possibly, even though I wanted him to, because if he had, he wouldn't have been Peer. You don't know him like I do. Bad things have happened to Peer before, and he's always, always faced up to them, even though he doesn't think he's brave. But he is brave. He's the bravest person I've ever met."

Astrid nodded gloomily. "I've always thought so."

Hilde stared at her. "I don't understand you, Astrid. Not one bit. How can you stick up for Gunnar, after everything he and Harald have done? You've told me a million lies. You wouldn't even try to help Peer. Yet you pretend you liked him."

"You're right." Astrid was icy. "You don't understand."

Hilde's lip curled. "Are you trying to tell me you love Gunnar?"

"Love him? I don't need to *love* him. He's my husband." Astrid shot out a thin, cold hand and gripped Hilde's wrist so tightly it hurt. "You don't get it, do you? *I'm married to Gunnar.* It's all right for you, whose father and mother are so soft they'll let you go off on a Viking ship just so you can decide who you really want to fall in love with. It wasn't like that for me. I said I wouldn't marry Gunnar, and my father threw me against the wall till my head bled. There's troll blood in my family. My father was desperate to get me off his hands before Gunnar found out. I'll say this for Gunnar, he's never laid a finger on me."

"You already spun me your long story about Erlend," said Hilde savagely. "So what about the first night we came here? I couldn't sleep, and I heard you talking to Gunnar. Telling him how to stop a ghost from walking – by sticking needles in a dead man's feet!"

Astrid eyes widened. "You heard that?"

"Yes! It didn't sound as though your dead lover meant much to you then."

Astrid went pale. "That had nothing to do with Erlend. We were talking about Thorolf."

"Thorolf?" Hilde felt her head was coming apart.

"Yes." With exaggerated patience, as if explaining to a child, Astrid said, "It's Thorolf's ghost Gunnar's afraid of. He told me the whole story, that night on the ship. Thorolf died under Gunnar's spear, but he put his dying curse on Gunnar first. *A cold life and a cold death.* Gunnar believes that Thorolf's ghost will come for him. They put the bodies into the *Long Serpent* and set her on fire, but she sank before everything burned. That was Gunnar's mistake. That's what you heard me telling him." She added earnestly, "A dead man can't follow you if you sew him up in a shroud and then break off the needle in the soles of his feet."

She saw Hilde's expression, and her own face went rigid. "I can't help what I know! Why should I care for Thorolf? I never knew him. And I cried for Erlend, but even if it *was* his ghost and not Thorolf's, I'd still help Gunnar. A live husband is better than a dead lover. I married Gunnar and I decided to make the best of it. What's wrong with that? Gunnar's all right, sometimes. You said so yourself! He's brave, and he's a good skipper, and the men like him. And—"

"Astrid," interrupted Hilde. "He *kills* people. *That's* what's wrong."

Astrid began to sob. "But mainly because of Harald. Nobody can control Harald, you know that. Harald would have got Peer in the end, whatever we did."

Hilde's voice rose. "And who made Harald the way he is? Gunnar, bringing him up to think he can do just as he likes!"

"No!" Astrid shook her head vehemently. "Haven't you heard Magnus talking? It wasn't Gunnar, it was Vardis – Harald's mother – she must have been a terrible woman. I'm not like that. It'll be different this time."

"But Gunnar's so proud of Harald..." Hilde trailed off. Her eyes flicked down to Astrid's stomach. Now she was looking for it she saw the shallow bulge at once.

"You're not. Are you—?"

Astrid gave a defiant tear-stained smile. "Yes! I am! I'm having Gunnar's baby."

Hilde was speechless. How had she missed something so obvious?

"Does Gunnar know? Have you told him?"

"Not yet. I wasn't sure, but I am now. I've been very careful. I know you're not supposed to run, or carry anything heavy."

Hilde remembered what she ought to have said. "That's wonderful, Astrid."

"I know." Astrid bit her lip and laughed suddenly. "A little rival for Harald. How annoyed he'll be. I'm so happy, Hilde." Her face shone. "A little baby, all of my own! I've wanted one for ages. Do you remember me cuddling Elli, at your parents' house? I was longing to take her with me."

Why not? Hilde thought. *You took the Nis*. She looked at Astrid's soft, flushed face, and remembered the weird little nursery rhyme she had chanted then. Something no human mother would sing. A troll's song.

What was it like to be Astrid?

Ma taught me ordinary things, milking and brewing, spinning and baking. Astrid's mother gave her a magic box and told her how to stop ghosts from walking.

What was it like to be Astrid, whose violent father regarded her troll blood as a shameful secret and married her off to a man as violent and as old as himself, instead of the young farmer she'd wanted?

And now she was happy, because she was going to have a little baby to love.

"What are you staring for?" Astrid asked abruptly. "Are you still angry?"

Hilde shook her head. Swallowing, she bent down and gave Astrid a kiss. Astrid's mouth trembled. Her arms went around Hilde. They hugged, hesitantly, then tightly.

"I'm sorry," Hilde muttered. "I've been stupid. It wasn't your fault."

"No, you were right. I am a liar. I wish I was like you, Hilde. But I'm all crooked inside..."

"No, you're not." They let go, both wiping their eyes.

"But what about Peer?" Astrid sniffed.

All the fear came rushing back. "Peer, oh, gods... Where is he? And he's hurt. His arm was bleeding. He never came back last night. I waited outside till dawn and I walked along the edge of the woods and called for him."

"Maybe I could find him," said Astrid slowly.

"You!" Hilde stared. "How?"

"If there's time... Run outside, Hilde, and tell me what the men are doing."

Hilde ran out into the dazzling sunshine and stared under her hand towards the shore. She saw figures wading with fish spears, and heard distant laughter.

"They're busy on the beach," she reported, coming back in.

"Good." Astrid emerged from the inner room with her goatskin bag. "Leave the door like that – just a bit open. Now then."

She darted her arm into the bag and drew out the little bone box that Hilde had seen before. Hilde's heart began to thump. More *seidr*?

"Keep an eye on the door," Astrid said. "I don't want the men to see."

"See what?"

"Something my mother showed me. When I was little, I used to sit and watch over her while she did this. It scared me. In case she never came back."

"What do you mean?" Hilde's mouth was dry, but she was excited too.

"You'll see," said Astrid impatiently. "No time to explain. Here, take the box." She shoved it at Hilde, who nearly dropped it.

"Careful!" hissed Astrid. "Now look. When you see me fall asleep, you must open it and *keep it open* until I come back. Understand?"

"Not really." Hilde flicked her plait over her shoulder. "What do—"

"And another thing. Don't touch me while I'm away. Don't call my name or try to speak to me."

"What if the men come back?"

"Keep them out."

Astrid swung her feet up on to the sheepskin-littered benches where the men slept. She lay back, closed her eyes and began muttering under her breath.

Hilde sat stiffly, clutching the little box. It felt warm and slippery. She glanced at Astrid, in time to see Astrid's mouth stretch open in the most enormous yawn. Her eyelids flickered up and her eyes rolled slowly upwards till only the whites showed. Her body went limp and relaxed.

The box vibrated. Hilde bit back a yelp. She prised and twisted with cold fingers, and the lid eased stiffly up. Underneath crouched a large, glittering fly – a delicate thing of green enamelling, and golden and black wires.

It moved its splayed black feet. The wings flirted and blurred. Hilde jerked. The box clattered to the ground. Buzzing, the fly rose, speeding to the open door. It flashed into the sunshine and was gone.

A fly? Was this some pointless joke? Hilde turned furiously, but the words died on her lips. Astrid looked dead. Her eyelids drooped, showing a line of white. Her lips were apart. Was she breathing? Hilde counted silently. At twenty-two she saw Astrid's chest slowly rise and subside.

Subdued, Hilde picked up the little box. The inside was smooth and empty.

You couldn't keep a fly in a box. So the fly was a *sending.* She'd heard it whispered of, the power of those skilled in *seidr* to send their spirits out in animal form. Could it work, this troll magic? And how long would it take?

She twisted uneasily this way and that. If she faced Astrid, she couldn't see the door. If she faced the door, she couldn't see Astrid: and there was something awful about the way she lay, neither alive nor properly dead. Her teeth showed. Her eyelids twitched, showing nothing but the whites, like hard-boiled eggs.

It was silly to be so afraid. She thought of the child Astrid shivering by her mother's bed. *If a little girl could do it, then so can I.*

Time passed, or crawled. The fire's bright rags fluttered quietly. Nothing else stirred. Hilde rubbed her face with sticky hands. *Oh Peer, please come back. Let us find you.*

A glittering green spark whirled in over her head and zoomed around the room, appearing and disappearing through the smoke. Hilde sprang for the little bone box and held it up without much hope that the fly would settle. Surely it wouldn't want to be shut up again in this tiny prison?

But the fly circled down on to the rim of the box. Hilde flinched. It was so big and confident. Deliberately it walked into the centre of the box, cleaned its head with two front legs, and sidled into a comfortable position. Hilde clapped the lid on.

With a second mighty yawn, Astrid pushed herself up. Hilde flew to her side. "Are you all right? Did it work, did you find him?"

Astrid's face was bloodless. Her lips smacked together clumsily. "I saw him," she mouthed. She sucked in another deep breath. "I saw him. It looks bad, Hilde. I think—"

The door scraped open and Gunnar's shadow filled it. Cursing under her breath, Hilde slipped the box into Astrid's bag and hid the bag behind her skirt.

"Done too much," Gunnar was muttering, standing in the doorframe, puffing. "Where's Astrid? What's this, what's this?" he added roughly as Astrid tried to get off the bench. "What's the matter, woman? Are you ill?" He turned to Hilde. "What's wrong with her?"

Hilde's wits deserted her. She gazed at him, blank and dumb. Astrid staggered to her feet. "Gunnar." Groggily she held out her arms. "I've got something to tell you, Gunnar. I'm having a baby!"

A slow, rare smile appeared on Gunnar's face. "Are you sure?"

When Astrid nodded, he turned around, threw open the door and bellowed, "You men get in here, and quickly!"

It was his sea-going voice, bound to be obeyed. Looking stronger than he had for weeks, he crossed the floor to Astrid and wound an arm around her. She drooped against him like a snowdrop. "Is this certain?" he demanded again, looking at Hilde.

"She says so." Hilde was grudgingly moved by Gunnar's delight. His chest expanded; his eyes seemed younger and brighter. For a moment it was possible to see that, once, he might have looked very like Harald.

The men crowded in with scuffling boots. Arne wasn't there. Except Harald, most of them looked apprehensive. Harald wore a slight frown, which altered to a scowl when he saw his father with Astrid.

"Good news, lads!" Gunnar squeezed Astrid's shoulders. "The very best. Astrid's having a baby!"

The men burst into cheers, catcalls and whistles. "Go, Gunnar!" "Good work, Gunnar!" "Well done, skipper!"

Gunnar raised his voice. "So much for the curse, eh?" he shouted joyfully. "So much for Thorolf!"

Hilde nearly choked. Gunnar admitted it! In front of everyone, he admitted responsibility for Thorolf's death. She saw with bitterness that no one looked surprised. Then what had Peer been fighting for?

Gunnar was repeating the curse. "*A cold wife and a cold bed.* Well, that part's wrong! So what's the rest of it worth now? Nothing!" He beckoned, sawing his short arm through the air in an excited gesture. "Where's Harald? Here, Harald. Stand with me."

Harald pushed to the front. His face was white as linen, but Gunnar did not notice. He flung his maimed arm round Harald's neck, linking his wife and his son.

"I've beaten the curse!"

He began to cry. Tears hung glistening in his sandy beard. "I've got it beat. I've a good wife and a fine son, and now another son coming. A son like Harald!"

He squeezed Astrid again. She stood tall beside him, face flushed, eyes bright.

"Give her a kiss!" bawled Magnus.

"Give her a kiss!" The men took up the shout as if, swept along by Gunnar's delight, they forgot they'd ever been wary of Astrid.

"Good idea!" Gunnar turned and pulled Astrid against him. He pressed his bristly lips against hers. Smack! Hilde winced, but Astrid was laughing. She cupped a hand to Gunnar's cheek and kissed him back.

"*Troll!*"

It was a high yell from Harald. The laughter and cheers thinned like smoke, and a bench fell over with a bang as someone backed off. Gunnar turned in amazement.

"Get off my father, troll!" Harald grabbed Astrid's arm and jerked her roughly towards him. Astrid shrieked.

"Tell him." Harald shook her. "Tell my father what you are." Again he shook her. "Tell him!"

"Stop it!" Hilde pulled Astrid away just as Harald shoved her aside. Astrid fell into Hilde's arms. Gunnar stared, bewildered and angry as a baited bear.

"She's a troll, Father," Harald panted. "I found out weeks ago. Couldn't bear to tell you. None of us could. She's deceived you. Troll magic, troll trickery. No wonder you've been ill. And now, this. Passing off some troll whelp as your son?"

Gunnar blinked painfully. He seemed to gather his wits. He said in a mild, pleading voice, "But Astrid's father is an old friend. Grimolf's daughter can't be a troll."

"No?" Harald snatched Astrid's goatskin bag and upended it, shaking the contents all over the floor. Astrid and Hilde both cried in protest, but everyone else craned to see. Out clattered the little bone box and cracked under Harald's foot. Out fell packages of herbs, balls of red and white thread, a spindle-whorl of rock crystal and another of jet.

"Look at this stuff." Harald ripped the packages and threw them down. "Poison, for all we know. Look!" He grabbed the spindles, holding up first the crystal and then the jet. "For spinning spells. White ones – and black! You haven't been getting any better, have you, Father? She wants to keep you ill, weak, womanish. Did you never wonder where she learned all this magic? She sucked it in with her mother's milk. Her mother was a troll, too. Of course Grimolf didn't tell you. It was the shame of his house. But ask any of the men, and they'll tell you. They call her the witch girl, the troll bitch. I've heard them talking."

Astrid choked. Hilde sprang to her feet. "Astrid's no troll!" She turned on Harald. "*You're* more of a troll than she is!"

Harald ignored her. He stared at Astrid. "You can actually see it when you look at her," he marvelled quietly. "Something about the eyes, I think."

Gunnar had gone a terrible colour, bluish red like undercooked meat. His pale eyes bulged. Between gritted teeth he said, "Astrid?"

Astrid faced him, bone-white. "I'm not a troll."

"And your mother?"

"There was troll blood in her family," said Astrid with difficulty. "Generations back."

"Troll blood will out," Harald sneered. "What will your baby be like, Astrid? Will it have a little – tail?"

"Gunnar!" cried Astrid. "Don't let him speak to me like that!"

Gunnar slapped her.

The blow landed with a loud crack. Astrid reeled and her fingers flew to her cheek. A bright scarlet print sprang out on her ear, mouth and cheekbone.

"You'll be sorry you did that," she said in a low, deadly voice.

They stared at each other. Gunnar looked away first. His gaze fell on the men standing goggle-eyed and open-mouthed. "What are you all staring at?" he shouted. "Get out of here!" The men broke for the door.

Gunnar turned away. After two steps he stumbled, and Harald was there, supporting him, leading him away towards the bedchamber. Astrid waited till they were in the doorway.

"You'll be sorry you did that, Gunnar Ingolfsson!" she screamed, and folded over on the sleeping bench, burying her face in the sheepskins and uttering gasping sobs. Hilde tried to comfort her. Astrid struck her arm away.

It was dark inside the house, now the door was shut. It must be nearly sunset. Slowly Hilde got down, and on hands and knees began picking up the torn packages that Harald had strewn across the floor. He came out of Gunnar's chamber while she was doing it and said, "Burn all of it."

His face was hard and pale, and Hilde wondered how he was enjoying his triumph. Didn't he realise he'd shamed Gunnar as well as Astrid?

He went out. Then Hilde saw the Nis, peeping from a crossbeam.

"It's safe to come out," she murmured, deathly tired. "He's gone."

The Nis ran down the wall. In big-eyed, solemn silence it picked up a few of the broken things. It kept glancing at Astrid, where she lay face down, with jerking shoulders. It sidled closer – and at last hopped up to crouch beside her. Timidly it reached out long, knobbly fingers to pat her hair.

Hilde's eyes blurred. She remembered making the same gesture with Peer – was it only yesterday? She remembered the touch of his hair, cool and thick and silky.

"I did find him." It was Astrid's voice, drenched in tears. She was sitting up at last, her eyes red with crying. The bruise on her cheekbone was turning a shiny purple.

"I did find Peer. But I think he was dying. I'm sorry, Hilde, I'm so, so sorry. I'm sure by now it will be too late."

CHAPTER 59

Down the Dark River

PEER WAKES... TO the sound of Loki barking. It's still night. His head pounds and his arm throbs. Loki barks again, angry growling barks as if he's holding something at bay. There's a dreadful smell, sweet and rotten. And a strange noise – twittering, giggling. Peer lifts himself painfully to see.

He's lying in a steep, secret gully, roofed with trees as thick as thatch. To his left, a few feet away, the creek pours past. To his right is the dark side of the gully, riddled with even darker, irregular holes, each with a spoilheap of earth at the mouth – some kind of animal lair.

But the nasty, shrill chattering noise from the holes doesn't sound like animals. Deep within, small eyes gleam white, like tiny pearls.

Loki dashes at them, then cries and yips. Stones rattle into his face. He bolts away, tail low. Next second Peer is hurled backwards. He cries out. The things scramble all over him, sniggering – scrawny things with puffed chests and nipped waists and cold scratching fingers. Their white eyes look sightless, like the eyes of a cooked fish. Pinching hands grip and roll him over. The stones graze his face. Again he's rolled, this time on to damp earth covered in twigs and pine needles.

And they fasten him down, forcing twigs into the soft

earth between every finger, stretching out his arms and legs, tugging back his hair. They ram a forked stick over his neck and use more to pin down his wrists and ankles. Peer struggles, but he's already weak, and there's so many of them crawling over him. Soon he can't lift a finger. He rolls his eyes and shouts, and one of them slips a sharp piece of wood into his mouth and twists it, propping his mouth wide open.

Peer gurgles and retches. Blood trickles down his throat. He prods his tongue at the wooden gag, but it's too tightly jammed to shift. His jaw aches already.

He waits in flinching horror. What will happen now? But the things, whatever they were, seem to have finished. One moment they're swarming over him; the next, they scuffle to get in through the entrance of the nearest hole. A sprinkle of earth is kicked out over him. And they've gone.

That's it? But they can't leave me like this!

Peer jerks and twitches at his bonds, but nothing gives. He tries to cry out, but can only manage a muffled, "Angh – ah!"

And who's going to hear?

He struggles again, then lies limp. Threads of saliva trickle from the corners of his mouth. Tears fill his eyes.

I don't want to die this way. Not like this. I should have let Harald kill me. Died fighting. I bet Thorolf didn't run.

His hurt arm throbs. Chilled, exhausted, he slides away into a world of dreams. He's with Hilde on the beach, and she says, "I love you too". He's back in the house, and he's just run Harald through with Gunnar's sword. Everyone cheers, everyone thinks he's a hero. He's sailing *Water Snake* into Trollsvik. Bjørn's there on the jetty, smiling his old smile. "Well done, Peer. I knew you could do it."

Lies.

Day comes. He wakes slowly, staring up at a brown tangle of interlaced branches, tipped with fringes of dark green. The sun shines through in white blinks. Surely it was all a bad dream?

But his mouth gapes open, wide, dry. He lies on the cold bank, pegged down. The water bounds past, chuckling and burbling, but he can't reach it or see it. A striped squirrel scampers down a tree, a dove coos, a crow calls harshly. Somewhere close, a lot of flies whirl and hum over the source of the bad smell. Peer doesn't want to think what it is. Sometimes, disturbed, they rise in a buzzing cloud. One big one finds Peer and explores his face, walking with tickling feet over his eyes, nose and mouth. Its body glints like green armour. He squints at it, helpless, unable even to puff it away.

Paws pad round his fallen body: a nose pushes into his face with a worried sigh that scares the fly off. *Poor Loki, that's all you can do. If only the Nis could come and set me free.*

It's cold. But Loki settles against Peer's side, and a little warmth creeps through. Peer drifts in and out of consciousness, woken sometimes by griping cramps. Once he hears an axe chopping, or perhaps it's only a woodpecker. Once when he wakes, Loki is not there, and he hears him drinking. And the long, slow, agonising day passes, and the pine trees huddle together overhead, and darkness returns.

Peer falls into a dream deeper than any he's had yet. He seems to be awake, sitting up, free of his bonds. The pain is gone. He hears splashing from the creek, looks around and sees without surprise the tall black dragonhead from the *Long Serpent* – alive, long bodied, writhing its way upstream with head raised, horns twitching, fiery eyes turned on him.

You're alive! Peer cries. *They didn't kill you after all.*

The dragon's jaws open in a long hiss. Then it speaks, using his father's voice. *Alive for you. Alive whenever you think of me.*

Peer is filled with joy. *Father! Where have you been all this time?*

In the land of the remembered dead, says the dragon gently.

It's wonderful not to be alone any more. There's so much to say, so much to tell, Peer doesn't know where to start. *Have you been with me, watching me? If only I'd known. I've kept trying, Father, really I have. But it's been so hard.*

I know only what you tell me, says the dragon, but Peer isn't listening. He pours it all out: *I came to find Thorolf, but Thorolf's dead. I fought Harald, but I ran away. I wasn't brave enough – I can't use a sword. And I've left Hilde behind, though I promised Ralf to look after her. And…*

Hush! The dragon shoots its long neck forwards and twines around him. Its wet, rough skin sizzles with life. Wherever it brushes against him, he feels a tingling shock.

What more could you do? it demands. *What did you leave undone?*

Nothing, says Peer slowly.

It touches him with a serpent's tongue, cold vivid kisses. *Then you did well.* It rears over him, fierce and glad, as it did on the prow of the longship. *You did all you could, Peer, Ulf's son. You faced your fear and kept faith with your friends.*

Peer is silent. At last he asks, *What happens now?*

Come with me.

The dragon loops, gliding down the bank into the water. *Come!*

Peer rises. Loki is nowhere to be seen, and for a moment that worries him, and reality, if this is reality, quivers like hot air over a fire. Impatiently the dragon shakes its fringed mane, and Peer hurries, wading into the creek. He puts his arm over the dragon's sinuous neck, and a moment later they are streaking downstream. The dragon's body lashes against him like a snake's, whipping around rocks, surging over little cascades where the spray flashes like ice. Enormous trees tower overhead. Their black branches reach into the sky like arms trying to tear down the stars. Their thick roots plunge deep into the river as if exploring to the bottom of the world.

And now the banks are becoming cliffs that lean over the water till they touch overhead, and all light vanishes. The noise of the river grows louder, growling and rumbling. Fear touches Peer like a drift of cold spray. *Where are we going?*

Away, says the dragon dreamily. *Away together, far from pain. Down the dark river.*

No! Peer frees his arm from the serpent's neck. Instantly the black water plucks him away. He fights the pull of the current, kicking fiercely. *I can't follow you, Father. Not yet. You're dead. I want to live. I want to live...*

And the tilt of the river steepens, and he's falling, falling over the waterfall, a long, slow tumble for ever and ever.

He wakes with a jolt, spreadeagled on his back. *Still here.* Every muscle in his body seems to be tearing itself away from the others. Each breath is shallow torture. How long can this go on?

Help me. Father. Somebody. Anybody, please, help me.

Loki growls low, vibrating against him. Panic flares through Peer's veins. Are those creatures coming back?

But something splashes, disturbing the rhythm of the creek. A stone plops. Black against the faint sheen of the water, shadows stoop and straighten, flitting towards him. A voice calls, cool and curious as a bird. Loki growls again, then whines and trembles.

An extraordinary face appears hanging over him, as thin as the blade of an axe. The eyes gleam, so closely set they look like a single green stone sticking through the narrow forehead. The face is almost all nose. A sharp, down-turned mouth looks comically disapproving. It warbles a rapid string of sounds that may be a question.

Peer tries to speak. Croaks. Hot and cold waves are washing up and down his body, and he seems to be shrinking, but at different rates. He feels very heavy, and very small. Yet his feet are miles away. His hands are useless cramped claws far off at the ends of his arms.

More of the thin faces peer down at him. Cold, gentle fingers prod and probe into his sore, cracked mouth. With an agonising twitch the wooden gag is pulled out, and tears of relief spring to his eyes as he tries to close his jaws over his swollen tongue. The Thin Faces uproot the forked sticks pinning him down, and toss them away.

An angry chittering comes from the holes in the side of the gully, but nothing emerges. Peer struggles to move. His rescuers drag him up, but he falls over. Loki circles anxiously.

The Thin Faces whistle quietly together. They range themselves on each side of him and pick him up. Their hands are cold and damp, but strong. They're not tall – only child-sized, and he finds himself bumping along close to the ground. A low singing starts up, "Hoi... hoi... hoi..." They stamp their feet in time, dancing down to the creek where they lower him into the water. The shock is delicious. He rolls over and buries his sore face in the swift coldness, sucking and lapping.

"Hoi... hoi... hoi..." Before he's had half-enough, the Thin Faces catch his arms and pull him up the opposite bank. Low fir branches shower needles into his hair, and his heels drag on the soft loose surface. They swing him up, running at a steady jog-trot. Peer hangs jolting, upside down, staring into the crooked sky-track above the trail. It streams past, pale with pre-dawn light, brushed with fingers of black yew, spruce and pine. Loki bounds along, keeping up with him, sometimes on one side, sometimes on the other.

Tiny clouds appear overhead like pink feathers. Birds call. Sixty feet up, the tips of the pines are brushed with gold. The Thin Faces glance uneasily at each other and warble. Their profiles are strong against the brightening sky. Their skin is brown with a bronze-green bloom, and their long lank hair is looped up in identical top-knots.

They stop and lower Peer to the earth. Heads hanging, they melt shyly away into the forest. The last one hesitates. It raises a slender arm and points up the trail. And then it's gone.

Returning blood jabs a million needles into Peer's hands and feet. His wounded arm throbs. He pushes himself into a crawling position, sits up. Loki watches, wagging his tail.

"Loki," Peer says with his sore tongue, and it feels like the first word he's ever uttered. "Loki, boy."

He can't begin to cope with what's happened. The dragon – the black river – he tucks it away inside himself to look at later.

The path slants along the side of a steep valley with a creek at the bottom. Peer can hear it below him, hidden by trees. He hobbles along, seized by unexpected crippling cramps. It may get warmer later, but it's cold down here in the shadows.

After an hour or so the trail steepens, curving away from the creek. The noise of the water fades. Peer climbs doggedly on. He comes out on to a ridge and the sun burns the back of his neck, though the air is still sharp. There's a view of more hills, pleating away in soft folds under a blue sky, covered with forest in which the endless green is already interrupted by autumn reds and golds. His heart sinks at the sight. Where in all this wilderness can he go?

The path fades downhill over dry ground till it vanishes under a litter of dead branches and undergrowth. Wherever he sets his foot, brown grasshoppers scramble and jump, and their *tick, tick, zizz* fills the air. He battles on, clambering over fallen trees, stumbling through ankle-deep moss. When he finds the trail again, he doesn't know if it's the same one. Or if it matters.

It dips into a ravine with a trickle of water at the bottom. The trickle becomes a brook, swirling over a series of waterfalls like deep steps. Peer stumbles on, not sure why, except that to stop moving is to give up hope entirely. But he has to rest more and more often, and each time it's harder to get up. Small goals become important. *I'll get to that bend in the stream before I stop. As far as that tree with the silver bark. As far as that overhanging rock.* At last he's not sure how long he's been wandering, or how many nights he's spent in the forest.

Once he almost steps on a little green snake lying in a patch of sun. It pokes out a scarlet tongue and shoots into the undergrowth. Once he finds a tangle of fruiting blackberries, and shoves the sweet berries into his bruised mouth till his fingers drip.

The path brings him to the top of a steep bank, thick with birches and aspens. The brook plunges over in a long horsetail, splashing off little ledges on the way down. At the bottom, between layers of golden leaves, is the silver glare of water. Echoing up from the water is childish laughter and splashing.

Children?

How? Whose? But it doesn't matter: there are people down there. He slithers downhill, Loki at his heels, skidding, sliding, catching hold of branches to check his descent. He tumbles out of the trees.

A stretch of open water spreads away, level and bright. Along the water's edge, against the fringe of the forest, is a village of conical huts or tents, constructed of tall poles propped together and wrapped in sheets of white and golden birchbark. There are fifteen, twenty of them. White smoke rises from cooking fires. Slender white boats lie drawn up on the shore, and a band of bare little black-haired children are chasing each other through the shallows.

Skraelings?

The word doesn't seem to fit the happy children and the white and golden village.

Then the children see him. They take one look at this pale, shambling, bloody creature and scatter, screaming. The village erupts. Dogs howl. Mothers run to snatch up their babies. Fathers scramble from their doorways and run yelling at Peer, shaking light axes and brandishing spears.

Peer sits down. In truth his legs have simply given way. But no one can think he's dangerous if he's sitting on the ground. And if they want to kill him, they'll do it anyway. And he's too tired to care. He grips Loki's collar and waits for them to come.

It works. A crowd of men and boys surrounds him, arguing loudly, threatening him with their spears but not touching him. Their dogs skulk around snarling, foxy-faced, with curling bushy tails. Peer looks up, beyond fear. Dark eyes glitter down at him, suspicious, doubtful. He sees details – a cluster of red feathers swinging from a brown earlobe; a long necklace of white beads; a chequerwork armband in black and blue and white. And then…

Can there be fair-haired Skraelings? A young boy scrabbles

his way to the front of the crowd. His chest is bare. He wears a breech cloth of soft leather. His shoulder-length, white-gold hair is braided at the front and tied with discs of white shell and bunches of little blue feathers. His round face, pale under the tan, is marked with paint – a black line drawn from his forehead down over his nose, and white diagonal streaks across each cheek. His blue eyes blaze at Peer, furious, incredulous, and more than a little scared.

"Who are you?" he demands, in clear, aggressive Norse. "Where have you come from?" The paint on his face wrinkles as he scowls. "Did Harald Silkenhair send you?"

CHAPTER 60

Thorolf the Seafarer

HILDE DREAMED. SHE thought she was running through the woods, trying to catch Peer, who was running ahead of her and wouldn't stop, although she called and called. He vanished into dark trees, leaving her alone and lost.

She woke, and the waking was as bad as the dream. She lay in the gloomy flicker of the fire hall, knowing that Peer was gone. Nothing good would ever happen again. Astrid lay asleep beside her, her arm over her face.

Gunnar had shut his door against Astrid, leaving the girls no choice but to sleep in the fire hall with the men. Hilde didn't know why it should be different from everyone sleeping together, as they had on the ship. But it was, and the men thought so too. There was a wide gap between herself and Tjørvi, the nearest sleeper.

Miserably she went over what Astrid had told her about Peer. He had fallen into some sort of trap; that was all she would say. When Hilde had pushed for details, Astrid got angry. She'd said, "It's too hard to explain. It's like looking through a tiny window, a peephole, at something bright and small. You can't see everything. In fact, you can't see much of anything."

"But you found him," Hilde burst out. "Then let's go and rescue him."

"But I don't know how to get there," Astrid said. "Oh Hilde, think about it. Think how a fly flies! I'd never find the way."

Hilde thought of it, the random career of a fly whirling through the woods, past tree after tree after tree... "You said he was trapped," she'd said at last, dreading the answer. "What sort of trap?"

Astrid wouldn't tell her for ages. And when she did, it was worse than Hilde could possibly have imagined. "He couldn't move. I think he was pegged down."

Pegged down!

She made a small noise, a groan of suppressed agony. Tomorrow Tjørvi and Arne would look for Peer again. She would go with them. But when Astrid's *sending* had found Peer, he had seemed to be dying, so by now he was probably dead. Perhaps there were things in the woods that weren't harmless like the little *wiklatmuj'ik*. Perhaps the elusive Skraelings had killed him... Her thoughts were running in frantic circles, when she was startled by an unexpected sound. A single muffled thump on the door.

Peer!

Her heart jumped into her throat.

It's him, it's got to be.

She sat up instantly, casting a look around the room. No one else had heard. They were all sleeping like the dead. Her bare feet touched the damp earth floor. Taking fast, shallow breaths, she tiptoed past the fire. *Peer's come back. He's waiting outside. It's him: he's safe.*

The relief, oh, the relief! The childhood reassurance was true after all: *It was only a bad dream. Everything would be all right. A second chance; we've got a second chance.*

There was another thud against the door, followed by a

strange scratching, like claws. Loki. Of course Loki would be with Peer; he never left him.

I'm coming, I'm coming…

He was so clear in her imagination, standing on the other side of the door. In a moment she would see him, speak to him, touch him. She seized the wooden bar that fastened the door at night. It was heavy, but she managed to lift it from its sockets without a sound and lay it quietly on the floor. Trembling with cold and excitement, she raised the latch and eased the door back.

A freezing wind whirled into her face, smelling of salt and seaweed. It blew her hair into her eyes. "Peer?"

The night was dark, cloudy, but surely there was someone on the threshold. Taller than Peer. A figure – or figures… She wiped her hair away and craned into the night with a cry of disappointment. Peer was not there.

The wind pushed into the house. It rushed up the room, sweeping the fire low. Along the walls, men raised sleepy heads, lifting themselves on their elbows. Hilde turned.

A wet trail crossed the floor, as though someone had run through the room with an armful of soaking washing. A person was disappearing through the door to the inner room – a big man, his clothes black and dripping. The door slapped shut.

There was a strangled wail from Floki. "Oh gods!"

His voice was drowned by Gunnar's waking yell of terror.

Hilde stumbled. Something squirmed between her feet. She looked down. The dragonhead lay there, inert, its blind eye staring at her, its mouth curled in a sardonic grin. She backed away from it, knuckles against her teeth.

It didn't move; it couldn't have moved.

But there it was. And how had it got there?

Frantic men scrambled from the blankets, grabbing axes, drawing knives. The dim end of the room filled with shadows as they threw themselves at the door of Gunnar's bedchamber. What a crowd they made. *Who were they all?* Breathless, she counted faces. There was Tjørvi, pressing against the door with Arne – but who was that hollow-cheeked fellow beside him, who ducked away as she looked? Between Floki and Magnus was someone whose head gleamed unpleasantly, like bald bone. And who was that, grinning most inappropriately over Halfdan's shoulder?

From beyond the door came a series of half-throttled screams.

"It's stuck!" Sweat poured down Tjørvi's face. "It's barred – on the inside!"

"Then break it down." Teeth bared, Harald swung round, his gold hair flying. "A log, quick. That one!"

"Not that one!" Hilde screeched. It was the dragonhead he was pointing at, and it was now much further up the room. "Don't touch it!"

Harald bent, stared, cursed. He grabbed an axe from the feeble hands of Floki and began attacking the door with huge hacking swipes.

Someone touched Hilde's elbow and she almost jumped out of her skin.

"What did you stop him for?" said Astrid viciously. The bruises on her face stood out. Her lips were parted and her breath came quickly.

"Nobody ought to touch that thing – not even Harald," said Hilde vehemently. She didn't know why. Then she did. *When the dead fight the living, I'm on the side of the living.* It was as simple as that.

Astrid pointed at the ruined dragonhead. "But you did.

You took it away. Where did you hide it?"

"In Thorolf's house."

"*Thorolf's house?*" Astrid began to laugh. "No wonder we have visitors. Can you see them, too? Poor fellows, they're not in very good shape any more – after sword and fire and seawater..."

Tjørvi had an axe now, and he and Harald were taking turns at the door, which shuddered and jumped. Splinters flew. They opened a long gash in the planks. Harald tossed the axe aside and called, "Father? Father!" The screaming had stopped. Harald ran desperate hands through his hair. "Astrid! Help him!"

"How?" said Astrid.

He seized her. "You're a troll, you've got troll powers, haven't you? Do something!"

Astrid showed her teeth. "And if I'm a troll, why should I help you or him? Maybe I did this! Maybe I let them in."

Harald grabbed a fistful of her bright hair. He jerked her head back and pressed his knife to her throat.

"No! Harald, she didn't." Hilde caught her friend's arm. "Astrid, everyone knows you're not a troll. Please help us. Please!"

Astrid's face twisted stubbornly. She looked at Harald out of the corners of her eyes and gasped, "Threaten away, Harald Silkenhair. I can't help Gunnar any more. You saw to that."

"What do you mean?" Harald yanked her hair.

Astrid laughed again, a high-pitched sound not far from weeping. "The soul has wings, Harald, did you know that? Even Gunnar's soul. So I hid it for him in an egg, a little bird's egg. And it was quite safe with me – till you stamped it into pieces this afternoon."

She lifted her voice and screamed, "Hear me, Gunnar, if

you can! You should have trusted me, not Harald. And now I wouldn't help you if you came crawling to me along the highway. *A cold wife and a cold bed. A cold life and a cold death to you, Gunnar Ingolfsson!*"

Harald flung her away. He hurled himself at the weakened door, and Tjørvi and Magnus joined him, throwing their shoulders against it.

It gave way, pitching them into the darkness beyond. "Bring torches!"

Hilde ran to the fire and plucked a burning stick from the embers then ran to the broken door. The men pushed in. Floki hung back, his mouth trembling – afraid to go in, afraid to stay in the fire hall by himself. Hilde held out her hand, and he gripped it tightly. Like children they tiptoed into the room together.

Gunnar lay uncovered on the bed. There were deep black marks on his bare throat. His skin ran with water; his hair was soaked. The air in the room smelled chill and shocked, as though a wave had burst through it. The bed linen dripped quietly on to the floor.

Floki's hand shook in Hilde's.

With a cry, Harald cast himself on the bed. He got an arm behind Gunnar's shoulders and heaved him up, cradling him. Gunnar's arms hung down and his eyes stared at nothing.

Thorolf the Seafarer had been – and gone.

They built up the fire till it blazed, and huddled around it, listening to Harald weeping behind the broken door.

"Harald's brave enough," Halfdan muttered once. "Sitting up with *that*."

The men nodded. After a while, and almost as though

he couldn't help it, Magnus said, "What if *Gunnar* won't lie quiet?"

That made everyone draw closer together – except Astrid, who sat alone and silent near the door.

When a little grey light crept through the smoke hole, Hilde began stiffly to set about stirring up some warm groute. She didn't ask Astrid to help: Astrid looked as though she might never move or speak again. Hilde set a small bowl aside for the Nis. It was frightened of ghosts. She hoped it was all right.

Harald came out of his father's room. The men jumped nervously as if expecting a monster. He paused in the doorway. "A funeral," he said coldly. "Build a pyre. We'll burn his body and raise a mound to cover his bones. Pull down the other house to make material for it. I don't want a turf or a hearthstone left in place. And from now on this bay will be called *Gunnar's Grave*. Where is the dragonhead? Has it been burned yet?"

"No," said Halfdan nervously. No one had liked to touch it. They all looked where it lay, halfway up the room.

"Put it on the pyre," said Harald. "Put it at his feet."

They built the pyre on the beach and carried Gunnar out on a board, wrapped in his cloak. Rain drove in from the sea. Out in the river, *Water Snake* tossed at her mooring. They stood in the cold wind, watching the flames. Astrid waited at a distance, her cloak and dress fluttering in the wind. She looked like a sort of ghost herself, Hilde thought. She had been "the skipper's wife". Then she had been "the troll girl". What was she, now? Widow, or faithless wife? Hilde was afraid for her – afraid of what Harald might do.

They went to the beach next day to recover the bones. The rain had beaten into the embers, and the fire was out. Raking through the debris, Floki gave a yelp of horror. The dragonhead thrust its snout out of the ashes, a long, black, staring, crooked thing, no more scorched than it had been before. Magnus turned it over with a flinching foot.

"Of course it won't burn," said Tjørvi angrily. "It's lain in the sea too long. Soaked in salt water – damp right through." Everyone nodded. No one believed it. They kicked it down to the tideline, where some winter storm might wash it away.

CHAPTER 61

War Dance

PEER'S BREATH SMOKED as he followed Kwimu and Ottar back to the wigwams. They'd been checking the traps around the beaver dam, and found two fine fat beavers, which had rashly triggered the deadfalls.

How quickly summer vanished! In a few brief weeks, since he'd been here, the trees had burned themselves up in a bonfire of colour – red, purple, gold. Now all that was left was bare black branches, and dark green firs, and bluish spruce. A powdering of snow had fallen, and Peer was glad of the warm moosehide wrap, as big as a blanket, which Nukumij had given him.

The still water above the beaver dam was already half frozen – thin shelves of ice spreading out from the edges. As they walked away, Kwimu said something that made Ottar laugh.

"Beavers build lodges and live in families like the People. Kwimu says if they were a tiny bit cleverer, they'd stick out their heads and talk to us. Then we'd have to stop hunting them."

When Ottar had finished translating, Kwimu grinned at Peer. Peer grinned back. It had been a long time since he'd had a friend of his own age, and you couldn't help liking Kwimu. With his long black hair, and strong, regular features, he was as handsome in his way as Harald Silkenhair, but there the comparison ended. Kwimu always had a smile ready, or a helping hand. Ottar adored him.

Peer was glad to be of use at last. The day he'd staggered out of the woods, he'd just managed to explain to Ottar that he wasn't an enemy, that Harald Silkenhair had driven him out. Then he'd collapsed, and lain ill for days. He remembered waking from dark dreams to see the fire flicker, smelling the strong green smell of broken fir branches. Crying out, struggling against the grip of hands, before realising that they meant only to poultice his arm, or tilt him up to pour odd-tasting drinks down his throat. Listening to human voices flowing over him like water. Then one night he'd woken to the sound of a light, shifting rattle, followed by the thud of a stick on a bark drum. Close by, someone began an intricate, flowing song that died away at the end of each breath and began again with renewed strength: "*Yah weh ah hah yay oh. Ah hah yay ah hay oh...*"

It was Grandmother, Nukumij, singing a medicine song to cure him. Its ever-changing rhythm seemed to bring back his spirit from where it was wandering. Soon he was sitting up and learning about the people who had helped him.

There was Grandmother, of course – so tiny she seemed almost lost in her voluminous deerskin robes, but whose skilful hands were always busy and whose bright eyes saw everything. There was Kwimu's father, Sinumkw, so stern and stately that Peer was nervous of him – until he smiled, when he looked just like Kwimu. There was Kwimu's quiet mother, and Plawej, a sweet-faced young woman with a plump, black-eyed baby, whose husband was away on a hunting trip. And Kwimu's little sister, Jipjawej – too shy even to look at Peer till, remembering a trick that charmed the children at home, he carved her a small wooden whistle. The first time he blew on it, she jumped. Then she took it with a quick, delighted smile.

Ottar watched her tooting on it as though he rather wanted one himself. "I'll show you how to make them," said Peer. "So if Jipjawej loses hers, you can make her another."

Ottar was no older than Sigurd. Cutting away at the whistle, he told Peer how he'd seen his father killed – how he'd climbed on the roof and hidden from the murderers – and watched them sail away, leaving him to die.

"And for nothing," he said bitterly. "For an argument about some furs. Pa set the traps and did the work, and then Harald claimed half of them. He said Pa and Gunnar had agreed to go halves on everything." His voice rose: "But that was a lie. Pa said they'd only agreed to share the expenses of setting out, and what we brought back was up to each of us. 'Then you won't give me the furs?' Harald said. He sounded really nasty. Up till then I'd liked Harald. He looks such a hero, and he used to say things that made me laugh." Ottar scowled and shivered.

"Next morning, while we were still getting up, we heard a dreadful yell from outside. I was eating breakfast and I nearly dropped the bowl. I didn't know if it was a man or a wolf. Pa said, 'What in thunder is that?' And the door burst open. They all had swords and axes." Ottar looked up with a tortured face. "How could they do it? They were supposed to be our friends."

All too easily, Peer thought. Prime fox and beaverskins sold at home for several silver pennies apiece. No wonder Gunnar could afford to buy Harald that expensive sword.

"And now he's back," Ottar stated. He swallowed. "Do you think I ought to try and kill him?"

"No," said Peer firmly.

"But it's my duty, isn't it? To avenge my father?"

"Do you really think your father would want you to fight

Harald?" Peer asked, and Ottar thought about it. "No," he admitted finally, looking relieved.

With Ottar's help, Peer told the family about his ordeal in the woods. The creatures who'd fastened him down were known as the Spreaders, and Ottar said that they ate rotten flesh. Peer remembered the sweet, fly-ridden stink of the gully, and shuddered. On the other hand, the Thin Faces were known to help lost travellers. "And Grandmother says they don't help bad people," Ottar said with a grin. "So you must be all right."

But when, shyly, Peer told them a little about the dream of the dragonhead, Grandmother's eyes snapped with excitement. She plunged into a long speech, and Ottar did his best. Grandmother was trying to tell Peer that his father's spirit had taken on the form of a *jipijka'm*. Peer got Ottar to say it again, and Grandmother nodded, repeating the word several times. So far as Ottar could explain, it was a sort of horned dragon, magical and dangerous, with powers to change and heal. "She says..." he stumbled, "the *jipijka'm* is your *tioml*. Your power, I think. Your strength."

Grandmother's whole face crinkled up into a smile, and she leaned forward and patted Peer's hand. She said something else, nodding again. "*Jipijka'm-kwis*," said Ottar. "That's what she'll call you. Dragon's son."

Dragon's son. A thrill of pride ran right through him. Then he thought of the Nis, and laughed a little. Nithing the Seafarer! Peer Dragon's Son! Peer Barelegs! What a difference a name could make.

It was snowing again, tiny white grains that swept across the ground without sticking. Peer transferred the beaver from one cold hand to the other, wishing he had mittens like Kwimu's. Kwimu lifted an eyebrow and said something with a teasing smile.

"Kwimu's asking about these girls that came on the ship with you," Ottar reported, his face a mixture of embarrassment and disdain. "He says, are they your wives?"

"My—?" Peer felt his jaw drop. "No, they're not!"

"He says, 'But you want them to be,'" Ottar mumbled.

"One of them." Peer bit his lip, grinned, and nodded.

Kwimu's eyes danced as he asked, and Ottar translated, "Is she pretty?"

"She's very pretty," said Peer.

But Ottar wriggled. "I'm going on ahead. I don't want to talk about girls any more." He ran off, throwing a stick for Loki.

Peer's smile faded. For the millionth time, he thought about Hilde. And for the millionth time he wondered what to do. The year was on the edge of winter. The sailing season was over. Back at Serpent's Bay they'd be dragging Water Snake up on to the shore on rollers. They'd take down the mast and lash the sail over her, leaving everything trim and snug, ready for months of snow and ice. The men would go out trapping for those precious furs. Hilde would be stuck indoors.

When will I see her? How can I let her know I'm still alive?

Even if he could find his way back to the bay and speak to Hilde secretly – even if she agreed to come with him – even if Sinumkw could be persuaded to take in another pale foreigner – what would be the use?

We still have to get home, and there's only one ship that can take us.

Sometimes he thought he should leave Hilde where she was. Gunnar and Harald weren't likely to harm a girl. That way, she'd have a chance of sailing home again – in about four years' time. *By then, she'll probably have married Arne. She'll think I'm dead.*

The pale cones of the wigwams loomed against the trees, and village smells blew on the wind: smoke and fish-oil and all the salty litter of human living. If he shut his eyes it reminded him of Trollsvik.

Oh, to be home. To be walking up past the brook, where the water ran sleek over the little stones, knowing that Gudrun and Hilde and the twins were all safe in the farmhouse waiting for him, with supper in the pot and old Alf thumping his tail in greeting—

Keen and close and shrill, a woman screamed.

Peer jumped, looking for danger in the early darkness and whipping wind. But the noise came from inside the thin birchbark walls. "*Akaia! Ah, ah, ah! Akaia!*"

Ottar shot into the wigwam like a rabbit into its hole. Kwimu and Peer ducked through the doorway after him.

"*Akaia!*"

Plawej knelt by the fire, doubled over, tearing at her hair and face. "*Ah, ah!*" she screamed, throwing herself backwards and forwards. All the women were crying, even Grandmother. *Someone's died,* Peer thought in horror. *Not the baby?* He looked, and saw Jipjawej hugging it, stiffly wrapped in its elaborate cradleboard, but alive all right. *No, not the baby, then. So, who?*

A dozen young men clustered at the far side of the fire, talking in angry, urgent voices. They saw Kwimu, grabbed him, and rattled off the story. Whatever it was, it made Kwimu's face harden till he looked years older.

Ottar slid out of the throng, and Peer caught him. "What's happened?"

"It's Kiunik," Ottar sounded shocked. "Kiunik, he's married

to Plawej. He's been found dead with his friend Tia'm. Killed. I can't believe it."

"Killed? You mean, deliberately? But—"

Peer broke off. A voice rang out of the past, Tjørvi's voice, rough with anger. *Skraelings. Just a couple of young fellows, cooking over a camp fire.*

Oh, no.

Ottar was still talking, "They've been away for weeks; Plawej was getting anxious. So their friends went looking for them..."

"Towards the sea?" Peer croaked. "Towards Serpent Bay? Down the river?"

"Yes." Ottar's eyes narrowed. "Kiunik wouldn't stop hunting there. He said we shouldn't be driven out. He said he'd hunt where he liked."

"Did he" – Peer's mouth was dry – "did either of them have a big bearclaw necklace?"

"Kiunik did!" Ottar grabbed him. "Why? Do you know something about it?"

Peer looked at Plawej. She wasn't wailing now. She was crushing charcoal from the fire between her palms, and methodically, drearily, blackening her face.

Two men murdered, and I haven't once thought about them since.

"I know what happened." Peer felt almost as guilty as if he'd done it himself. "Harald killed them."

Ottar's face scrunched up. He flung himself at Kwimu, tugging his arm and shouting. Everything quieted for a second. Even Plawej raised her blotched and blackened face. Sinumkw turned slowly.

Peer quailed. Sinumkw surveyed him as an eagle might, looking down on a man from some great height or icy mountain. His severe face was carved with lines of authority, and, now, of sorrow and distrust. His black hair was knotted with painted strings; on his breast his knife hung from a cord, and looped about his neck was row after row of beads, strung with copper discs and pearl-shell. He looked more like a leader of men than Gunnar ever had.

He spoke slowly, coldly, emphatically.

"He says, 'Why didn't you tell us this before?'" Ottar almost spat the words.

Excuses whirled through Peer's head. *I heard about it, but I didn't see it. So much else has happened since. I was shocked, but it happened to "Skraelings" and I hadn't met any. I didn't know Kiunik was missing. I've been ill.*

He met Sinumkw's dark eyes, and knew that not one of these sly, shameful answers was possible. "I ought to have told you," he said quietly. "I forgot. There's no excuse."

Sinumkw's face remained stern. He paused, and asked something.

"He wants you to say what happened," Ottar said.

Peer explained what he knew, even to the theft of the bearclaw necklace. Ottar translated. The young men murmured angrily. Sinumkw held Peer's gaze, searching him for the truth. Peer faced him, sweating but steady. At last Sinumkw gave a slow, stiff nod. He began to speak, a few sentences at a time, waiting for Ottar to translate.

"He says you were ill, and didn't know Kiunik or Tia'm. He says you were not to blame for their deaths. He says he already guessed who killed them, because they were so close to the Place of Ghosts. He says he warned Kiunik not to go there, but Kiunik went, because he was brave" – Ottar's voice wobbled and caught – "and proud, like a warrior. He says Kiunik was right."

Sinumkw stepped to the centre of the wigwam, to the swept earth floor around the fire. He lifted his voice for everyone to hear, and went on speaking, more rapidly.

"He says, when he heard that the pale people had come back, he wasn't sure what to do," Ottar whispered. "He didn't want to fight them, because there are not many of them, and they took Summer Bay out of ignorance, not knowing it was ours. He says our lands are wide. If they wanted to live in the Place of Ghosts, he thought they could do that without troubling us, even though they are bad men who kill each other. But now, he says, two of our own young men have been killed. He says…" Ottar chewed his lip, nearly in tears. "He says they killed Kiunik and Tia'm and left their bodies to be eaten by animals. Muin and Kopit, who found them, could hardly recognise them. But they wrapped them in bark and left them on a – a sort of platform, a scaffold in the woods, to keep them safe, and soon we'll go and take them to the burying place. But before that, Sinumkw says, we have a – a duty to them. Their ghosts are waiting outside in the dark right now, to see what we will do. He says they will be angry if we don't send them on their way with honour. They need revenge."

The warriors yelled – a crash of approval. "*Heh!*"

"'Let us give it to them.'"

"*Heh!*"

"'We will go to the Place of Ghosts.'"

"*Heh!*"

Ottar's face was sharp and glowing. "'We will pull down their houses and leave not one alive.'"

"*Heh!*"

"And he says – yes! He says we'll rip off the scalp of the boy with the long golden hair and dry it in the smoke, and

Kiunik and Tia'm will take it with them on their journey! Hooray!"

"*Heh! Heh! Heh!*" the young men roared. Kwimu stepped forward with a shallow birchbark bowl. Sinumkw dipped his fingers in and brought them out covered with thick red pigment. Deliberately, ceremoniously, he smeared it over his face.

"War!" Ottar whispered.

"*Heh!*" shouted Kwimu. He too dipped in his hand and dragged red fingers across his face.

"*Heh!*" shrieked Ottar.

Even Peer felt the surge of excitement. Harald, the bully with the sword – if he could see what was coming to him!

"*Hey! Hey!*" he yelled in unison with the other young men. Everyone was crowding to redden their faces. Peer found himself waiting in line. The pat-pat-pat of a drum started up – a stick knocking on a thick roll of birchbark. The men began a dance step, heads high, arms held out with clenched fists. They sang and stamped.

Kwimu's eyes were hot and bright; his face was taut under the disfiguring pigment. He held out the bowl to Peer. There wasn't much left, but Peer scooped some out and touched it to his face.

The young men swept him into the dance. It wasn't difficult – a step forward and a step back. Stamp, step, round and round. Stamp, step, round and round. Stamp…

What had Sinumkw said? *We will pull down their houses and leave not one alive?*

He staggered out of the dance and crouched on the fir boughs that lined the floor, taking deep breaths. Ottar danced past, and Peer thrust out a foot to trip him.

"What's that for?" the boy cried angrily.

"Wait, Ottar – it's important." Peer grabbed his arm as Ottar tried to pull away. "What are we thinking? We can't do this. We can't attack the houses."

"Why not?" demanded Ottar. "Harald deserves to die!"

"But what about the others? The girls? My friend Hilde, and her friend Astrid? And—" *And Tjørvi and Arne*, he was about to say, who didn't even sail with Gunnar before. *And Magnus and Floki and Halfdan – I don't want any of them to die...*

He looked into Ottar's indifferent face and realised that to him, they would be only a string of names.

"I expect you can save the women," Ottar said. "We can ask Sinumkw, if you like. About the others, I don't care. They didn't care about Kiunik, did they? Or Pa?"

"What if they surrender?" Peer demanded.

Ottar stared. "Harald and Gunnar won't surrender! And I don't want them to. They killed my pa, and I want them to die!" He wrenched himself free and whirled off into the dance, singing.

Peer rubbed his face, wiping his red fingers on the fresh green fir branches, and looked at the dancing men with sudden loathing. What was all this singing about? Who were these people – these *Skraelings*, who danced and sang about going to war?

Someone touched his arm. It was Nukumij – Grandmother. She sat down beside him and pointed to his face and then at the dancers. She shook her head, and made an eloquent gesture, which took in the war dance, the fire, the sad figure of Plawej with her woeful, besmeared face.

Peer thought he understood. *Killing people,* she seemed to say, *is such a terrible thing that we have to work ourselves up to it.* Making a ceremony out of it – did that make it better?

Better than Harald's casual killings?

These weren't people who disregarded life. Those beavers he and Kwimu had trapped – every scrap would be used: the meat, the fur, even the chisel teeth. Then the bones would be placed respectfully in running water, so the dogs couldn't chew them. Far in the woods, Ottar told him, was the wigwam of the Man Who Brings Back Animals. He would sing his song of power to bring the bones to life, so there would always be beavers for the people to hunt.

That was what they believed.

Harald Silkenhair had killed two young men with no ceremony at all, and left their bodies lying.

Why should Sinumkw care about Magnus or Tjørvi? Why should anybody care about someone else whom they'd never met?

But I care. I'm in the middle. I know them all. Probably Harald deserves it. But nobody else does. I can't let them die.

He groaned, and Grandmother reached out and took his hand. Her fingers were a bunch of slender bones covered in wrinkled brown skin. His own were pale in comparison, even after a summer out of doors, stained with red streaks. She squeezed gently and let go. They sat quietly together.

Ottar flung himself down beside them, flushed and panting.

"Hear them singing?" he asked. "Want to know what it means?

"Death I make, singing.

Heh! Ey!

Bones I break, singing.

Heh! Ey!

Death I make, singing!"

CHAPTER 62

The Fight in the House

SINUMKW CALLED A halt in an open glade, a tilted clearing on a hill shoulder, facing east towards the sea. A wind sharp as a skinning knife sliced between the trees, ruffling the black fur of pines and spruce, moaning through the skeletal arms of oaks, chestnuts and maples.

Peer looked at the war band. Nearly fifty men had set out from the village for the two-day walk to the shore. All wore red on their faces. All were wrapped in thick clothes against the cold: double layers of beaver robes, long leggings and hide boots. All moved easily over the snow on wide, flat snowshoes, which they tied to their feet.

"There's no shelter here," he said in a low voice to Ottar. Ottar had insisted on coming. The young men treated him as a favoured little brother with a right to be here.

"There soon will be," said Ottar confidently. "Like this!" He kicked off one of his snowshoes and started using it as a shovel to scoop a hollow from the snow. Kwimu and Peer joined in, flinging out snow to make a hole four feet deep and seven or eight feet across. All the men were digging shelters. They broke branches from the fir trees and threw them in to layer the bottoms of the holes with a springy criss-cross. Larger boughs partly roofed the shelters. And soon, small fires were spiralling upwards.

The shelter had a cosy feel, like a snow nest. The wind sped by overhead but couldn't reach them. Peer leaned back on the branches, fed Loki a strip of dried meat, and, chewing on one himself, stretched out his feet to the fire.

While the other young men chatted, checking their bows, axes and clubs, Peer worried about tomorrow. He'd volunteered to carry Sinumkw's declaration of war. Anything could happen in an attack. Sinumkw had agreed not to harm the girls, but Hilde would certainly defend herself, and then what? This gave him a chance to explain to her what was going on. But it meant walking openly into the house.

Grimly he foresaw how his news would be received. *Even if Harald doesn't skewer me straight off, Gunnar won't let the girls leave. He won't trust me, and he certainly won't trust the "Skraelings", and he'll never give up Harald.*

They'd be killed in the end, of course – eight men against fifty. But their steel-edged weapons would do some damage first. He pictured Kwimu or Ottar sliced down by Harald's sword. Blood spreading in the snow. Death and injuries and pain and misery. What was the point?

The stars looked like frost crystals in the black sky. In the light of the small fire, the young men's painted faces glowed a startling, fearsome red. Some had cut their hair short, or shaved it right off to leave a single long lock falling from the crown. But their expressions were thoughtful as they talked together. He wished he could join in. These could be friends – if they weren't going to war against his other friends.

Ottar turned to Peer. "Do you believe in Valhalla, Peer? Where do you think we go to when we die? Kwimu says the People walk along the Ghost Road to the Land of Souls. Look, you can see it up there."

Kwimu pointed upwards. A-glimmer above the trees was

the line of the Milky Way, spangled and studded with stars. A royal road for the feet of the dead. Peer's breath caught.

"I don't know," he answered. "My father used to say we cross over a bridge."

"It looks like a bridge, doesn't it?" said Ottar, staring up. "I hope it's the same one. Wherever Kwimu goes, I want to go there too."

Crossing a bridge… floating away down a dark river… Perhaps all the journeys ended at the same bourne. Peer thought of his father and was comforted.

Shadowy snowflakes whirled into the fire like moths. Peer's breath smoked. The wind wailed. Or was it a wolf or some other animal, crying?

Kwimu sat up, listening. He took off the fox-skin pouch, which usually dangled from his belt. It had the face and paws and tail all attached, and Peer had sometimes seen him playing with it, stroking it and pretending to make it pounce. Now Kwimu scrambled lithely out of the shelter and disappeared into the snow. He came back almost immediately, without the pouch, and lay down. The others followed suit.

"What's that about?" Peer whispered.

Ottar yawned. "It's all right. He's leaving Fox on a tree branch not far away. To warn us of danger."

"Fox? You mean his *pouch?*"

Ottar scowled. "It's his *tioml.* His power. You don't notice much, Peer. Haven't you seen how it comes alive?"

"But…" Peer shut his mouth. He wasn't sure of anything. And about midnight, after the fires had gone out, they were woken by a yapping bark from close above. Loki stirred and grumbled.

On the cold wind came a distant howl, a lonely, hungry sound. It drew nearer. Beside him, Peer saw Ottar's eyes gleam wide.

Out of the woods, into the clearing, a moose came leaping in an arc of snow – running for its life. Peer rose to see better. It lifted over the shelter in a single bound, kicked a freezing dust of powder snow into his hair, and galloped into the trees. After it something came rushing, with crashing of undergrowth and explosive cracks of branches. It must be enormous to make such a noise. Wolves? Bears? Impossible. *Here it comes, and it's big. It's very big—*

"Down! Get down!" Ottar hissed. In disbelief Peer saw the tops of the pine trees shiver and sway apart. He sat down hard. It was overhead – a striding shadow against the stars – a yell that threw them to the ground – a double shock of mighty footsteps leaping over them.

It was gone. The woods swallowed it. An odd, musky smell blew back on the wind.

And a small animal slunk light-footed over the edge of the snow shelter, dashed to Kwimu and disappeared under his cloak.

In the eerie snowlight, men poured from the dugouts like ants from disturbed anthills. Peer too scrambled up into the cold. Ottar dragged him over to a great shapeless treadmark stamped into the snow on the very edge of one of the other shelters. They grouped around it, excited and afraid.

"*Jenu*," Peer heard. "*Jenu*..." He turned to see Kwimu standing sombrely, staring into the trees. The fox pouch hung limp from his belt, dark-eyed and grinning.

"What was it?" Peer asked quietly.

"A sort of – ice giant." Ottar's teeth rattled. "That's the s-second time I've seen one. I'll t-tell you about it – but not out here."

With the dawn, they clambered out of their snow holes. It was a bad omen for the day ahead. Peer hoped they might give up and go back to the village. But his companions were strapping on their snowshoes and setting off, and with a heavy heart he knelt to do the same. As Kwimu bent beside him, Peer got a good look at the fox pouch. Whatever it had done in the night, it was definitely not alive now. The eyes were made of little black shells.

And the day passed in trudging along slanting hillsides, under the lee of rocky ridges and over open tracts where fire had swept through the woods and the charred treestumps poked through the snow like black teeth. Peer couldn't recognise anything from his autumn journey. Apart from their own passing – the creak of the snowshoes, and the swish of robes – the woods were silent. Snow spread endlessly under the trees till the woods looked like a white cavern held up by dark pillars. His eyes ached from the whiteness, and his ears ached from the lack of sound.

In the blue dusk, they descended one last slope. At the bottom, snow curled over the banks of a river, frozen over except for black cores and sink-holes out in the middle where the ice was still treacherous. Following the bank, they came to frozen marshlands where the wind swept the snow like dust before a broom. Beyond the marshlands, Peer heard the pounding of the sea.

Serpent's Bay! It looked different. Ottar pushed alongside, staring. "What have they done?" he said hoarsely. "They've pulled down our old house." Only Gunnar's house was left. Peer stared hungrily at it. Hilde was there. So close!

The sky was clear and very cold. In the south west a fingernail moon clung, setting into the trees. Sinumkw led the war party silently along the edge of the wood, leaving the frozen flats to their left, till they came to the spot where in summer the brook rushed down the slope. Now it was a white cascade of leaping ice.

From here, with Thorolf's house gone, there was a clear view to Gunnar's. Sinumkw signed his men to stop. It was a good position, uphill from the house, and camouflaged against the trees.

Ottar shivered – with old memories, Peer thought, not with cold. Kwimu put an arm around him. Sinumkw turned to Peer. Peer couldn't read his face under the dark war paint, but his eyes gleamed. Ottar translated. "Sinumkw says, 'Now do what you came for. Carry our challenge. Tell them who they killed and why we have come.' And he says if you can get the girls out, do it before the moon sets. That's when we'll attack."

"It's mighty cold tonight," said Arne to Hilde. He wiped the last of the broth from his bowl with a lump of bread. "It will be a long winter."

"I know," said Hilde, rousing herself with an effort.

Astrid sat on the floor close to the hearth, mending clothes in the firelight. At the other end of the fire, Harald sprawled moodily in his father's chair, a low trestle table in front of him. He ignored his food, playing with his knife, twiddling it on its point and catching it before it fell over. The rest of the men were eating silently, heads down. Sometimes one of them coughed, or nudged his neighbour to pass the bread. Floki had a bad cold, and sniffed steadily – juicy, bubbling sniffs. "Can't you stop doing that?" Magnus grumbled. No one else spoke.

Somewhere in the rafters, Hilde supposed, the Nis perched, swinging a leg and watching them. If it wasn't dying of boredom.

Arne watched her. He cleared his throat. "It would be easier, maybe, if we two could help each other."

She turned drearily. "What do you mean?"

"Peer's not coming back, Hilde," Arne said quietly. "Not after all this time. I know you were fond of him – but aren't you fond of me, too? If you'll marry me, I'll take care of you. I won't let you worry about anything."

Hilde felt a twisting sensation inside her chest, as though he had taken her heart in both his hands and wrung it out. She met his clear blue eyes and remembered Astrid's words: *Arne's quite ordinary.* It was true. Nice, yes, but ordinary. She wondered why it taken her so long to notice.

"Of course I like you, Arne, but you can't 'take care' of me."

"I'd like to try."

"You don't understand." She closed her eyes and saw, as if by flashes of lightning, pictures against the darkness. Peer on the ship, gripping her arm and dashing off to deal with the Nis. Peer telling Harald the lie about the seagull. Peer facing Harald down not once, but many times, armed only with his wits, and, finally, with a burned dragonhead. She opened her eyes. Dammed-up tears spilled out. "Peer never tried to take care of me. He just took it for granted we'd do things together. You say you'd look after me. But in all this time, the only person who's stood up to Harald – the only person brave enough – has been Peer. And I miss him – so much."

Arne rubbed his eyes. On the back of his wrist Hilde saw the scar where he'd turned aside Harald's harpoon. "I'm sorry," she added. "But it's no good, Arne. Don't ask me."

"I see it's no good asking you now," said Arne. "I spoke too soon. Don't worry, I'll wait."

Though he looked sorry for her, she sensed he was

confident that she'd change her mind. She began to protest, and fell silent. What was the use? Maybe he was right. Maybe Astrid was right. If the person you wanted died, you just had to accept it and move on. Didn't you?

No, she thought passionately. *No!*

"Floki," said Harald in a cutting voice. "Will you stop that revolting sniffing? You sound like a pig."

A ripple went down the room – men lifting their heads and then deciding not to look. Floki smeared his nose with the back of his hand. "Sorry," he muttered, and sniffed again almost at once.

"Gods!" Harald stared at him in disgust. "You're like a human water clock. We ought to stand you in a corner and keep time by the drips."

Now that, thought Hilde, is the sort of remark that used to make Floki giggle. *See how he likes it when it happens to him.*

This time there were no smothered chuckles. The men ate on steadily, pretending not to notice. There'd been a lot of this lately: everyone tiptoeing around, afraid of setting Harald off. Since Gunnar died his moods had become dangerously unpredictable and his mocking tongue was sharper than ever.

Floki, who had been struggling not to sniff, gave up the battle. "*Sssnnnfff!*"

Harald heaved a cold sigh. "Someone should make a poem about you, Floki. Though I wonder if anyone could do you justice. Let's see. *Indoors, Floki's nose drips into the pot. Outside, it sprouts an icicle of snot.*" He showed his teeth. "How's that? Not bad, I feel, on the spur of the moment."

"I've got a cold," Floki muttered. "I can't help it."

"I know that, Floki," Harald said soothingly. "I know you can't help it." Floki's worried forehead cleared, but Harald wasn't finished. "But tell me something. Is there anything you can help?"

Floki looked this way and that.

"Answer the question," said Harald pleasantly. "You look like a pig, you sound like a pig. Granted. But do you have to be as stupid as one? Do you have to be a bandy-legged, red-faced, useless idiot?"

Floki tried to grin, but there were tears in his eyes.

Magnus growled, "Come on, Harald, stop picking on the lad. Like he told you, he can't help having a cold."

"Ah!" Harald's blue eyes flicked to Magnus. "Magnus, rushing in to look after Floki, as usual." He spun his knife and caught it. "You should be in petticoats. You fuss over him like an old woman, don't you? Why is that, Magnus?"

Magnus flushed a slow, angry red.

With widening eyes, Floki plastered his fingers to his face and exploded into a huge, wet sneeze. "*Aaaarcchoooo!*"

Harald grabbed his cup. "Get out of my sight, you fool!" he yelled, and threw it. It bounced off Floki's head, splashing Magnus with weak ale. Floki squealed in pain. Magnus jumped up.

"Right! I'm sick of your sneering ways, Harald. I stood by while you drove one young lad to his death, and I'll not stand by while you start on Floki. Who gave you the right to push us all around?" He glared at Harald. "Your dad was all right, but I can't stick the sight of you. If you was old enough, I'd pick you up and break you in half."

"Shut up!" Harald's voice slashed like a whip. "Tuck Floki into bed and kiss him goodnight. That's what you're good at, isn't it?"

With an incoherent roar Magnus launched himself at Harald's throat. Harald stood. The trestle table collapsed between them. Harald put his chin over Magnus's shoulder, hugging him close. His right arm jerked, once, twice. He stepped back. His knife was covered in wet blood. Magnus slid to the ground.

It happened too fast for anyone else to move. Hilde stopped breathing. All around the table were open mouths and horrified eyes.

"Oh, gods. Magnus!" A wail from Floki broke the silence. He scurried round the table and dropped to his knees, grabbing Magnus's arm, rolling him over. "Oh, gods!" He patted Magnus desperately. "Wake up, wake up! Oh gods, Magnus!"

Hilde stared at Magnus. There was a blood-stained slit in his shirt. His mouth hung slack, showing his missing teeth, and his eyes were setting in his head.

Floki looked up. "Tjørvi!" He threw himself at Tjørvi, grabbing fistfuls of his clothes with trembling urgency. "The life-stone, Tjørvi, give it to me, quick!"

Big Tjørvi gaped. "What?"

"That life-stone," Floki shrieked. "The one you told us about. The one your friend got from the eagle. You can have it back later. We need it for Magnus. Quickly, he's dying!"

Tjørvi's face twisted in shocked understanding. "There isn't any life-stone, Floki. It was just a story."

Floki stared at him, panting. "But – we need it."

"There isn't any life-stone," Tjørvi repeated.

Floki dragged his hands down his face, staring at Tjørvi with wild eyes. He fell down beside Magnus again, shaking him. "Magnus – Magnus…"

"He's dead," said Harald drily. The bloody knife was still in his hand.

"Oh, gods." Tears poured down Floki's face. His nose ran. "You killed him. You killed Magnus."

He got up, arms and legs scrabbling as though he could hardly control them. "Then I'll kill you! I'll kill you," he screamed, and snatched a knife from the table. His hands were shaking so hard that he fumbled and dropped it. Harald laughed, but the others were coming out of their shock.

"That was murder," Arne yelled.

"Aye!" Tjørvi growled, and there was a chorus of agreement.

Harald flicked the knife into his left hand and drew his sword with a scrape of steel. "Come and tell me so," he taunted. "Come on!" He threw back his head to make his hair shake. "Who's first? Who wants to meet Bone-Biter? Come and kill me, Floki!"

Sobbing, Floki tried to fling himself forward, but Tjørvi grappled him back. Harald laughed again, shrill and loud. He stepped across Magnus's body and began to chant, beating time on his chest with the fist that held the dagger.

"My name is Harald Silkenhair!
I am the son of Gunnar One Hand.
He gave me my blade, Bone-Biter.
Ha!

I was bred for battle.
My mother fed me on wolf meat.
She gave me knives to play with,
To teach me the sharpness of swords.
Ha!

I will dance between the spearpoints.
I will split skulls.
Who dares to meet me?"

The men hung back. To get to Harald they had to get past three feet of pointed steel.

Under Harald's feet, poor Magnus lay sprawled in death. Floki was weeping in awful, shrill whimpers. A haze of shame and defeat floated in the room.

Astrid backed up close to Hilde and spoke between her teeth. "You threw a bucket of water over him once. Could we try it again?"

"He didn't have his sword then," Hilde answered. But Astrid was right, they had to think of something, fast. She could see Arne creeping forward, and Tjørvi shifting his balance. Harald was watching with pin-prick eyes, laughing silently, his sword braced.

What would Peer do? Distract him somehow. There was a chirrup from overhead. The Nis! Her gaze flew upwards. Could the Nis distract Harald? The Nis was beside itself with excitement. It teetered on the edge of the rafter, eyes popping, pursing its lips in an exaggerated *Sshh!* Sure of their attention, it jumped from beam to beam till it crouched directly over the clothes Astrid had been mending by the fire, and jabbed a long forefinger downwards.

Hilde stared. *A cloak, a couple of tunics, some leggings?* And now the Nis was pointing excitedly at Harald…

Astrid's face came alive. She clutched Hilde's arm, sprang forward, snatched up an armful of clothes, and threw them over Harald's sword and sword-arm. The blade sagged, muffled in fabric. Harald jumped back, swearing, trying to shake off the clothes, but Hilde tore a blanket from the sleeping bench and sent it sailing at him.

The girls went crazy. They grabbed everything they could off the benches and sent cloaks, jerkins, blankets, socks – a snowstorm of clothes – whirling at Harald. The Nis squeaked deliriously.

Harald staggered. A pair of Floki's trousers hung drunkenly over one eye. His sword was tangled in the folds of Tjørvi's heaviest cloak. Arne leaped on him, bearing him to the ground. Tjørvi followed. They pinned him down, and wrenched the sword from his hand.

Astrid and Hilde leaned together, laughing and crying. The men dragged Harald to his feet. The floor was a mess of clothes. Magnus's feet stuck out from under it. Hilde sobered abruptly. Rough, cheerful Magnus was dead, and their little victory couldn't change that. Floki, weeping like a rainstorm, went on his knees to clear the clothes from Magnus's face.

Tjørvi looked down at him, and then at Harald, whose face was ugly with rage. "What shall we do with him?" he asked heavily.

"Take your hands off me," Harald spat. Then his eyes went black with shock, and he stared past them, down the room, at something behind them – something that could not be happening.

The house door scraped slowly open, revealing a wedge of black night and white snow. Someone walked stiffly in. Someone – or something. The clothes were strange, and covered in painted symbols. The face was stained with blood, but it looked familiar.

Hilde went cold. It was Peer's face.

It was Peer's ghost.

CHAPTER 63

Death in the Snow

PEER BLINKED. HE'D expected surprise, but not this. Every person in the room stood in stiff, arrested positions, gaping in terror. He stepped forwards, and they all stepped back. Tjørvi let go of Harald. Floki jumped to his feet. "It wasn't us!" he yelled. "You can't blame us, it wasn't us. It was him! Take Harald, not us, it wasn't us..."

Peer looked at Hilde. Her hand had flown to her mouth and she was gazing at him in apparent horror, her eyes huge. He swallowed. "Hilde. It's me. I'm back."

Hilde clutched Astrid for support. "Peer?" It was a breath of a word, her lips barely moving. "Peer?"

Loki nosed his way around the door. He saw Hilde, flattened his ears, and threw himself at her with a yelp of joy. Hilde shrieked. "It is you! It's Loki! Oh, Peer!"

She fell on her knees and gathered Loki into her arms, pressing her face against his fur. He wriggled ecstatically, licked her face, tore himself away to dash around the room greeting people, and returned to Hilde again. But by this time, Hilde was on her feet, locked into Peer's arms, her face buried in his shoulder.

Peer thought he could stand there for ever, happiness blazing through him like a pillar of fire.

She looked up. "What's on your face? Blood? Are you hurt?"

He'd forgotten how he must look. No wonder they'd been staring. "Warpaint," he answered, rubbing at it. "I'll explain later." He looked around, realising for the first time something was going on. Why was Floki crying? "Where's Gunnar? I've got a message for you all."

Hilde drew a deep, deep breath. "Gunnar's dead." By now the rest of the room was coming to life. No one could think Loki was a ghost. The men looked at Peer with delight and disbelief. Tjørvi was beaming, Arne shaking his head.

"Gunnar's dead?" Peer exclaimed.

"*Magnus is dead, too-oo-oo.*" It was a dog-like howl of misery from Floki. Peer's scalp crawled. The men began yelling, "That's right!"

"Harald killed him! Stabbed him to death in front of us..."

"Just now, before you came in. Look, he's there on the floor."

Shock punched through Peer. Magnus sprawled on his back at the other end of the hearth, staring at nothing. His hands curled half open. His big toe stuck through a hole in one of his socks.

"*What message, Barelegs?*"

Peer swung round.

Harald had picked up his sword. He was standing on the other side of the hearth, staring across the flames at Peer. His head jerked, and his mouth twitched. The fire danced in his eyes.

"Why did you let him go?" Halfdan yelled at Tjørvi.

"Why didn't you get rid of his sword?" Tjørvi shouted. Peer ignored them. He knew better than to take his eyes off Harald.

He spoke loudly. "I've been living with the Skraelings.

They sheltered me, took me in. But you killed two of them, Harald. Their names were Kiunik and Tia'm. Their people have found out, and they want your blood."

He raised his voice over the growing murmur. "They'll not hurt the girls. The rest of you could try and surrender. There's a war band out there, fifty of them, with bows and spears and axes. If you surrender, I'll do what I can to help you. But they're angry. They've got a right to be, their kinsmen were murdered…"

Harald's voice lifted over the hubbub. "Traitor! You led them here!"

Peer laughed at him. "Led them? I couldn't have found my way without them. They know these woods, Harald – we're the strangers."

Harald threw his head back. "*Hooo-ooo!* Skraelings! Hear him, lads? Are we a match for them? Are we men?"

"Peer," Tjørvi bellowed. "If we surrender, will they harm us?"

"I don't know." He had to be honest. "They don't like cowards. But there's so many, if you fight you'll die anyway…"

"They don't like cowards?" Tjørvi said bleakly. "Who does? All right, if we've got to die, let's take a few of them with us."

"No!" Peer yelled.

But the others were nodding. "Aye!" "Die like men!" "Like heroes!"

"I don't want to die," sobbed Floki.

Harald kicked him. "Get up, Floki, you son of a pig. Find yourself a weapon and act like a Norseman." He faced the men, sword uplifted. "Who's your leader?"

There was a confused murmur.

"Harald?"

"No, no..."

"Yes – Harald – we need him..."

"Harald Silkenhair!"

"Who's with me?" Harald shouted.

"We are! We all are!"

"I DON'T BELIEVE IT!" screamed Hilde. "Harald just killed Magnus, and now you want him to lead you?"

"Who else can do it?" Halfdan snarled. "We need a leader – a war leader. We can sort out the stuff about Magnus later."

"There won't be any later!" Peer shouted.

"Not for you," said Harald, and he sprang at Peer, over the fire.

For an endless second Peer saw him coming, his golden hair floating out, underlit by the firelight, his mouth opening in a war cry.

"Run!" Astrid screamed.

Peer ducked under Harald's sword stroke and bolted for the door. *Here I go again*, he had time to think. Would it always, always come down to this: *He's got a sword, and I haven't?*

The wind bit his face. Loose snow smoked along the ground. The thin moon was touching the crest of the hill. The forested slope was a dark wall under it. He ran for the trees and the safety of Sinumkw's men. It was further than it looked... His foot plunged into a hole under the snow and he pitched forwards, hitting the rock-hard ground with an impact that drove the breath from his lungs.

He writhed on to his back, pulling up his knees, trying to suck in air, while tingling stars popped and blistered in front of his eyes. A bare foot crunched into the snow beside his head. Harald had run out into the snow after him without boots. Unable to breathe or speak, Peer twisted to see a sword-point inches from his nose. It looked enormous, dwindling upwards to Harald's fist, and finally his far-off face, dark against the sky.

"If you've never killed anyone, Barelegs…"

Peer wheezed. A thread of air wound into his lungs. Nothing like enough. He doubled up. If he could get one breath, one, before Harald killed him.

"… you won't know…" Harald paused. "You won't know how good life truly tastes. You can't know at all."

The sword point pulled back from his face. "And now for a good death," whispered Harald. He sounded happy. Peer set his teeth and waited for the blow.

With a whirr and a thump, something struck Harald and spun him round. He staggered, clawing at his right shoulder where a slim shaft bristled. He ripped at it. Blood ran down his arm and dripped dark into the snow. Harald threw back his head, opened his mouth and howled at the stars.

"*Ahoooooooooooooh!*"

It was a cry to melt your bones, a fluid shriek that rose and fell and trailed off into unending loneliness. Peer cringed into the snow, while all the hairs on his neck rose. Still the expected blow did not fall. Harald stepped away.

Icy air rushed into Peer's lungs. He pushed himself up, coughing.

Another arrow hissed past his shoulder, burying itself in the snow. A string of dark figures detached from the edge of the wood and rushed out over the white flats, whooping. In the pale snowlight, Peer couldn't see faces, but he knew that Kwimu and Sinumkw were leading them. Harald raced barefoot to meet them, his pale hair streaming, throwing his sword into the air and catching it. He howled again, and the hillside echoed: "*Ahooooooooooooh! Hoo, hoo, hoo!*"

"Come on, lads!" Tjørvi, Arne and Halfdan pounded out of the house, waving axes.

"Arne! Halfdan!" Peer shouted in despair.

"Peer!" With a rush of skirts, Hilde threw herself down in the snow alongside him, panting and actually laughing. He turned on her in fury. "What are you doing? You could get killed!"

"I don't care." Her eyes were bright. "I'm not losing you twice."

He flung an arm over her shoulders and kissed her. She kissed him back. Her mouth was cold, then warm. The wind hurled snow into their faces, as fine as salt. They clung to each other.

Harald began a series of sharp yipping barks, climbing to another fearsome howl. Peer half rose. Hilde dragged him down. "Stay with me!"

They heard the echo from the woods. How could the hillside twist the sound like that, to fling it back clearer, longer, louder?

That's not an echo. It's an answer.

He jumped up, heedless of flying arrows. "Sinumkw! Kwimu! Up there on the ridge! Behind you!"

It didn't matter that he was using his own language. His urgent voice and pointing arm did it all. Black on the crest of the ridge, something impossibly tall stalked long-legged against the moonglow, a flickering shape behind the trees, now visible, now gone. It raised long, angular arms above its head and screamed, a scream to shred your nerves and tear the top of your head off and rip open your brain. Then it jumped below the skyline. The trees shook as it crashed downhill.

The war party turned, scattering and reforming to face the woods.

"Tjørvi! Arne!" Peer bellowed between his hands. "Look out!"

The Norsemen flung themselves down. The *jenu* burst out of the woods in an avalanche of frozen clods and broken branches. It stopped at the base of the slope, one arm hooked around the top of a bending pine, and leaned out, swivelling this way and that as if searching for someone.

"What *is* it?" Hilde's voice rose.

"Get back to the house—" Peer stopped. It was all open ground between here and the house. If Hilde ran, the *jenu* could catch her in a few strides, and he was sure it would chase anything that ran away.

"Keep down." He grabbed her arm and towed her towards the war band.

She struggled. "They're Skraelings!"

"No, they're friends." It sounded stupid: friends didn't attack with arrows. He added firmly, "Safety in numbers."

He hoped it was true. The war party crouched in a ragged arc, bows and spears at the ready. Peer and Hilde scurried into the band of warriors. Friends... it *was* true. Muin, and Kopit, and Ki'kwaju – he knew all their names. Kwimu, kneeling with bent bow, flicked Peer a single glance of welcome and turned back to concentrate on the foe.

They were nearer, now. Peer could see more. The thing had the horrifying proportions of a stick man: long exaggerated arms and legs, with swollen joints and splayed fingers. The naked body reflected the snowlight as it stared about with huge, rolling, almost fish-like eyes. It opened a lipless gash of a mouth and howled like the north wind.

"*Owooooooooooohhh!*"

Harald Silkenhair screamed in answer.

Hilde gripped Peer's arm. "It'll see him! Is he mad?"

Harald had been standing in the snow, transfixed. Now he was running towards the *jenu*, his pale hair floating. With a yell he whirled his sword and threw himself at the monster.

Peer saw the sword carve a dark slash in the creature's thin thigh. The *jenu* bellowed. Its raking fingers came down and plucked Harald from the ground. Struggling, Harald swung the sword again, stabbing at the creature's face. The *jenu* tore the sword from his hand and threw it away. It brought up a bony knee and snapped him over it like a stick of firewood.

Hilde clapped her hands over her face. Sinumkw shouted. The warriors loosed their bows. Arrows rushed through the air, and some of them stuck in the *jenu's* side. It brushed at them clumsily, as if they were thorns.

Tjørvi crawled through the snow, worming along on his elbows. He reached Peer and gripped his arm with steely fingers. "What can we do?"

Peer shook his head.

The *jenu* began to cough. It threw Harald into the snow, where he lay like a broken doll. It retched, and finally gobbed something out into its hands, pale and slippery, the size of a newborn baby shaped out of ice. The *jenu* stared at it for a moment. Then it pushed its heart back into its mouth and gulped. It grabbed Harald and crouched down, growling. *It's going to eat him*, Peer thought, sickened. *And then it will start on us.*

There was a shrill yell from the direction of the houses. Splashes of bright fire like living gold came jerking and weaving over the grey, frozen ground. Two figures bounded through the snow, waving fiery torches. Loki raced ahead of them, barking.

The *jenu* sprang upright, snarling, clutching Harald's

broken body to its chest. Kwimu yelled. Tjørvi and Arne shouted. Ottar screamed.

Floki came panting up, a blazing torch in each hand. He held one out, and Kwimu snatched it. Astrid ran up, her wild hair the same colour as the flames. Sinumkw leaped at her, seized both her torches and ran at the *jenu*, whooping. His warriors streamed after him. Peer grabbed Hilde's hand. Madly, together, everyone charged with Sinumkw, hurling spears and waving torches.

For a second Peer thought the *jenu* would fight. It bent over them, hissing, and they choked on its musky stench, sweet and stale. Cradled in its sinewy arms, Harald lolled lifeless, his long hair trailing.

Then, like a dog protecting its bone, the *jenu* turned. They saw the nicked ridge of its spine, its thin buttocks and long bony legs scissoring away in ground-swallowing strides, heading for the river. It faded rapidly in the grey light. It leaped across the river and disappeared into the far woods. They heard one last distant shriek of rage and loneliness. And it was gone.

Ottar ran up, dragging something heavy along with him. "It's Harald's sword," he sobbed. "I've got his sword." He stared over the dim marshes towards the river and the black, watching woods, and let the sword drop into the snow. He looked up at Peer and tears ran down his cheeks. "I hated him. I hated him. But he was brave, wasn't he, Peer? He *was* brave."

"Yes, he was brave," said Peer slowly. "But I'm afraid that's all he was."

CHAPTER 64

Peace Pipe

"HOW DID YOU guess the thing could be driven away by fire?" asked Tjørvi in admiration.

Astrid and Floki looked at each other. "We didn't," said Astrid.

Floki shook his head. "Nah. We just thought, what's worse? Fighting with the rest of you, or hiding in the house waiting for it to come and get us?"

"And there weren't any weapons left," Astrid added. "So the Nis said—"

"Aha – the Nis!" Tjørvi interrupted, glancing up. There were no secrets left. The Nis sat openly on a beam overhead, guzzling a bowlful of hot groute. "That was the Nis's idea, was it? I wish I'd known we had a Nis with us all this time."

"Wait," Ottar interrupted. "Let me tell the others all that." He turned and began to translate.

Peer drew Hilde against him. She whispered, "It's a full house."

It was. Sinumkw's warriors sat cross-legged on the floor by the fire, or sprawled on the sleeping benches. The firelight shone on their oiled black hair and brown faces, still smudged with war paint. Peer smiled as he looked around. Trades and swaps were happening already. Halfdan had a tuft of blue feathers in his hair. Tjørvi was sporting Kopit's beartooth necklace, and

Kopit had slung Tjørvi's steel knife around his neck. Both looked very happy with their bargains.

"So the Nis suggested the torches?" Peer tipped his head back. "Well done!"

The Nis was licking its messy fingers, and a splash of groute dripped into Peer's hair. "I has lots of good ideas," it boasted. "Has you heard how we threw the clothes at Harald?"

"Hilde's told me." Peer wished he could have seen Harald struggling to fight a rain of socks and trousers.

"What name suits me best, Peer Ulfsson?" the Nis enquired. It upended the basin and stuck its entire face inside to lick out the bottom. "'Nithing the Seafarer' – or 'Nithing the Warrior'?"

"Oh well – erm..."

"It was brave of you and Floki to come out," Hilde said to Astrid. "Weren't you afraid of hurting the baby, running like that?"

"It was time I did something to help." Astrid pressed a hand to her stomach. "He's fine. I can feel him kicking."

Sinumkw spoke to her across the fire, his dark eyes gleaming. Astrid raised her brows and turned to Ottar. "What does he say?"

"He says a brave mother makes a brave son," said Ottar.

Astrid's eyes filled.

"Don't cry," Hilde said softly.

"I'm not," Astrid muttered, dashing a hand across her face. "Well, yes I am. I'm thinking of Gunnar. He'll never see his son now. If it is a boy, I mean. *A son like Harald.* And I promised I'd save him, and I harmed him instead."

"You didn't harm him," Hilde protested.

"Yes, I did. I was so angry when he slapped me. I wanted revenge. I could have warned Harald not to crush the egg, but I didn't. I'm not a nice person like you. It's true about troll blood, you see. It always comes out in the end. And my son will inherit it from me. He'll be the same."

"How can you say that?" Hilde began, but there was an outburst of excitement in the roof. The Nis knocked its empty bowl off the beam, just missing Peer's head, and scrabbled in an angle of the rafters, scattering straw and dust.

"See, see?" It tossed something light into Astrid's lap. A tiny hollow egg.

"I finds it on the floor when I is tidying up," the Nis chirped. "When Harald Silkenhair makes all that mess and leaves it for the Nis to clear away. And I thinks, a *thrush egg*! I keeps it, I puts it in my den to look pretty, in my nice nest up in the roof." It looked down at Astrid with sharp eyes. "It's empty," it added.

Astrid's hand closed around it. "Harald didn't smash it after all," she breathed. "Then – it didn't matter..."

"Oh, Astrid," said Hilde impatiently. "Gunnar died because of what *he* did – not because of what you did. Do stop going on about your troll blood. Take my advice. Don't tell your baby anything about it, and he'll grow up fine."

Astrid looked at her with slowly dawning relief. "Do you think – if *I'd* never known...?" She took a deep breath. "I could forget about it. I could be just like anyone else..."

The Nis cracked its knuckles gleefully. "Always, always the Nis finds the answer. Maybe I should be 'Nithing the Clever'..."

Troll blood, Peer thought. *What does it mean to have troll blood?* He remembered, all those years ago, how his two bullying uncles had turned into trolls after drinking troll beer. But they'd been trolls on the inside all along. Perhaps being a troll was more to do with how you behaved than the blood you inherited. If you howled to the *jenu*, the *jenu* would howl back.

And tomorrow, thought Peer, *we'll give Harald's sword to Sinumkw. Kiunik and Tia'm can take it with them on the Ghost Road, on their long journey to the Land of Souls.*

He looked at Floki, who sat silently with lowered head. "Hey, Floki." Floki looked up out of red-rimmed eyes. Peer leaned across. "It was great, the way you ran out with the torches. Magnus would be so proud."

Floki didn't speak. But his rough, freckled hand came out to grip Peer's. He sniffed.

There was a shrill yap, a screech, and a roar of laughter. The Nis shot into the rafters, chittering hysterically. Hilde stifled giggles. "Did you see that? The Nis got the nerve to creep up behind Kwimu, and it got too near that pet fox of his." She looked more closely. "It's not a fox, is it? What on earth…?"

Kwimu smiled across at them. For a second, Peer was sure the fox winked. But a moment later, Kwimu lifted it, and it was just a fur pouch, with the mask and paws and tail of a fox attached. He plunged his hand into it and pulled out a pipe. He lit it and handed it to his father.

The noise and chatter died. The Norsemen watched curiously.

"He's swallowing fire!"

"They'll never believe this at home."

"It's a sign of friendship," said Peer. "Isn't it, Ottar? If he gives the pipe to you, make sure you take it."

Sinumkw blew out a thin flutter of smoke. He rose ceremoniously and passed the pipe to Peer. Peer drew down a mouthful of sweet smoke.

"Arne…" He held out the pipe. Arne looked at it without moving. Then he scratched his head. "A sign of friendship, eh? All right, I'll give it a go." He took the pipe, sucked on it, and coughed. "Not bad!" he said with watering eyes, handing it on to Tjørvi. He added gruffly, "I'm glad you're not dead."

"Thanks," said Peer. They looked at each other with uncertain smiles.

With jokes and back-slapping, the pipe passed around the room. Up in the rafters, the Nis spluttered, pretending to be annoyed by the smoke. Considering it spent most of its time in the haze of woodsmoke floating about the rafters, that was rich, Peer thought. He stood on tiptoe and whispered, "Here's a good name. How about 'Nithing the Wise Warrior'?" The Nis purred.

"What are you thinking?" Hilde asked Peer as he sat down.

He stretched. "Oh, lots of things. What to do next. How to spend the winter. When to go home. Whether Ottar will come with us. And who's going to decide it all? Now Gunnar's gone, who's going to lead us?"

"You, I should think," said Hilde.

"Me?" He stared at her.

"Yes, you." Hilde grinned at him. "Who else will do all the thinking?" She leaned against him and whispered into his ear, "So go on. What's going to happen to us?"

Peer dropped his arm around her shoulders. He thought of the months of cold ahead; the blizzards; the creatures like the *jenu* lurking in the woods. He thought of trying to cross the immense ocean dividing them from home, with no Gunnar to guide them, and only five men to sail the ship. He remembered the storms and icebergs of the voyage out. He looked down at Hilde, and saw his own fears in her eyes.

"The winter will pass," he whispered back. "Perhaps we'll stay here in the house for the whole of it. Or, if they'll let us, we'll go back to the village with Kwimu and the People, and go hunting and trapping with them. Astrid's baby will be born there, and she'll have lots of women to help her, not just you by yourself. And then the spring will come. The ice will melt, and the buds will thicken on the trees. We'll take *Water Snake* out of her winter quarters and push her down into the sea. And we'll sail away.

"It'll take us a long time, weeks and weeks, but we'll sight Greenland and the Islands of Sheep. We'll follow the whales home. And one day, we'll see our own mountain again. Troll Fell.

"I wonder if it will be sunrise. Or sunset, or raining, or foggy even. Maybe we'll meet Bjørn in his faering, coming out to the fishing grounds. But anyway, we'll sail in to the jetty and walk up through Trollsvik. And we'll see the farmhouse, with the smoke rising from the roof. And Gudrun will dash out to meet us, and Ralf will come running from the field..."

Hilde was smiling, though her eyes were full of tears.

"And I'll say, 'Here we are. We're back. And we want to get married.'"

"That will be such a happy ending," Hilde sighed.

"There's never any ending," said Peer softly. "Life goes on."

The background to Troll Blood

Over a thousand years ago (and five hundred years before Columbus), in the year 985 or 986, a young man called Bjarni Herjolfsson who'd been trying to sail from Iceland to Greenland, was driven south and west in a gale that lasted several days. When he eventually sighted land, it wasn't the icy mountains of Greenland, but a strange wooded country with low hills.

Bjarni wasn't interested in going ashore. He didn't want to discover new lands; he wanted to get where he'd been going, so he and his men sailed northwards, hopping up the coast, and finally across what is now known as the Davis Strait to Greenland.

Fifteen years later, Leif Eiriksson of Greenland bought Bjarni's ship (possibly on the principle that it had been there once and could find the way again) and set out to retrace Bjarni's voyage in the opposite direction. He did so with spectacular success, naming three lands on his way south: Helluland, which means "Slab land", a stony, glaciated landscape; Markland, or "Forest land", a flat woody country; and finally a grassy, wooded peninsular where he and his men built houses and overwintered, naming the country Vinland for the grapes they said they found there. Later, more voyages were made by Leif's brother Thorvald, his sister Freydis, and his relative Thorfinn Karlsefni.

No one doubts now that Helluland, Markland and Vinland were parts of the north-eastern coast of America. The most likely candidates are Baffin Island, Labrador and Newfoundland respectively. Traces of a Viking settlement at

L'Anse aux Meadows in Newfoundland may actually be the place where Leif built his houses.

Two sagas, *The Greenland Saga* and *Eirik the Red's Saga* tell how Leif, Freydis and Thorfinn met "Skraelings", a scornful and dismissive term used indiscriminately by the Norsemen for all the Native Americans they met, including the northern Inuit. Though some trading took place, relations were pretty unstable. Both sagas tell of battles between the Norse and the Skraelings. Partly these were due to misunderstandings, but some were triggered by murders. When Leif's brother Thorvald came across nine Skraelings asleep under their canoes, he and his men promptly killed eight of them. He paid the price for his aggressive behaviour. The ninth Skraeling escaped to raise the alarm. A fleet of canoes attacked, and Thorvald died from an arrow wound. Incidents like this go a long way towards explaining why the Norse never formed permanent settlements in Vinland. Their iron and steel weapons, such as swords, axes and spears might have given them an edge – literally – over the flint-tipped weapons of the indigenous peoples, but not that much of an edge. And there were far more Native Americans than there were Norsemen.

So who were these "Skraelings"? The Native American people of Newfoundland were named the Beothuk. It's known that they painted their clothes and bodies with red ochre, because they thought of red as a sacred colour. (Their neighbours called them the Red People. Europeans would call them Red Indians.) The Beothuk saw off the Vikings, but not the later arrival of the French and the British, whose diseases and guns drove them to extinction. In 1829, the last of the Beothuk, a woman named Shaw-na-dith-it, died of tuberculosis in captivity. And with her died the last chance of learning the Beothuk's language, beliefs and customs. Only a few scraps of information remain – nothing like enough to build a book upon.

So, since the Norsemen would certainly have explored beyond Newfoundland, I chose to base my account of Kwimu and his People not on the Beothuk, but on the Mi'kmaq people of New Brunswick – only a step further south – who still live in the land of their ancestors, and many of whose beliefs, customs and stories have either been documented or are a matter of living and proud tradition. To them I owe a debt of admiration – and my apologies for errors.

For those interested in geography, I've imagined that Gunnar and Thorolf built their houses somewhere along the north shore of the Baie des Chaleurs, on the Gaspé Peninsula, between New Brunswick and Quebec. But I've not been too precise. And though most of the Native American references are to Mi'kmaq customs and lore, I have occasionally borrowed from their neighbours, the Passamaquoddy, Abenaki, Montaignais and other Algonquian peoples. After all, the story is set at a time 500 years earlier than the French missionaries who, even as they set about trying to change them, wrote accounts of the manners, customs and beliefs of the Mi'kmaq people. I hope I will be forgiven a certain amount of imaginative licence.

I didn't invent any of the magical creatures in *Troll Blood*. From the Nis to the *jenu*, they are my interpretations of creatures which have all been believed in by real people at some point in history. I wanted to write about the world in which such beliefs were possible – a world in which ordinary men and women co-existed with spirits and ghosts, both helpful and harmful. I've tried my best to imagine how the Norsemen and Kwimu's People lived and thought. I did lots of research; I even had the tremendous fun of spending a week learning how to sail a reconstruction of a real Viking ship on a Danish fjord. But, at the end of the day, *Troll Blood* is fantasy, not history.

Six hundred years ago, the London printer William Caxton published Sir Thomas Malory's story of King Arthur; *Le Morte d'Arthur*. I feel I can't do better than to pass on Caxton's warning to his readers:

"And for to pass the time, this book shall be pleasant to read in. But for to give faith and believe that all is true that is set herein, ye be at your liberty."

Glossary

All the Native American words in the book are from the Mi'kmaq language. Here is a rough guide to pronunciation. As a rule of thumb, 'k' is pronounced as a hard 'g', and 't' as a light 'd'.

eula'qmeujit (ey-oo-**lahk**-may-oo-jeet)	starvation
jenu (**jen**-oo)	ice giant, once a human being
ji'j (**jeej**)	small (a suffix)
jipijka'm (jee-**peej**-gahm)	horned serpent
jipjawej (**jeep**-ja-wedge)	robin
kewasu'nukwej (gee-wa-**soo**-nook-wage)	invisible Other One who chops trees
kiunik (gee-**oon**-ig)	otter
kopit (**go**-peed)	beaver
kwimu (**gwee**-moo)	loon, a diving water bird
kwetejk (gwed-edge-k)	St Lawrence Iroquois people
muin (moo-**een**)	bear
n'kwis (en-**gwees**)	my son
nukumij (noo-**goo**-meej)	my grandmother
nuji'j (noo-jeej)	my grandchild
nujj (en-**oodge**)	my father
plawej (pl-**ow**-wedge)	partridge
sinumkw (seh-**num**-k)	wild goose
skite'kmuj (es-kuh-**deg**-uh-mooj)	ghost
skus (es-**koos**)	weasel
sqoljk (es-**holch**-ig)	frogs
tia'm (dee-**ahm**)	moose
tioml (**dee**-oh-mull)	powerful animal totem
wiklatmu'jk (week-laht-**moo**-jig)	race of tiny Persons who inhabit the shore

'Langrish is a first-rate storyteller.'
The Times

KATHERINE LANGRISH

Wolf is on the run, lost on Devil's Edge, a hill riddled with old mine shafts and said to be infested with ghosts, boggarts, elves, and perhaps even the Devil himself. Luckily, Wolf meets a local knight out hunting, who offers him work and shelter in his castle, and introduces him to his daughter, Nest. But together Wolf and Nest become embroiled in a mystery which leads them into the very darkest depths of Devil's Edge…

ISBN 978-0-00-721489-1

HarperCollins *Children's Books*

The enthralling sequel to
THE WEIRDSTONE OF BRISINGAMEN

THE MOON OF GOMRATH

It is the Eve of Gomrath – the night of the year when the Old Magic is aroused. Had Colin and Susan known this, they would never have lighted a fire on the Beacon, thereby releasing the uncontrollable ferocity of the Wild Hunt. Soon they are inextricably caught up in the struggle between their friend, the Wizard Cadellin silverbrow, and the evil Morrigan.

But the children too are in great danger.
They will need all their strength and courage, just to survive…

"Not only powerful but full of wild and whirling adventure… the reader is drawn right into the midst of it all."
The Times

ISBN 978-0-00-712787-0

HarperCollins *Children's Books*